CLUB KICK OUT! 1

★★★ INTO THE RING ★★★

STEPH MIDED

HARPER alley

An Imprint of HarperCollinsPublishers

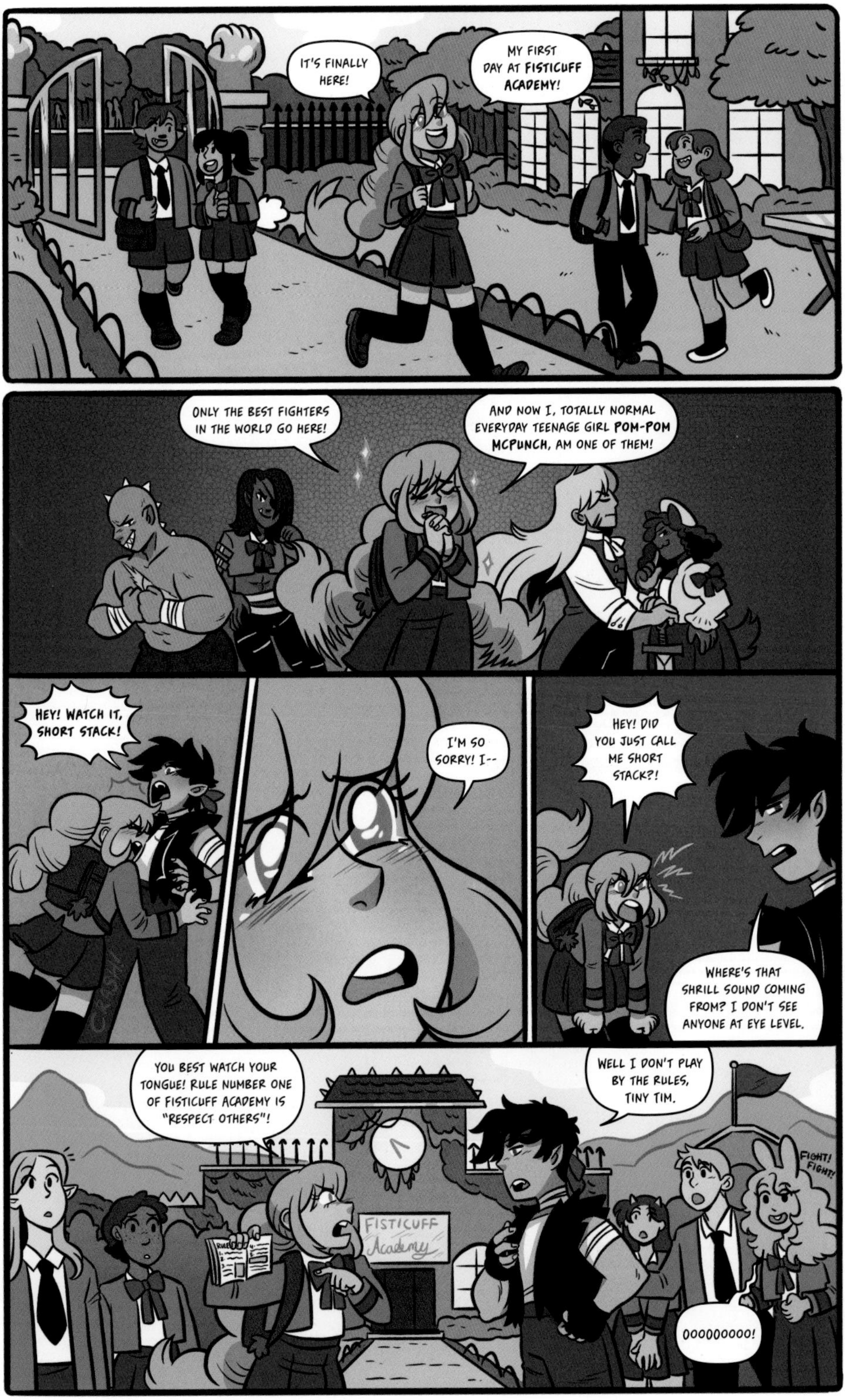

IT'S FINALLY HERE!
MY FIRST DAY AT FISTICUFF ACADEMY!
ONLY THE BEST FIGHTERS IN THE WORLD GO HERE!
AND NOW I, TOTALLY NORMAL EVERYDAY TEENAGE GIRL POM-POM MCPUNCH, AM ONE OF THEM!
HEY! WATCH IT, SHORT STACK!
I'M SO SORRY! I--
HEY! DID YOU JUST CALL ME SHORT STACK?!
WHERE'S THAT SHRILL SOUND COMING FROM? I DON'T SEE ANYONE AT EYE LEVEL.
YOU BEST WATCH YOUR TONGUE! RULE NUMBER ONE OF FISTICUFF ACADEMY IS "RESPECT OTHERS"!
WELL I DON'T PLAY BY THE RULES, TINY TIM.
FISTICUFF Academy
FIGHT! FIGHT!
OOOOOOOOO!

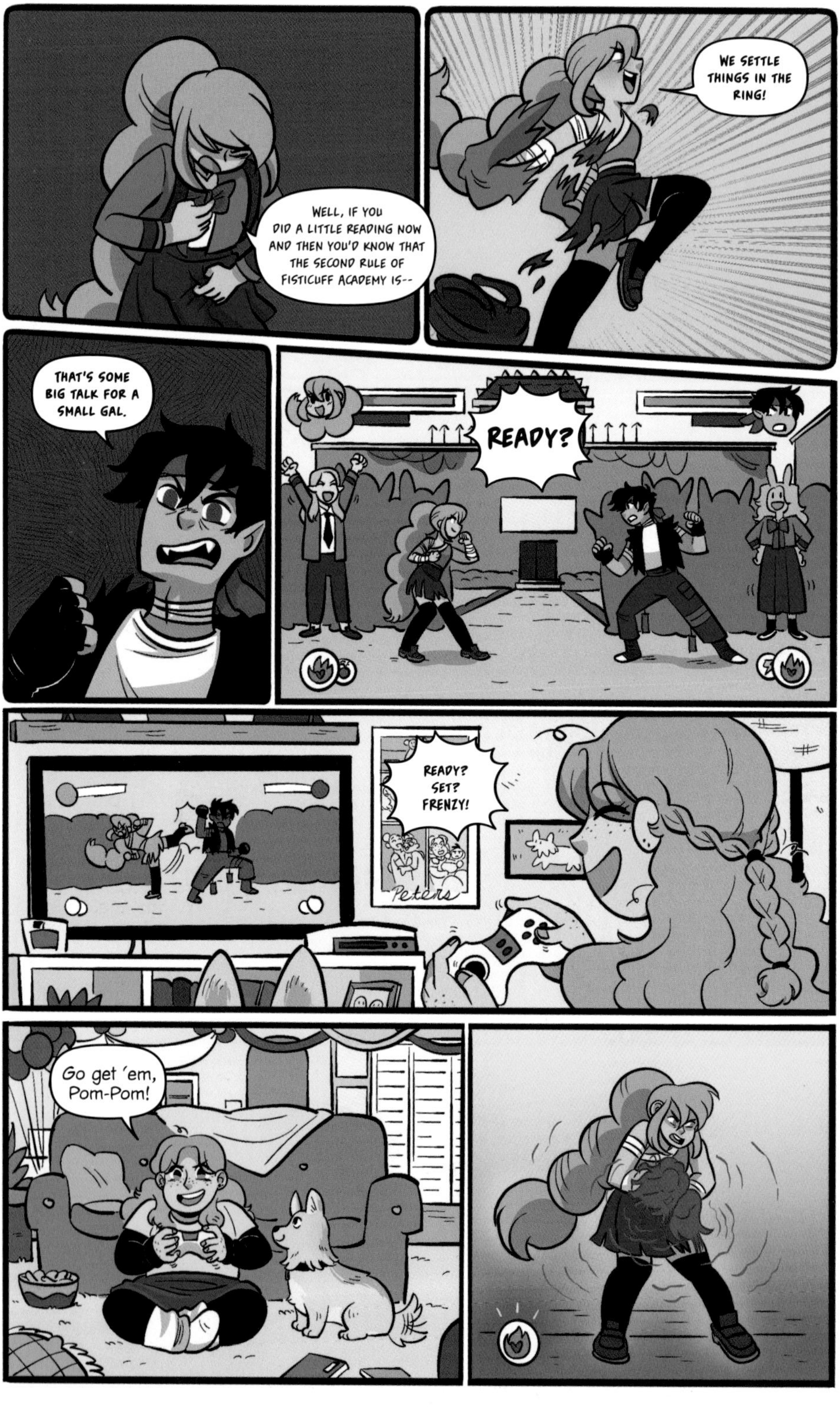
WELL, IF YOU DID A LITTLE READING NOW AND THEN YOU'D KNOW THAT THE SECOND RULE OF FISTICUFF ACADEMY IS--
WE SETTLE THINGS IN THE RING!
THAT'S SOME BIG TALK FOR A SMALL GAL.
READY?
READY? SET? FRENZY!
Peters
Go get 'em, Pom-Pom!

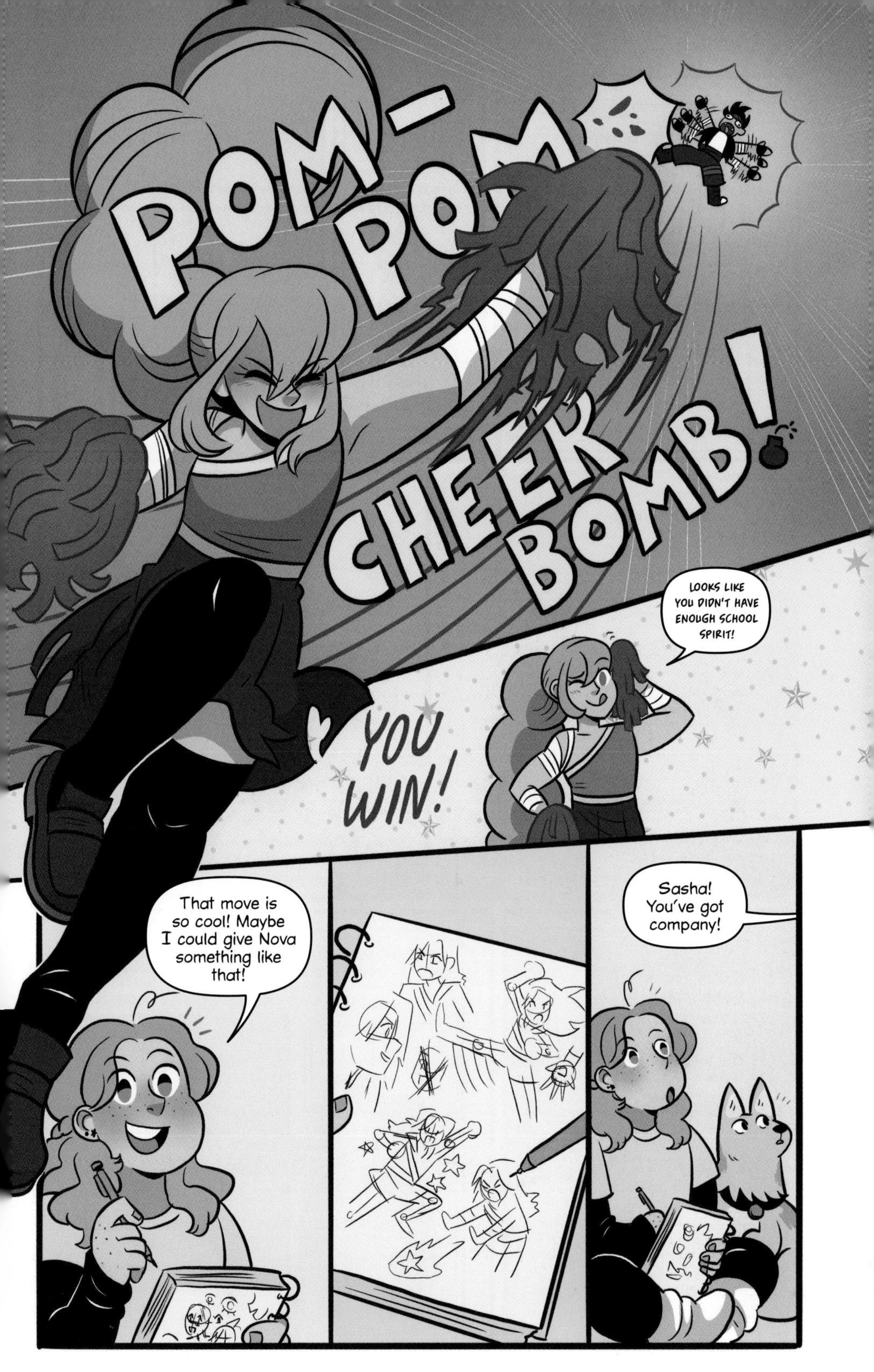
POM-POM
CHEER BOMB!
LOOKS LIKE YOU DIDN'T HAVE ENOUGH SCHOOL SPIRIT!
YOU WIN!
That move is so cool! Maybe I could give Nova something like that!
Sasha! You've got company!

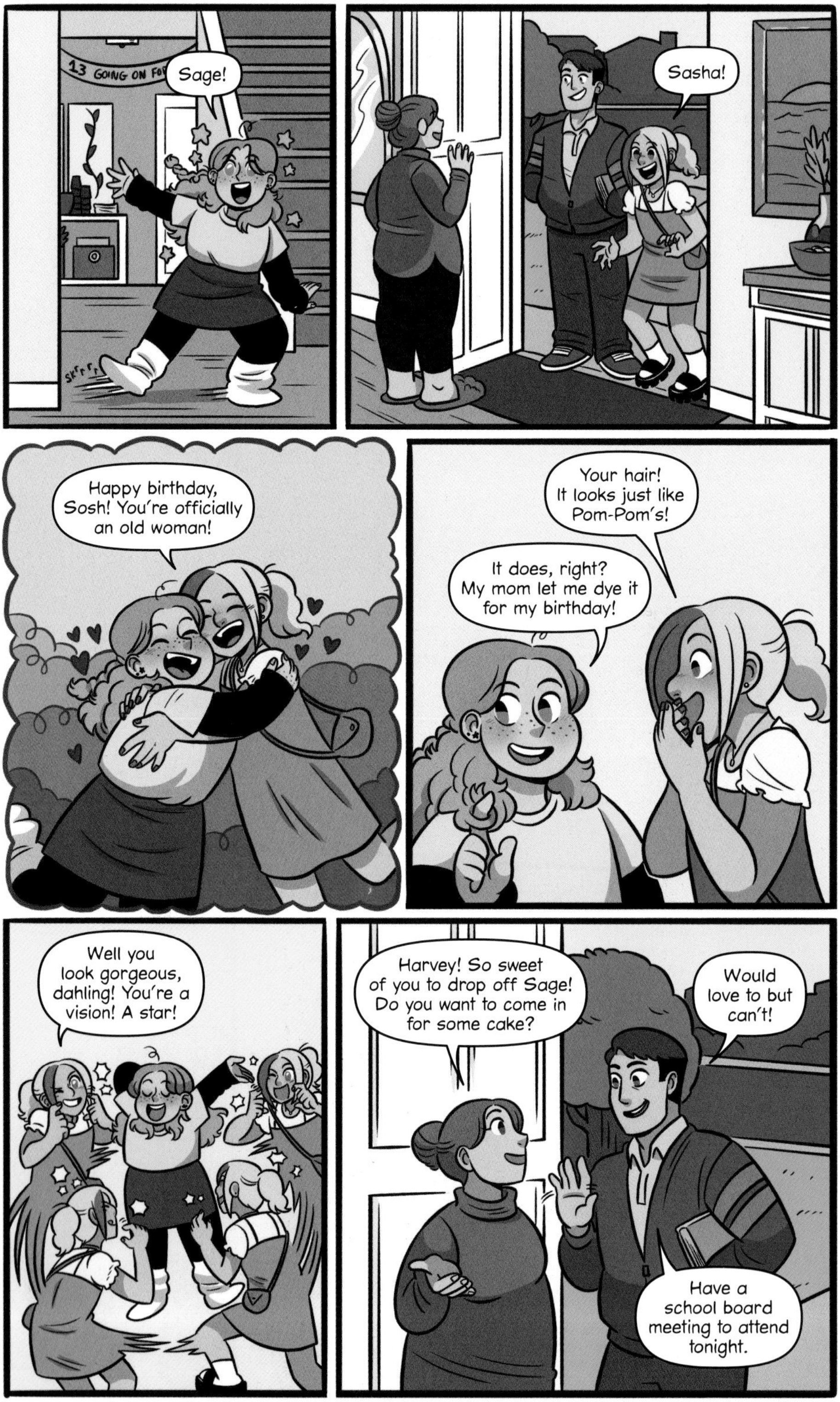
13 GOING ON FO
Sage!
SKrrr
Sasha!
Happy birthday, Sosh! You're officially an old woman!
Your hair! It looks just like Pom-Pom's!
It does, right? My mom let me dye it for my birthday!
Well you look gorgeous, dahling! You're a vision! A star!
Harvey! So sweet of you to drop off Sage! Do you want to come in for some cake?
Would love to but can't!
Have a school board meeting to attend tonight.

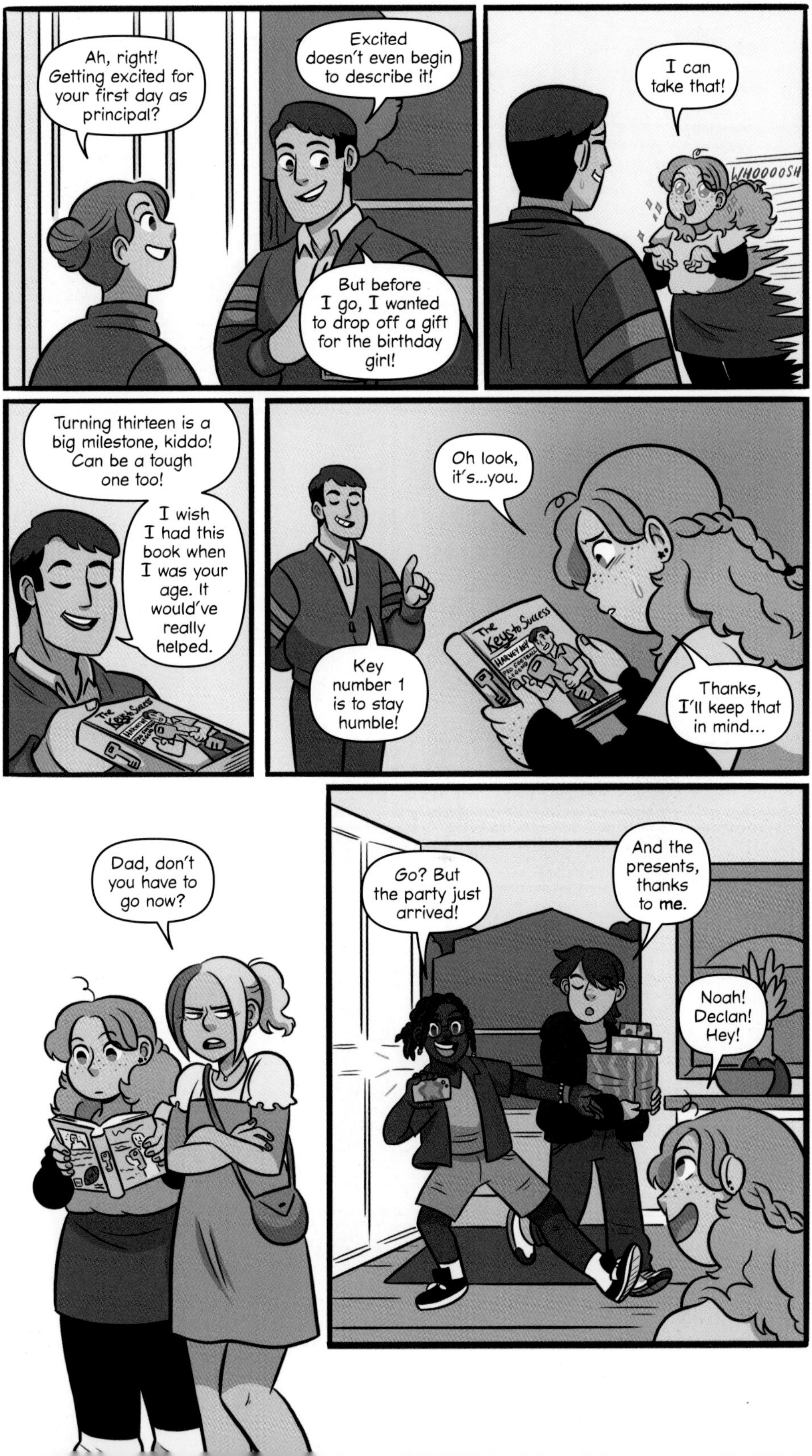
Ah, right! Getting excited for your first day as principal?
Excited doesn't even begin to describe it!
But before I go, I wanted to drop off a gift for the birthday girl!
I can take that!
WHOOOOSH
Turning thirteen is a big milestone, kiddo! Can be a tough one too!
I wish I had this book when I was your age. It would've really helped.
Oh look, it's...you.
Key number 1 is to stay humble!
Thanks, I'll keep that in mind...
Dad, don't you have to go now?
Go? But the party just arrived!
And the presents, thanks to **me**.
Noah! Declan! Hey!

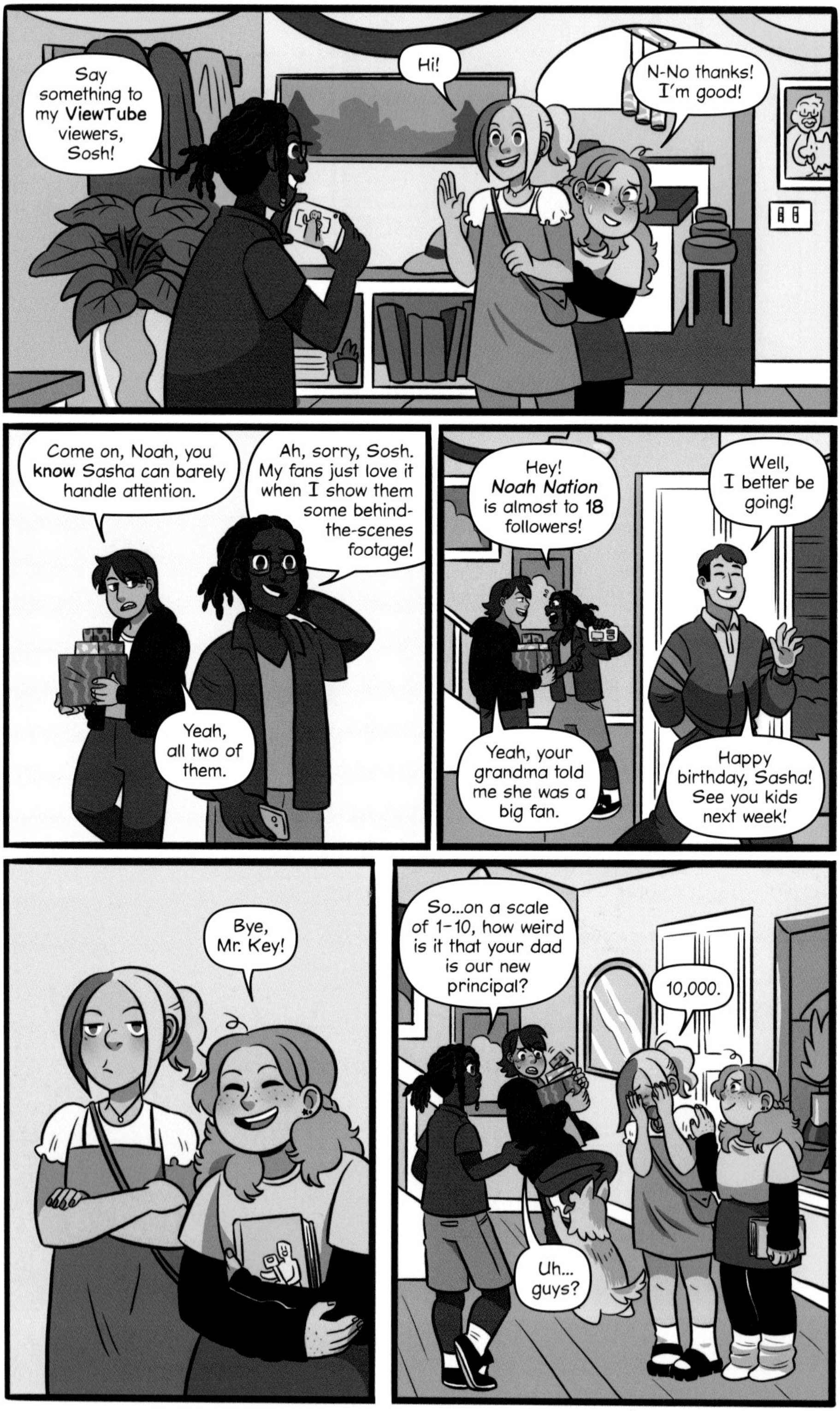
Say something to my ViewTube viewers, Sosh!
Hi!
N-No thanks! I'm good!
Come on, Noah, you know Sasha can barely handle attention.
Ah, sorry, Sosh. My fans just love it when I show them some behind-the-scenes footage!
Yeah, all two of them.
Hey! Noah Nation is almost to 18 followers!
Yeah, your grandma told me she was a big fan.
Well, I better be going!
Happy birthday, Sasha! See you kids next week!
Bye, Mr. Key!
So...on a scale of 1-10, how weird is it that your dad is our new principal?
10,000.
Uh... guys?

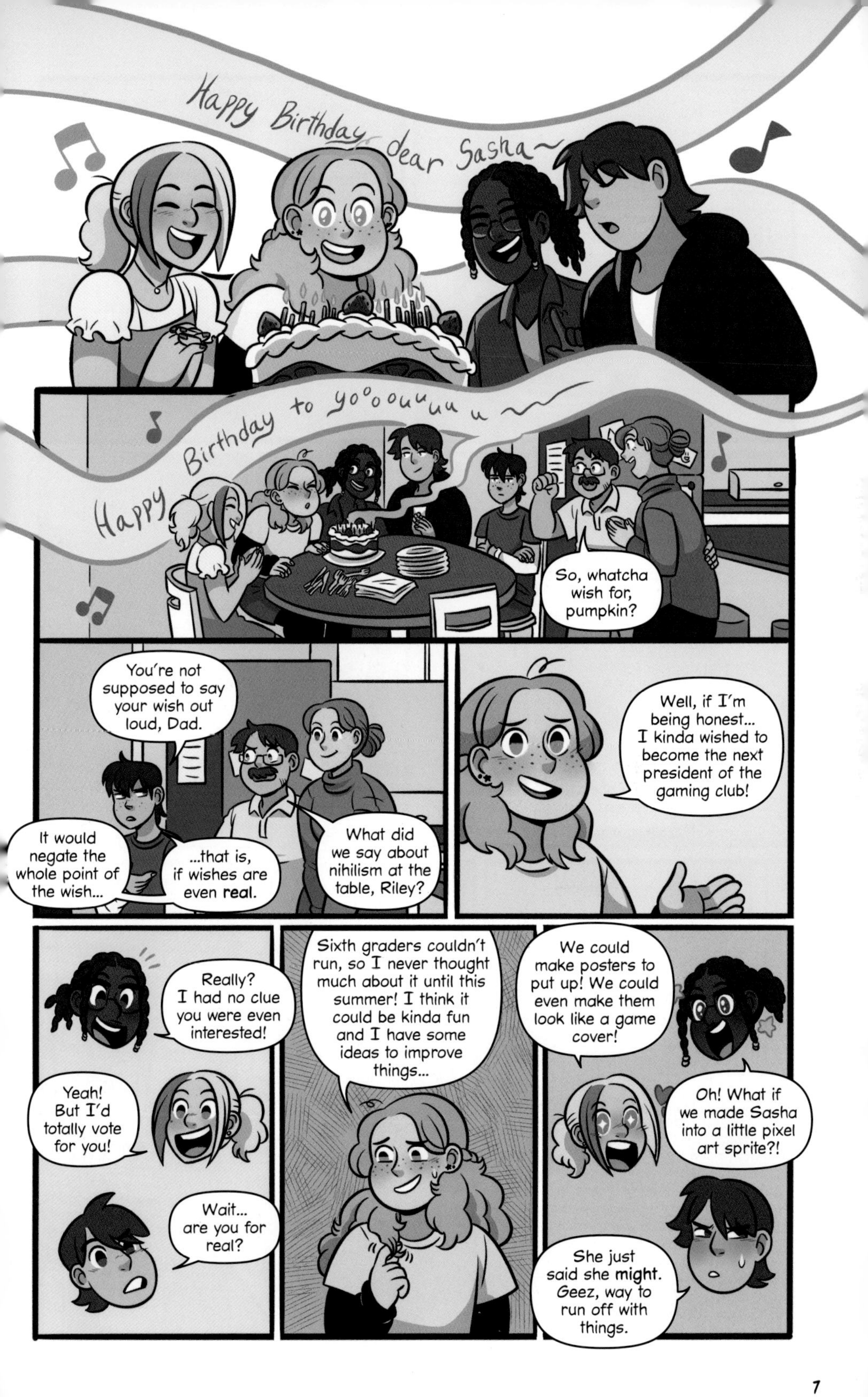
Happy Birthday dear Sasha~
Happy Birthday to yoooouuuu u ~~
So, whatcha wish for, pumpkin?
You're not supposed to say your wish out loud, Dad.
It would negate the whole point of the wish...
...that is, if wishes are even real.
What did we say about nihilism at the table, Riley?
Well, if I'm being honest... I kinda wished to become the next president of the gaming club!
Really? I had no clue you were even interested!
Yeah! But I'd totally vote for you!
Wait... are you for real?
Sixth graders couldn't run, so I never thought much about it until this summer! I think it could be kinda fun and I have some ideas to improve things...
We could make posters to put up! We could even make them look like a game cover!
Oh! What if we made Sasha into a little pixel art sprite?!
She just said she might. Geez, way to run off with things.

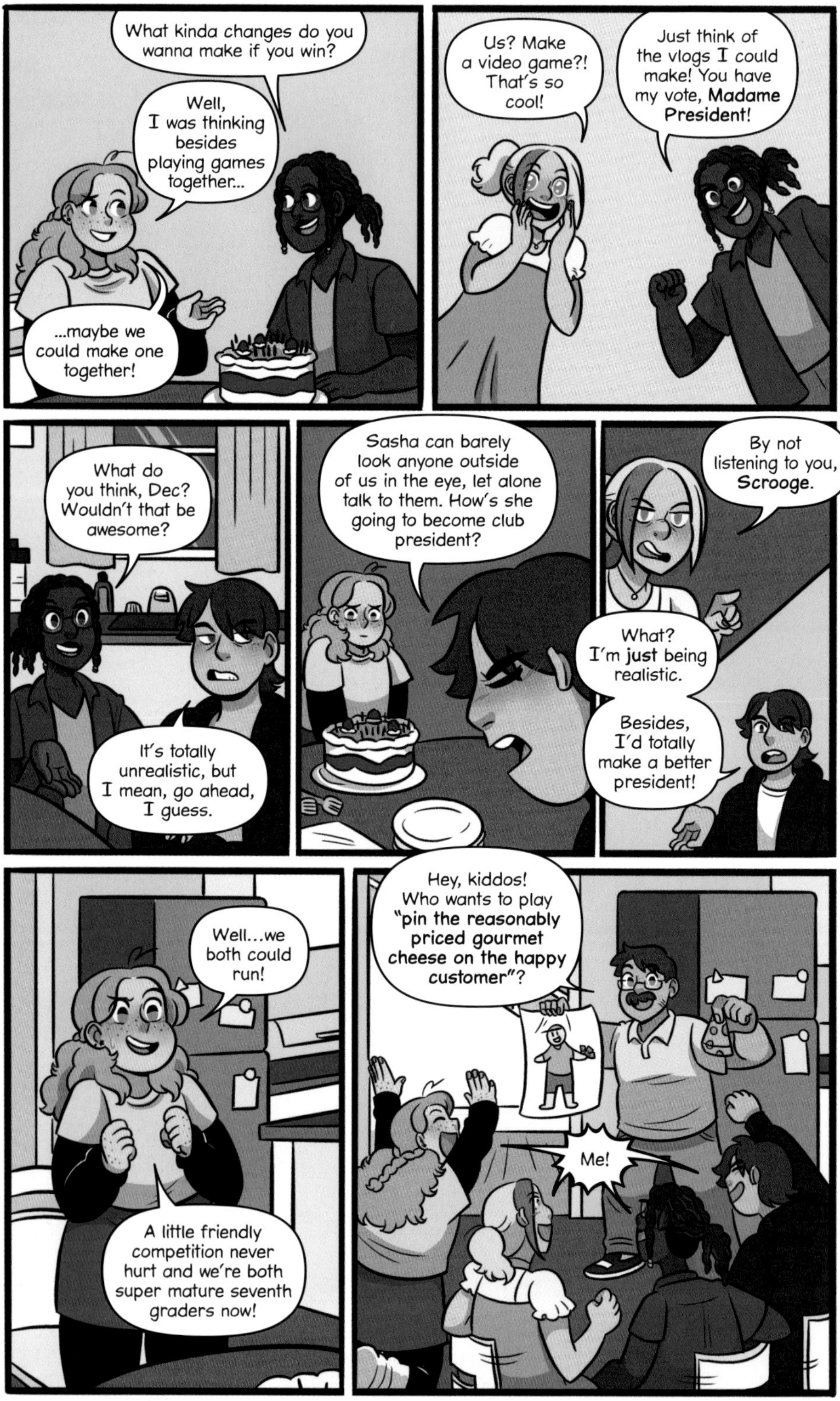
What kinda changes do you wanna make if you win?
Well, I was thinking besides playing games together...
...maybe we could make one together!
Us? Make a video game?! That's so cool!
Just think of the vlogs I could make! You have my vote, **Madame President**!
What do you think, Dec? Wouldn't that be awesome?
It's totally unrealistic, but I mean, go ahead, I guess.
Sasha can barely look anyone outside of us in the eye, let alone talk to them. How's she going to become club president?
By not listening to you, **Scrooge**.
What? I'm **just** being realistic.
Besides, I'd totally make a better president!
Well...we both could run!
A little friendly competition never hurt and we're both super mature seventh graders now!
Hey, kiddos! Who wants to play **"pin the reasonably priced gourmet cheese on the happy customer"**?
Me!

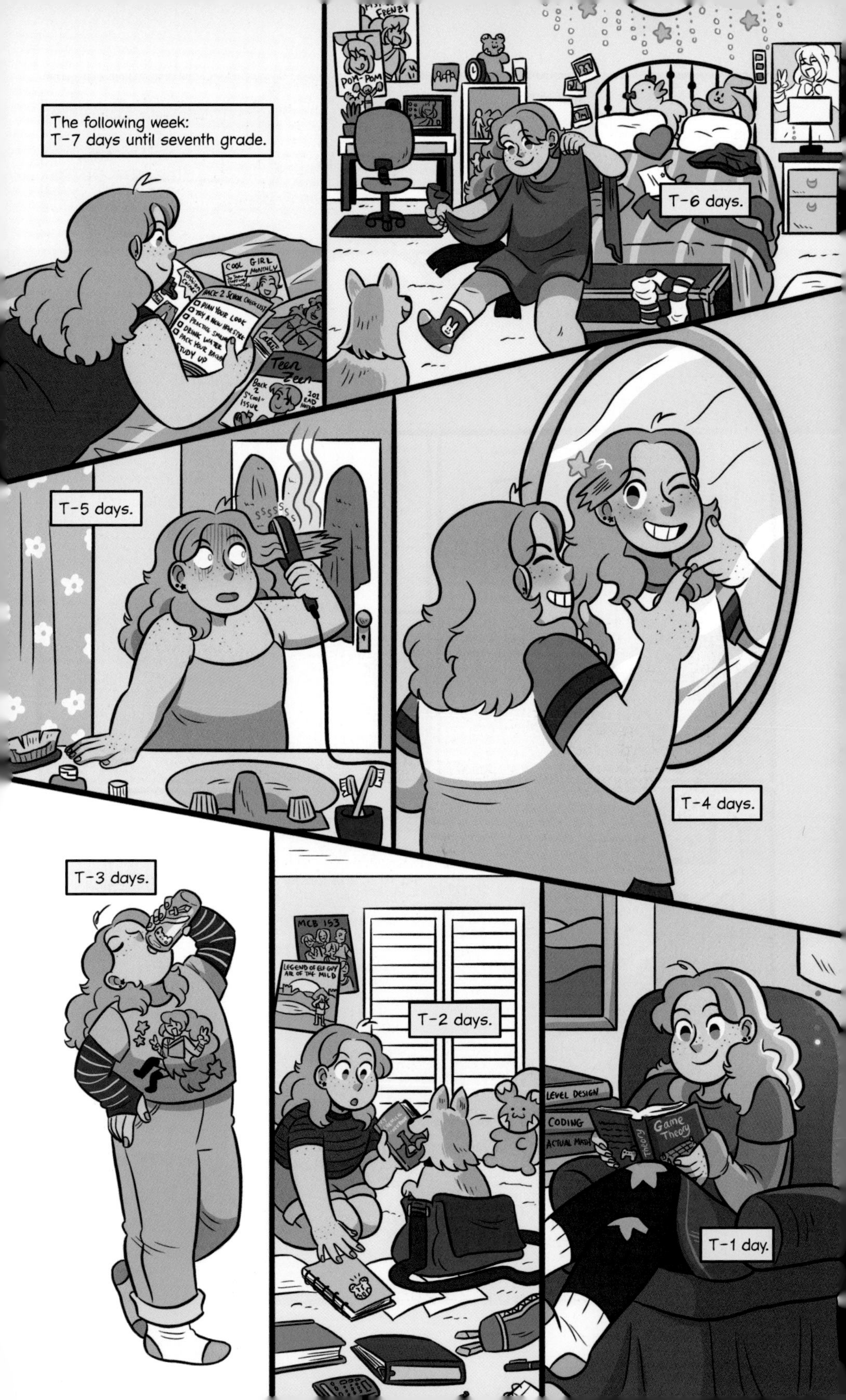
The following week:
T-7 days until seventh grade.
COOL GIRL MONTHLY
BACK 2 SCHOOL CHECKLIST
PLAN YOUR LOOK
TRY A NEW HAIRSTYLE
PRACTICE SMILING
DRINK WATER
PACK YOUR BAG
STUDY UP
Teen Zeen
POM-POM
T-6 days.
T-5 days.
SSSSSS
T-4 days.
T-3 days.
MCB 153
LEGEND OF ELF GUY AIR OF THE MILD
T-2 days.
LEVEL DESIGN
CODING
ACTUAL MATH
Game Theory
T-1 day.

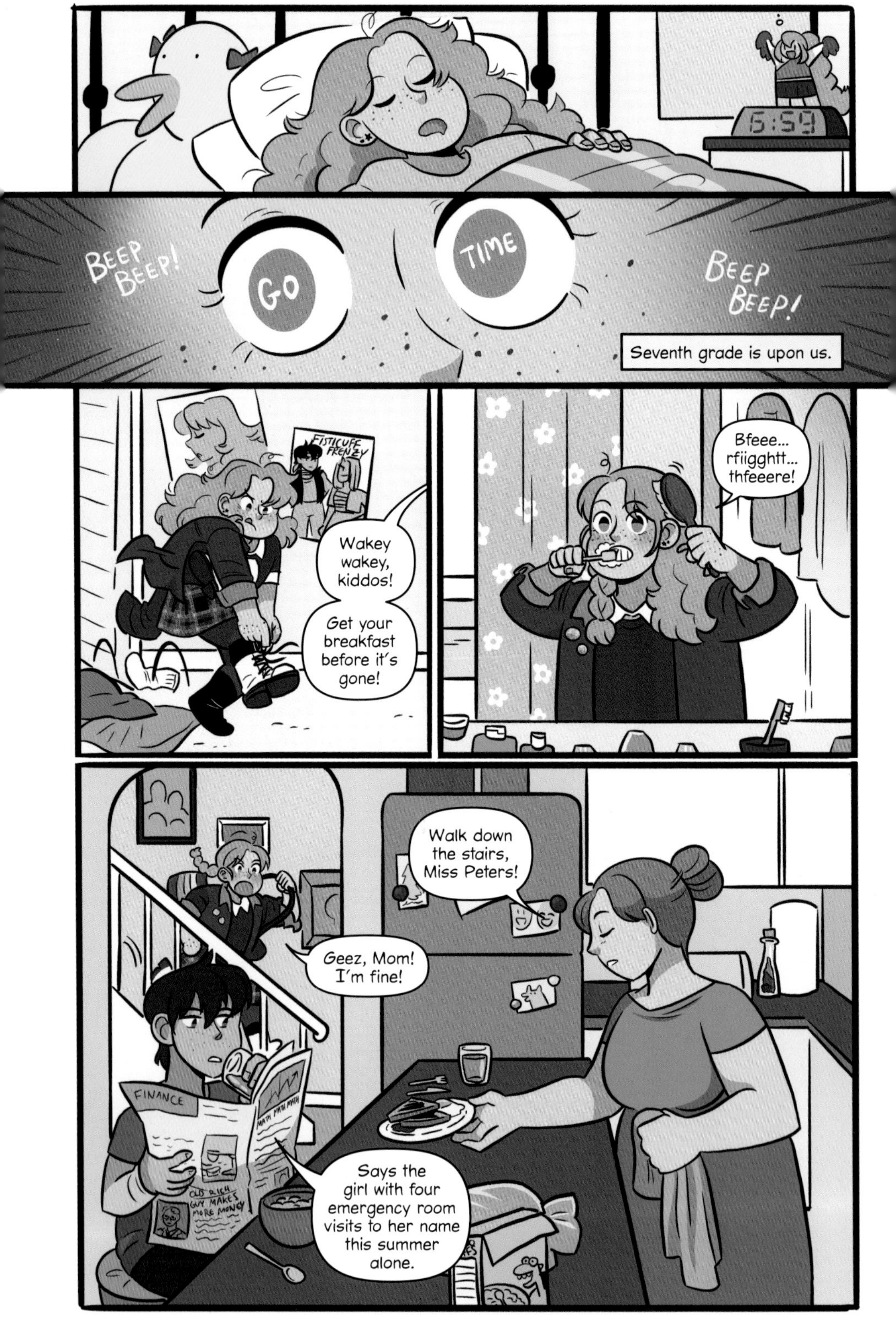
5:59
BEEP BEEP!
GO
TIME
BEEP BEEP!
Seventh grade is upon us.
FISTICUFF FRENZY
Wakey wakey, kiddos!
Get your breakfast before it's gone!
Bfeee... rfiigghtt... thfeeere!
Walk down the stairs, Miss Peters!
Geez, Mom! I'm fine!
FINANCE
MATH MATH MATH
OLD RICH GUY MAKES MORE MONEY
Says the girl with four emergency room visits to her name this summer alone.

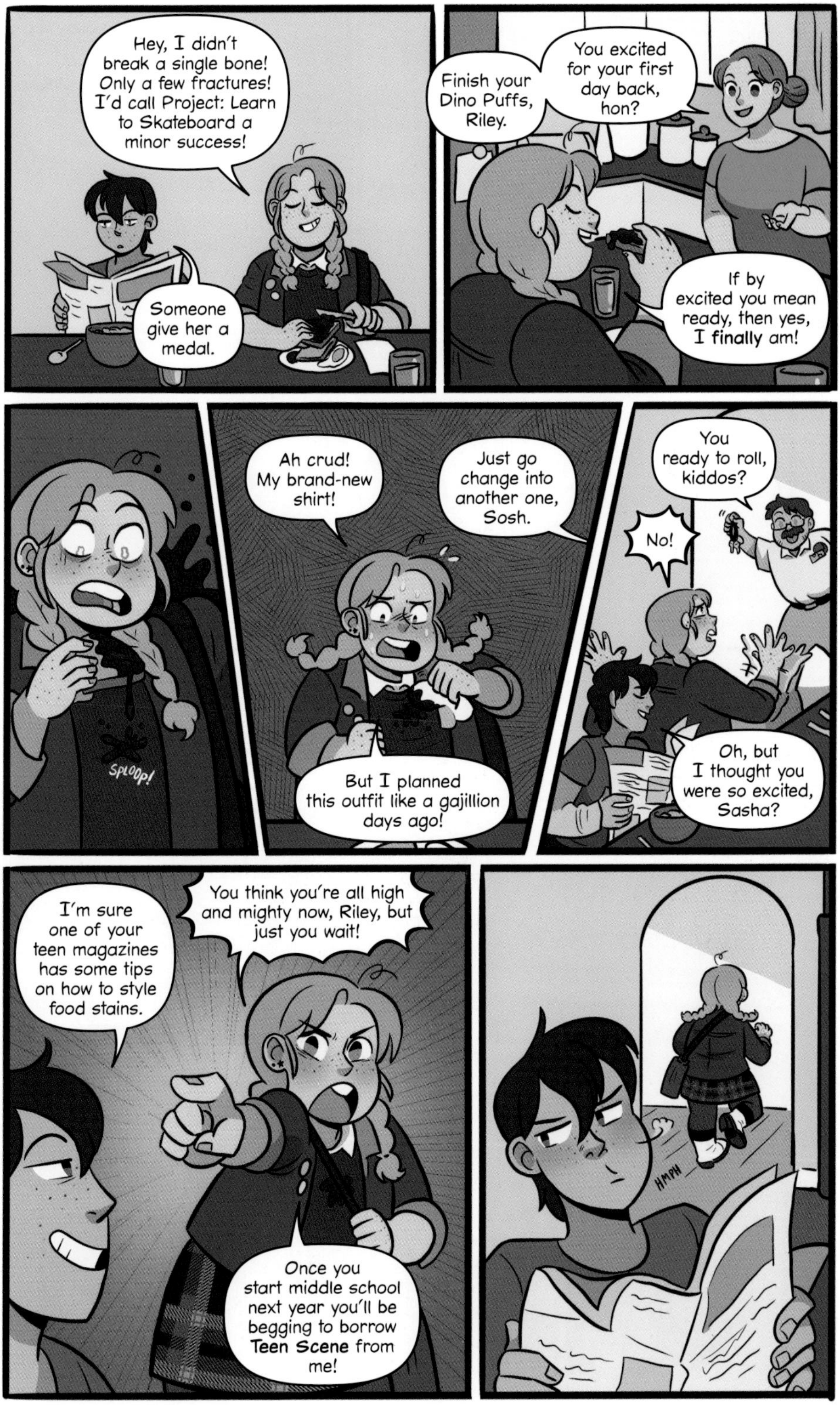
Hey, I didn't break a single bone! Only a few fractures! I'd call Project: Learn to Skateboard a minor success!
Someone give her a medal.
Finish your Dino Puffs, Riley.
You excited for your first day back, hon?
If by excited you mean ready, then yes, I **finally** am!
SPLOOP!
Ah crud! My brand-new shirt!
Just go change into another one, Sosh.
But I planned this outfit like a gajillion days ago!
You ready to roll, kiddos?
No!
Oh, but I thought you were so excited, Sasha?
I'm sure one of your teen magazines has some tips on how to style food stains.
You think you're all high and mighty now, Riley, but just you wait!
Once you start middle school next year you'll be begging to borrow **Teen Scene** from me!
HMPH

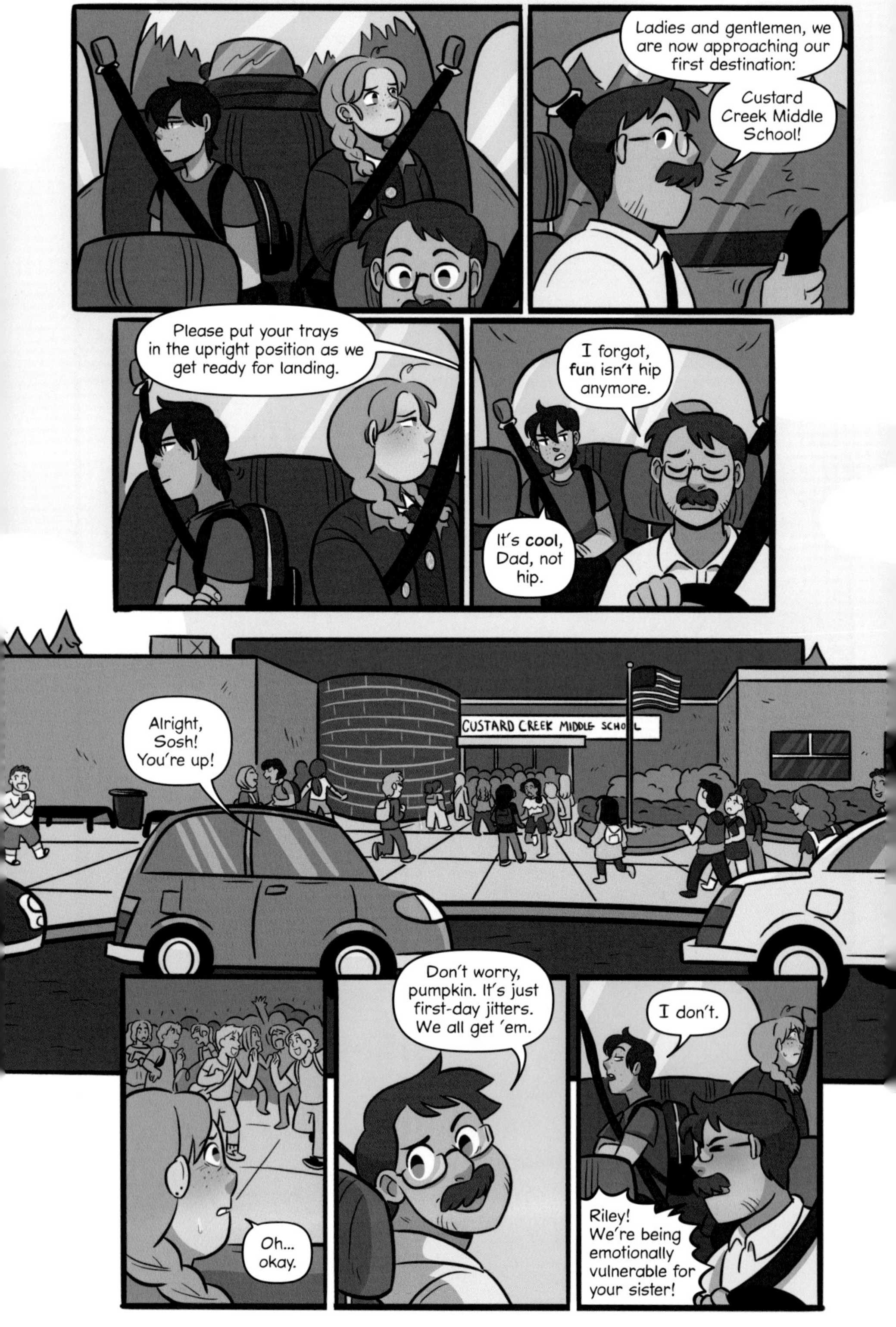

Ladies and gentlemen, we are now approaching our first destination:
Custard Creek Middle School!
Please put your trays in the upright position as we get ready for landing.
I forgot, **fun** isn't hip anymore.
It's **cool**, Dad, not hip.
CUSTARD CREEK MIDDLE SCHOOL
Alright, Sosh! You're up!
Oh... okay.
Don't worry, pumpkin. It's just first-day jitters. We all get 'em.
I don't.
Riley! We're being emotionally vulnerable for your sister!

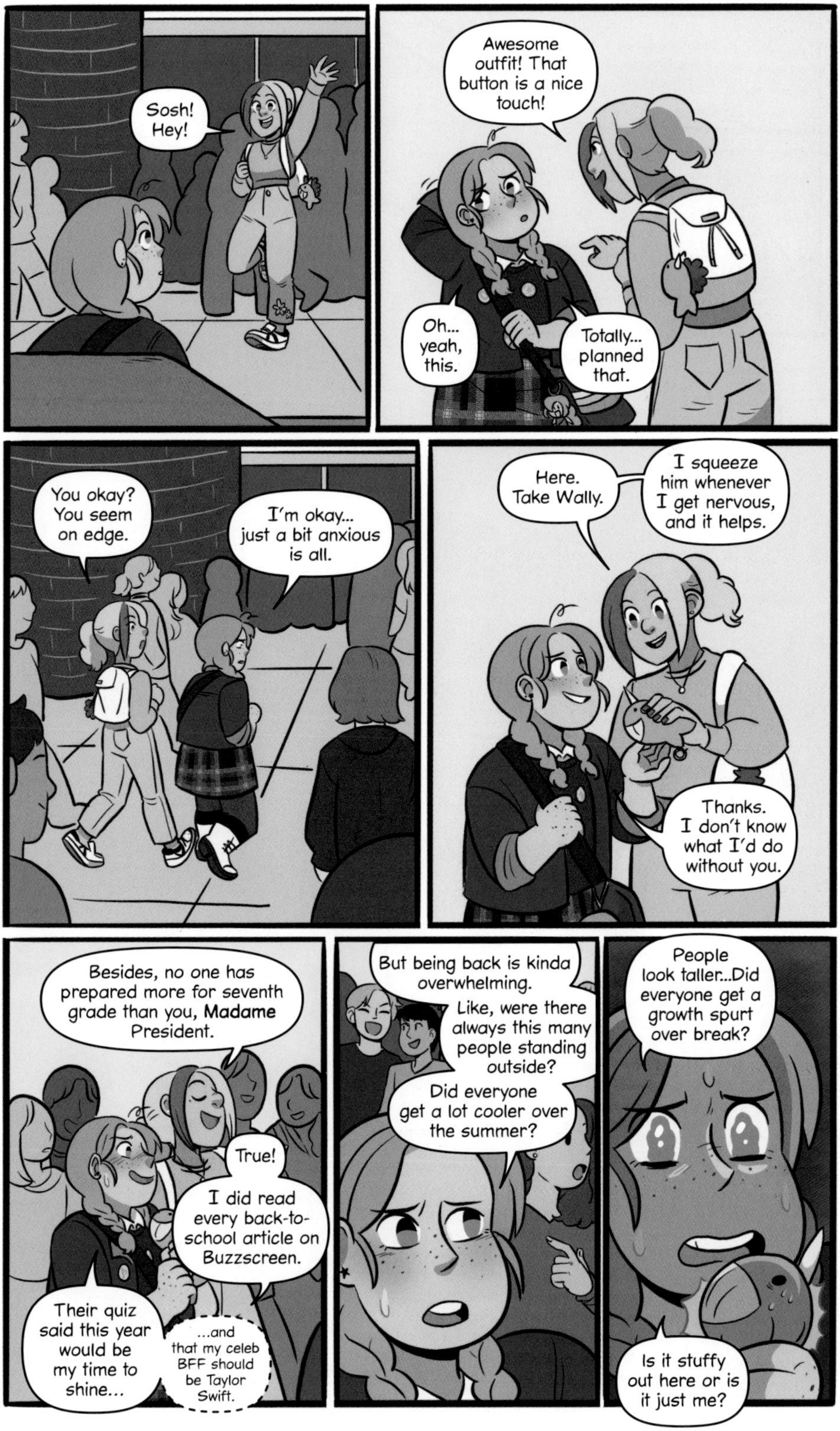
Sosh! Hey!
Awesome outfit! That button is a nice touch!
Oh... yeah, this.
Totally... planned that.
You okay? You seem on edge.
I'm okay... just a bit anxious is all.
Here. Take Wally.
I squeeze him whenever I get nervous, and it helps.
Thanks. I don't know what I'd do without you.
Besides, no one has prepared more for seventh grade than you, **Madame** President.
True!
I did read every back-to-school article on Buzzscreen.
Their quiz said this year would be my time to shine...
...and that my celeb BFF should be Taylor Swift.
But being back is kinda overwhelming.
Like, were there always this many people standing outside?
Did everyone get a lot cooler over the summer?
People look taller...Did everyone get a growth spurt over break?
Is it stuffy out here or is it just me?

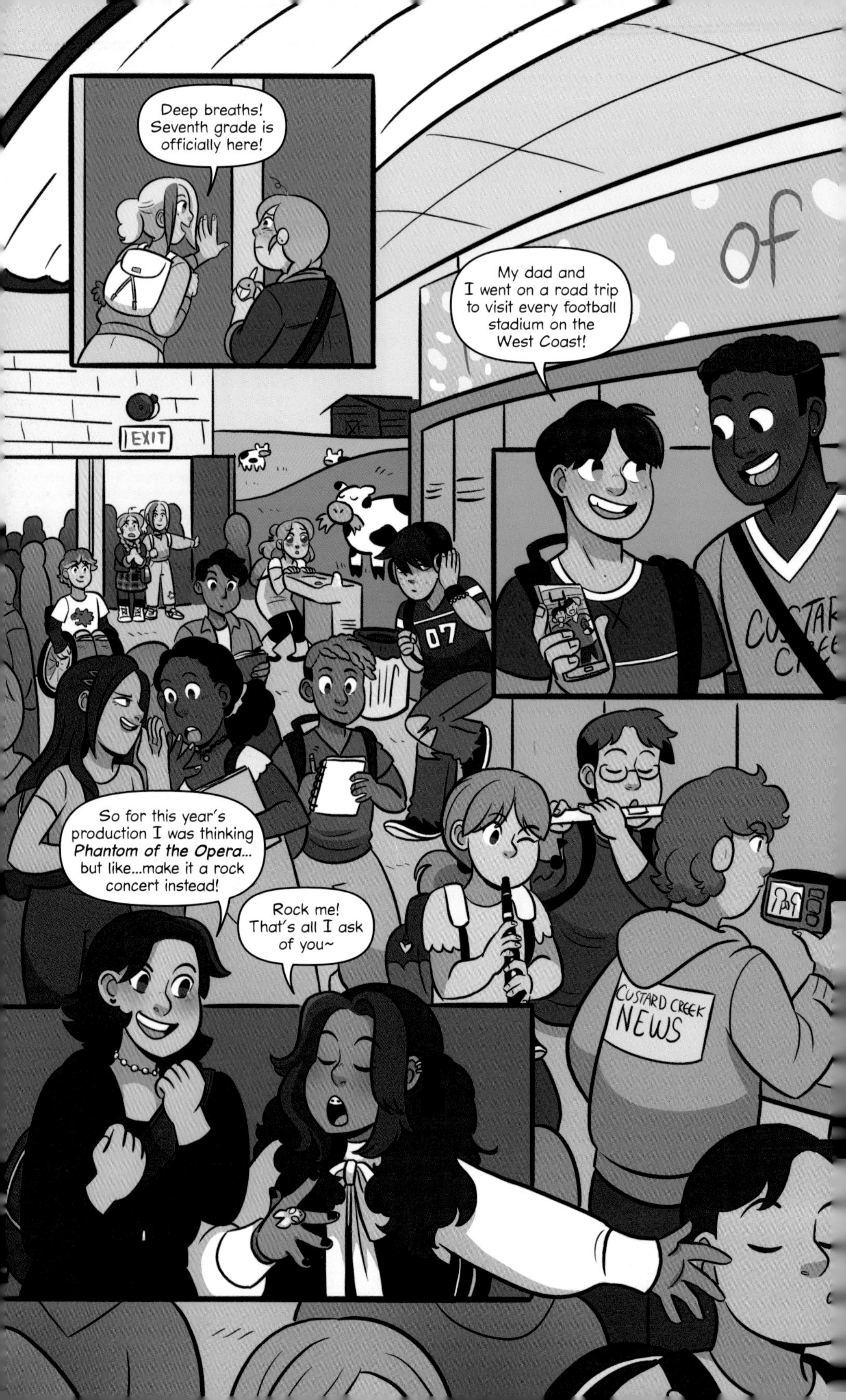
Deep breaths! Seventh grade is officially here!
EXIT
My dad and I went on a road trip to visit every football stadium on the West Coast!
07
So for this year's production I was thinking *Phantom of the Opera*... but like...make it a rock concert instead!
Rock me! That's all I ask of you~
CUSTARD CREEK NEWS

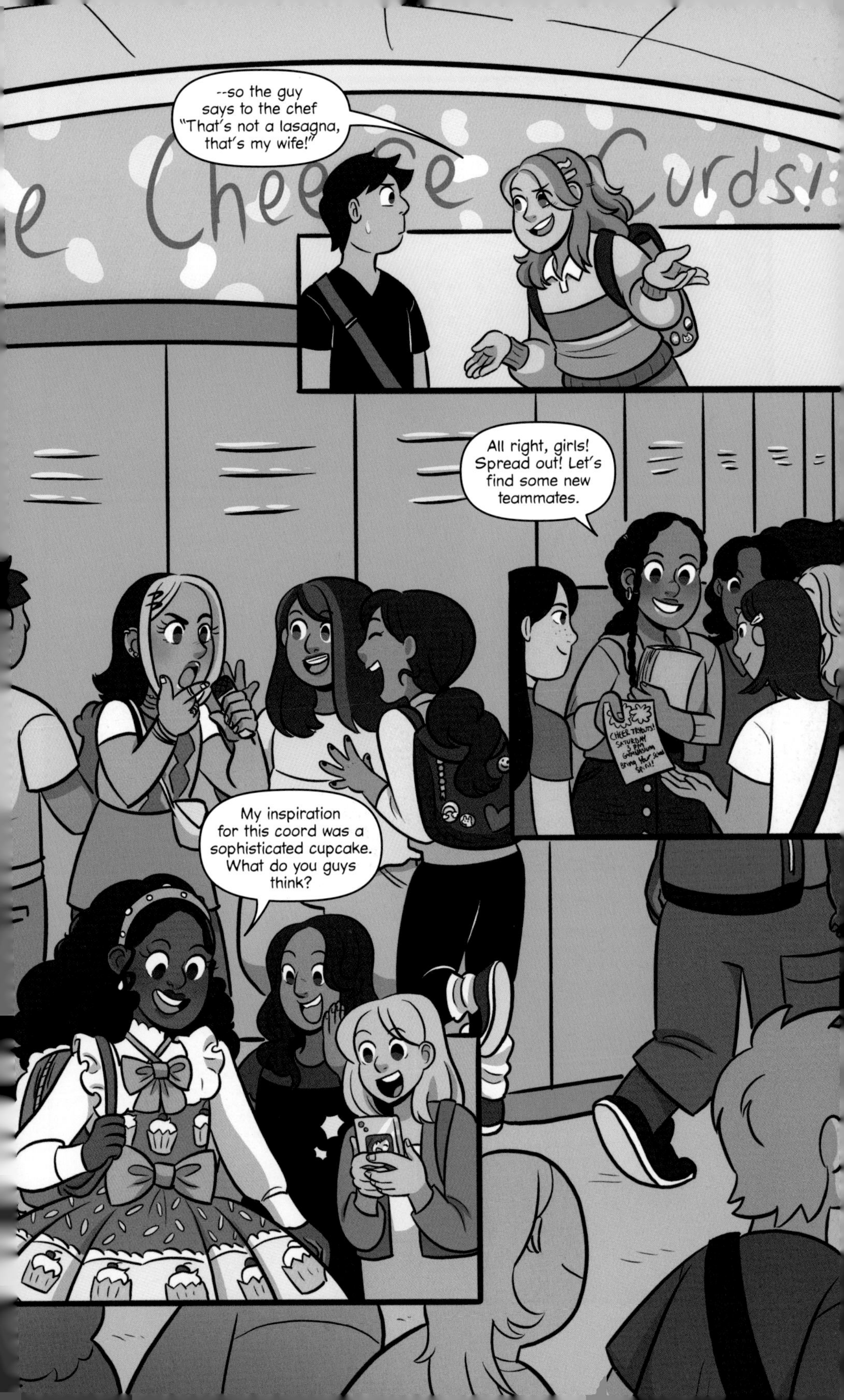

--so the guy says to the chef "That's not a lasagna, that's my wife!"
All right, girls! Spread out! Let's find some new teammates.
CHEER TRYOUTS! SATURDAY 3 PM
My inspiration for this coord was a sophisticated cupcake. What do you guys think?

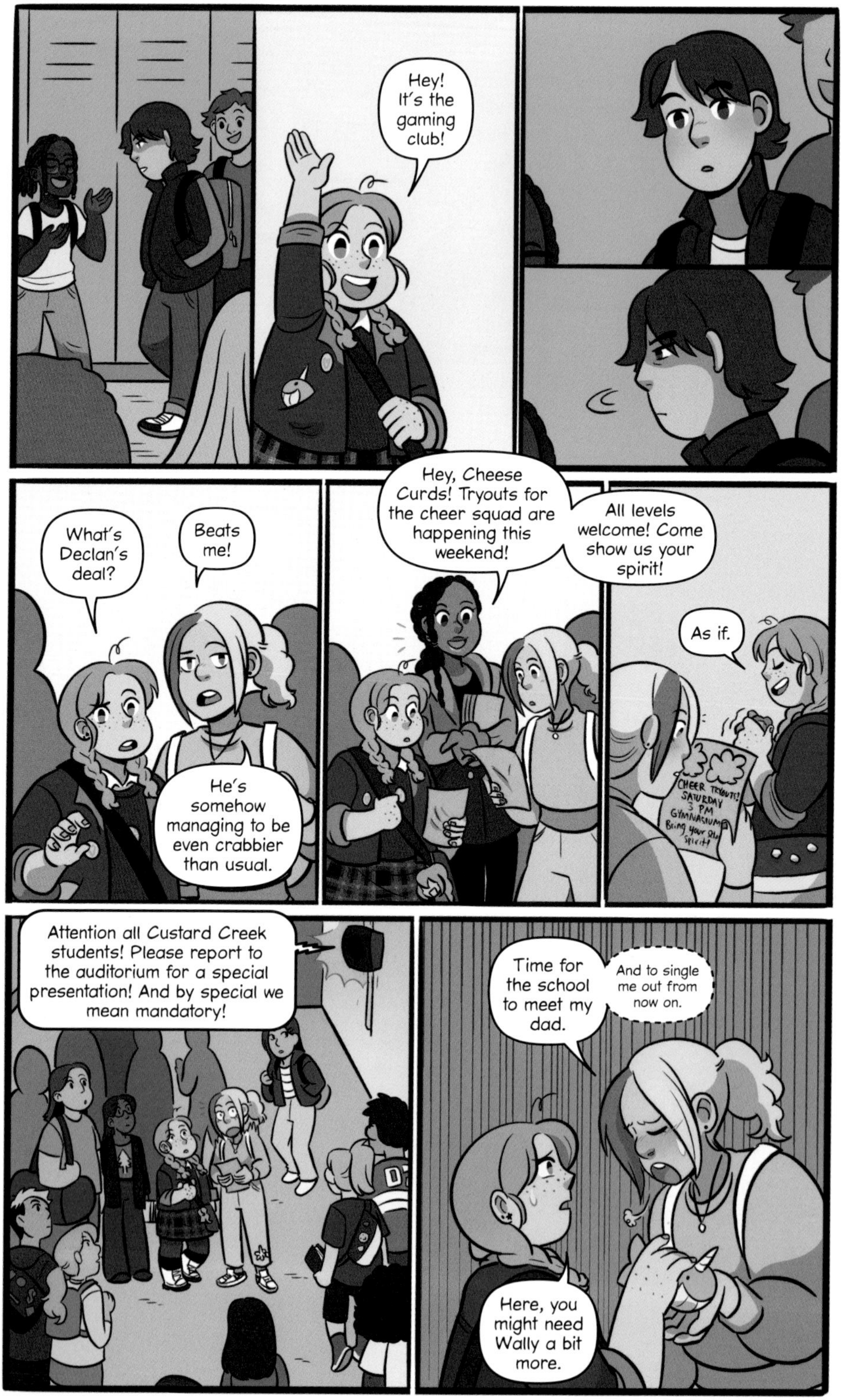
Hey! It's the gaming club!
What's Declan's deal?
Beats me!
He's somehow managing to be even crabbier than usual.
Hey, Cheese Curds! Tryouts for the cheer squad are happening this weekend!
All levels welcome! Come show us your spirit!
As if.
CHEER TRYOUTS! SATURDAY 3 PM GYMNASIUM
Attention all Custard Creek students! Please report to the auditorium for a special presentation! And by special we mean mandatory!
Time for the school to meet my dad.
And to single me out from now on.
Here, you might need Wally a bit more.

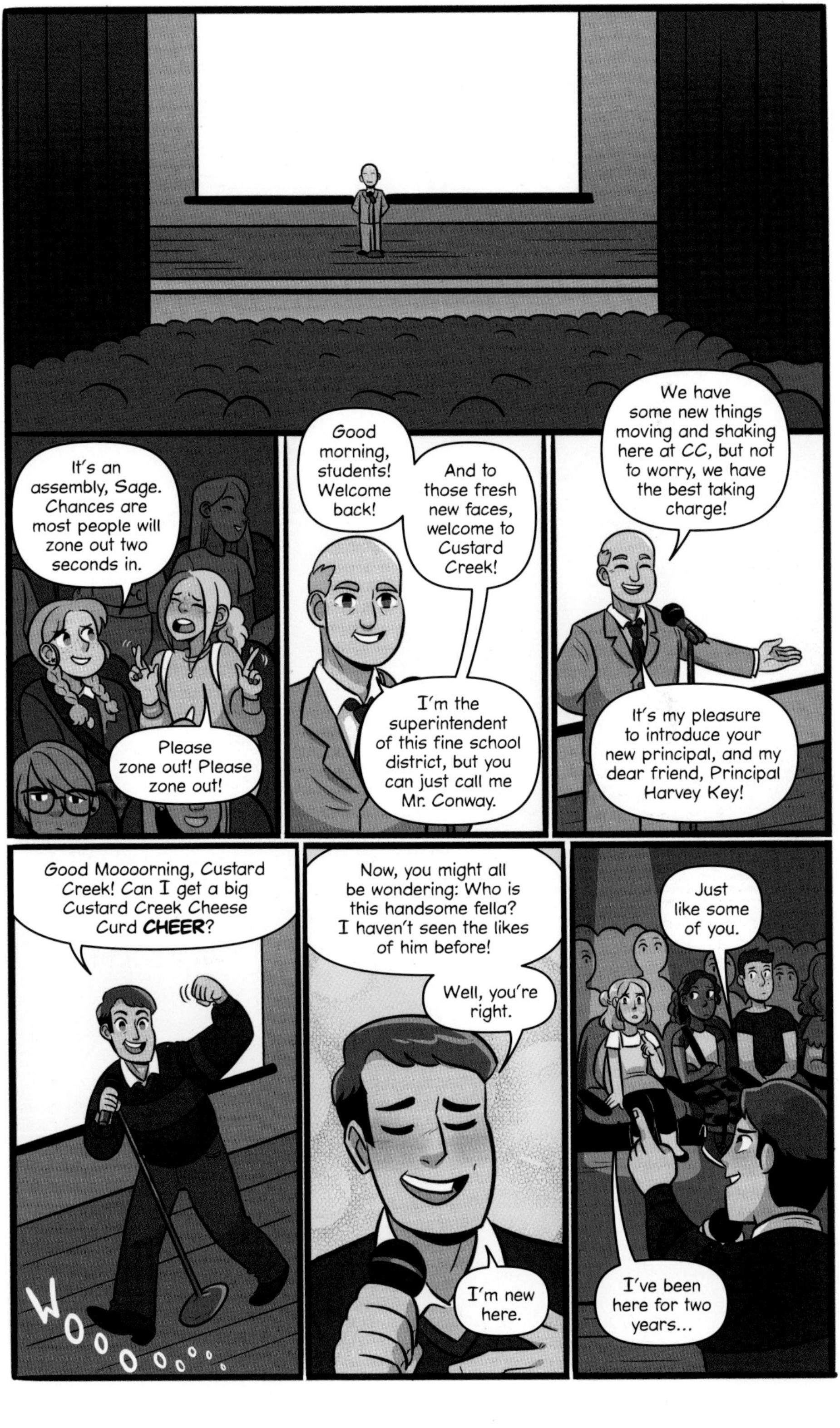
It's an assembly, Sage. Chances are most people will zone out two seconds in.
Please zone out! Please zone out!
Good morning, students! Welcome back!
And to those fresh new faces, welcome to Custard Creek!
I'm the superintendent of this fine school district, but you can just call me Mr. Conway.
We have some new things moving and shaking here at CC, but not to worry, we have the best taking charge!
It's my pleasure to introduce your new principal, and my dear friend, Principal Harvey Key!
Good Moooorning, Custard Creek! Can I get a big Custard Creek Cheese Curd **CHEER**?
Wooooo...
Now, you might all be wondering: Who is this handsome fella? I haven't seen the likes of him before!
Well, you're right.
I'm new here.
Just like some of you.
I've been here for two years...

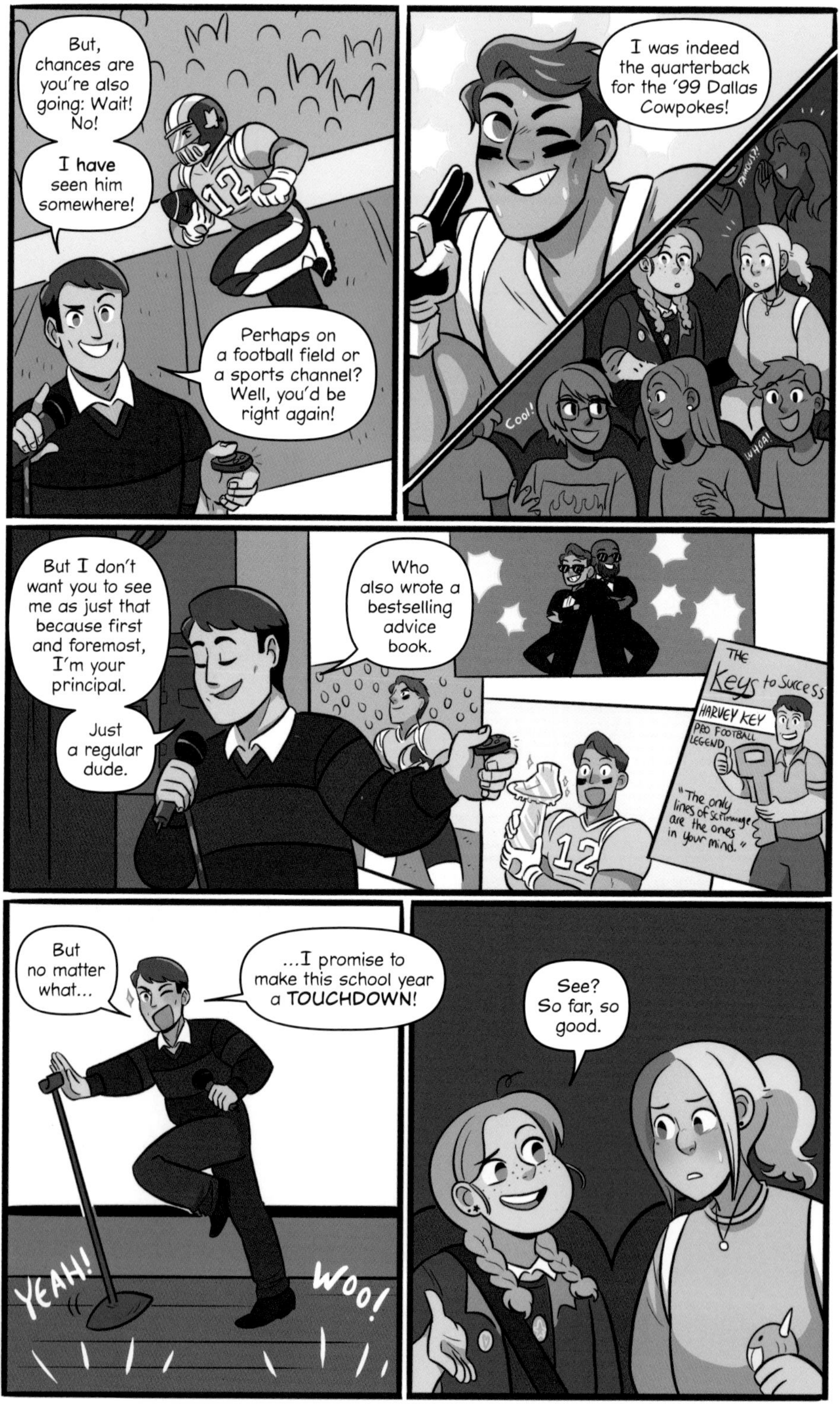
But, chances are you're also going: Wait! No!
I have seen him somewhere!
Perhaps on a football field or a sports channel? Well, you'd be right again!
I was indeed the quarterback for the '99 Dallas Cowpokes!
FAMOUS?!
COOL!
WHOA!
But I don't want you to see me as just that because first and foremost, I'm your principal.
Just a regular dude.
Who also wrote a bestselling advice book.
THE Keys to Success
HARVEY KEY
PRO FOOTBALL LEGEND
"The only lines of scrimmage are the ones in your mind."
But no matter what...
...I promise to make this school year a TOUCHDOWN!
YEAH!
WOO!
See? So far, so good.

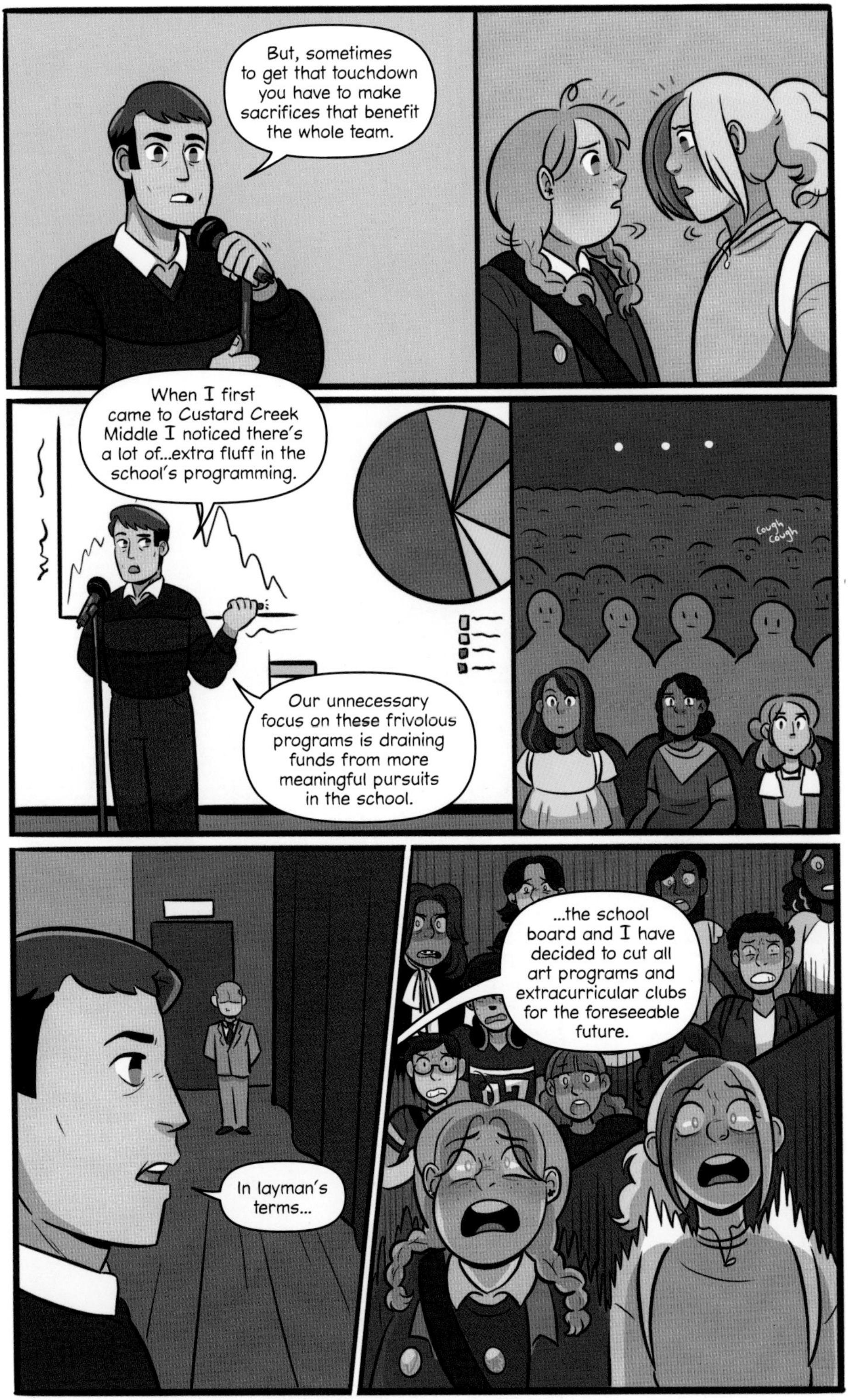
But, sometimes to get that touchdown you have to make sacrifices that benefit the whole team.
When I first came to Custard Creek Middle I noticed there's a lot of...extra fluff in the school's programming.
Our unnecessary focus on these frivolous programs is draining funds from more meaningful pursuits in the school.
cough cough
In layman's terms...
...the school board and I have decided to cut all art programs and extracurricular clubs for the foreseeable future.

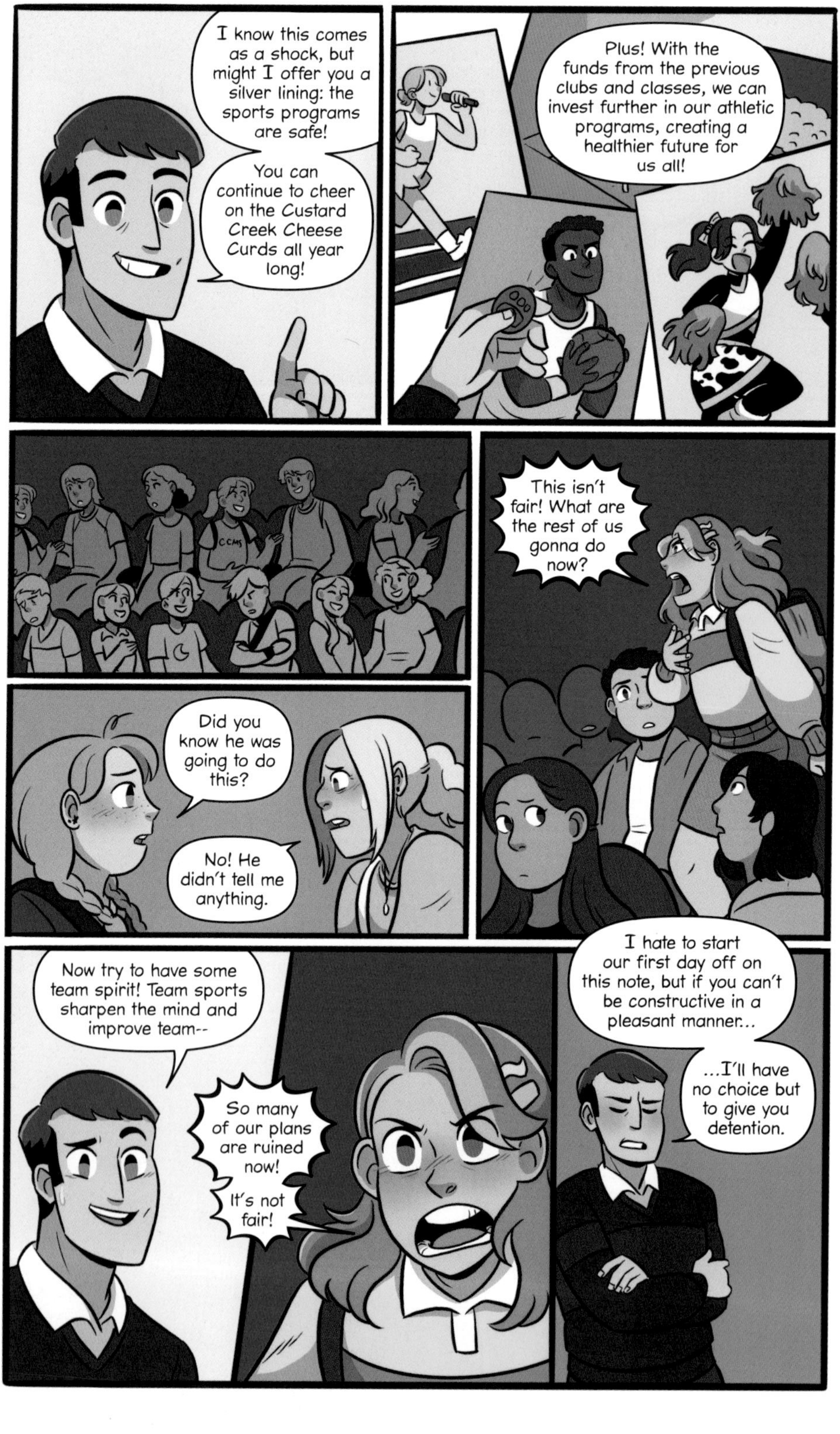
I know this comes as a shock, but might I offer you a silver lining: the sports programs are safe!
You can continue to cheer on the Custard Creek Cheese Curds all year long!
Plus! With the funds from the previous clubs and classes, we can invest further in our athletic programs, creating a healthier future for us all!
CCMS
This isn't fair! What are the rest of us gonna do now?
Did you know he was going to do this?
No! He didn't tell me anything.
Now try to have some team spirit! Team sports sharpen the mind and improve team--
So many of our plans are ruined now!
It's not fair!
I hate to start our first day off on this note, but if you can't be constructive in a pleasant manner...
...I'll have no choice but to give you detention.

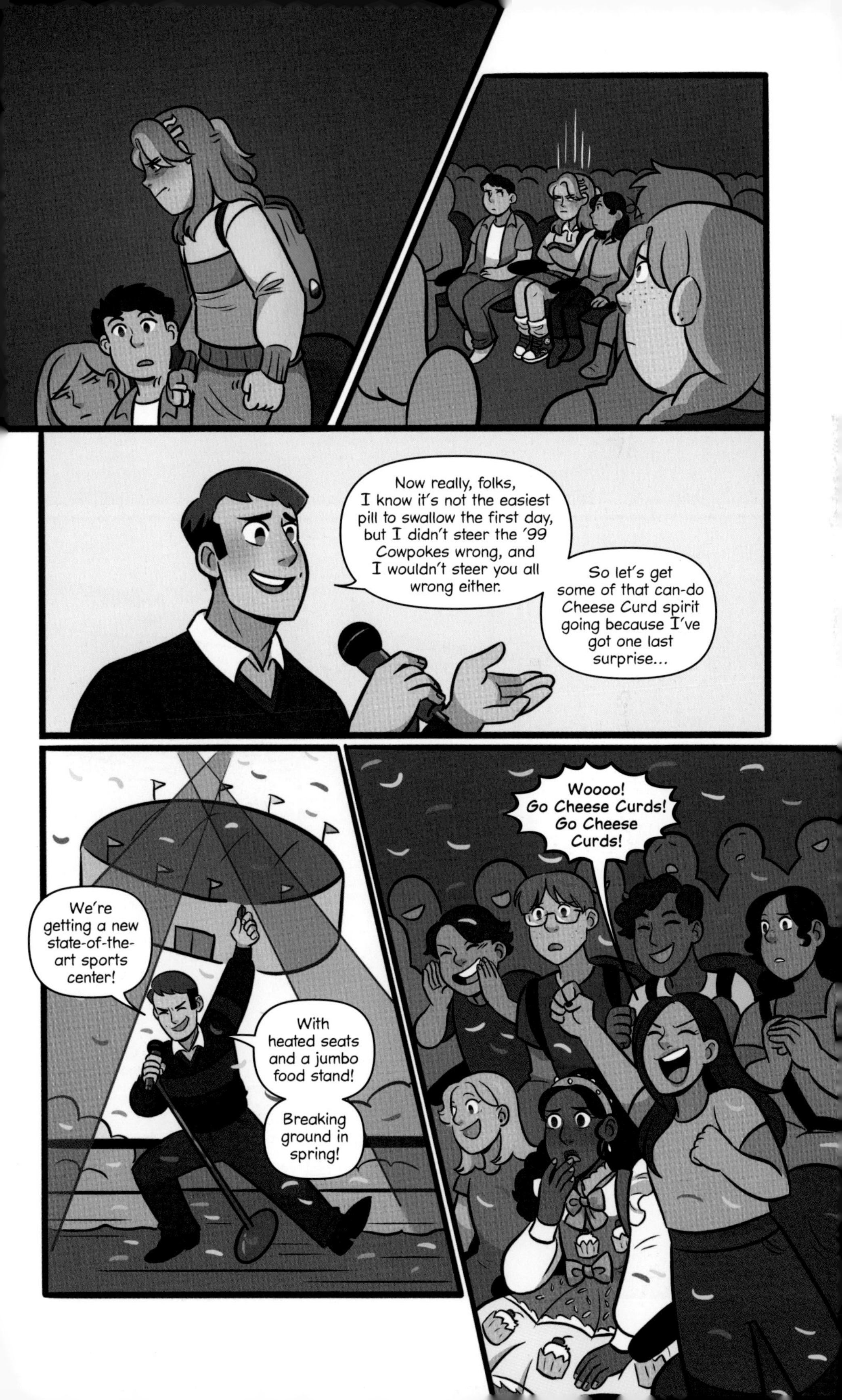
Now really, folks, I know it's not the easiest pill to swallow the first day, but I didn't steer the '99 Cowpokes wrong, and I wouldn't steer you all wrong either.
So let's get some of that can-do Cheese Curd spirit going because I've got one last surprise...
We're getting a new state-of-the-art sports center!
With heated seats and a jumbo food stand!
Breaking ground in spring!
Woooo! Go Cheese Curds! Go Cheese Curds!

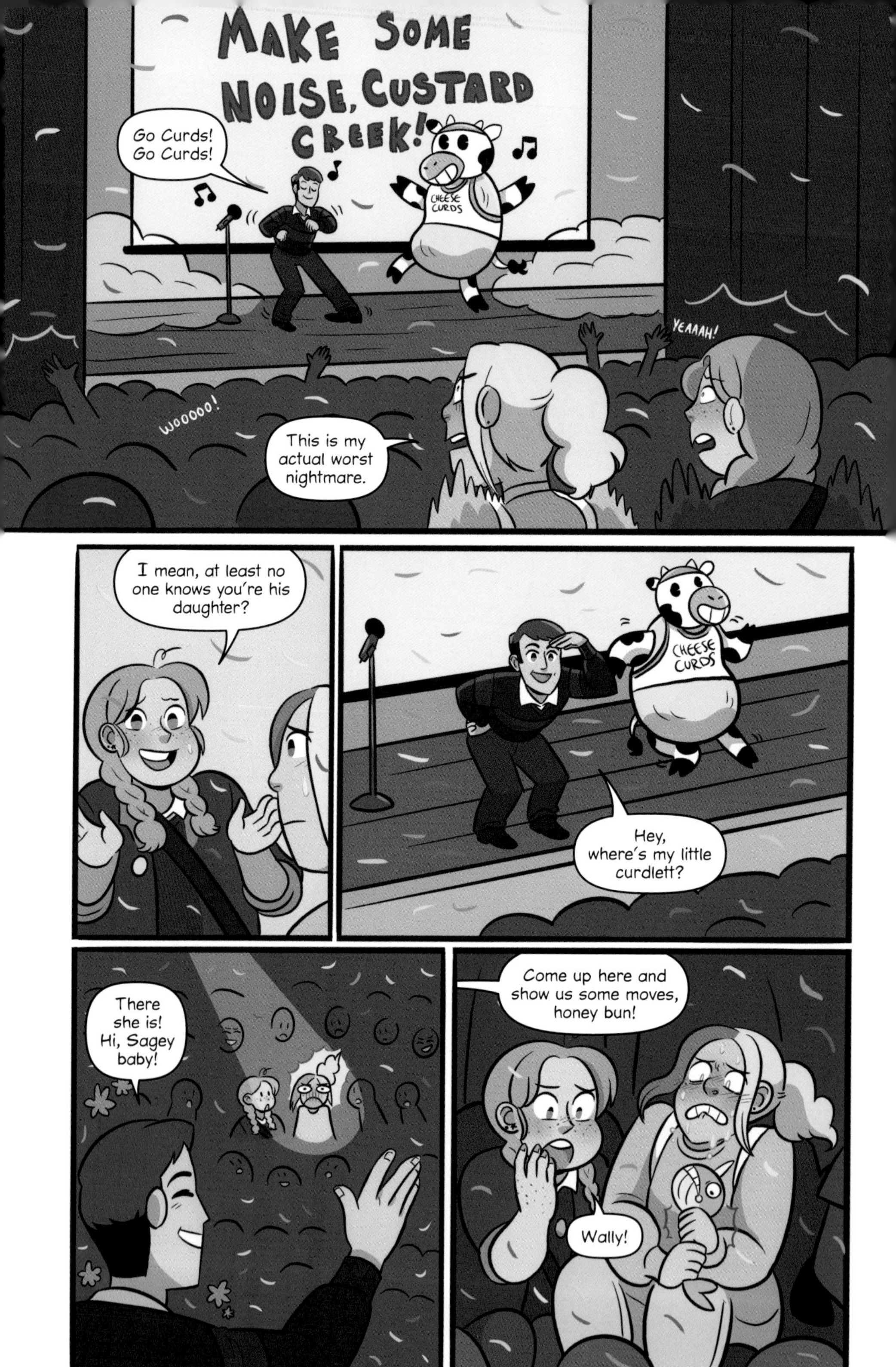
MAKE SOME NOISE, CUSTARD CREEK!
Go Curds! Go Curds!
CHEESE CURDS
YEAAAH!
WOOOOO!
This is my actual worst nightmare.
I mean, at least no one knows you're his daughter?
CHEESE CURDS
Hey, where's my little curdlett?
There she is! Hi, Sagey baby!
Come up here and show us some moves, honey bun!
Wally!

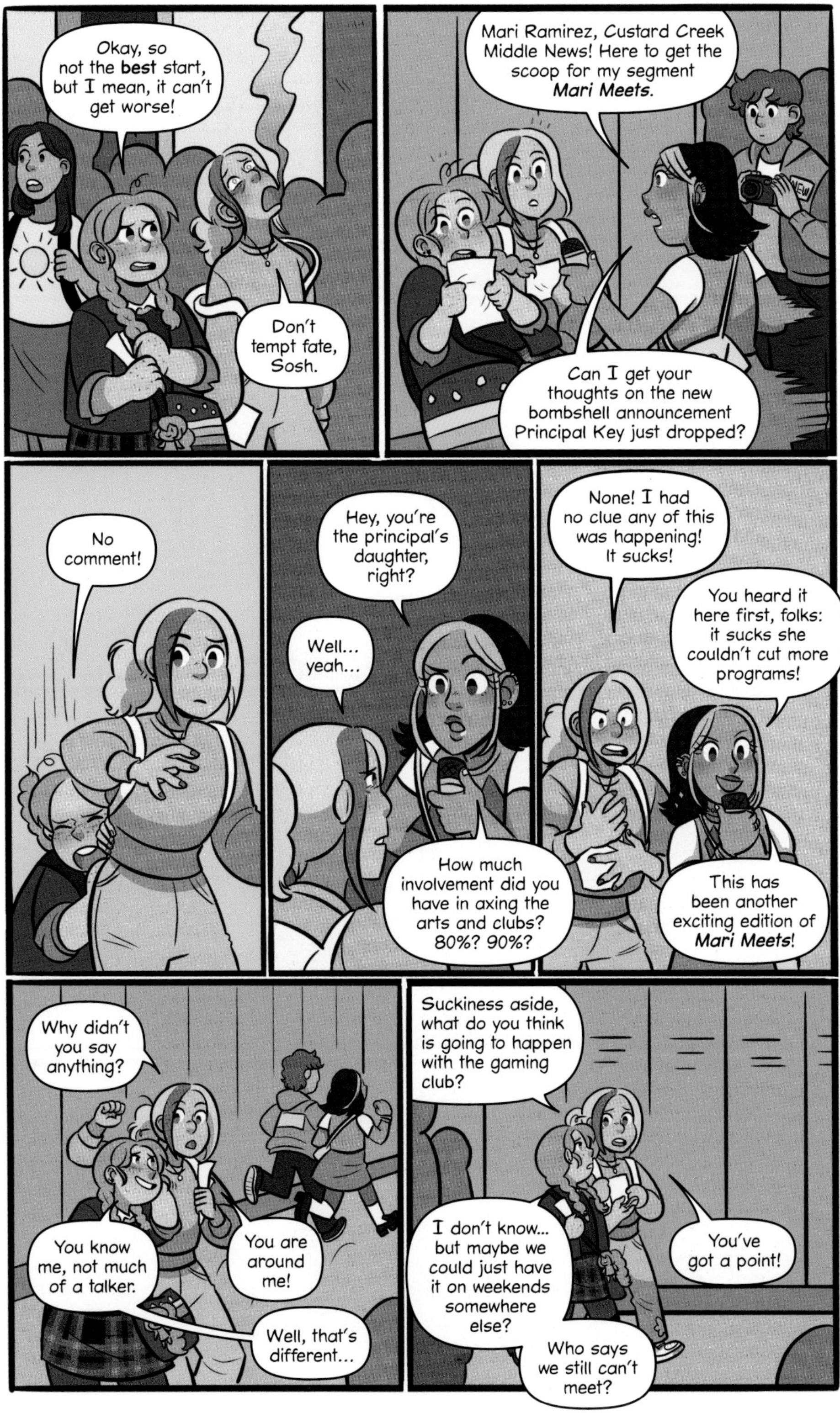
Okay, so not the **best** start, but I mean, it can't get worse!
Don't tempt fate, Sosh.
Mari Ramirez, Custard Creek Middle News! Here to get the scoop for my segment *Mari Meets*.
Can I get your thoughts on the new bombshell announcement Principal Key just dropped?
No comment!
Hey, you're the principal's daughter, right?
Well... yeah...
How much involvement did you have in axing the arts and clubs? 80%? 90%?
None! I had no clue any of this was happening! It sucks!
You heard it here first, folks: it sucks she couldn't cut more programs!
This has been another exciting edition of *Mari Meets*!
Why didn't you say anything?
You know me, not much of a talker.
You are around me!
Well, that's different...
Suckiness aside, what do you think is going to happen with the gaming club?
I don't know... but maybe we could just have it on weekends somewhere else?
Who says we still can't meet?
You've got a point!

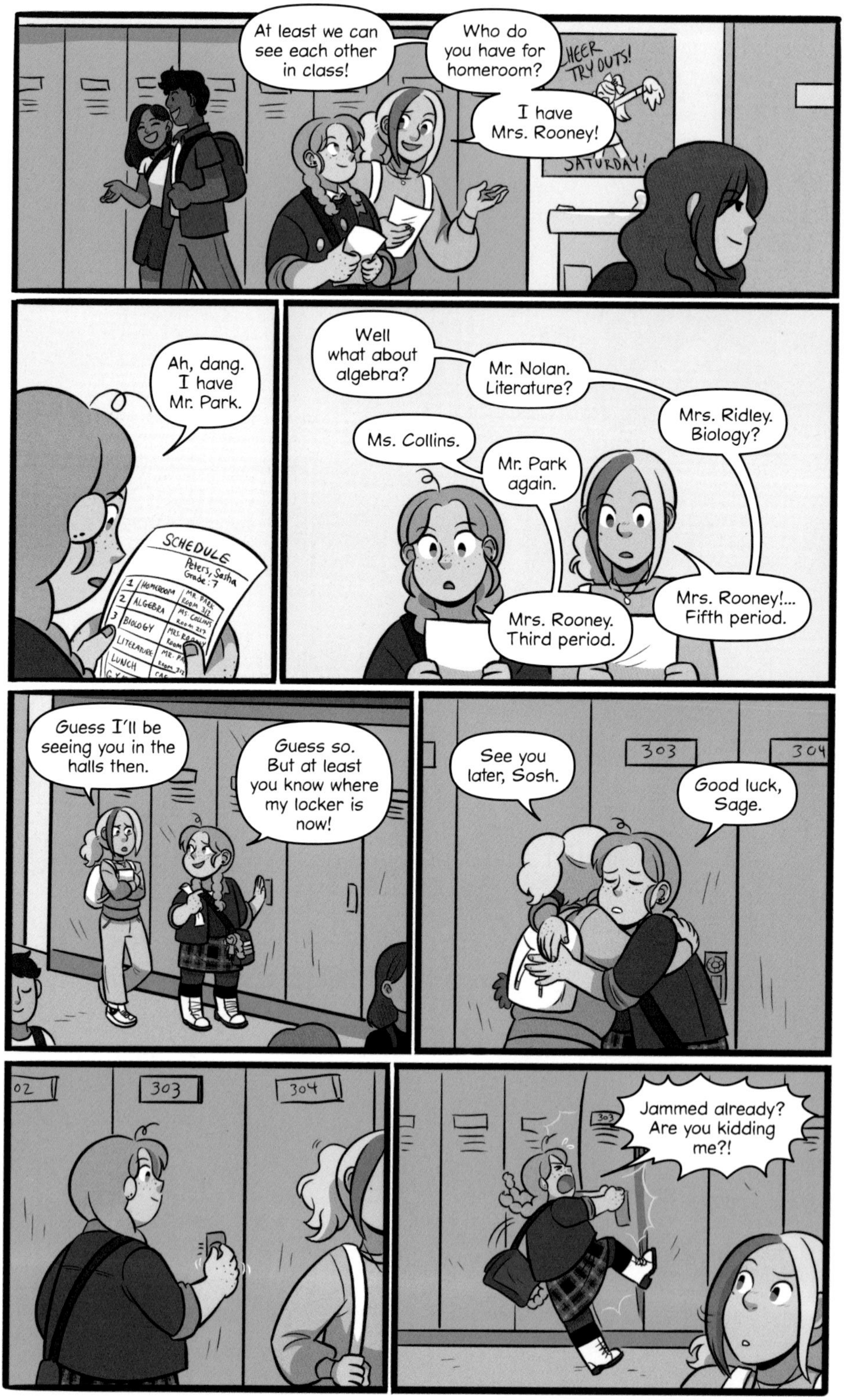
At least we can see each other in class!
Who do you have for homeroom?
I have Mrs. Rooney!
CHEER TRY OUTS!
SATURDAY!
Ah, dang. I have Mr. Park.
SCHEDULE
Peters, Sasha
Grade: 7
HOMEROOM
ALGEBRA
BIOLOGY
LITERATURE
LUNCH
Well what about algebra?
Mr. Nolan. Literature?
Mrs. Ridley. Biology?
Ms. Collins.
Mr. Park again.
Mrs. Rooney. Third period.
Mrs. Rooney!... Fifth period.
Guess I'll be seeing you in the halls then.
Guess so. But at least you know where my locker is now!
303
304
See you later, Sosh.
Good luck, Sage.
303
304
Jammed already? Are you kidding me?!

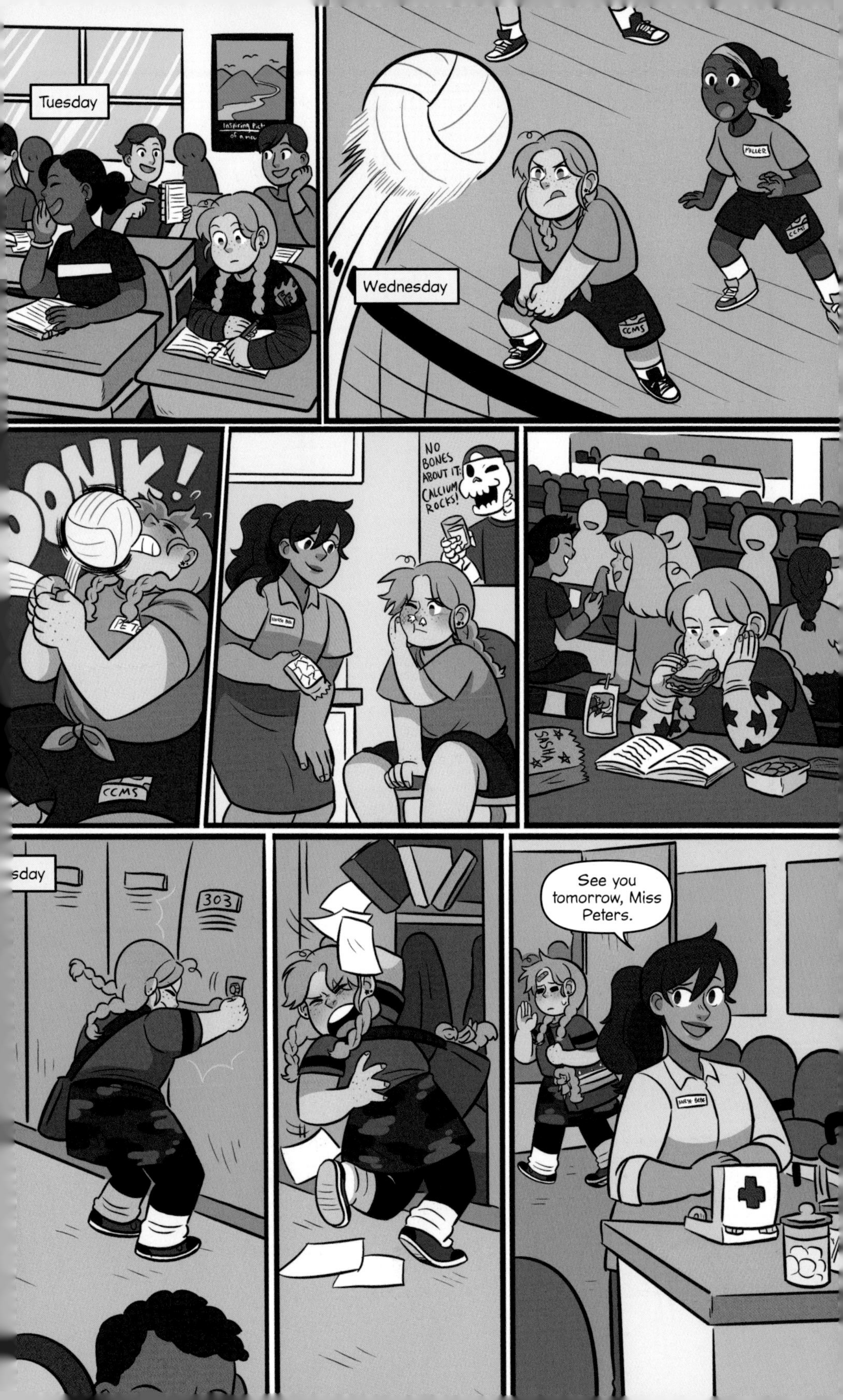
Tuesday
Wednesday
DONK!
NO BONES ABOUT IT: CALCIUM ROCKS!
SASHA
sday
303
See you tomorrow, Miss Peters.

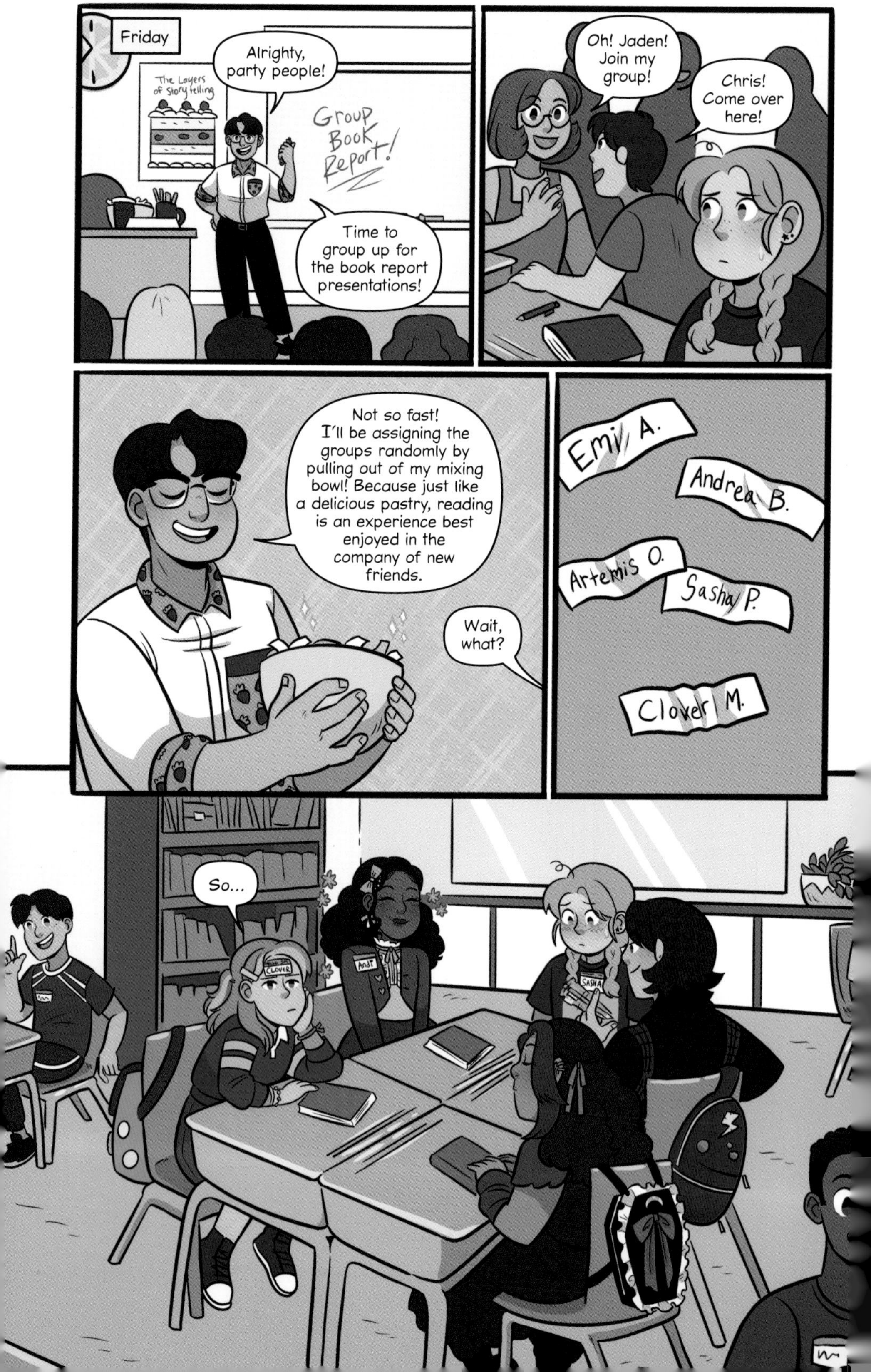
Friday
The Layers of Story telling
Alrighty, party people!
Group Book Report!
Time to group up for the book report presentations!
Oh! Jaden! Join my group!
Chris! Come over here!
Not so fast! I'll be assigning the groups randomly by pulling out of my mixing bowl! Because just like a delicious pastry, reading is an experience best enjoyed in the company of new friends.
Wait, what?
Emi A.
Andrea B.
Artemis O.
Sasha P.
Clover M.
So...
CLOVER
SASHA

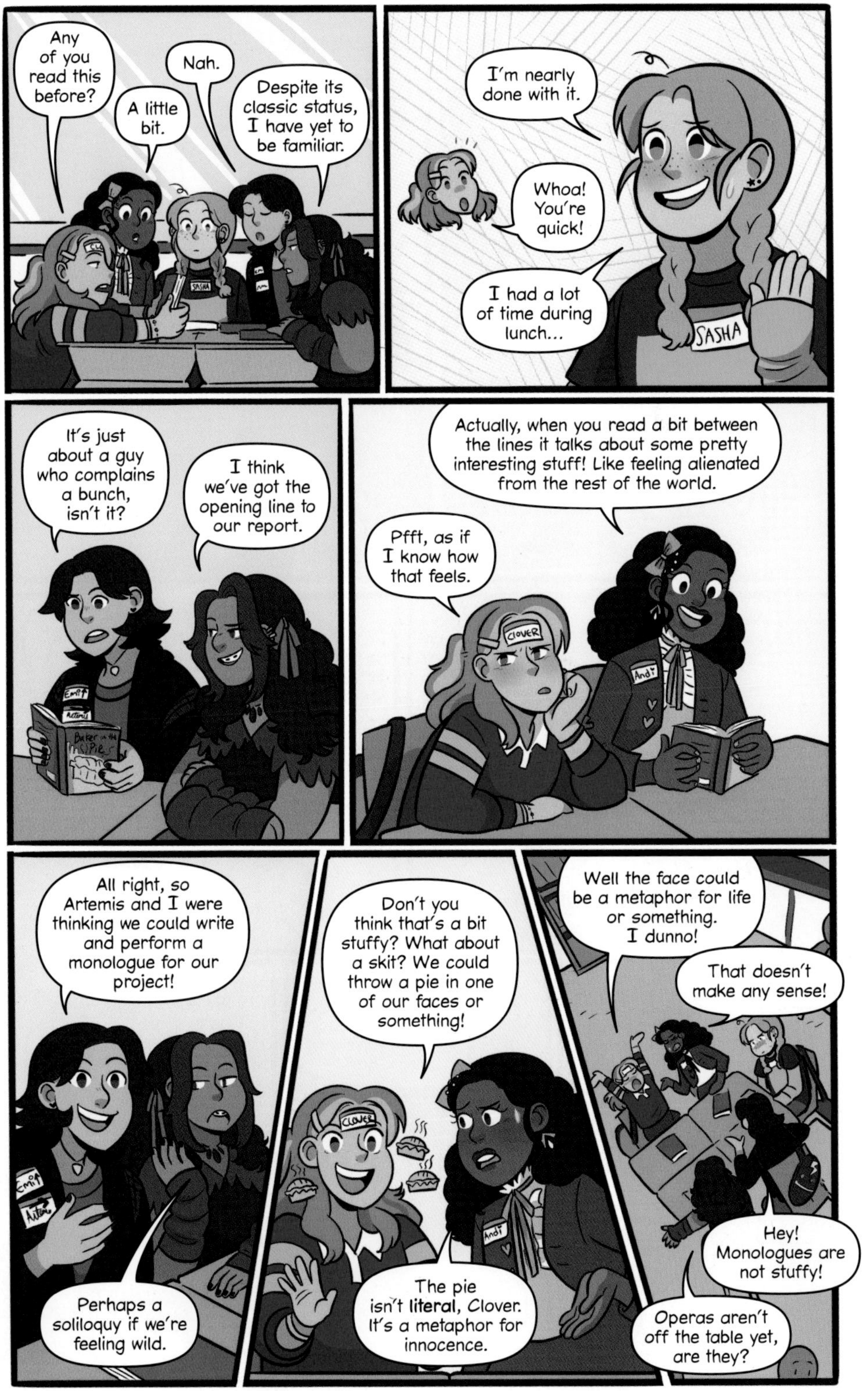
Any of you read this before?
A little bit.
Nah.
Despite its classic status, I have yet to be familiar.
I'm nearly done with it.
Whoa! You're quick!
I had a lot of time during lunch...
It's just about a guy who complains a bunch, isn't it?
I think we've got the opening line to our report.
Actually, when you read a bit between the lines it talks about some pretty interesting stuff! Like feeling alienated from the rest of the world.
Pfft, as if I know how that feels.
All right, so Artemis and I were thinking we could write and perform a monologue for our project!
Perhaps a soliloquy if we're feeling wild.
Don't you think that's a bit stuffy? What about a skit? We could throw a pie in one of our faces or something!
The pie isn't **literal**, Clover. It's a metaphor for innocence.
Well the face could be a metaphor for life or something. I dunno!
That doesn't make any sense!
Hey! Monologues are not stuffy!
Operas aren't off the table yet, are they?

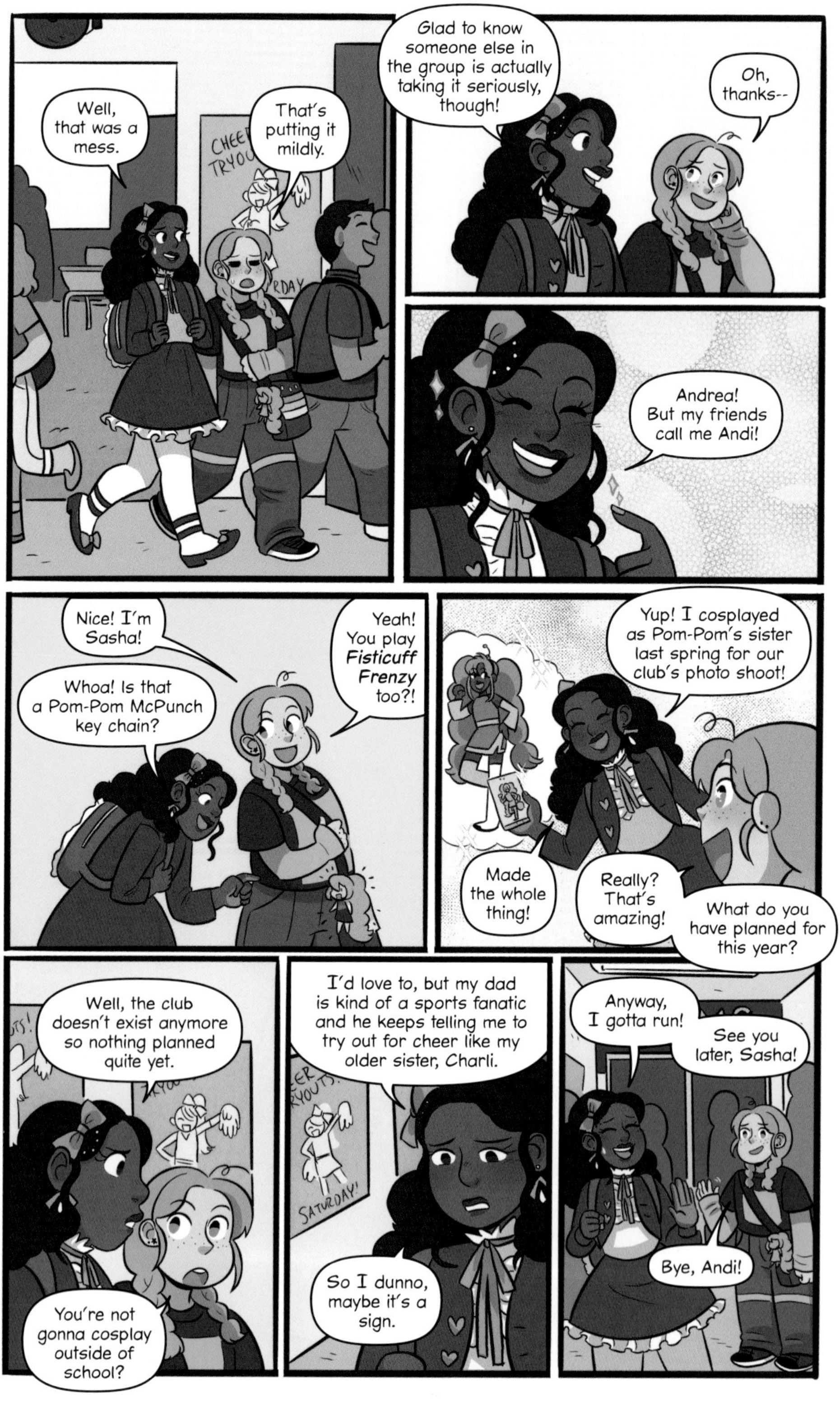
Well, that was a mess.
That's putting it mildly.
CHEER TRYOUTS
Glad to know someone else in the group is actually taking it seriously, though!
Oh, thanks--
Andrea! But my friends call me Andi!
Nice! I'm Sasha!
Whoa! Is that a Pom-Pom McPunch key chain?
Yeah! You play *Fisticuff Frenzy* too?!
Yup! I cosplayed as Pom-Pom's sister last spring for our club's photo shoot!
Made the whole thing!
Really? That's amazing!
What do you have planned for this year?
Well, the club doesn't exist anymore so nothing planned quite yet.
You're not gonna cosplay outside of school?
I'd love to, but my dad is kind of a sports fanatic and he keeps telling me to try out for cheer like my older sister, Charli.
SATURDAY!
So I dunno, maybe it's a sign.
Anyway, I gotta run!
See you later, Sasha!
Bye, Andi!

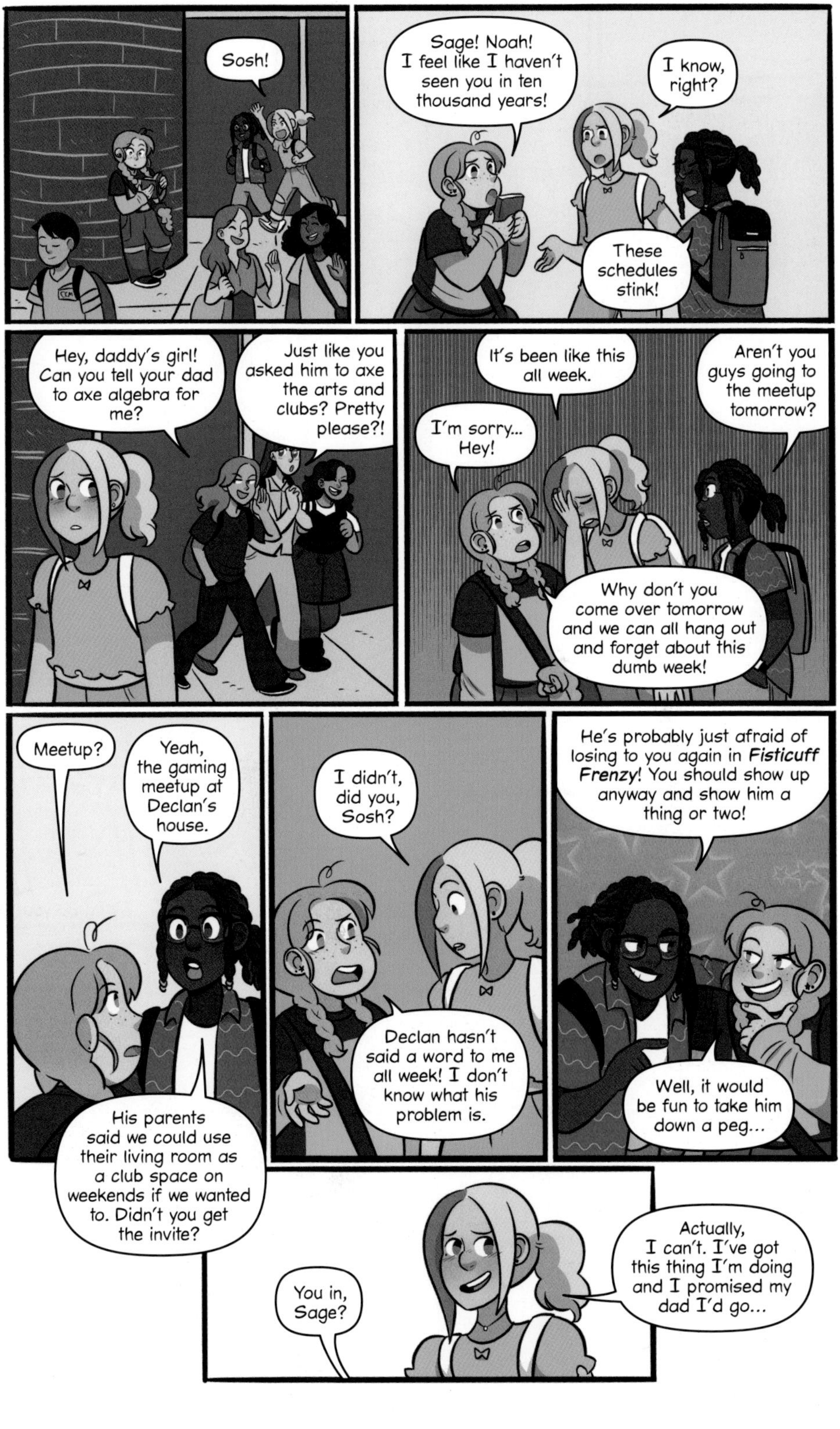

Sosh!
Sage! Noah! I feel like I haven't seen you in ten thousand years!
I know, right?
These schedules stink!
Hey, daddy's girl! Can you tell your dad to axe algebra for me?
Just like you asked him to axe the arts and clubs? Pretty please?!
It's been like this all week.
I'm sorry... Hey!
Aren't you guys going to the meetup tomorrow?
Why don't you come over tomorrow and we can all hang out and forget about this dumb week!
Meetup?
Yeah, the gaming meetup at Declan's house.
His parents said we could use their living room as a club space on weekends if we wanted to. Didn't you get the invite?
I didn't, did you, Sosh?
Declan hasn't said a word to me all week! I don't know what his problem is.
He's probably just afraid of losing to you again in *Fisticuff Frenzy*! You should show up anyway and show him a thing or two!
Well, it would be fun to take him down a peg...
You in, Sage?
Actually, I can't. I've got this thing I'm doing and I promised my dad I'd go...

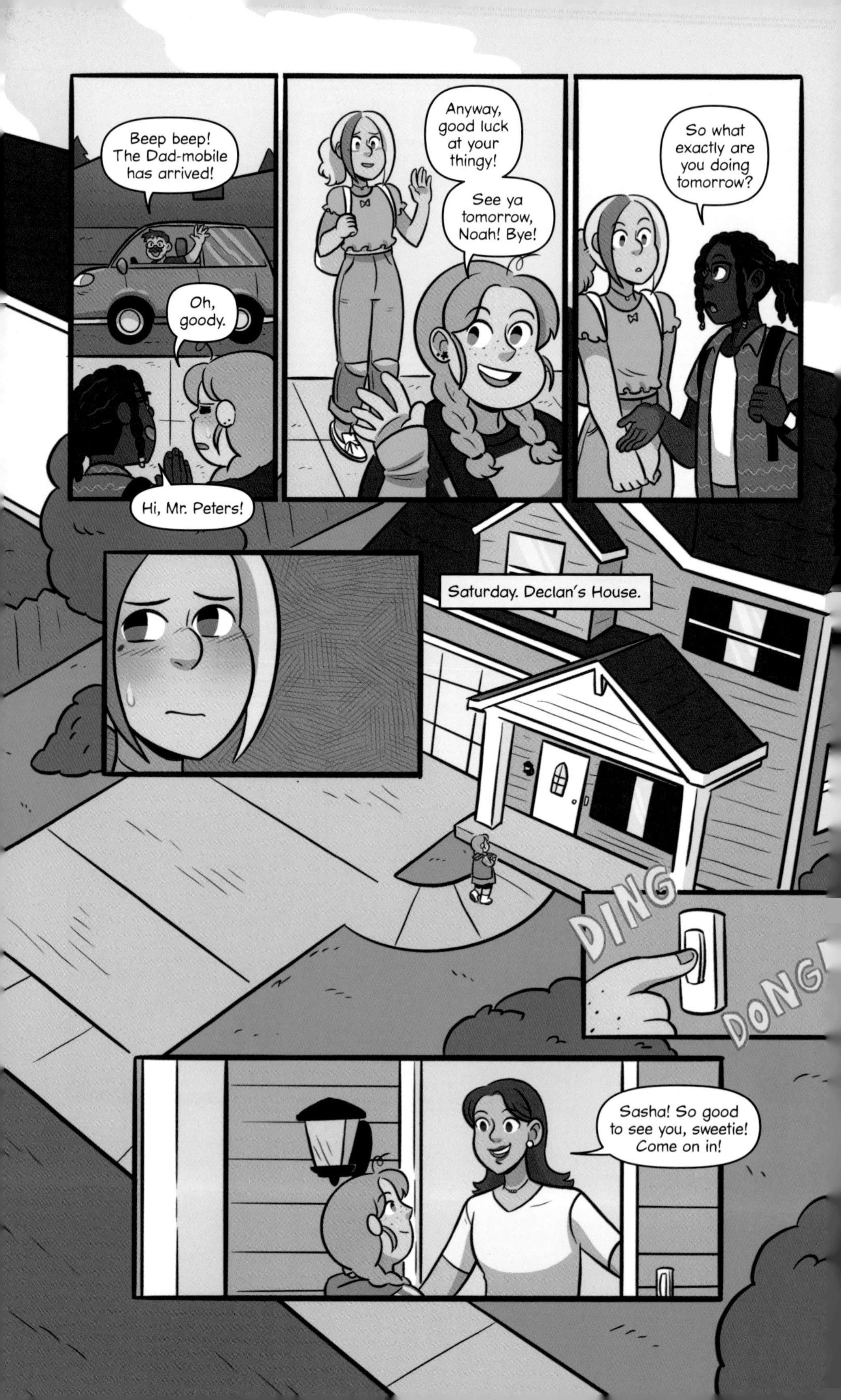

Beep beep! The Dad-mobile has arrived!
Oh, goody.
Hi, Mr. Peters!
Anyway, good luck at your thingy!
See ya tomorrow, Noah! Bye!
So what exactly are you doing tomorrow?
Saturday. Declan's House.
DING
DONG
Sasha! So good to see you, sweetie! Come on in!

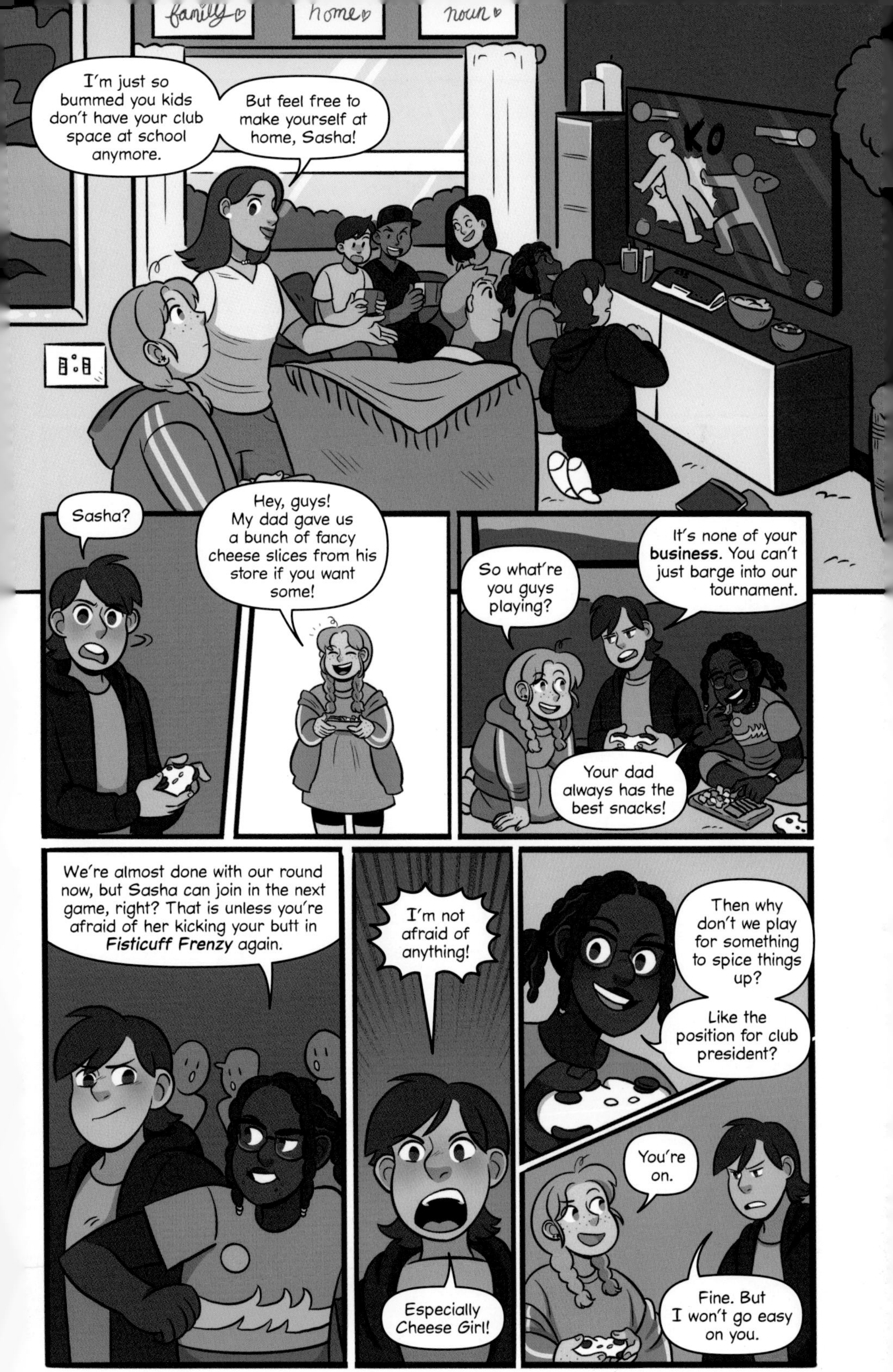
family
home
noun
I'm just so bummed you kids don't have your club space at school anymore.
But feel free to make yourself at home, Sasha!
KO
Sasha?
Hey, guys! My dad gave us a bunch of fancy cheese slices from his store if you want some!
So what're you guys playing?
It's none of your **business**. You can't just barge into our tournament.
Your dad always has the best snacks!
We're almost done with our round now, but Sasha can join in the next game, right? That is unless you're afraid of her kicking your butt in *Fisticuff Frenzy* again.
I'm not afraid of anything!
Especially Cheese Girl!
Then why don't we play for something to spice things up?
Like the position for club president?
You're on.
Fine. But I won't go easy on you.

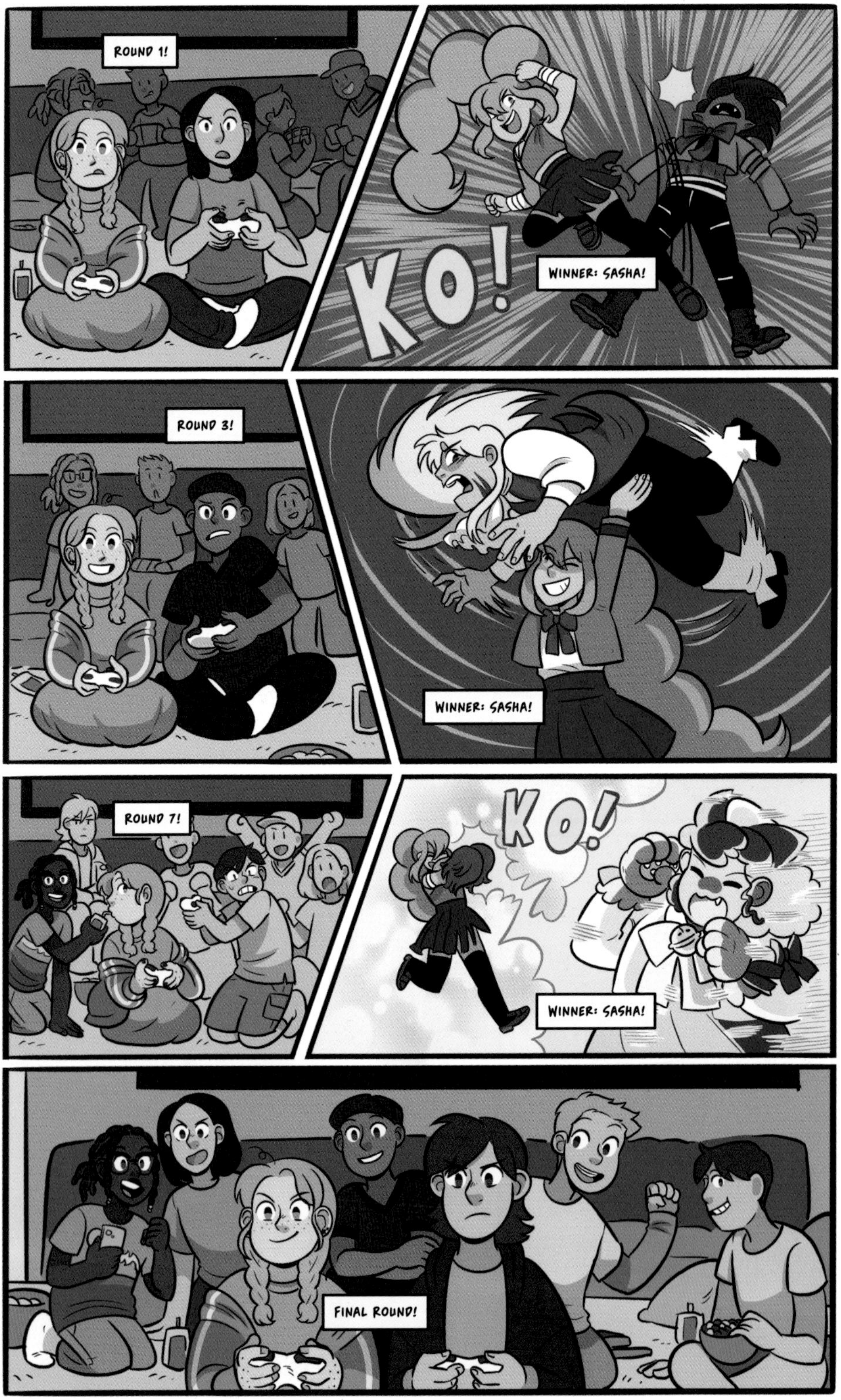
ROUND 1!
KO!
WINNER: SASHA!
ROUND 3!
WINNER: SASHA!
ROUND 7!
KO!
WINNER: SASHA!
FINAL ROUND!

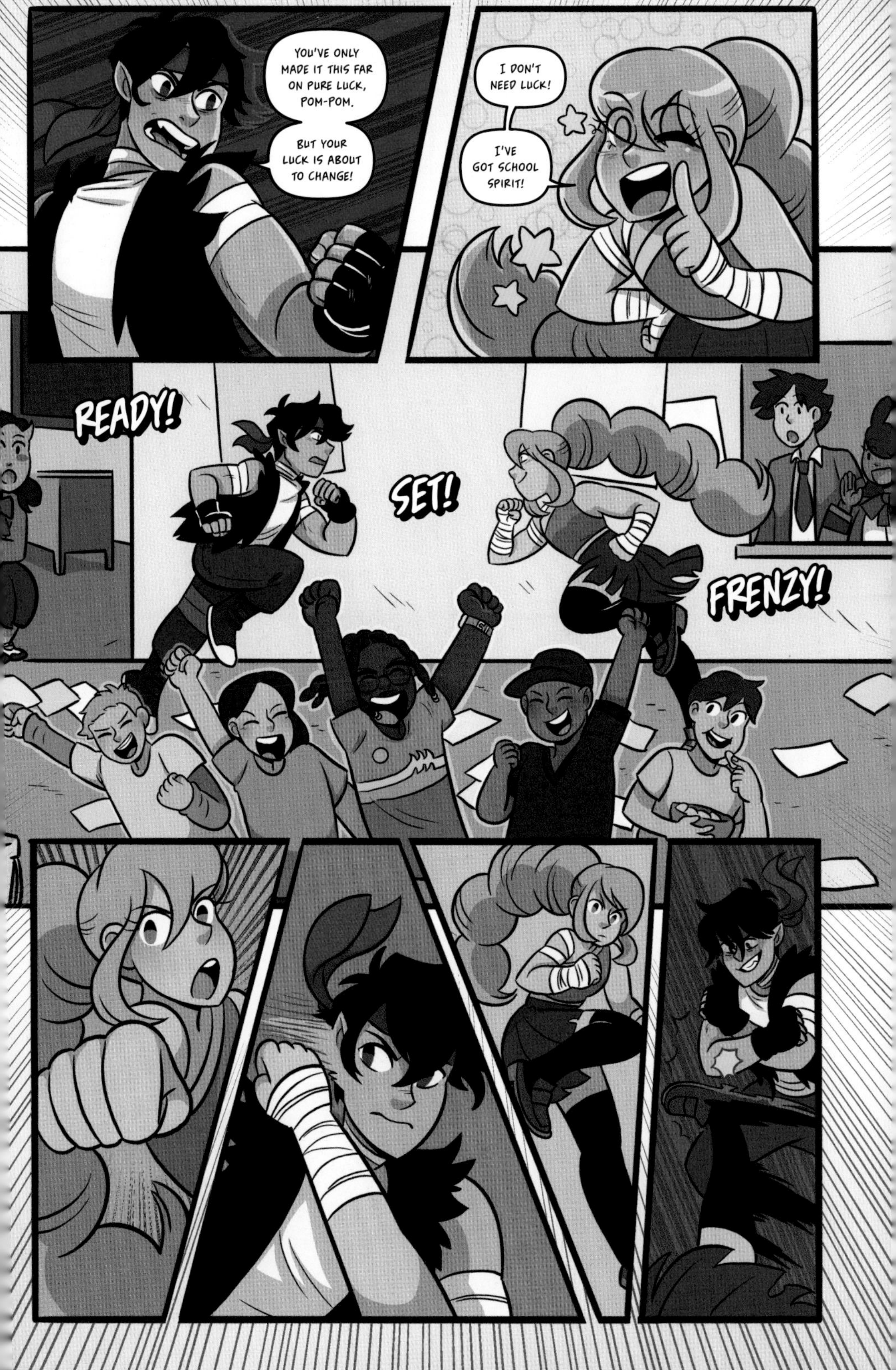
YOU'VE ONLY MADE IT THIS FAR ON PURE LUCK, POM-POM.
BUT YOUR LUCK IS ABOUT TO CHANGE!
I DON'T NEED LUCK!
I'VE GOT SCHOOL SPIRIT!
READY!
SET!
FRENZY!

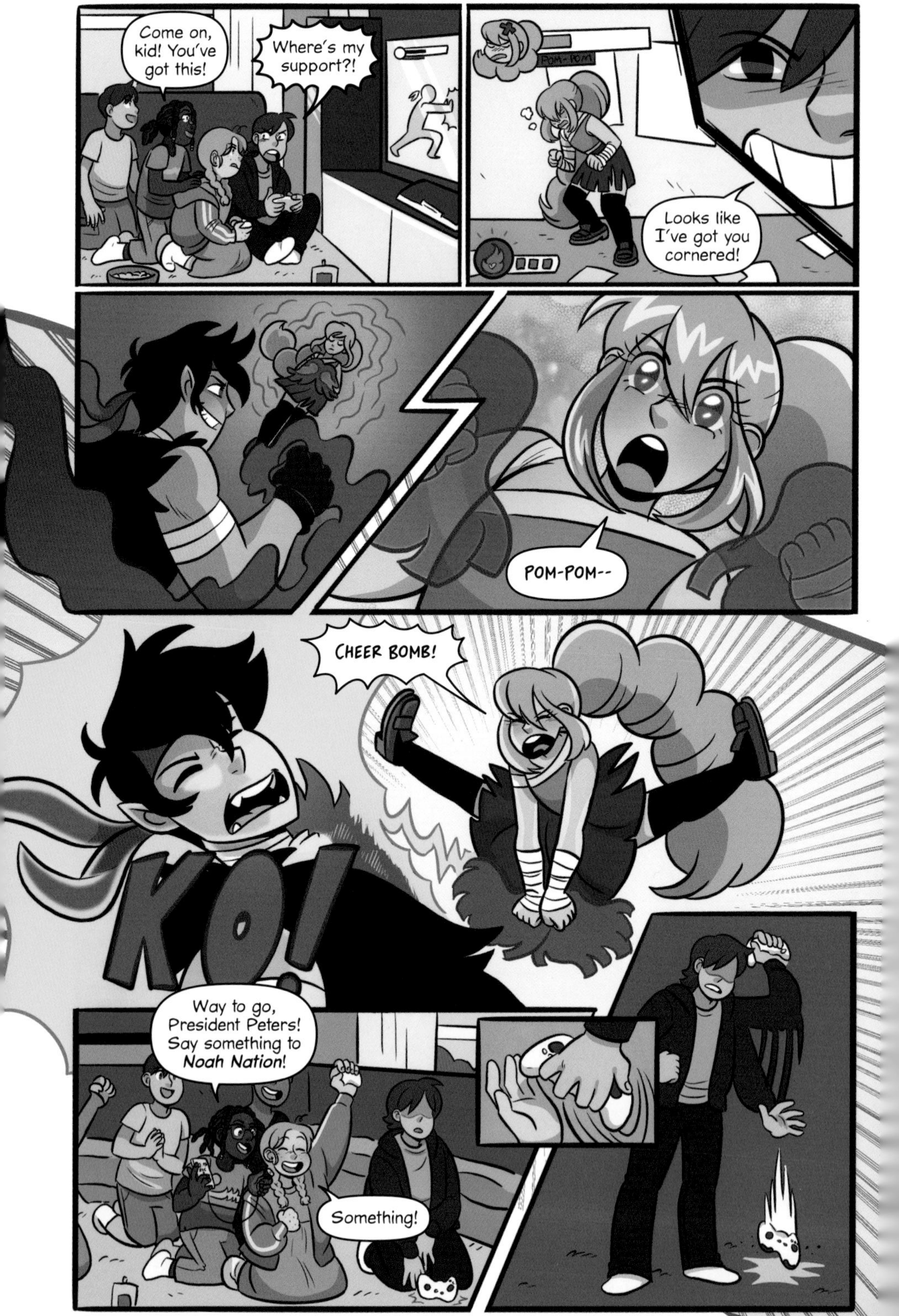
Come on, kid! You've got this!
Where's my support?!
POM-POM
Looks like I've got you cornered!
POM-POM--
CHEER BOMB!
KO!
Way to go, President Peters! Say something to *Noah Nation*!
Something!

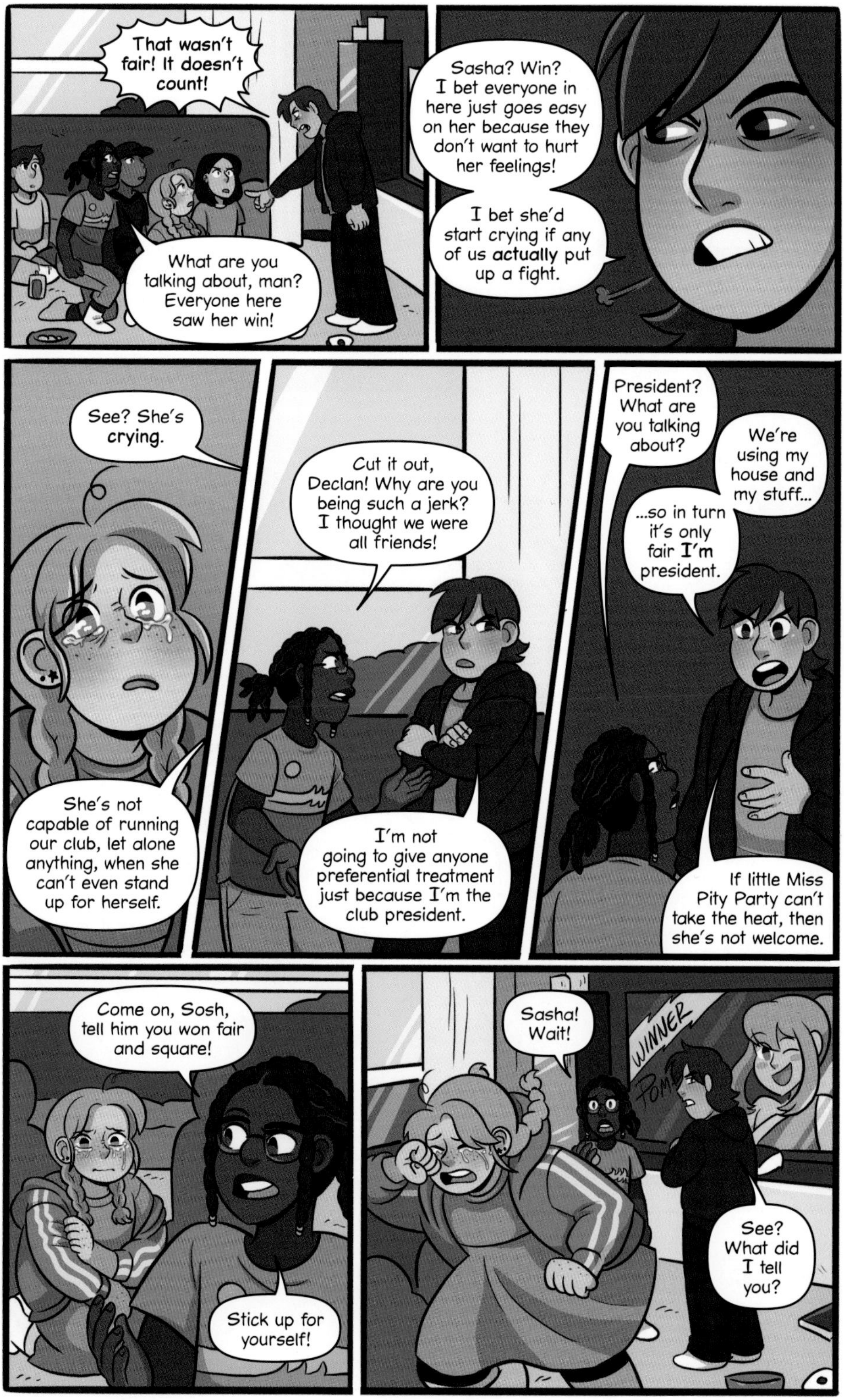
That wasn't fair! It doesn't count!
What are you talking about, man? Everyone here saw her win!
Sasha? Win? I bet everyone in here just goes easy on her because they don't want to hurt her feelings!
I bet she'd start crying if any of us **actually** put up a fight.
See? She's **crying.**
She's not capable of running our club, let alone anything, when she can't even stand up for herself.
Cut it out, Declan! Why are you being such a jerk? I thought we were all friends!
I'm not going to give anyone preferential treatment just because I'm the club president.
President? What are you talking about?
We're using my house and my stuff...
...so in turn it's only fair **I'm** president.
If little Miss Pity Party can't take the heat, then she's not welcome.
Come on, Sosh, tell him you won fair and square!
Stick up for yourself!
Sasha! Wait!
WINNER
POM
See? What did I tell you?

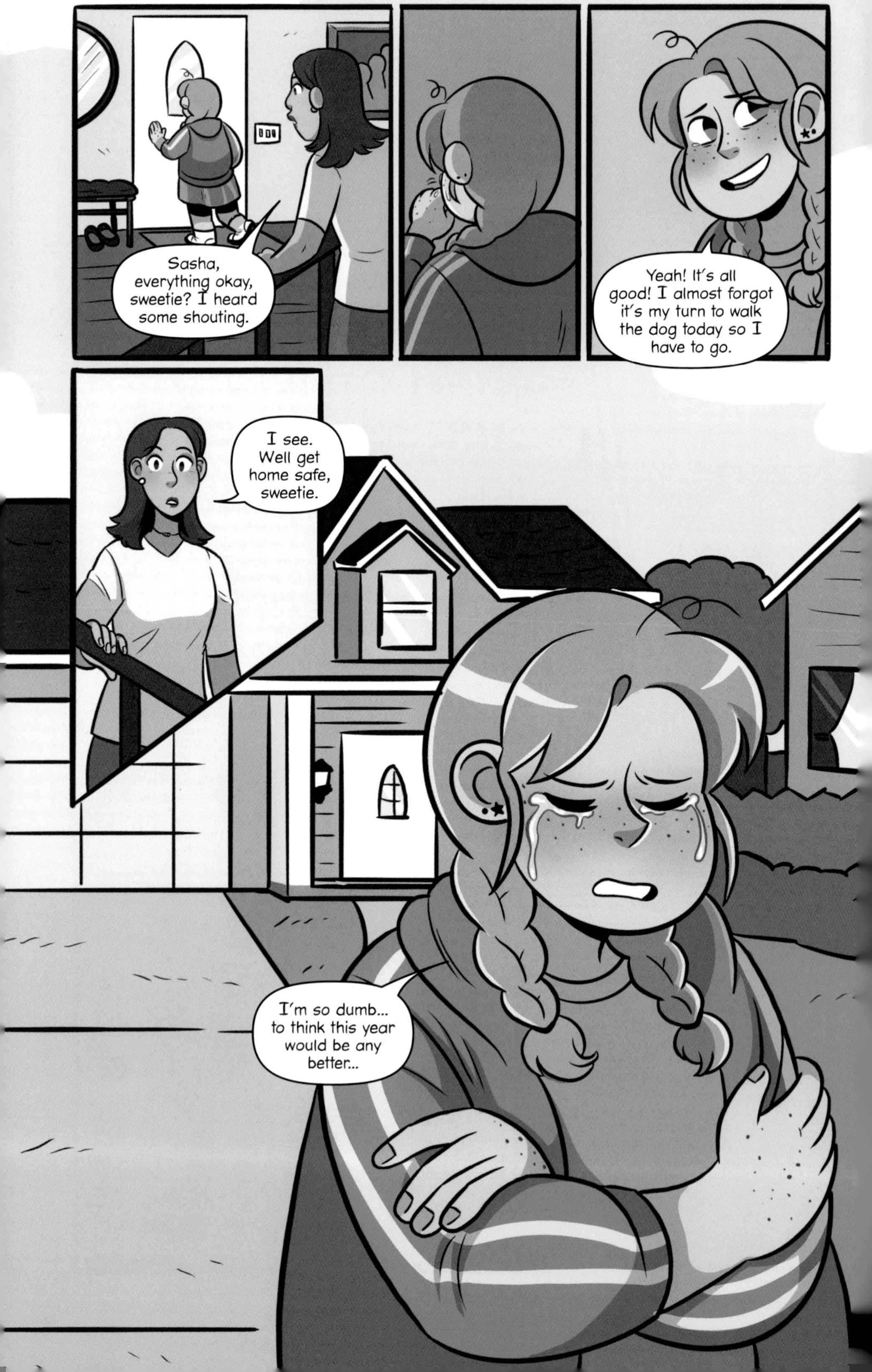
Sasha, everything okay, sweetie? I heard some shouting.
Yeah! It's all good! I almost forgot it's my turn to walk the dog today so I have to go.
I see. Well get home safe, sweetie.
I'm so dumb... to think this year would be any better...

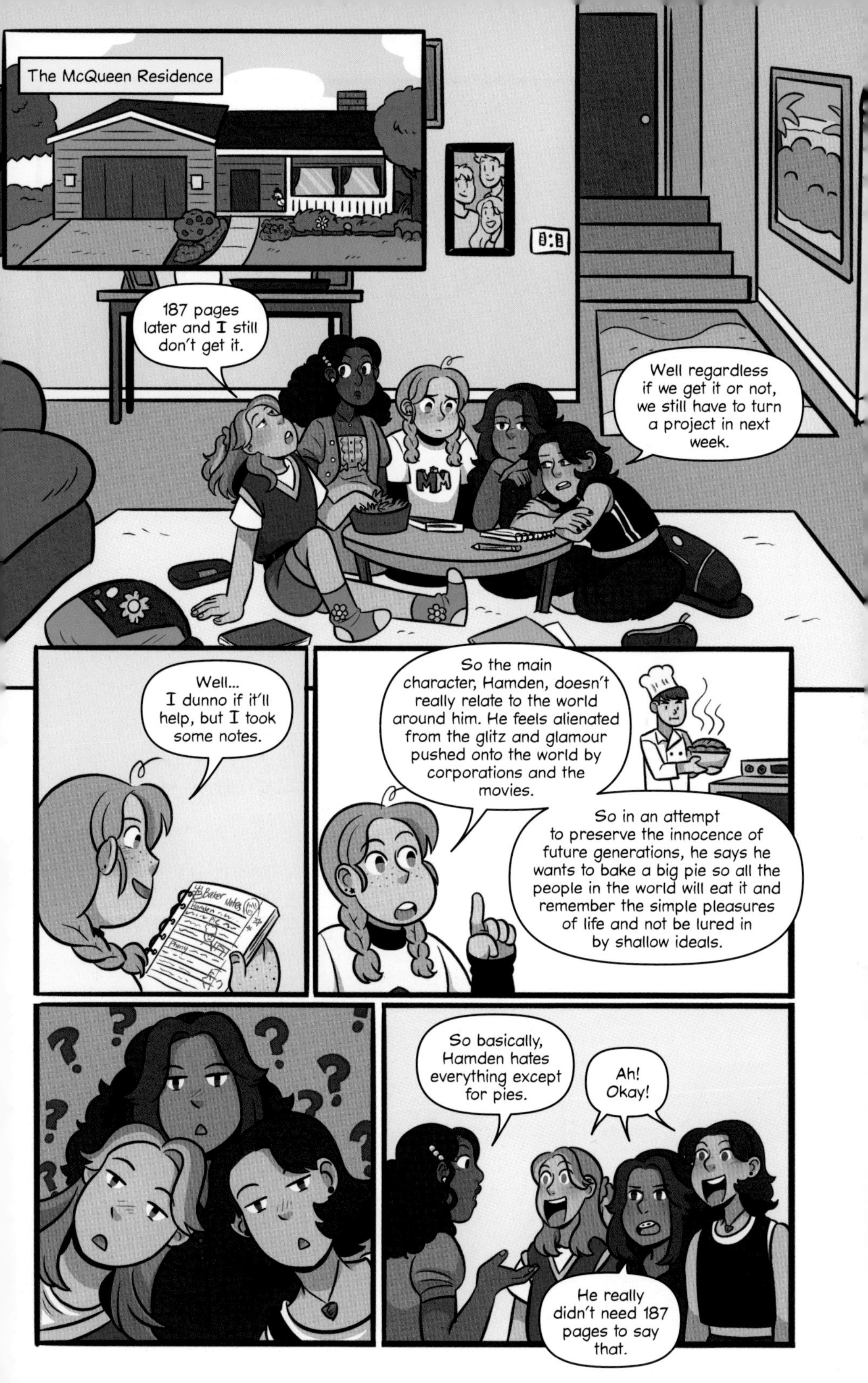

The McQueen Residence
187 pages later and I still don't get it.
Well regardless if we get it or not, we still have to turn a project in next week.
Well... I dunno if it'll help, but I took some notes.
So the main character, Hamden, doesn't really relate to the world around him. He feels alienated from the glitz and glamour pushed onto the world by corporations and the movies.
So in an attempt to preserve the innocence of future generations, he says he wants to bake a big pie so all the people in the world will eat it and remember the simple pleasures of life and not be lured in by shallow ideals.
So basically, Hamden hates everything except for pies.
Ah! Okay!
He really didn't need 187 pages to say that.

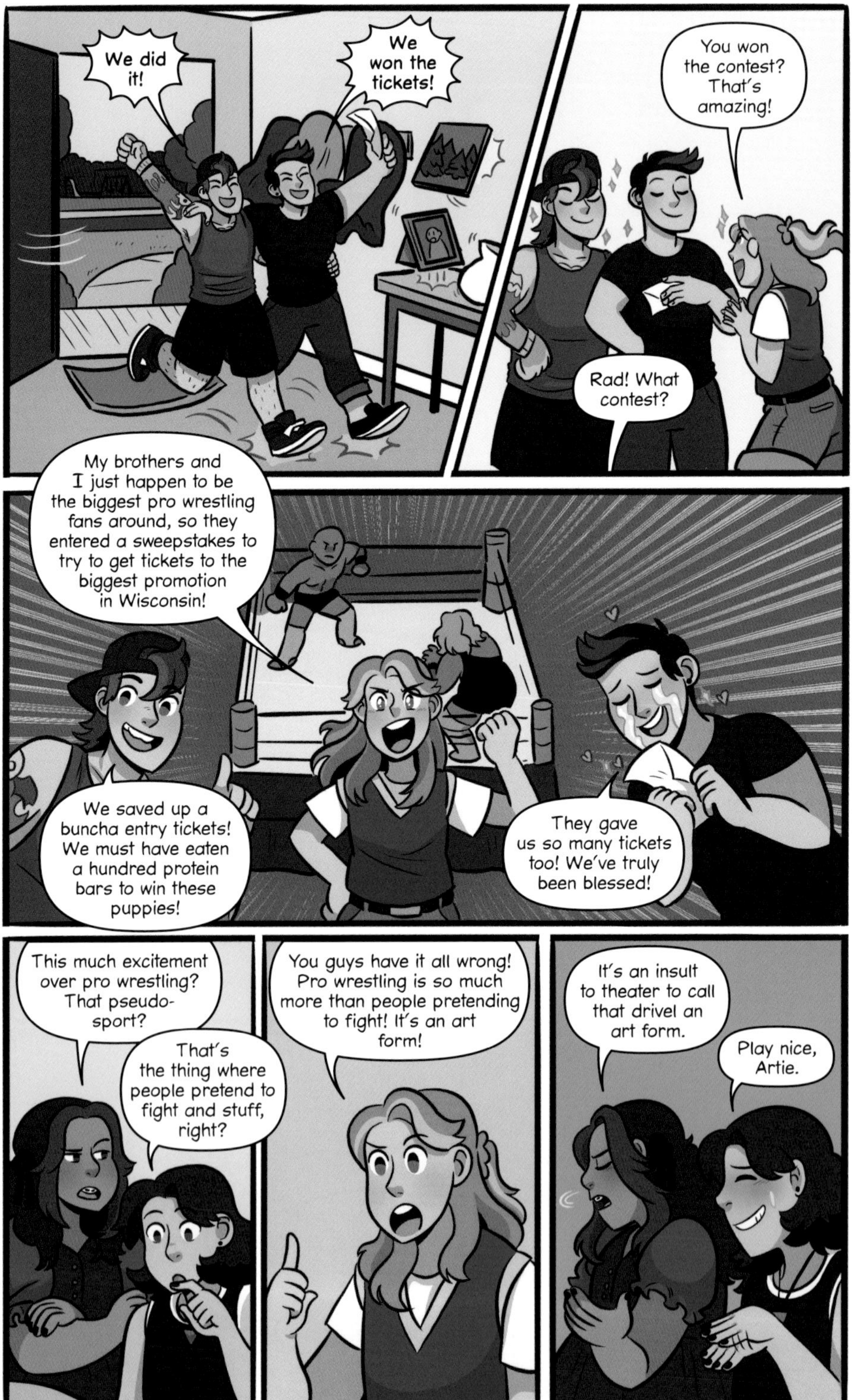

We did it!
We won the tickets!
You won the contest? That's amazing!
Rad! What contest?
My brothers and I just happen to be the biggest pro wrestling fans around, so they entered a sweepstakes to try to get tickets to the biggest promotion in Wisconsin!
We saved up a buncha entry tickets! We must have eaten a hundred protein bars to win these puppies!
They gave us so many tickets too! We've truly been blessed!
This much excitement over pro wrestling? That pseudo-sport?
That's the thing where people pretend to fight and stuff, right?
You guys have it all wrong! Pro wrestling is so much more than people pretending to fight! It's an art form!
It's an insult to theater to call that drivel an art form.
Play nice, Artie.

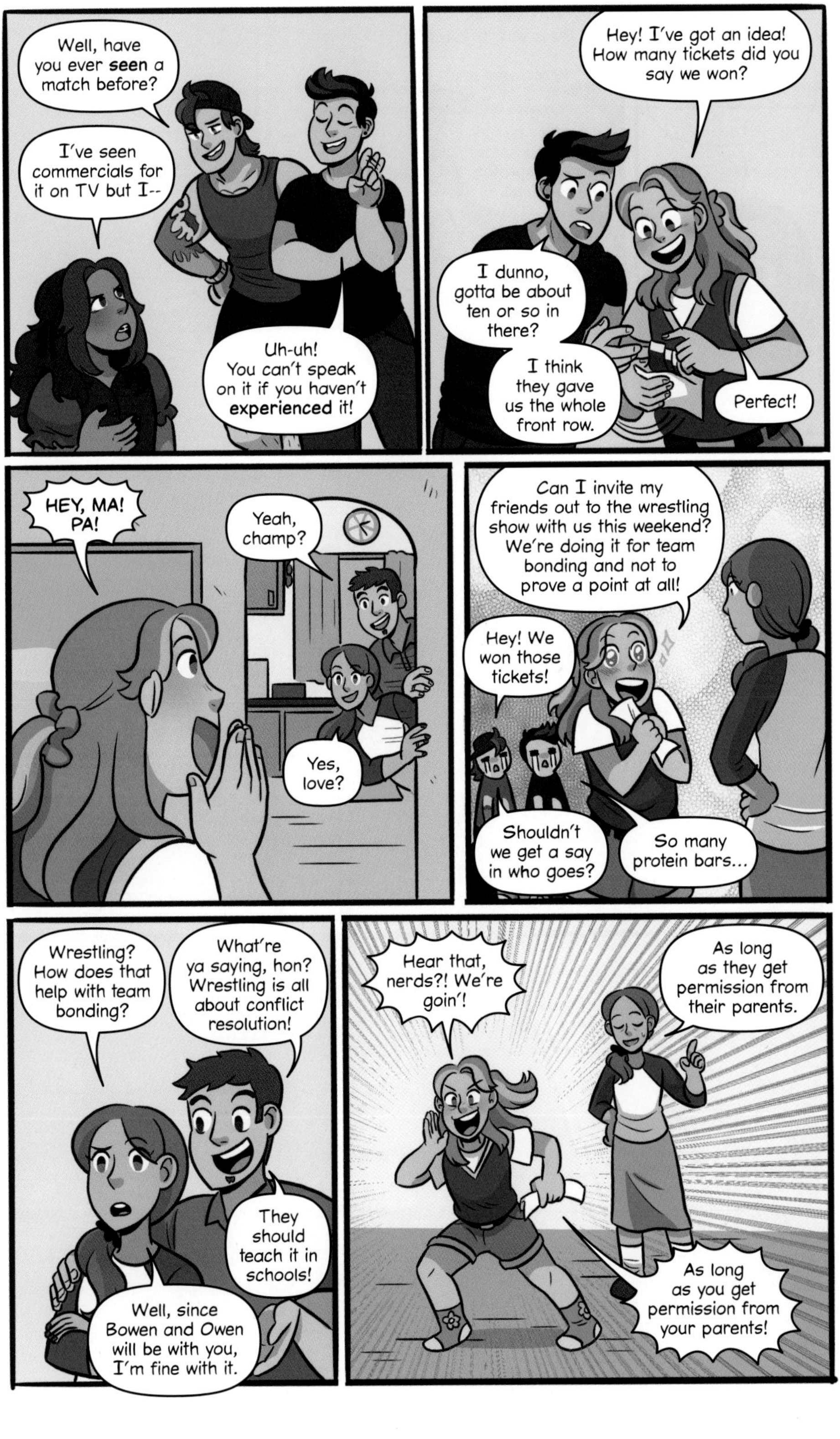

Well, have you ever **seen** a match before?
I've seen commercials for it on TV but I--
Uh-uh! You can't speak on it if you haven't **experienced** it!
Hey! I've got an idea! How many tickets did you say we won?
I dunno, gotta be about ten or so in there?
I think they gave us the whole front row.
Perfect!
HEY, MA! PA!
Yeah, champ?
Yes, love?
Can I invite my friends out to the wrestling show with us this weekend? We're doing it for team bonding and not to prove a point at all!
Hey! We won those tickets!
Shouldn't we get a say in who goes?
So many protein bars...
Wrestling? How does that help with team bonding?
What're ya saying, hon? Wrestling is all about conflict resolution!
They should teach it in schools!
Well, since Bowen and Owen will be with you, I'm fine with it.
Hear that, nerds?! We're goin'!
As long as they get permission from their parents.
As long as you get permission from your parents!

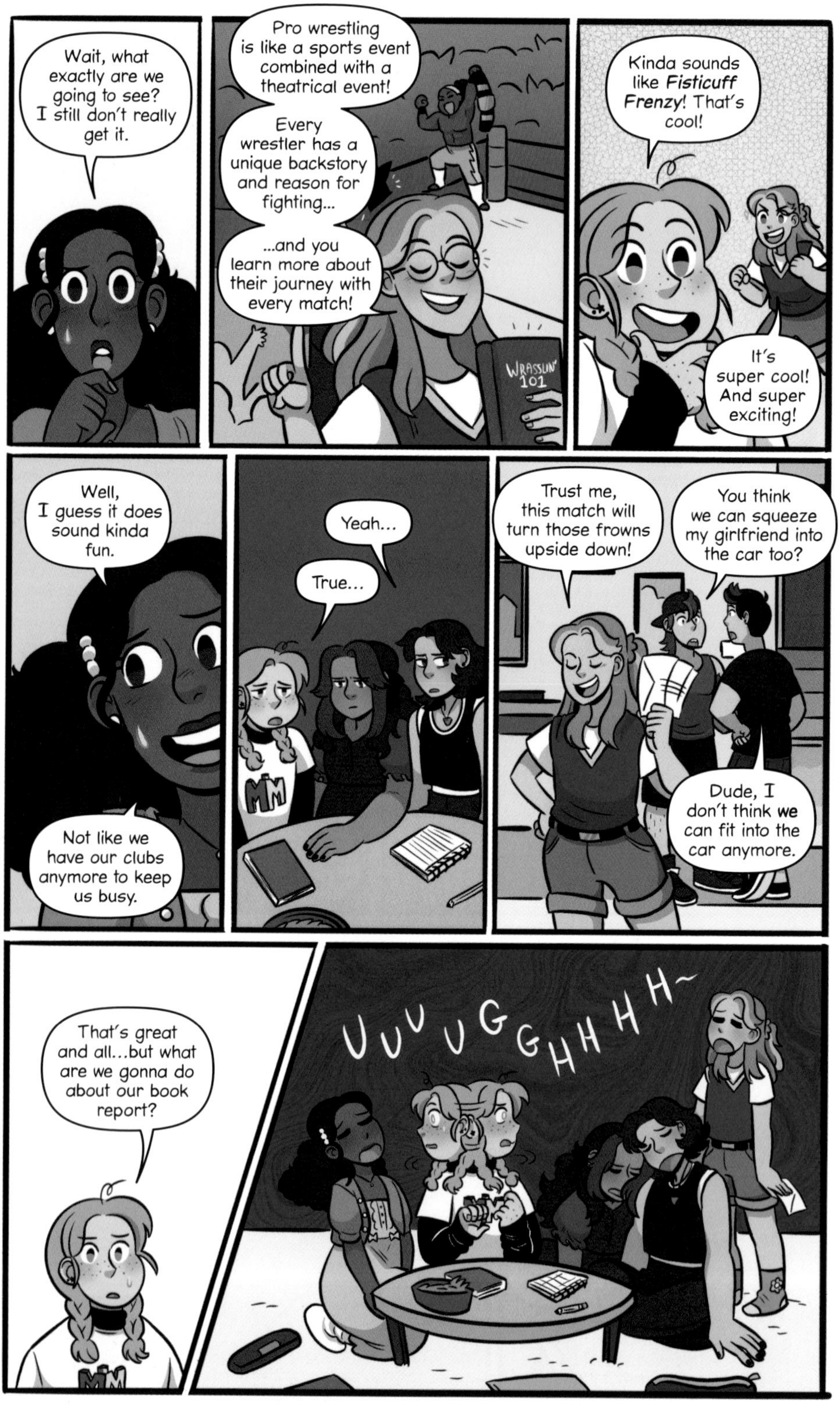
Wait, what exactly are we going to see? I still don't really get it.
Pro wrestling is like a sports event combined with a theatrical event!
Every wrestler has a unique backstory and reason for fighting...
...and you learn more about their journey with every match!
WRASSLIN' 101
Kinda sounds like *Fisticuff Frenzy*! That's cool!
It's super cool! And super exciting!
Well, I guess it does sound kinda fun.
Not like we have our clubs anymore to keep us busy.
Yeah...
True...
Trust me, this match will turn those frowns upside down!
You think we can squeeze my girlfriend into the car too?
Dude, I don't think **we** can fit into the car anymore.
That's great and all...but what are we gonna do about our book report?
UUUUGGHHHH~

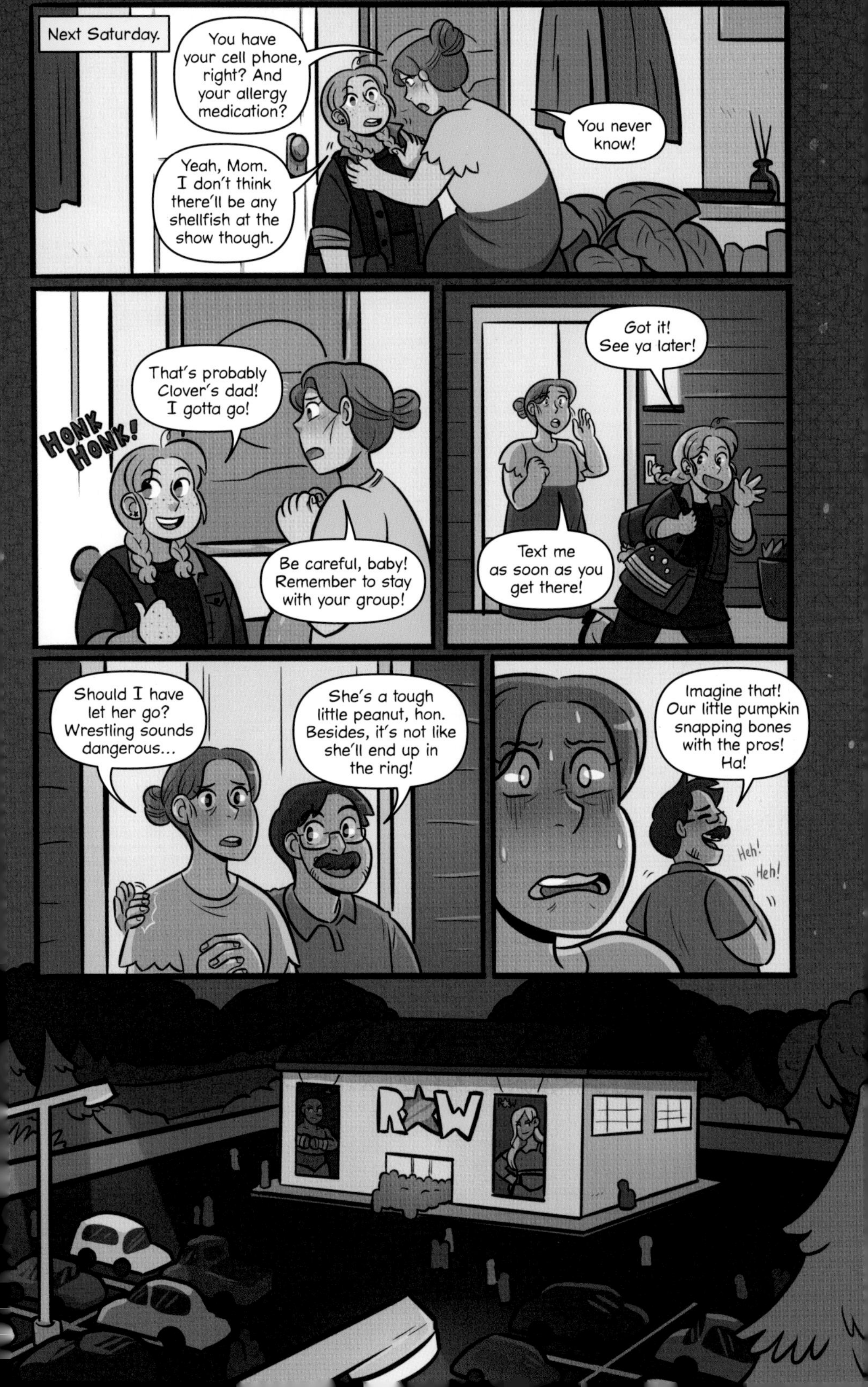
Next Saturday.
You have your cell phone, right? And your allergy medication?
You never know!
Yeah, Mom. I don't think there'll be any shellfish at the show though.
HONK HONK!
That's probably Clover's dad! I gotta go!
Be careful, baby! Remember to stay with your group!
Got it! See ya later!
Text me as soon as you get there!
Should I have let her go? Wrestling sounds dangerous...
She's a tough little peanut, hon. Besides, it's not like she'll end up in the ring!
Imagine that! Our little pumpkin snapping bones with the pros! Ha!
Heh! Heh!
R★W

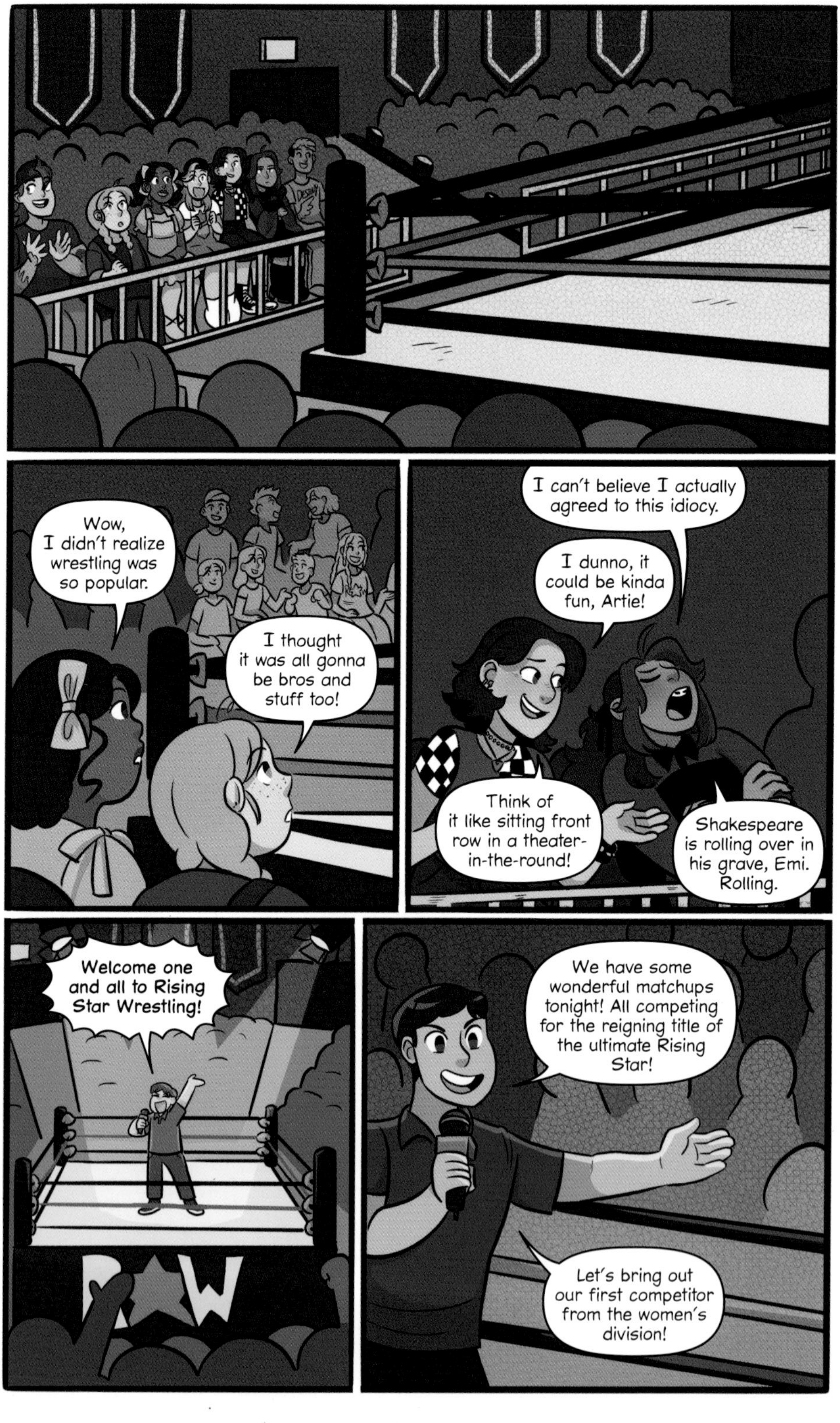

Wow, I didn't realize wrestling was so popular.
I thought it was all gonna be bros and stuff too!
I can't believe I actually agreed to this idiocy.
I dunno, it could be kinda fun, Artie!
Think of it like sitting front row in a theater-in-the-round!
Shakespeare is rolling over in his grave, Emi. Rolling.
Welcome one and all to Rising Star Wrestling!
We have some wonderful matchups tonight! All competing for the reigning title of the ultimate Rising Star!
Let's bring out our first competitor from the women's division!

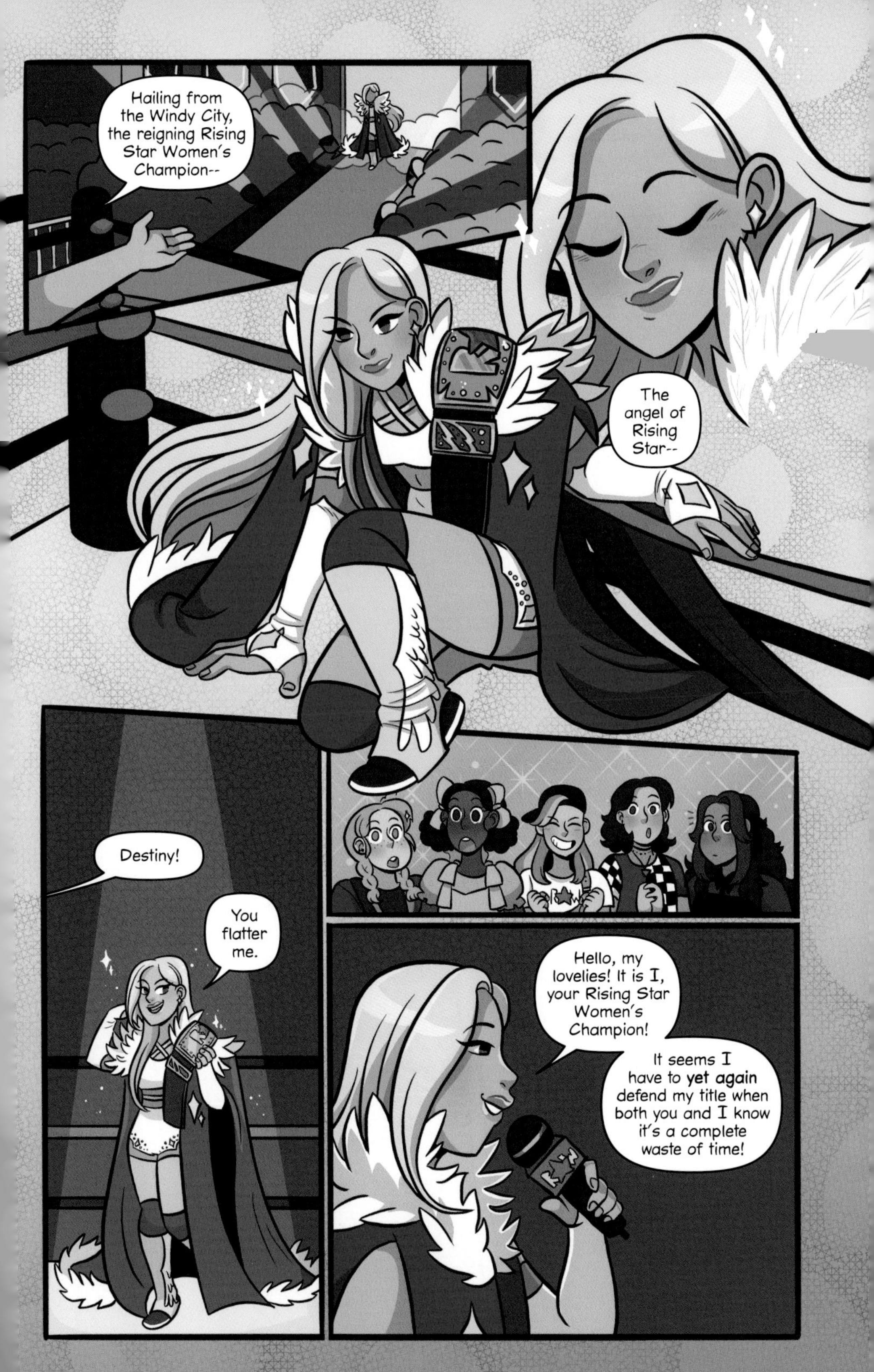

Hailing from the Windy City, the reigning Rising Star Women's Champion--
The angel of Rising Star--
Destiny!
You flatter me.
Hello, my lovelies! It is I, your Rising Star Women's Champion!
It seems I have to **yet again** defend my title when both you and I know it's a complete waste of time!

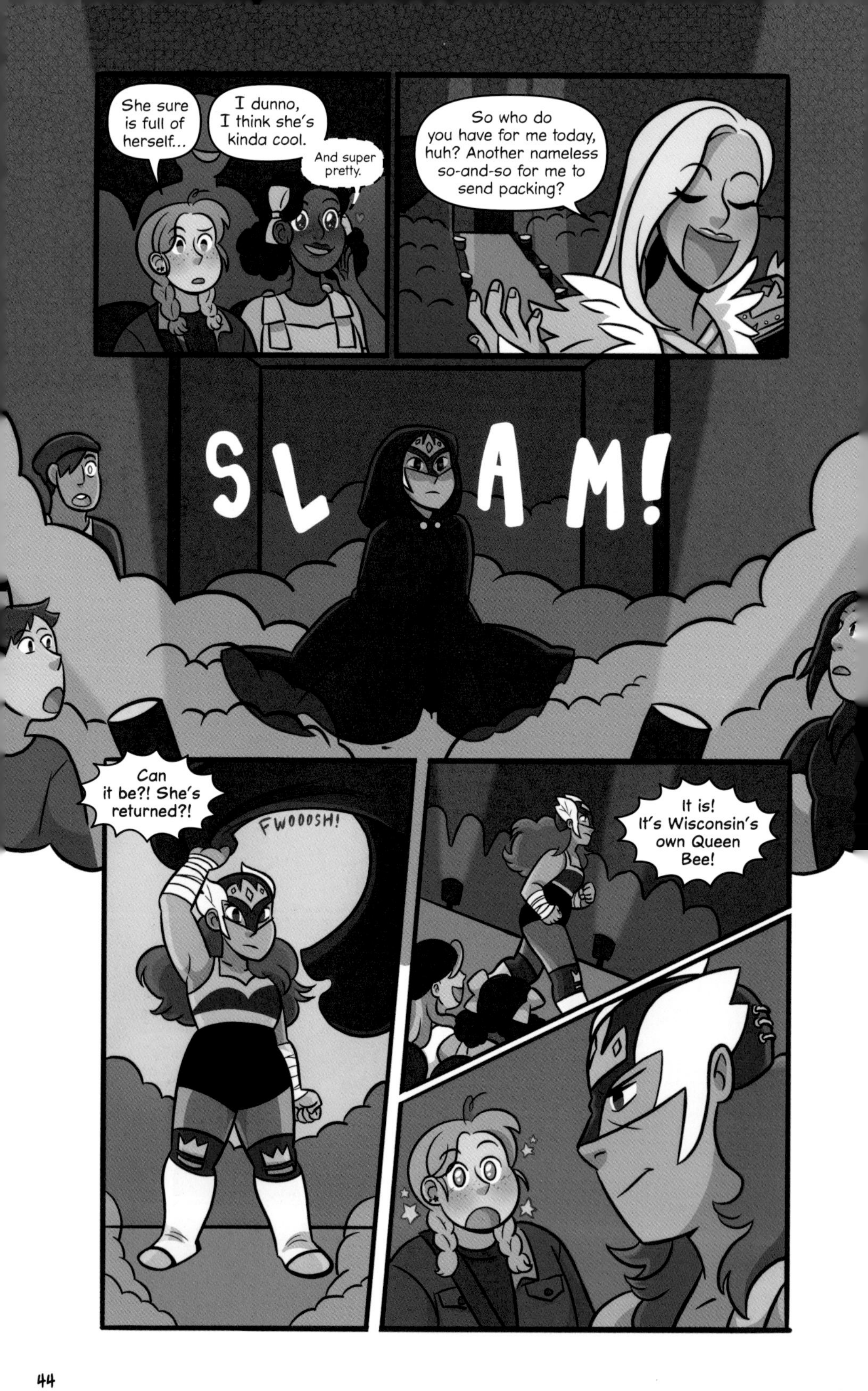

She sure is full of herself...
I dunno, I think she's kinda cool.
And super pretty.
So who do you have for me today, huh? Another nameless so-and-so for me to send packing?
SLAM!
Can it be?! She's returned?!
FWOOOSH!
It is! It's Wisconsin's own Queen Bee!

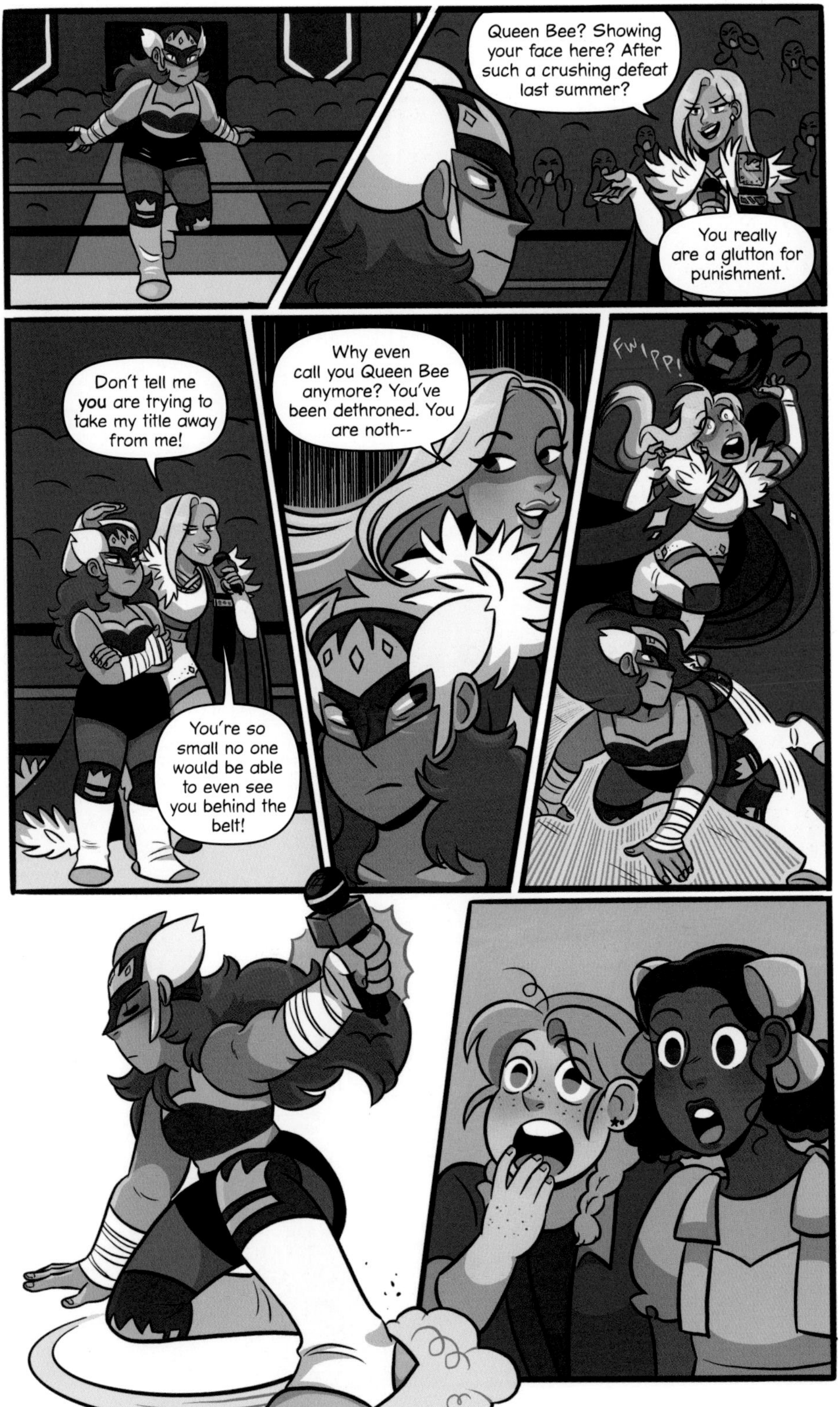
Queen Bee? Showing your face here? After such a crushing defeat last summer?
You really are a glutton for punishment.
Don't tell me **you** are trying to take my title away from me!
You're so small no one would be able to even see you behind the belt!
Why even call you Queen Bee anymore? You've been dethroned. You are noth--
FWIPP!

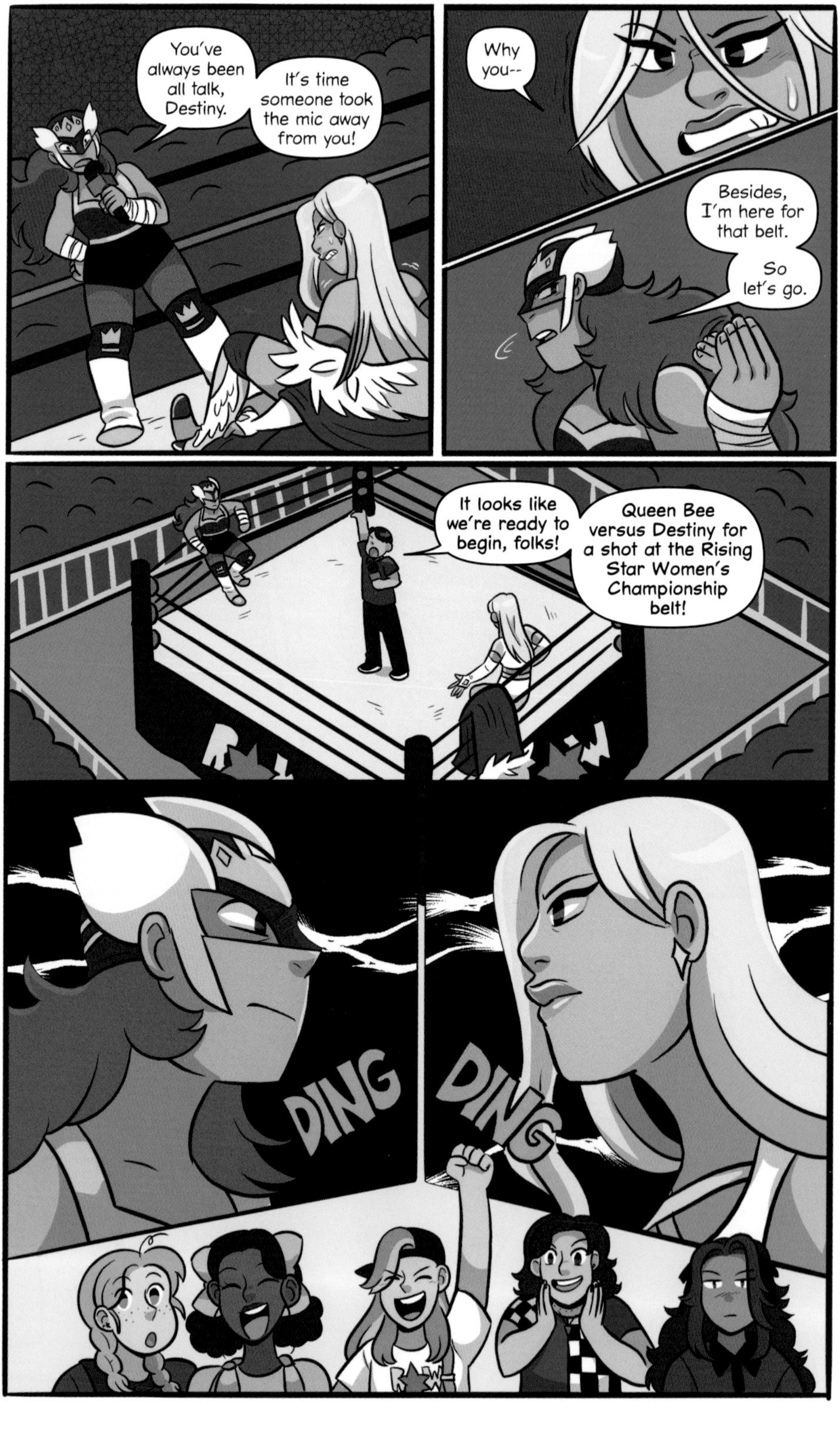
You've always been all talk, Destiny.
It's time someone took the mic away from you!
Why you--
Besides, I'm here for that belt.
So let's go.
It looks like we're ready to begin, folks!
Queen Bee versus Destiny for a shot at the Rising Star Women's Championship belt!
DING
DING

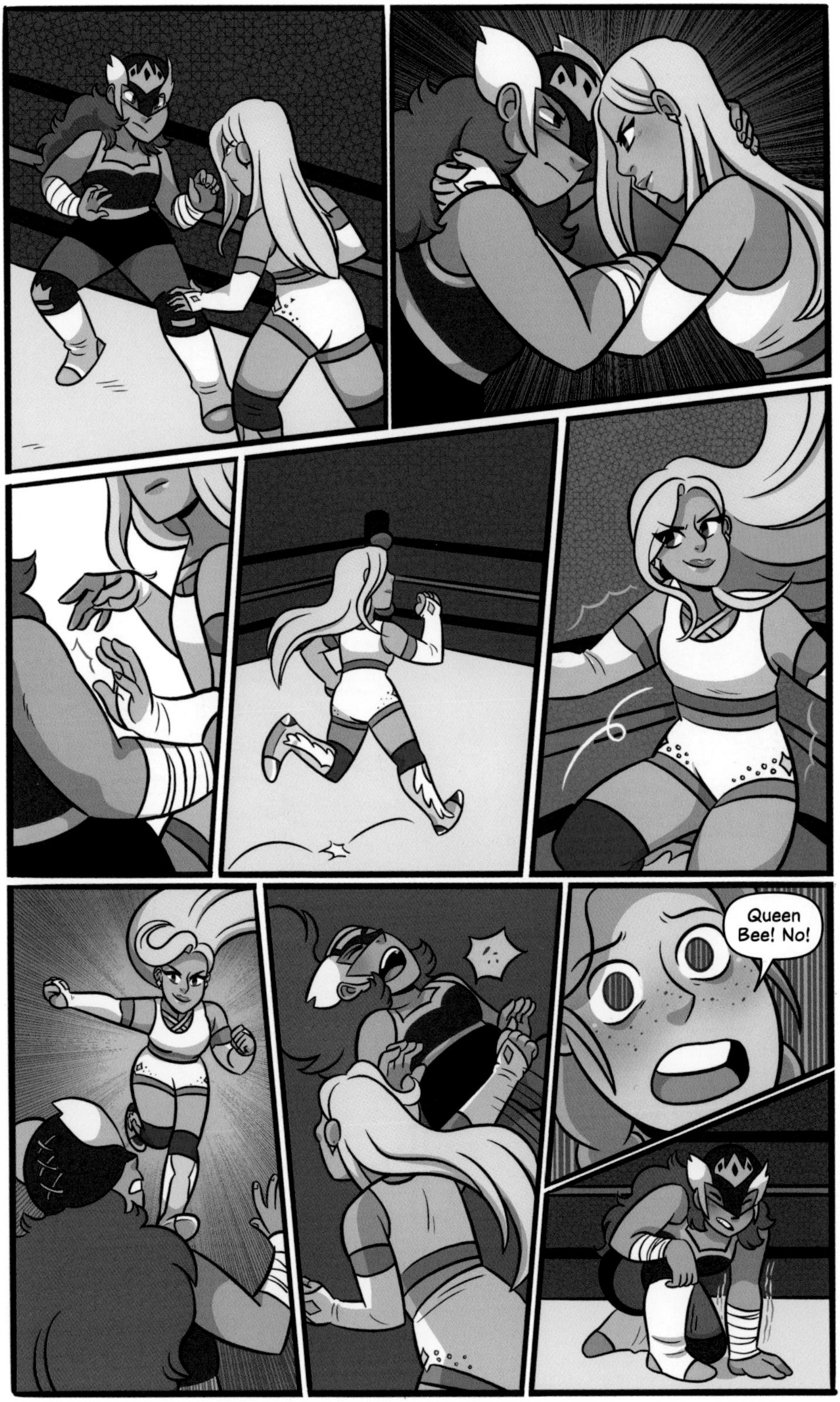
Queen
Bee! No!

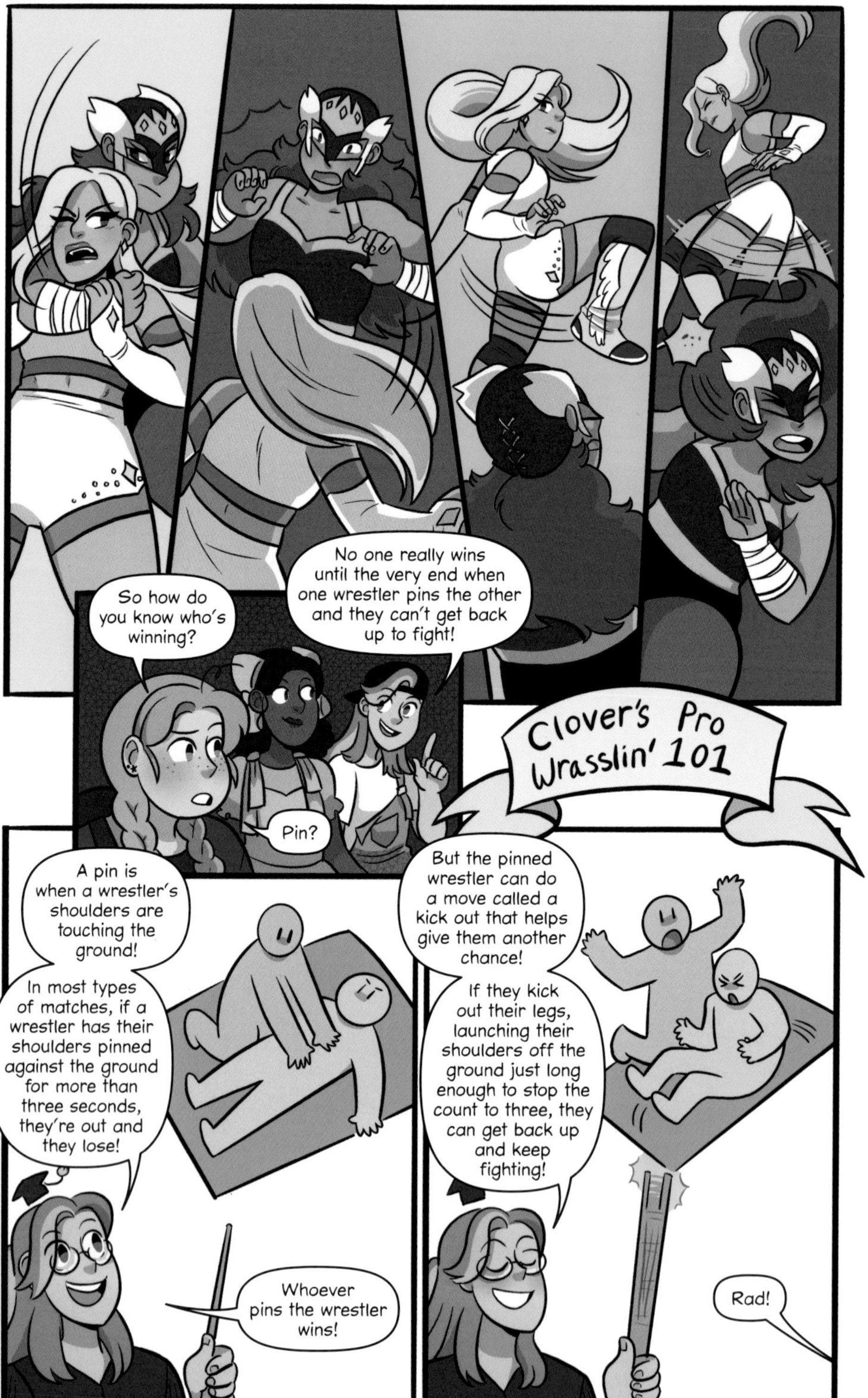

So how do you know who's winning?
No one really wins until the very end when one wrestler pins the other and they can't get back up to fight!
Pin?
Clover's Pro Wrasslin' 101
A pin is when a wrestler's shoulders are touching the ground!
In most types of matches, if a wrestler has their shoulders pinned against the ground for more than three seconds, they're out and they lose!
Whoever pins the wrestler wins!
But the pinned wrestler can do a move called a kick out that helps give them another chance!
If they kick out their legs, launching their shoulders off the ground just long enough to stop the count to three, they can get back up and keep fighting!
Rad!

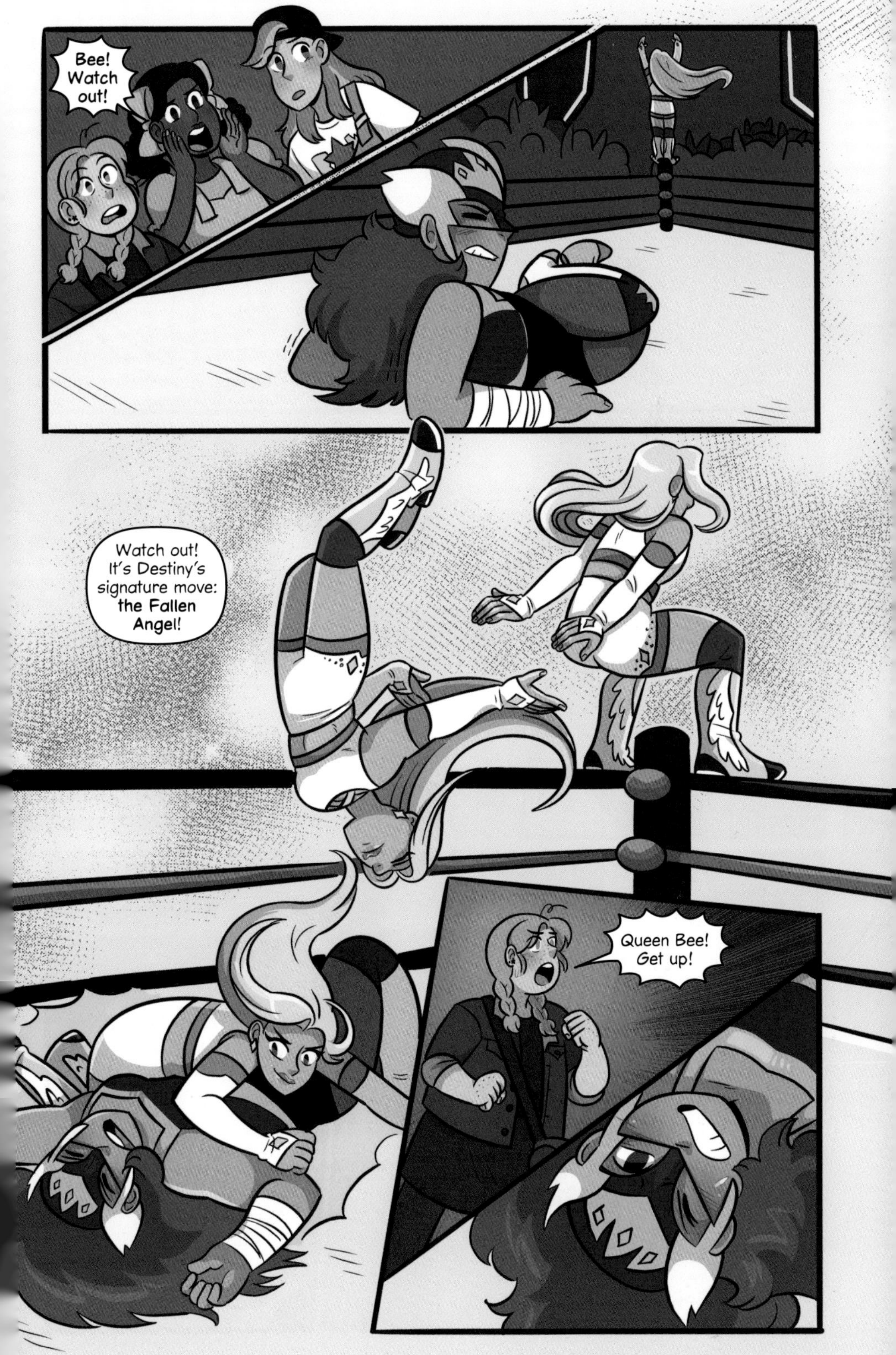
Bee! Watch out!
Watch out! It's Destiny's signature move: **the Fallen Angel!**
Queen Bee! Get up!

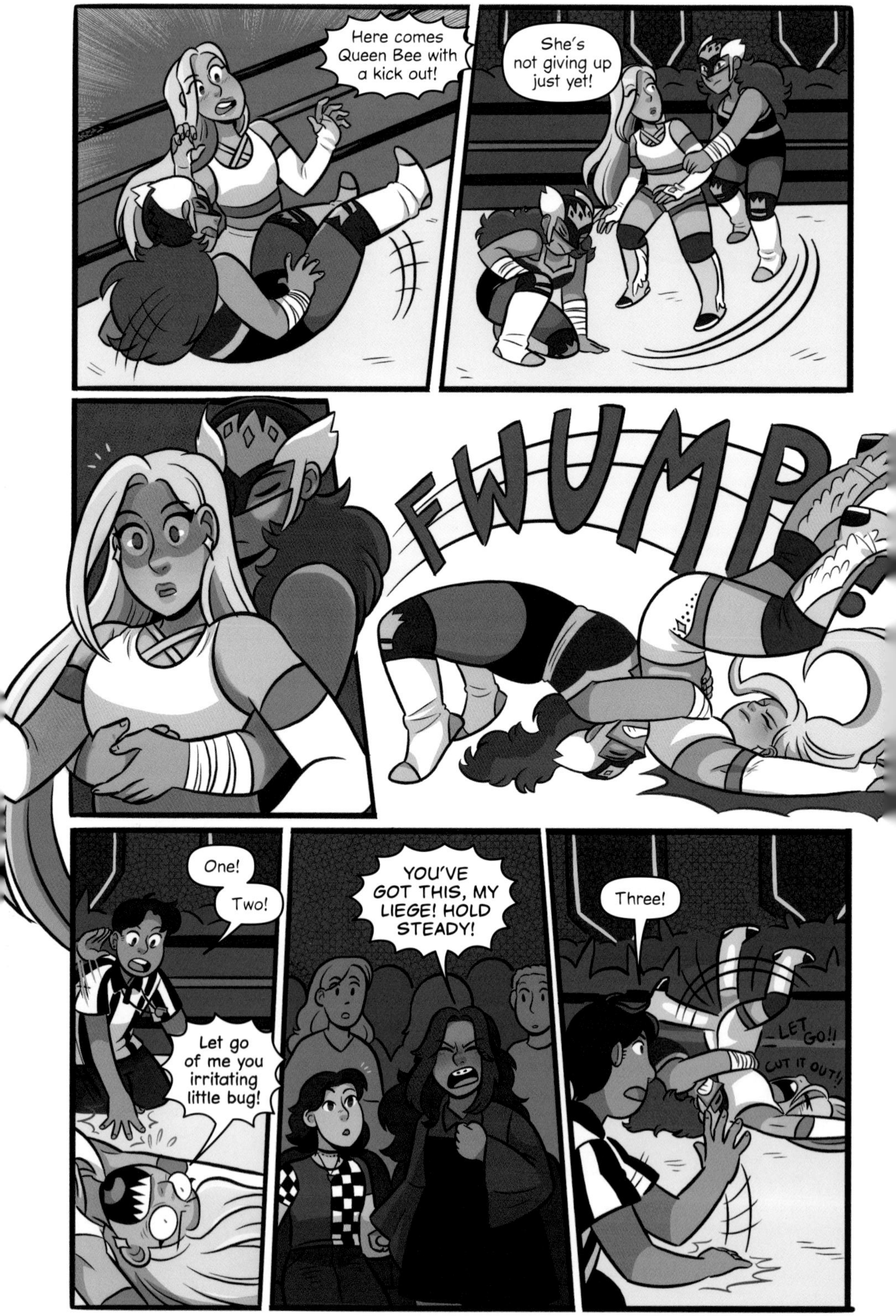

Here comes Queen Bee with a kick out!
She's not giving up just yet!
FWUMP
One!
Two!
Let go of me you irritating little bug!
YOU'VE GOT THIS, MY LIEGE! HOLD STEADY!
Three!
LET GO!!
CUT IT OUT!!

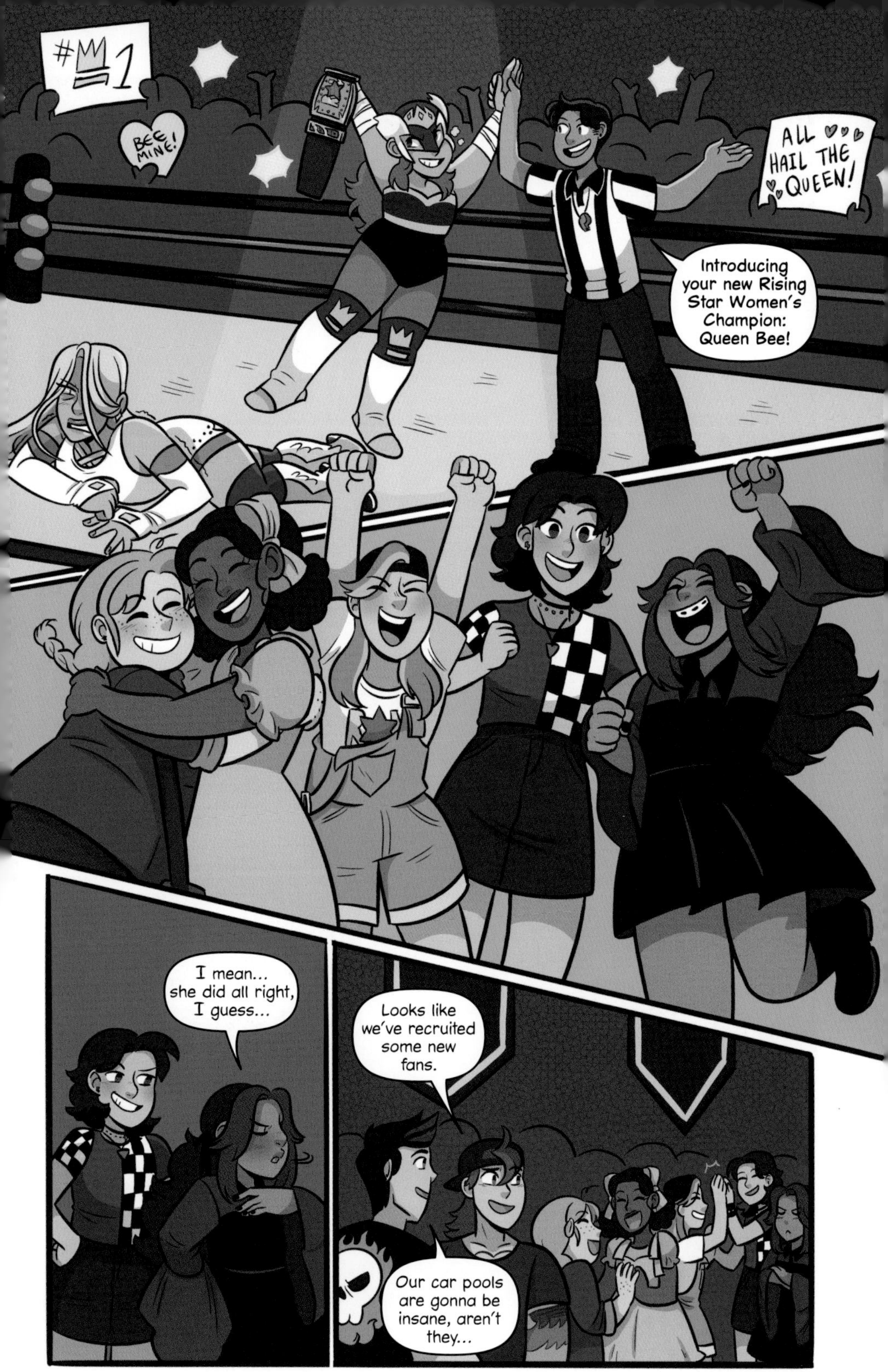
#1
BEE MINE!
ALL HAIL THE QUEEN!
Introducing your new Rising Star Women's Champion: Queen Bee!
I mean... she did all right, I guess...
Looks like we've recruited some new fans.
Our car pools are gonna be insane, aren't they...

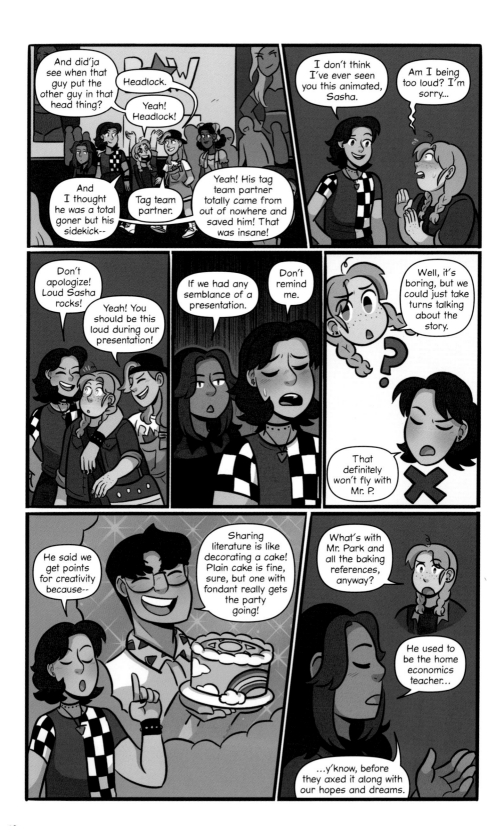

And did'ja see when that guy put the other guy in that head thing?

Headlock.

Yeah! Headlock!

And I thought he was a total goner but his sidekick--

Tag team partner.

Yeah! His tag team partner totally came from out of nowhere and saved him! That was insane!

I don't think I've ever seen you this animated, Sasha.

Am I being too loud? I'm sorry...

Don't apologize! Loud Sasha rocks!

Yeah! You should be this loud during our presentation!

If we had any semblance of a presentation.

Don't remind me.

Well, it's boring, but we could just take turns talking about the story.

That definitely won't fly with Mr. P.

He said we get points for creativity because--

Sharing literature is like decorating a cake! Plain cake is fine, sure, but one with fondant really gets the party going!

What's with Mr. Park and all the baking references, anyway?

He used to be the home economics teacher...

...y'know, before they axed it along with our hopes and dreams.

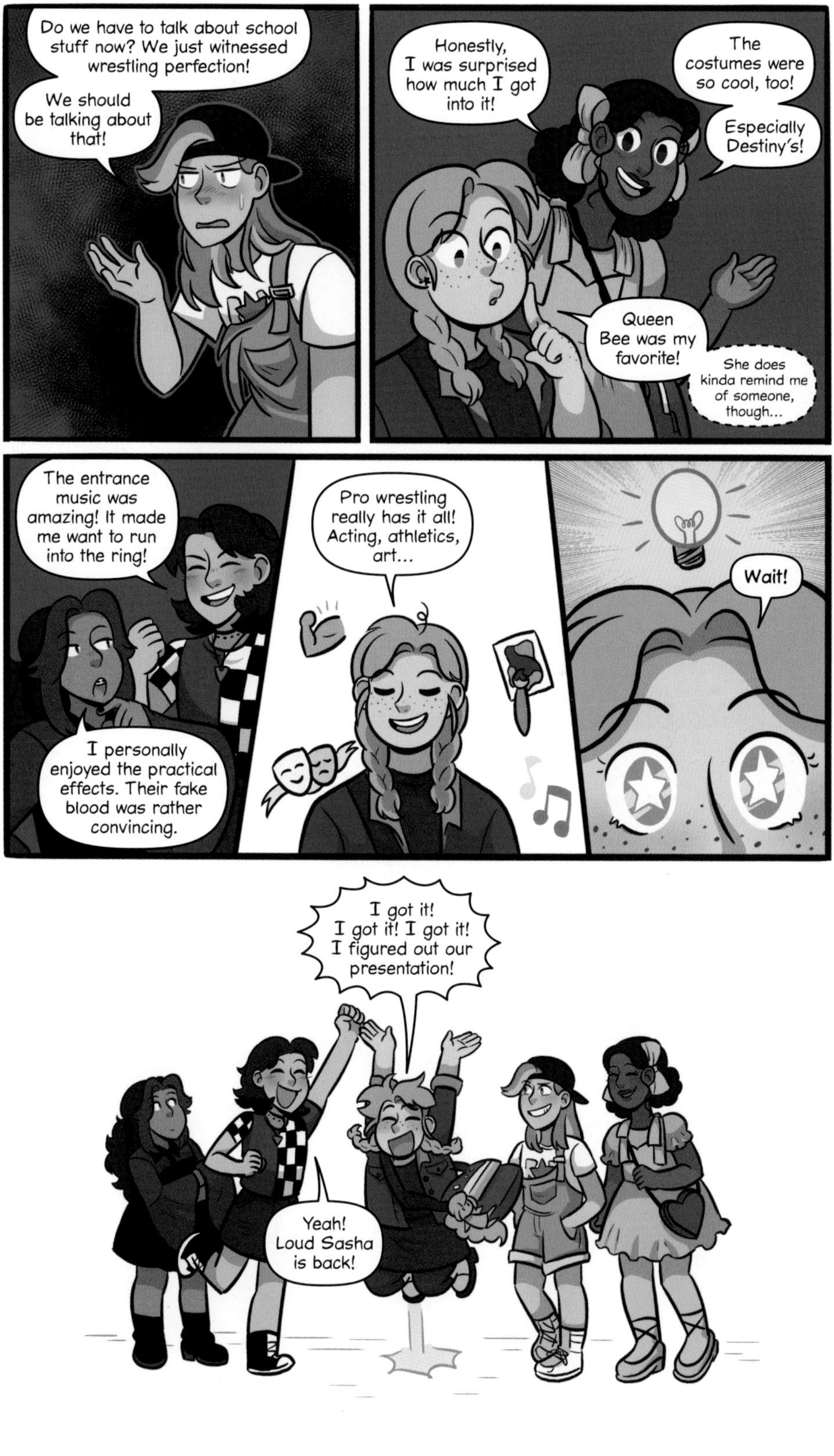
Do we have to talk about school stuff now? We just witnessed wrestling perfection!
We should be talking about that!
Honestly, I was surprised how much I got into it!
The costumes were so cool, too!
Especially Destiny's!
Queen Bee was my favorite!
She does kinda remind me of someone, though...
The entrance music was amazing! It made me want to run into the ring!
I personally enjoyed the practical effects. Their fake blood was rather convincing.
Pro wrestling really has it all! Acting, athletics, art...
Wait!
I got it! I got it! I got it! I figured out our presentation!
Yeah! Loud Sasha is back!

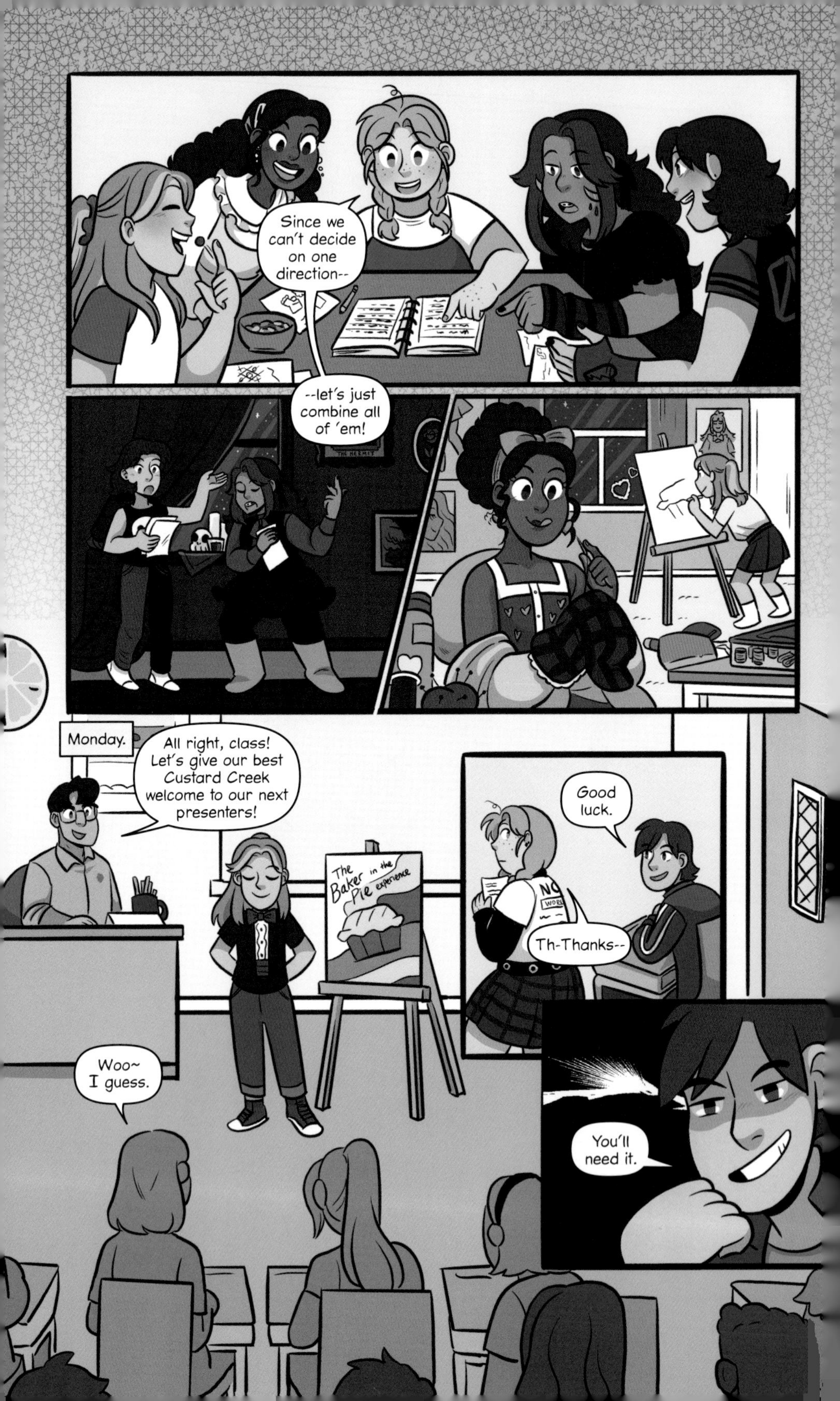
Since we can't decide on one direction--
--let's just combine all of 'em!
THE HERMIT
Monday.
All right, class! Let's give our best Custard Creek welcome to our next presenters!
The Baker in the Pie experience
Good luck.
Th-Thanks--
Woo~ I guess.
You'll need it.

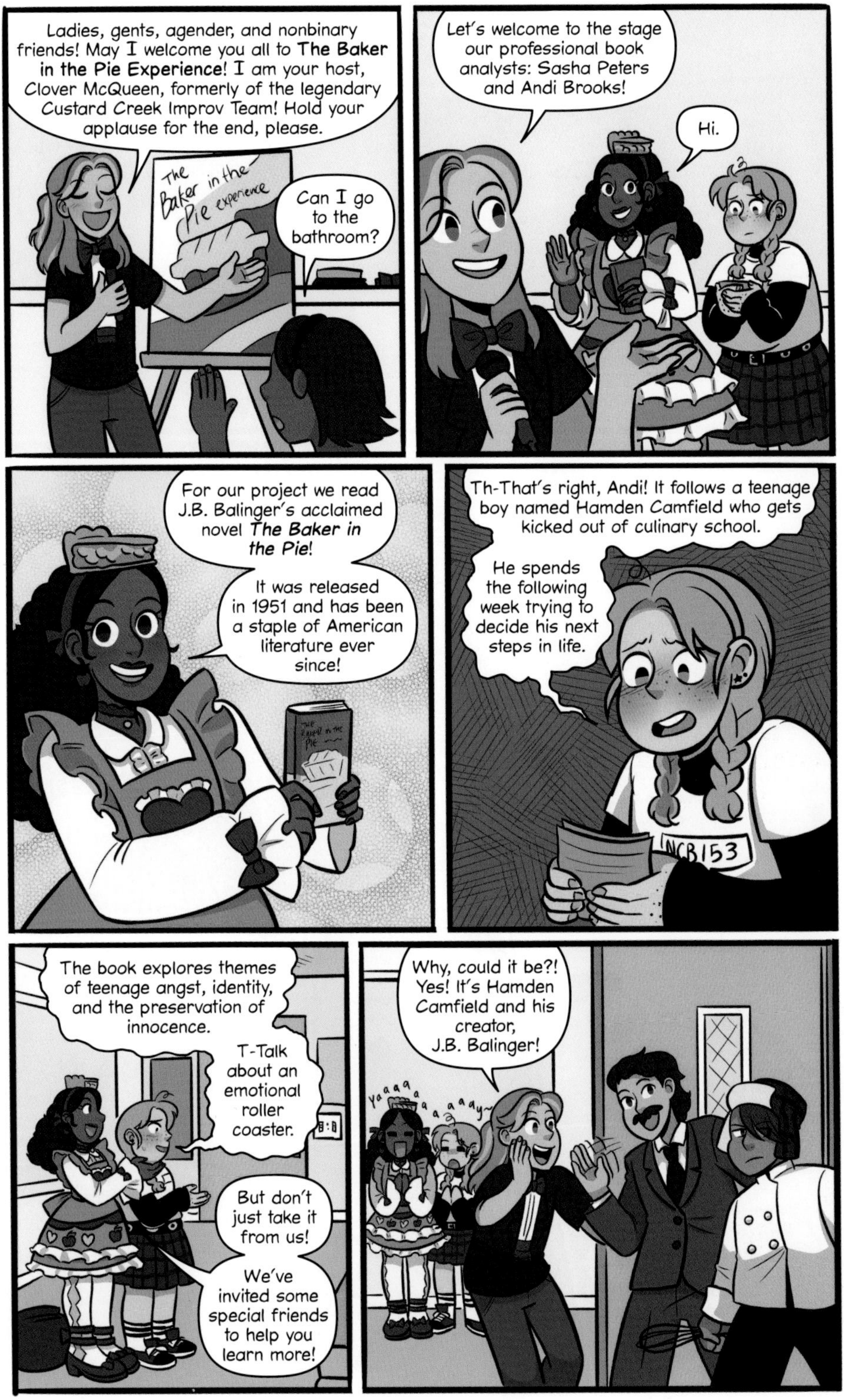
Ladies, gents, agender, and nonbinary friends! May I welcome you all to The Baker in the Pie Experience! I am your host, Clover McQueen, formerly of the legendary Custard Creek Improv Team! Hold your applause for the end, please.
The Baker in the Pie experience
Can I go to the bathroom?
Let's welcome to the stage our professional book analysts: Sasha Peters and Andi Brooks!
Hi.
For our project we read J.B. Balinger's acclaimed novel The Baker in the Pie!
It was released in 1951 and has been a staple of American literature ever since!
Th-That's right, Andi! It follows a teenage boy named Hamden Camfield who gets kicked out of culinary school.
He spends the following week trying to decide his next steps in life.
NCB153
The book explores themes of teenage angst, identity, and the preservation of innocence.
T-Talk about an emotional roller coaster.
But don't just take it from us!
We've invited some special friends to help you learn more!
Why, could it be?! Yes! It's Hamden Camfield and his creator, J.B. Balinger!
Yaaaaaaaaady~

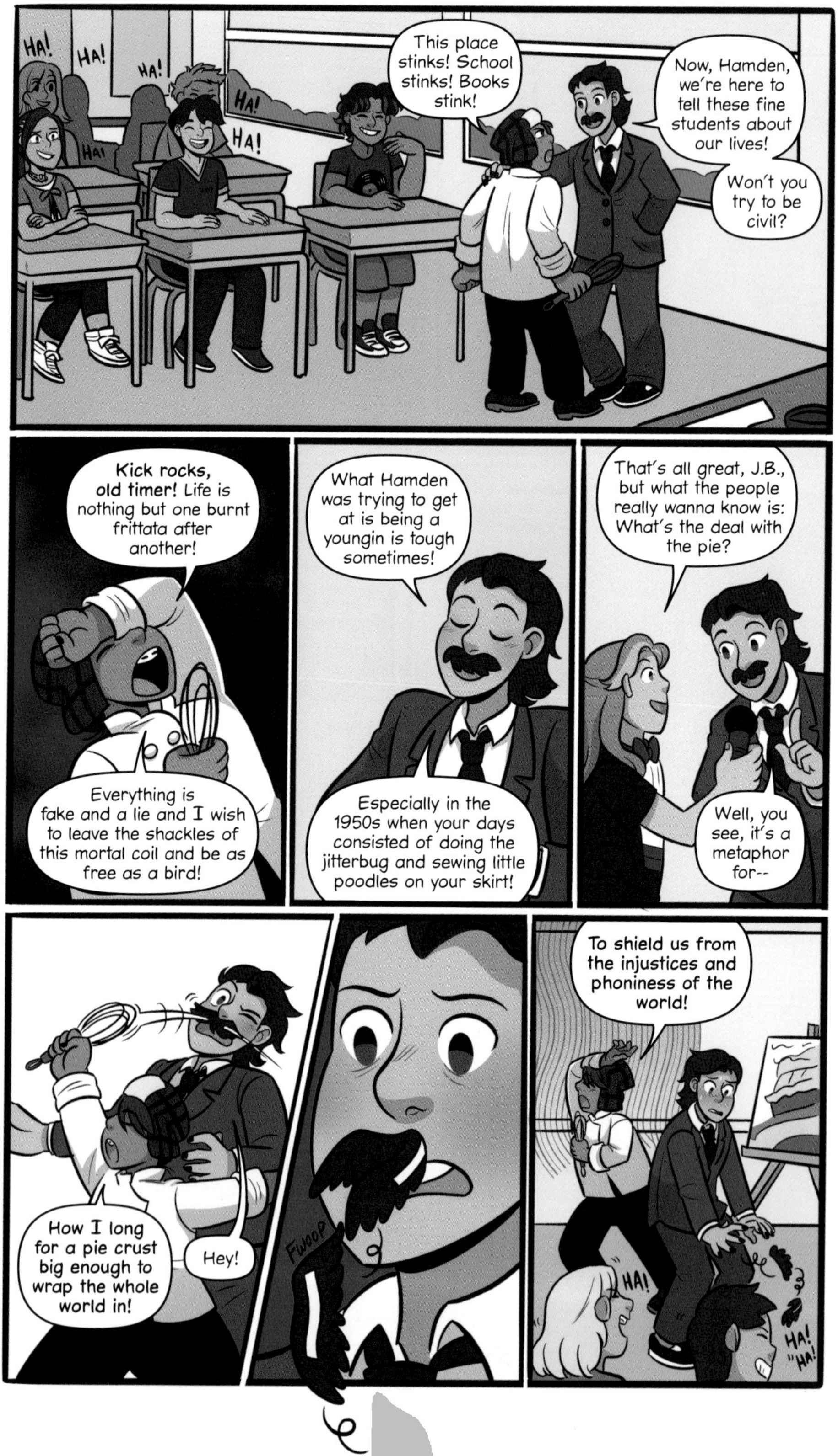
HA!
HA!
HA!
HA!
HA!
HA!
This place stinks! School stinks! Books stink!
Now, Hamden, we're here to tell these fine students about our lives!
Won't you try to be civil?
Kick rocks, old timer! Life is nothing but one burnt frittata after another!
Everything is fake and a lie and I wish to leave the shackles of this mortal coil and be as free as a bird!
What Hamden was trying to get at is being a youngin is tough sometimes!
Especially in the 1950s when your days consisted of doing the jitterbug and sewing little poodles on your skirt!
That's all great, J.B., but what the people really wanna know is: What's the deal with the pie?
Well, you see, it's a metaphor for--
How I long for a pie crust big enough to wrap the whole world in!
Hey!
FWOOP
To shield us from the injustices and phoniness of the world!
HA!
HA!
HA!

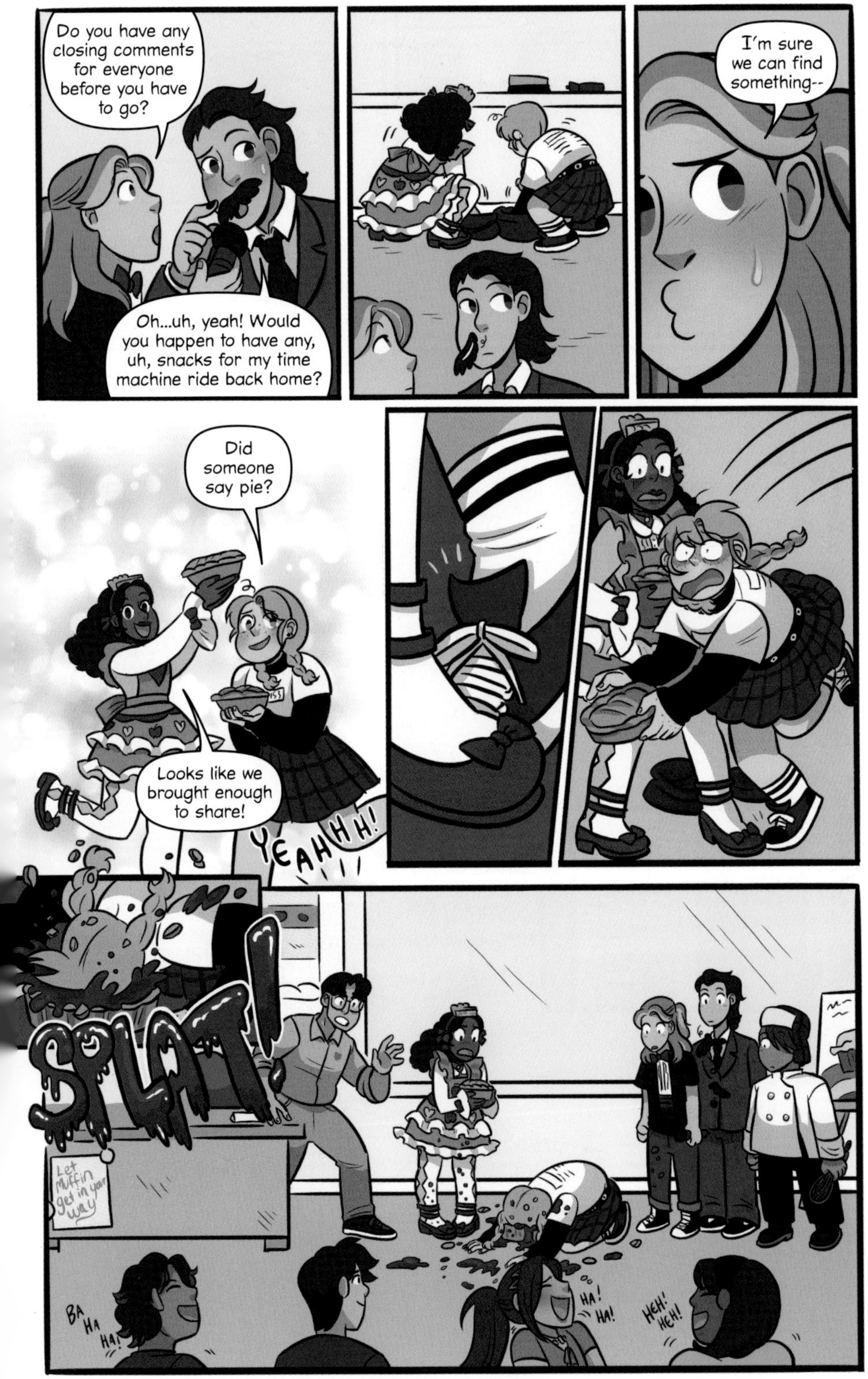
Do you have any closing comments for everyone before you have to go?
Oh...uh, yeah! Would you happen to have any, uh, snacks for my time machine ride back home?
I'm sure we can find something--
Did someone say pie?
Looks like we brought enough to share!
YEAHHH!
SPLAT!
Let Muffin get in your way
BA HA HA!
HA! HA!
HEH! HEH!

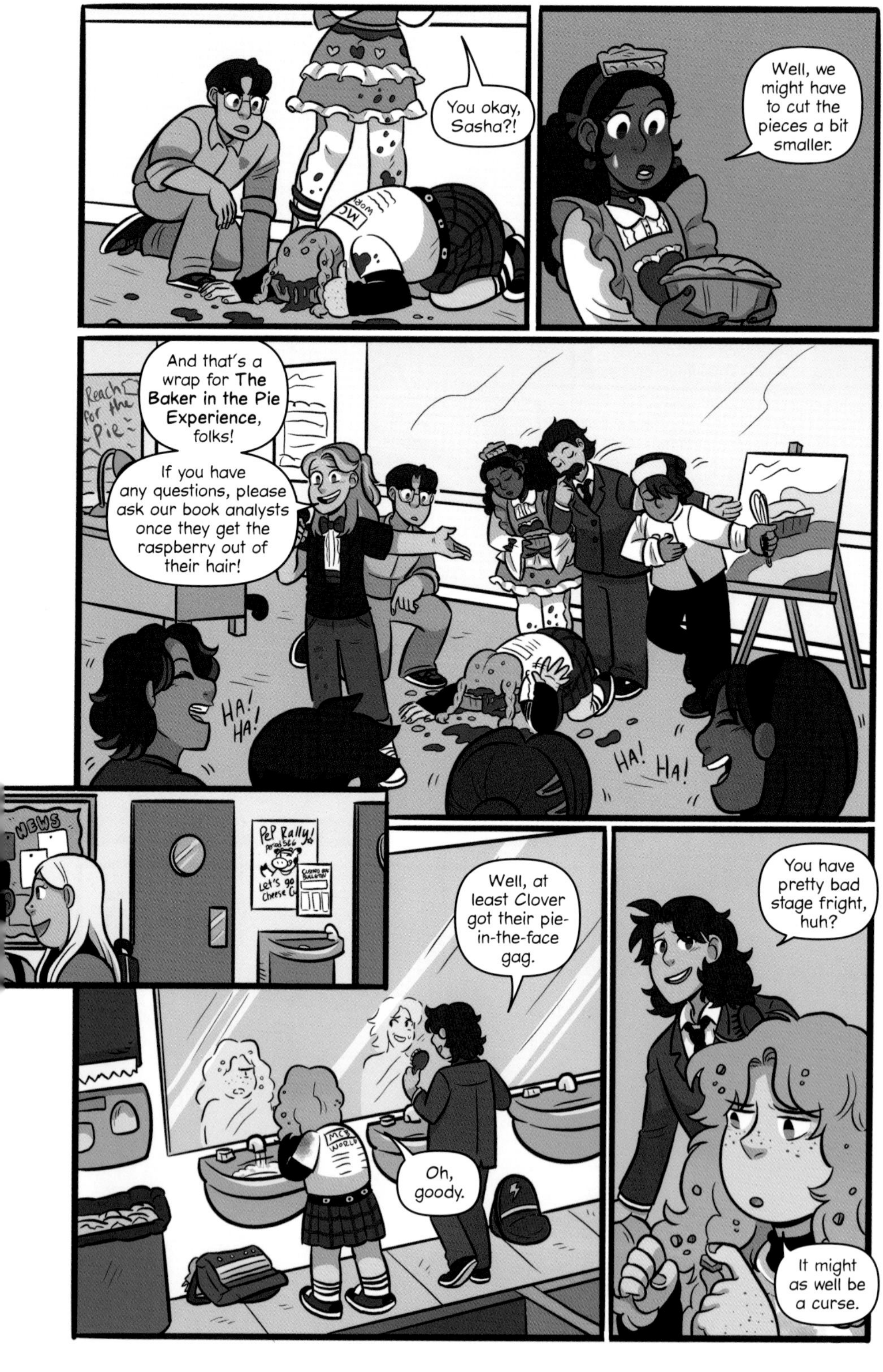

You okay, Sasha?!
Well, we might have to cut the pieces a bit smaller.
Reach for the Pie
And that's a wrap for **The Baker in the Pie Experience,** folks!
If you have any questions, please ask our book analysts once they get the raspberry out of their hair!
HA! HA!
HA! HA!
NEWS
Pep Rally!
period 5&6
Let's go Cheese
Well, at least Clover got their pie-in-the-face gag.
Oh, goody.
You have pretty bad stage fright, huh?
It might as well be a curse.

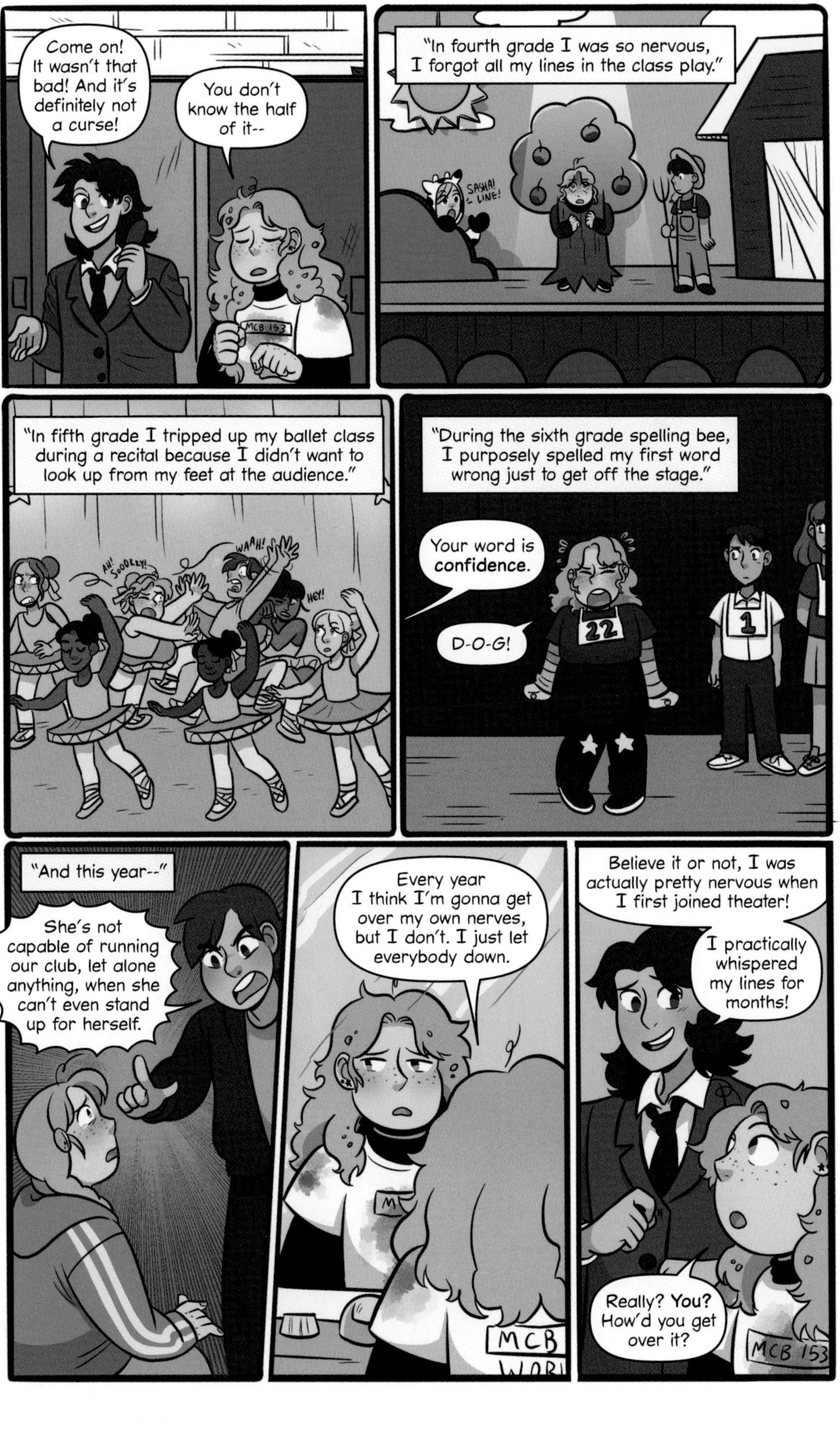
Come on! It wasn't that bad! And it's definitely not a curse!
You don't know the half of it--
MCB 153
"In fourth grade I was so nervous, I forgot all my lines in the class play."
SASHA! LINE!
"In fifth grade I tripped up my ballet class during a recital because I didn't want to look up from my feet at the audience."
AH! SOORRY!
WAAH!
HEY!
"During the sixth grade spelling bee, I purposely spelled my first word wrong just to get off the stage."
Your word is **confidence.**
D-O-G!
22
1
"And this year--"
She's not capable of running our club, let alone anything, when she can't even stand up for herself.
Every year I think I'm gonna get over my own nerves, but I don't. I just let everybody down.
MCB WORL
Believe it or not, I was actually pretty nervous when I first joined theater!
I practically whispered my lines for months!
Really? **You?** How'd you get over it?
MCB 153

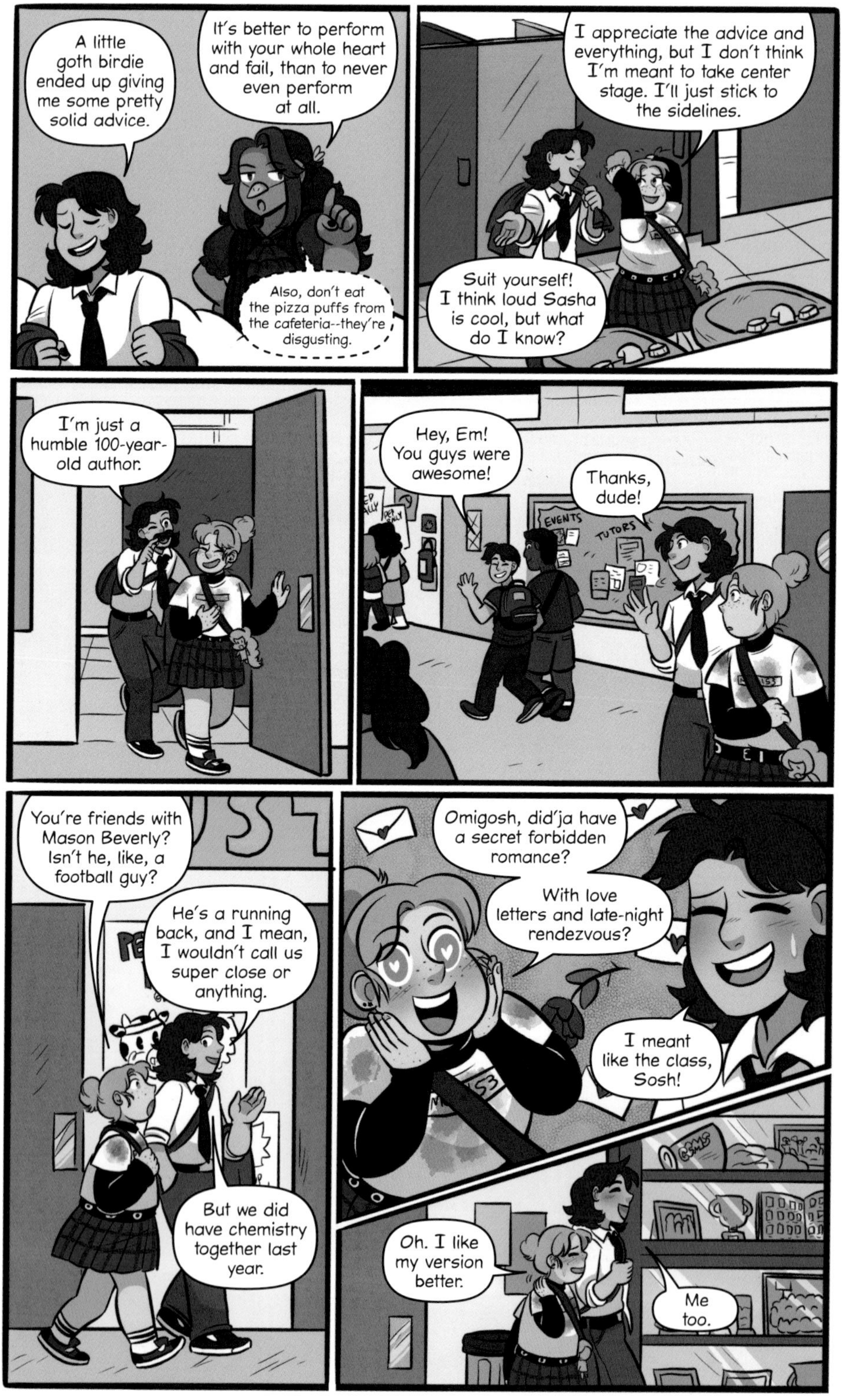
A little goth birdie ended up giving me some pretty solid advice.
It's better to perform with your whole heart and fail, than to never even perform at all.
Also, don't eat the pizza puffs from the cafeteria--they're disgusting.
I appreciate the advice and everything, but I don't think I'm meant to take center stage. I'll just stick to the sidelines.
Suit yourself! I think loud Sasha is cool, but what do I know?
I'm just a humble 100-year-old author.
Hey, Em! You guys were awesome!
Thanks, dude!
EVENTS
TUTORS
You're friends with Mason Beverly? Isn't he, like, a football guy?
He's a running back, and I mean, I wouldn't call us super close or anything.
But we did have chemistry together last year.
Omigosh, did'ja have a secret forbidden romance?
With love letters and late-night rendezvous?
I meant like the class, Sosh!
Oh. I like my version better.
Me too.

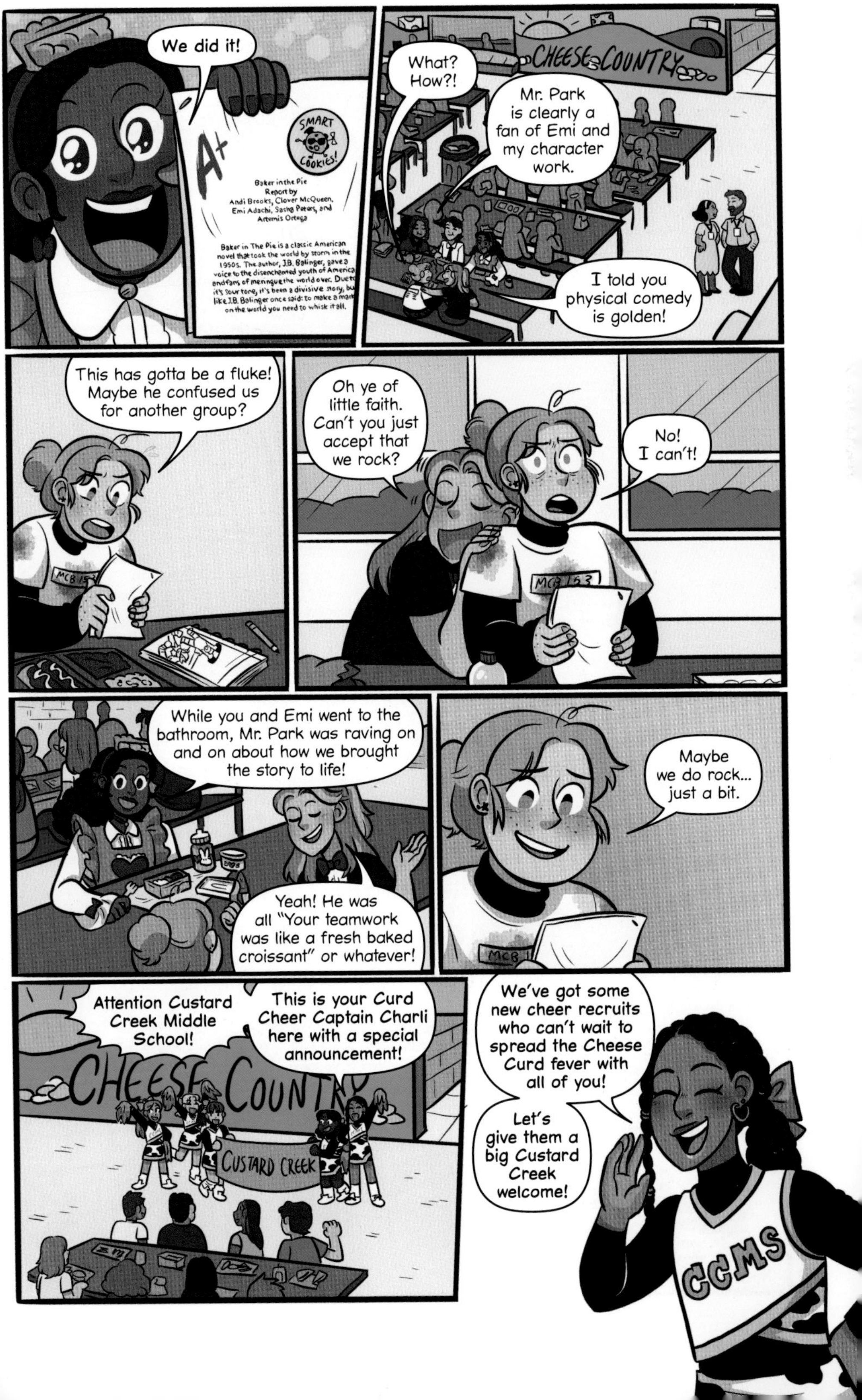
We did it!
A+
SMART COOKIES!
Baker in the Pie
Report by
Andi Brooks, Clover McQueen,
Emi Adachi, Sasha Peters, and
Artemis Ortega
Baker in The Pie is a classic American novel that took the world by storm in the 1950s. The author, J.B. Balinger, gave a voice to the disenchanted youth of America and fans of meringue the world over. Due t it's sour tone, it's been a divisive story, bu like J.B. Balinger once said: to make a mar on the world you need to whisk it all.
CHEESE COUNTRY
What? How?!
Mr. Park is clearly a fan of Emi and my character work.
I told you physical comedy is golden!
This has gotta be a fluke! Maybe he confused us for another group?
Oh ye of little faith. Can't you just accept that we rock?
No! I can't!
While you and Emi went to the bathroom, Mr. Park was raving on and on about how we brought the story to life!
Yeah! He was all "Your teamwork was like a fresh baked croissant" or whatever!
Maybe we do rock... just a bit.
Attention Custard Creek Middle School!
This is your Curd Cheer Captain Charli here with a special announcement!
CHEESE COUNTRY
CUSTARD CREEK
We've got some new cheer recruits who can't wait to spread the Cheese Curd fever with all of you!
Let's give them a big Custard Creek welcome!
CCMS

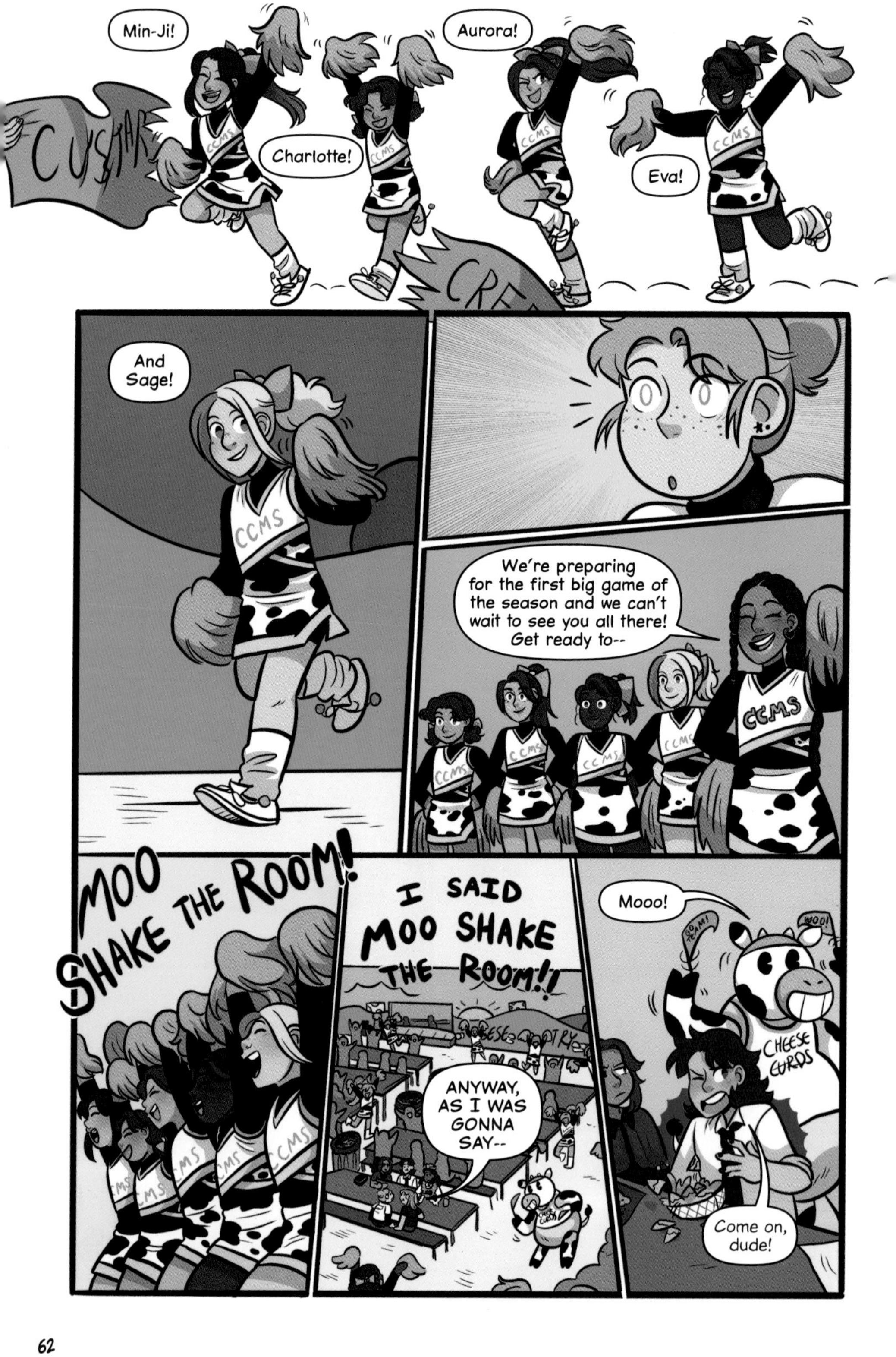
Min-Ji!
Charlotte!
Aurora!
Eva!
And Sage!
We're preparing for the first big game of the season and we can't wait to see you all there! Get ready to--
CCMS
MOO SHAKE THE ROOM!
I SAID MOO SHAKE THE ROOM!!
ANYWAY, AS I WAS GONNA SAY--
Mooo!
CHEESE CURDS
Come on, dude!

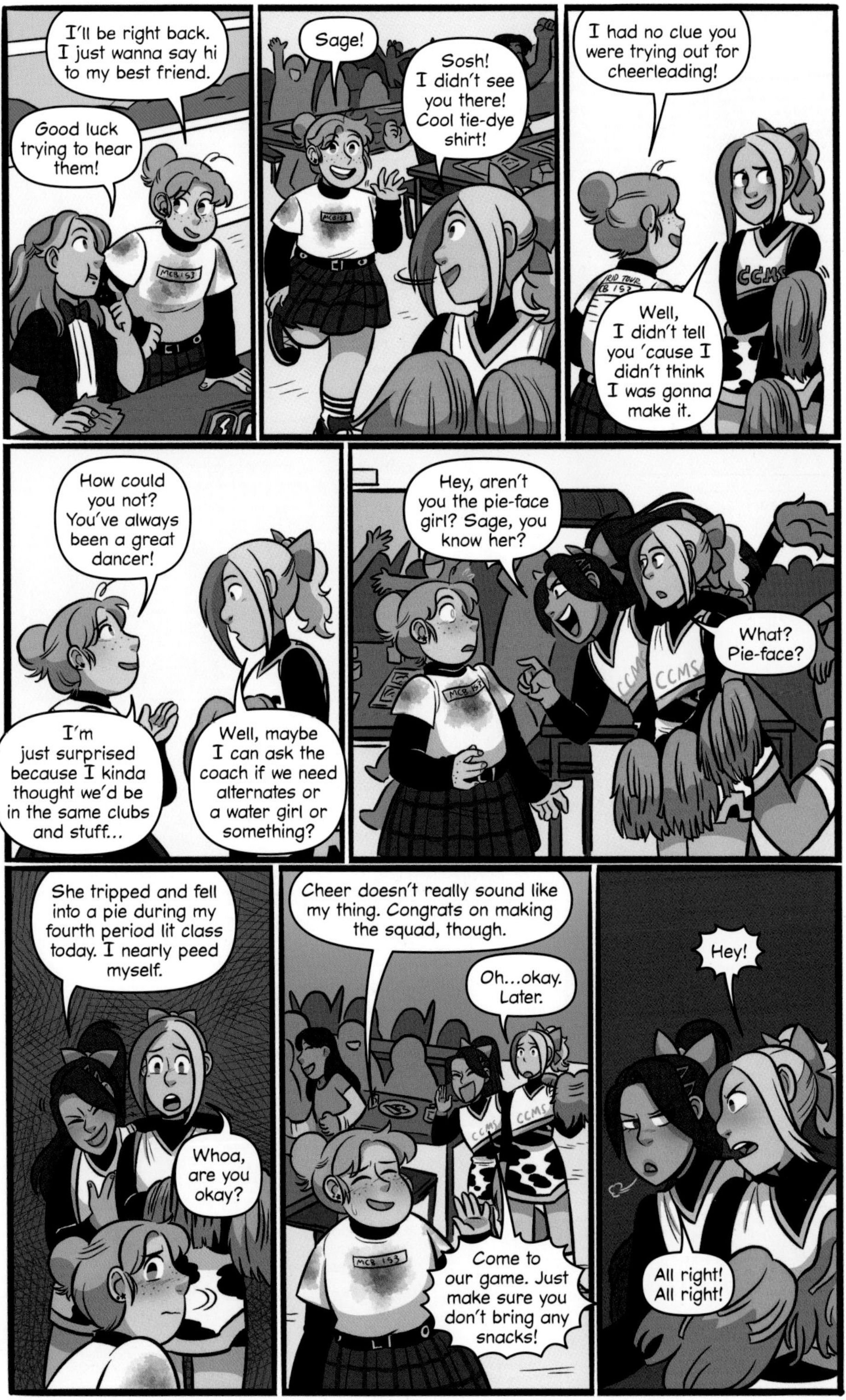

I'll be right back. I just wanna say hi to my best friend.
Good luck trying to hear them!
MCB 153
Sage!
Sosh! I didn't see you there! Cool tie-dye shirt!
I had no clue you were trying out for cheerleading!
CCMS
Well, I didn't tell you 'cause I didn't think I was gonna make it.
How could you not? You've always been a great dancer!
I'm just surprised because I kinda thought we'd be in the same clubs and stuff...
Well, maybe I can ask the coach if we need alternates or a water girl or something?
Hey, aren't you the pie-face girl? Sage, you know her?
What? Pie-face?
She tripped and fell into a pie during my fourth period lit class today. I nearly peed myself.
Whoa, are you okay?
Cheer doesn't really sound like my thing. Congrats on making the squad, though.
Oh...okay. Later.
Come to our game. Just make sure you don't bring any snacks!
Hey!
All right! All right!

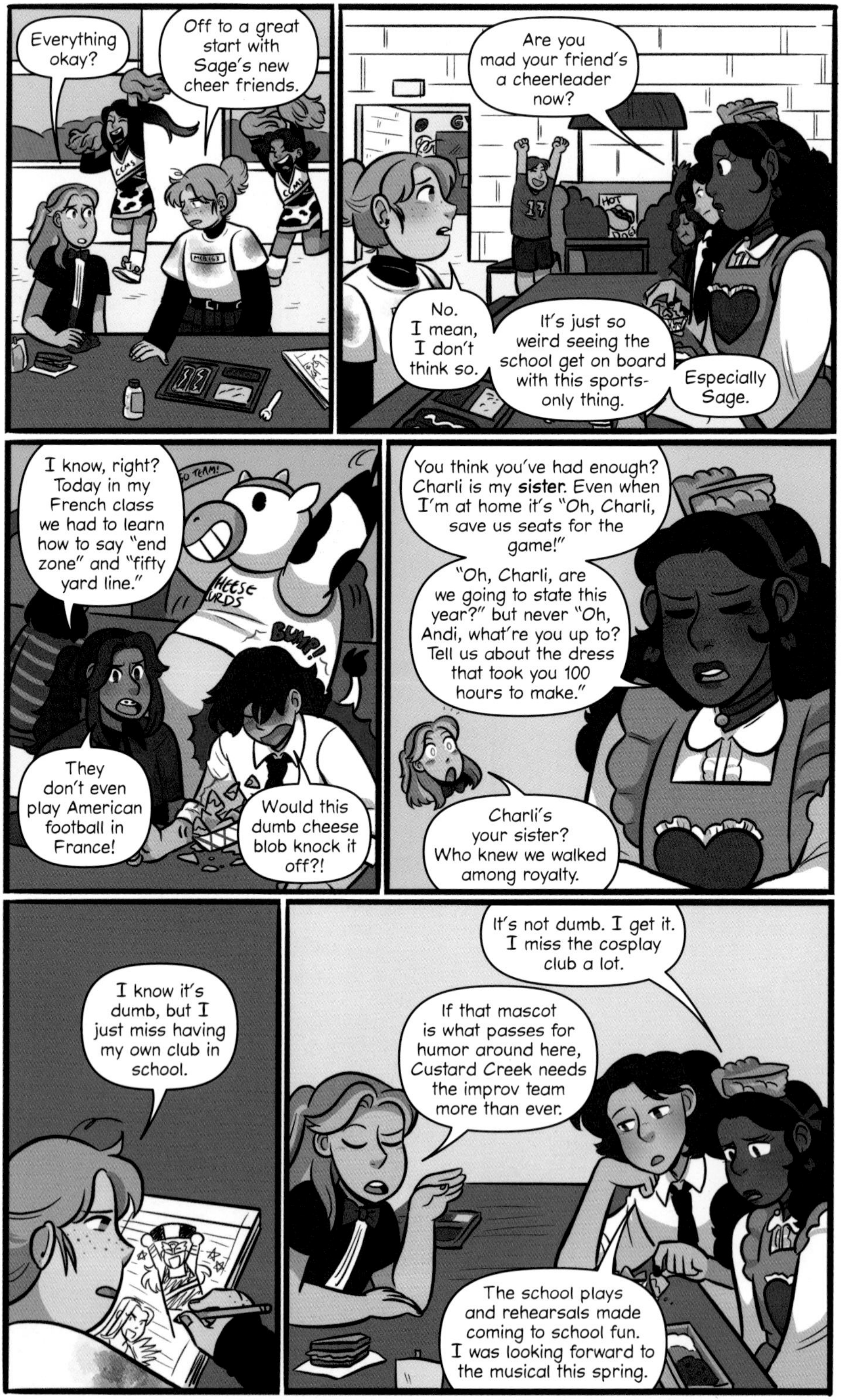
Everything okay?
Off to a great start with Sage's new cheer friends.
Are you mad your friend's a cheerleader now?
No. I mean, I don't think so.
It's just so weird seeing the school get on board with this sports-only thing.
Especially Sage.
I know, right? Today in my French class we had to learn how to say "end zone" and "fifty yard line."
GO TEAM!
CHEESE CURDS
BUMP!
They don't even play American football in France!
Would this dumb cheese blob knock it off?!
You think you've had enough? Charli is my **sister**. Even when I'm at home it's "Oh, Charli, save us seats for the game!"
"Oh, Charli, are we going to state this year?" but never "Oh, Andi, what're you up to? Tell us about the dress that took you 100 hours to make."
Charli's your sister? Who knew we walked among royalty.
I know it's dumb, but I just miss having my own club in school.
It's not dumb. I get it. I miss the cosplay club a lot.
If that mascot is what passes for humor around here, Custard Creek needs the improv team more than ever.
The school plays and rehearsals made coming to school fun. I was looking forward to the musical this spring.

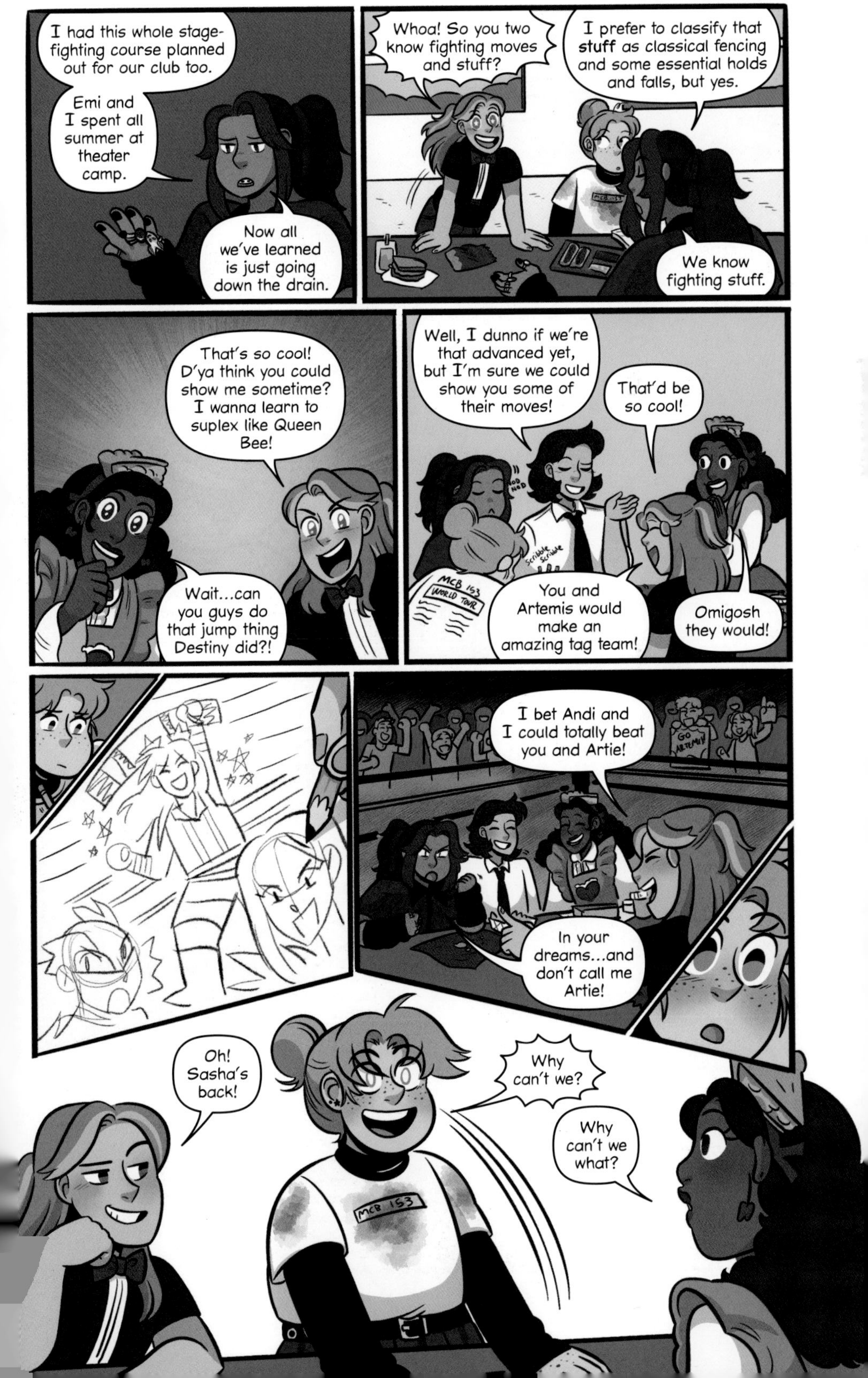

I had this whole stage-fighting course planned out for our club too.
Emi and I spent all summer at theater camp.
Now all we've learned is just going down the drain.
Whoa! So you two know fighting moves and stuff?
I prefer to classify that **stuff** as classical fencing and some essential holds and falls, but yes.
We know fighting stuff.
That's so cool! D'ya think you could show me sometime? I wanna learn to suplex like Queen Bee!
Wait...can you guys do that jump thing Destiny did?!
Well, I dunno if we're that advanced yet, but I'm sure we could show you some of their moves!
That'd be so cool!
NOD NOD
Scribble Scribble
MCB 153 WORLD TOUR
You and Artemis would make an amazing tag team!
Omigosh they would!
I bet Andi and I could totally beat you and Artie!
GO ARTEMIS
In your dreams...and don't call me Artie!
Oh! Sasha's back!
Why can't we?
Why can't we what?
MCB 153

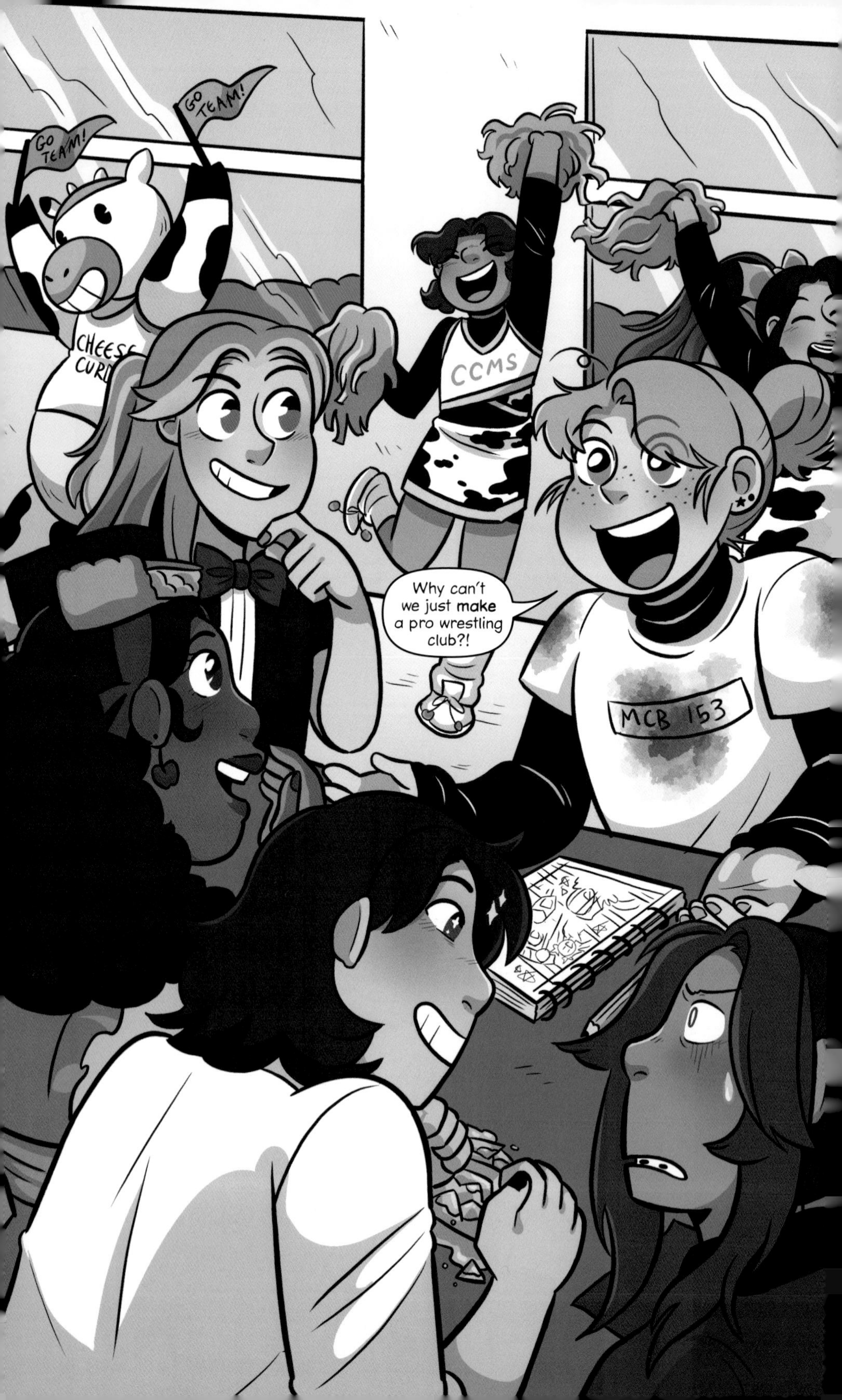
GO TEAM!
GO TEAM!
CCMS
Why can't we just **make** a pro wrestling club?!
MCB 153

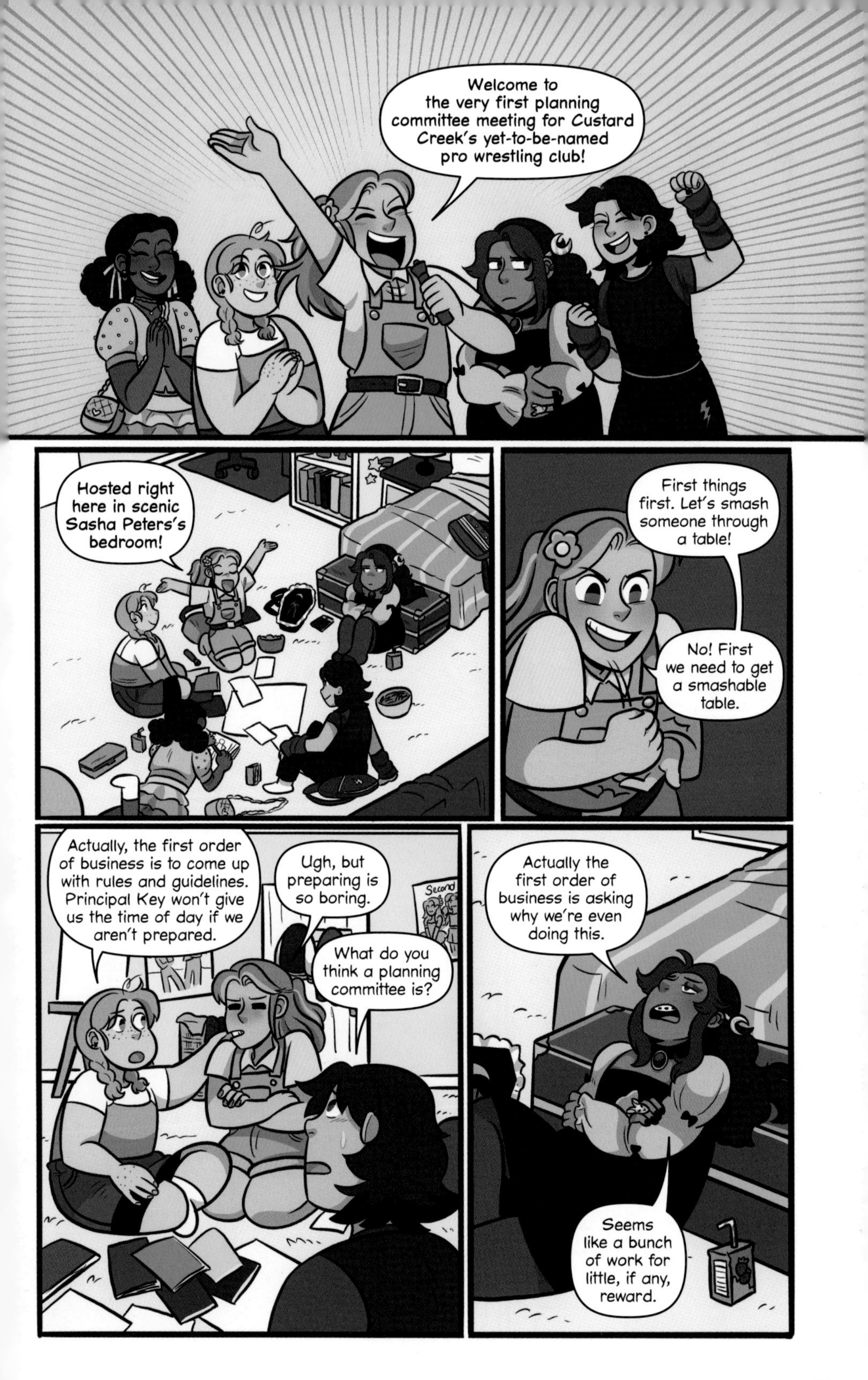

Welcome to the very first planning committee meeting for Custard Creek's yet-to-be-named pro wrestling club!
Hosted right here in scenic Sasha Peters's bedroom!
First things first. Let's smash someone through a table!
No! First we need to get a smashable table.
Actually, the first order of business is to come up with rules and guidelines. Principal Key won't give us the time of day if we aren't prepared.
Ugh, but preparing is so boring.
What do you think a planning committee is?
Actually the first order of business is asking why we're even doing this.
Seems like a bunch of work for little, if any, reward.

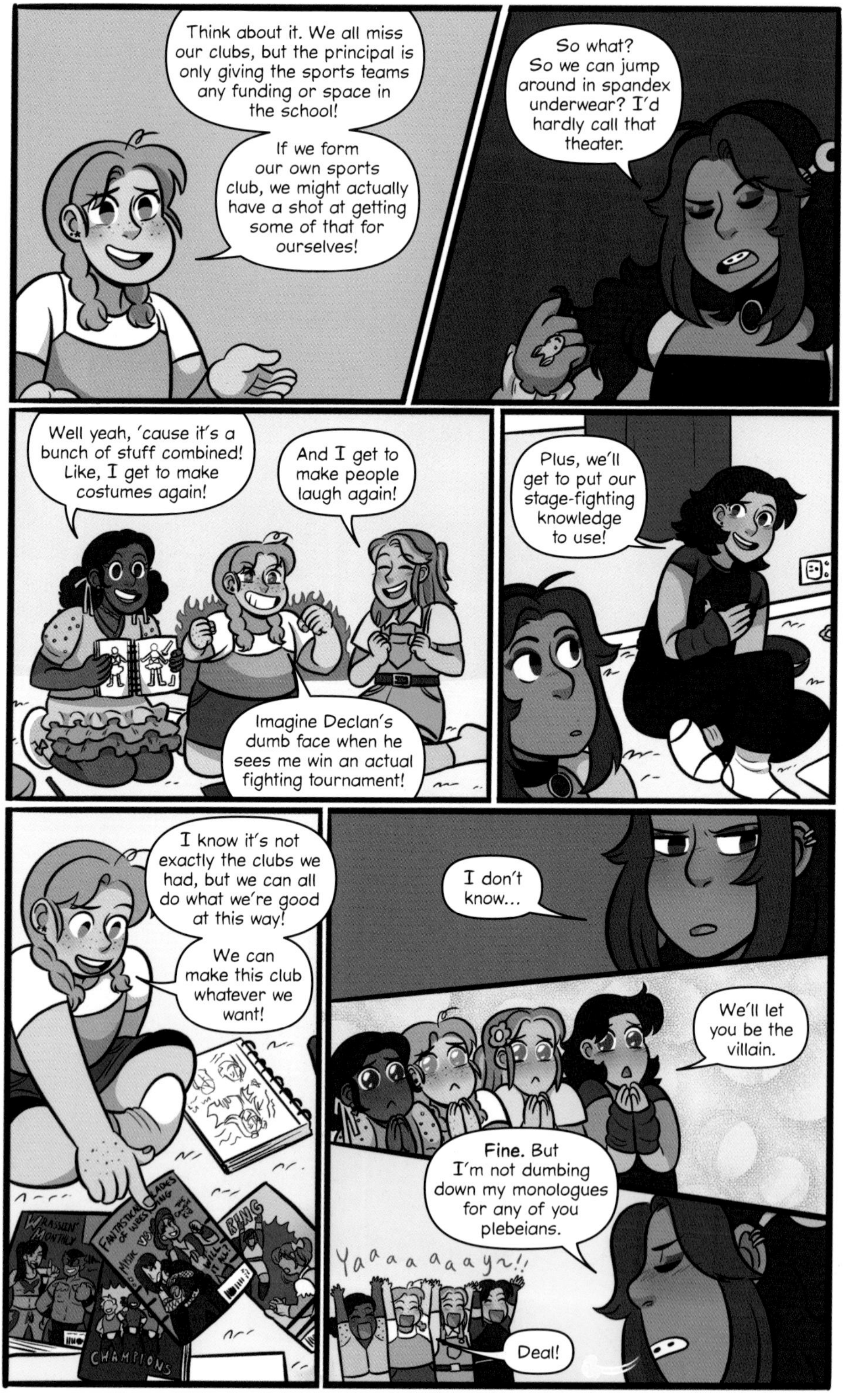
Think about it. We all miss our clubs, but the principal is only giving the sports teams any funding or space in the school!
If we form our own sports club, we might actually have a shot at getting some of that for ourselves!
So what? So we can jump around in spandex underwear? I'd hardly call that theater.
Well yeah, 'cause it's a bunch of stuff combined! Like, I get to make costumes again!
And I get to make people laugh again!
Imagine Declan's dumb face when he sees me win an actual fighting tournament!
Plus, we'll get to put our stage-fighting knowledge to use!
I know it's not exactly the clubs we had, but we can all do what we're good at this way!
We can make this club whatever we want!
RING
CHAMPIONS
I don't know...
We'll let you be the villain.
Fine. But I'm not dumbing down my monologues for any of you plebeians.
Yaaaaaaay~!!
Deal!

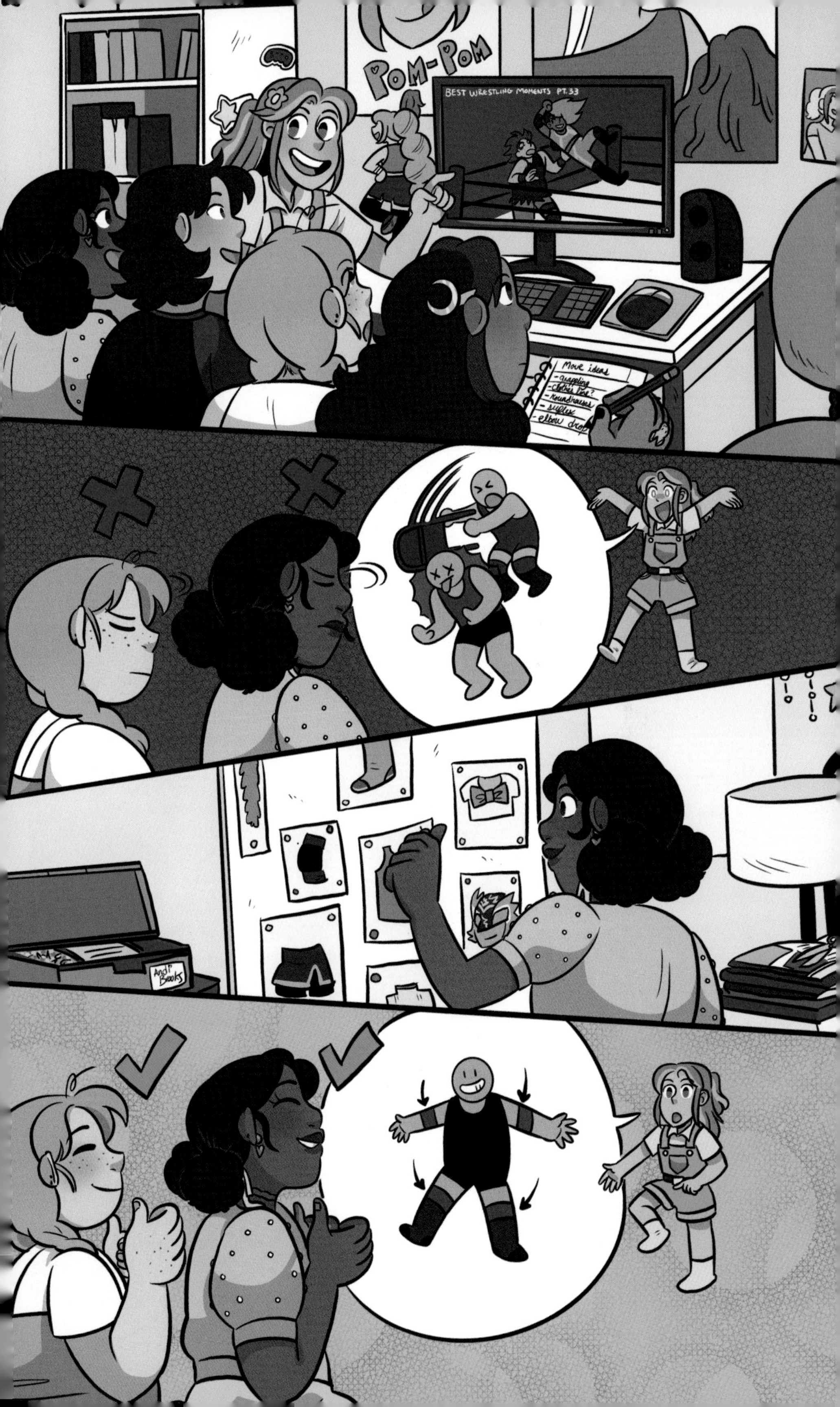
POM-POM
BEST WRESTLING MOMENTS PT. 33
Move ideas
-grappling
-clothes line?
-roundhouses
-suplex
-elbow drop
Andi P Books

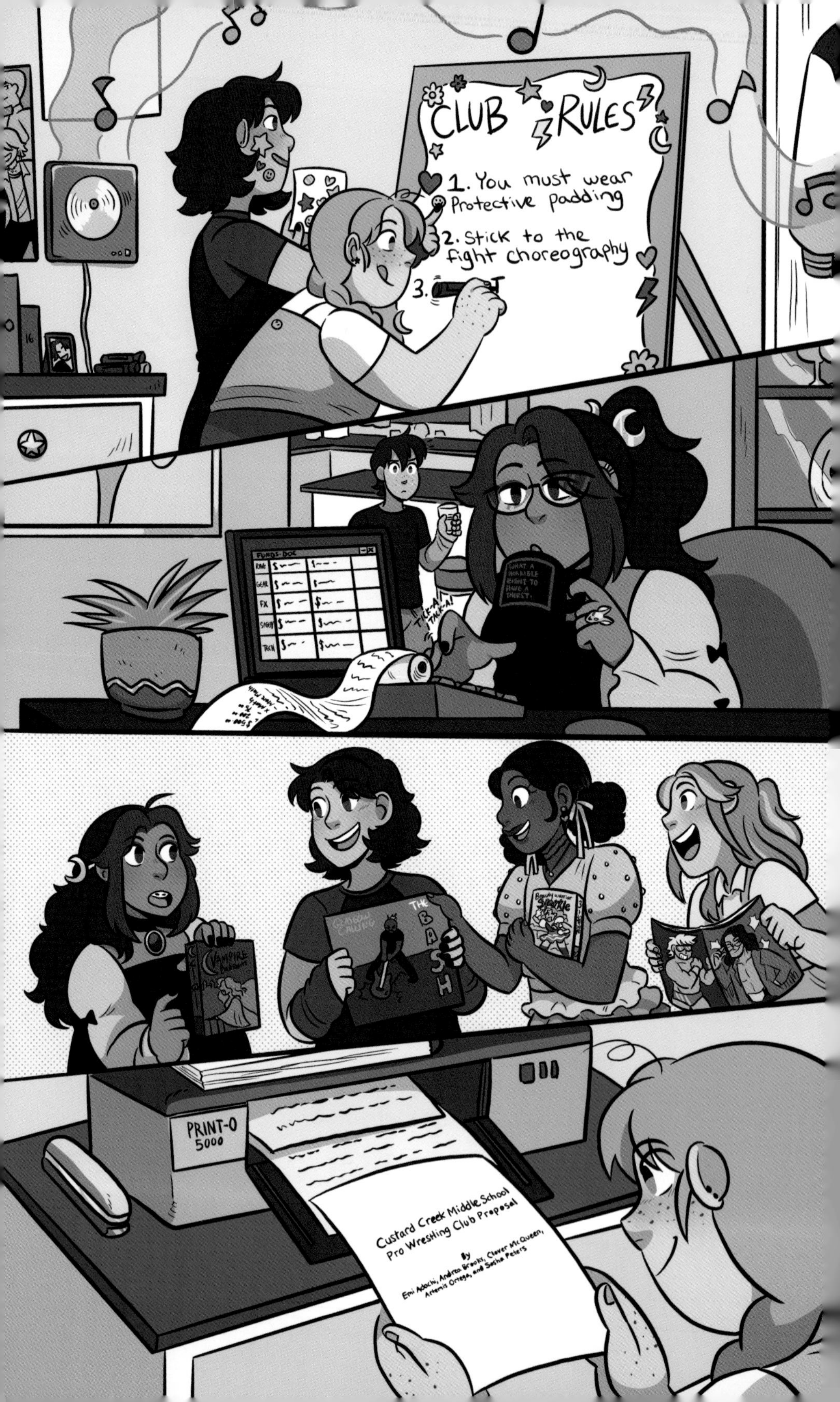

CLUB RULES
1. You must wear Protective padding
2. Stick to the fight choreography
3.
FUNDS.DOC
RING
GEAR
FX
TECH
TICK-A TACK-A!
WHAT A HORRIBLE NIGHT TO HAVE A THIRST.
VAMPIRE
THE BASH
Beauty warrior Sparkle
PRINT-O 5000
Custard Creek Middle School
Pro Wrestling Club Proposal
By
Emi Adachi, Andrea Brooks, Clover McQueen,
Artemis Ortega, and Sasha Peters

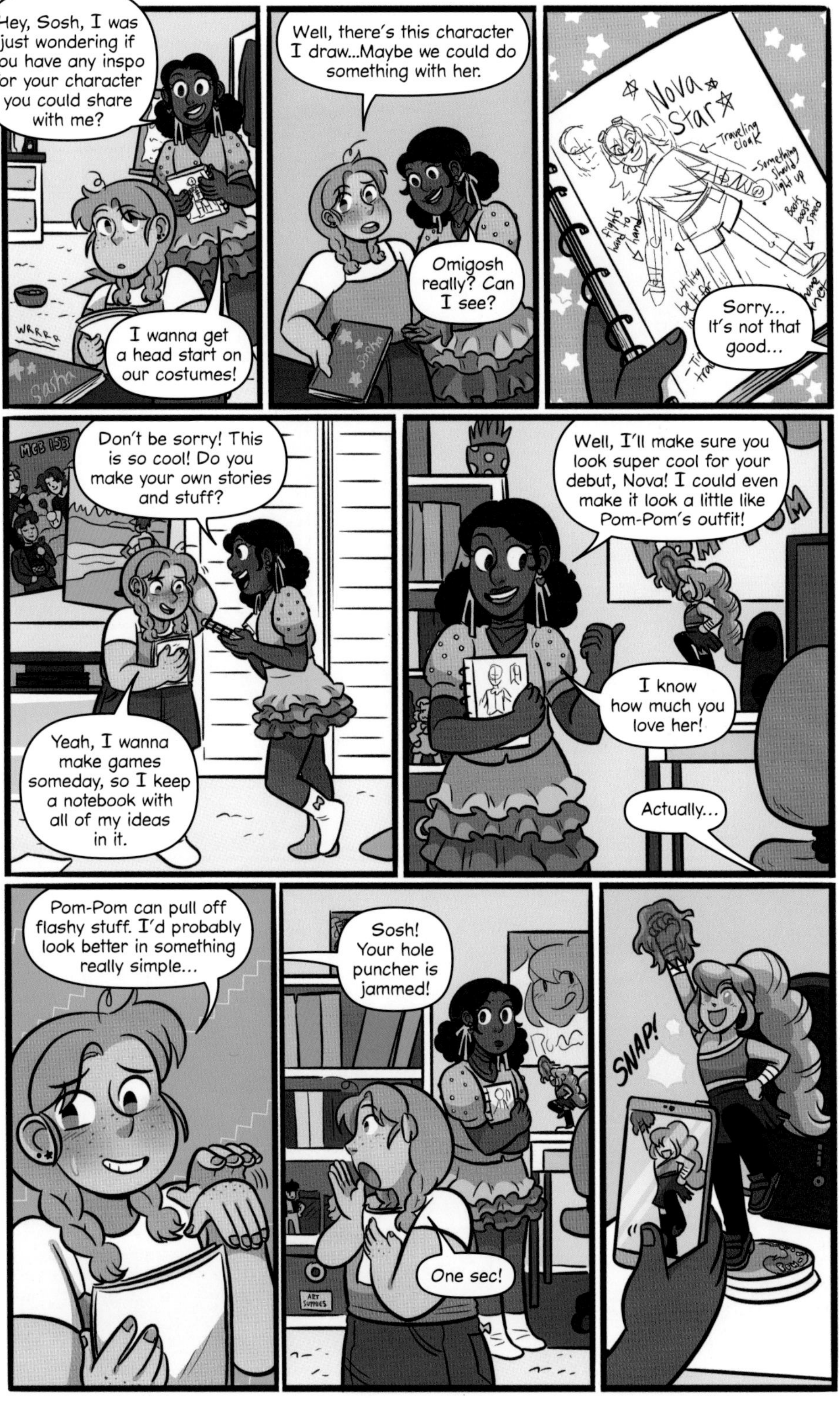

Hey, Sosh, I was just wondering if you have any inspo for your character you could share with me?
I wanna get a head start on our costumes!
WRRRR
Sasha
Well, there's this character I draw...Maybe we could do something with her.
Omigosh really? Can I see?
Sosha
Nova Star
Traveling cloak
Something should light up
Boots boost speed
fights hand to hand
Sorry... It's not that good...
MGB 153
Don't be sorry! This is so cool! Do you make your own stories and stuff?
Yeah, I wanna make games someday, so I keep a notebook with all of my ideas in it.
Well, I'll make sure you look super cool for your debut, Nova! I could even make it look a little like Pom-Pom's outfit!
I know how much you love her!
Actually...
Pom-Pom can pull off flashy stuff. I'd probably look better in something really simple...
Sosh! Your hole puncher is jammed!
One sec!
ART SUPPLIES
SNAP!

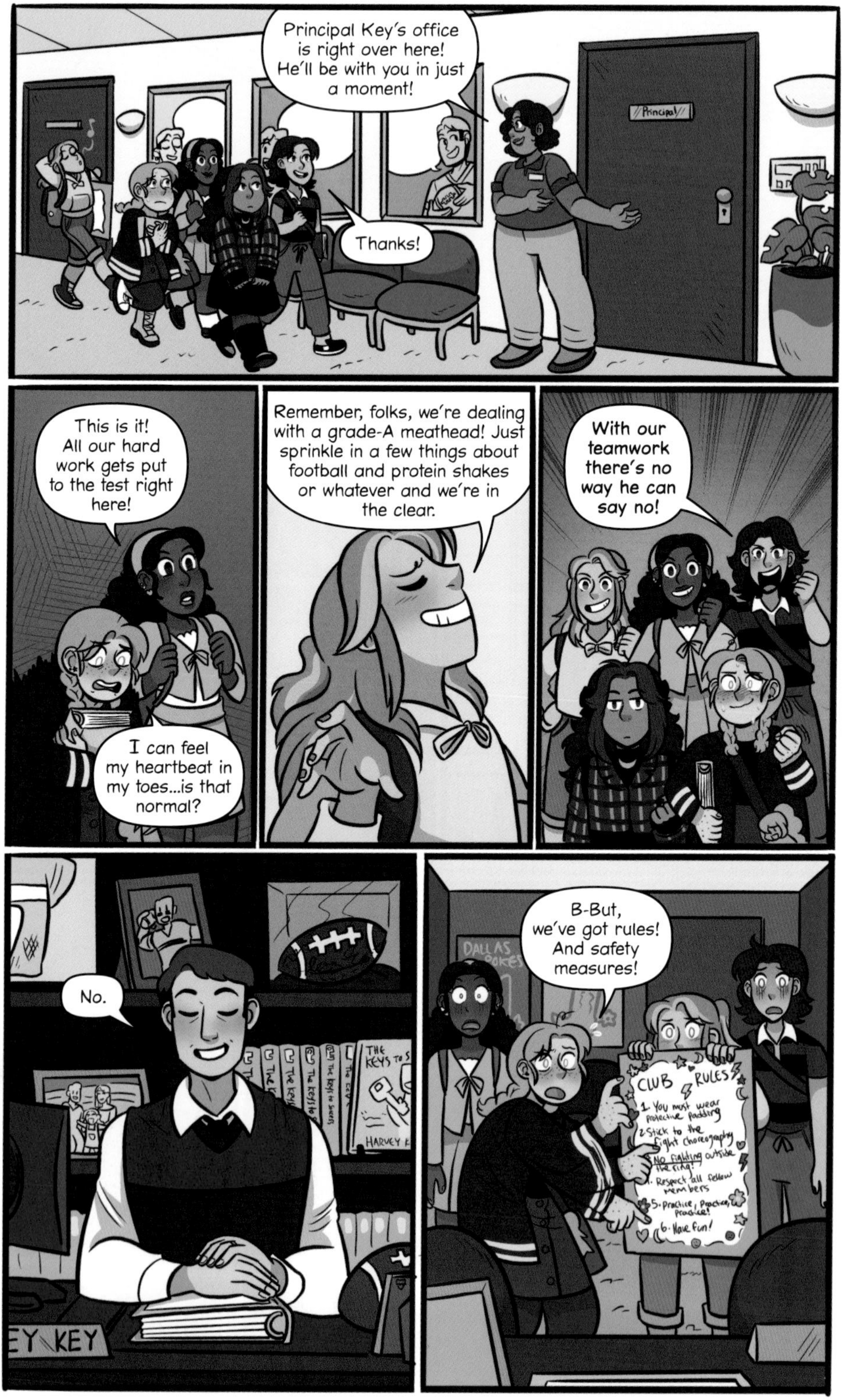
Principal Key's office is right over here! He'll be with you in just a moment!
Principal
Thanks!
This is it! All our hard work gets put to the test right here!
I can feel my heartbeat in my toes...is that normal?
Remember, folks, we're dealing with a grade-A meathead! Just sprinkle in a few things about football and protein shakes or whatever and we're in the clear.
With our teamwork there's no way he can say no!
No.
B-But, we've got rules! And safety measures!
CLUB RULES
1. You must wear protective padding
2. Stick to the fight choreography
No fighting outside the ring!
4. Respect all fellow members
5. Practice, Practice, Practice!
6. Have fun!

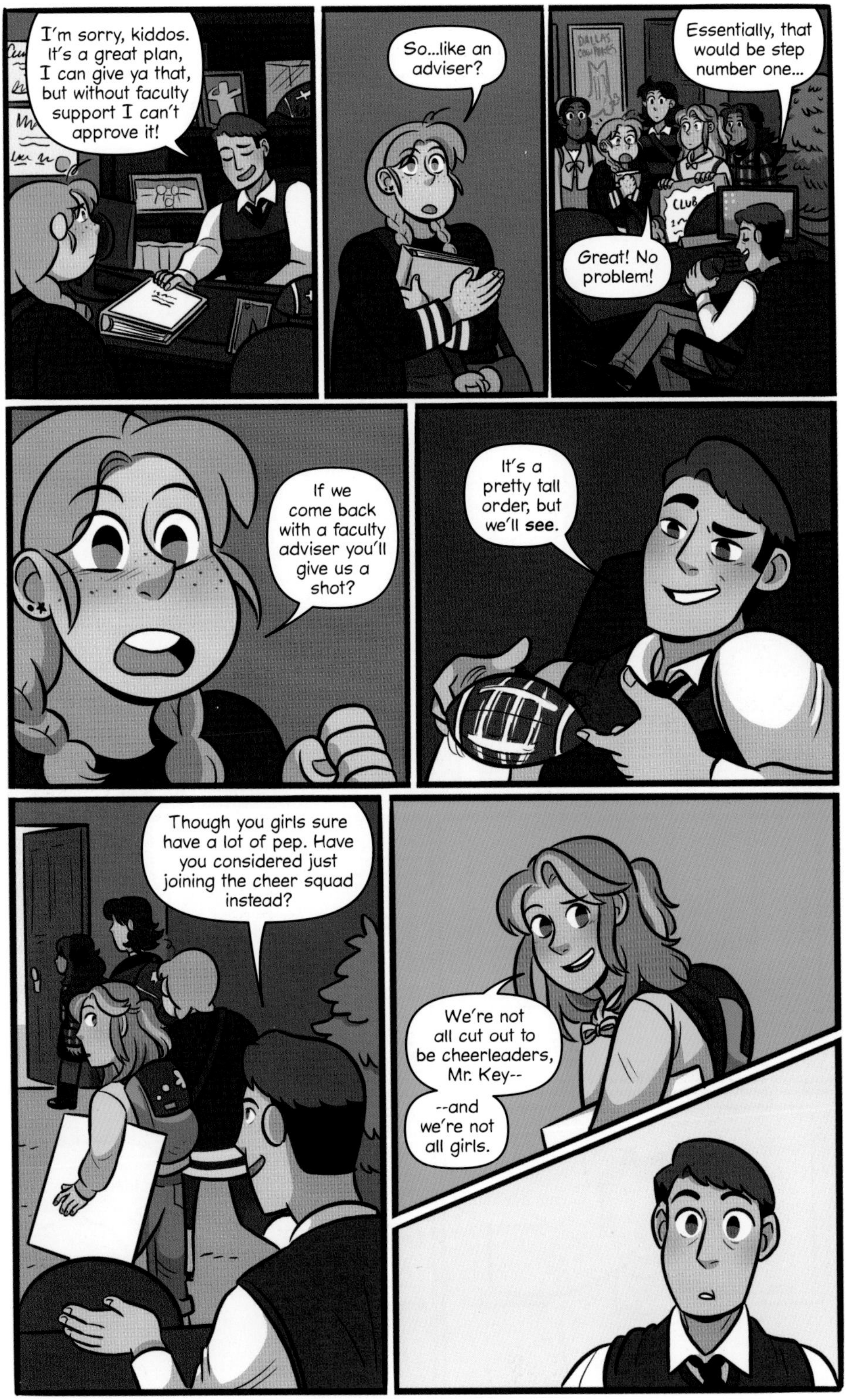
I'm sorry, kiddos. It's a great plan, I can give ya that, but without faculty support I can't approve it!
So...like an adviser?
Essentially, that would be step number one...
Great! No problem!
If we come back with a faculty adviser you'll give us a shot?
It's a pretty tall order, but we'll **see**.
Though you girls sure have a lot of pep. Have you considered just joining the cheer squad instead?
We're not all cut out to be cheerleaders, Mr. Key--
--and we're not all girls.

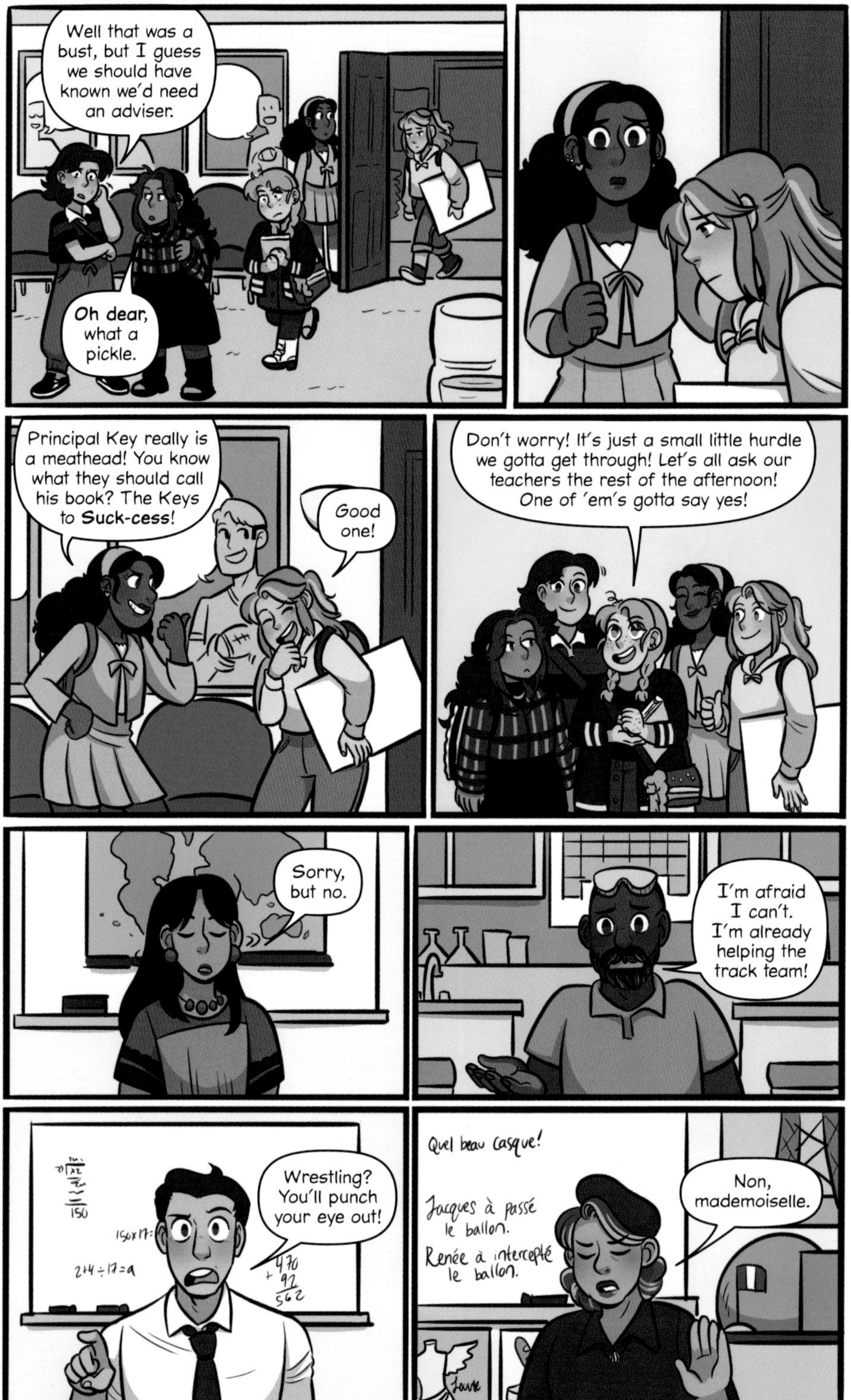
Well that was a bust, but I guess we should have known we'd need an adviser.
Oh dear, what a pickle.
Principal Key really is a meathead! You know what they should call his book? The Keys to **Suck-cess**!
Good one!
Don't worry! It's just a small little hurdle we gotta get through! Let's all ask our teachers the rest of the afternoon! One of 'em's gotta say yes!
Sorry, but no.
I'm afraid I can't. I'm already helping the track team!
Wrestling? You'll punch your eye out!
Quel beau casque!
Jacques à passé le ballon.
Renée à intercepté le ballon.
Non, mademoiselle.

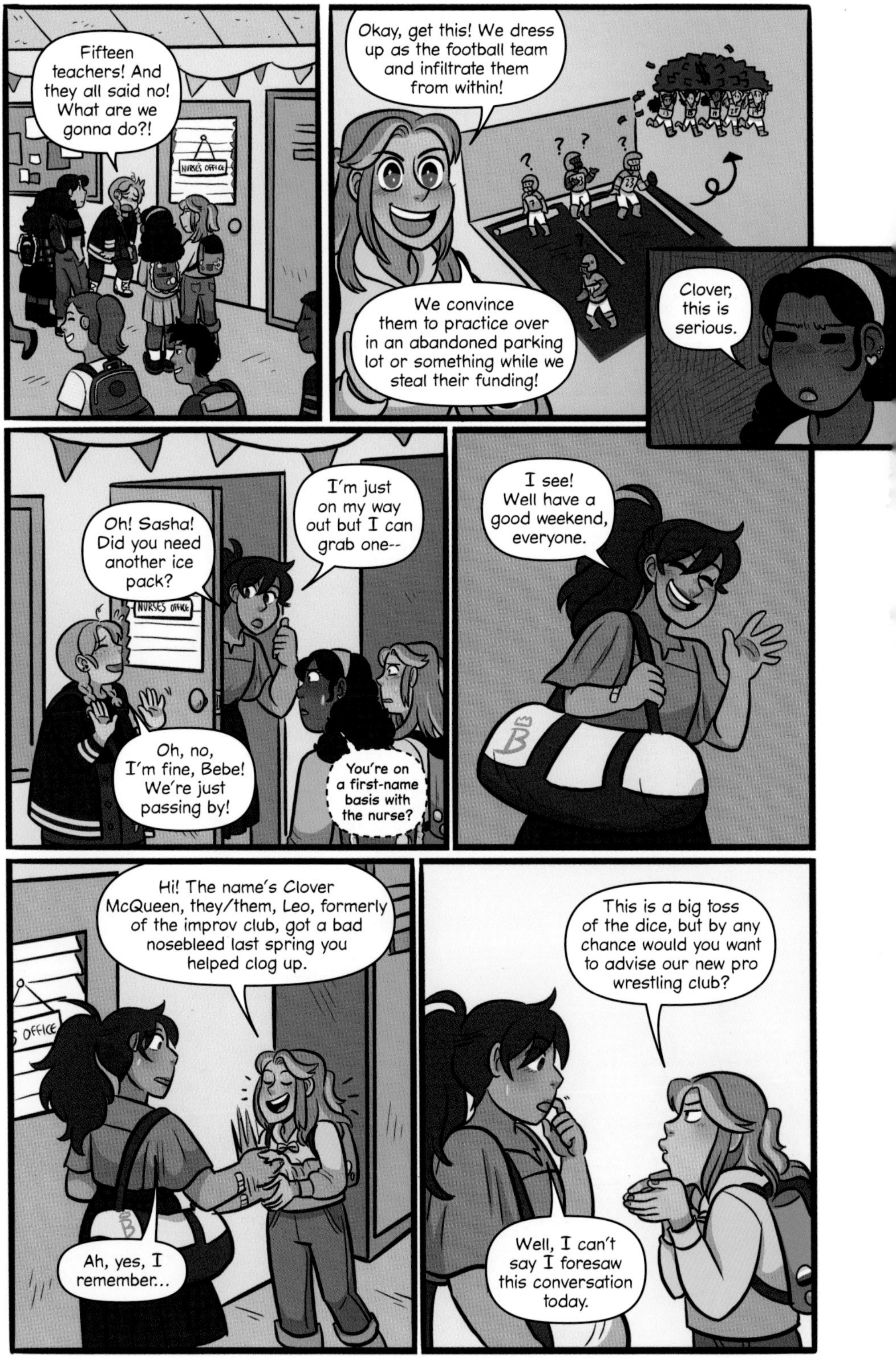
Fifteen teachers! And they all said no! What are we gonna do?!
NURSE'S OFFICE
Okay, get this! We dress up as the football team and infiltrate them from within!
We convince them to practice over in an abandoned parking lot or something while we steal their funding!
Clover, this is serious.
Oh! Sasha! Did you need another ice pack?
NURSE'S OFFICE
I'm just on my way out but I can grab one--
Oh, no, I'm fine, Bebe! We're just passing by!
You're on a first-name basis with the nurse?
I see! Well have a good weekend, everyone.
Hi! The name's Clover McQueen, they/them, Leo, formerly of the improv club, got a bad nosebleed last spring you helped clog up.
Ah, yes, I remember...
This is a big toss of the dice, but by any chance would you want to advise our new pro wrestling club?
Well, I can't say I foresaw this conversation today.

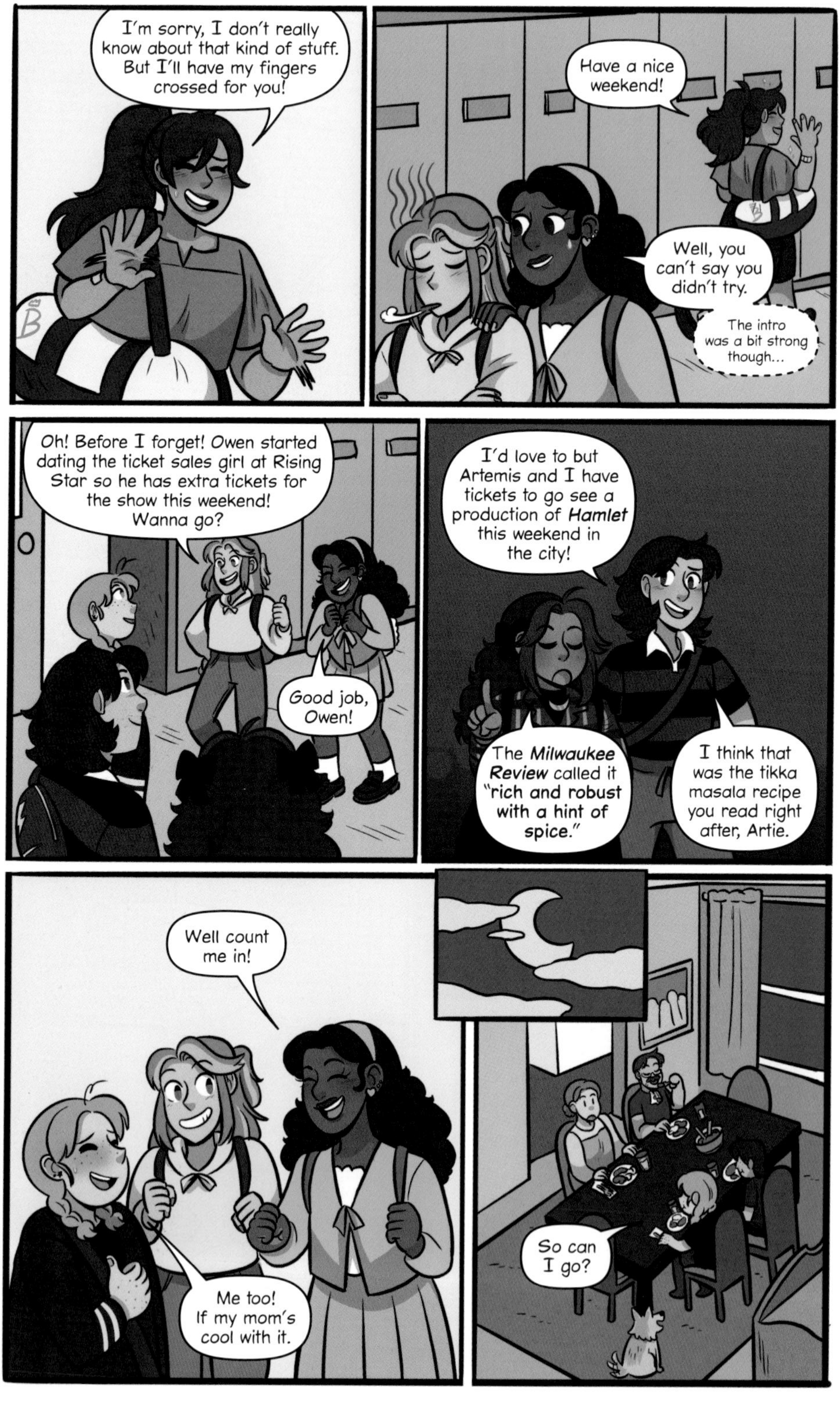
I'm sorry, I don't really know about that kind of stuff. But I'll have my fingers crossed for you!
Have a nice weekend!
Well, you can't say you didn't try.
The intro was a bit strong though...
Oh! Before I forget! Owen started dating the ticket sales girl at Rising Star so he has extra tickets for the show this weekend! Wanna go?
Good job, Owen!
I'd love to but Artemis and I have tickets to go see a production of **Hamlet** this weekend in the city!
The *Milwaukee Review* called it **"rich and robust with a hint of spice."**
I think that was the tikka masala recipe you read right after, Artie.
Well count me in!
Me too! If my mom's cool with it.
So can I go?

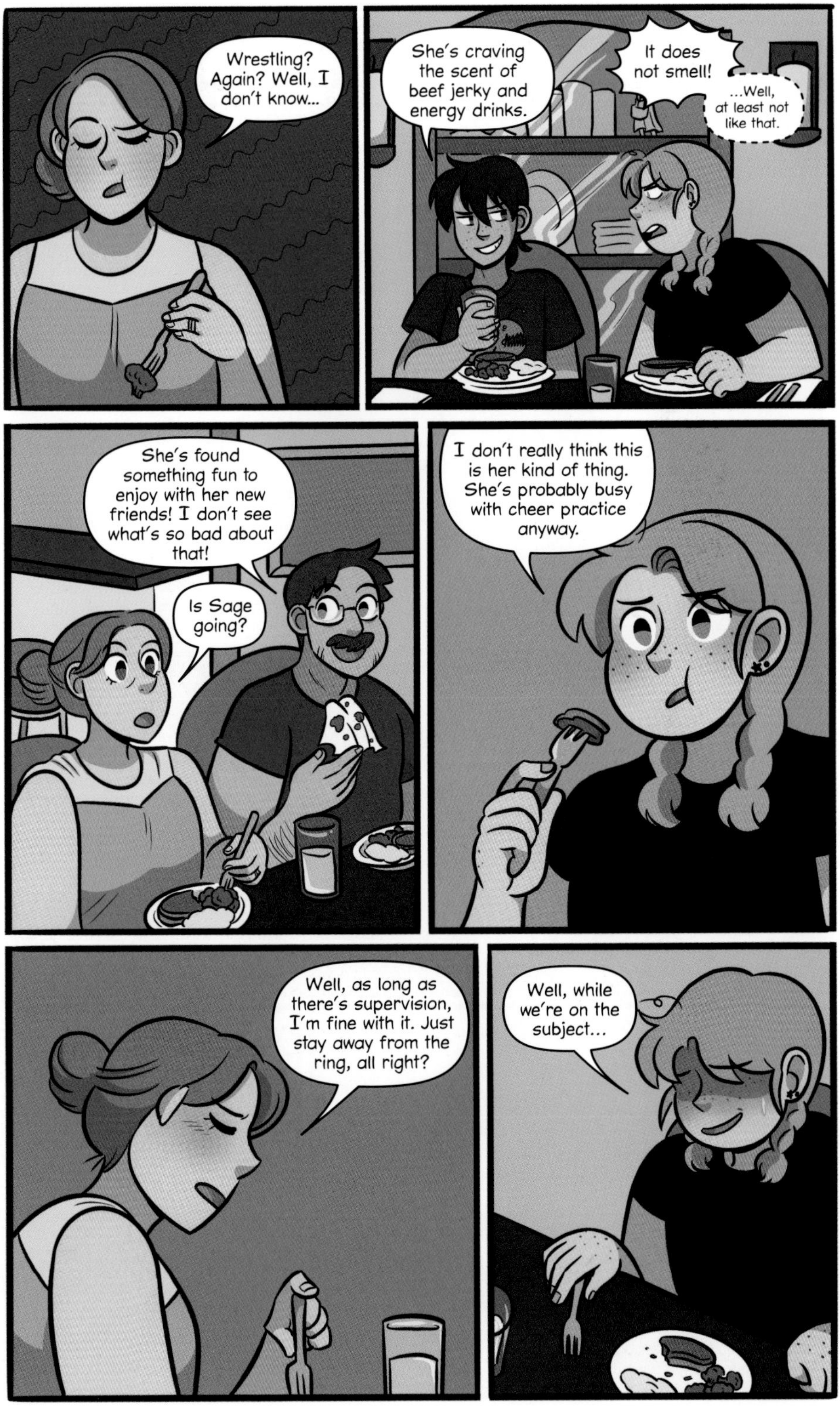
Wrestling? Again? Well, I don't know...
She's craving the scent of beef jerky and energy drinks.
It does not smell!
...Well, at least not like that.
She's found something fun to enjoy with her new friends! I don't see what's so bad about that!
Is Sage going?
I don't really think this is her kind of thing. She's probably busy with cheer practice anyway.
Well, as long as there's supervision, I'm fine with it. Just stay away from the ring, all right?
Well, while we're on the subject...

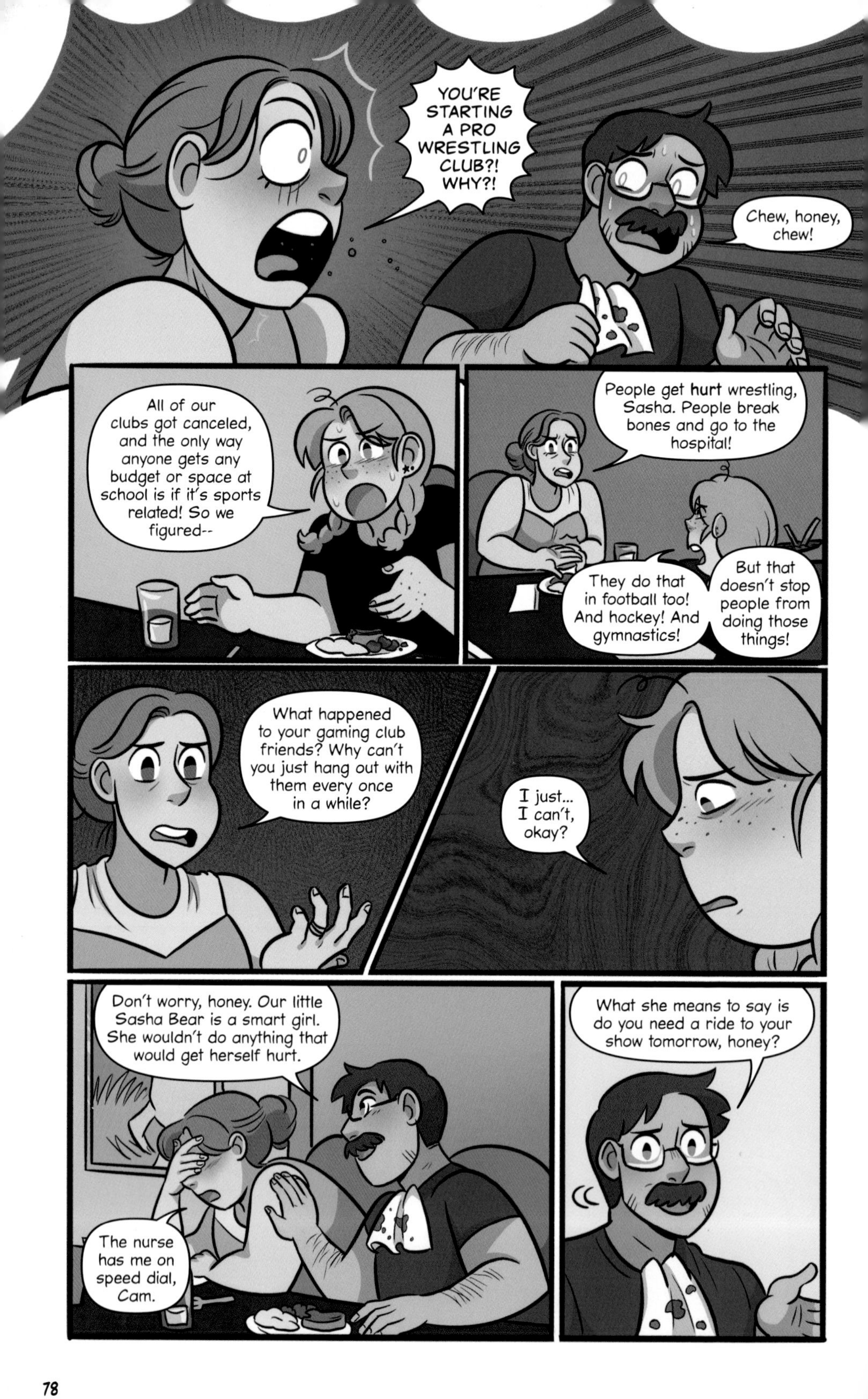
YOU'RE STARTING A PRO WRESTLING CLUB?! WHY?!
Chew, honey, chew!
All of our clubs got canceled, and the only way anyone gets any budget or space at school is if it's sports related! So we figured--
People get **hurt** wrestling, Sasha. People break bones and go to the hospital!
They do that in football too! And hockey! And gymnastics!
But that doesn't stop people from doing those things!
What happened to your gaming club friends? Why can't you just hang out with them every once in a while?
I just... I can't, okay?
Don't worry, honey. Our little Sasha Bear is a smart girl. She wouldn't do anything that would get herself hurt.
The nurse has me on speed dial, Cam.
What she means to say is do you need a ride to your show tomorrow, honey?

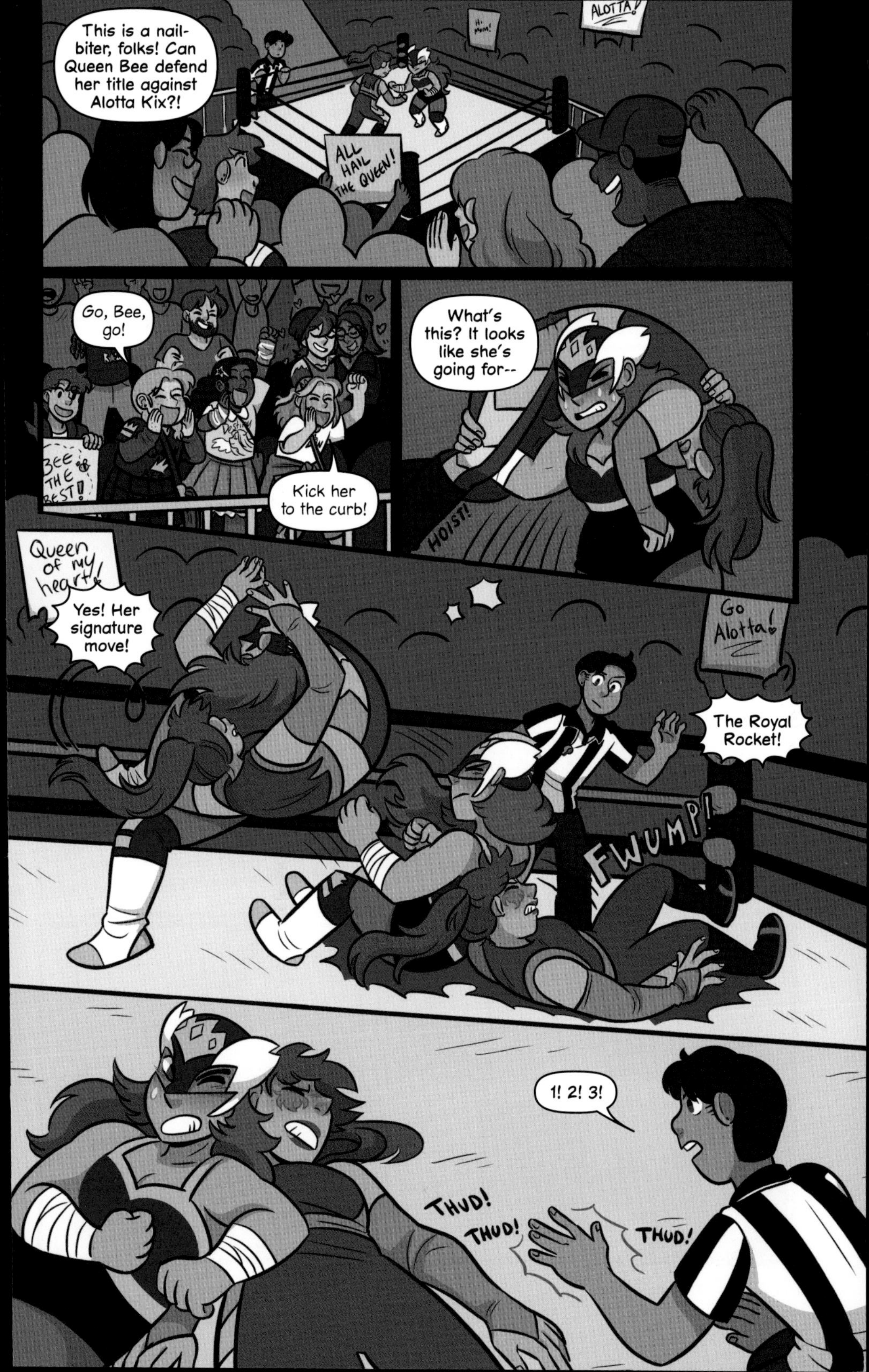
ALOTTA!
Hi Mom!
This is a nail-biter, folks! Can Queen Bee defend her title against Alotta Kix?!
ALL HAIL THE QUEEN!
Go, Bee, go!
BEE THE BEST!
Kick her to the curb!
What's this? It looks like she's going for--
HOIST!
Queen of my heart!
Yes! Her signature move!
Go Alotta!
The Royal Rocket!
FWUMP!
1! 2! 3!
THUD!
THUD!
THUD!

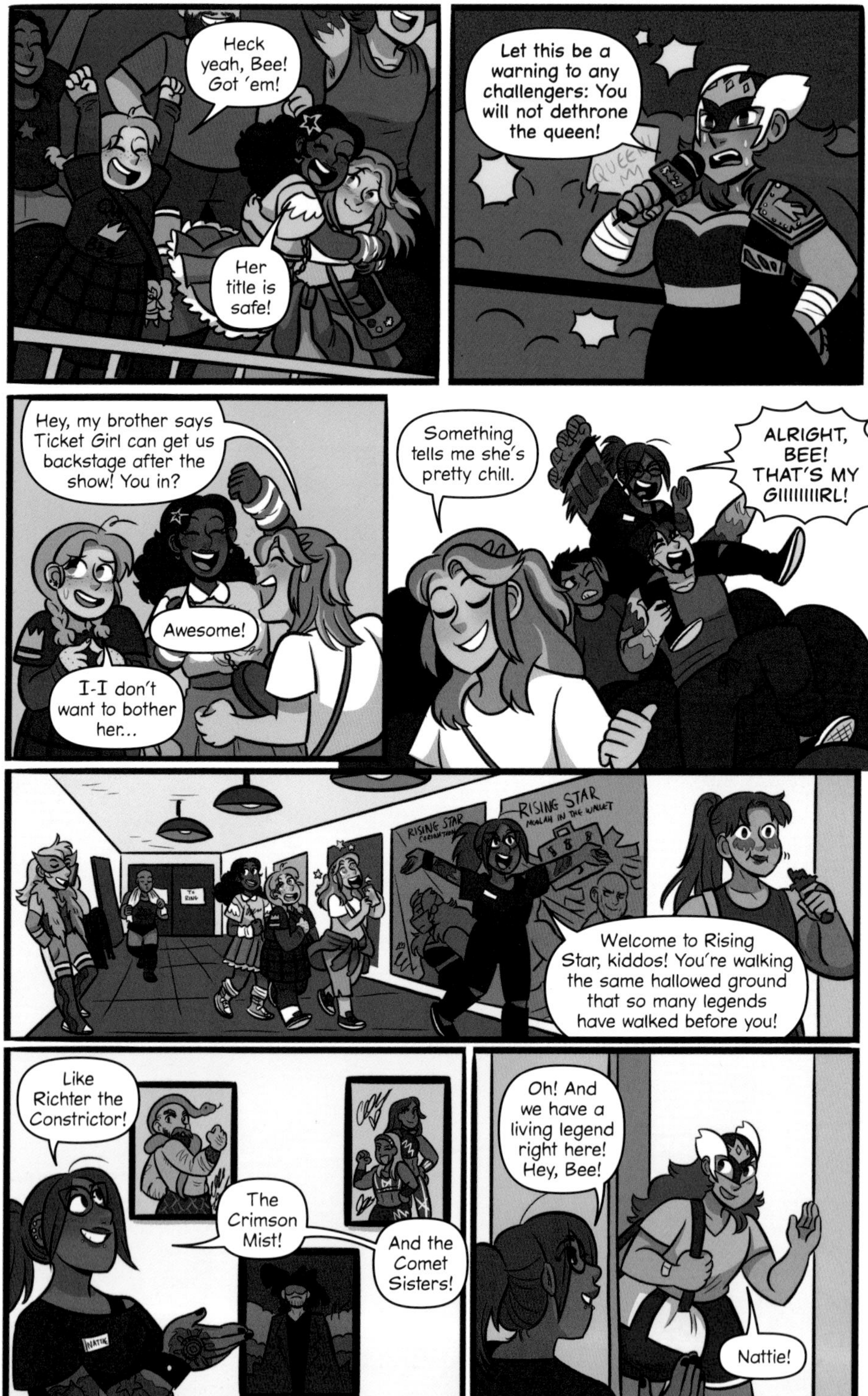
Heck yeah, Bee! Got 'em!
Her title is safe!
Let this be a warning to any challengers: You will not dethrone the queen!
QUEEN
Hey, my brother says Ticket Girl can get us backstage after the show! You in?
Awesome!
I-I don't want to bother her...
Something tells me she's pretty chill.
ALRIGHT, BEE! THAT'S MY GIIIIIIIRL!
RISING STAR
RISING STAR
TO RING
Welcome to Rising Star, kiddos! You're walking the same hallowed ground that so many legends have walked before you!
Like Richter the Constrictor!
The Crimson Mist!
And the Comet Sisters!
NATTIE
Oh! And we have a living legend right here! Hey, Bee!
Nattie!

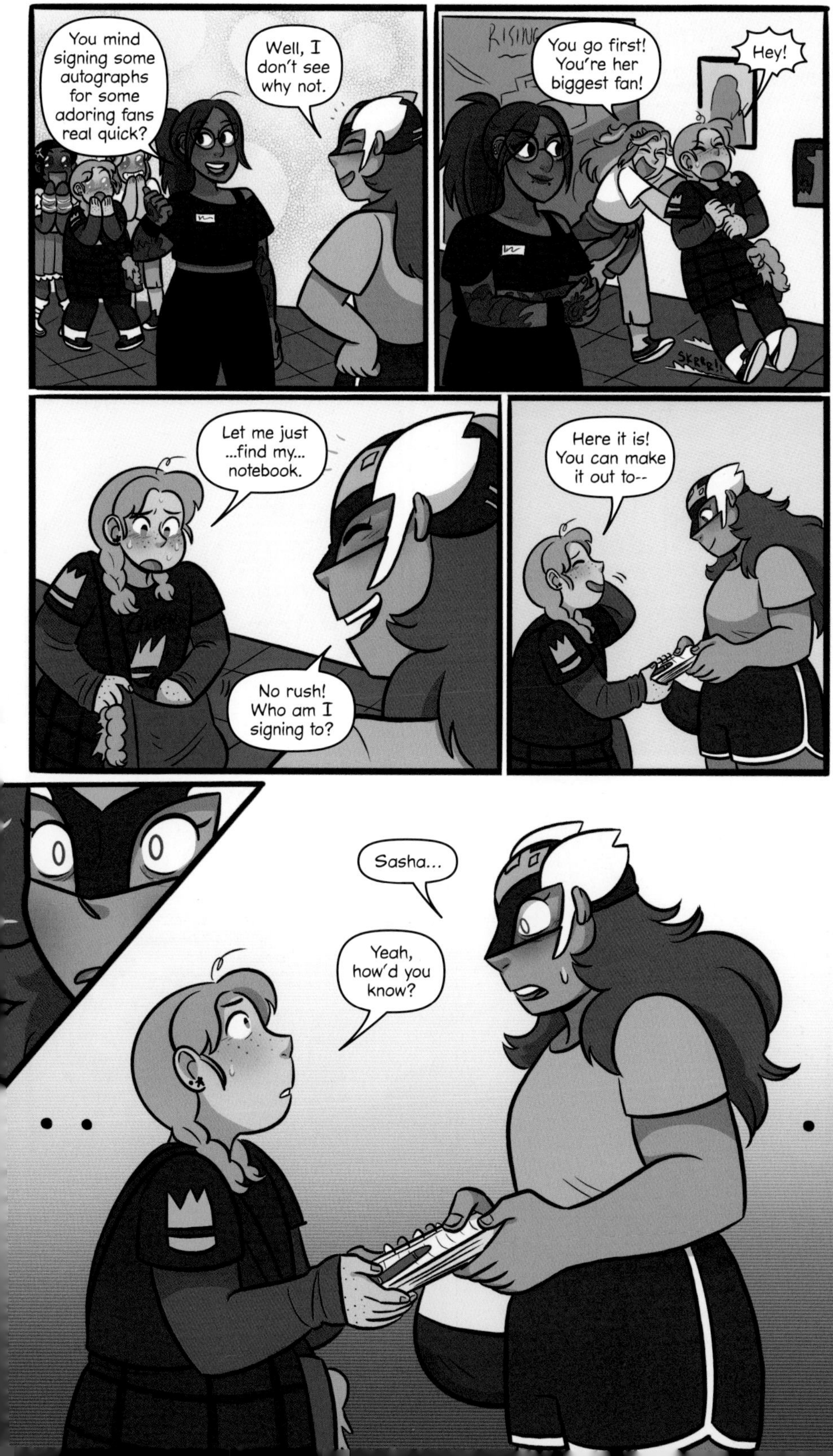
You mind signing some autographs for some adoring fans real quick?
Well, I don't see why not.
RISING
You go first! You're her biggest fan!
Hey!
SKRRR!!
Let me just ...find my... notebook.
No rush! Who am I signing to?
Here it is! You can make it out to--
Sasha...
Yeah, how'd you know?
• •
• •

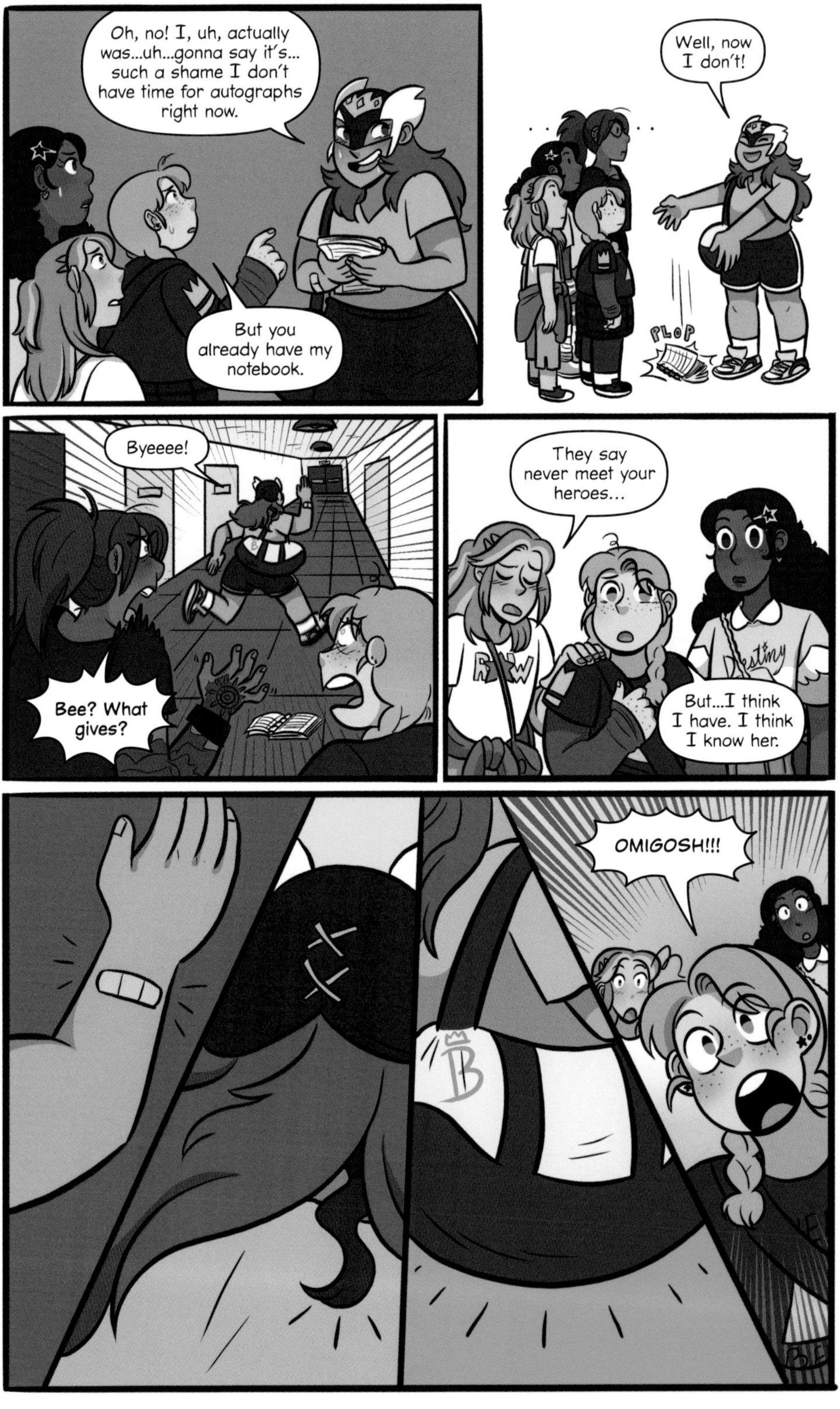
Oh, no! I, uh, actually was...uh...gonna say it's... such a shame I don't have time for autographs right now.
But you already have my notebook.
Well, now I don't!
PLOP
Byeeee!
Bee? What gives?
They say never meet your heroes...
But...I think I have. I think I know her.
OMIGOSH!!!

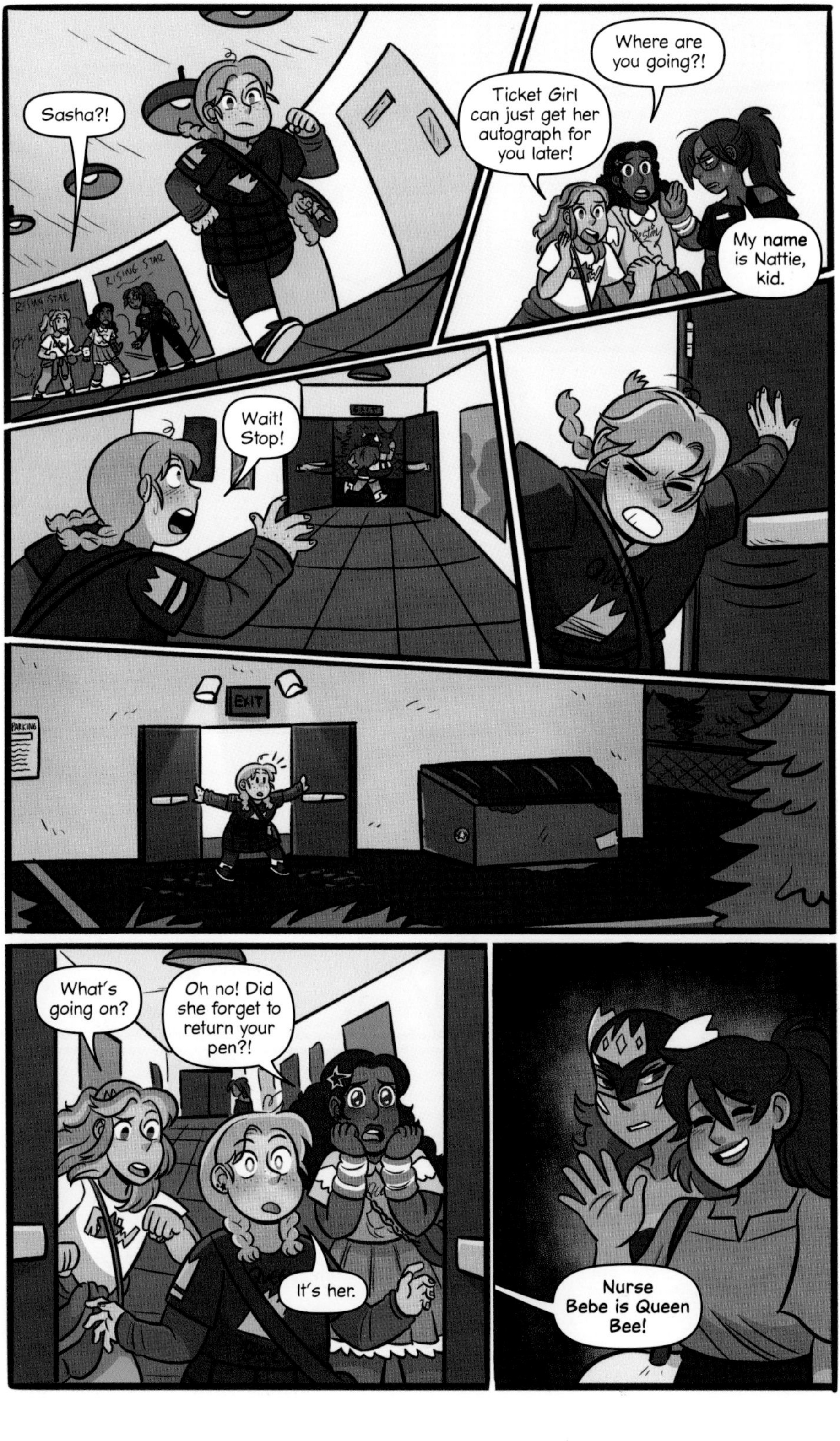
Sasha?!
Where are you going?!
Ticket Girl can just get her autograph for you later!
My name is Nattie, kid.
RISING STAR
RISING STAR
Wait! Stop!
EXIT
PARKING
What's going on?
Oh no! Did she forget to return your pen?!
It's her.
Nurse Bebe is Queen Bee!

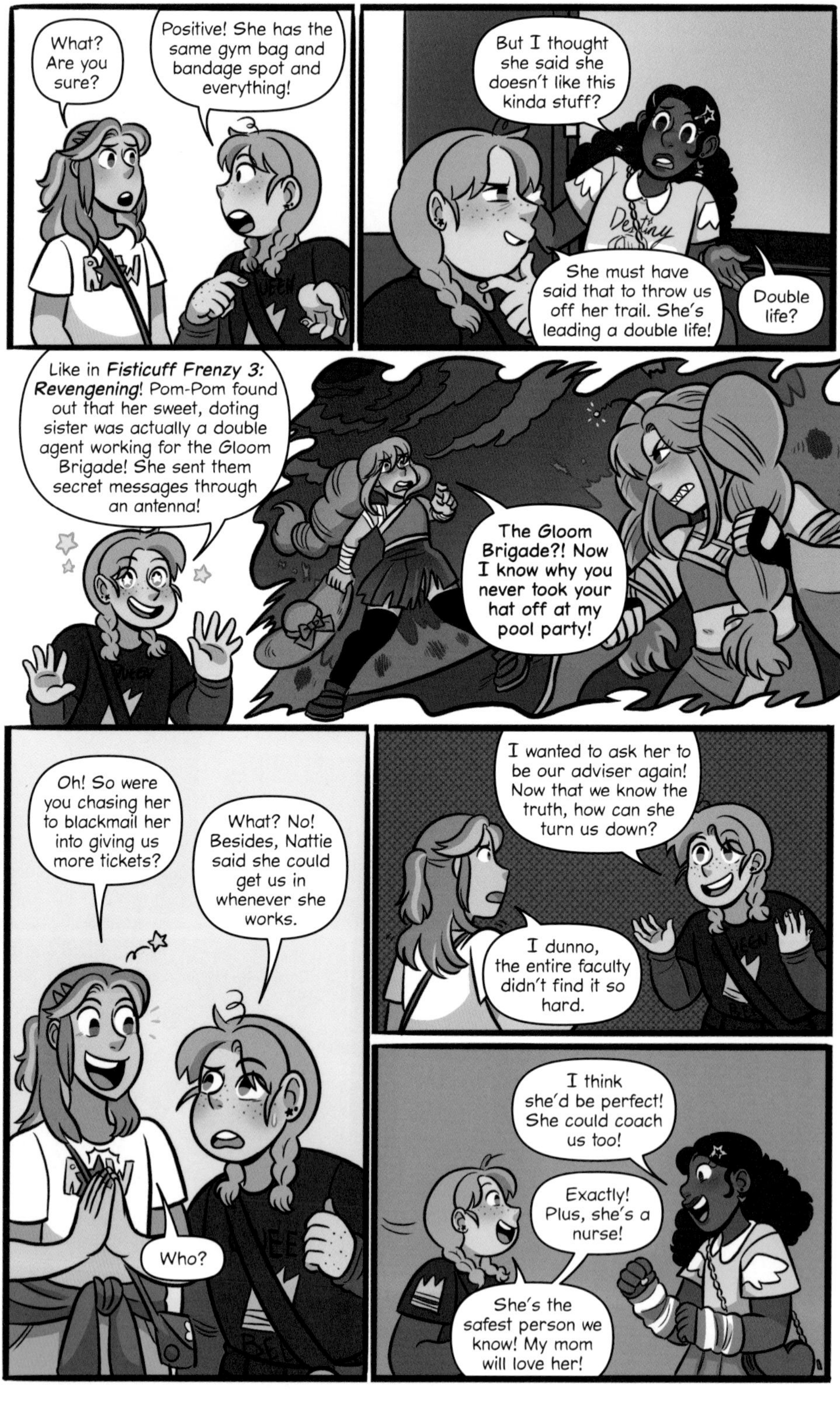

What? Are you sure?
Positive! She has the same gym bag and bandage spot and everything!
But I thought she said she doesn't like this kinda stuff?
She must have said that to throw us off her trail. She's leading a double life!
Double life?
Like in ***Fisticuff Frenzy 3: Revengening***! Pom-Pom found out that her sweet, doting sister was actually a double agent working for the Gloom Brigade! She sent them secret messages through an antenna!
The Gloom Brigade?! Now I know why you never took your hat off at my pool party!
Oh! So were you chasing her to blackmail her into giving us more tickets?
What? No! Besides, Nattie said she could get us in whenever she works.
Who?
I wanted to ask her to be our adviser again! Now that we know the truth, how can she turn us down?
I dunno, the entire faculty didn't find it so hard.
I think she'd be perfect! She could coach us too!
Exactly! Plus, she's a nurse!
She's the safest person we know! My mom will love her!

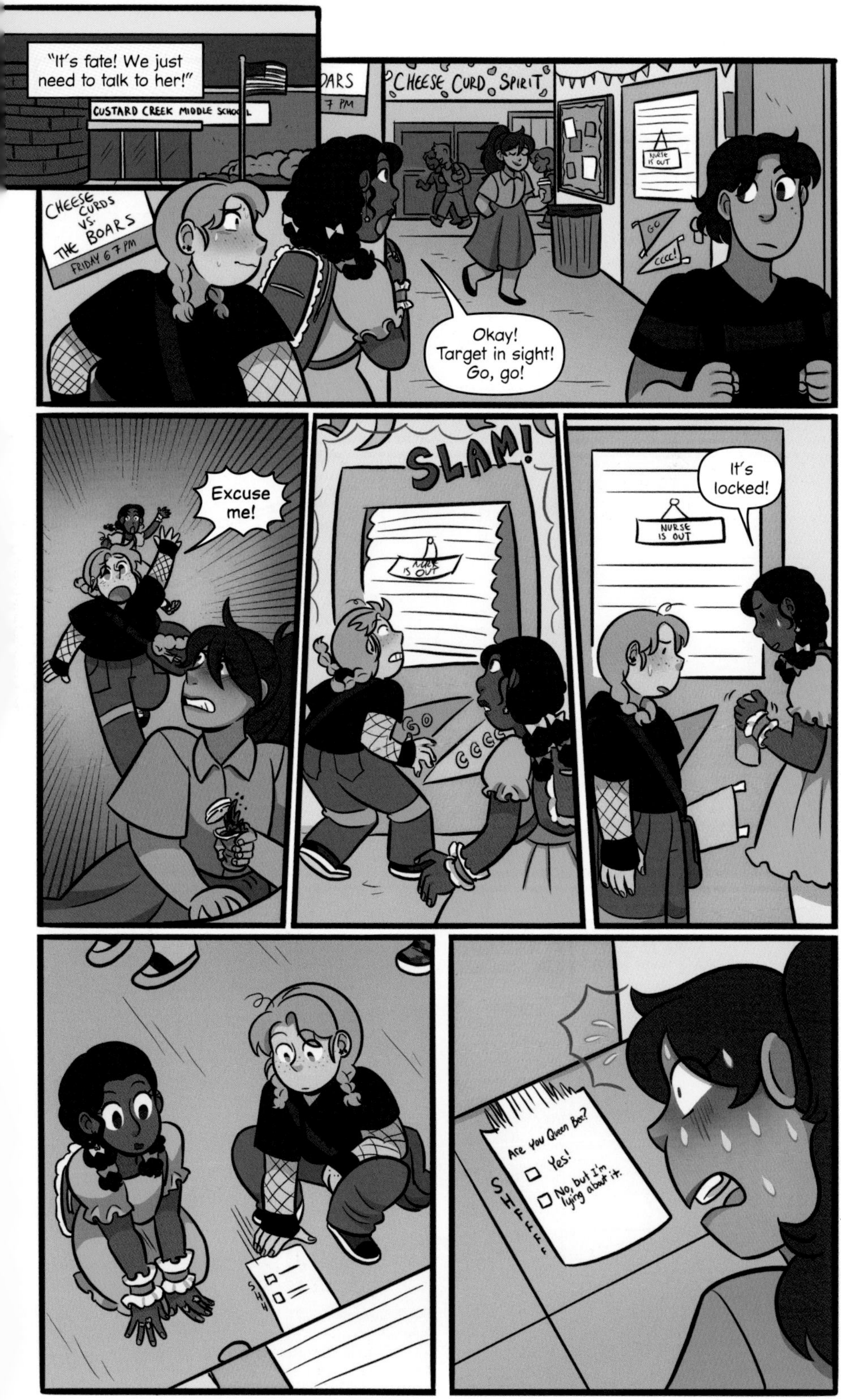
"It's fate! We just need to talk to her!"
CUSTARD CREEK MIDDLE SCHOOL
CHEESE CURDS VS. THE BOARS
FRIDAY 6-7 PM
CHEESE CURD SPIRIT
NURSE IS OUT
GO
CCCC!
Okay! Target in sight! Go, go!
Excuse me!
SLAM!
It's locked!
NURSE IS OUT
Are You Queen Bee?
Yes!
No, but I'm lying about it.
SHFFFF

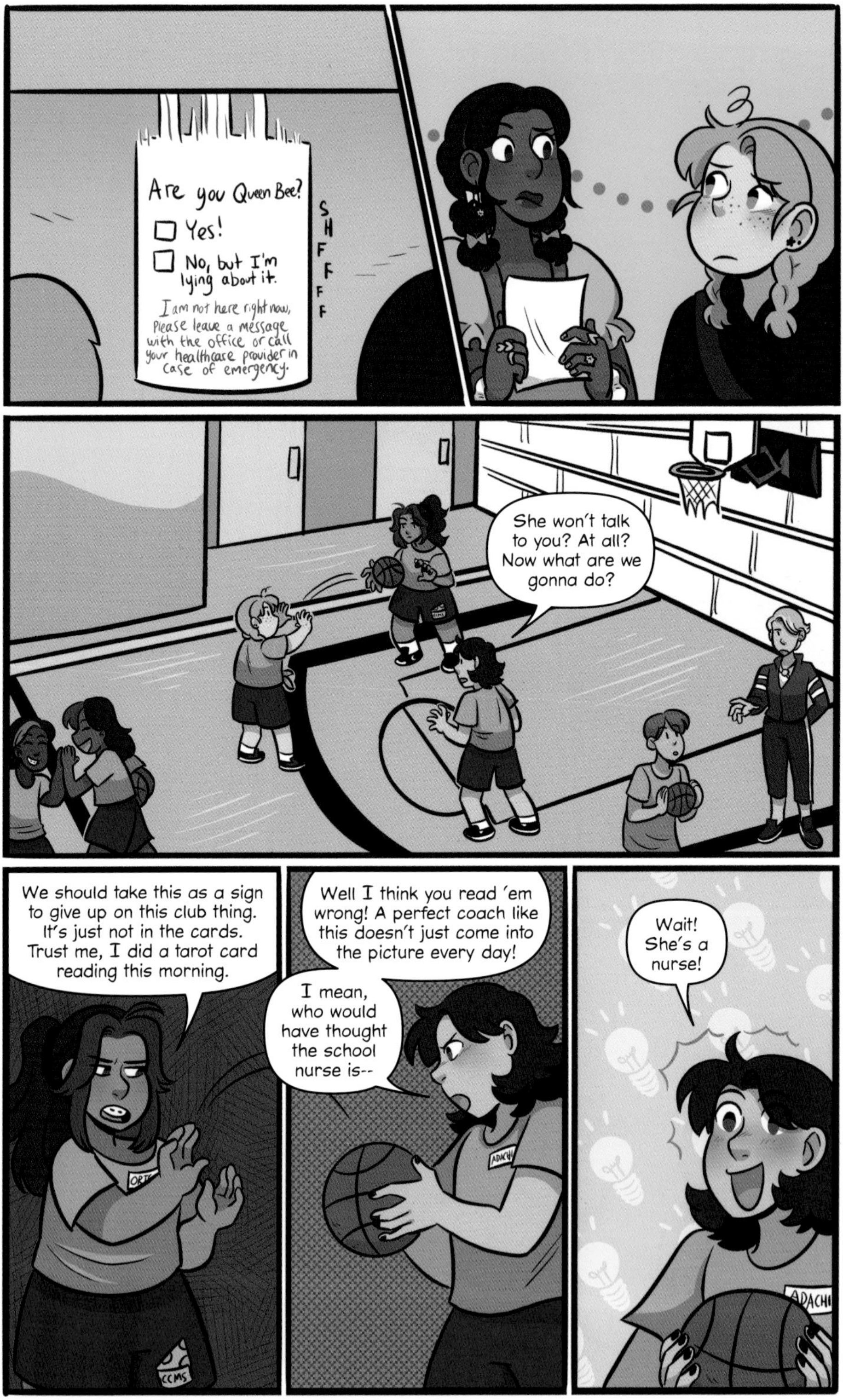
Are you Queen Bee?
Yes!
No, but I'm lying about it.
I am not here right now, Please leave a message with the office or call your healthcare provider in case of emergency.
SHFFFF
She won't talk to you? At all? Now what are we gonna do?
We should take this as a sign to give up on this club thing. It's just not in the cards. Trust me, I did a tarot card reading this morning.
Well I think you read 'em wrong! A perfect coach like this doesn't just come into the picture every day!
I mean, who would have thought the school nurse is--
Wait! She's a nurse!

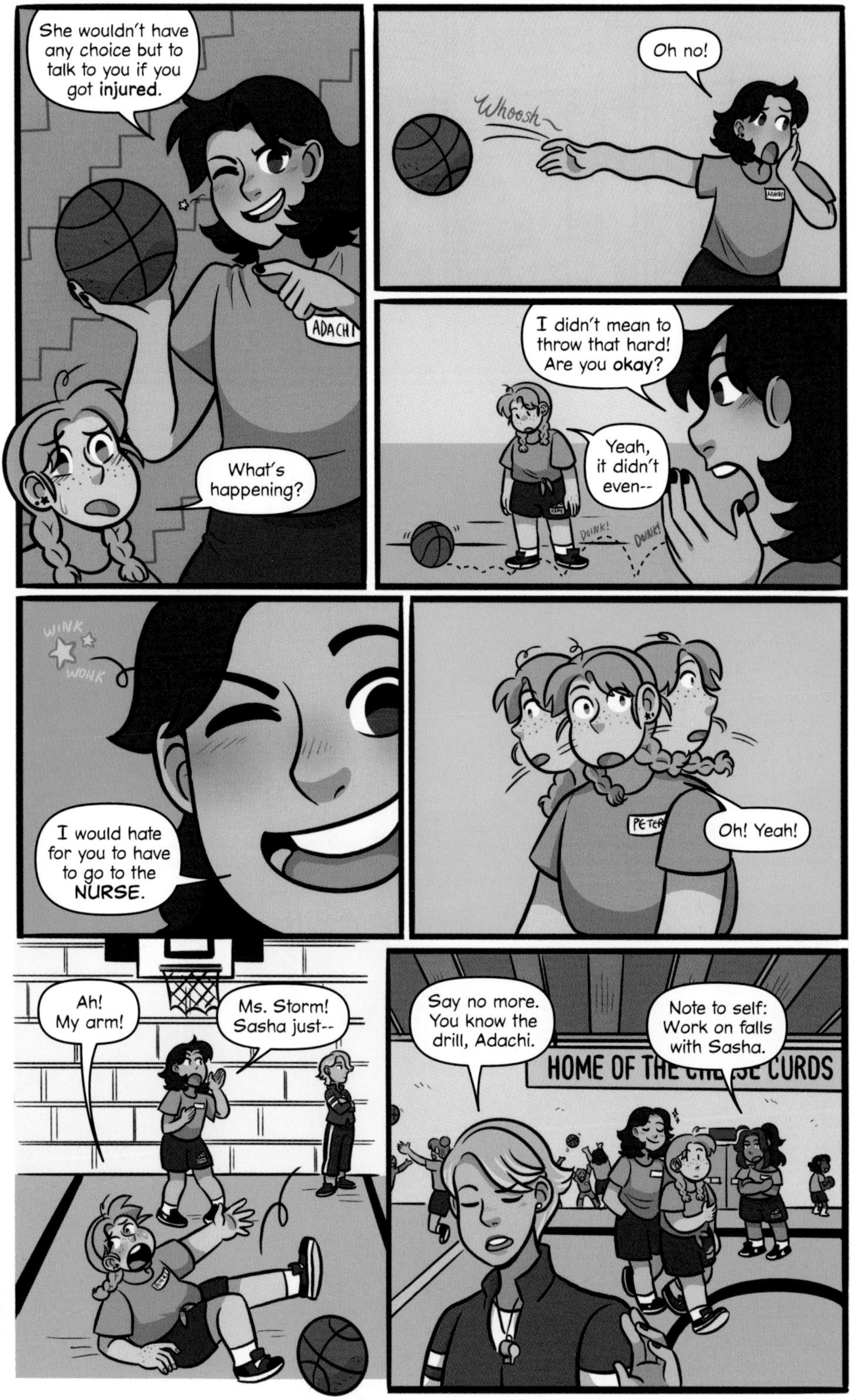

She wouldn't have any choice but to talk to you if you got **injured**.
What's happening?
ADACHI
Oh no!
Whoosh
I didn't mean to throw that hard! Are you **okay**?
Yeah, it didn't even--
DOINK!
DOINK!
WINK
WONK
I would hate for you to have to go to the **NURSE**.
PETER
Oh! Yeah!
Ah! My arm!
Ms. Storm! Sasha just--
Say no more. You know the drill, Adachi.
Note to self: Work on falls with Sasha.

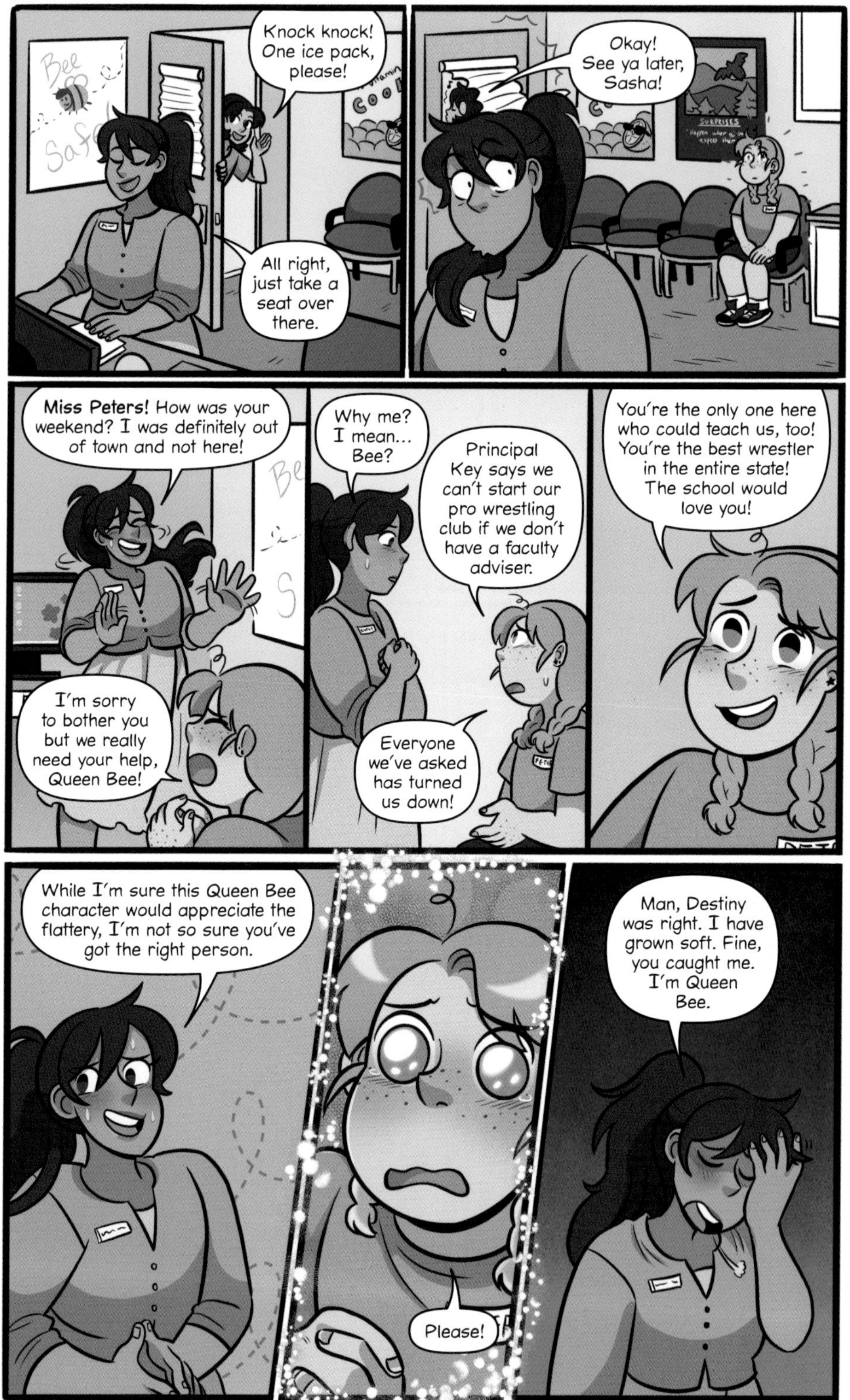
Knock knock! One ice pack, please!
All right, just take a seat over there.
Okay! See ya later, Sasha!
SURPRISES
Miss Peters! How was your weekend? I was definitely out of town and not here!
I'm sorry to bother you but we really need your help, Queen Bee!
Why me? I mean... Bee?
Principal Key says we can't start our pro wrestling club if we don't have a faculty adviser.
Everyone we've asked has turned us down!
You're the only one here who could teach us, too! You're the best wrestler in the entire state! The school would love you!
While I'm sure this Queen Bee character would appreciate the flattery, I'm not so sure you've got the right person.
Please!
Man, Destiny was right. I have grown soft. Fine, you caught me. I'm Queen Bee.

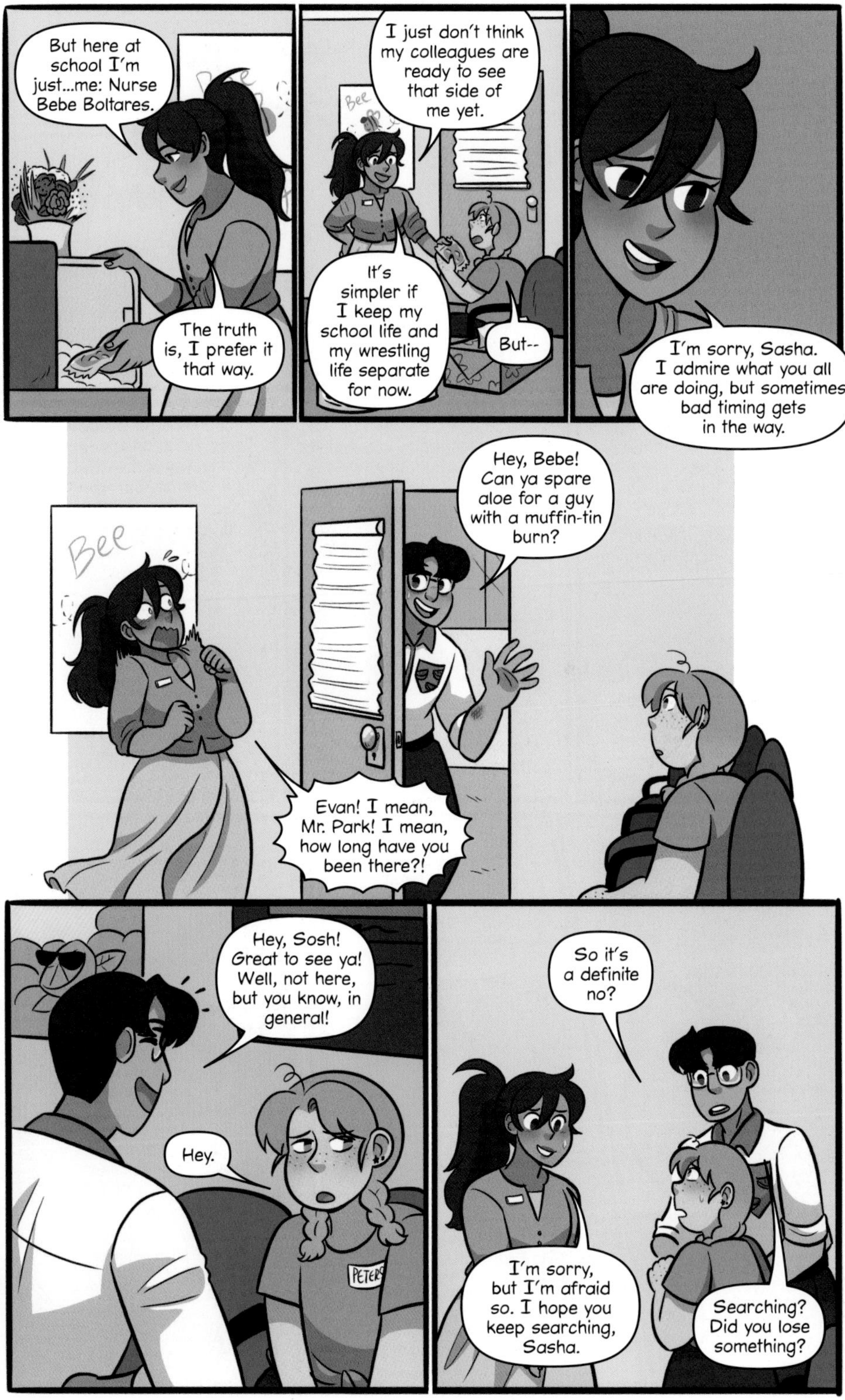
But here at school I'm just...me: Nurse Bebe Boltares.
The truth is, I prefer it that way.
I just don't think my colleagues are ready to see that side of me yet.
It's simpler if I keep my school life and my wrestling life separate for now.
But--
I'm sorry, Sasha. I admire what you all are doing, but sometimes bad timing gets in the way.
Bee
Hey, Bebe! Can ya spare aloe for a guy with a muffin-tin burn?
Evan! I mean, Mr. Park! I mean, how long have you been there?!
Hey, Sosh! Great to see ya! Well, not here, but you know, in general!
Hey.
PETERS
So it's a definite no?
I'm sorry, but I'm afraid so. I hope you keep searching, Sasha.
Searching? Did you lose something?

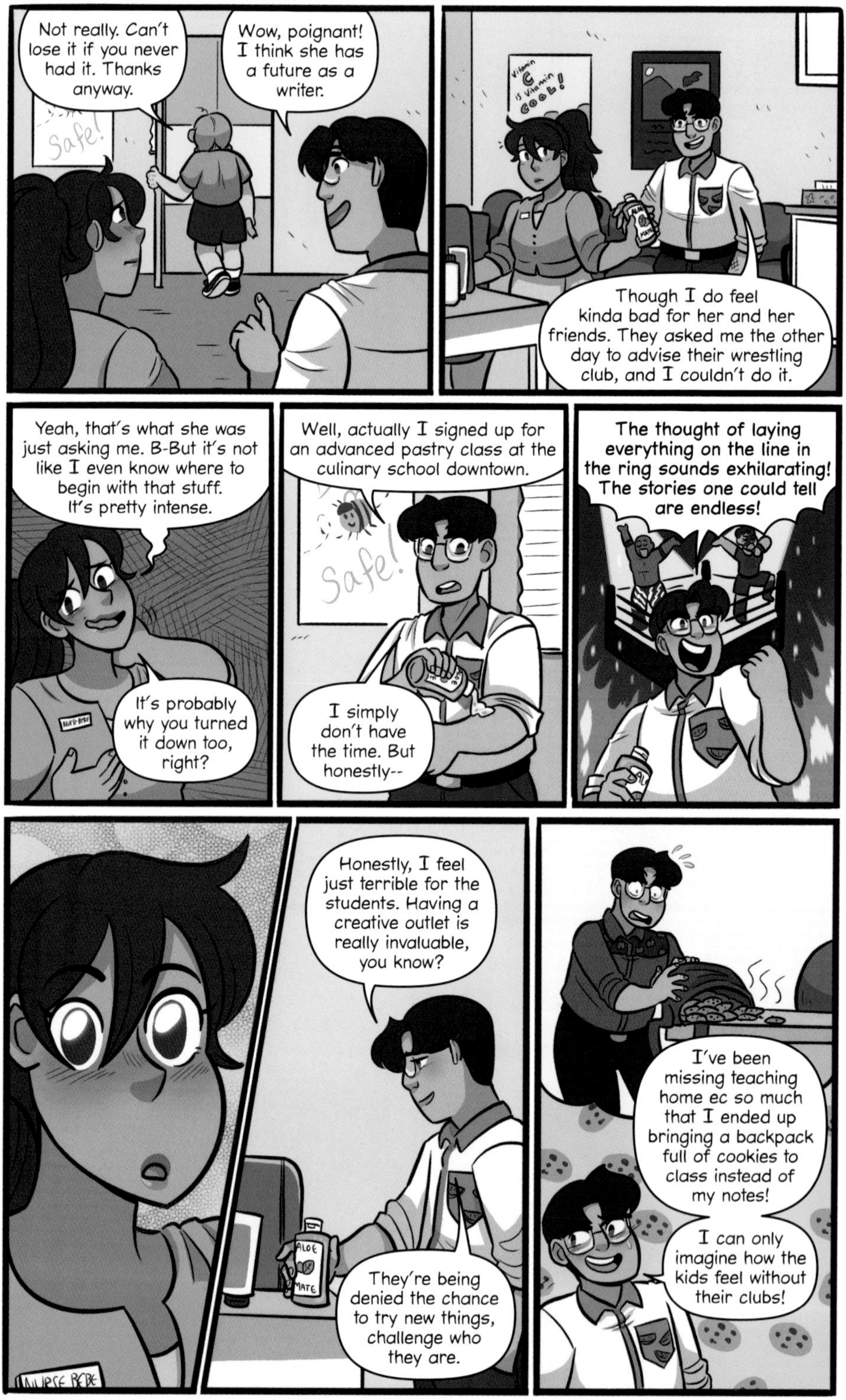
Not really. Can't lose it if you never had it. Thanks anyway.
Wow, poignant! I think she has a future as a writer.
Safe!
Vitamin C is Vitamin COOL!
Though I do feel kinda bad for her and her friends. They asked me the other day to advise their wrestling club, and I couldn't do it.
Yeah, that's what she was just asking me. B-But it's not like I even know where to begin with that stuff. It's pretty intense.
It's probably why you turned it down too, right?
Well, actually I signed up for an advanced pastry class at the culinary school downtown.
Safe!
I simply don't have the time. But honestly--
The thought of laying everything on the line in the ring sounds exhilarating! The stories one could tell are endless!
Honestly, I feel just terrible for the students. Having a creative outlet is really invaluable, you know?
ALOE MATE
They're being denied the chance to try new things, challenge who they are.
NURSE BEBE
I've been missing teaching home ec so much that I ended up bringing a backpack full of cookies to class instead of my notes!
I can only imagine how the kids feel without their clubs!

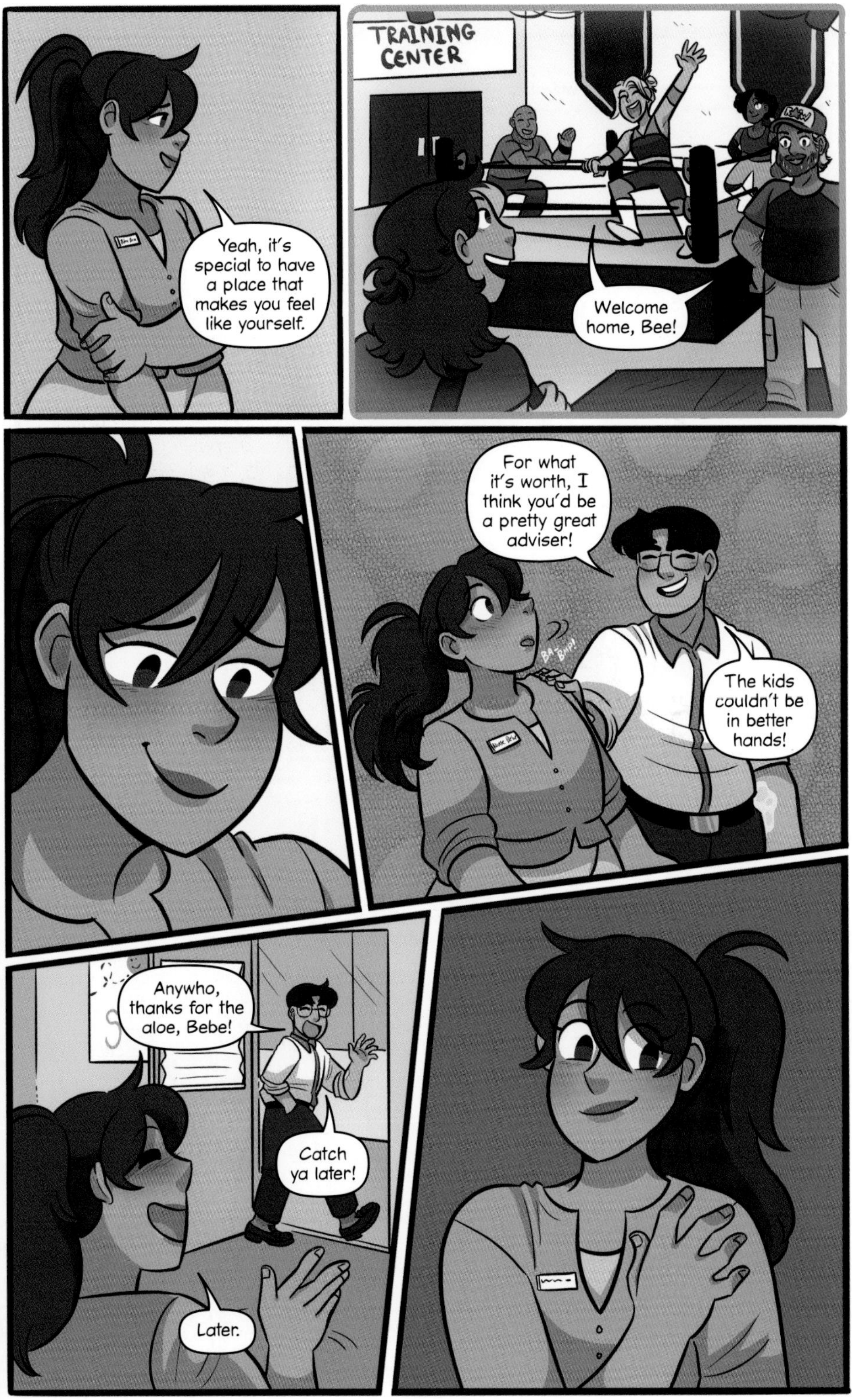
Yeah, it's special to have a place that makes you feel like yourself.
TRAINING CENTER
Welcome home, Bee!
For what it's worth, I think you'd be a pretty great adviser!
BA-BMP!
The kids couldn't be in better hands!
Anywho, thanks for the aloe, Bebe!
Catch ya later!
Later.

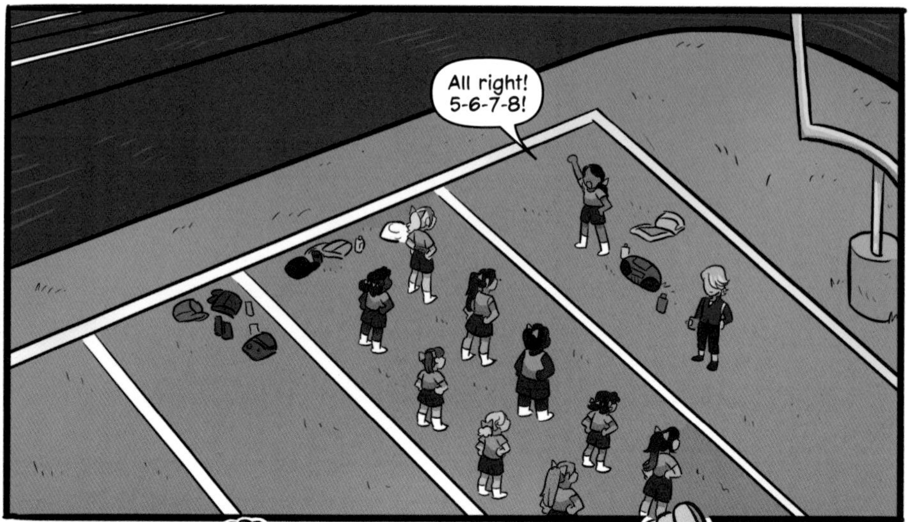
All right!
5-6-7-8!

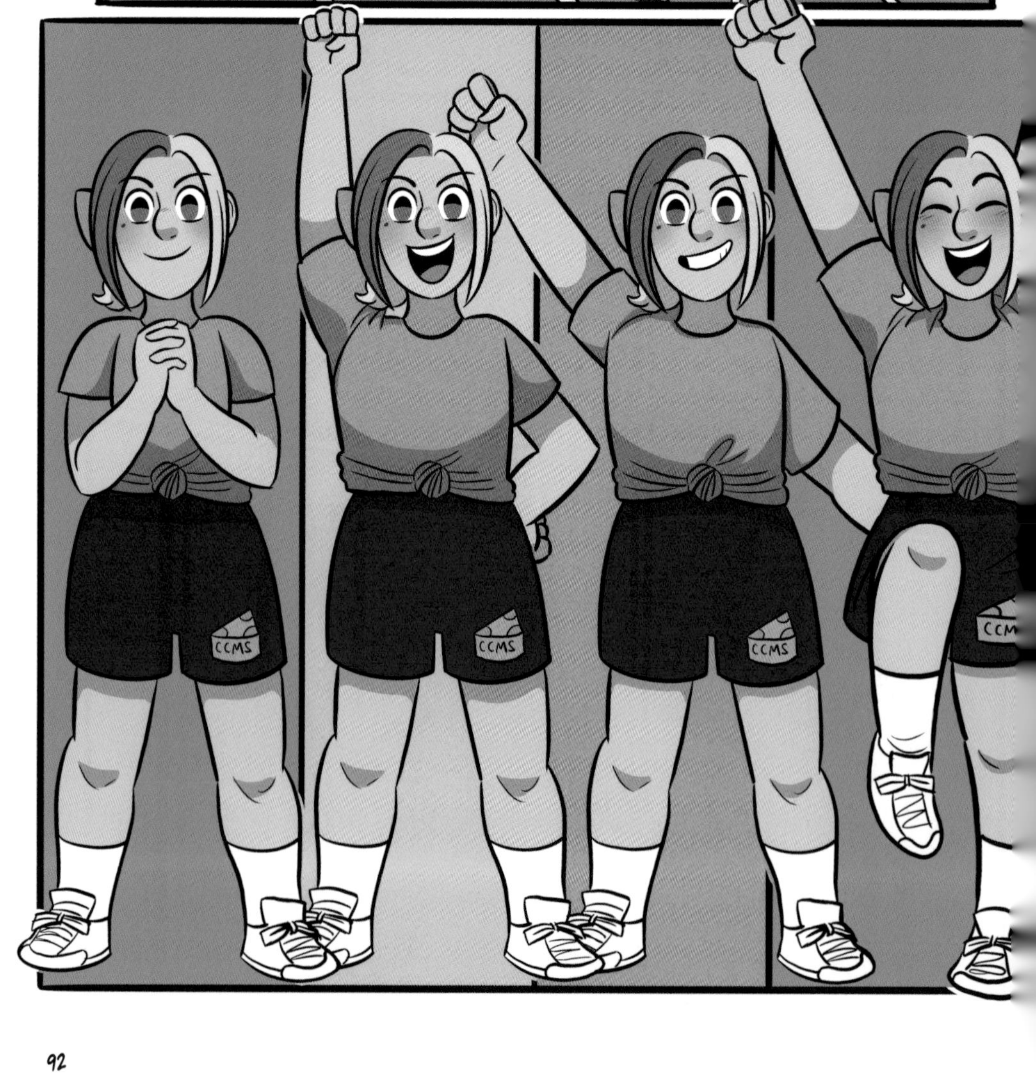
CCMS
CCMS
CCMS

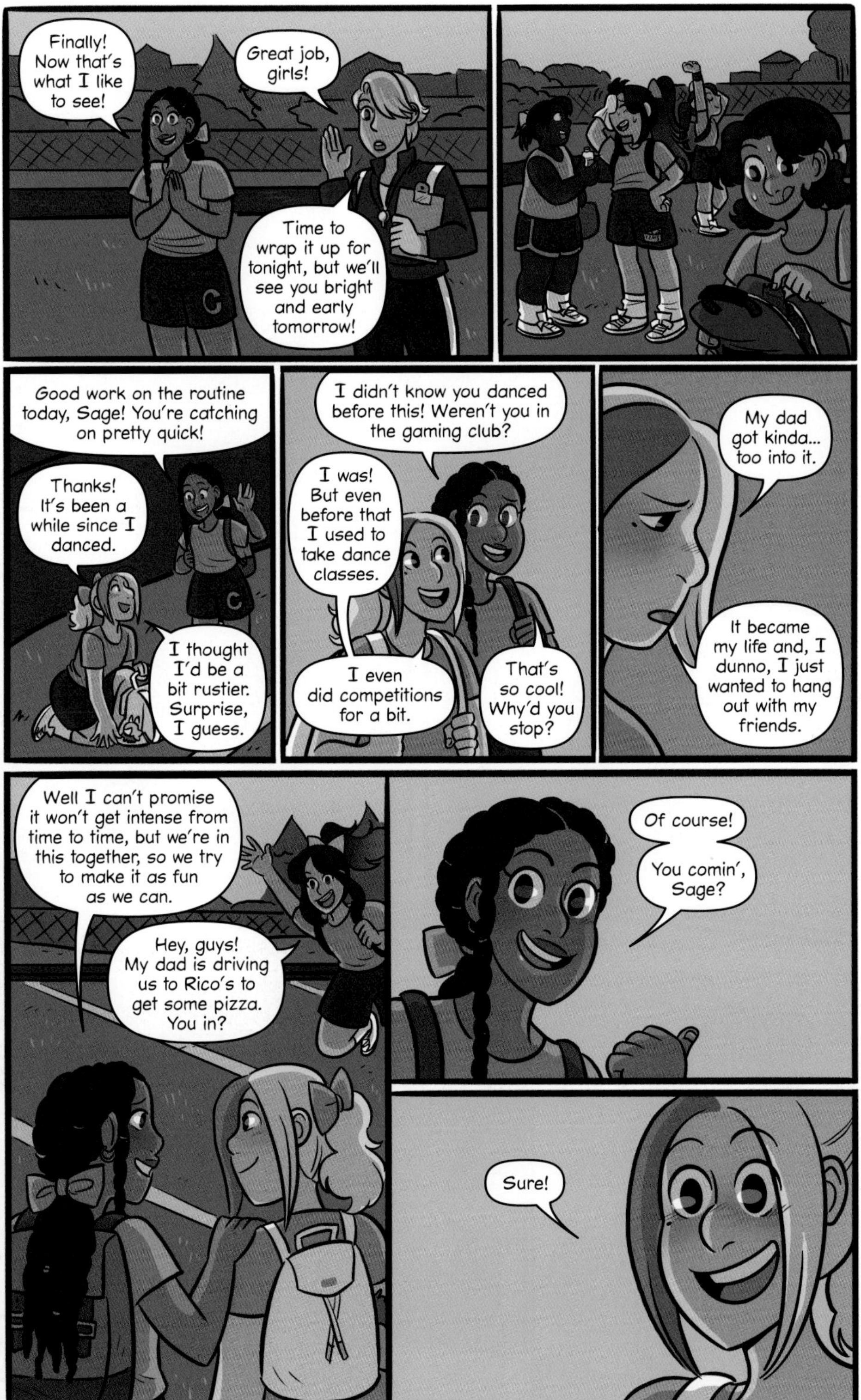
Finally! Now that's what I like to see!
Great job, girls!
Time to wrap it up for tonight, but we'll see you bright and early tomorrow!
Good work on the routine today, Sage! You're catching on pretty quick!
Thanks! It's been a while since I danced.
I thought I'd be a bit rustier. Surprise, I guess.
I didn't know you danced before this! Weren't you in the gaming club?
I was! But even before that I used to take dance classes.
I even did competitions for a bit.
That's so cool! Why'd you stop?
My dad got kinda... too into it.
It became my life and, I dunno, I just wanted to hang out with my friends.
Well I can't promise it won't get intense from time to time, but we're in this together, so we try to make it as fun as we can.
Hey, guys! My dad is driving us to Rico's to get some pizza. You in?
Of course!
You comin', Sage?
Sure!

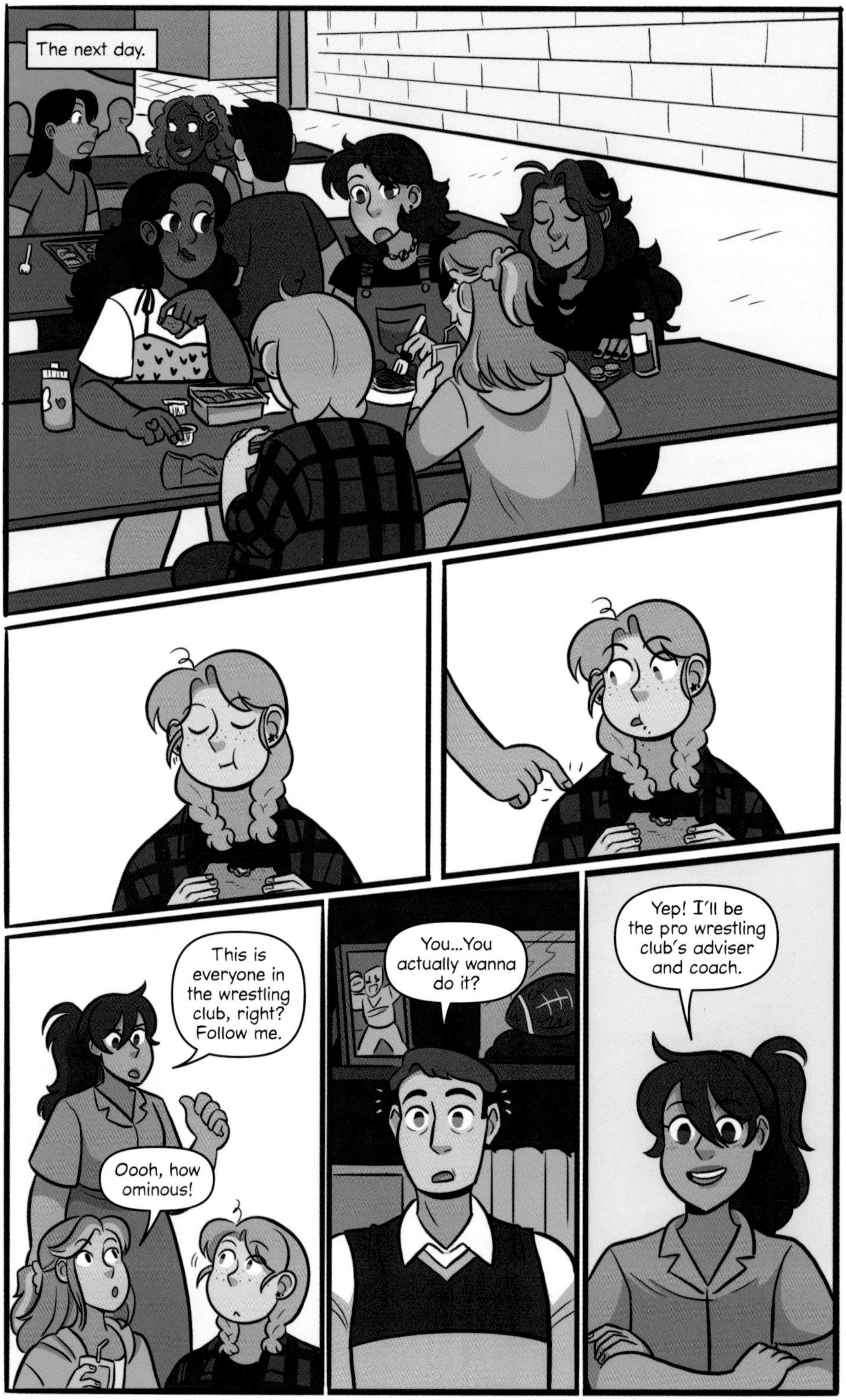

The next day.
This is everyone in the wrestling club, right? Follow me.
Oooh, how ominous!
You...You actually wanna do it?
Yep! I'll be the pro wrestling club's adviser and coach.

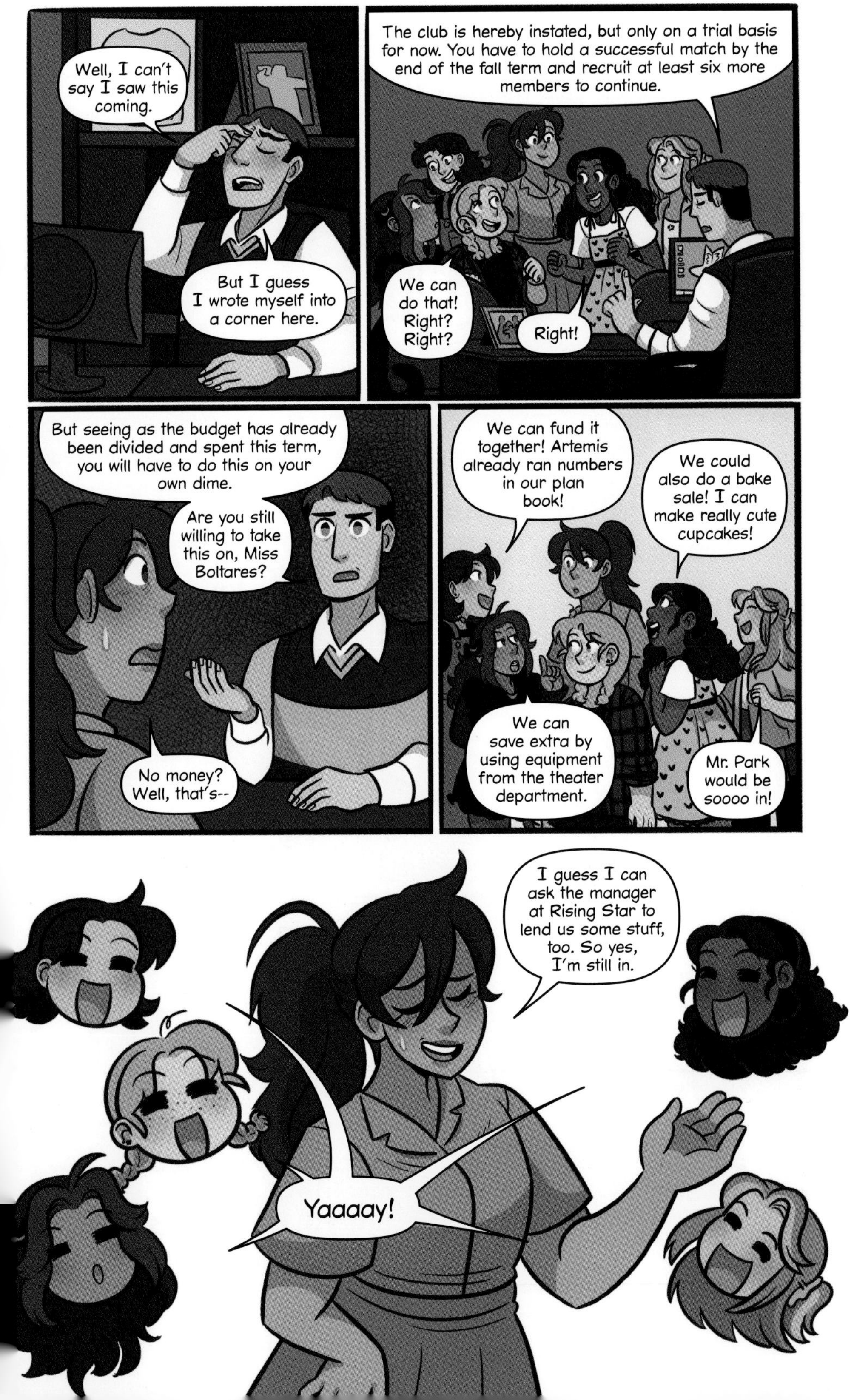
Well, I can't say I saw this coming.
But I guess I wrote myself into a corner here.
The club is hereby instated, but only on a trial basis for now. You have to hold a successful match by the end of the fall term and recruit at least six more members to continue.
We can do that! Right? Right?
Right!
But seeing as the budget has already been divided and spent this term, you will have to do this on your own dime.
Are you still willing to take this on, Miss Boltares?
No money? Well, that's--
We can fund it together! Artemis already ran numbers in our plan book!
We could also do a bake sale! I can make really cute cupcakes!
We can save extra by using equipment from the theater department.
Mr. Park would be soooo in!
I guess I can ask the manager at Rising Star to lend us some stuff, too. So yes, I'm still in.
Yaaaay!

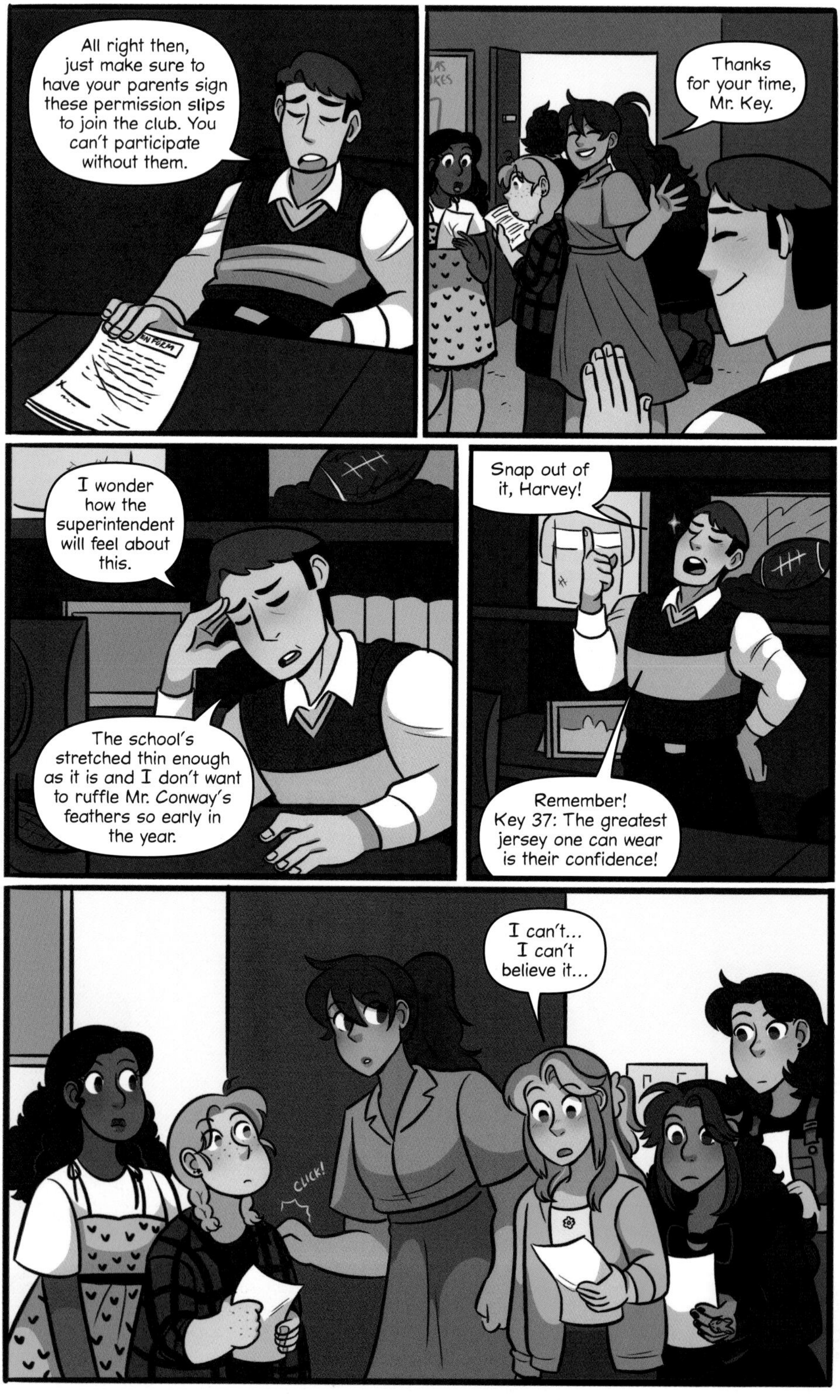
All right then, just make sure to have your parents sign these permission slips to join the club. You can't participate without them.
Thanks for your time, Mr. Key.
I wonder how the superintendent will feel about this.
The school's stretched thin enough as it is and I don't want to ruffle Mr. Conway's feathers so early in the year.
Snap out of it, Harvey!
Remember! Key 37: The greatest jersey one can wear is their confidence!
I can't... I can't believe it...
CLICK!

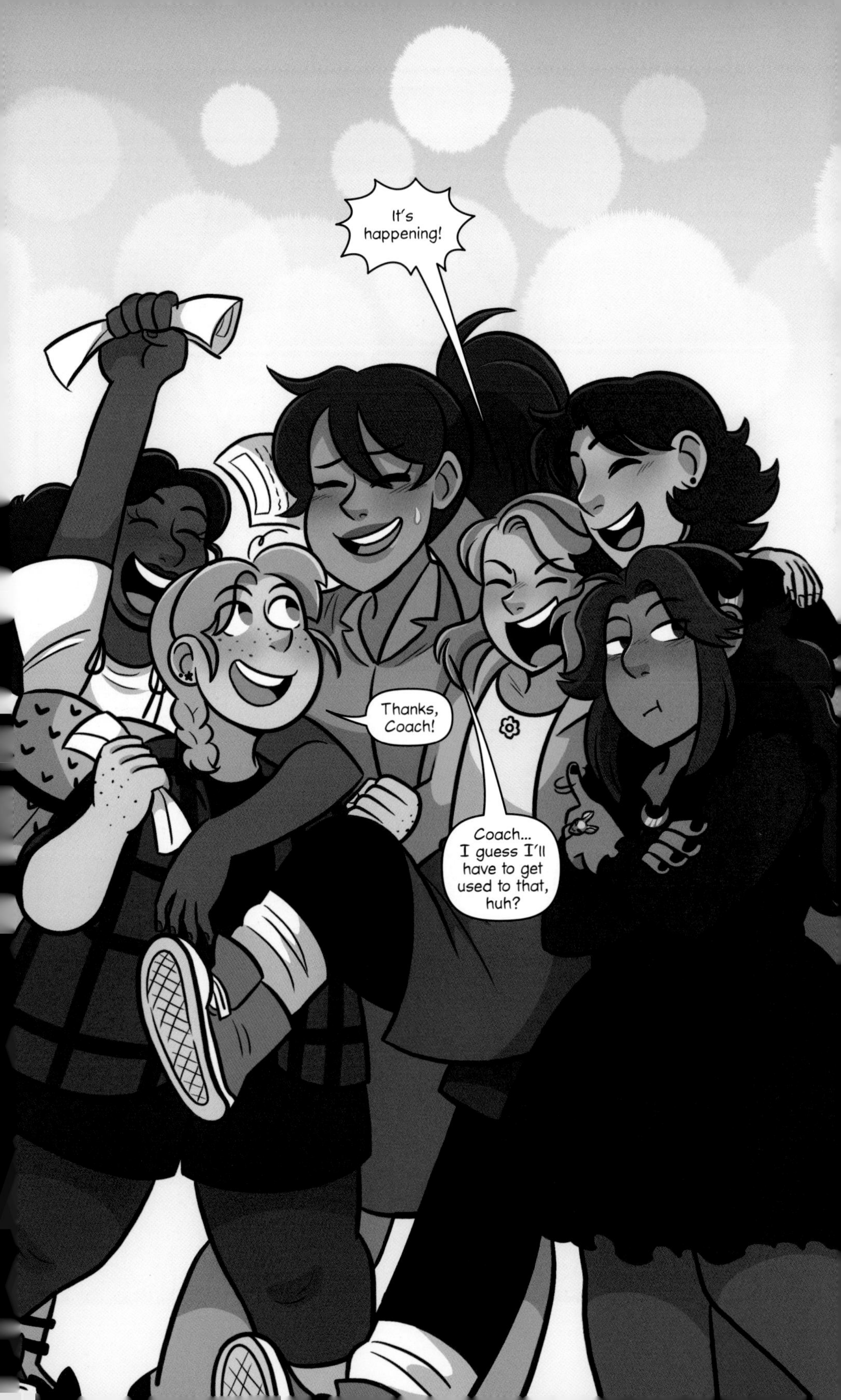
It's happening!
Thanks, Coach!
Coach... I guess I'll have to get used to that, huh?

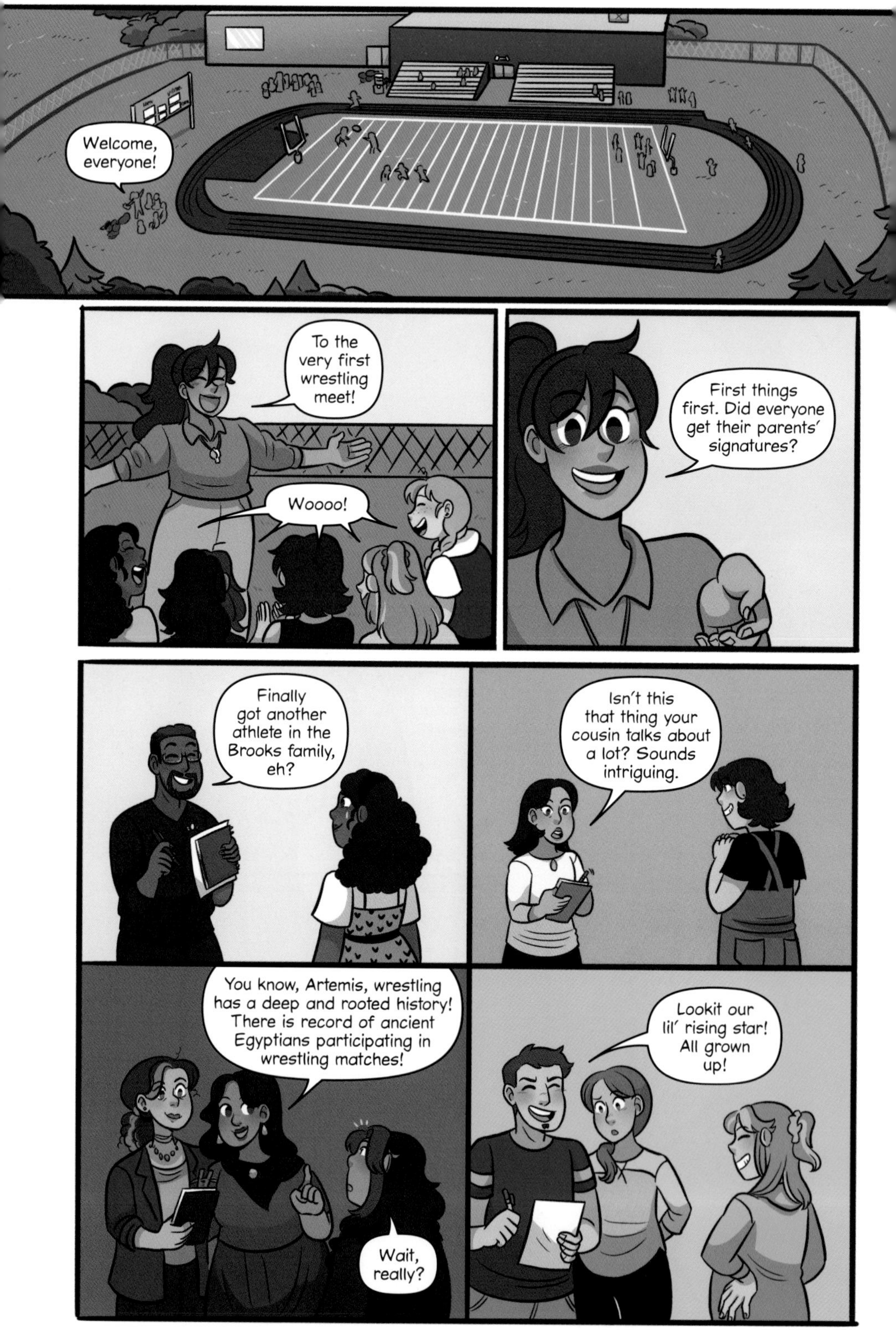

Welcome, everyone!
To the very first wrestling meet!
Woooo!
First things first. Did everyone get their parents' signatures?
Finally got another athlete in the Brooks family, eh?
Isn't this that thing your cousin talks about a lot? Sounds intriguing.
You know, Artemis, wrestling has a deep and rooted history! There is record of ancient Egyptians participating in wrestling matches!
Wait, really?
Lookit our lil' rising star! All grown up!

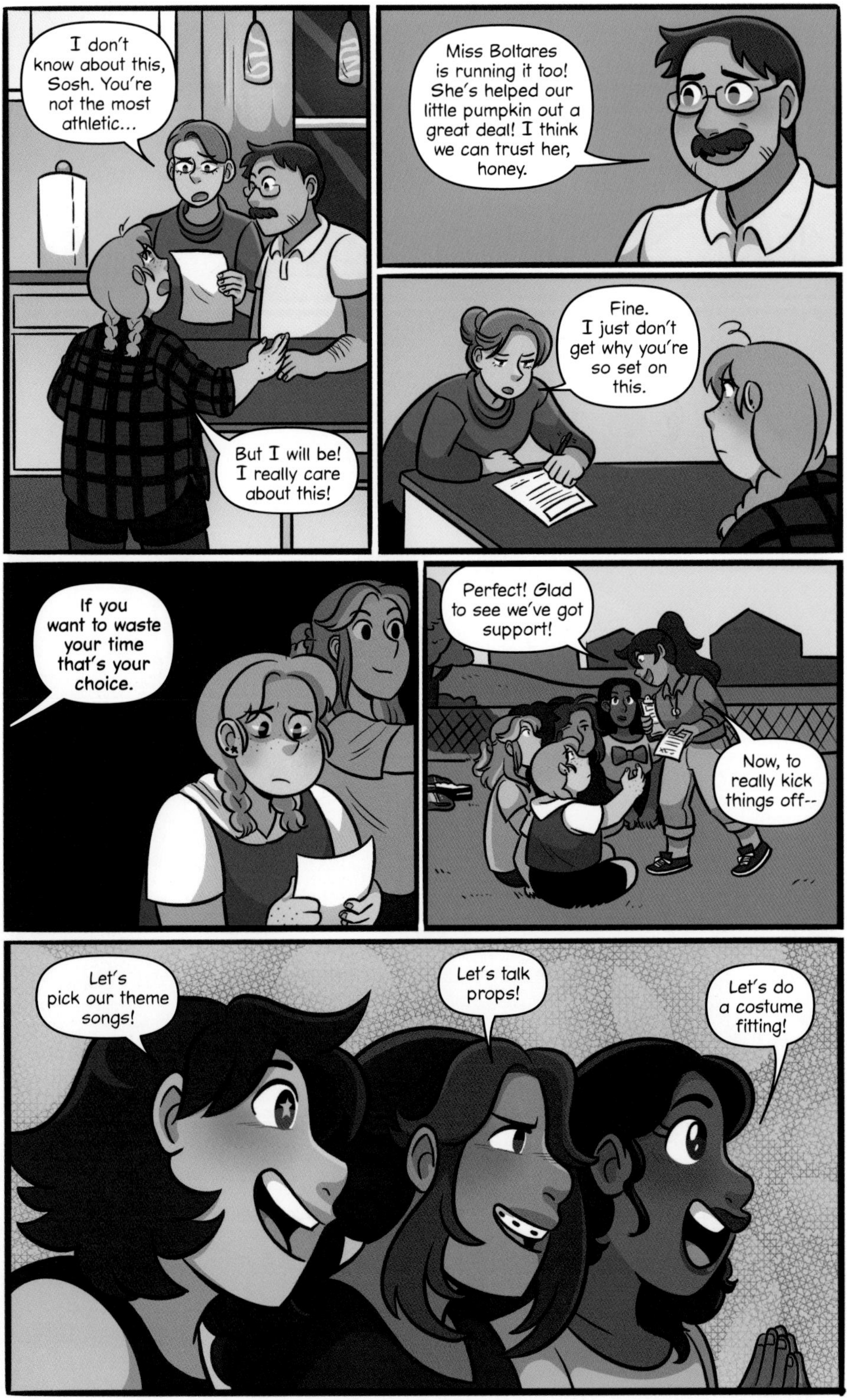
I don't know about this, Sosh. You're not the most athletic...
But I will be! I really care about this!
Miss Boltares is running it too! She's helped our little pumpkin out a great deal! I think we can trust her, honey.
Fine. I just don't get why you're so set on this.
If you want to waste your time that's your choice.
Perfect! Glad to see we've got support!
Now, to really kick things off--
Let's pick our theme songs!
Let's talk props!
Let's do a costume fitting!

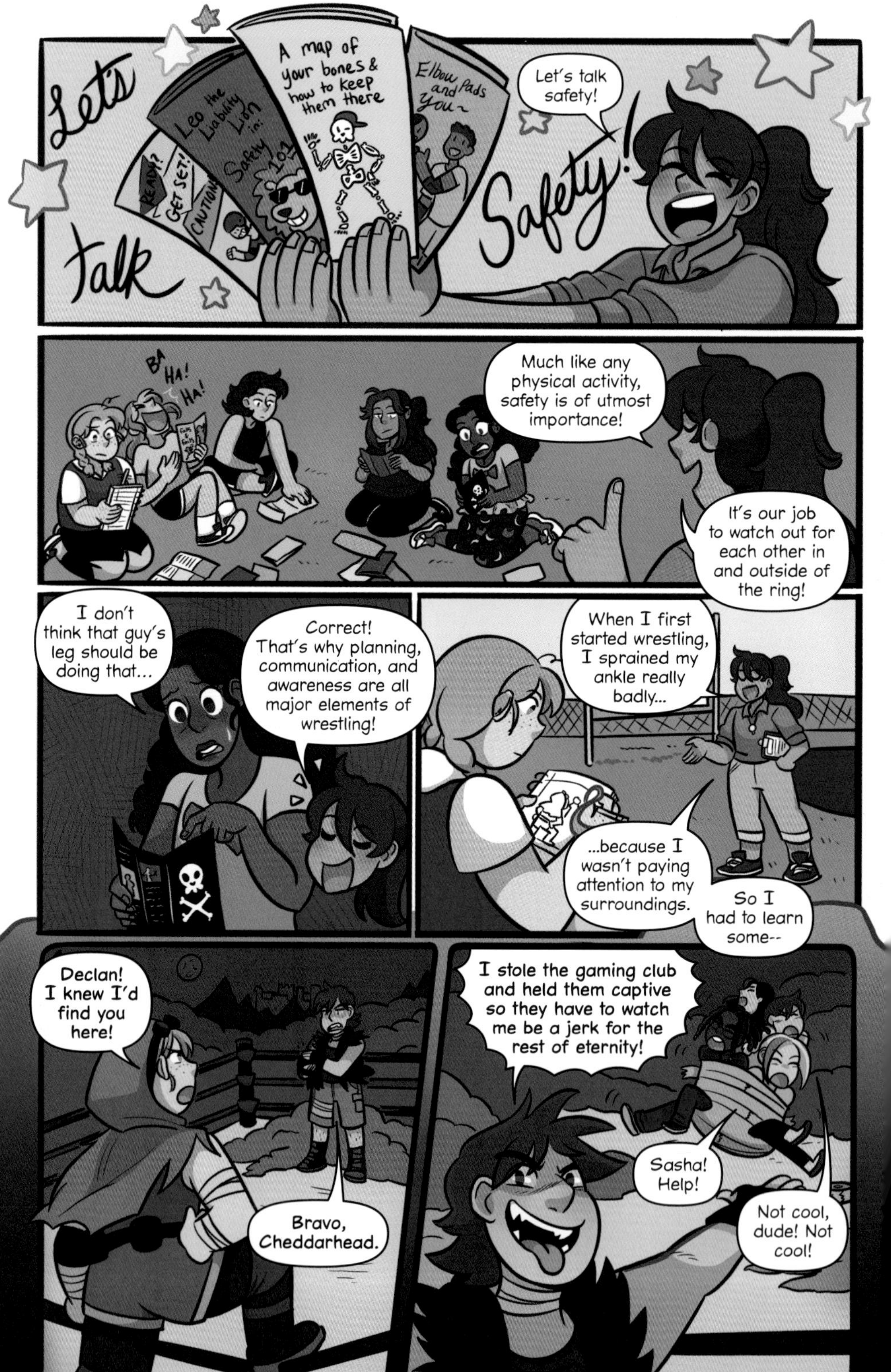
Let's Talk Safety!
READY? GET SET! CAUTION
Leo the Liability Lion in: Safety 101
A map of your bones & how to keep them there
Elbow Pads and You~
Let's talk safety!
BA HA! HA!
Much like any physical activity, safety is of utmost importance!
It's our job to watch out for each other in and outside of the ring!
I don't think that guy's leg should be doing that...
Correct! That's why planning, communication, and awareness are all major elements of wrestling!
When I first started wrestling, I sprained my ankle really badly...
...because I wasn't paying attention to my surroundings.
So I had to learn some--
Declan! I knew I'd find you here!
Bravo, Cheddarhead.
I stole the gaming club and held them captive so they have to watch me be a jerk for the rest of eternity!
Sasha! Help!
Not cool, dude! Not cool!

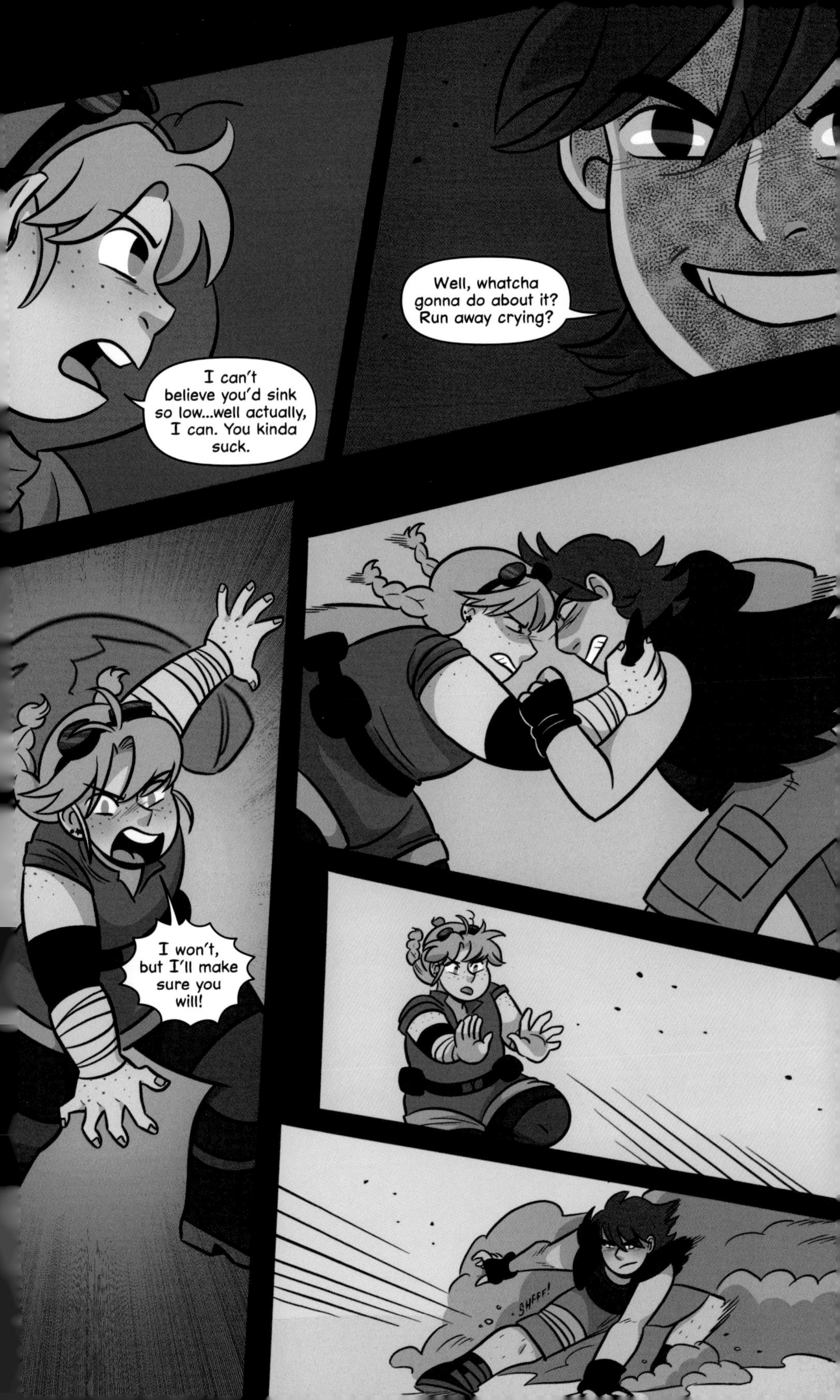
I can't believe you'd sink so low...well actually, I can. You kinda suck.
Well, whatcha gonna do about it? Run away crying?
I won't, but I'll make sure you will!
SHFFF!

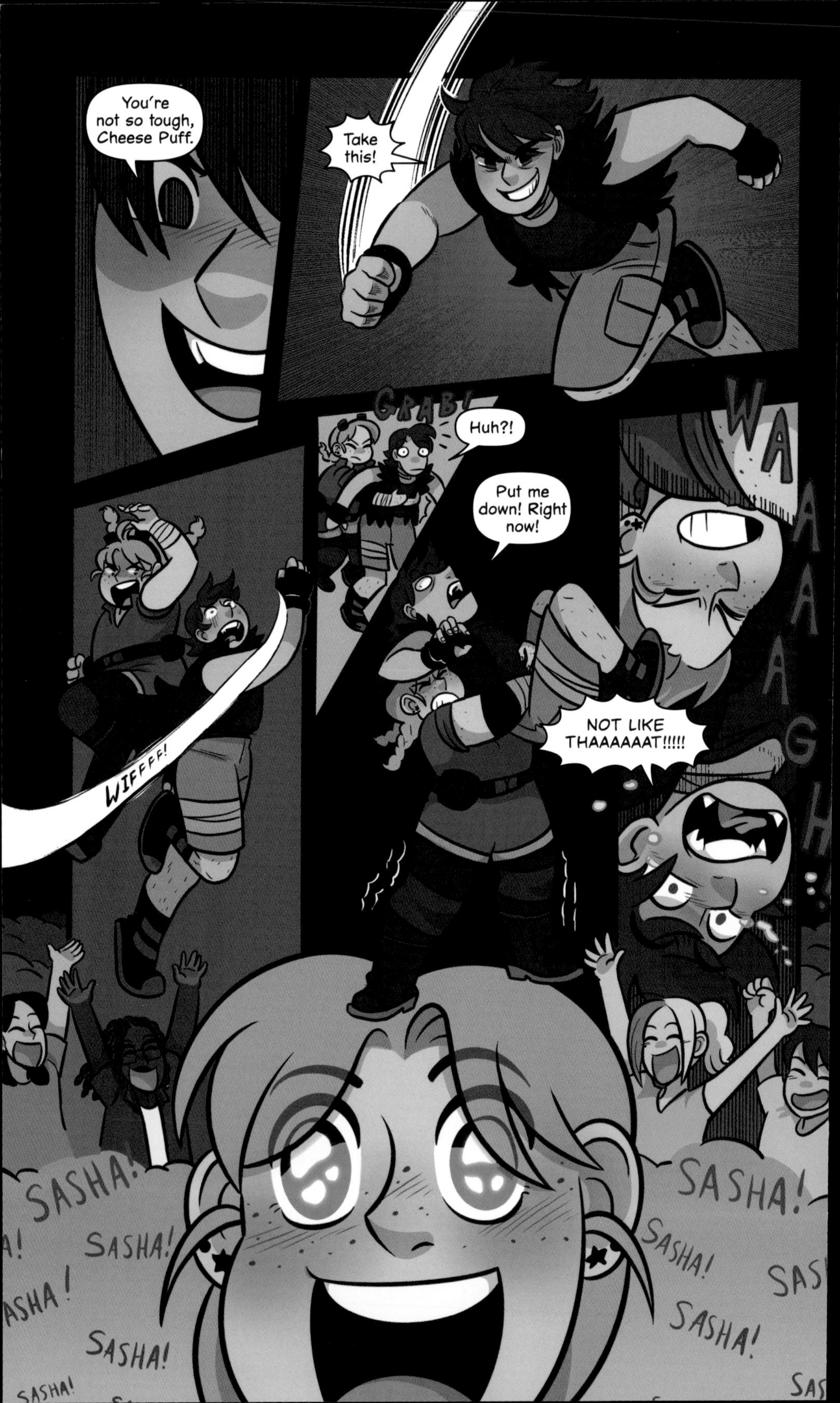

You're not so tough, Cheese Puff.
Take this!
WIFFFF!
GRAB!
Huh?!
Put me down! Right now!
WAAAAAGH!
NOT LIKE THAAAAAAT!!!!!
SASHA!
SASHA!
SASHA!
SASHA!
SASHA!
SASHA!
SASHA!

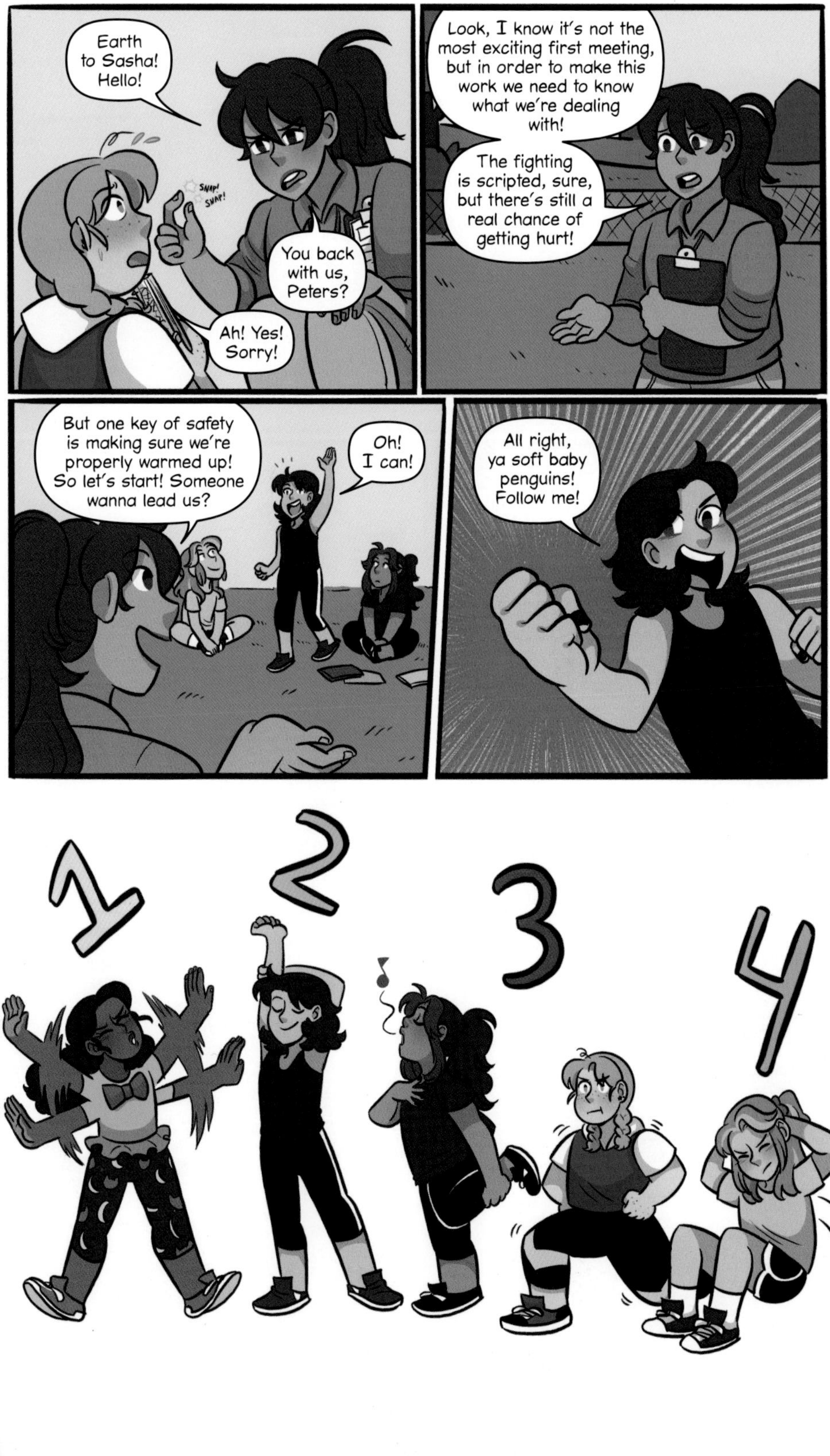
Earth to Sasha! Hello!
SNAP! SNAP!
You back with us, Peters?
Ah! Yes! Sorry!
Look, I know it's not the most exciting first meeting, but in order to make this work we need to know what we're dealing with!
The fighting is scripted, sure, but there's still a real chance of getting hurt!
But one key of safety is making sure we're properly warmed up! So let's start! Someone wanna lead us?
Oh! I can!
All right, ya soft baby penguins! Follow me!
1
2
3
4

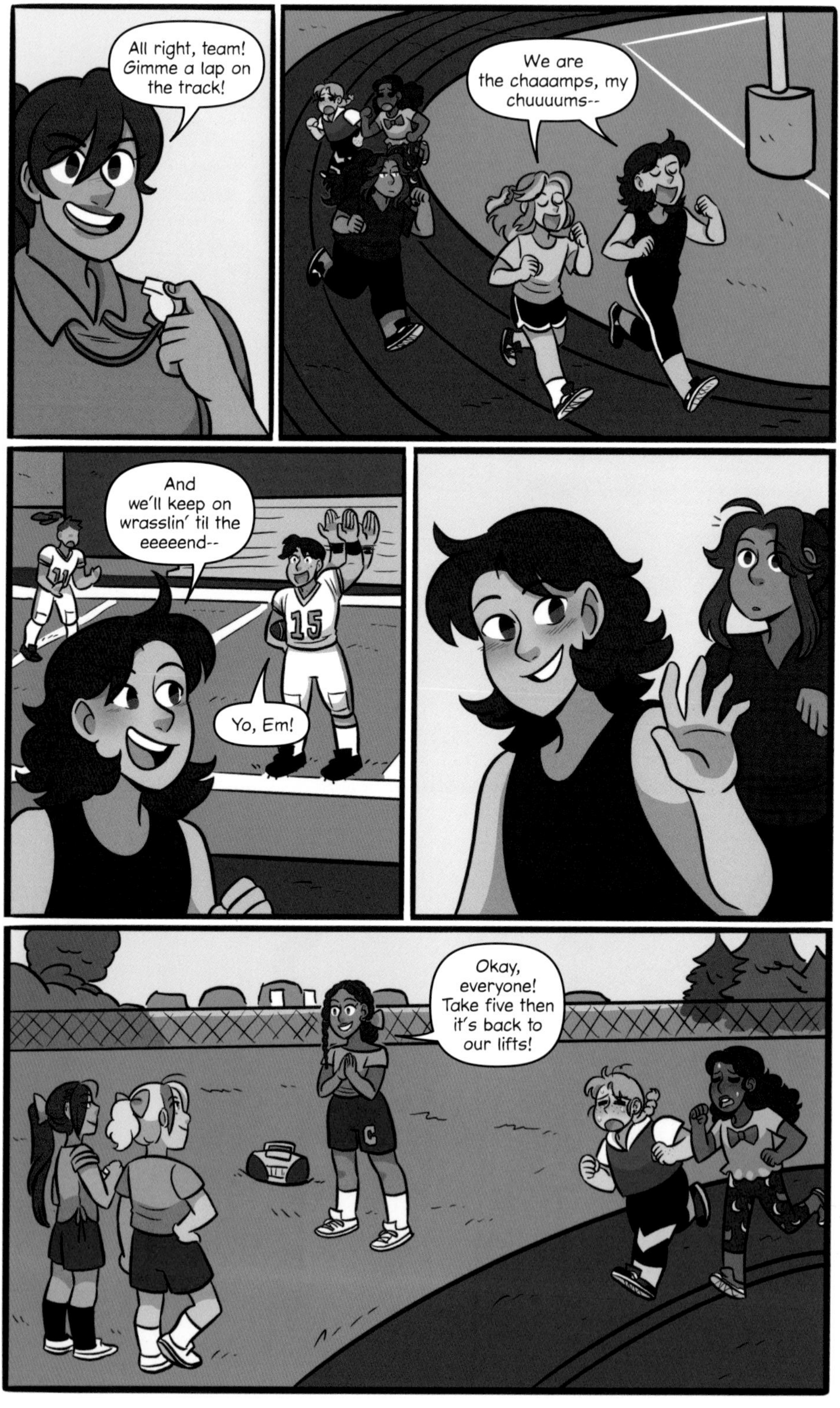
All right, team! Gimme a lap on the track!
We are the chaaamps, my chuuuums--
And we'll keep on wrasslin' til the eeeeend--
Yo, Em!
Okay, everyone! Take five then it's back to our lifts!

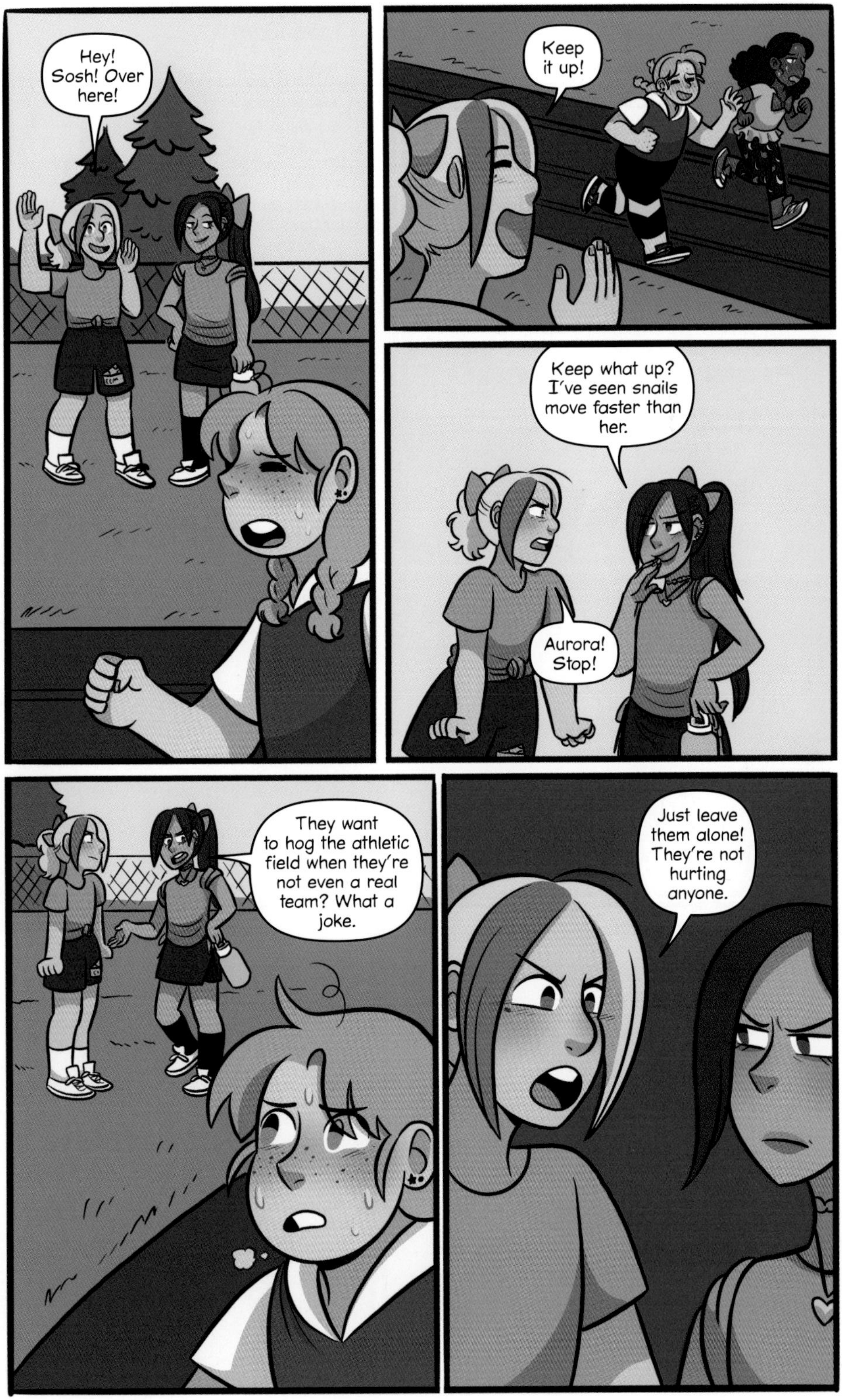
Hey! Sosh! Over here!
Keep it up!
Keep what up? I've seen snails move faster than her.
Aurora! Stop!
They want to hog the athletic field when they're not even a real team? What a joke.
Just leave them alone! They're not hurting anyone.

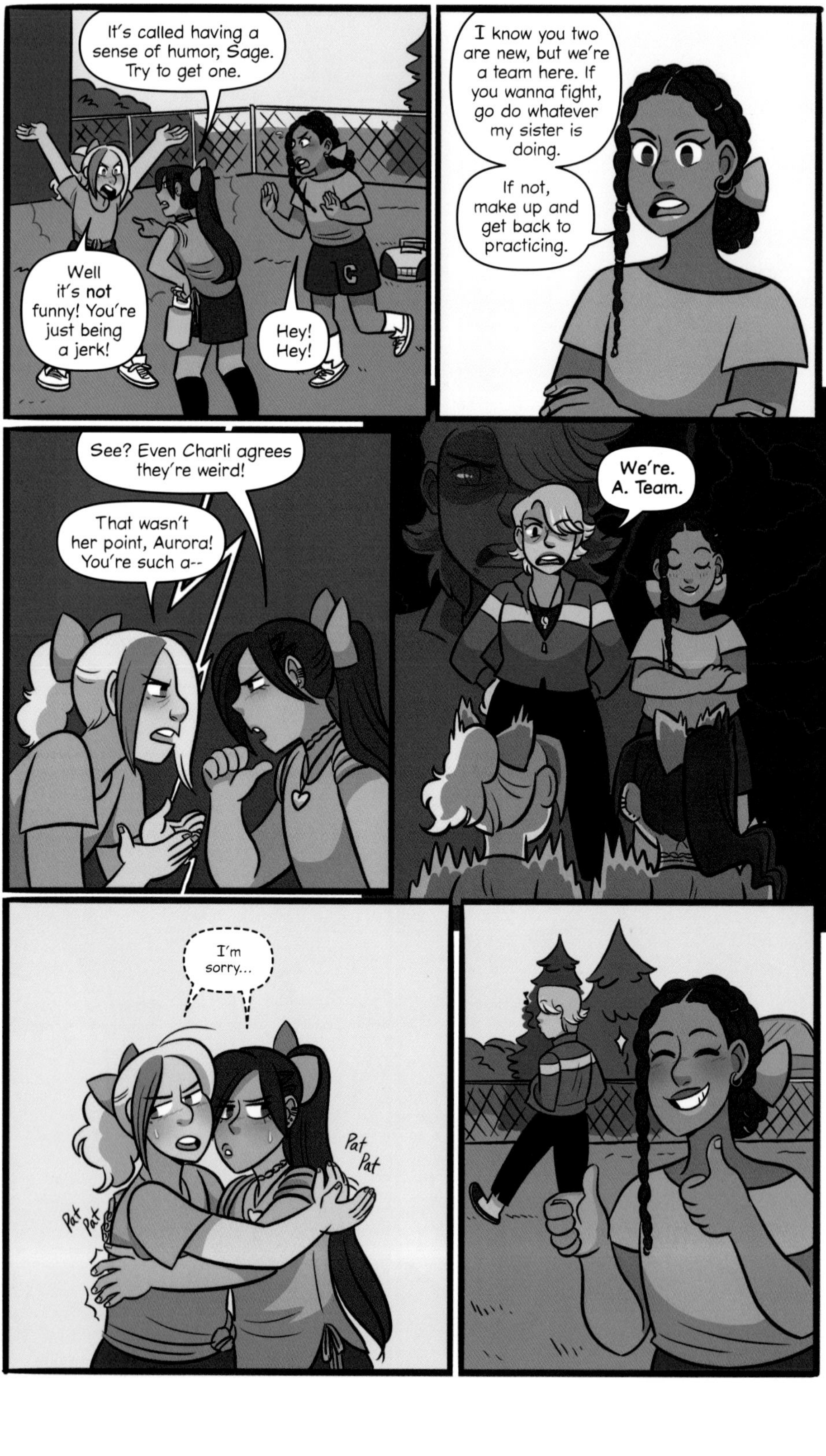
It's called having a sense of humor, Sage. Try to get one.
Well it's not funny! You're just being a jerk!
Hey! Hey!
I know you two are new, but we're a team here. If you wanna fight, go do whatever my sister is doing.
If not, make up and get back to practicing.
See? Even Charli agrees they're weird!
That wasn't her point, Aurora! You're such a--
We're. A. Team.
I'm sorry...
Pat Pat
Pat Pat

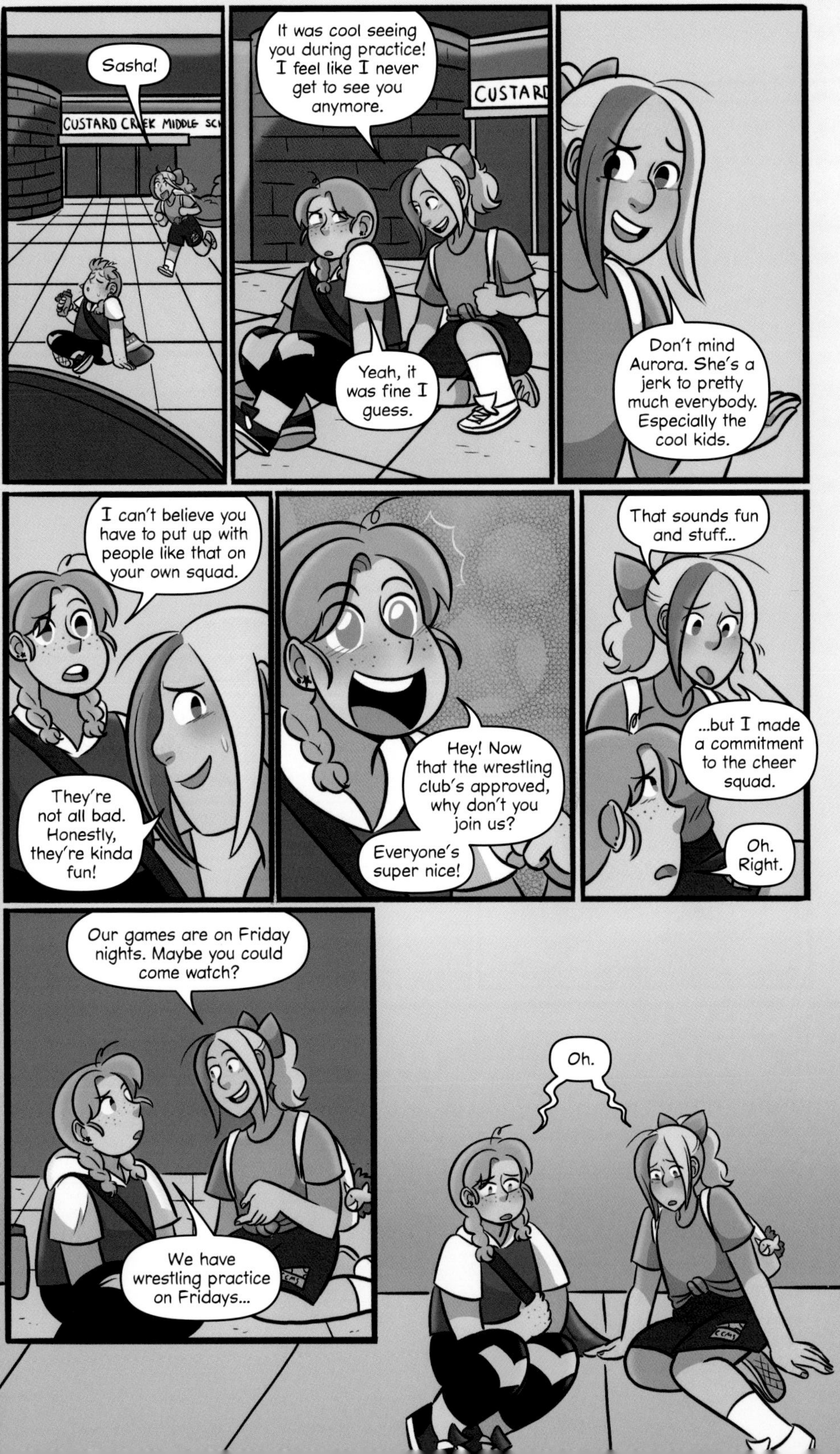
Sasha!
CUSTARD CREEK MIDDLE SCH
It was cool seeing you during practice! I feel like I never get to see you anymore.
CUSTARD
Yeah, it was fine I guess.
Don't mind Aurora. She's a jerk to pretty much everybody. Especially the cool kids.
I can't believe you have to put up with people like that on your own squad.
They're not all bad. Honestly, they're kinda fun!
Hey! Now that the wrestling club's approved, why don't you join us?
Everyone's super nice!
That sounds fun and stuff...
...but I made a commitment to the cheer squad.
Oh. Right.
Our games are on Friday nights. Maybe you could come watch?
We have wrestling practice on Fridays...
Oh.

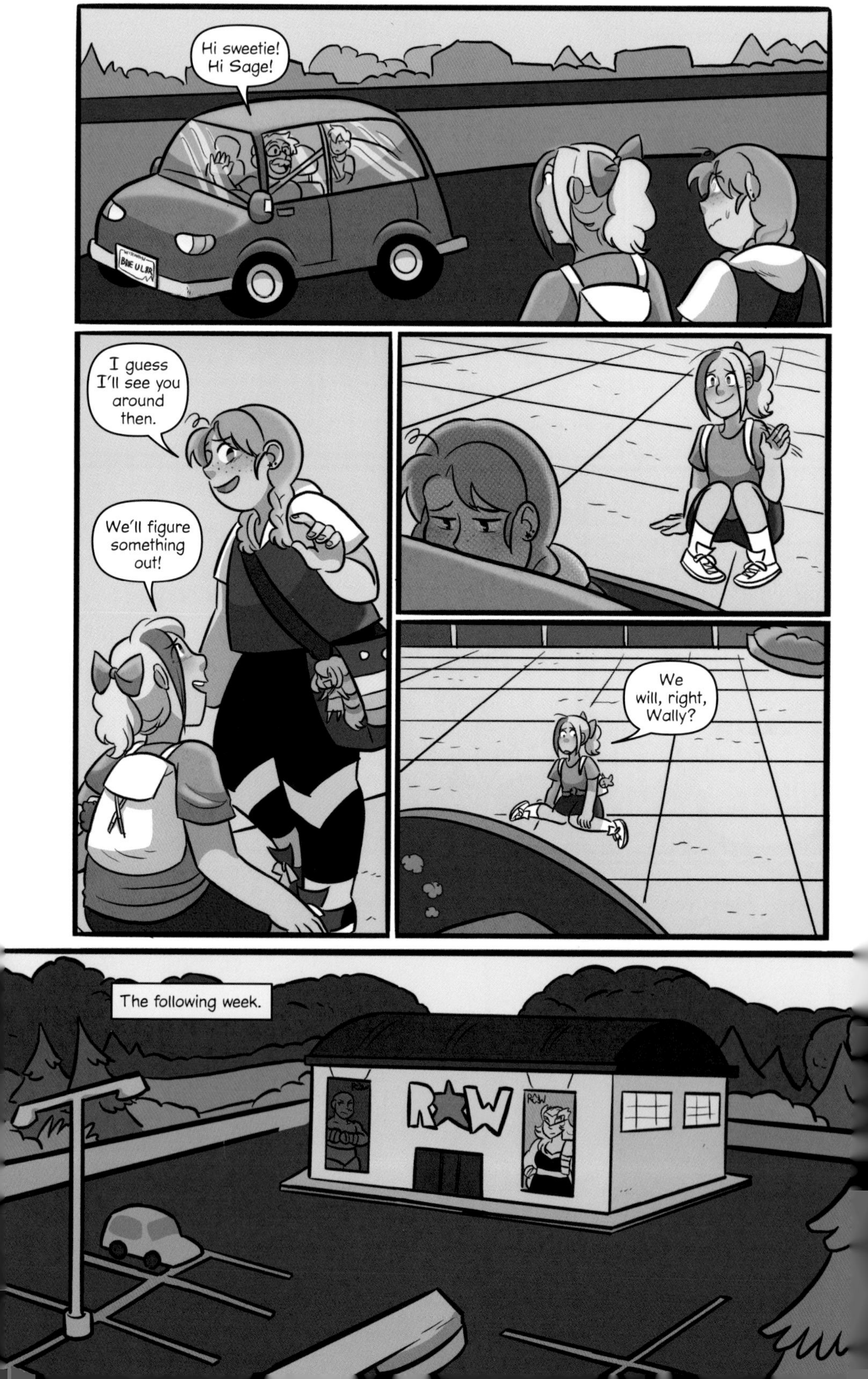
Hi sweetie! Hi Sage!
I guess I'll see you around then.
We'll figure something out!
We will, right, Wally?
The following week.

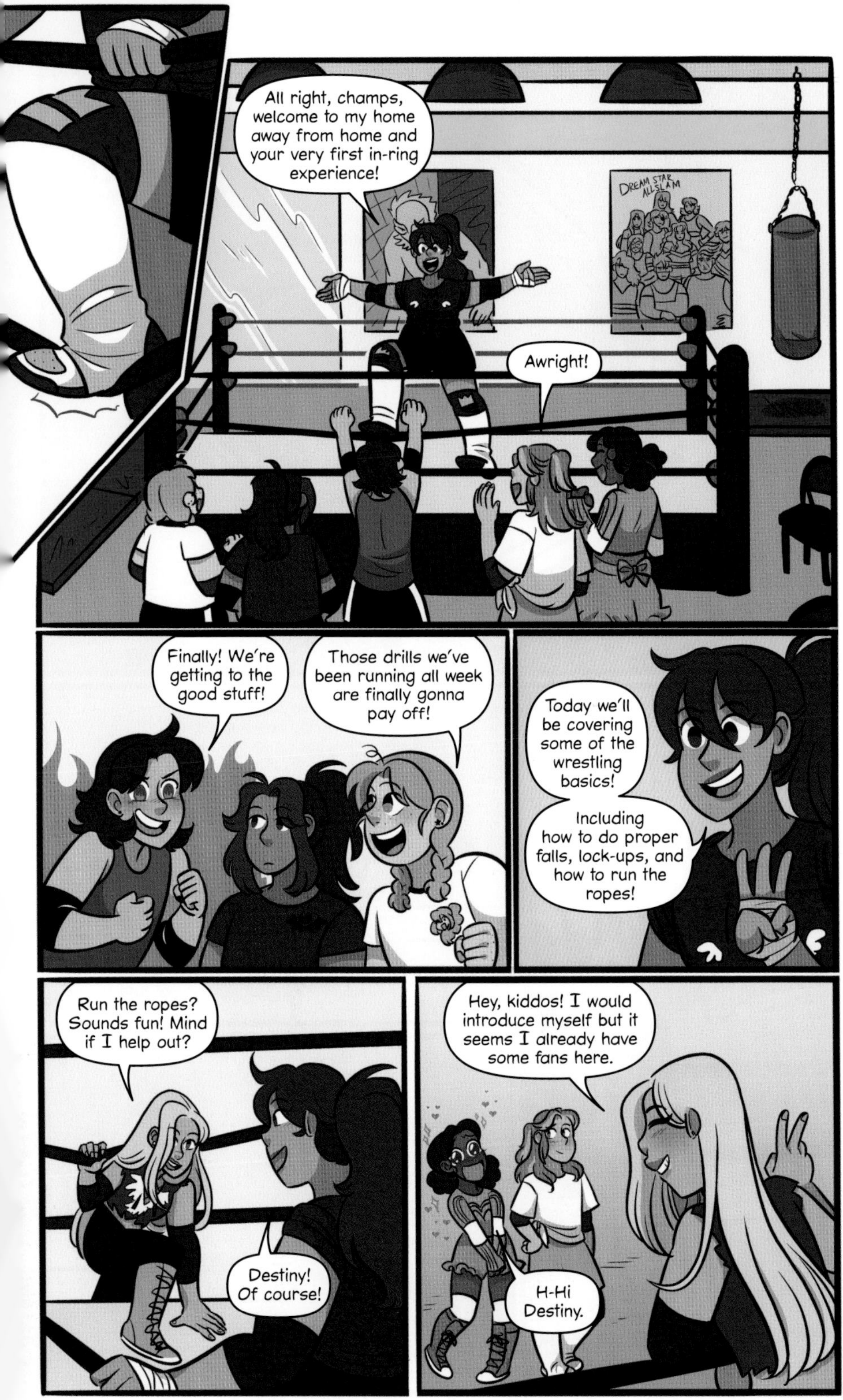

All right, champs, welcome to my home away from home and your very first in-ring experience!
DREAM STAR ALLSLAM
Awright!
Finally! We're getting to the good stuff!
Those drills we've been running all week are finally gonna pay off!
Today we'll be covering some of the wrestling basics!
Including how to do proper falls, lock-ups, and how to run the ropes!
Run the ropes? Sounds fun! Mind if I help out?
Destiny! Of course!
Hey, kiddos! I would introduce myself but it seems I already have some fans here.
H-Hi Destiny.

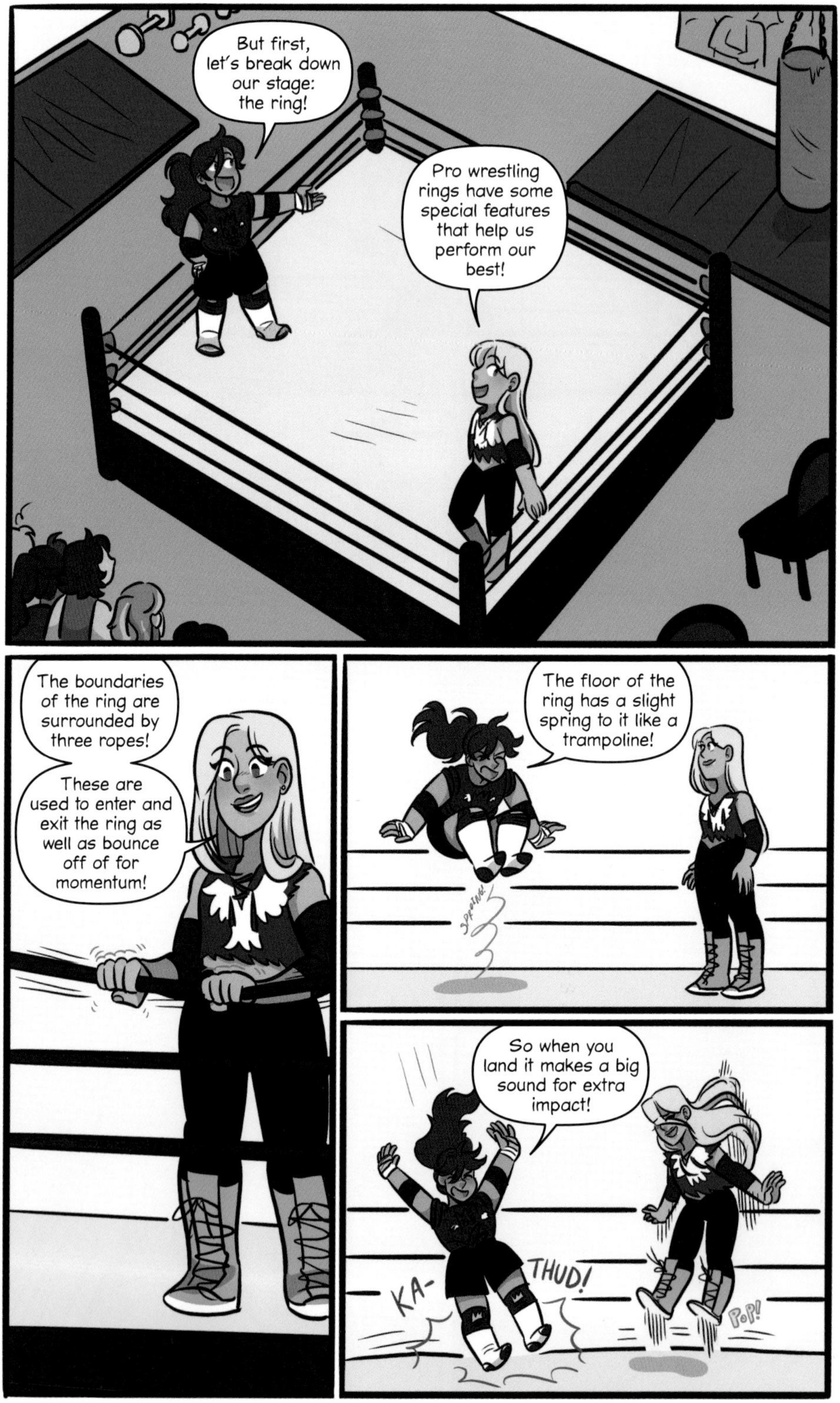

But first, let's break down our stage: the ring!
Pro wrestling rings have some special features that help us perform our best!
The boundaries of the ring are surrounded by three ropes!
These are used to enter and exit the ring as well as bounce off of for momentum!
The floor of the ring has a slight spring to it like a trampoline!
SPRING!
So when you land it makes a big sound for extra impact!
KA-
THUD!
POP!

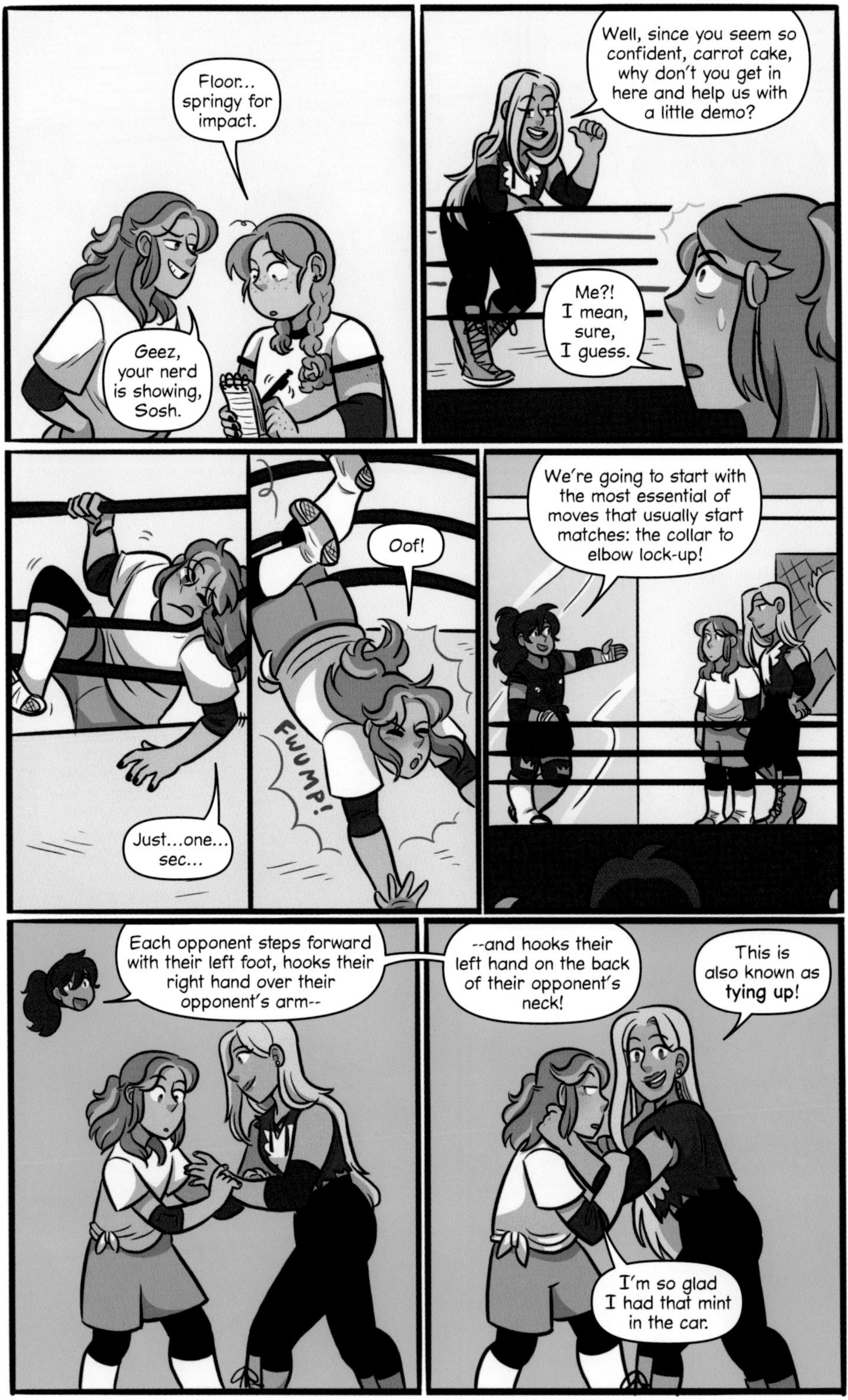

Floor... springy for impact.
Geez, your nerd is showing, Sosh.
Well, since you seem so confident, carrot cake, why don't you get in here and help us with a little demo?
Me?! I mean, sure, I guess.
Just...one... sec...
Oof!
FWUMP!
We're going to start with the most essential of moves that usually start matches: the collar to elbow lock-up!
Each opponent steps forward with their left foot, hooks their right hand over their opponent's arm--
--and hooks their left hand on the back of their opponent's neck!
This is also known as **tying up!**
I'm so glad I had that mint in the car.

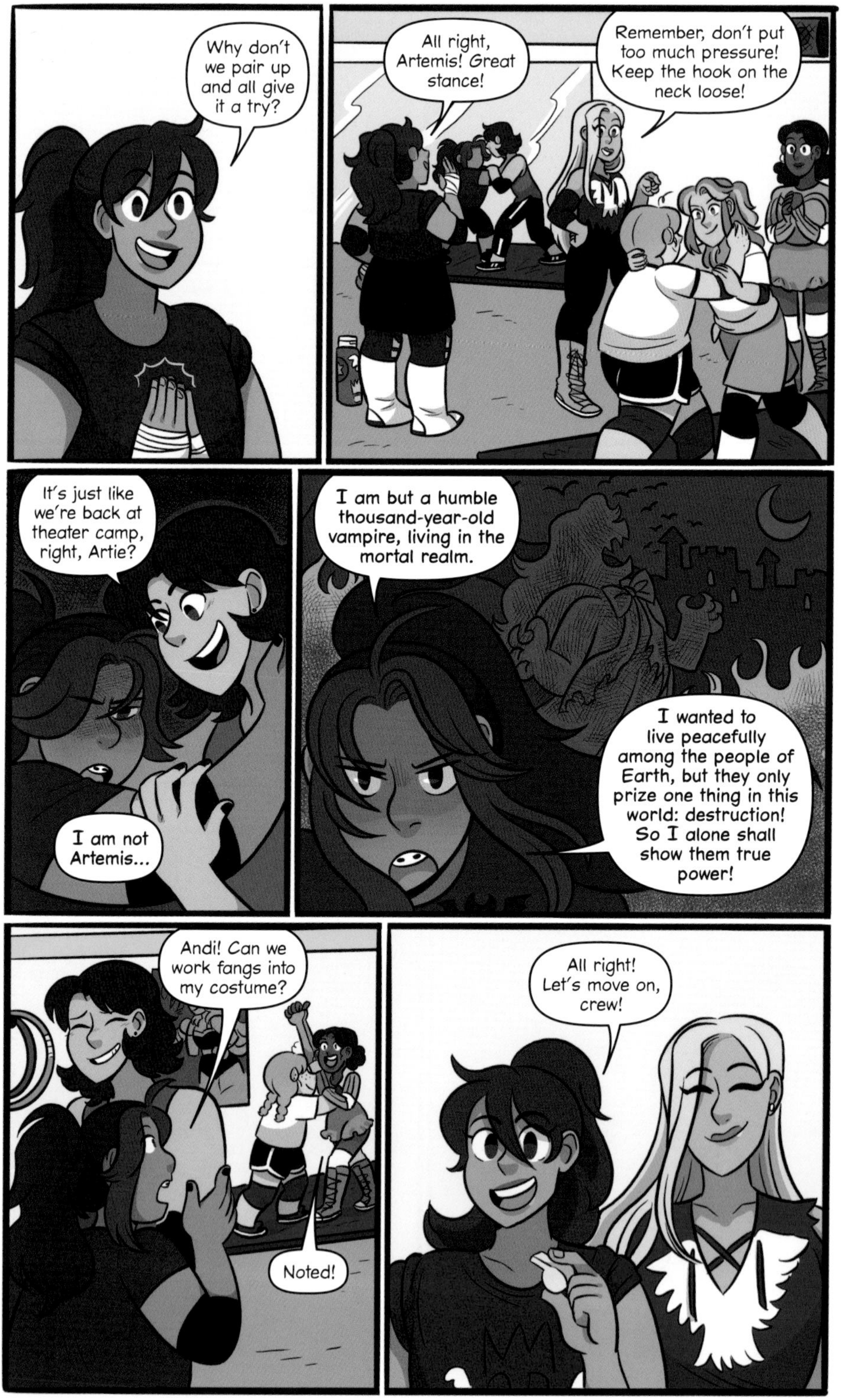
Why don't we pair up and all give it a try?
All right, Artemis! Great stance!
Remember, don't put too much pressure! Keep the hook on the neck loose!
It's just like we're back at theater camp, right, Artie?
I am not Artemis...
I am but a humble thousand-year-old vampire, living in the mortal realm.
I wanted to live peacefully among the people of Earth, but they only prize one thing in this world: destruction! So I alone shall show them true power!
Andi! Can we work fangs into my costume?
Noted!
All right! Let's move on, crew!

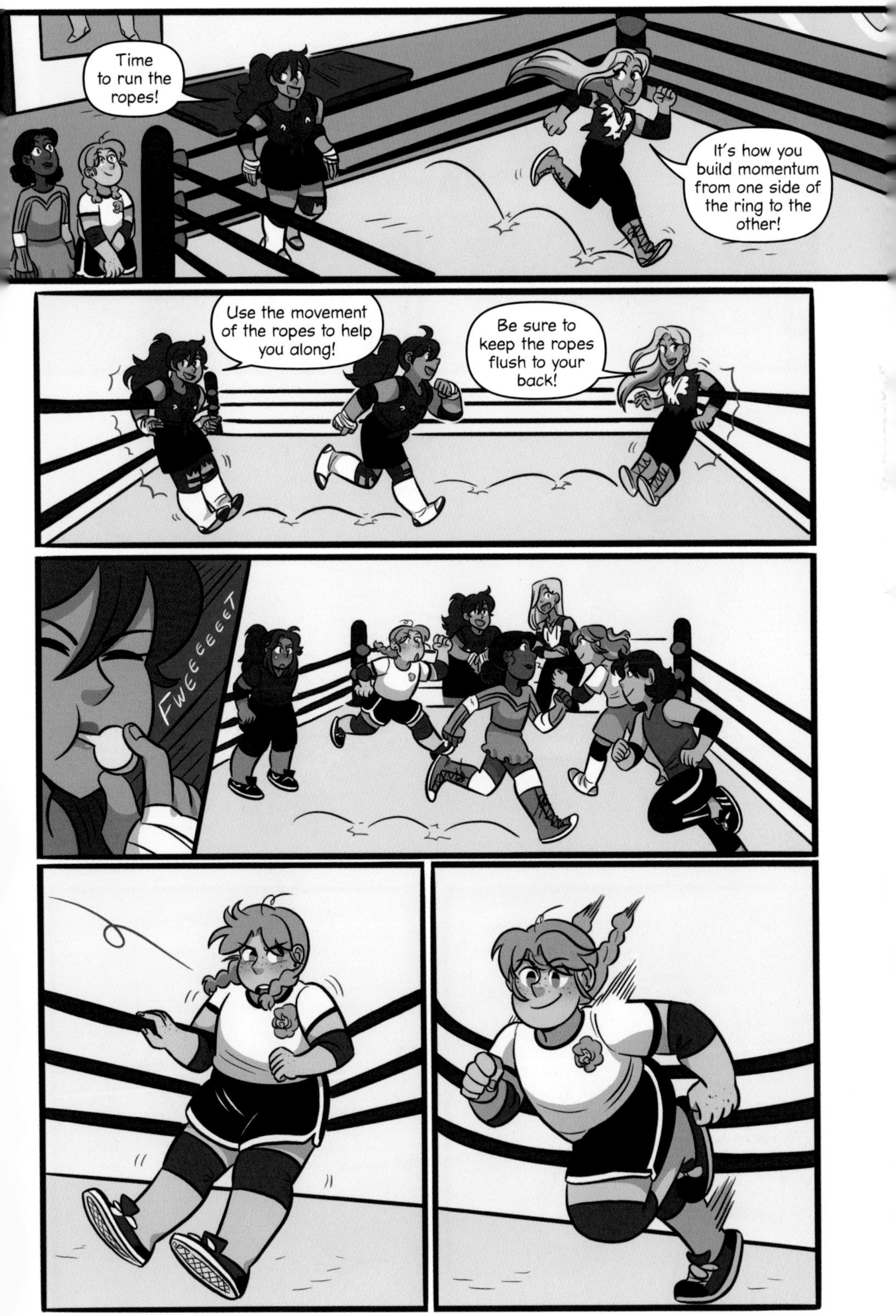
Time to run the ropes!
It's how you build momentum from one side of the ring to the other!
Use the movement of the ropes to help you along!
Be sure to keep the ropes flush to your back!
FWEEEEEET

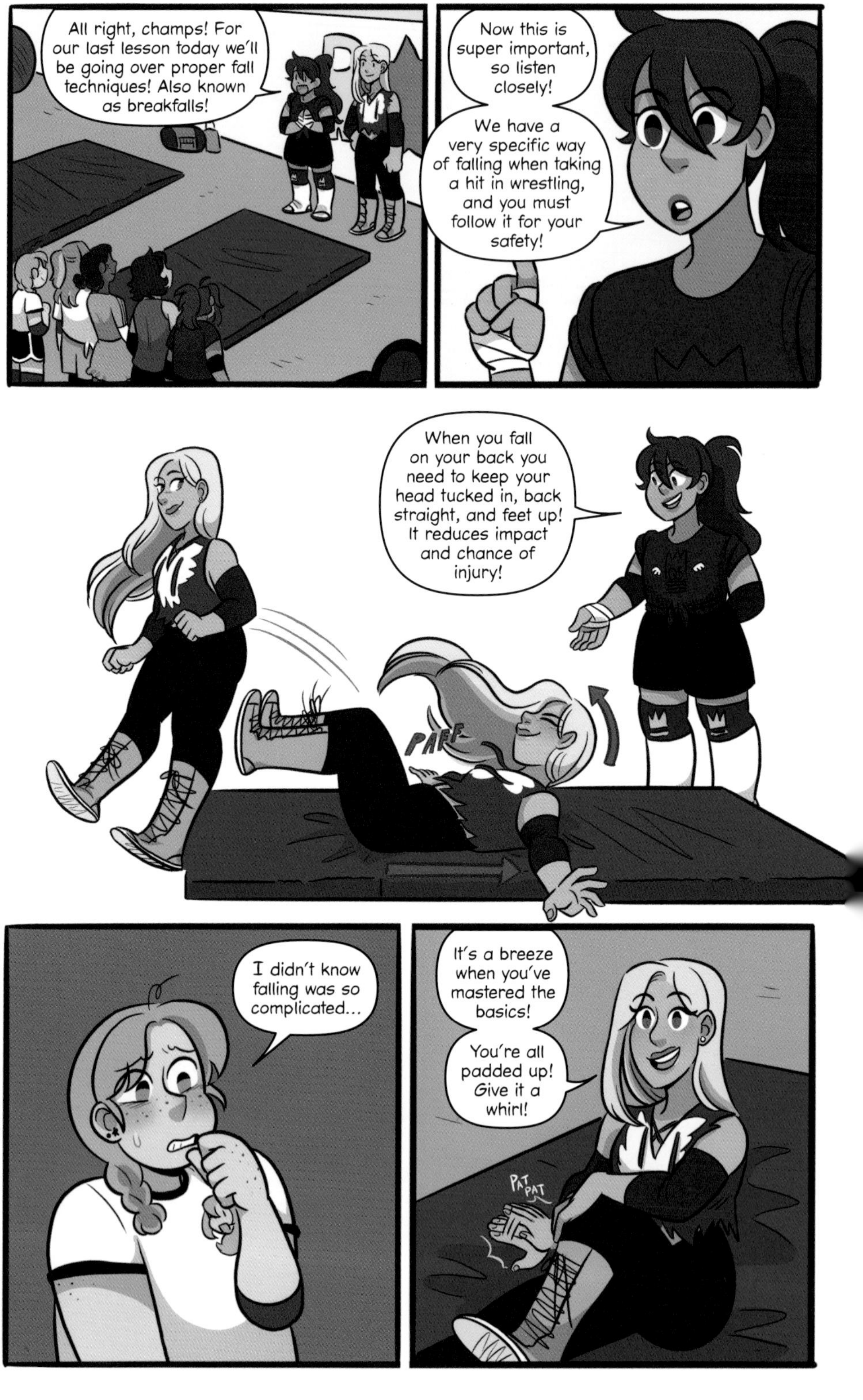
All right, champs! For our last lesson today we'll be going over proper fall techniques! Also known as breakfalls!
Now this is super important, so listen closely!
We have a very specific way of falling when taking a hit in wrestling, and you must follow it for your safety!
When you fall on your back you need to keep your head tucked in, back straight, and feet up! It reduces impact and chance of injury!
PAFF
I didn't know falling was so complicated...
It's a breeze when you've mastered the basics!
You're all padded up! Give it a whirl!
PAT PAT

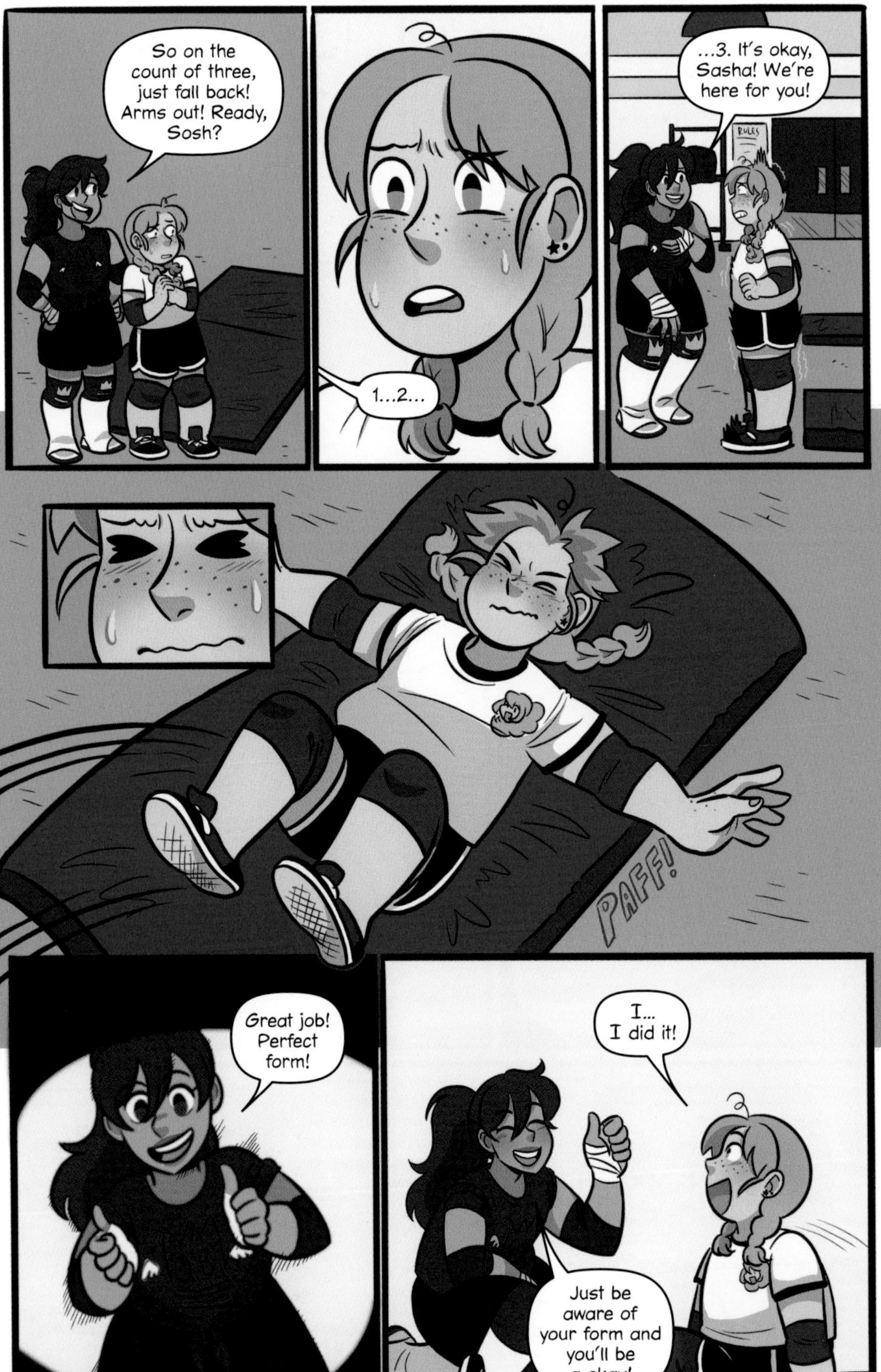
So on the count of three, just fall back! Arms out! Ready, Sosh?
1...2...
...3. It's okay, Sasha! We're here for you!
RULES
PAFF!
Great job! Perfect form!
I... I did it!
Just be aware of your form and you'll be a-okay!

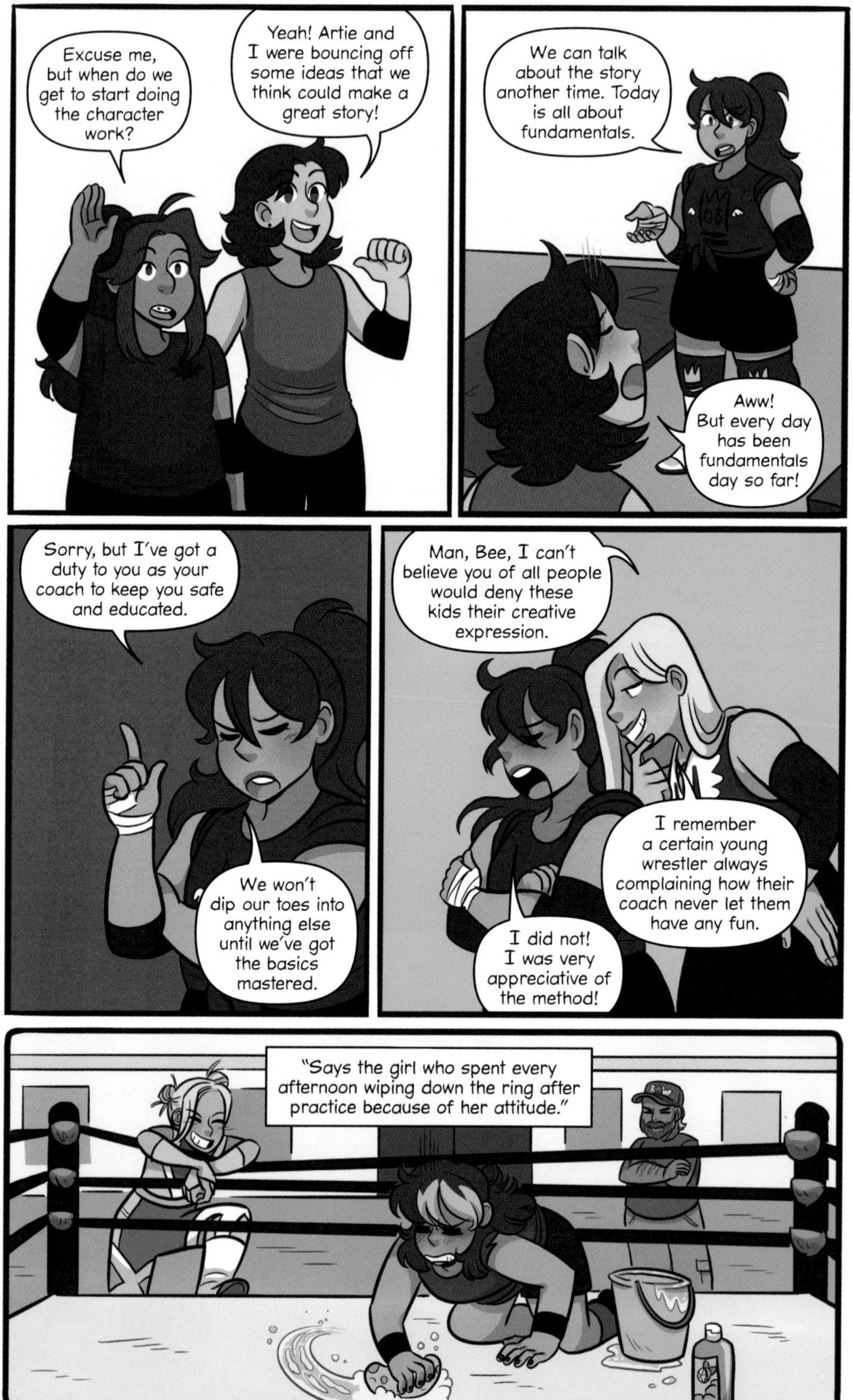
Excuse me, but when do we get to start doing the character work?
Yeah! Artie and I were bouncing off some ideas that we think could make a great story!
We can talk about the story another time. Today is all about fundamentals.
Aww! But every day has been fundamentals day so far!
Sorry, but I've got a duty to you as your coach to keep you safe and educated.
We won't dip our toes into anything else until we've got the basics mastered.
Man, Bee, I can't believe you of all people would deny these kids their creative expression.
I remember a certain young wrestler always complaining how their coach never let them have any fun.
I did not! I was very appreciative of the method!
"Says the girl who spent every afternoon wiping down the ring after practice because of her attitude."

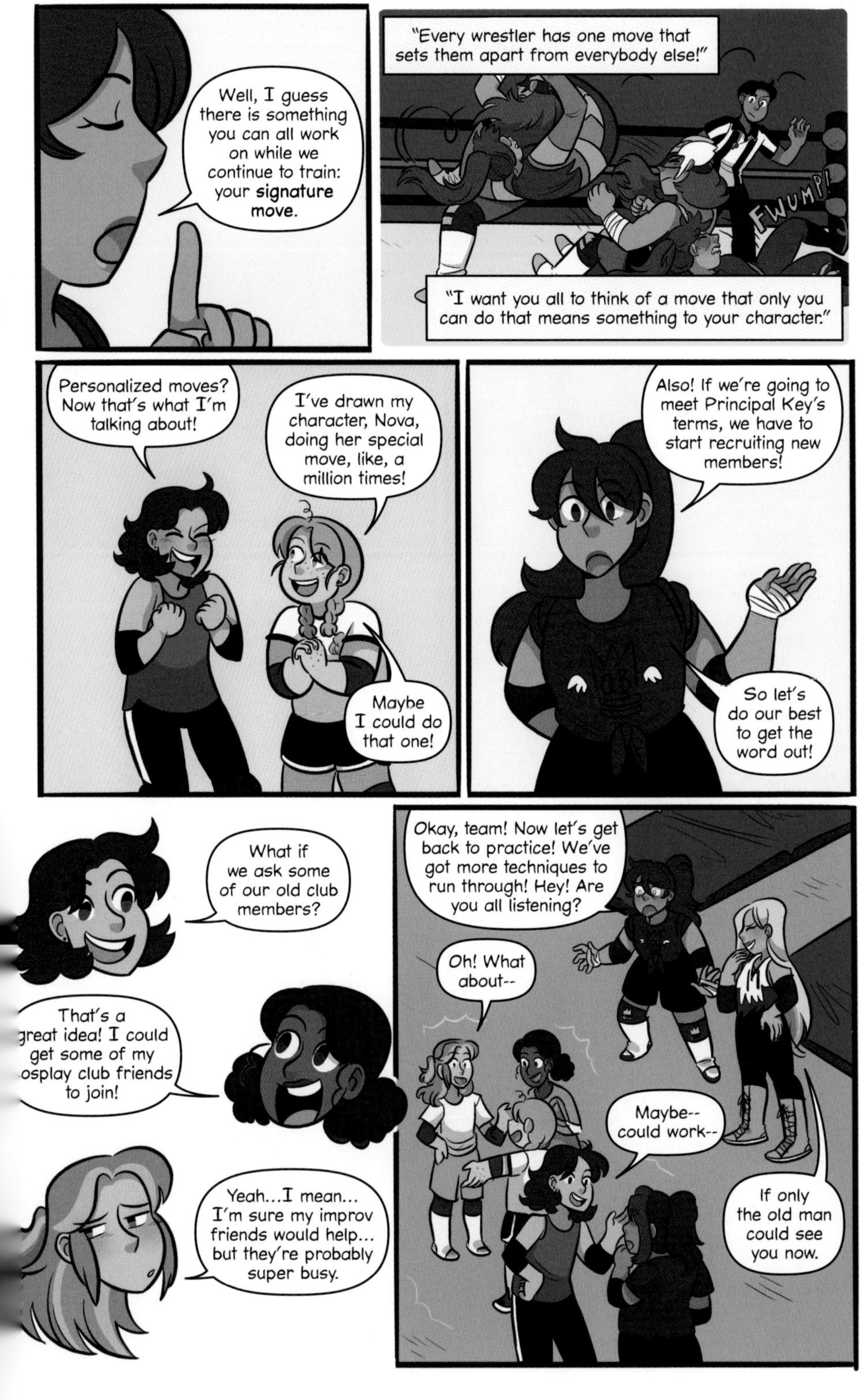

Well, I guess there is something you can all work on while we continue to train: your **signature move**.
"Every wrestler has one move that sets them apart from everybody else!"
FWUMP!
"I want you all to think of a move that only you can do that means something to your character."
Personalized moves? Now that's what I'm talking about!
I've drawn my character, Nova, doing her special move, like, a million times!
Maybe I could do that one!
Also! If we're going to meet Principal Key's terms, we have to start recruiting new members!
So let's do our best to get the word out!
What if we ask some of our old club members?
That's a great idea! I could get some of my cosplay club friends to join!
Yeah...I mean... I'm sure my improv friends would help... but they're probably super busy.
Okay, team! Now let's get back to practice! We've got more techniques to run through! Hey! Are you all listening?
Oh! What about--
Maybe-- could work--
If only the old man could see you now.

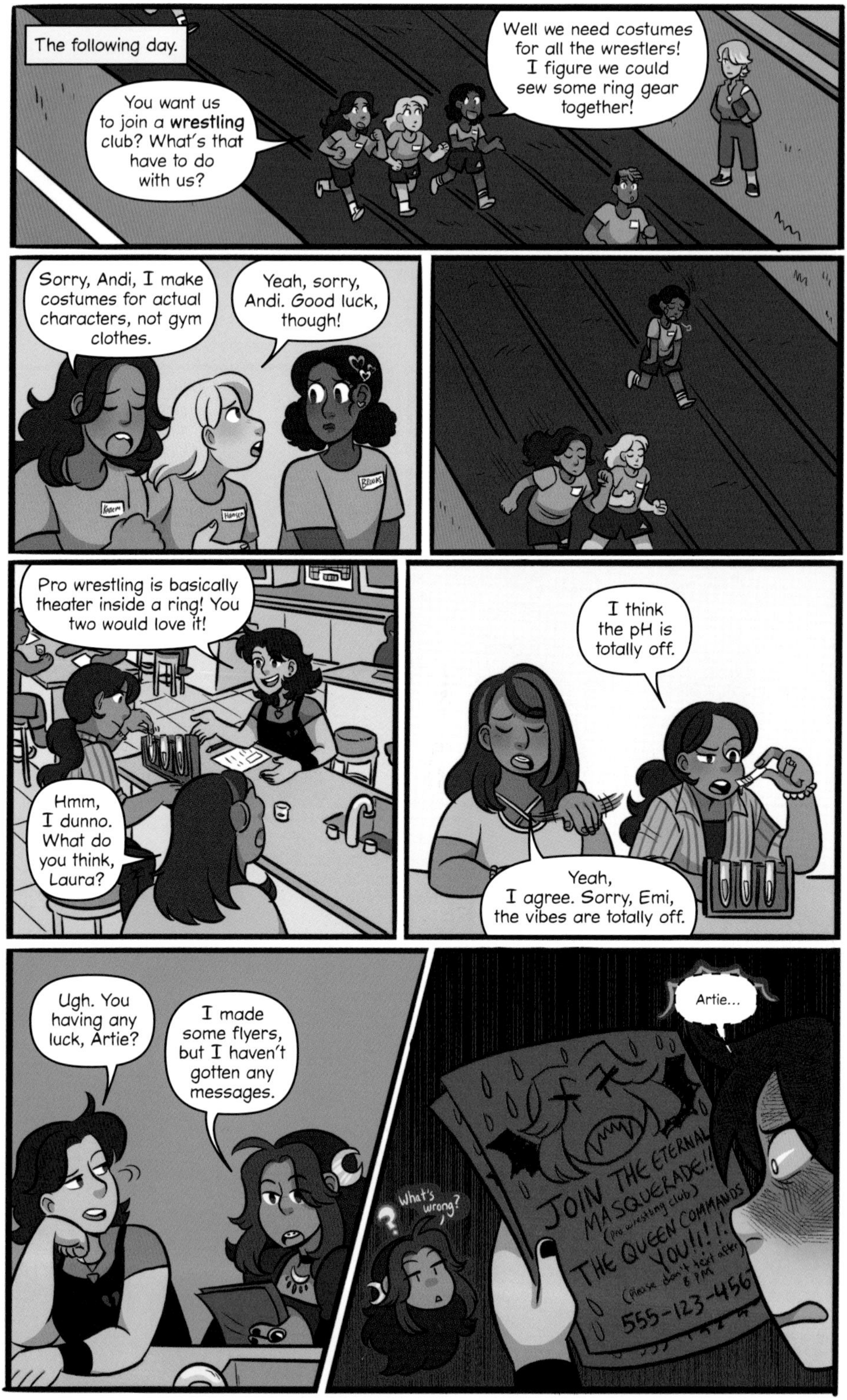

The following day.
You want us to join a **wrestling** club? What's that have to do with us?
Well we need costumes for all the wrestlers! I figure we could sew some ring gear together!
Sorry, Andi, I make costumes for actual characters, not gym clothes.
Yeah, sorry, Andi. Good luck, though!
Pro wrestling is basically theater inside a ring! You two would love it!
Hmm, I dunno. What do you think, Laura?
I think the pH is totally off.
Yeah, I agree. Sorry, Emi, the vibes are totally off.
Ugh. You having any luck, Artie?
I made some flyers, but I haven't gotten any messages.
Artie...
What's wrong?
JOIN THE ETERNAL MASQUERADE!!
(Pro wrestling club)
THE QUEEN COMMANDS YOU!!!!
(please don't text after 8 PM)
555-123-4567

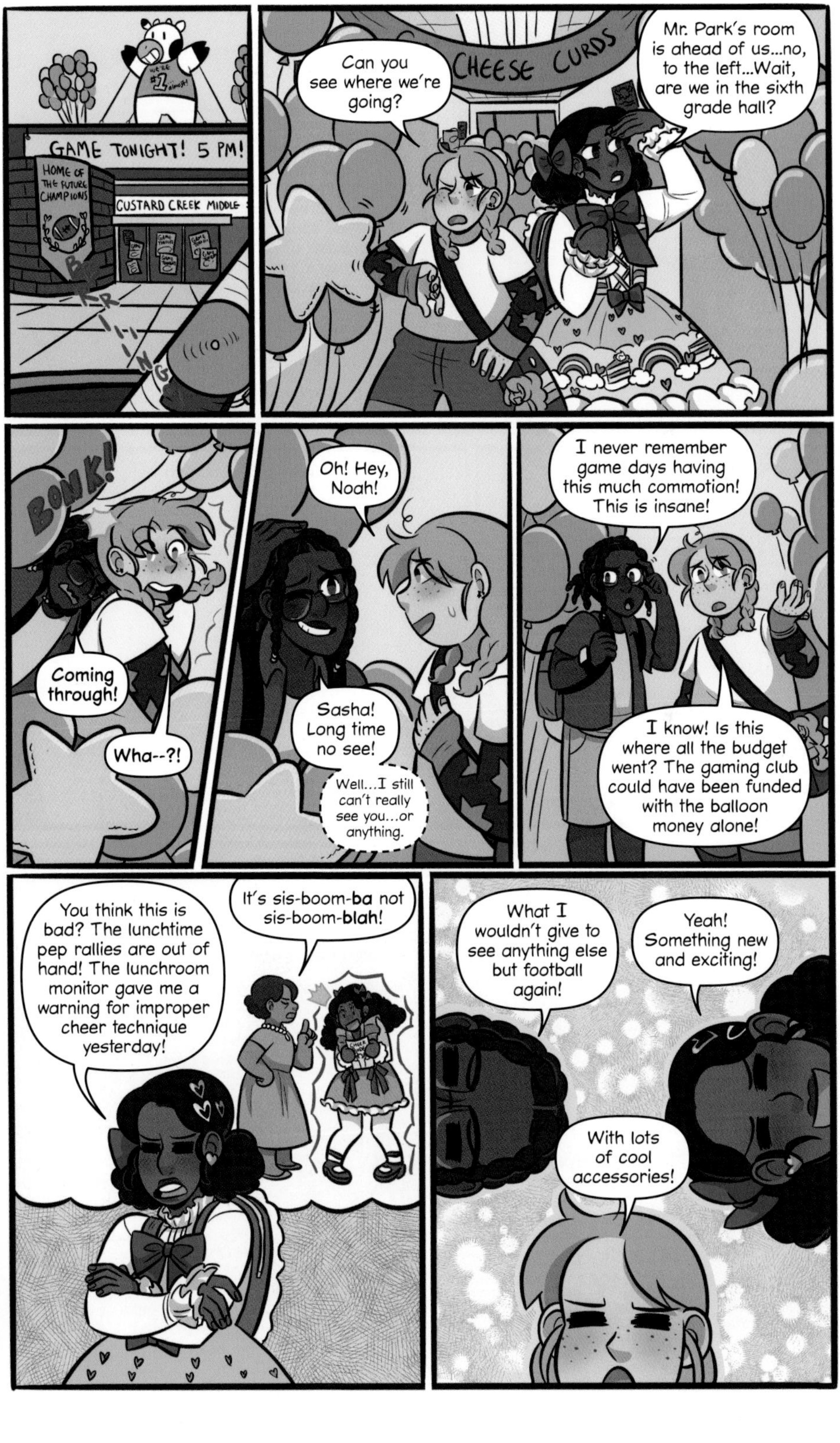
WE'RE #1 almost!
GAME TONIGHT! 5 PM!
HOME OF THE FUTURE CHAMPIONS
CUSTARD CREEK MIDDLE
B-R-I-I-ING
CHEESE CURDS
Can you see where we're going?
Mr. Park's room is ahead of us...no, to the left...Wait, are we in the sixth grade hall?
BONK!
Coming through!
Wha--?!
Oh! Hey, Noah!
Sasha! Long time no see!
Well...I still can't really see you...or anything.
I never remember game days having this much commotion! This is insane!
I know! Is this where all the budget went? The gaming club could have been funded with the balloon money alone!
You think this is bad? The lunchtime pep rallies are out of hand! The lunchroom monitor gave me a warning for improper cheer technique yesterday!
It's sis-boom-**ba** not sis-boom-**blah**!
What I wouldn't give to see anything else but football again!
Yeah! Something new and exciting!
With lots of cool accessories!

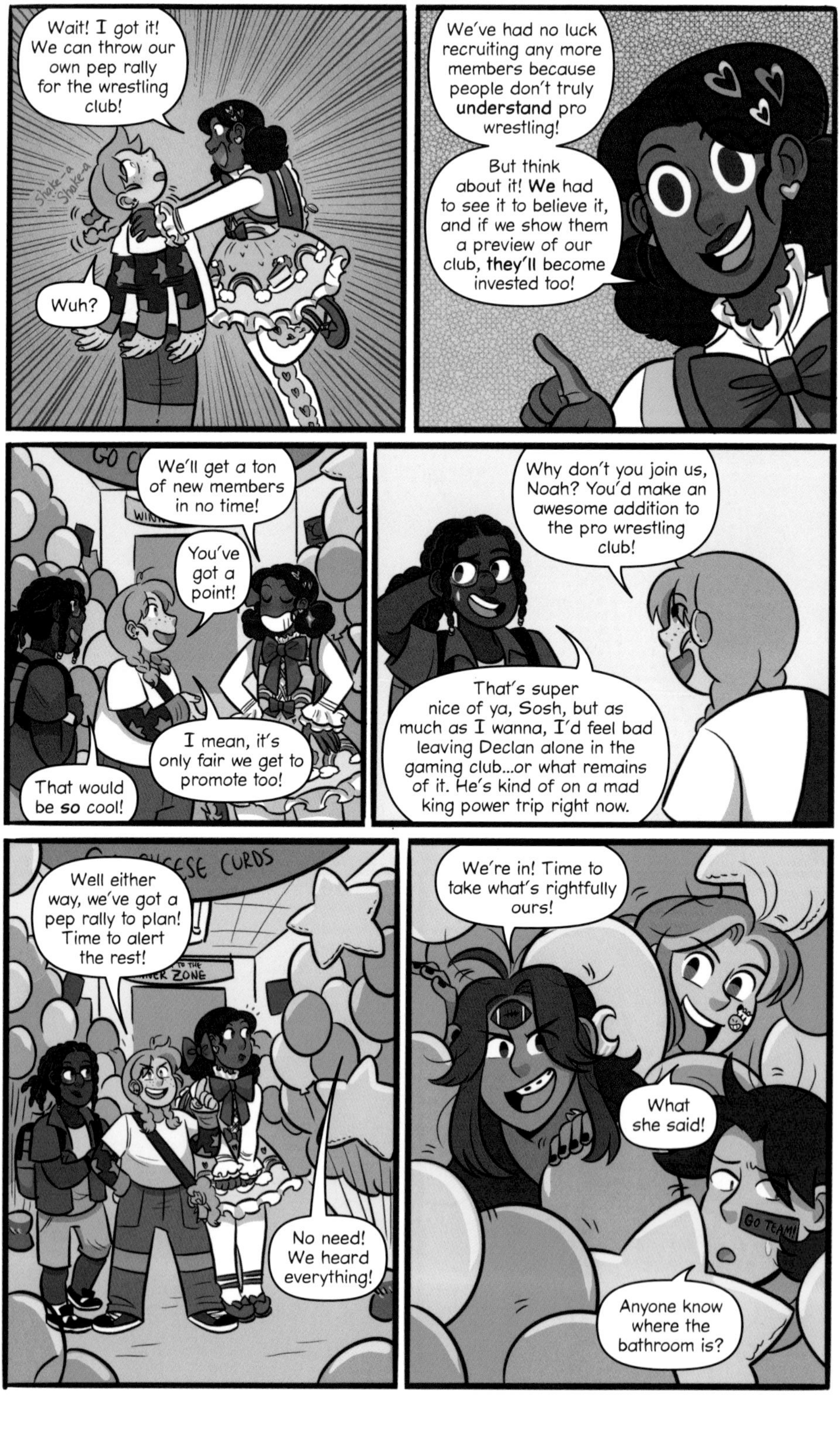

Wait! I got it! We can throw our own pep rally for the wrestling club!
Shake-a Shake-a
Wuh?
We've had no luck recruiting any more members because people don't truly **understand** pro wrestling!
But think about it! **We** had to see it to believe it, and if we show them a preview of our club, **they'll** become invested too!
We'll get a ton of new members in no time!
You've got a point!
I mean, it's only fair we get to promote too!
That would be **so** cool!
Why don't you join us, Noah? You'd make an awesome addition to the pro wrestling club!
That's super nice of ya, Sosh, but as much as I wanna, I'd feel bad leaving Declan alone in the gaming club...or what remains of it. He's kind of on a mad king power trip right now.
Well either way, we've got a pep rally to plan! Time to alert the rest!
No need! We heard everything!
We're in! Time to take what's rightfully ours!
What she said!
GO TEAM!
Anyone know where the bathroom is?

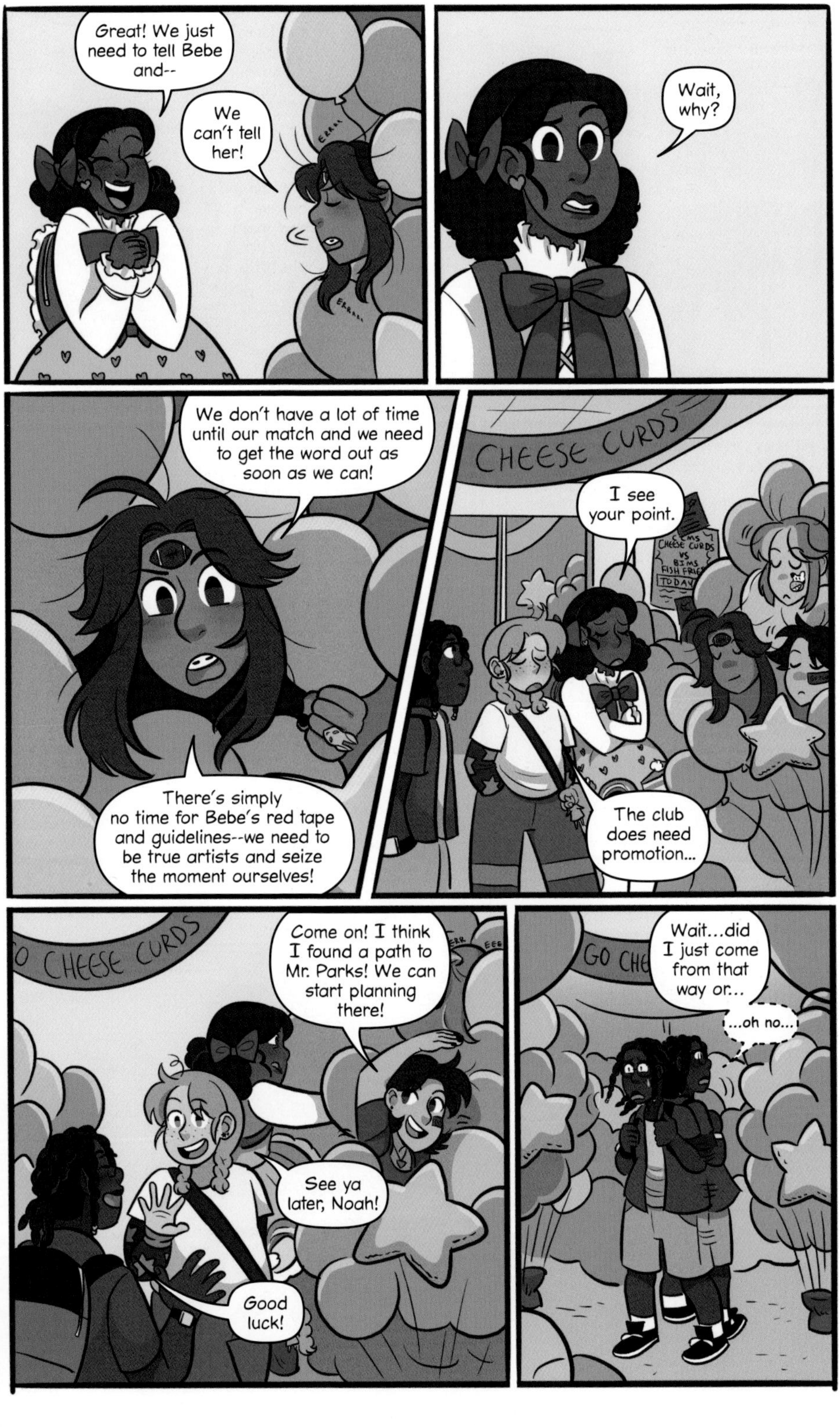
Great! We just need to tell Bebe and--
We can't tell her!
Wait, why?
We don't have a lot of time until our match and we need to get the word out as soon as we can!
There's simply no time for Bebe's red tape and guidelines--we need to be true artists and seize the moment ourselves!
CHEESE CURDS
I see your point.
The club does need promotion...
Come on! I think I found a path to Mr. Parks! We can start planning there!
See ya later, Noah!
Good luck!
Wait...did I just come from that way or...
...oh no...

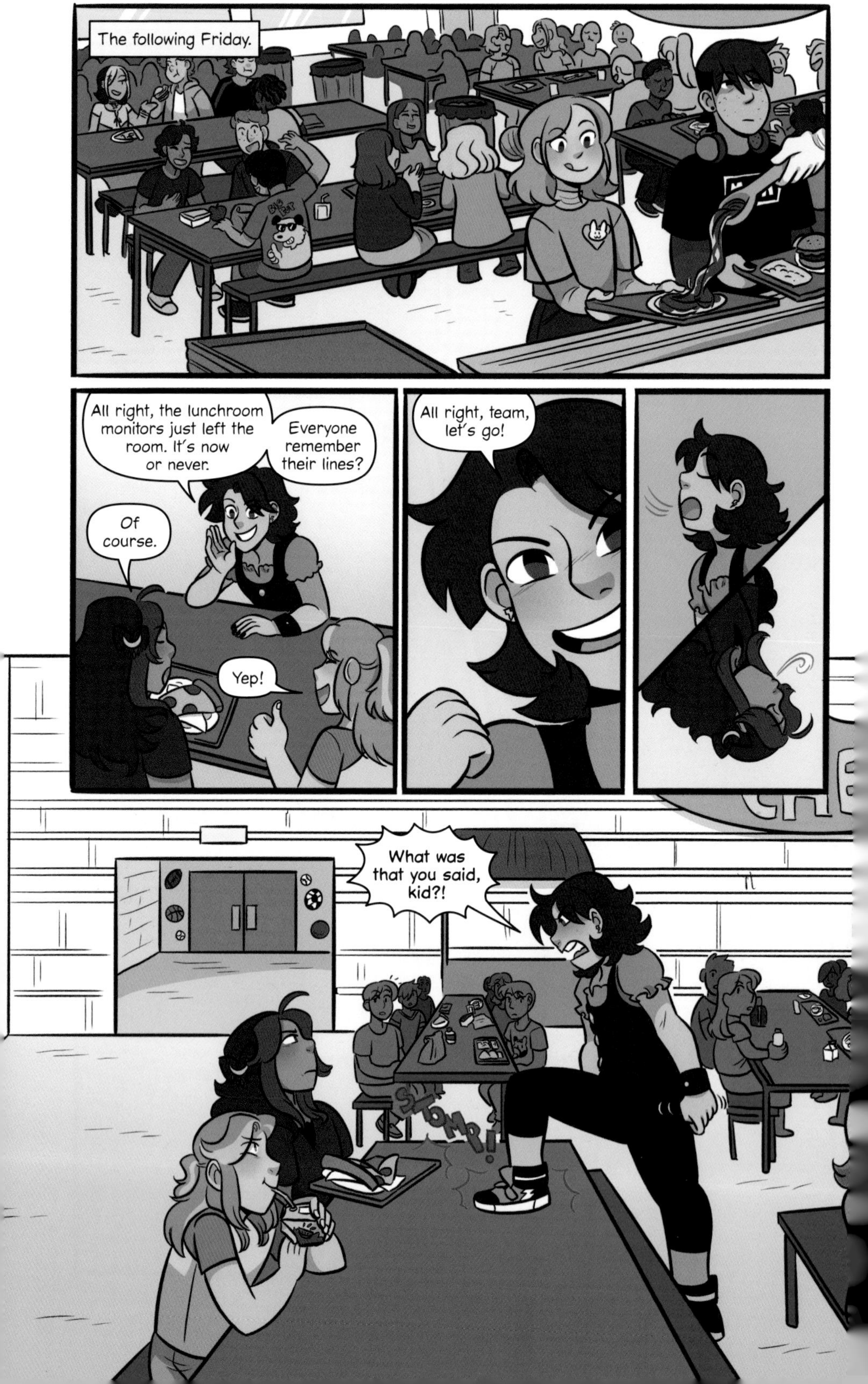
The following Friday.
All right, the lunchroom monitors just left the room. It's now or never.
Everyone remember their lines?
Of course.
Yep!
All right, team, let's go!
What was that you said, kid?!
STOMP!

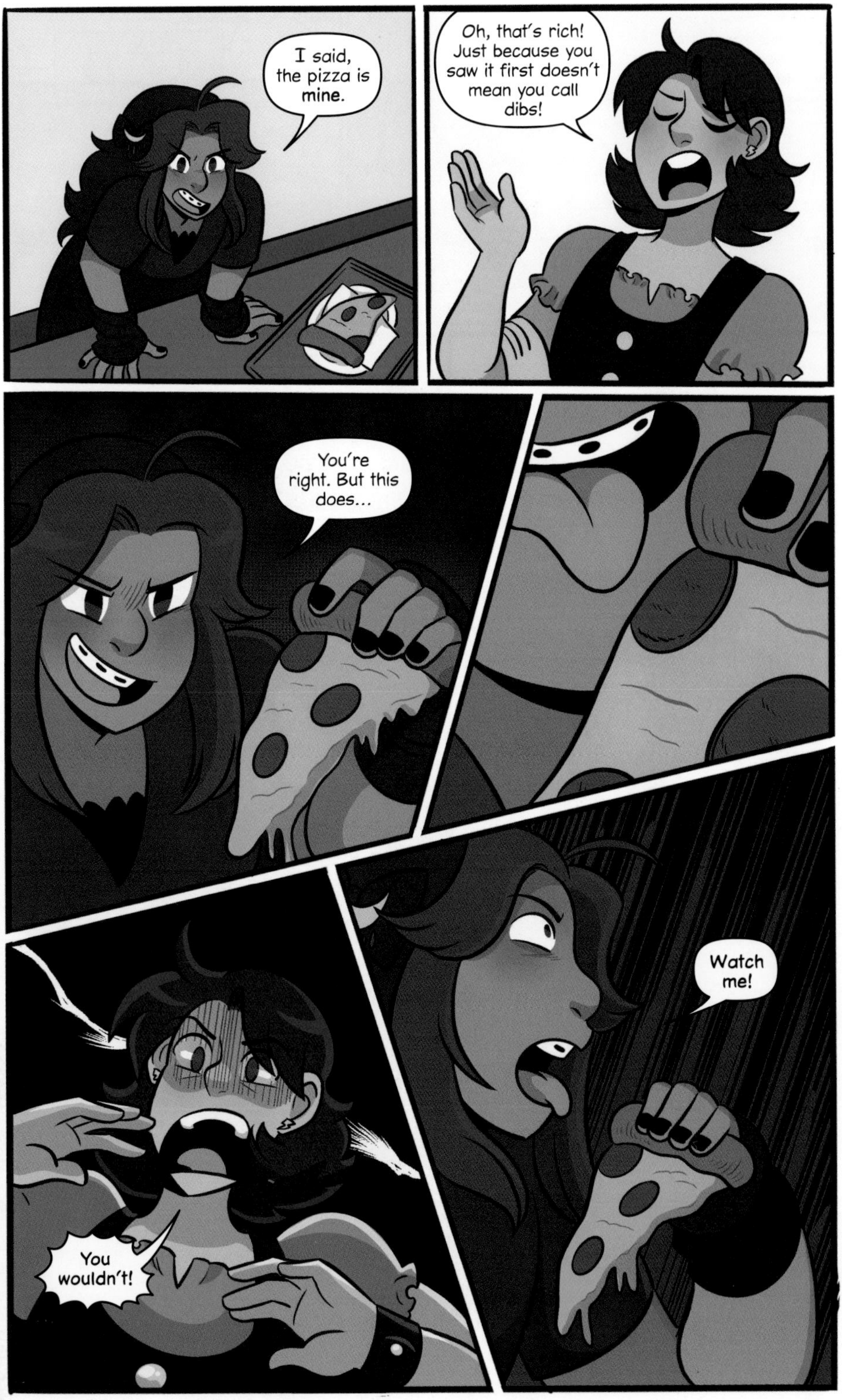
I said, the pizza is mine.
Oh, that's rich! Just because you saw it first doesn't mean you call dibs!
You're right. But this does...
Watch me!
You wouldn't!

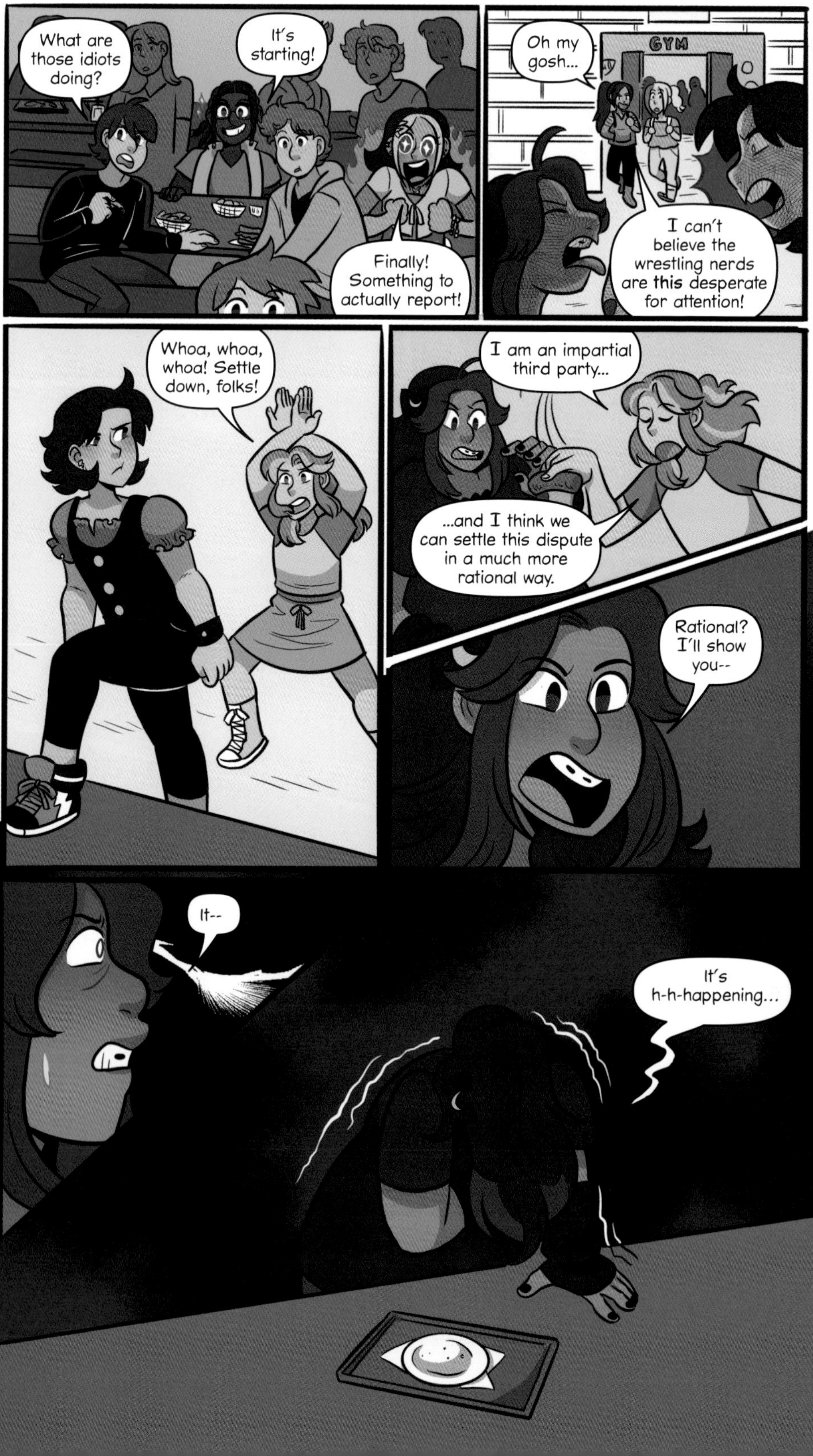
What are those idiots doing?
It's starting!
Finally! Something to actually report!
Oh my gosh...
GYM
I can't believe the wrestling nerds are **this** desperate for attention!
Whoa, whoa, whoa! Settle down, folks!
I am an impartial third party...
...and I think we can settle this dispute in a much more rational way.
Rational? I'll show you--
It--
It's h-h-happening...

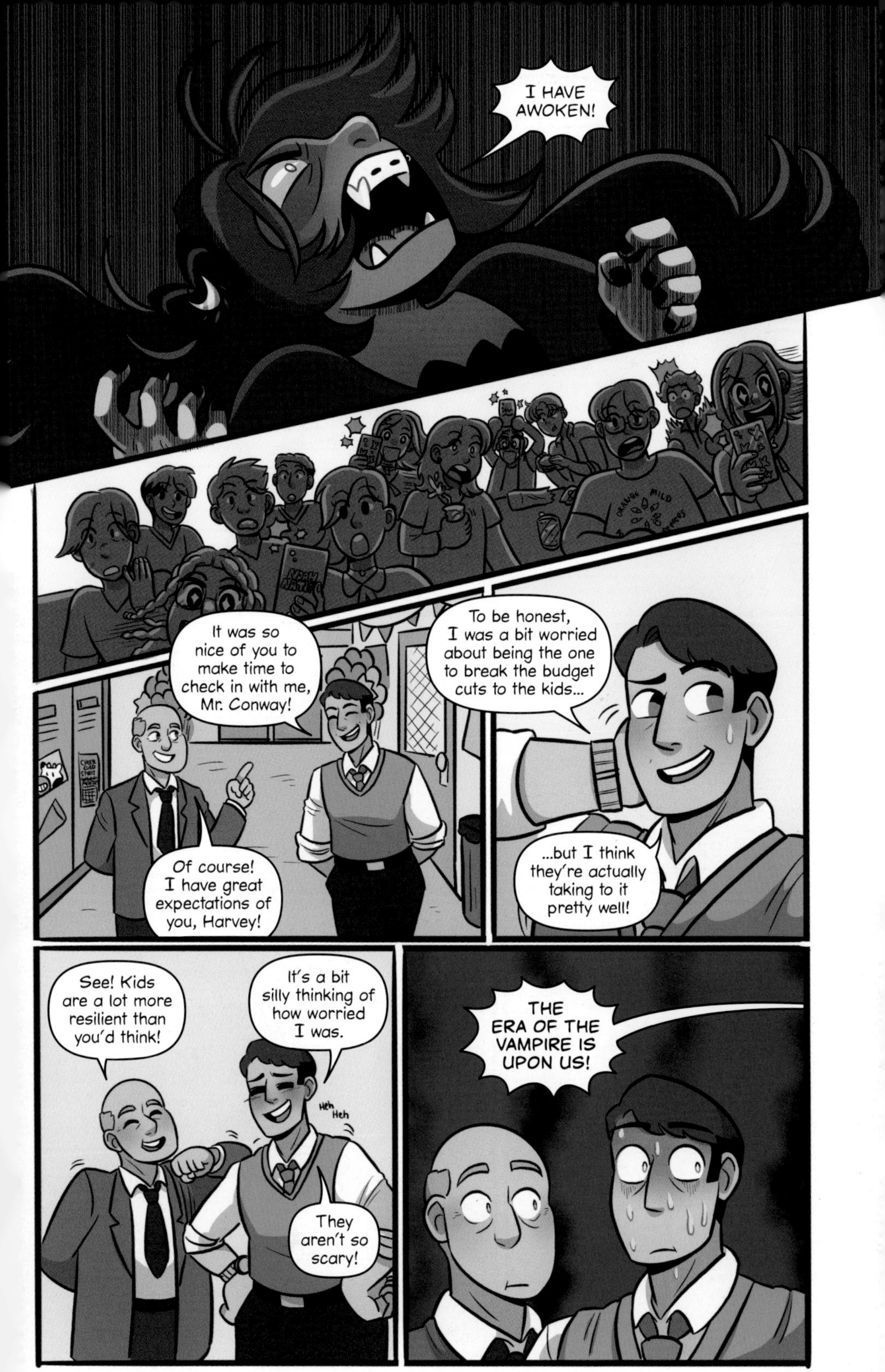
I HAVE AWOKEN!
It was so nice of you to make time to check in with me, Mr. Conway!
Of course! I have great expectations of you, Harvey!
To be honest, I was a bit worried about being the one to break the budget cuts to the kids...
...but I think they're actually taking to it pretty well!
See! Kids are a lot more resilient than you'd think!
It's a bit silly thinking of how worried I was.
Heh Heh
They aren't so scary!
THE ERA OF THE VAMPIRE IS UPON US!

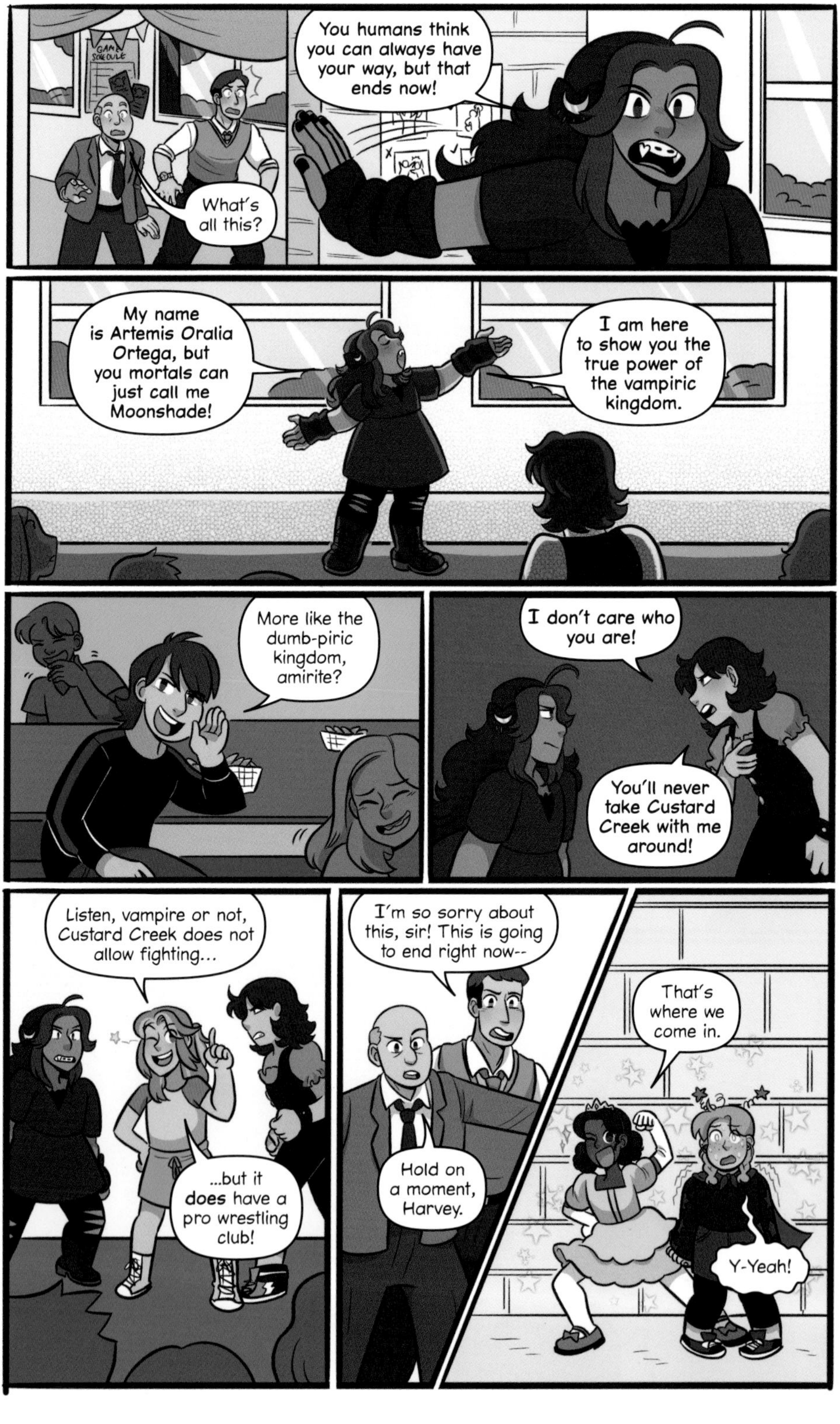
What's all this?
You humans think you can always have your way, but that ends now!
My name is Artemis Oralia Ortega, but you mortals can just call me Moonshade!
I am here to show you the true power of the vampiric kingdom.
More like the dumb-piric kingdom, amirite?
I don't care who you are!
You'll never take Custard Creek with me around!
Listen, vampire or not, Custard Creek does not allow fighting...
...but it **does** have a pro wrestling club!
I'm so sorry about this, sir! This is going to end right now--
Hold on a moment, Harvey.
That's where we come in.
Y-Yeah!

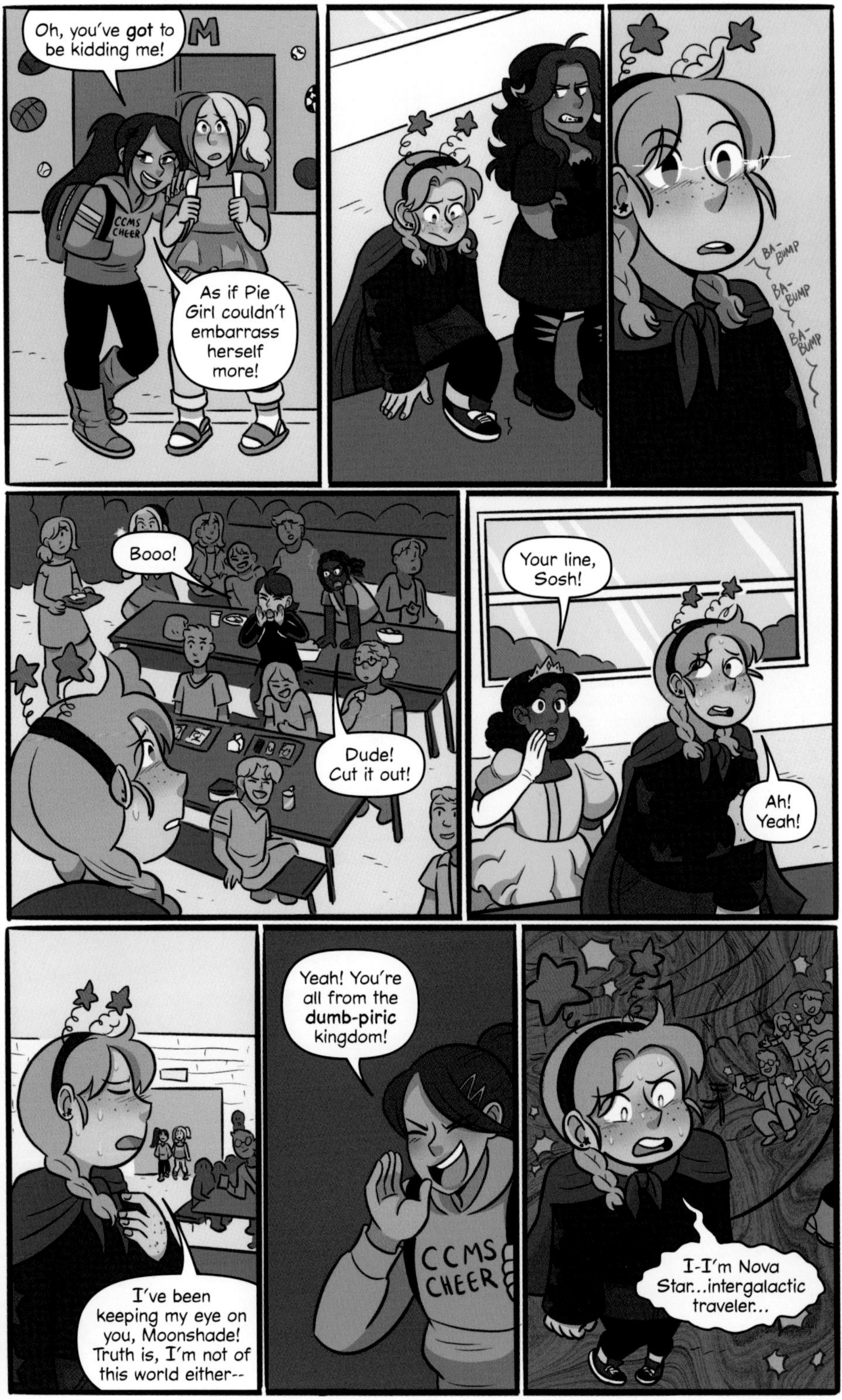
Oh, you've **got** to be kidding me!
As if Pie Girl couldn't embarrass herself more!
CCMS CHEER
BA-BUMP
BA-BUMP
BA-BUMP
Booo!
Dude! Cut it out!
Your line, Sosh!
Ah! Yeah!
I've been keeping my eye on you, Moonshade! Truth is, I'm not of this world either--
Yeah! You're all from the **dumb-piric** kingdom!
CCMS CHEER
I-I'm Nova Star...intergalactic traveler...

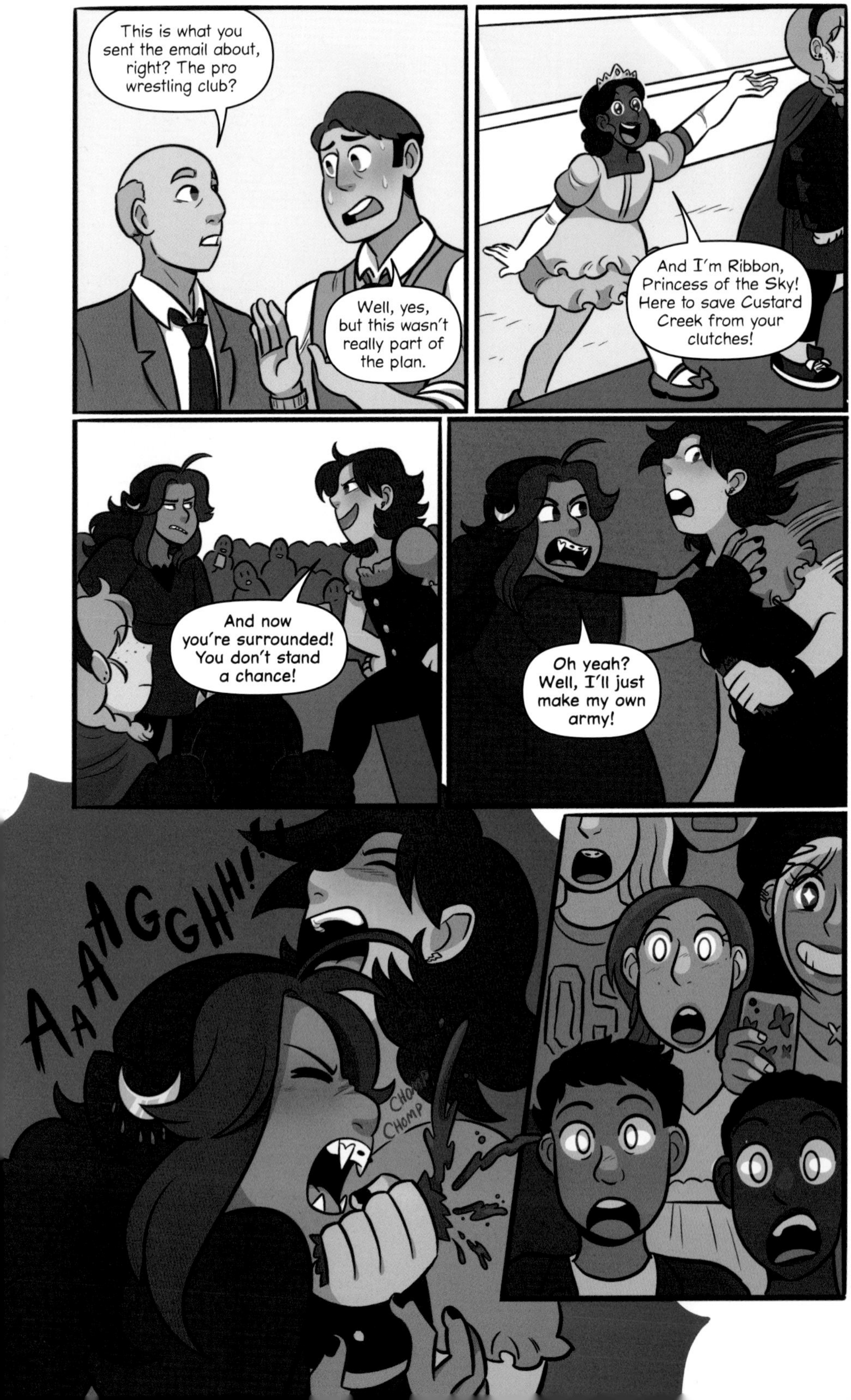
This is what you sent the email about, right? The pro wrestling club?
Well, yes, but this wasn't really part of the plan.
And I'm Ribbon, Princess of the Sky! Here to save Custard Creek from your clutches!
And now you're surrounded! You don't stand a chance!
Oh yeah? Well, I'll just make my own army!
AAAAGGHH!!
CHOMP CHOMP

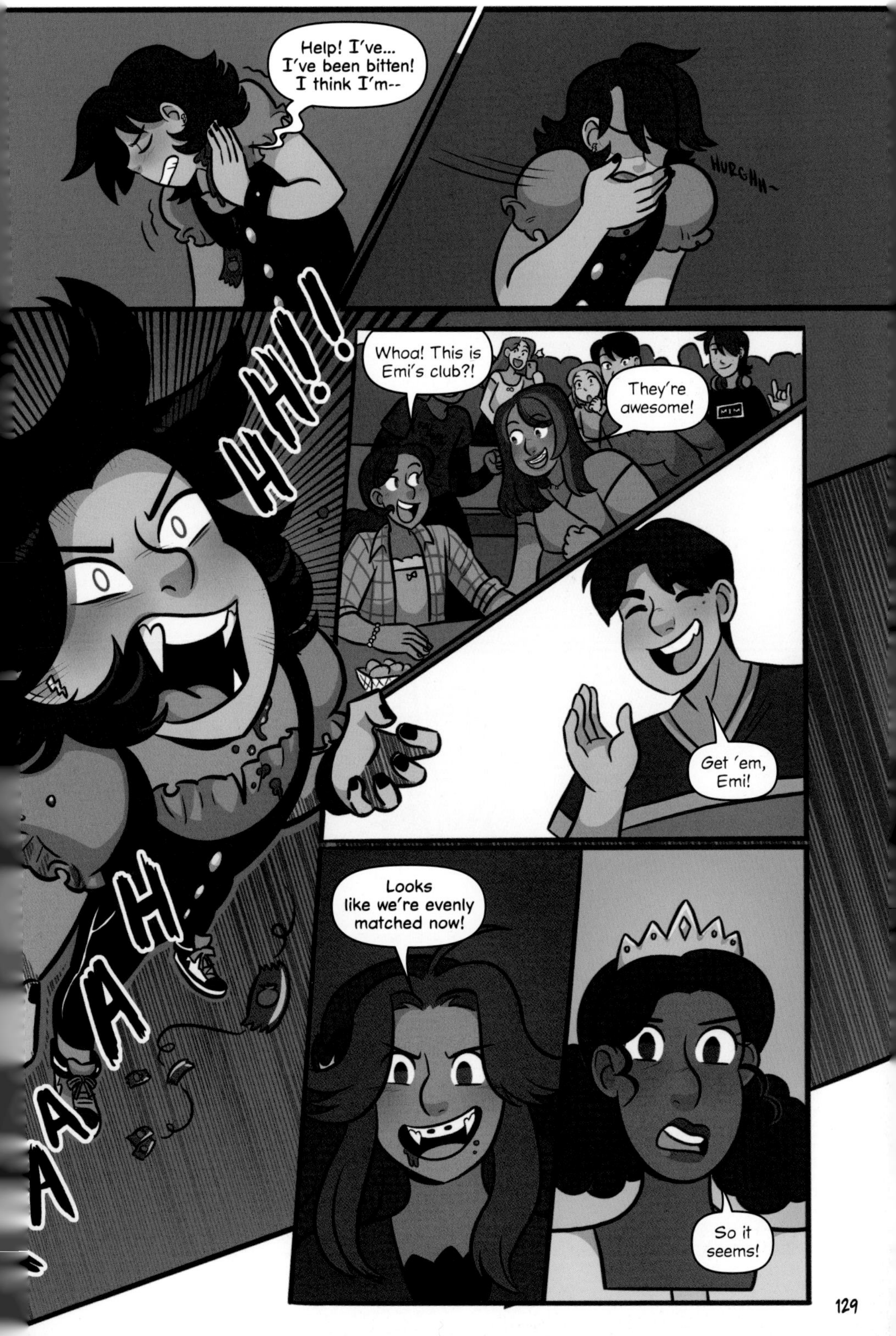
Help! I've... I've been bitten! I think I'm--
HURGHH~
AAAHHH!!
Whoa! This is Emi's club?!
They're awesome!
Get 'em, Emi!
Looks like we're evenly matched now!
So it seems!

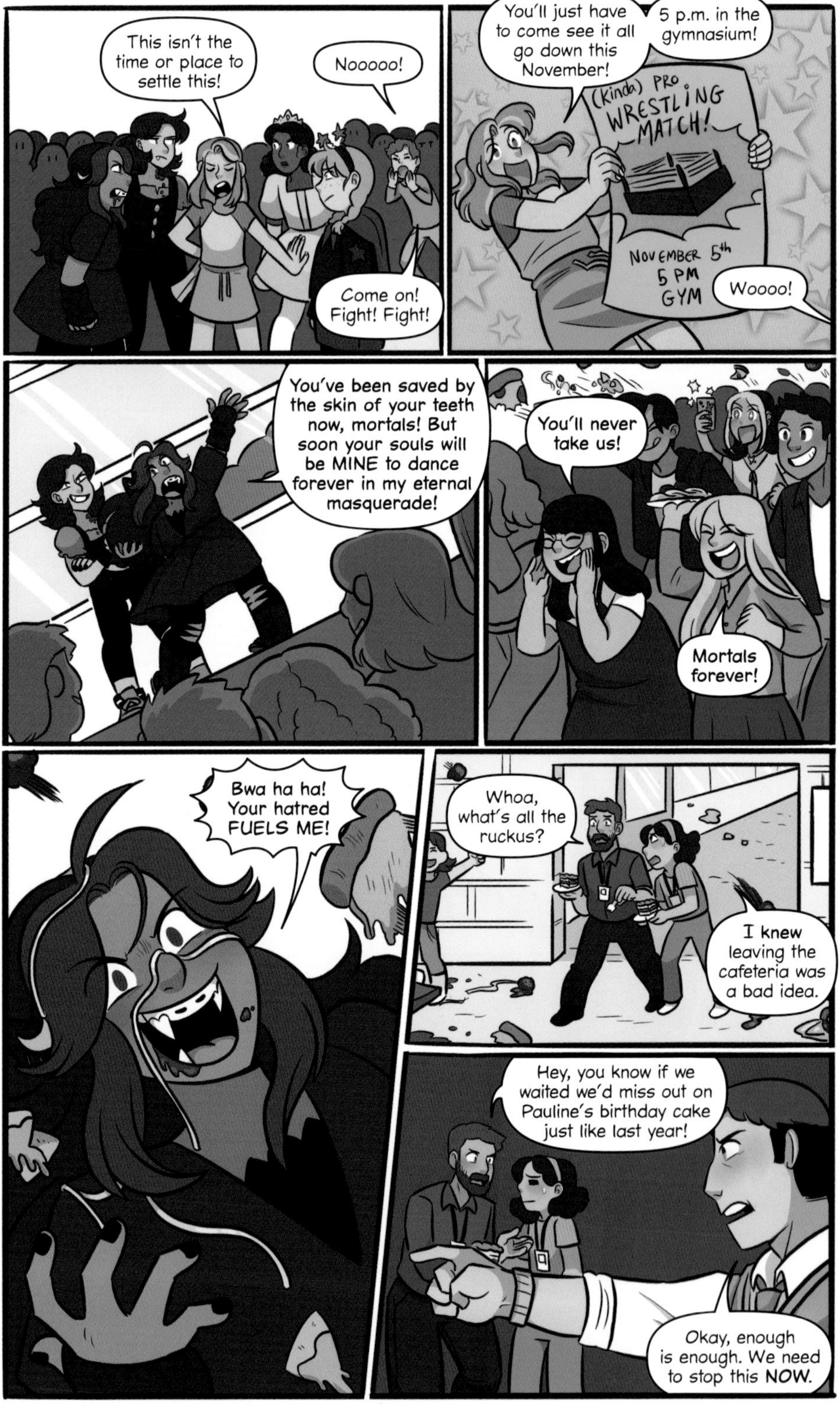
This isn't the time or place to settle this!
Nooooo!
Come on! Fight! Fight!
You'll just have to come see it all go down this November!
5 p.m. in the gymnasium!
(Kinda) PRO WRESTLING MATCH!
NOVEMBER 5th 5 PM GYM
Woooo!
You've been saved by the skin of your teeth now, mortals! But soon your souls will be MINE to dance forever in my eternal masquerade!
You'll never take us!
Mortals forever!
Bwa ha ha! Your hatred FUELS ME!
Whoa, what's all the ruckus?
I knew leaving the cafeteria was a bad idea.
Hey, you know if we waited we'd miss out on Pauline's birthday cake just like last year!
Okay, enough is enough. We need to stop this NOW.

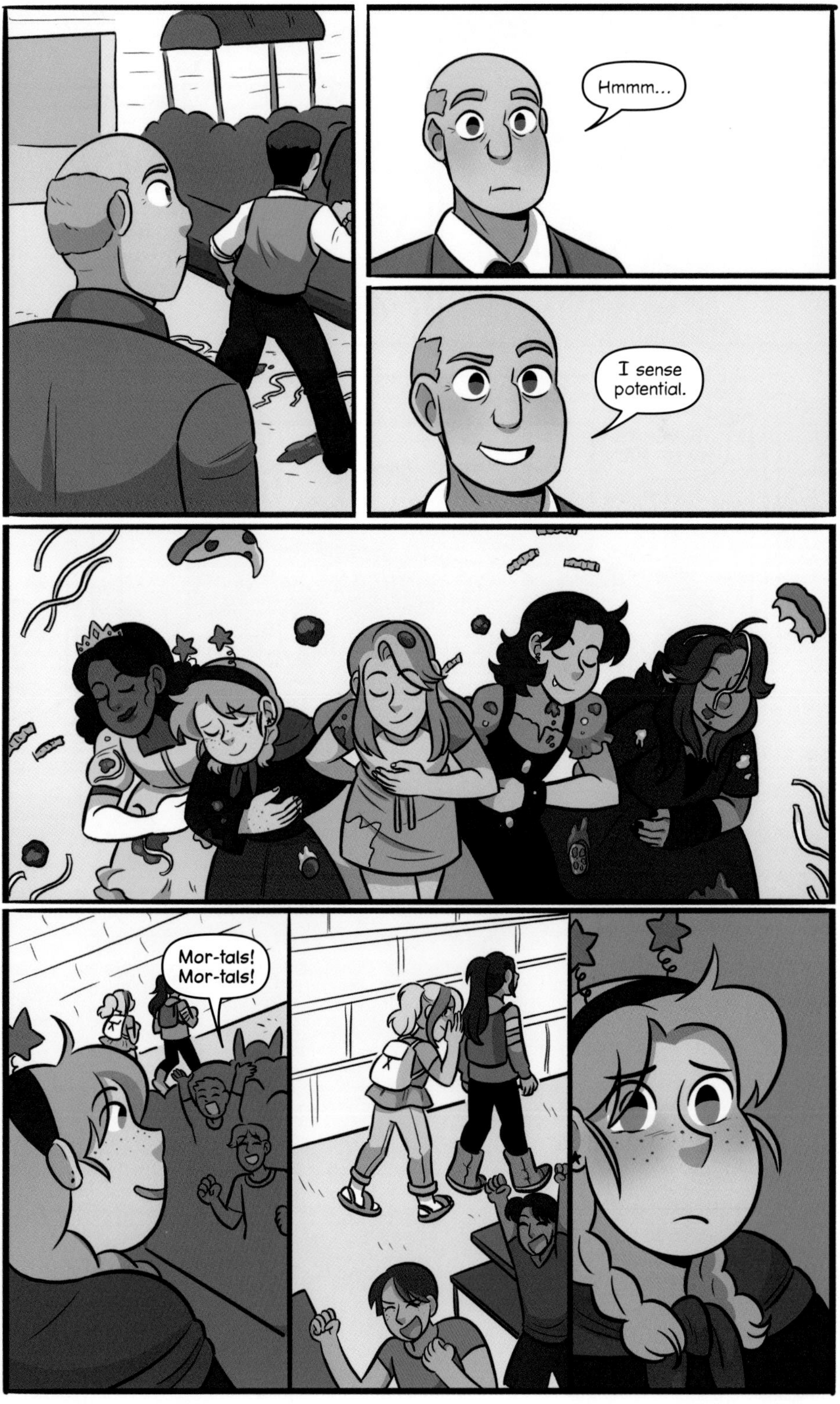

Hmmm...
I sense potential.
Mor-tals!
Mor-tals!

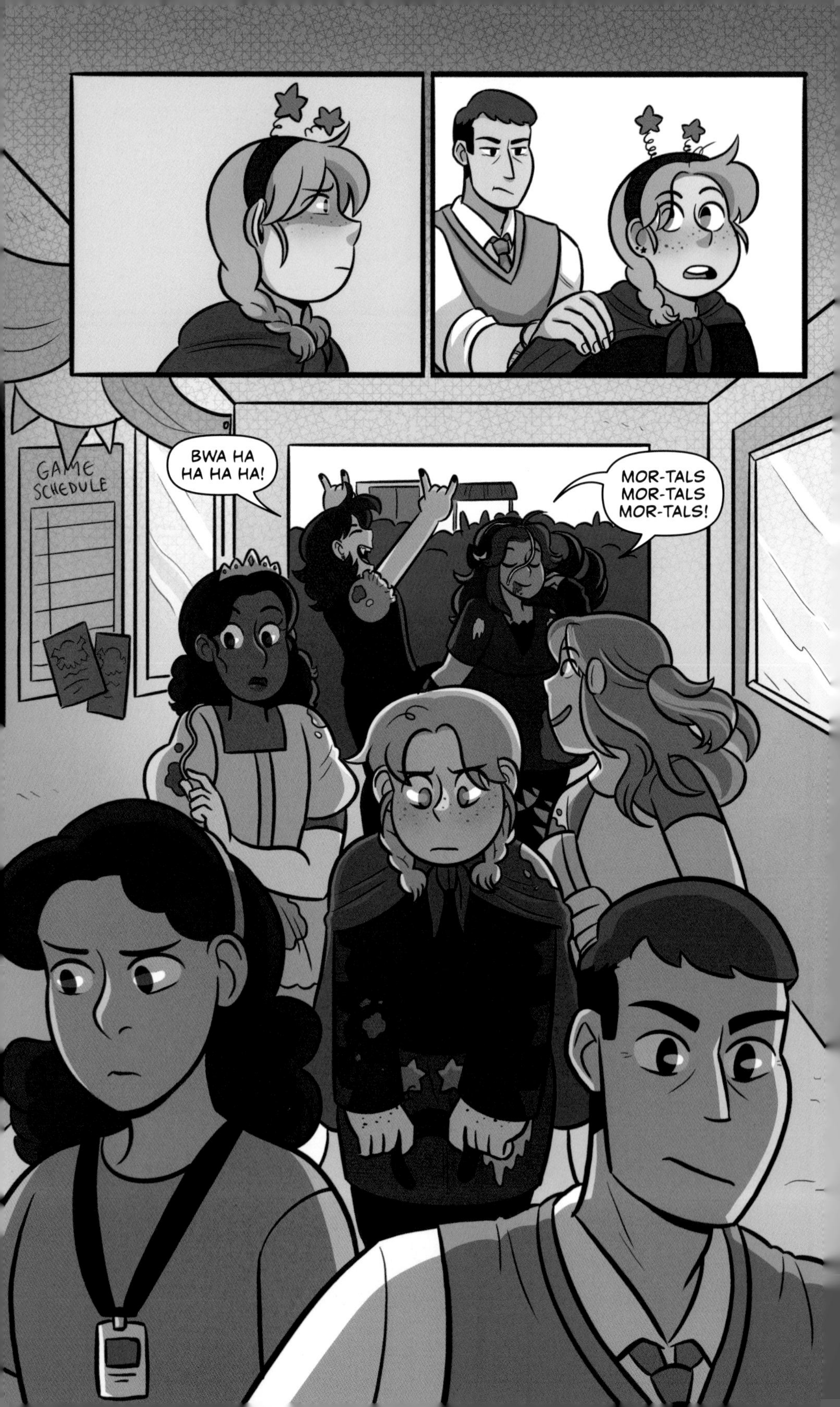
GAME SCHEDULE
BWA HA HA HA HA!
MOR-TALS MOR-TALS MOR-TALS!

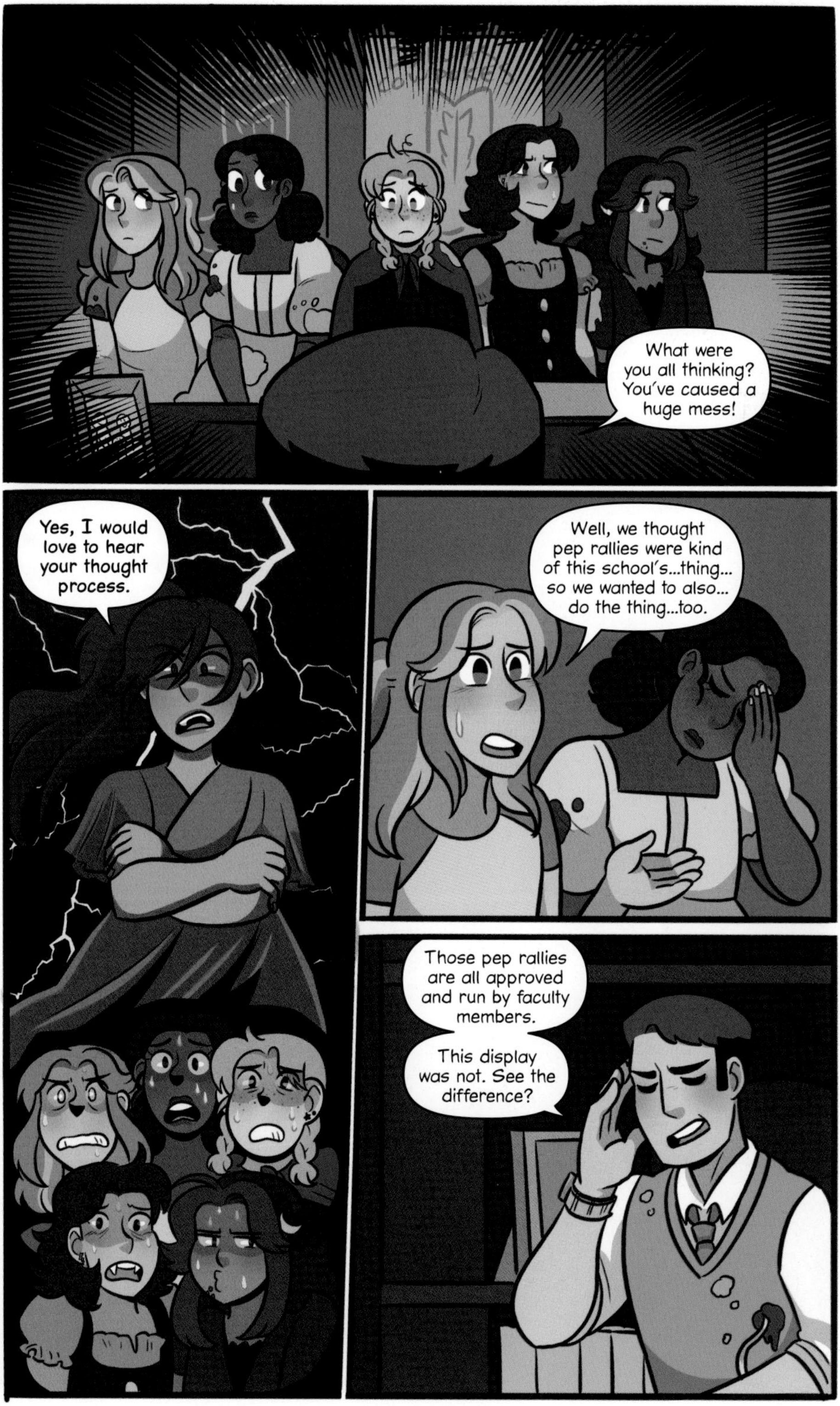
What were you all thinking? You've caused a huge mess!
Yes, I would love to hear your thought process.
Well, we thought pep rallies were kind of this school's...thing... so we wanted to also... do the thing...too.
Those pep rallies are all approved and run by faculty members.
This display was not. See the difference?

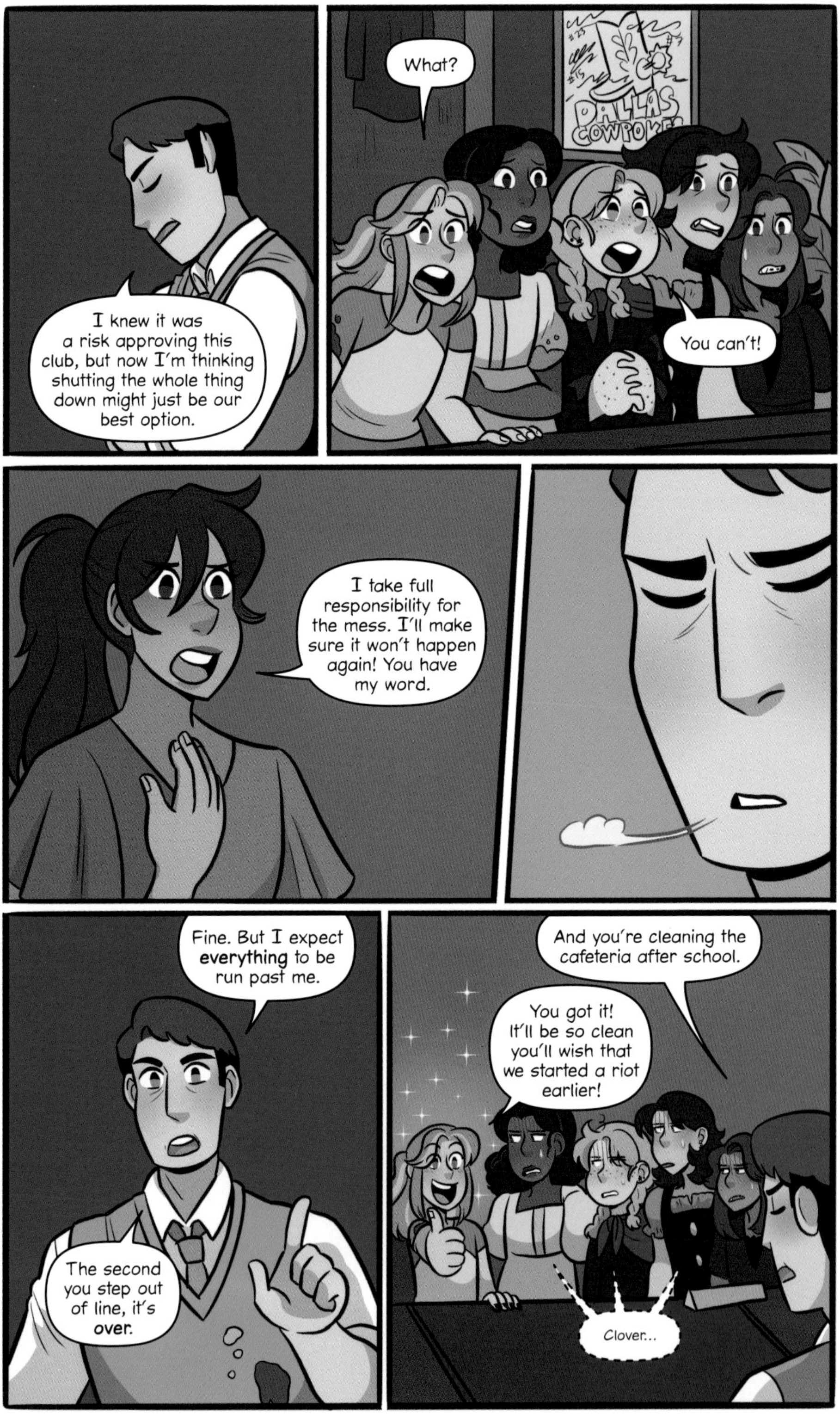
I knew it was a risk approving this club, but now I'm thinking shutting the whole thing down might just be our best option.
What?
DALLAS COWPOKES
You can't!
I take full responsibility for the mess. I'll make sure it won't happen again! You have my word.
Fine. But I expect **everything** to be run past me.
The second you step out of line, it's **over**.
And you're cleaning the cafeteria after school.
You got it! It'll be so clean you'll wish that we started a riot earlier!
Clover...

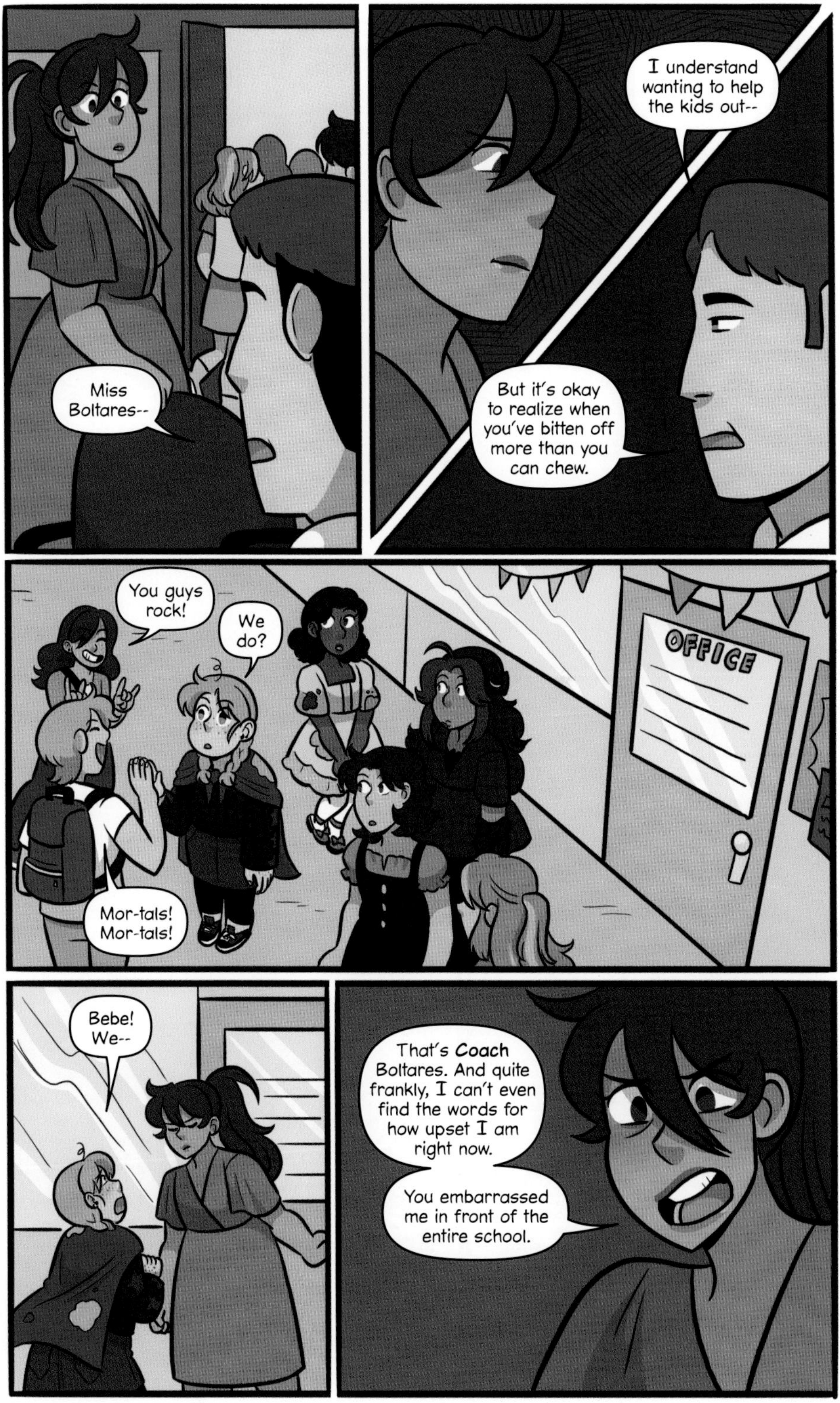
Miss
Boltares--
I understand wanting to help the kids out--
But it's okay to realize when you've bitten off more than you can chew.
You guys rock!
We do?
OFFICE
Mor-tals! Mor-tals!
Bebe! We--
That's **Coach** Boltares. And quite frankly, I can't even find the words for how upset I am right now.
You embarrassed me in front of the entire school.

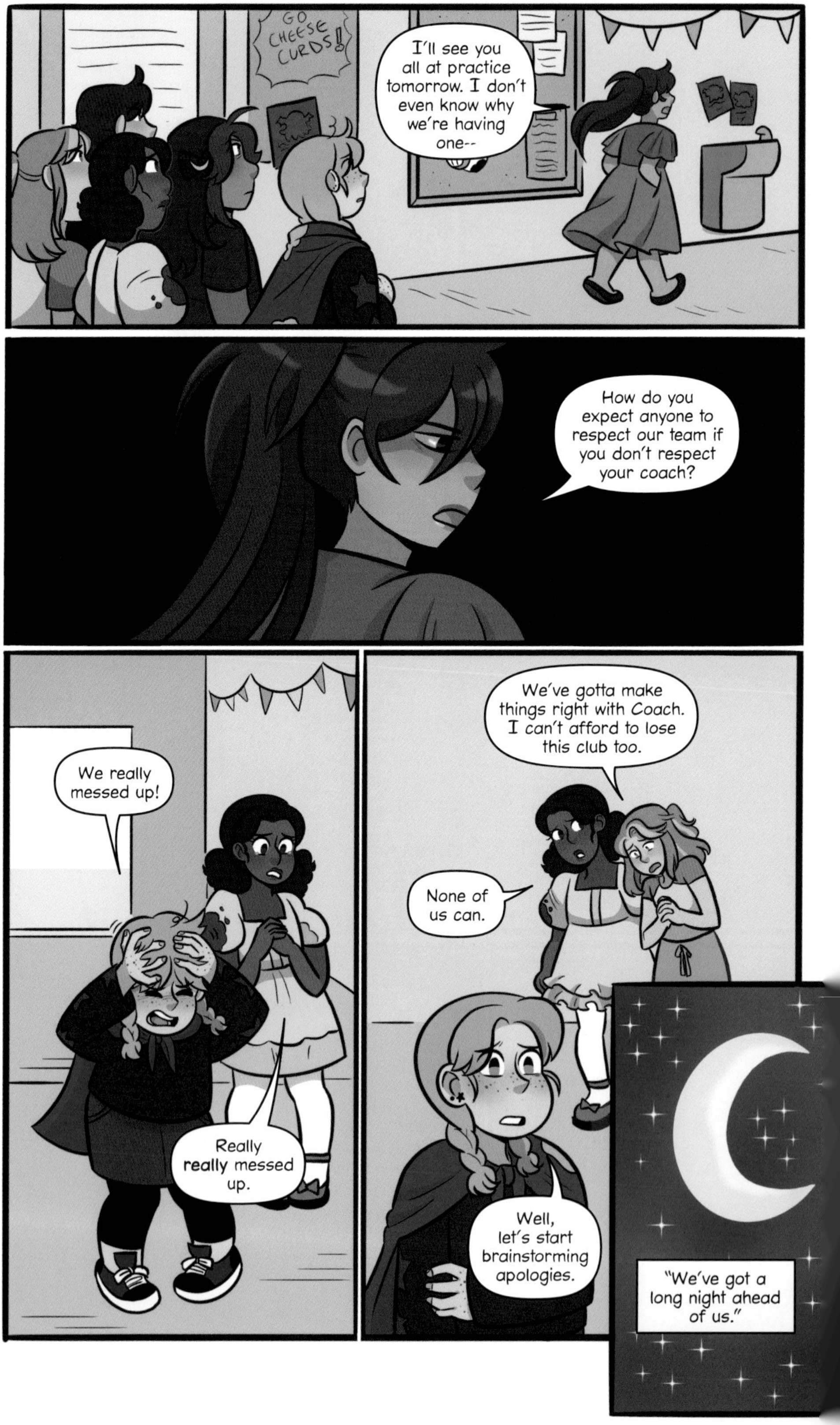
GO CHEESE CURDS!!
I'll see you all at practice tomorrow. I don't even know why we're having one--
How do you expect anyone to respect our team if you don't respect your coach?
We really messed up!
Really **really** messed up.
We've gotta make things right with Coach. I can't afford to lose this club too.
None of us can.
Well, let's start brainstorming apologies.
"We've got a long night ahead of us."

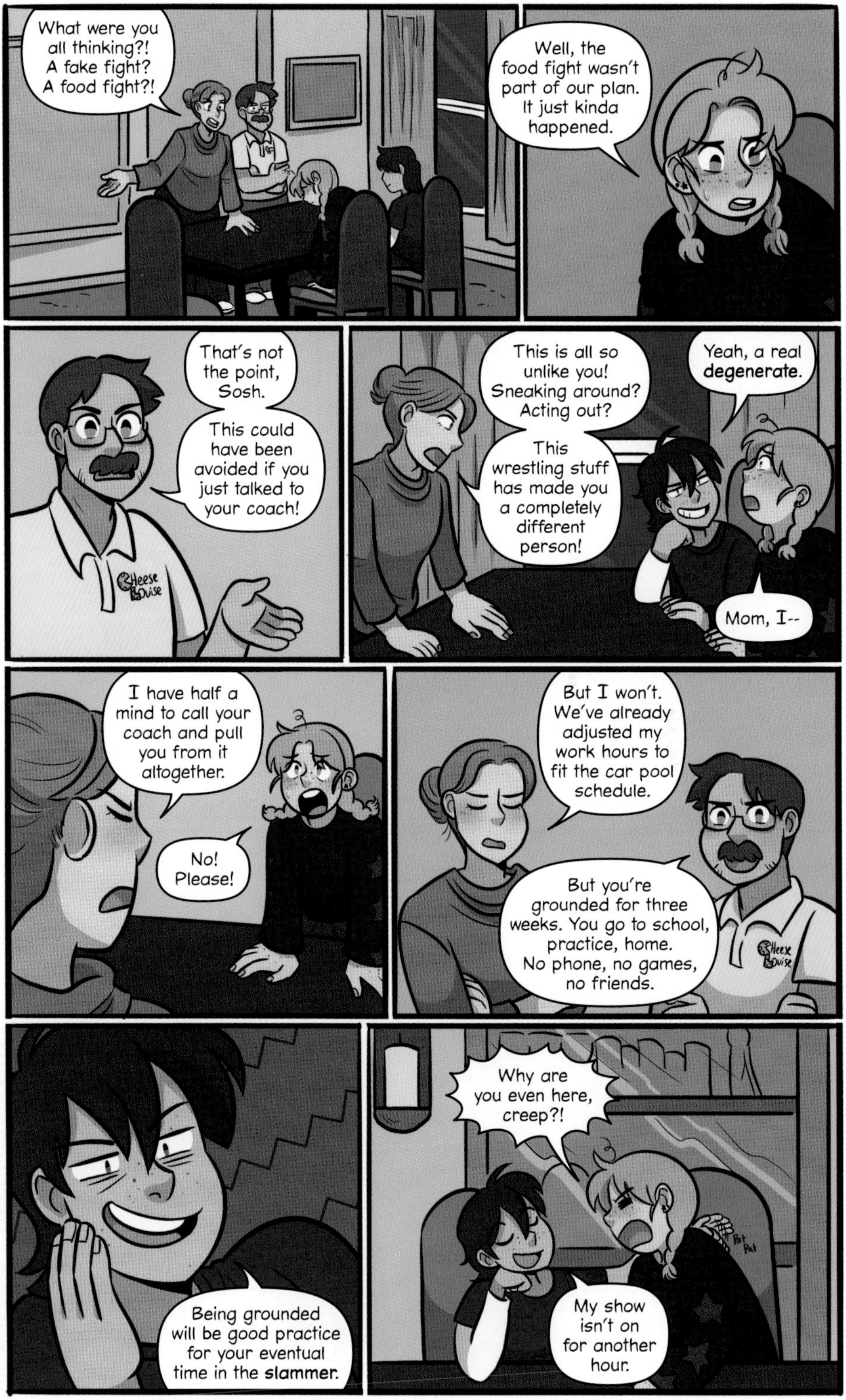

What were you all thinking?! A fake fight? A food fight?!
Well, the food fight wasn't part of our plan. It just kinda happened.
That's not the point, Sosh.
This could have been avoided if you just talked to your coach!
This is all so unlike you! Sneaking around? Acting out?
This wrestling stuff has made you a completely different person!
Yeah, a real **degenerate**.
Mom, I--
I have half a mind to call your coach and pull you from it altogether.
No! Please!
But I won't. We've already adjusted my work hours to fit the car pool schedule.
But you're grounded for three weeks. You go to school, practice, home. No phone, no games, no friends.
Being grounded will be good practice for your eventual time in the **slammer**.
Why are you even here, creep?!
My show isn't on for another hour.

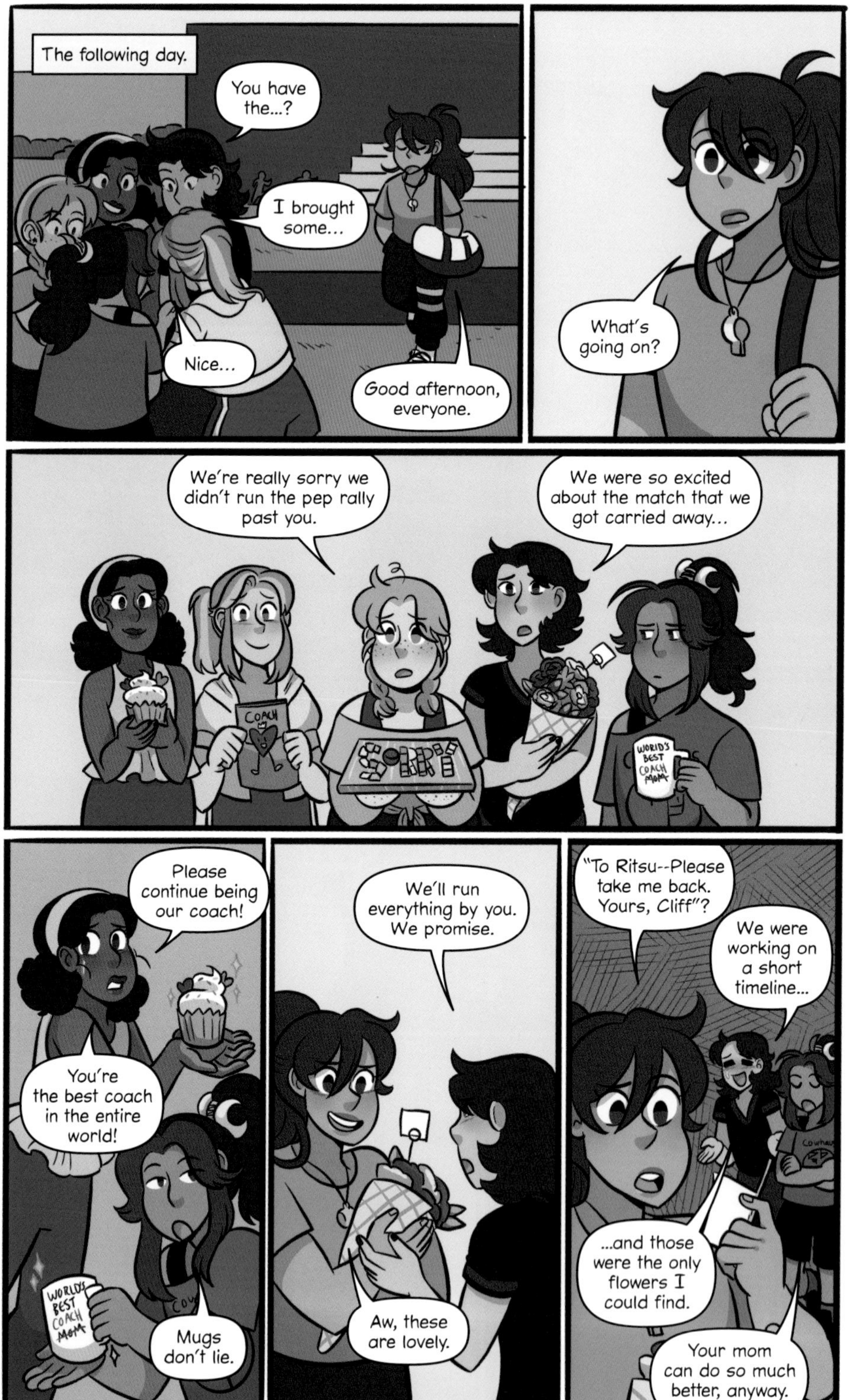
The following day.
You have the...?
I brought some...
Nice...
Good afternoon, everyone.
What's going on?
We're really sorry we didn't run the pep rally past you.
We were so excited about the match that we got carried away...
COACH
SORRY
WORLD'S BEST COACH MOM
Please continue being our coach!
You're the best coach in the entire world!
WORLD'S BEST COACH MOM
Mugs don't lie.
We'll run everything by you. We promise.
Aw, these are lovely.
"To Ritsu--Please take me back. Yours, Cliff"?
We were working on a short timeline...
...and those were the only flowers I could find.
Your mom can do so much better, anyway.

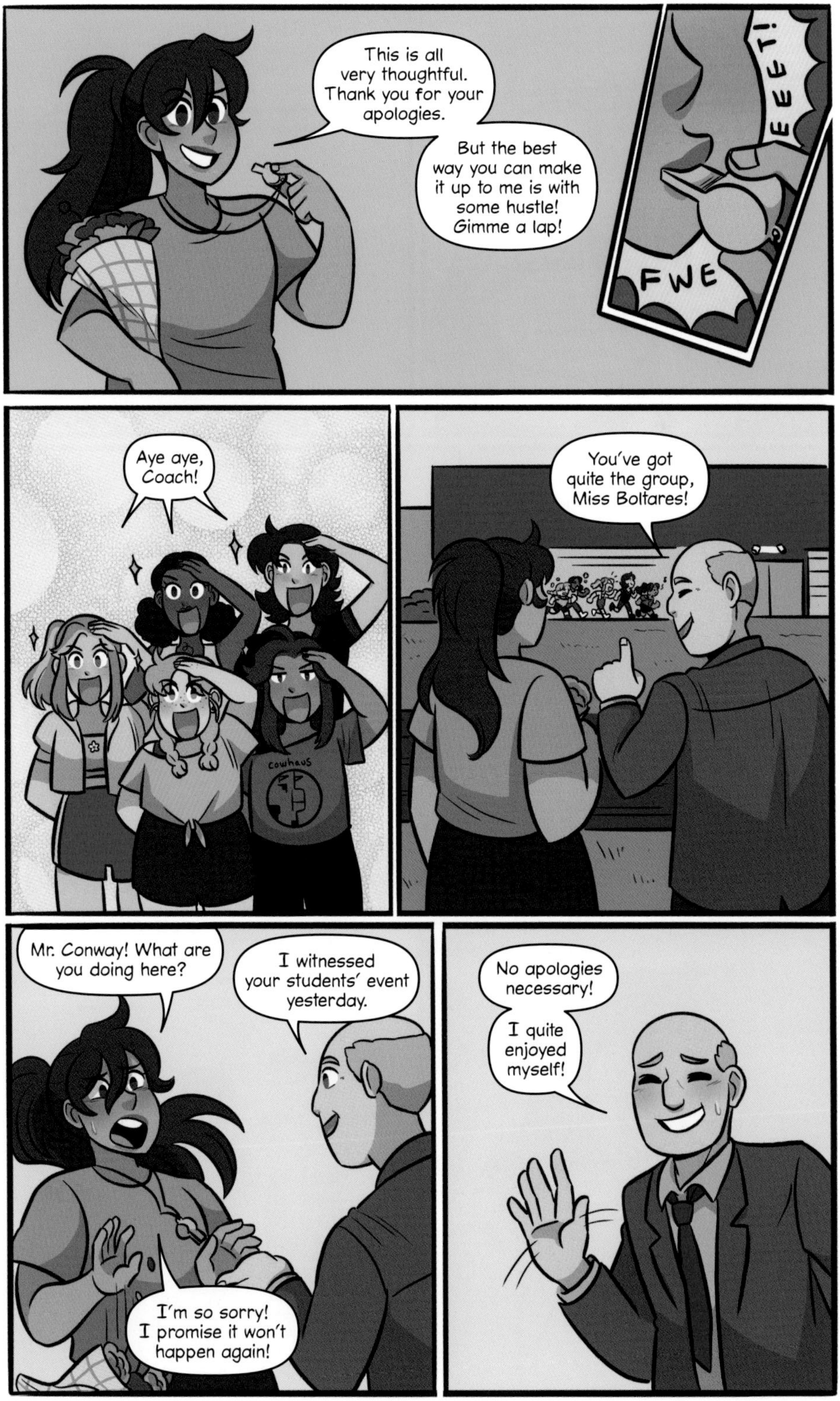
This is all very thoughtful. Thank you for your apologies.
But the best way you can make it up to me is with some hustle! Gimme a lap!
FWEEEET!!
Aye aye, Coach!
COWHAUS
You've got quite the group, Miss Boltares!
Mr. Conway! What are you doing here?
I witnessed your students' event yesterday.
I'm so sorry! I promise it won't happen again!
No apologies necessary!
I quite enjoyed myself!

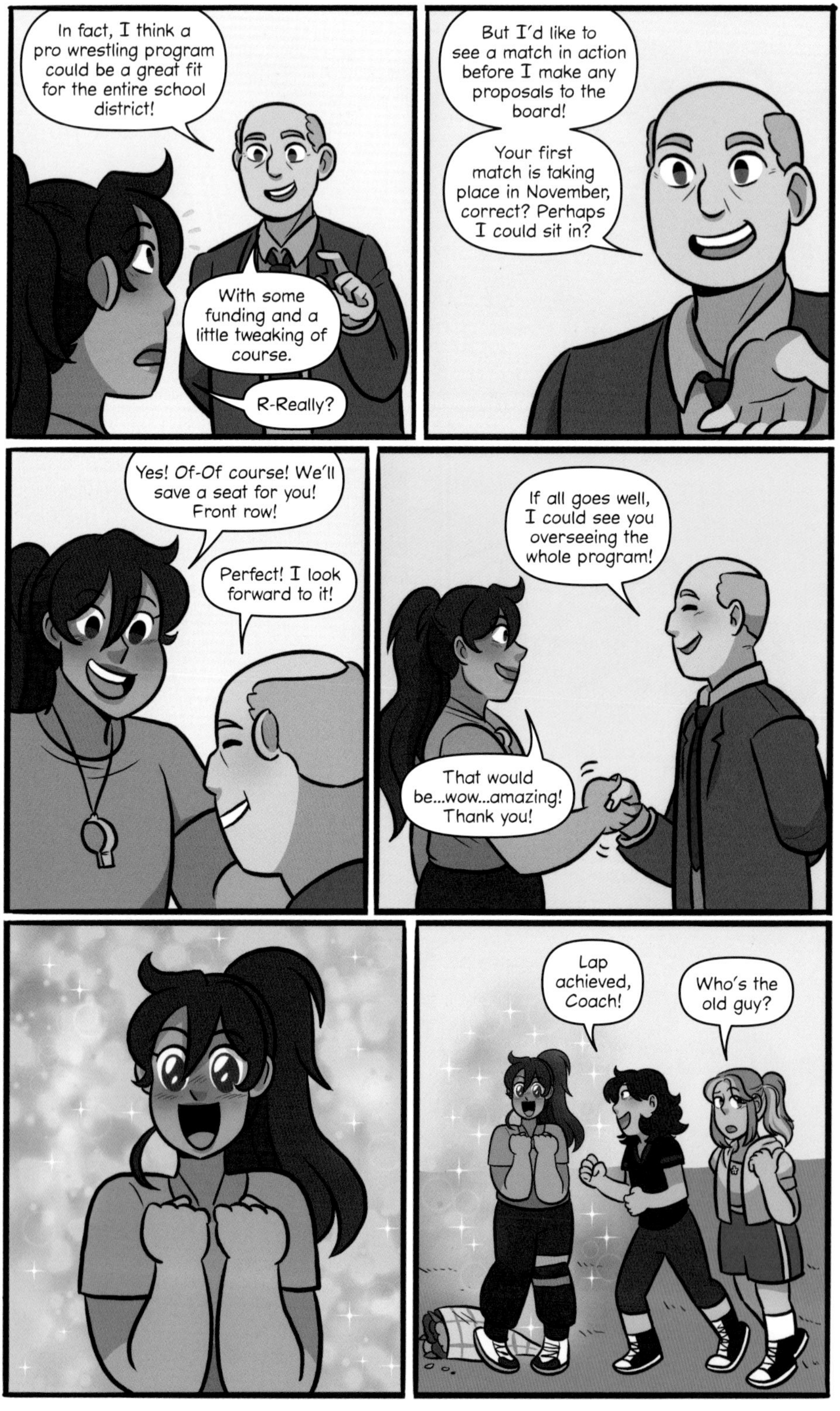
In fact, I think a pro wrestling program could be a great fit for the entire school district!
With some funding and a little tweaking of course.
R-Really?
But I'd like to see a match in action before I make any proposals to the board!
Your first match is taking place in November, correct? Perhaps I could sit in?
Yes! Of-Of course! We'll save a seat for you! Front row!
Perfect! I look forward to it!
If all goes well, I could see you overseeing the whole program!
That would be...wow...amazing! Thank you!
Lap achieved, Coach!
Who's the old guy?

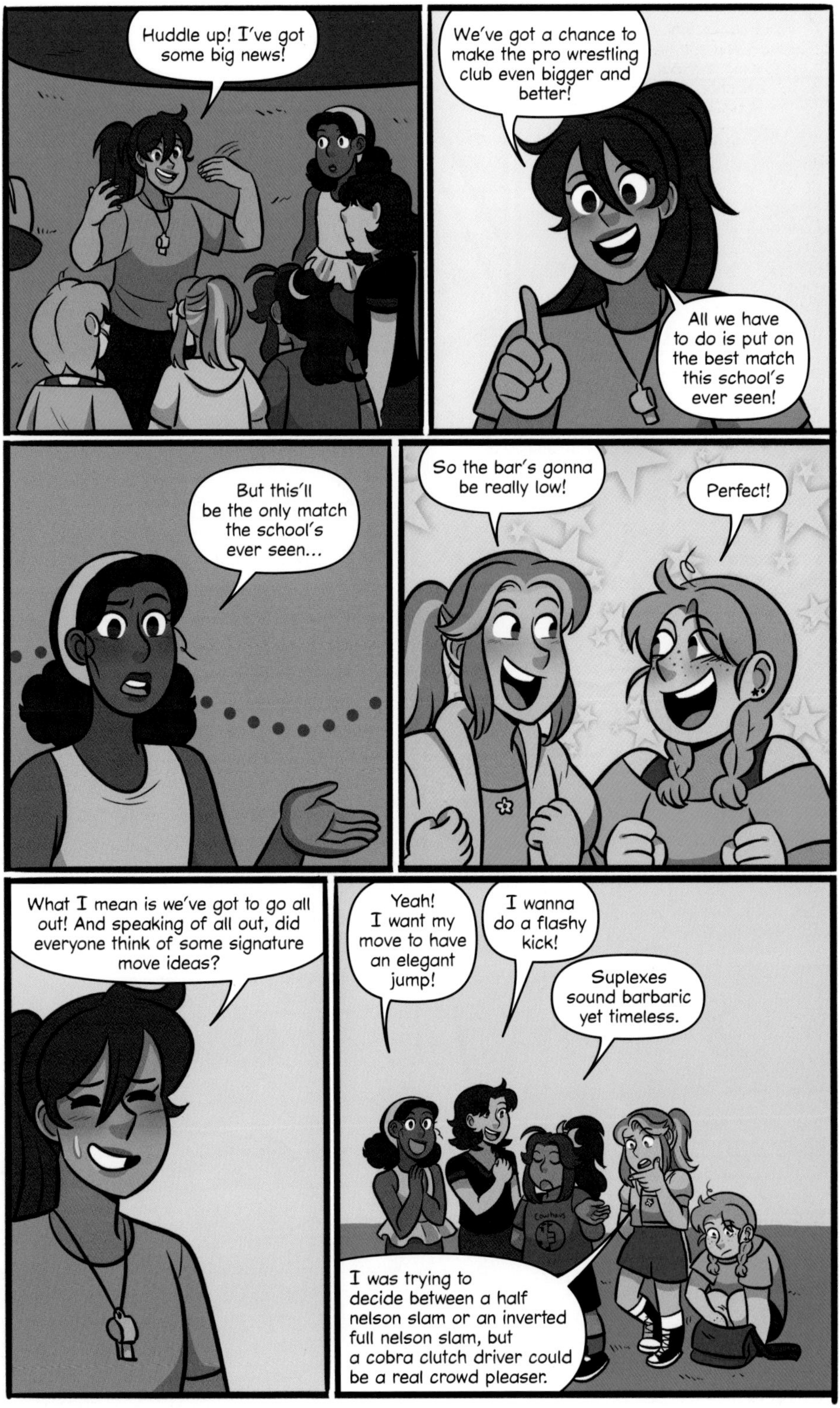
Huddle up! I've got some big news!
We've got a chance to make the pro wrestling club even bigger and better!
All we have to do is put on the best match this school's ever seen!
But this'll be the only match the school's ever seen...
So the bar's gonna be really low!
Perfect!
What I mean is we've got to go all out! And speaking of all out, did everyone think of some signature move ideas?
Yeah! I want my move to have an elegant jump!
I wanna do a flashy kick!
Suplexes sound barbaric yet timeless.
I was trying to decide between a half nelson slam or an inverted full nelson slam, but a cobra clutch driver could be a real crowd pleaser.

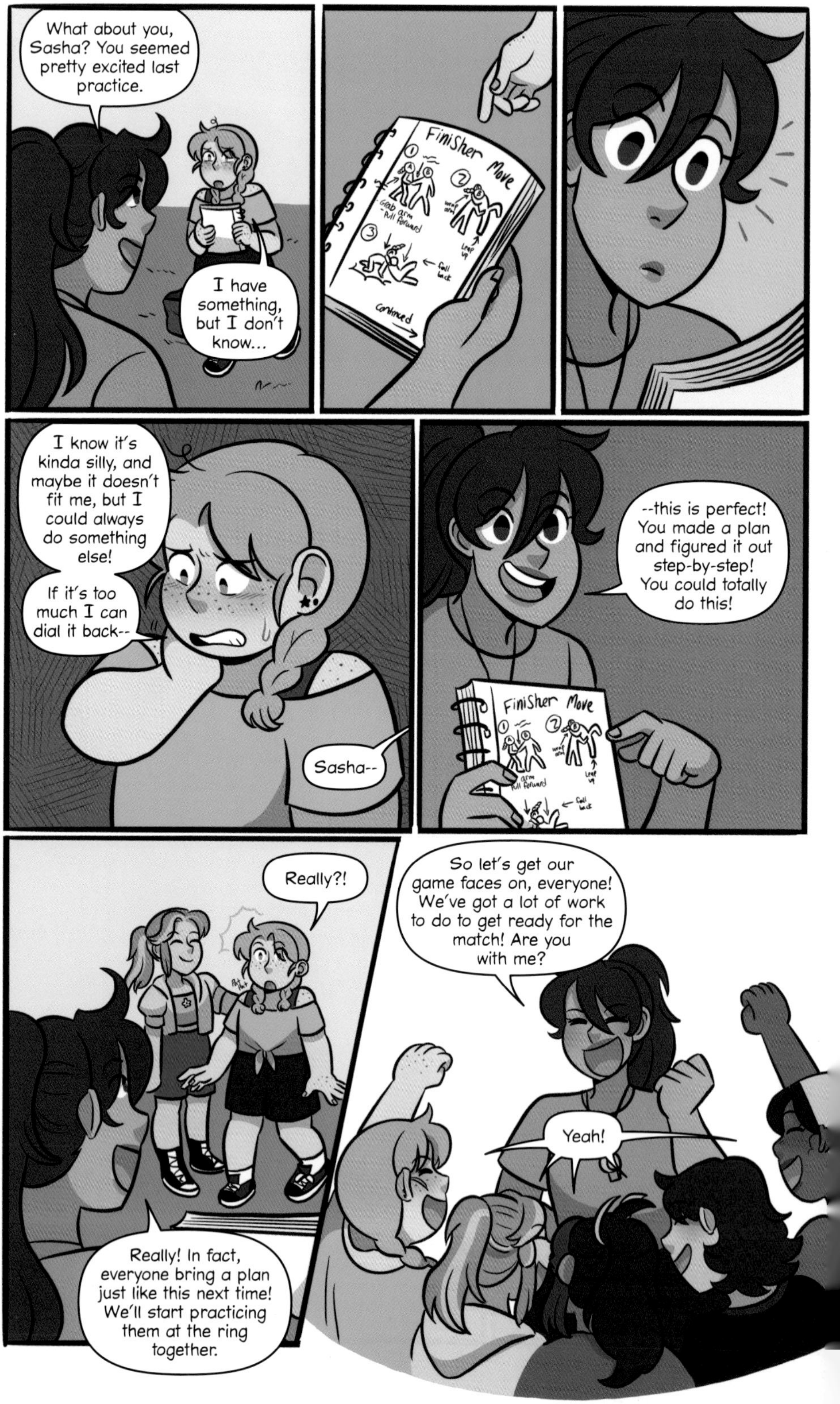
What about you, Sasha? You seemed pretty excited last practice.
I have something, but I don't know...
Finisher Move
Grab arm pull forward
wrap arm
Leap up
fall back
continued
I know it's kinda silly, and maybe it doesn't fit me, but I could always do something else!
If it's too much I can dial it back--
Sasha--
--this is perfect! You made a plan and figured it out step-by-step! You could totally do this!
Finisher Move
Really?!
Really! In fact, everyone bring a plan just like this next time! We'll start practicing them at the ring together.
So let's get our game faces on, everyone! We've got a lot of work to do to get ready for the match! Are you with me?
Yeah!

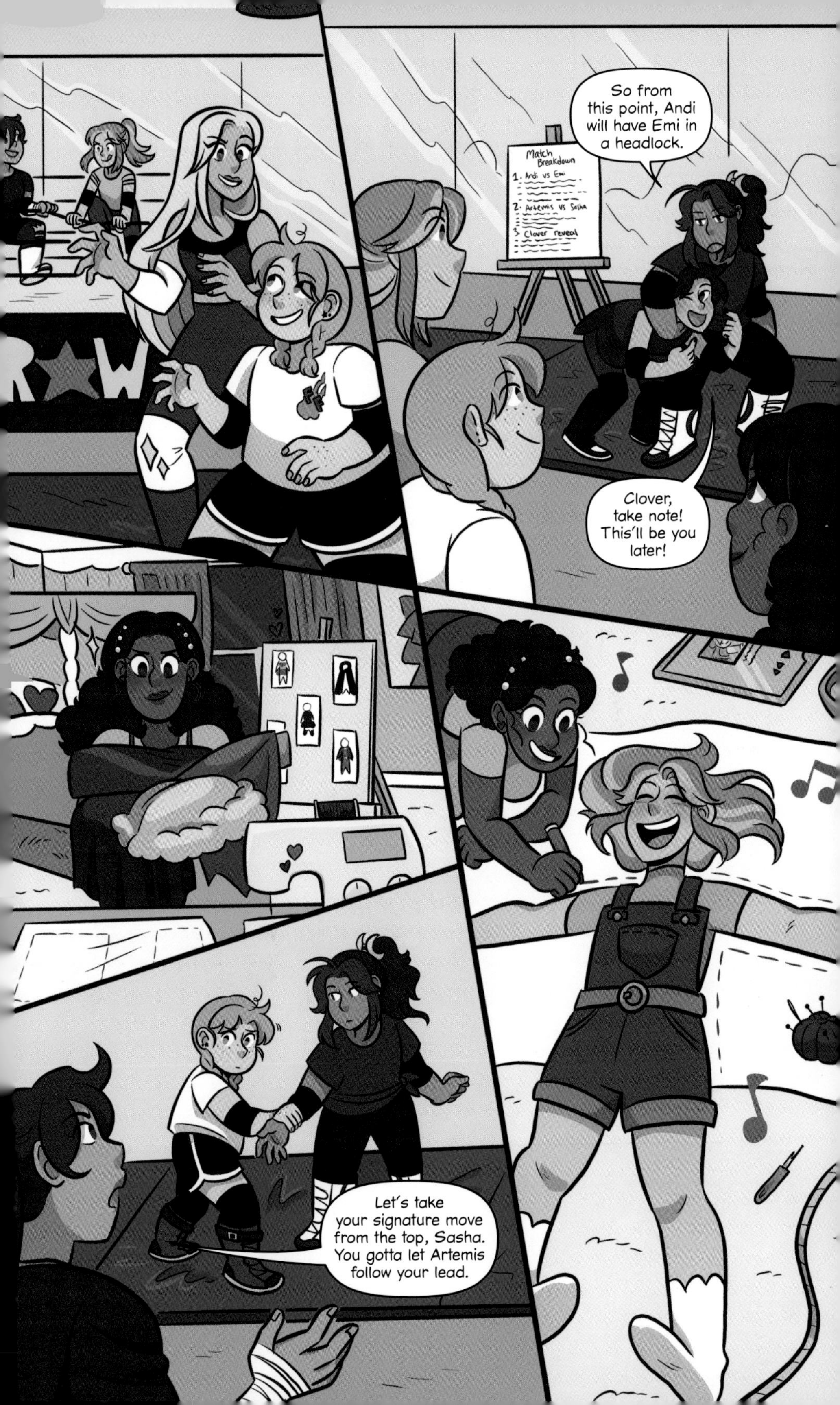
So from this point, Andi will have Emi in a headlock.
Match Breakdown
1. Andi vs Emi
2. Artemis vs Sasha
3. Clover reveal
Clover, take note! This'll be you later!
Let's take your signature move from the top, Sasha. You gotta let Artemis follow your lead.

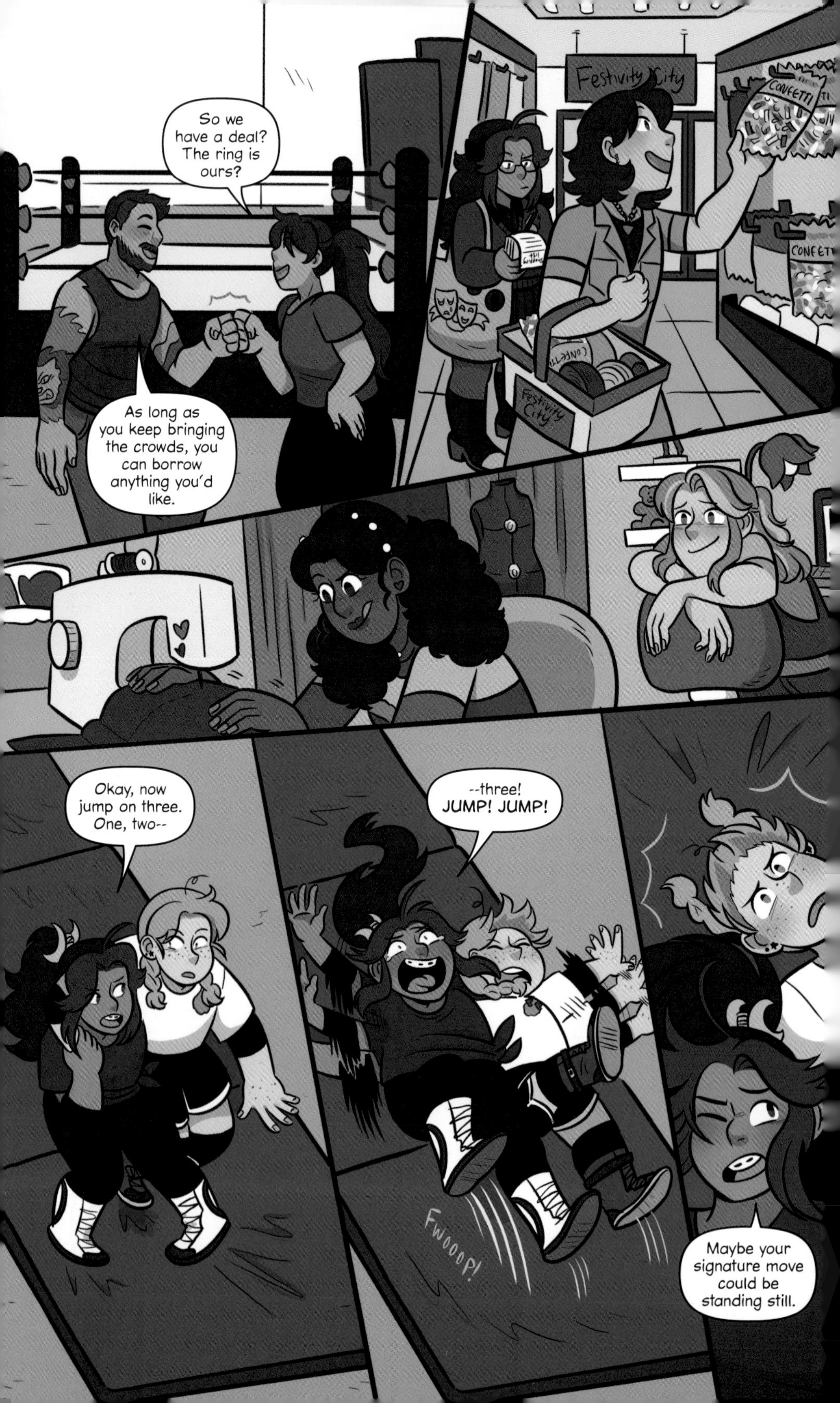
So we have a deal? The ring is ours?
As long as you keep bringing the crowds, you can borrow anything you'd like.
Festivity City
CONFETTI
CONFETTI
Festivity City
Okay, now jump on three. One, two--
--three! JUMP! JUMP!
Fwooop!
Maybe your signature move could be standing still.

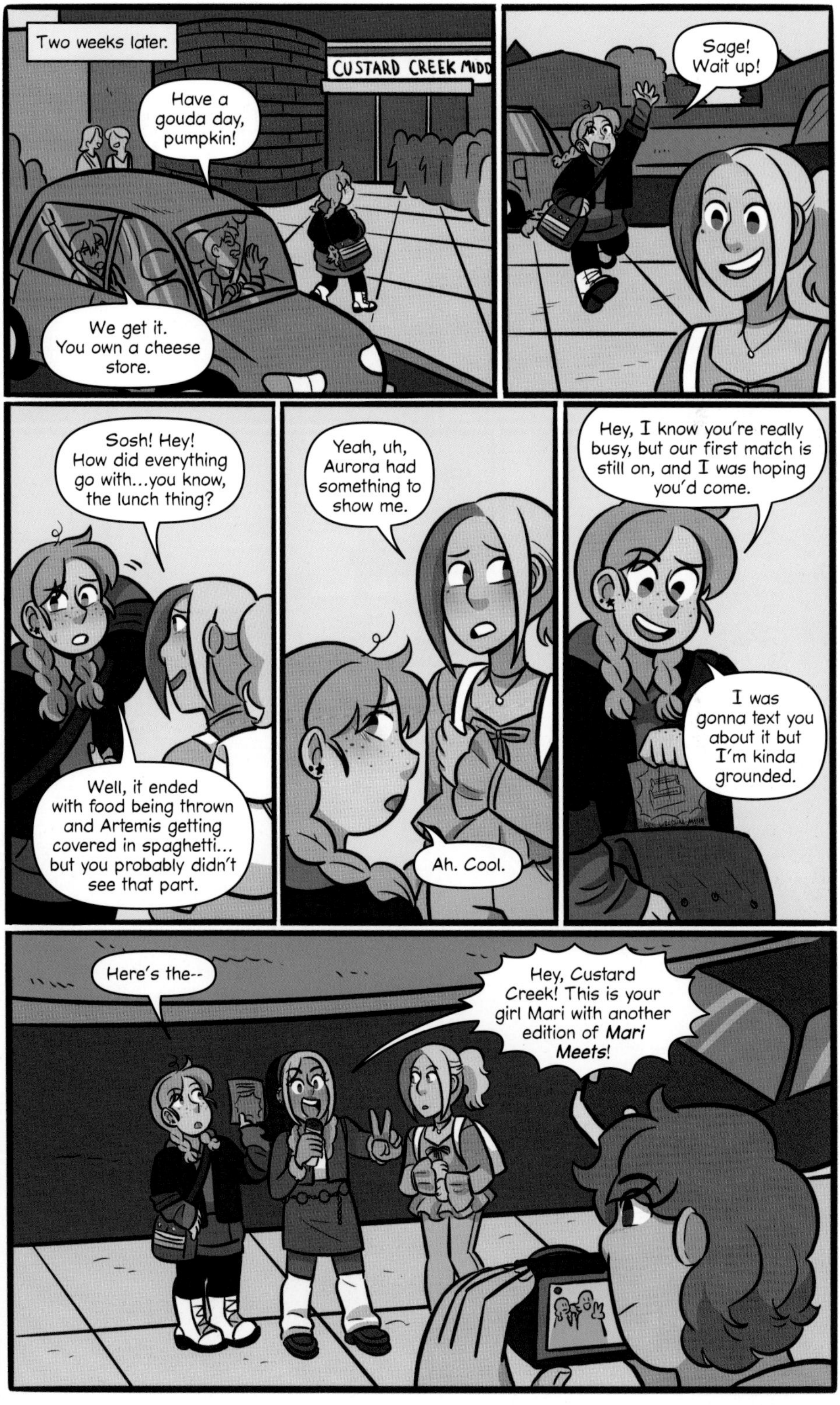
Two weeks later.
CUSTARD CREEK MIDD
Have a gouda day, pumpkin!
We get it. You own a cheese store.
Sage! Wait up!
Sosh! Hey! How did everything go with...you know, the lunch thing?
Well, it ended with food being thrown and Artemis getting covered in spaghetti... but you probably didn't see that part.
Yeah, uh, Aurora had something to show me.
Ah. Cool.
Hey, I know you're really busy, but our first match is still on, and I was hoping you'd come.
I was gonna text you about it but I'm kinda grounded.
Here's the--
Hey, Custard Creek! This is your girl Mari with another edition of *Mari Meets*!

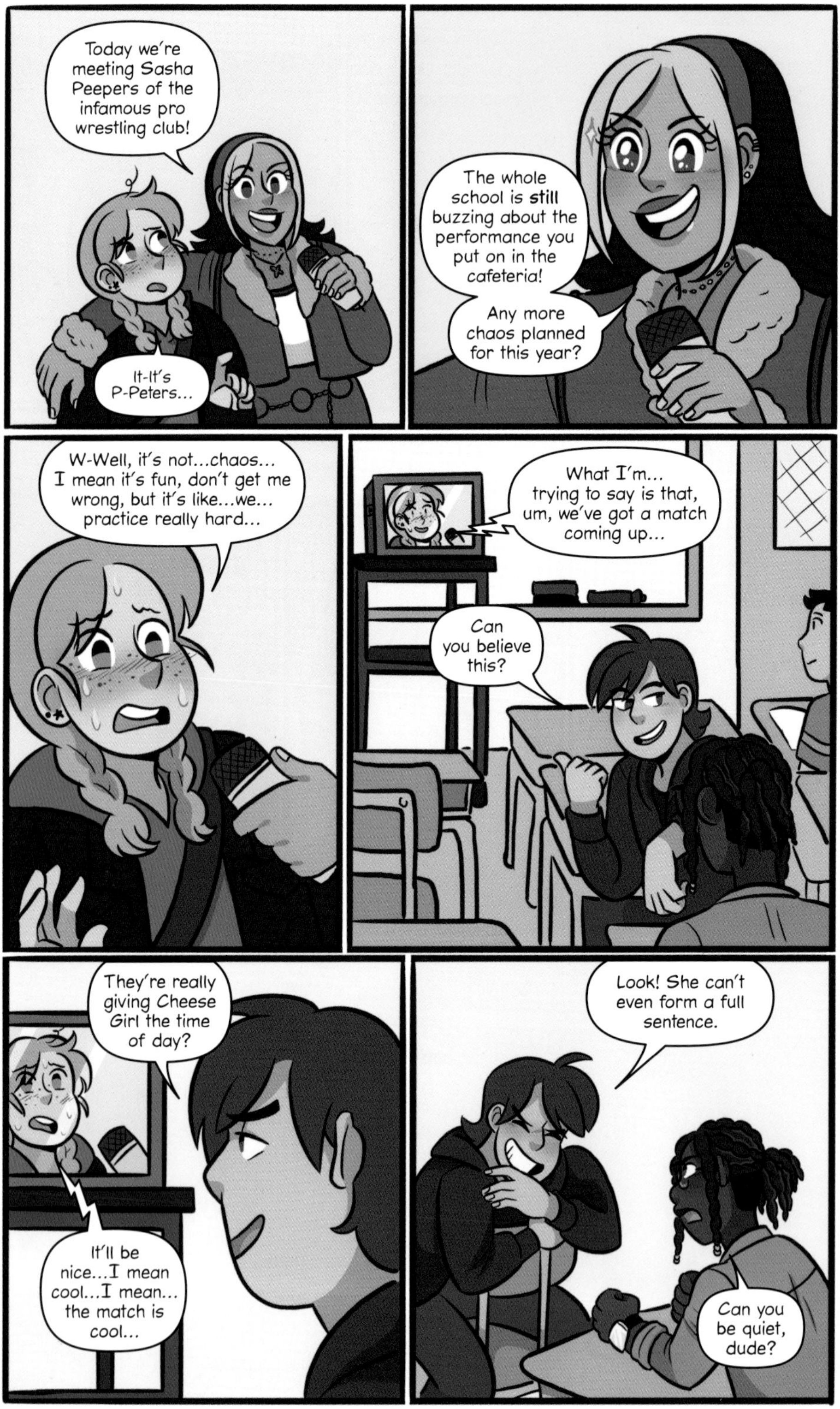

Today we're meeting Sasha Peepers of the infamous pro wrestling club!
It-It's P-Peters...
The whole school is **still** buzzing about the performance you put on in the cafeteria!
Any more chaos planned for this year?
W-Well, it's not...chaos... I mean it's fun, don't get me wrong, but it's like...we... practice really hard...
What I'm... trying to say is that, um, we've got a match coming up...
Can you believe this?
They're really giving Cheese Girl the time of day?
It'll be nice...I mean cool...I mean... the match is cool...
Look! She can't even form a full sentence.
Can you be quiet, dude?

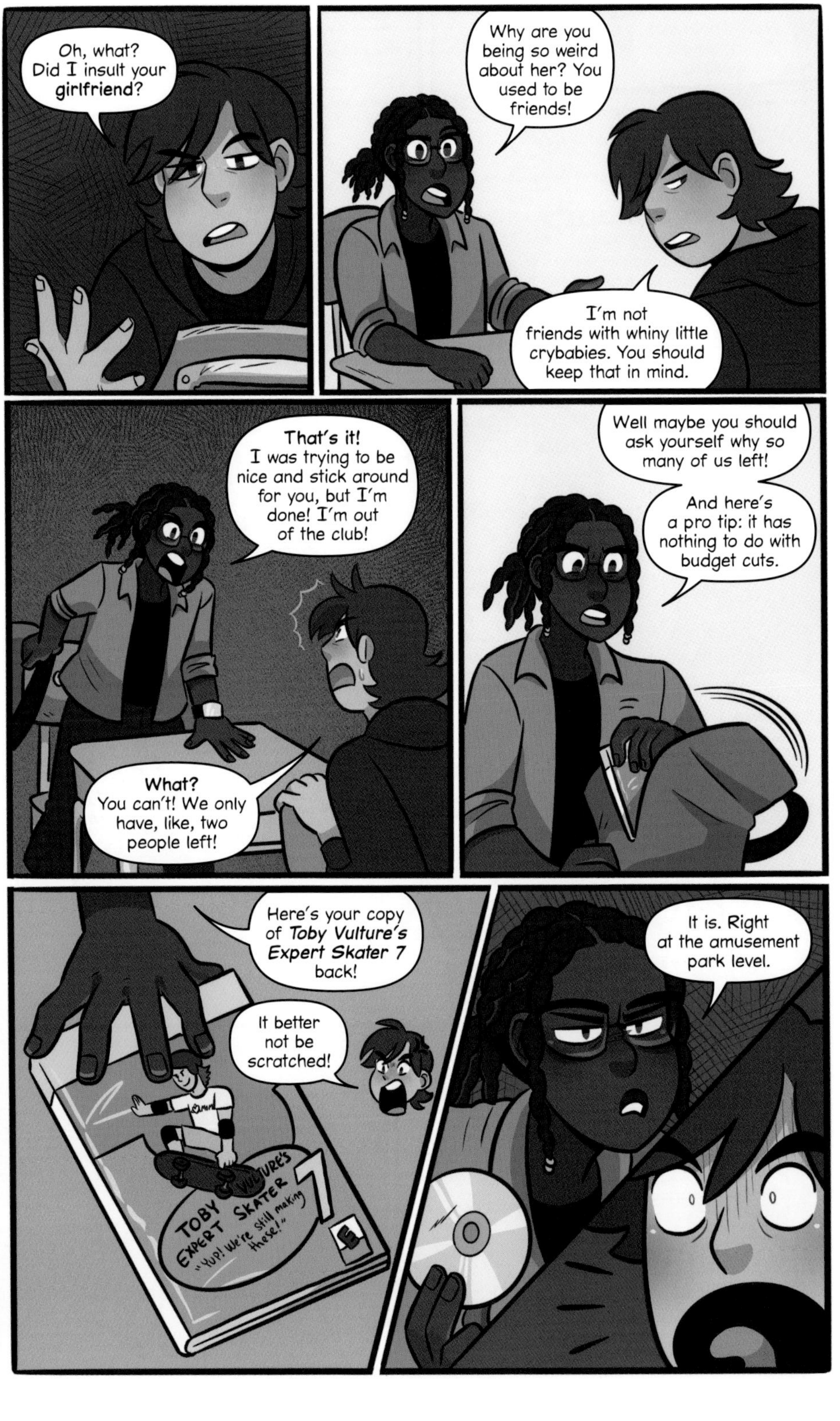
Oh, what? Did I insult your girlfriend?
Why are you being so weird about her? You used to be friends!
I'm not friends with whiny little crybabies. You should keep that in mind.
That's it! I was trying to be nice and stick around for you, but I'm done! I'm out of the club!
What? You can't! We only have, like, two people left!
Well maybe you should ask yourself why so many of us left!
And here's a pro tip: it has nothing to do with budget cuts.
Here's your copy of Toby Vulture's Expert Skater 7 back!
It better not be scratched!
TOBY VULTURE'S EXPERT SKATER 7
"Yup! We're still making these!"
It is. Right at the amusement park level.

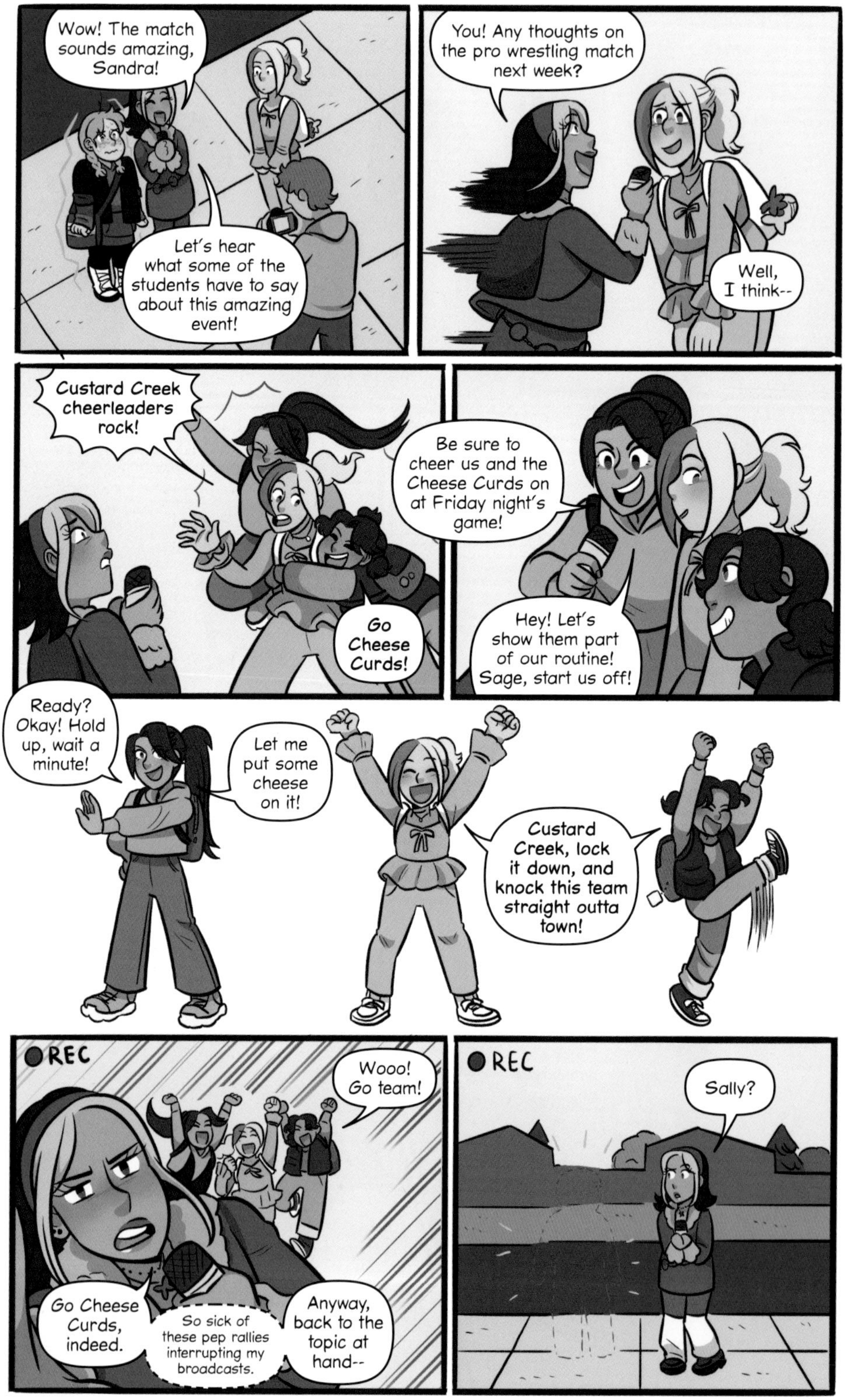
Wow! The match sounds amazing, Sandra!
Let's hear what some of the students have to say about this amazing event!
You! Any thoughts on the pro wrestling match next week?
Well, I think--
Custard Creek cheerleaders rock!
Go Cheese Curds!
Be sure to cheer us and the Cheese Curds on at Friday night's game!
Hey! Let's show them part of our routine! Sage, start us off!
Ready? Okay! Hold up, wait a minute!
Let me put some cheese on it!
Custard Creek, lock it down, and knock this team straight outta town!
REC
Wooo! Go team!
Go Cheese Curds, indeed.
So sick of these pep rallies interrupting my broadcasts.
Anyway, back to the topic at hand--
REC
Sally?

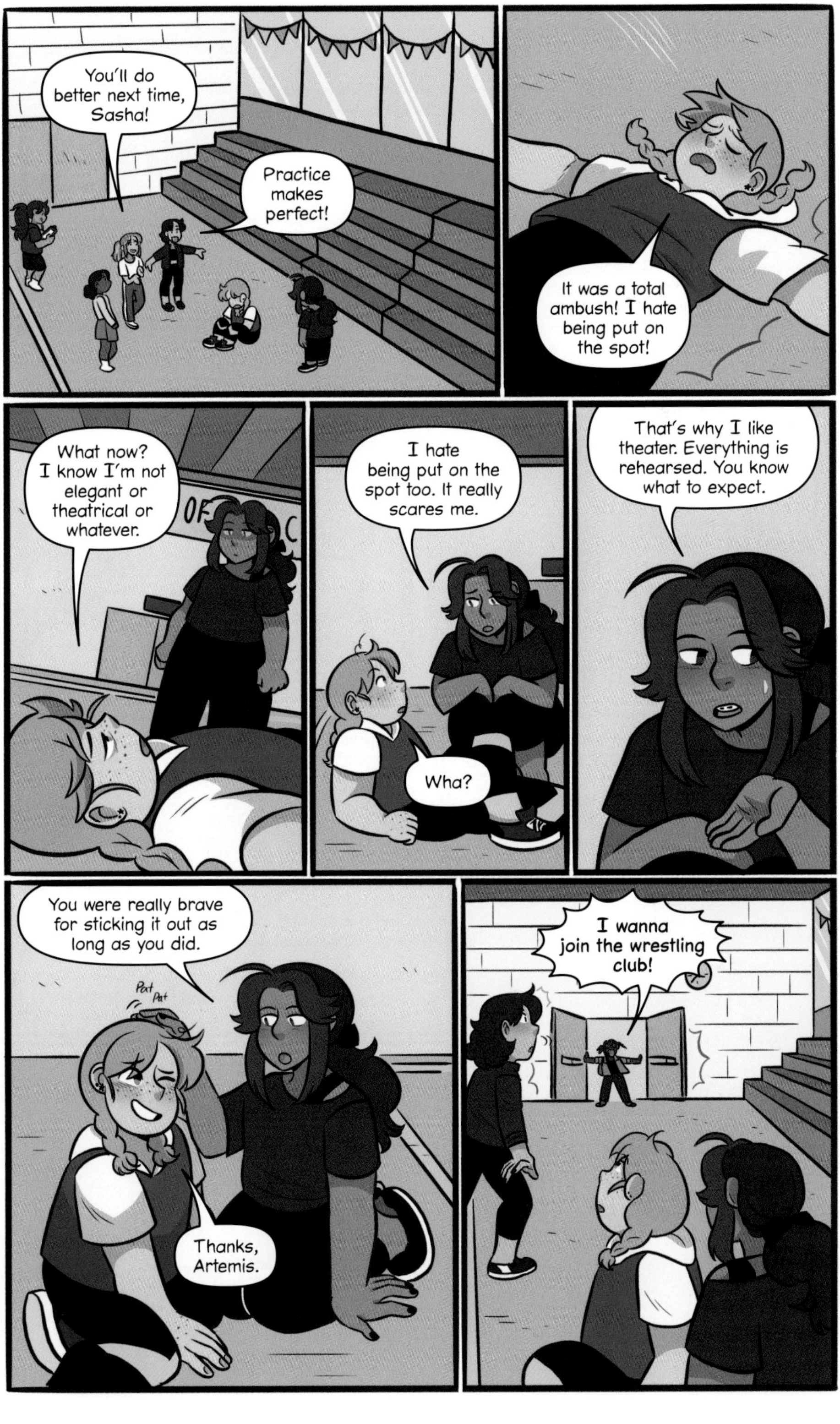
You'll do better next time, Sasha!
Practice makes perfect!
It was a total ambush! I hate being put on the spot!
What now? I know I'm not elegant or theatrical or whatever.
I hate being put on the spot too. It really scares me.
Wha?
That's why I like theater. Everything is rehearsed. You know what to expect.
You were really brave for sticking it out as long as you did.
Pat Pat
Thanks, Artemis.
I wanna join the wrestling club!

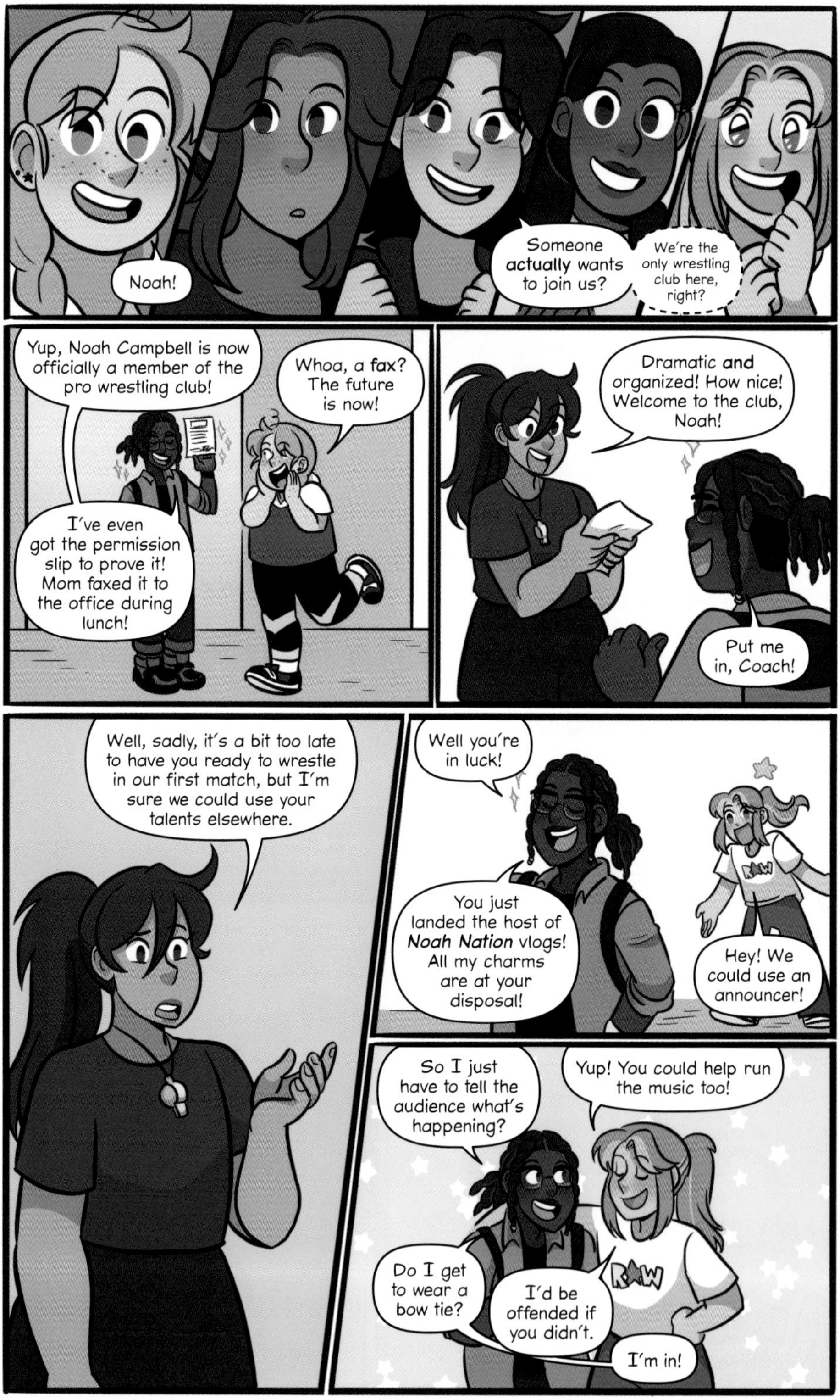

Noah!
Someone **actually** wants to join us?
We're the only wrestling club here, right?
Yup, Noah Campbell is now officially a member of the pro wrestling club!
I've even got the permission slip to prove it! Mom faxed it to the office during lunch!
Whoa, a **fax**? The future is now!
Dramatic **and** organized! How nice! Welcome to the club, Noah!
Put me in, Coach!
Well, sadly, it's a bit too late to have you ready to wrestle in our first match, but I'm sure we could use your talents elsewhere.
Well you're in luck!
You just landed the host of ***Noah Nation*** vlogs! All my charms are at your disposal!
RAW
Hey! We could use an announcer!
So I just have to tell the audience what's happening?
Yup! You could help run the music too!
Do I get to wear a bow tie?
RAW
I'd be offended if you didn't.
I'm in!

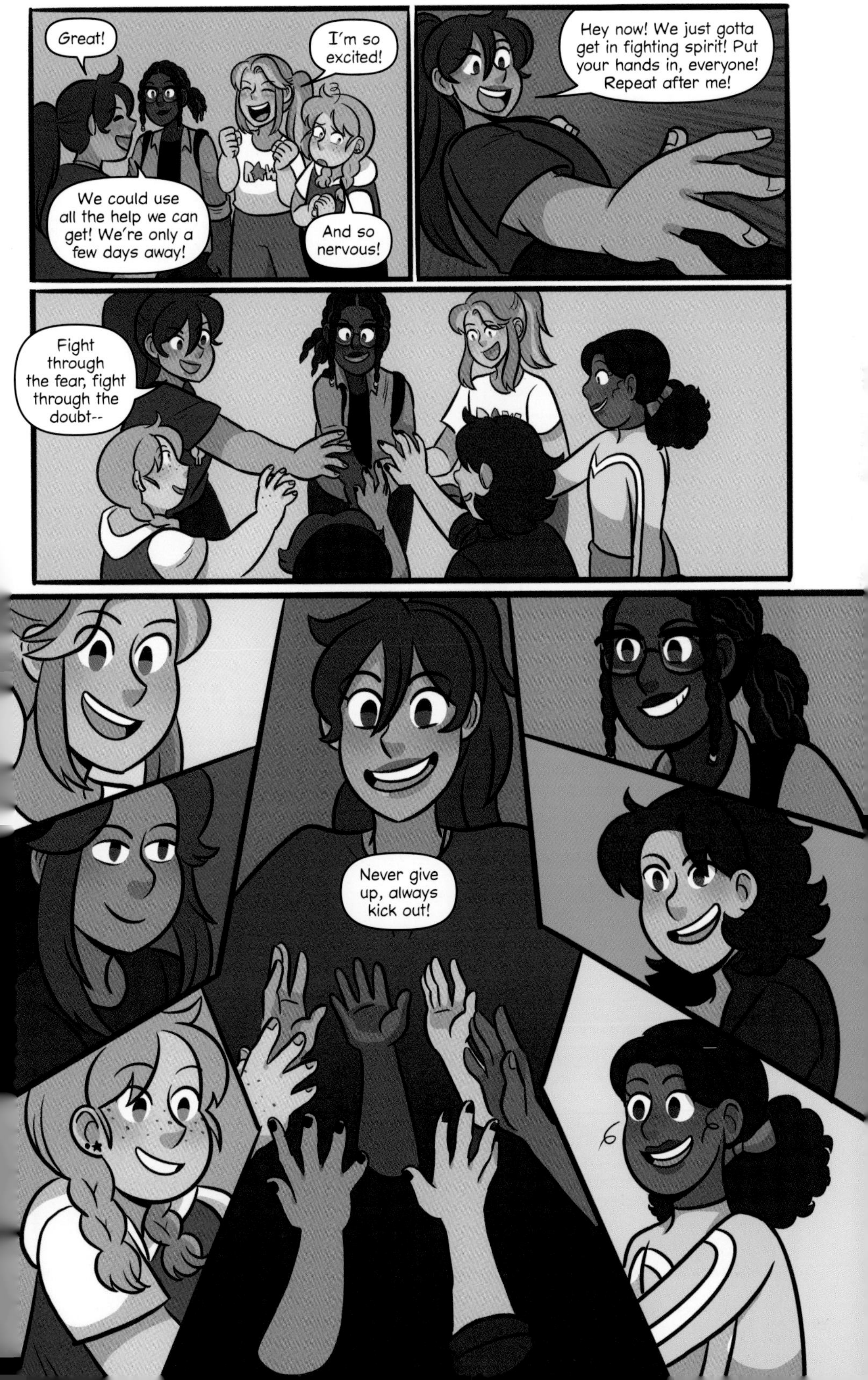
Great!
I'm so excited!
We could use all the help we can get! We're only a few days away!
And so nervous!
Hey now! We just gotta get in fighting spirit! Put your hands in, everyone! Repeat after me!
Fight through the fear, fight through the doubt--
Never give up, always kick out!

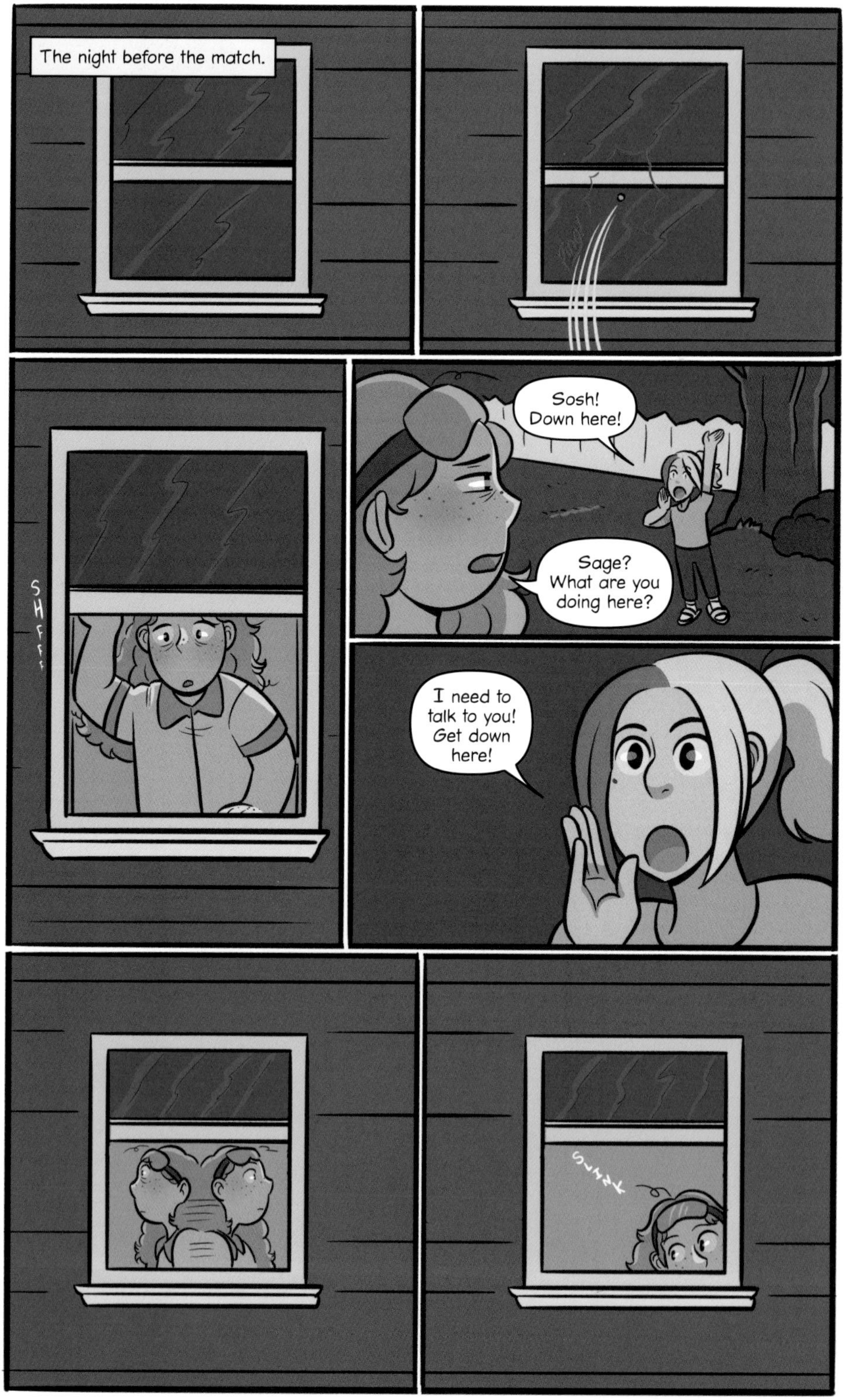

The night before the match.
SHFFF
Sosh! Down here!
Sage? What are you doing here?
I need to talk to you! Get down here!

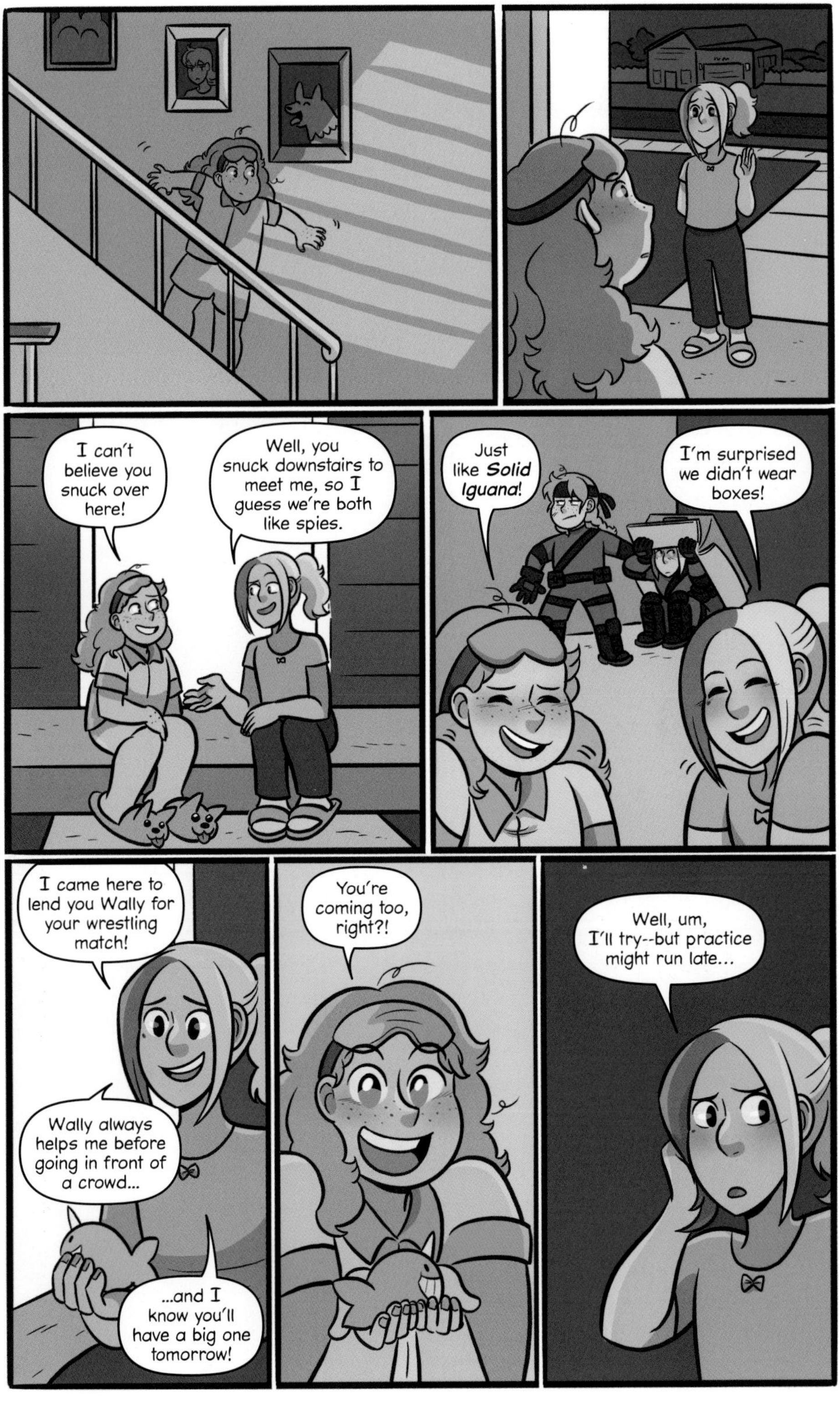
I can't believe you snuck over here!
Well, you snuck downstairs to meet me, so I guess we're both like spies.
Just like **Solid Iguana**!
I'm surprised we didn't wear boxes!
I came here to lend you Wally for your wrestling match!
Wally always helps me before going in front of a crowd...
...and I know you'll have a big one tomorrow!
You're coming too, right?!
Well, um, I'll try--but practice might run late...

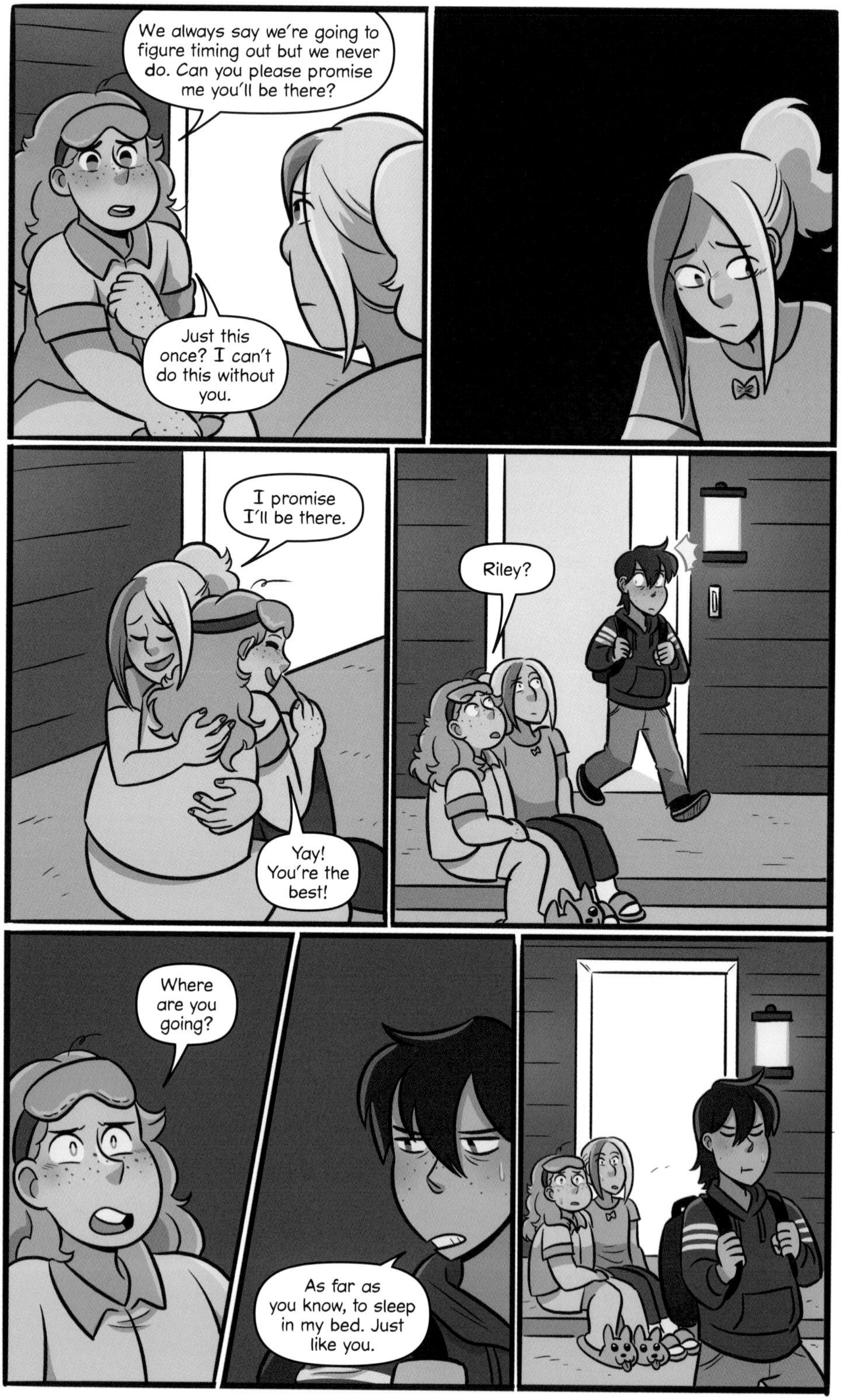
We always say we're going to figure timing out but we never do. Can you please promise me you'll be there?
Just this once? I can't do this without you.
I promise I'll be there.
Yay! You're the best!
Riley?
Where are you going?
As far as you know, to sleep in my bed. Just like you.

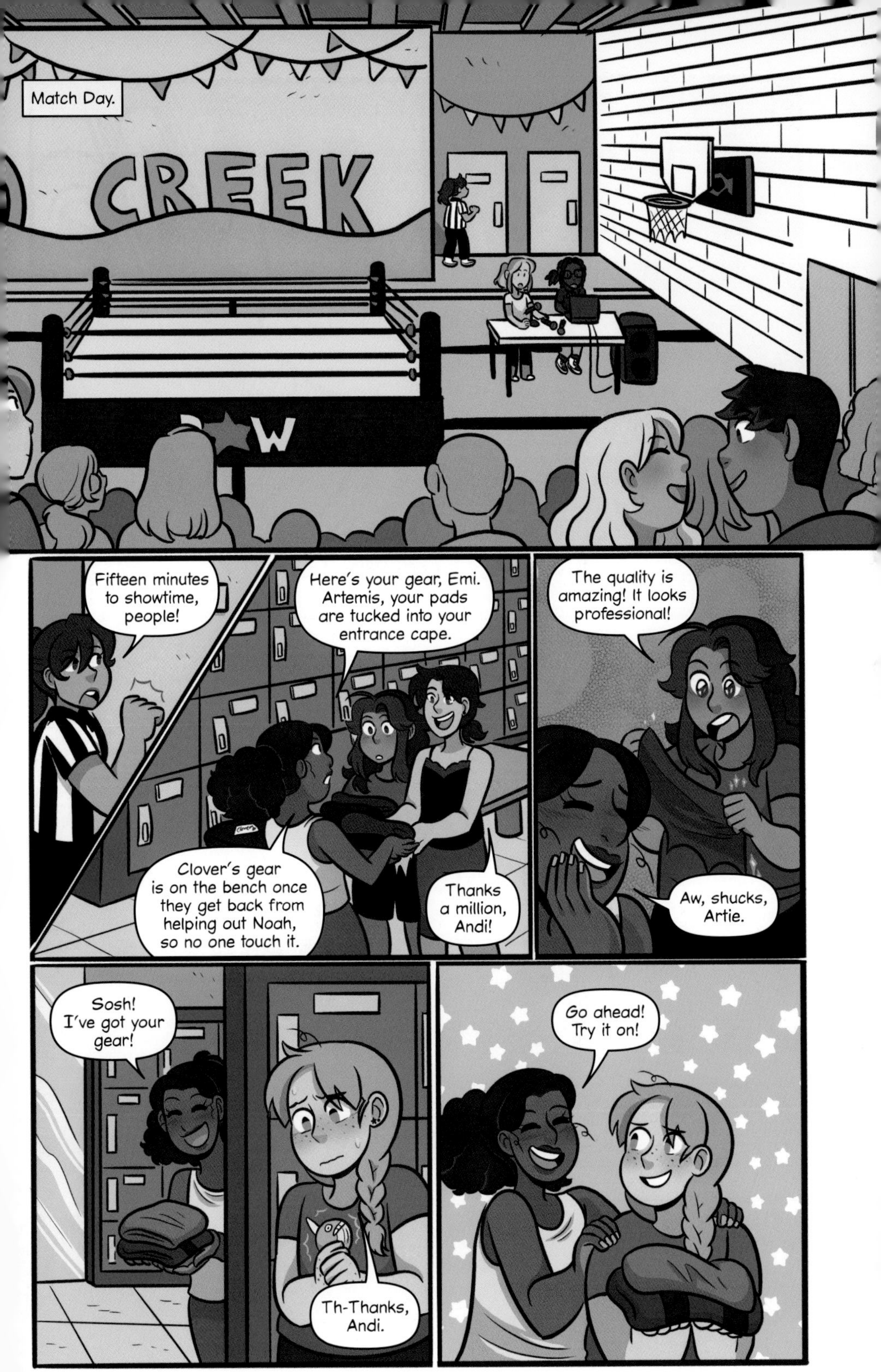
Match Day.
CREEK
W
Fifteen minutes to showtime, people!
Here's your gear, Emi. Artemis, your pads are tucked into your entrance cape.
Clover's gear is on the bench once they get back from helping out Noah, so no one touch it.
Thanks a million, Andi!
The quality is amazing! It looks professional!
Aw, shucks, Artie.
Sosh! I've got your gear!
Th-Thanks, Andi.
Go ahead! Try it on!

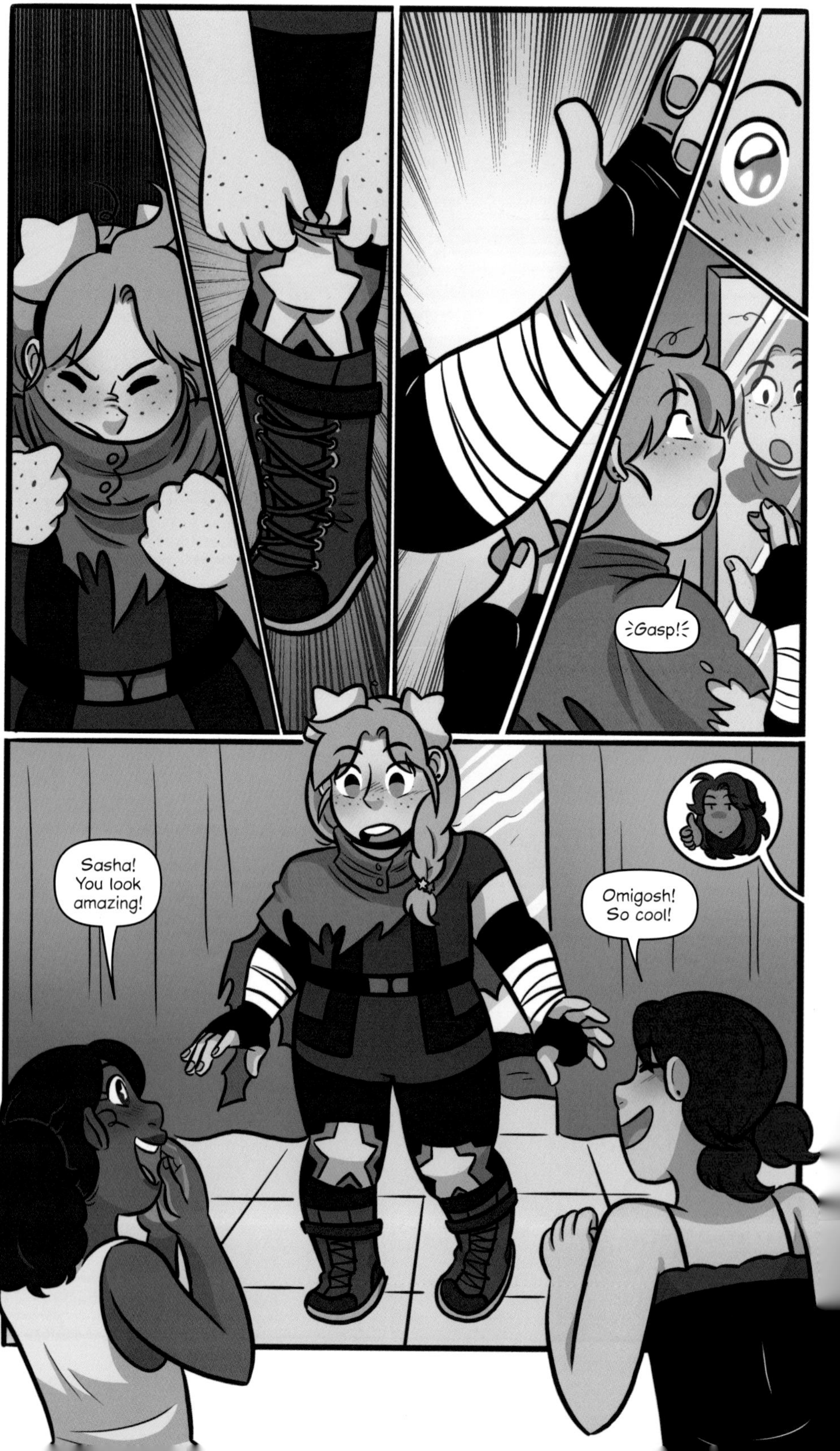
Gasp!
Sasha! You look amazing!
Omigosh! So cool!

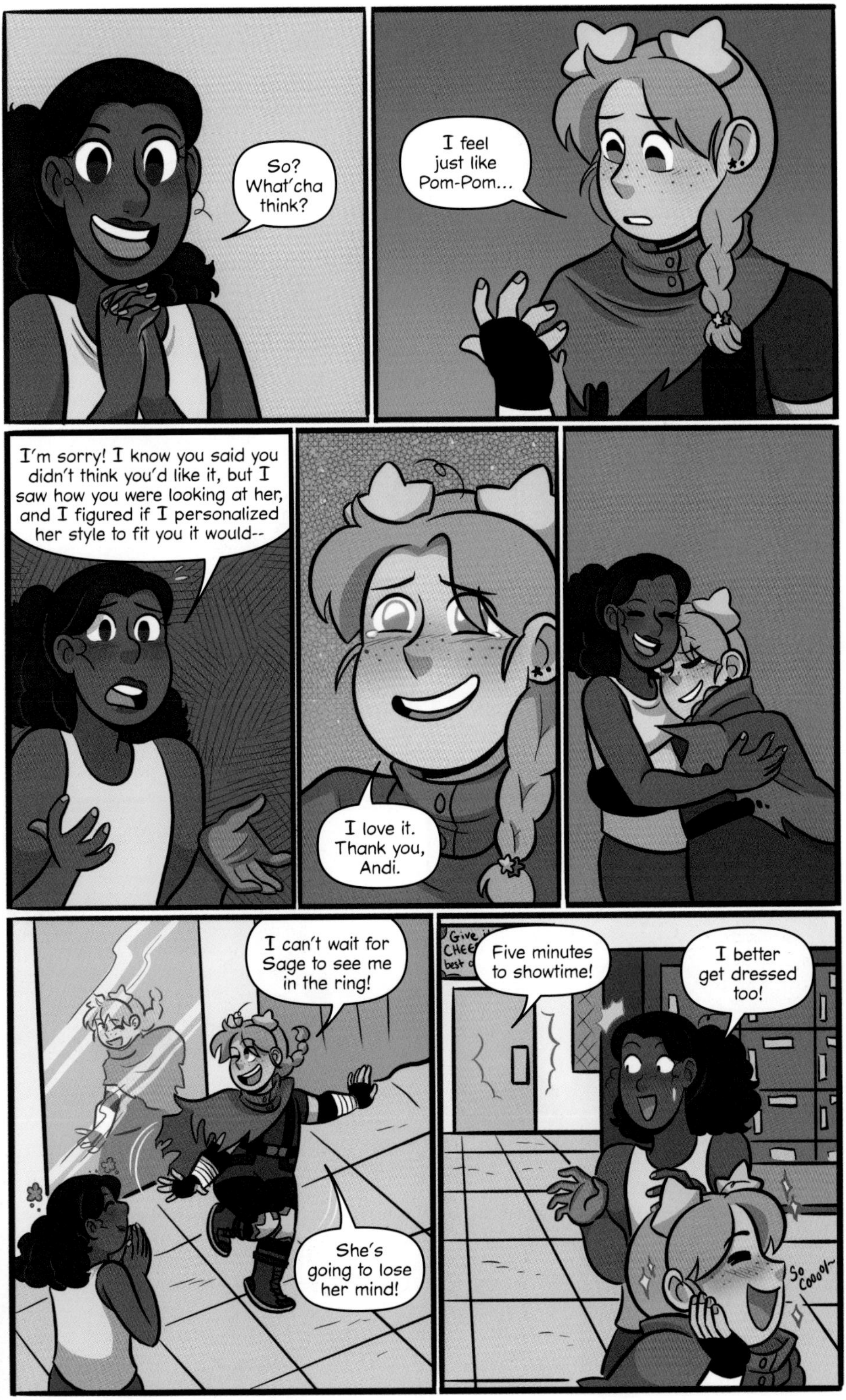

So? What'cha think?
I feel just like Pom-Pom...
I'm sorry! I know you said you didn't think you'd like it, but I saw how you were looking at her, and I figured if I personalized her style to fit you it would--
I love it. Thank you, Andi.
I can't wait for Sage to see me in the ring!
She's going to lose her mind!
Five minutes to showtime!
I better get dressed too!
So cooool~

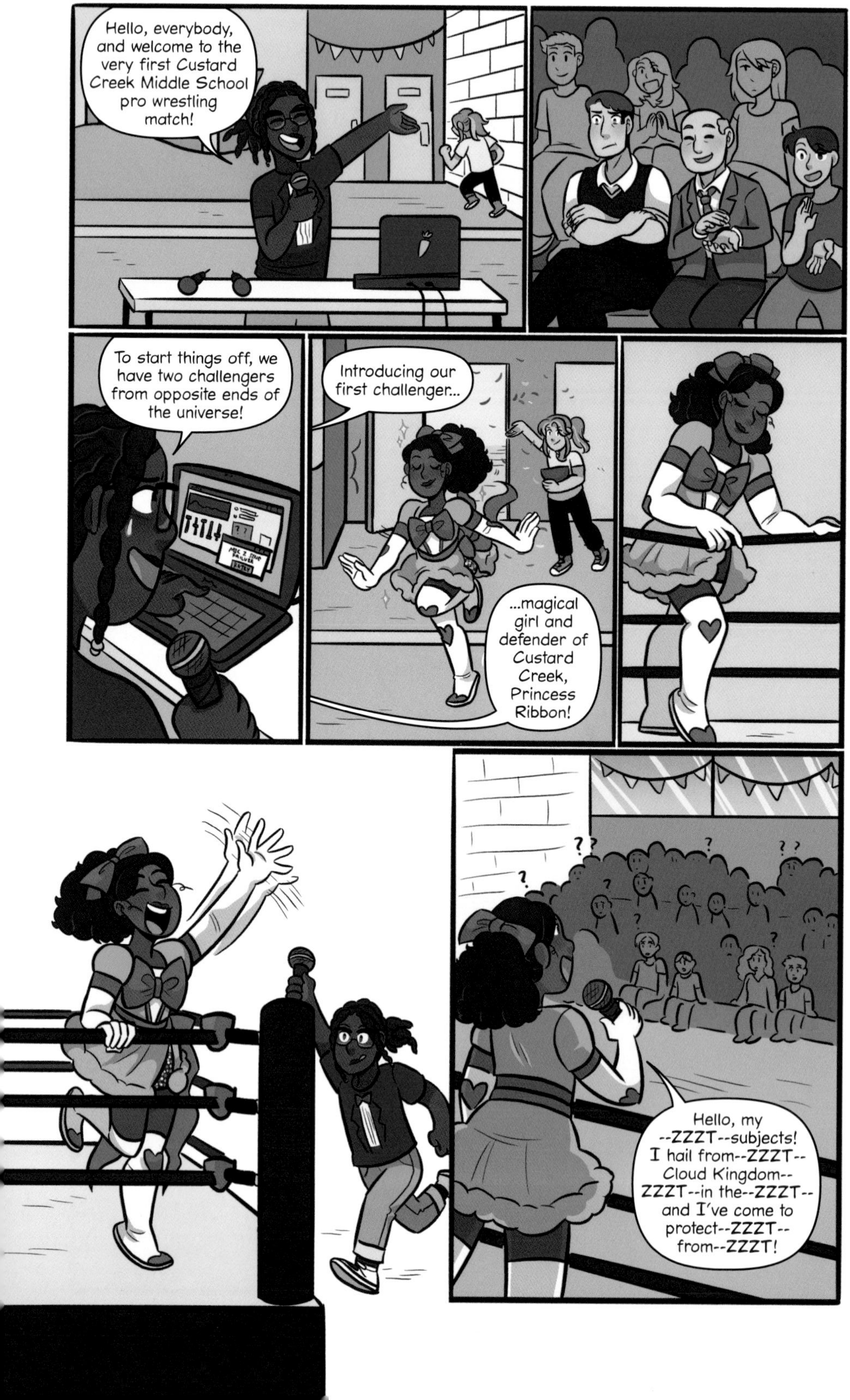
Hello, everybody, and welcome to the very first Custard Creek Middle School pro wrestling match!
To start things off, we have two challengers from opposite ends of the universe!
Introducing our first challenger...
...magical girl and defender of Custard Creek, Princess Ribbon!
Hello, my --ZZZT--subjects! I hail from--ZZZT-- Cloud Kingdom-- ZZZT--in the--ZZZT-- and I've come to protect--ZZZT-- from--ZZZT!

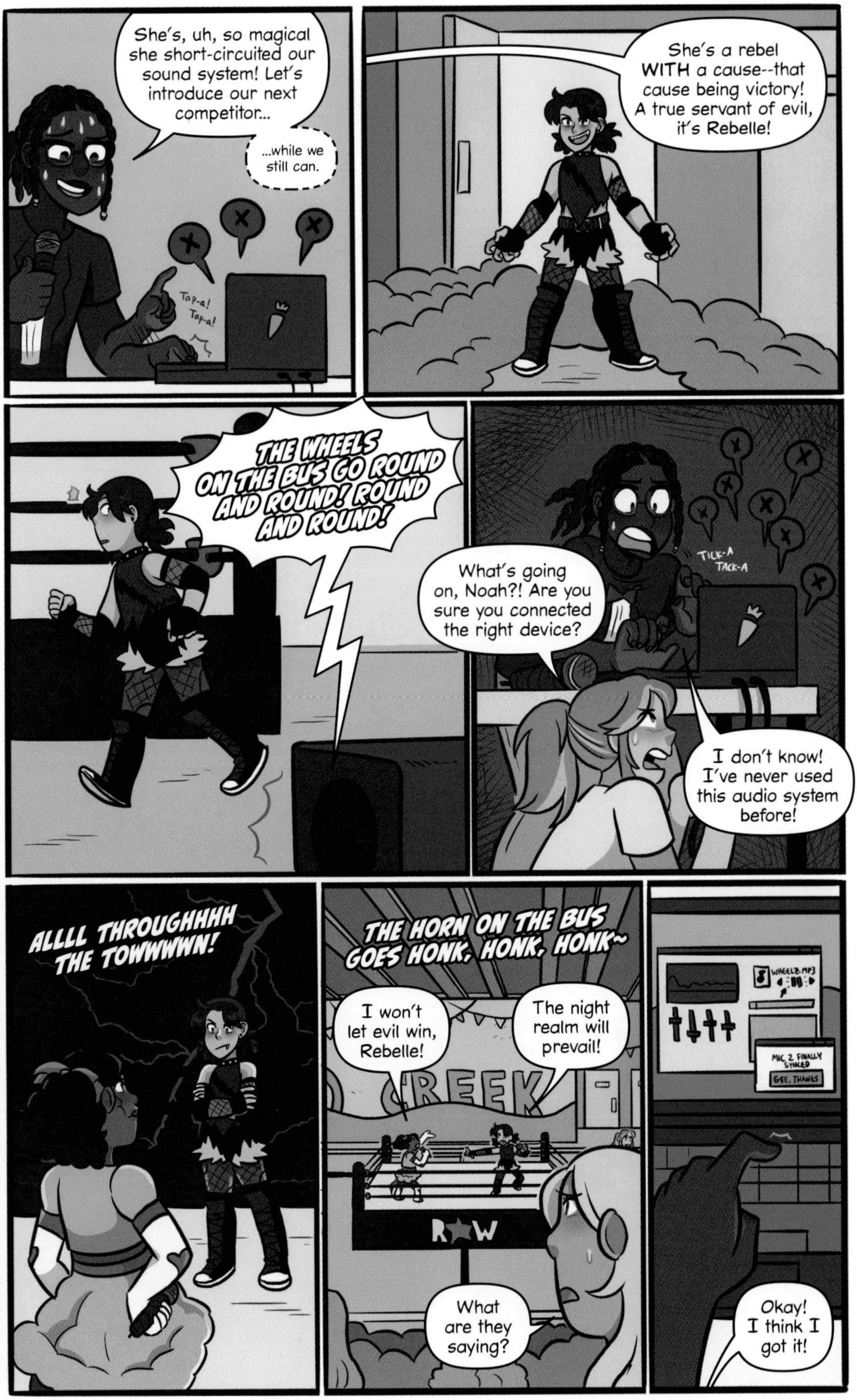
She's, uh, so magical she short-circuited our sound system! Let's introduce our next competitor...
...while we still can.
Tap-a! Tap-a!
She's a rebel WITH a cause--that cause being victory! A true servant of evil, it's Rebelle!
THE WHEELS ON THE BUS GO ROUND AND ROUND! ROUND AND ROUND!
What's going on, Noah?! Are you sure you connected the right device?
TICK-A TACK-A
I don't know! I've never used this audio system before!
ALLLL THROUGHHHH THE TOWWWWN!
THE HORN ON THE BUS GOES HONK, HONK, HONK~
I won't let evil win, Rebelle!
The night realm will prevail!
CREEK
What are they saying?
WHEELZ.MP3
MIC 2 FINALLY SYNCED
GEE, THANKS
Okay! I think I got it!

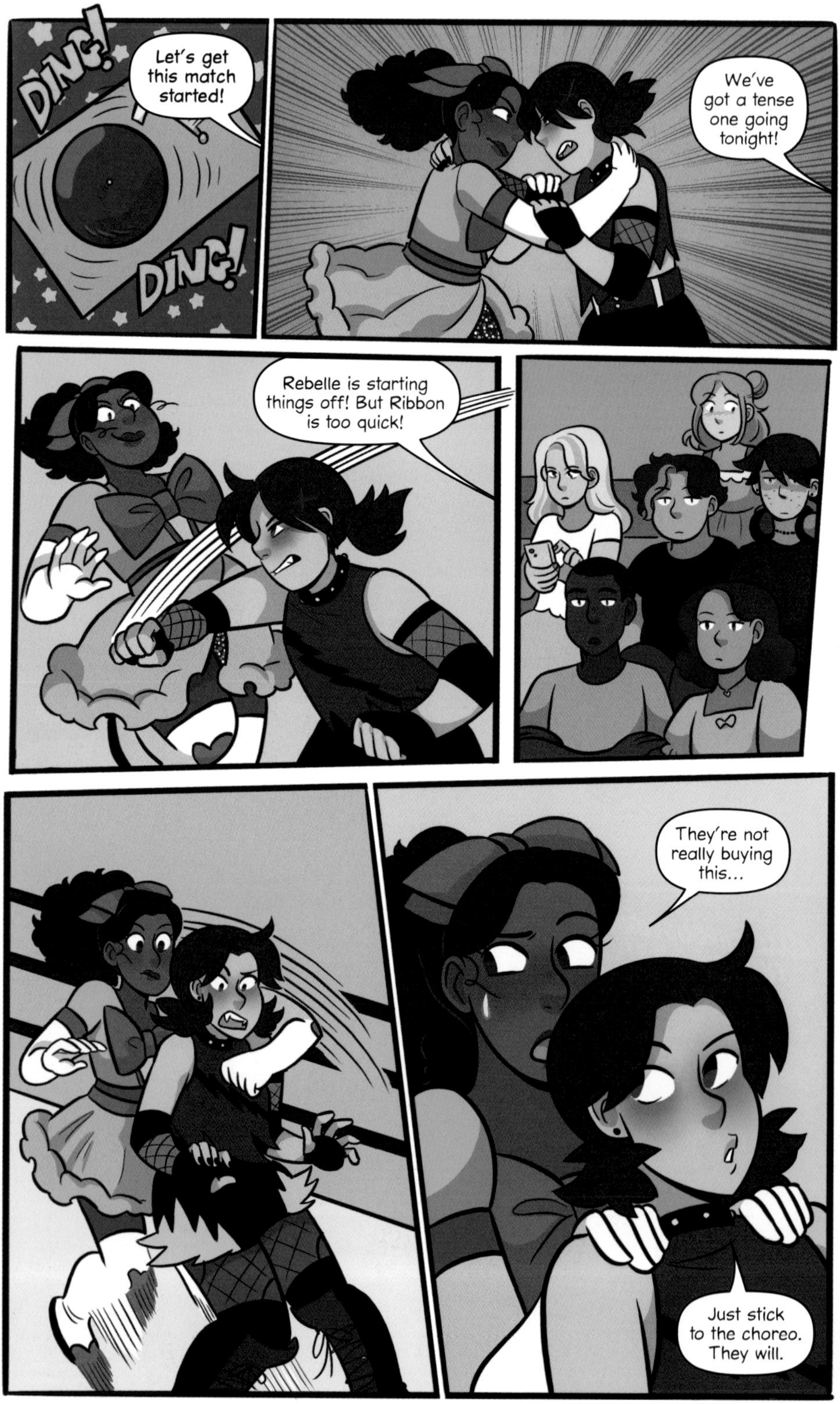
DING!
Let's get this match started!
DING!
We've got a tense one going tonight!
Rebelle is starting things off! But Ribbon is too quick!
They're not really buying this...
Just stick to the choreo. They will.

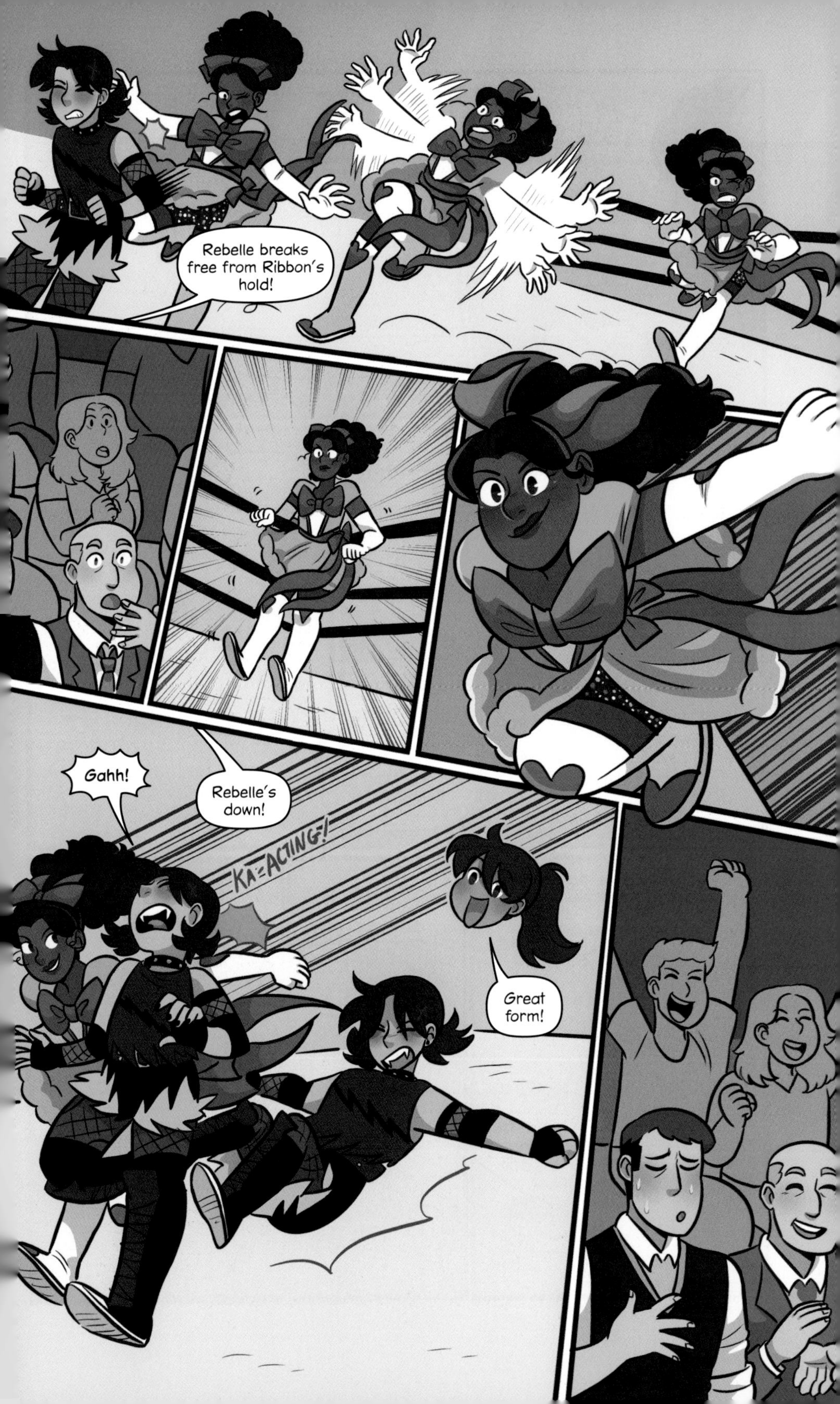
Rebelle breaks free from Ribbon's hold!
Gahh!
Rebelle's down!
KA-ACTING!
Great form!

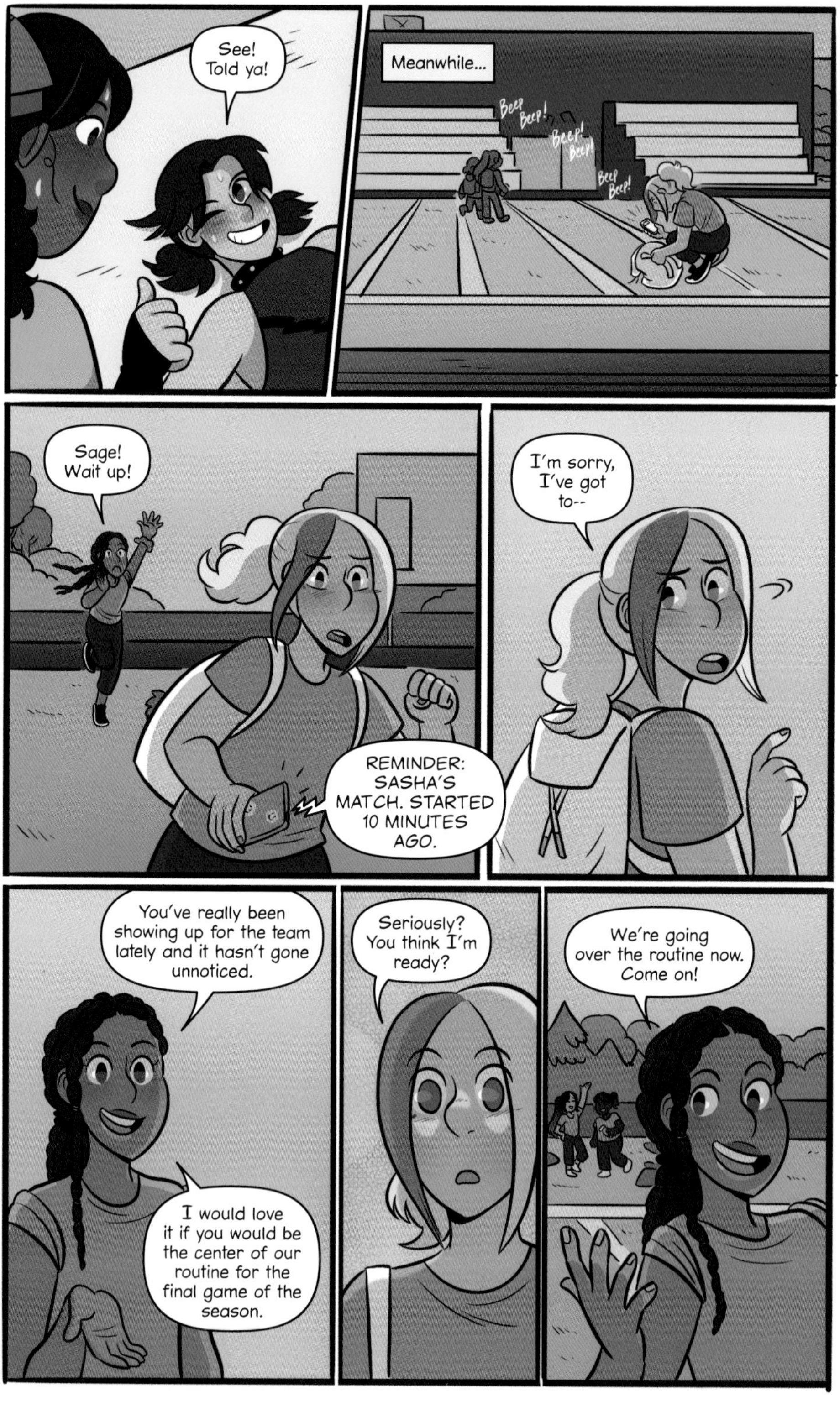
See! Told ya!
Meanwhile...
Beep Beep!
Beep! Beep!
Beep Beep!
Sage! Wait up!
REMINDER: SASHA'S MATCH. STARTED 10 MINUTES AGO.
I'm sorry, I've got to--
You've really been showing up for the team lately and it hasn't gone unnoticed.
I would love it if you would be the center of our routine for the final game of the season.
Seriously? You think I'm ready?
We're going over the routine now. Come on!

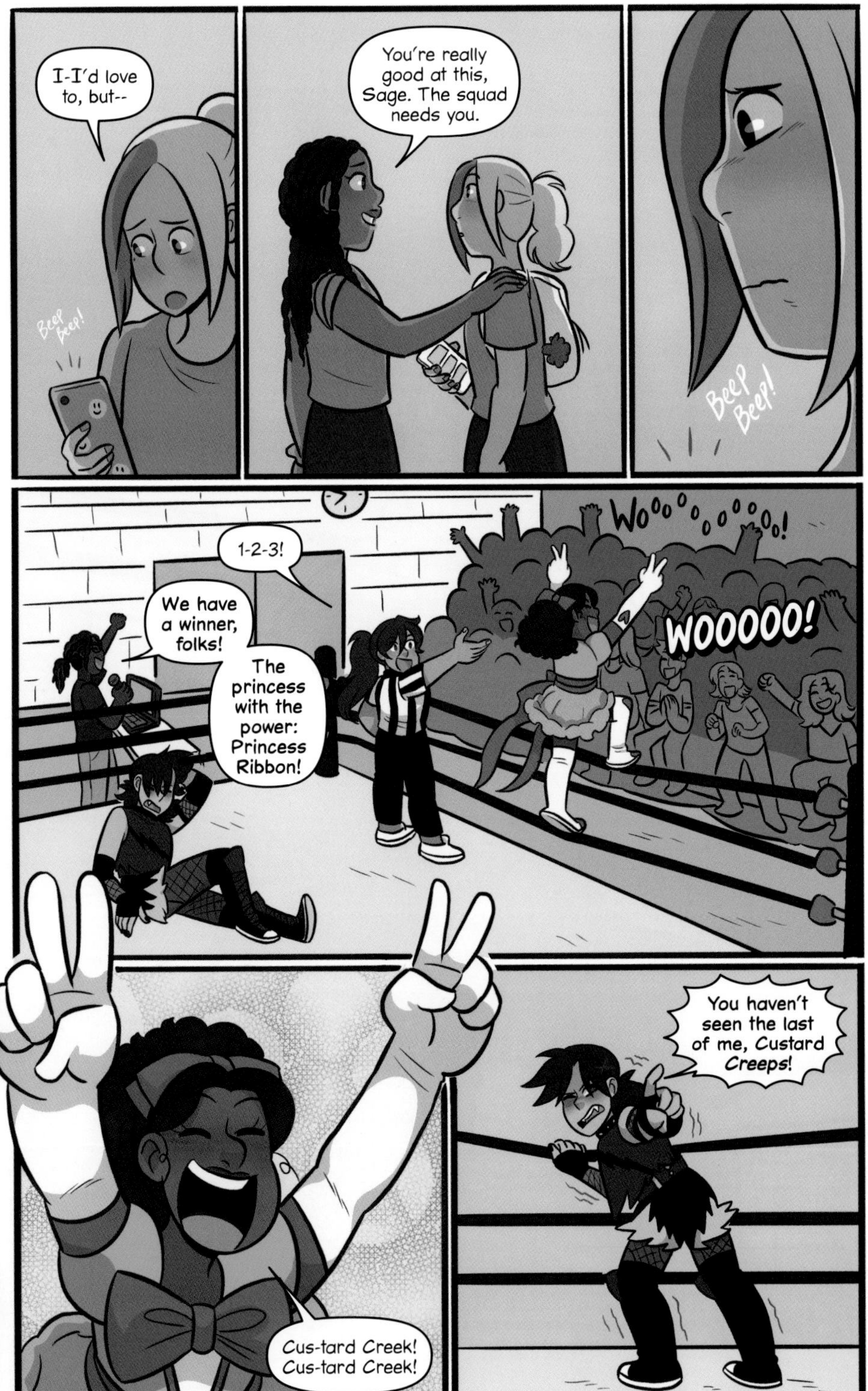
I-I'd love to, but--
Beep Beep!
You're really good at this, Sage. The squad needs you.
Beep Beep!
Wo o o o o o o o o o!
1-2-3!
We have a winner, folks!
The princess with the power: Princess Ribbon!
WOOOOO!
Cus-tard Creek! Cus-tard Creek!
You haven't seen the last of me, Custard Creeps!

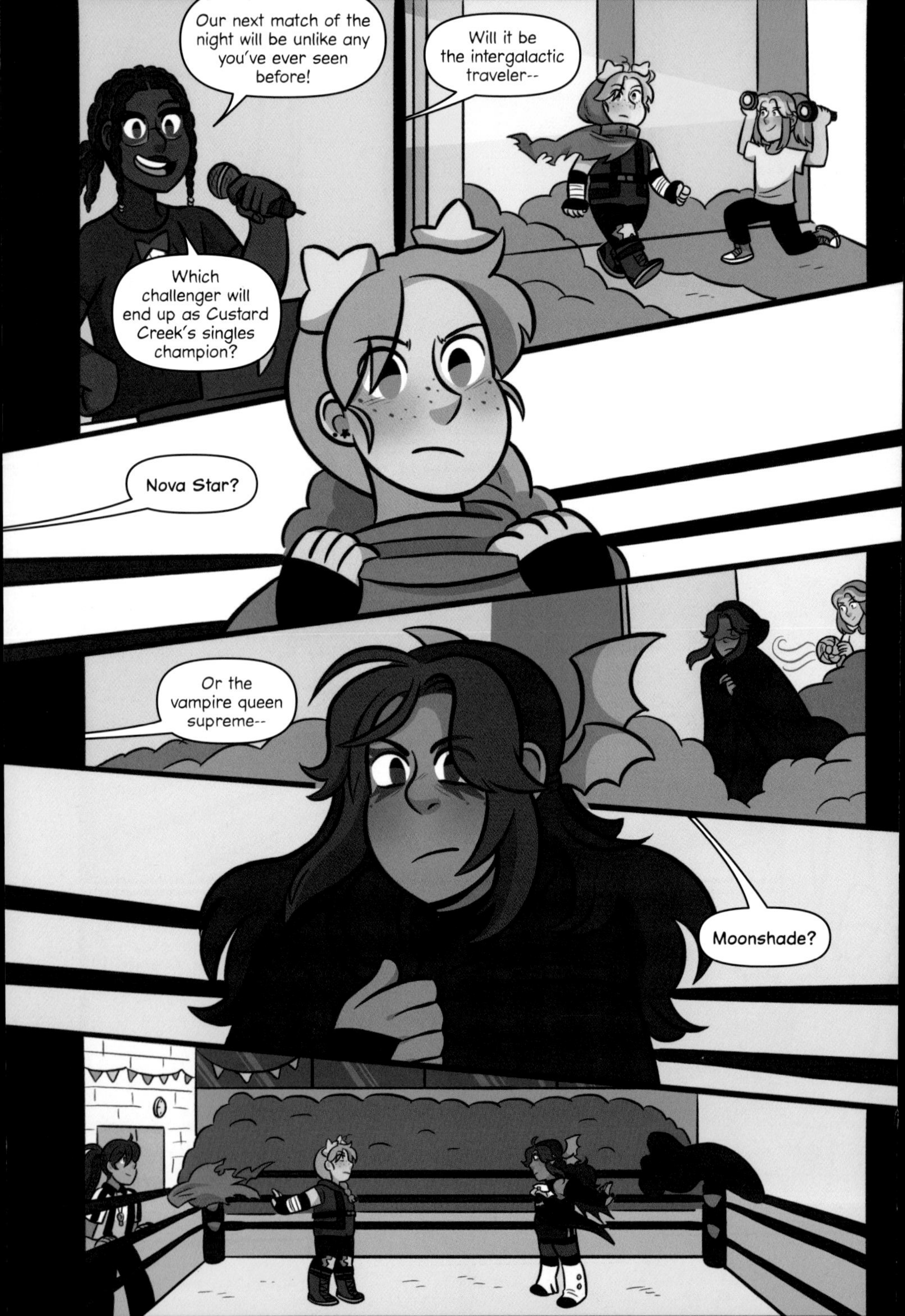
Our next match of the night will be unlike any you've ever seen before!
Will it be the intergalactic traveler--
Which challenger will end up as Custard Creek's singles champion?
Nova Star?
Or the vampire queen supreme--
Moonshade?

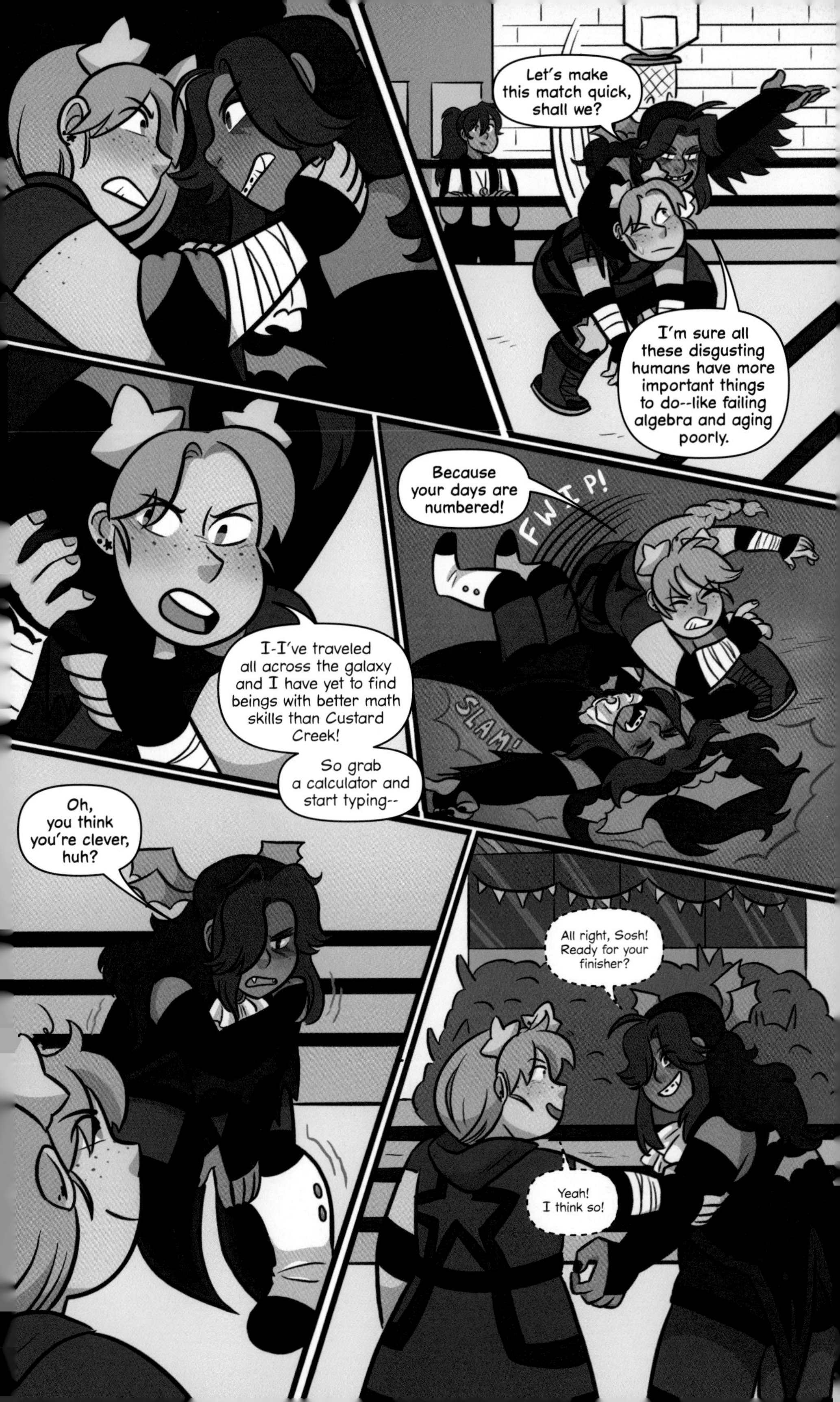
Let's make this match quick, shall we?
I'm sure all these disgusting humans have more important things to do--like failing algebra and aging poorly.
I-I've traveled all across the galaxy and I have yet to find beings with better math skills than Custard Creek!
So grab a calculator and start typing--
Because your days are numbered!
FWIP!
SLAM!
Oh, you think you're clever, huh?
All right, Sosh! Ready for your finisher?
Yeah! I think so!

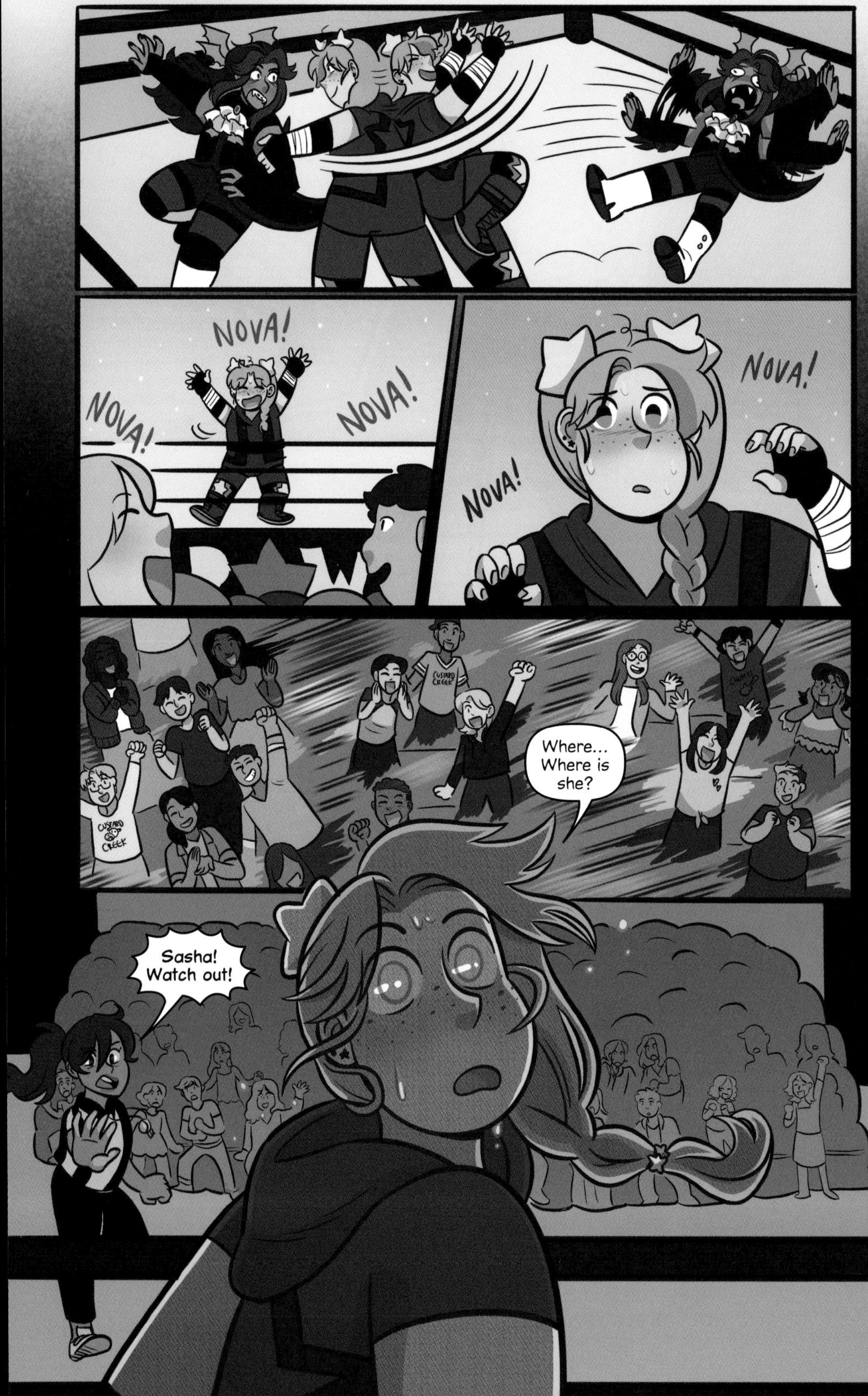
NOVA!
NOVA!
NOVA!
NOVA!
NOVA!
Where... Where is she?
Sasha! Watch out!

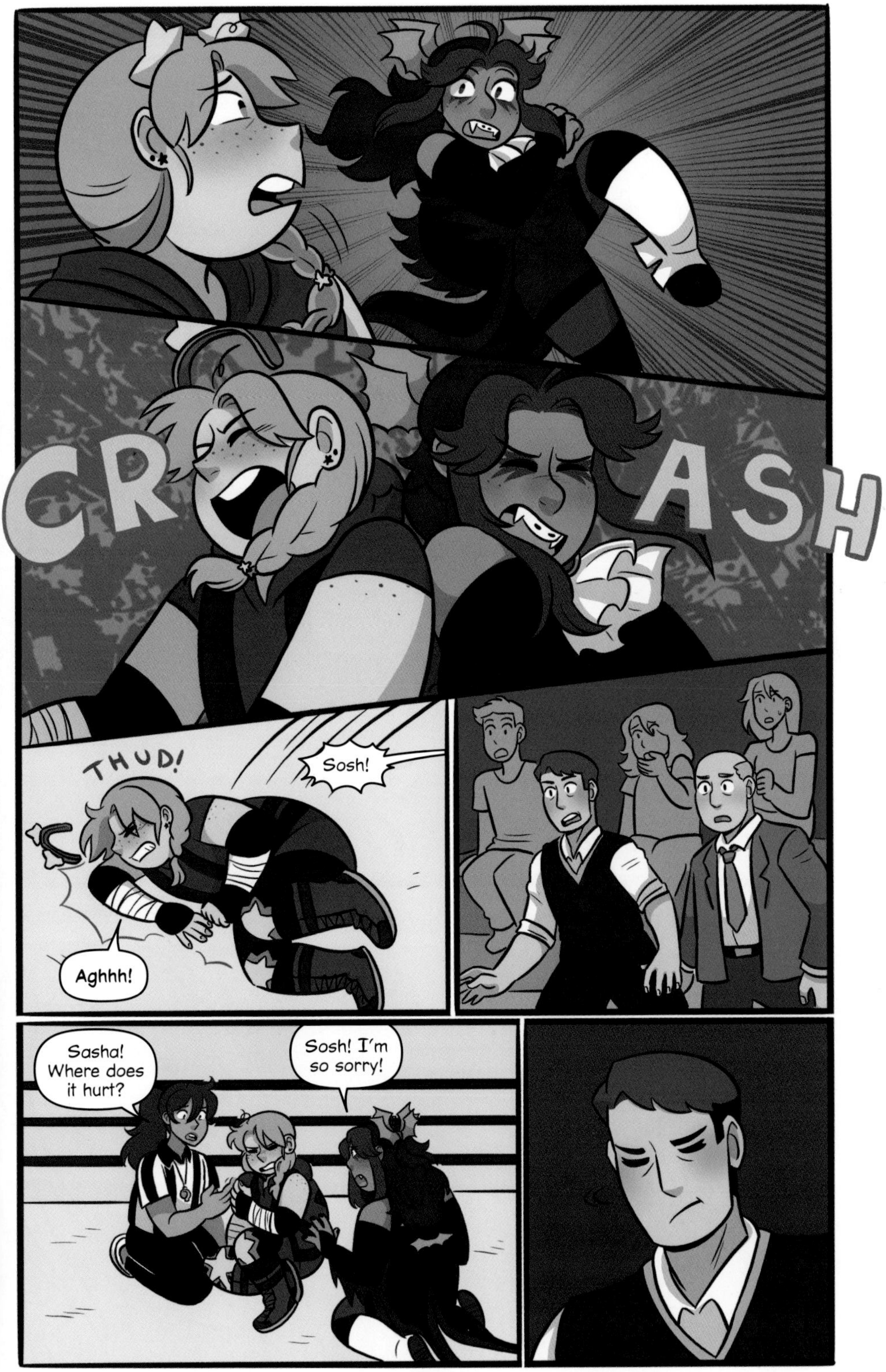
CR
ASH
THUD!
Sosh!
Aghhh!
Sasha! Where does it hurt?
Sosh! I'm so sorry!

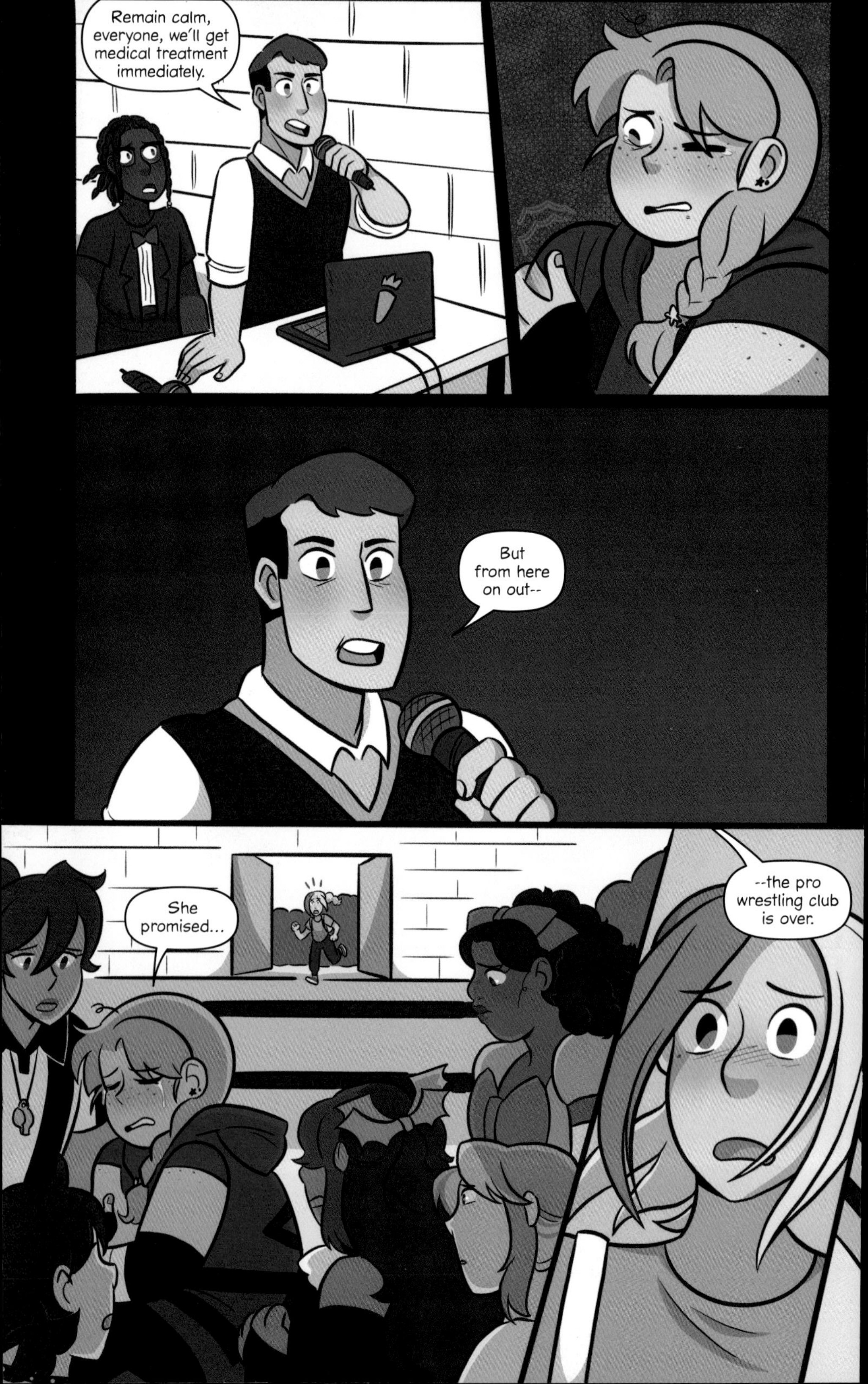
Remain calm, everyone, we'll get medical treatment immediately.
But from here on out--
She promised...
--the pro wrestling club is over.

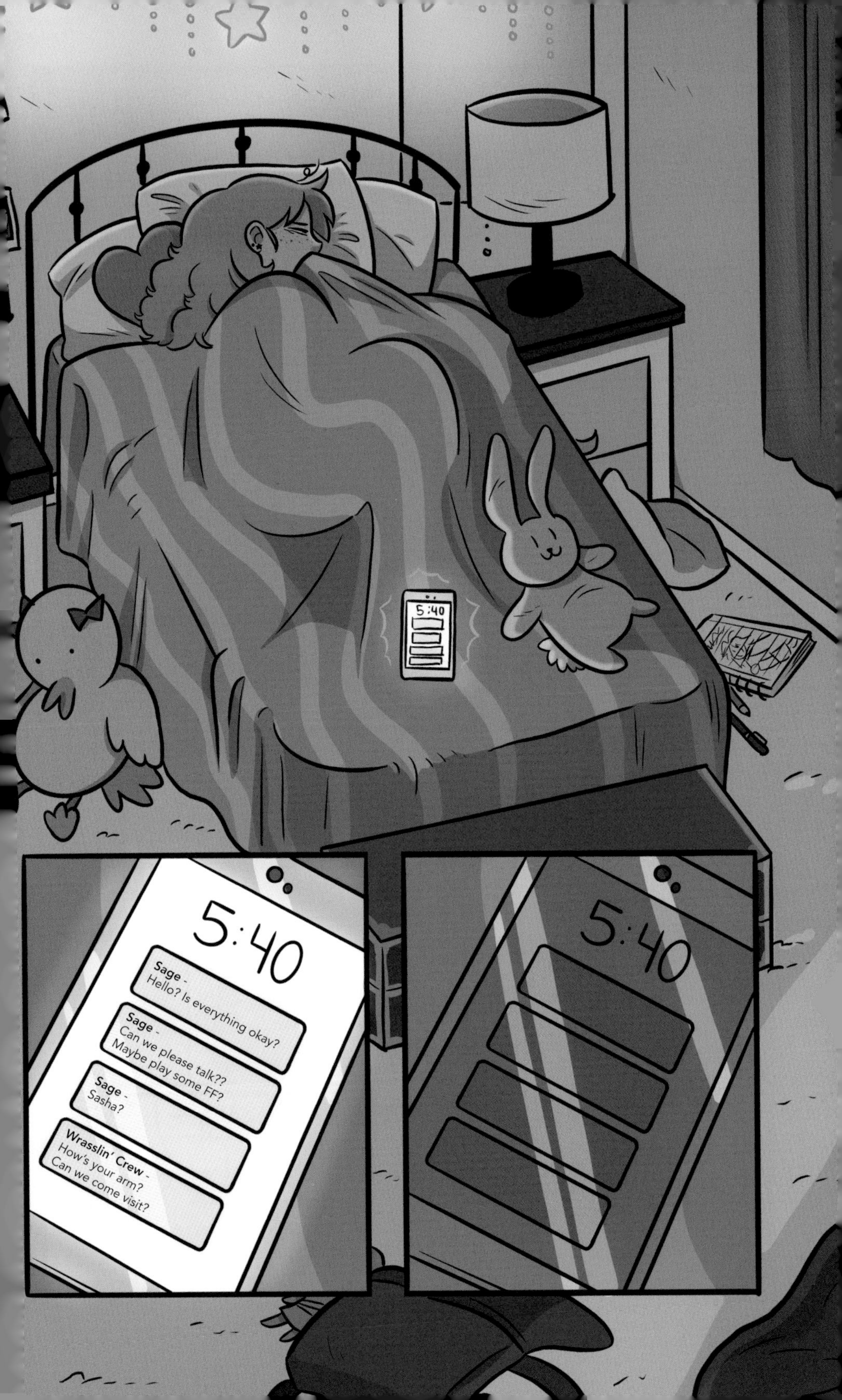

5:40
5:40
Sage -
Hello? Is everything okay?
Sage -
Can we please talk??
Maybe play some FF?
Sage -
Sasha?
Wrasslin' Crew -
How's your arm?
Can we come visit?
5:40

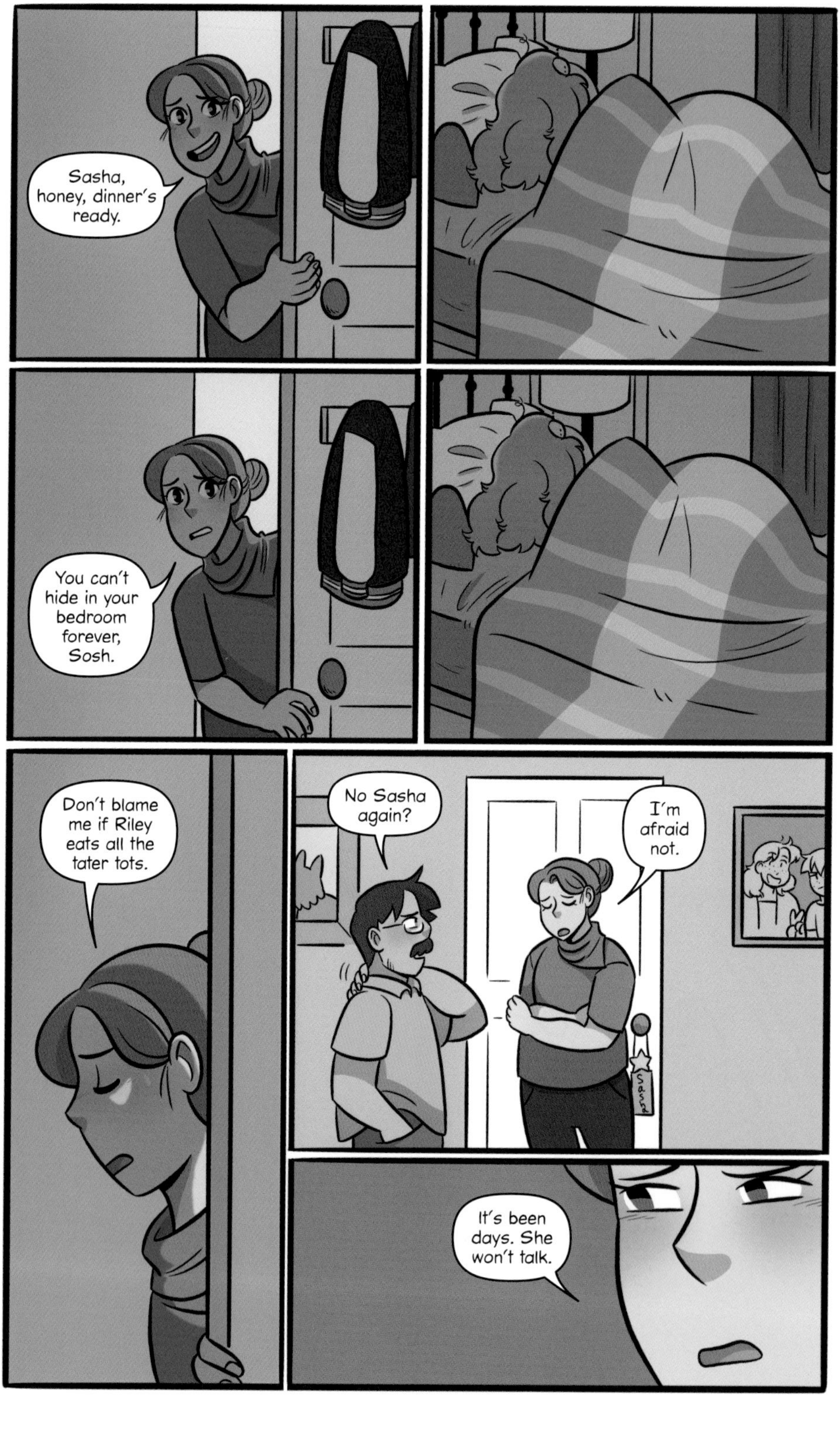
Sasha, honey, dinner's ready.
You can't hide in your bedroom forever, Sosh.
Don't blame me if Riley eats all the tater tots.
No Sasha again?
I'm afraid not.
It's been days. She won't talk.

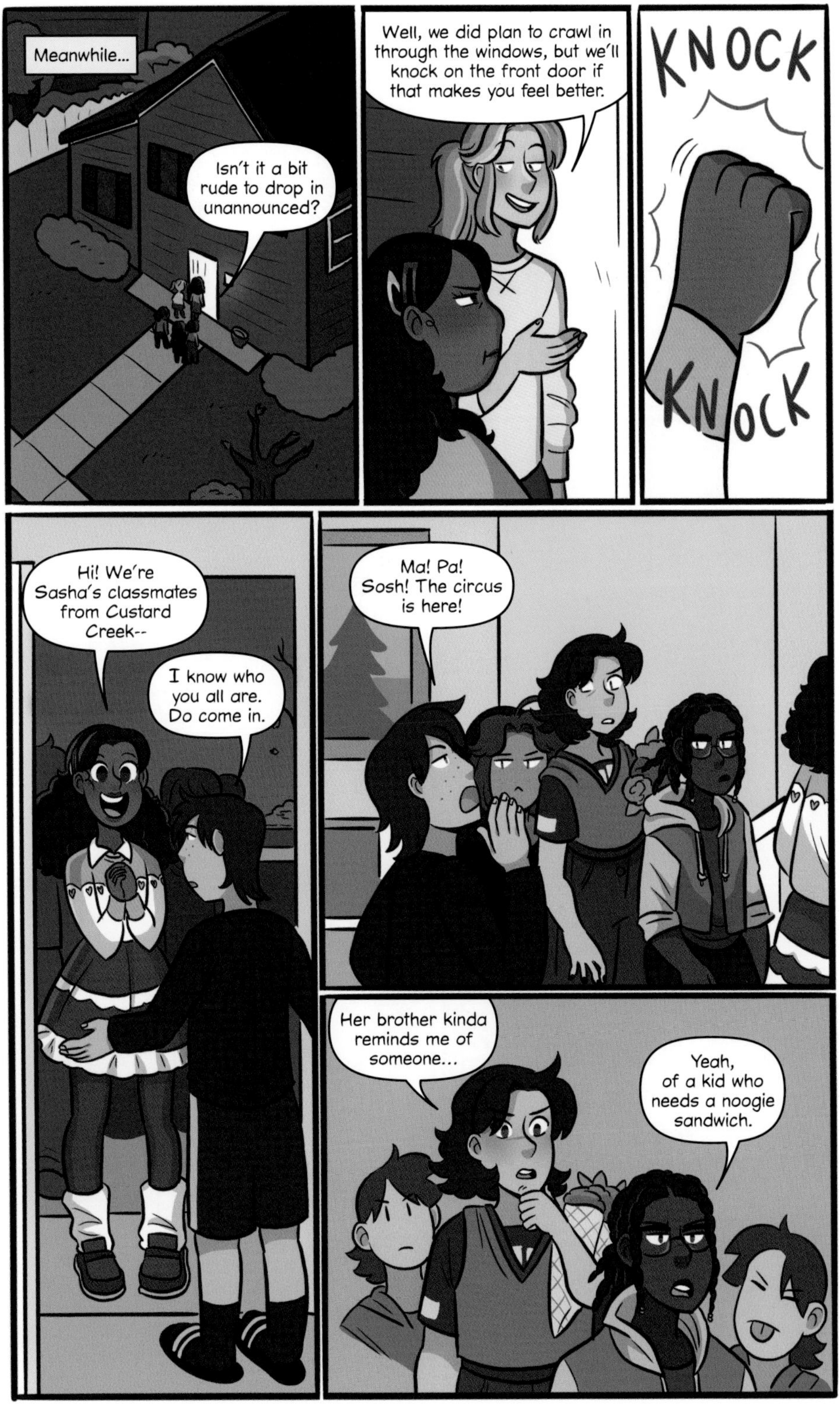
Meanwhile...
Isn't it a bit rude to drop in unannounced?
Well, we did plan to crawl in through the windows, but we'll knock on the front door if that makes you feel better.
KNOCK
KNOCK
Hi! We're Sasha's classmates from Custard Creek--
I know who you all are. Do come in.
Ma! Pa! Sosh! The circus is here!
Her brother kinda reminds me of someone...
Yeah, of a kid who needs a noogie sandwich.

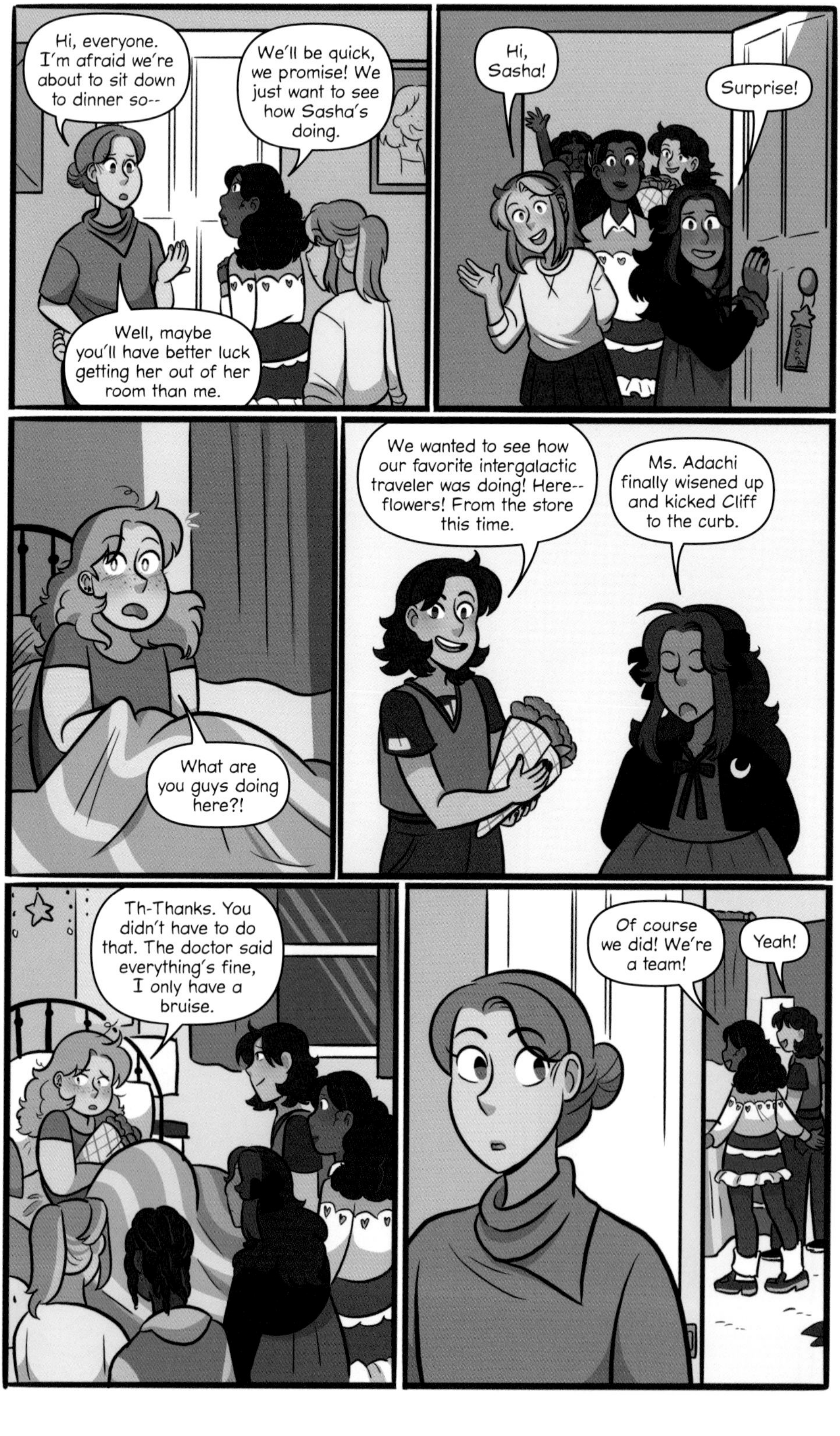
Hi, everyone. I'm afraid we're about to sit down to dinner so--
We'll be quick, we promise! We just want to see how Sasha's doing.
Well, maybe you'll have better luck getting her out of her room than me.
Hi, Sasha!
Surprise!
What are you guys doing here?!
We wanted to see how our favorite intergalactic traveler was doing! Here-- flowers! From the store this time.
Ms. Adachi finally wisened up and kicked Cliff to the curb.
Th-Thanks. You didn't have to do that. The doctor said everything's fine, I only have a bruise.
Of course we did! We're a team!
Yeah!

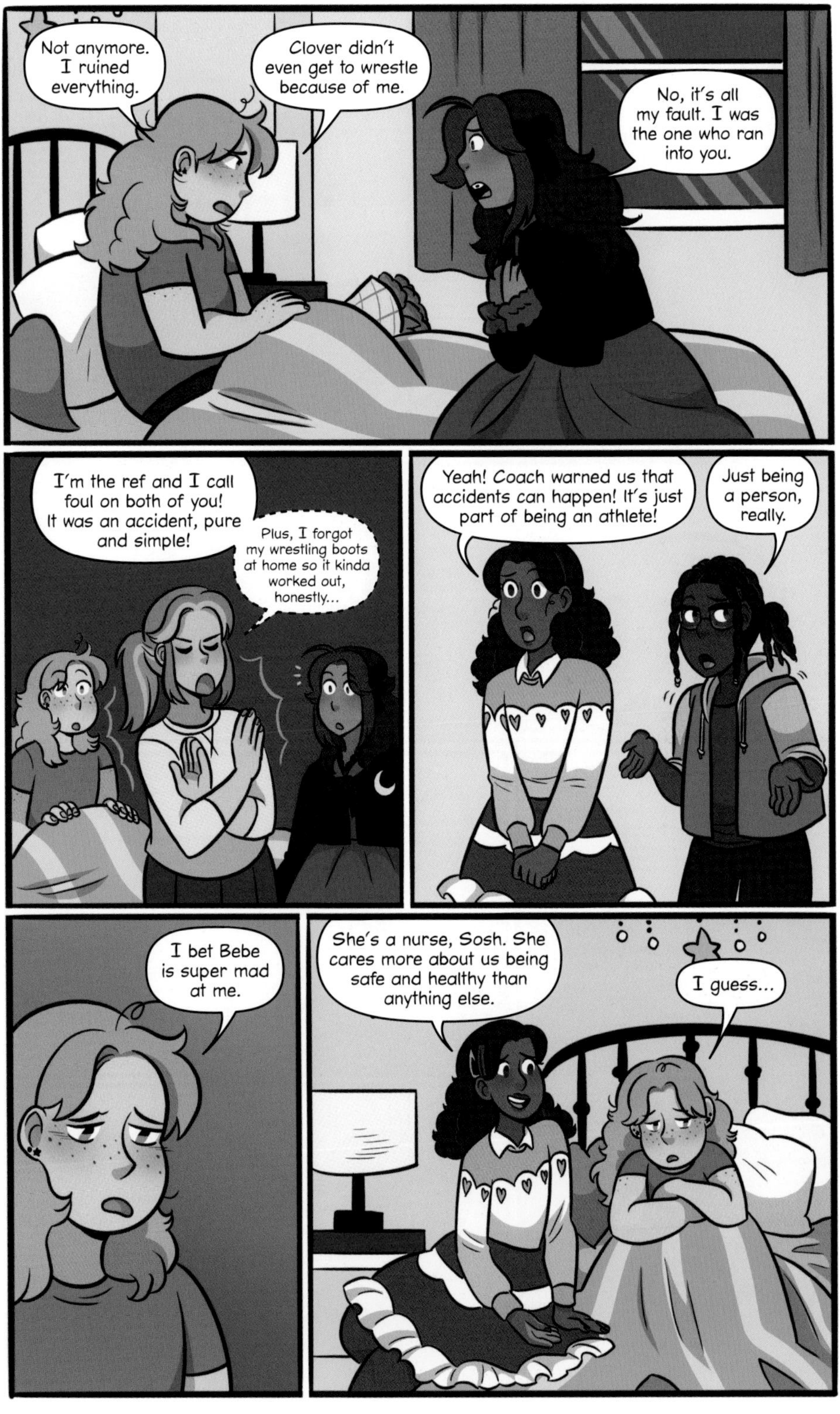

Not anymore. I ruined everything.
Clover didn't even get to wrestle because of me.
No, it's all my fault. I was the one who ran into you.
I'm the ref and I call foul on both of you! It was an accident, pure and simple!
Plus, I forgot my wrestling boots at home so it kinda worked out, honestly...
Yeah! Coach warned us that accidents can happen! It's just part of being an athlete!
Just being a person, really.
I bet Bebe is super mad at me.
She's a nurse, Sosh. She cares more about us being safe and healthy than anything else.
I guess...

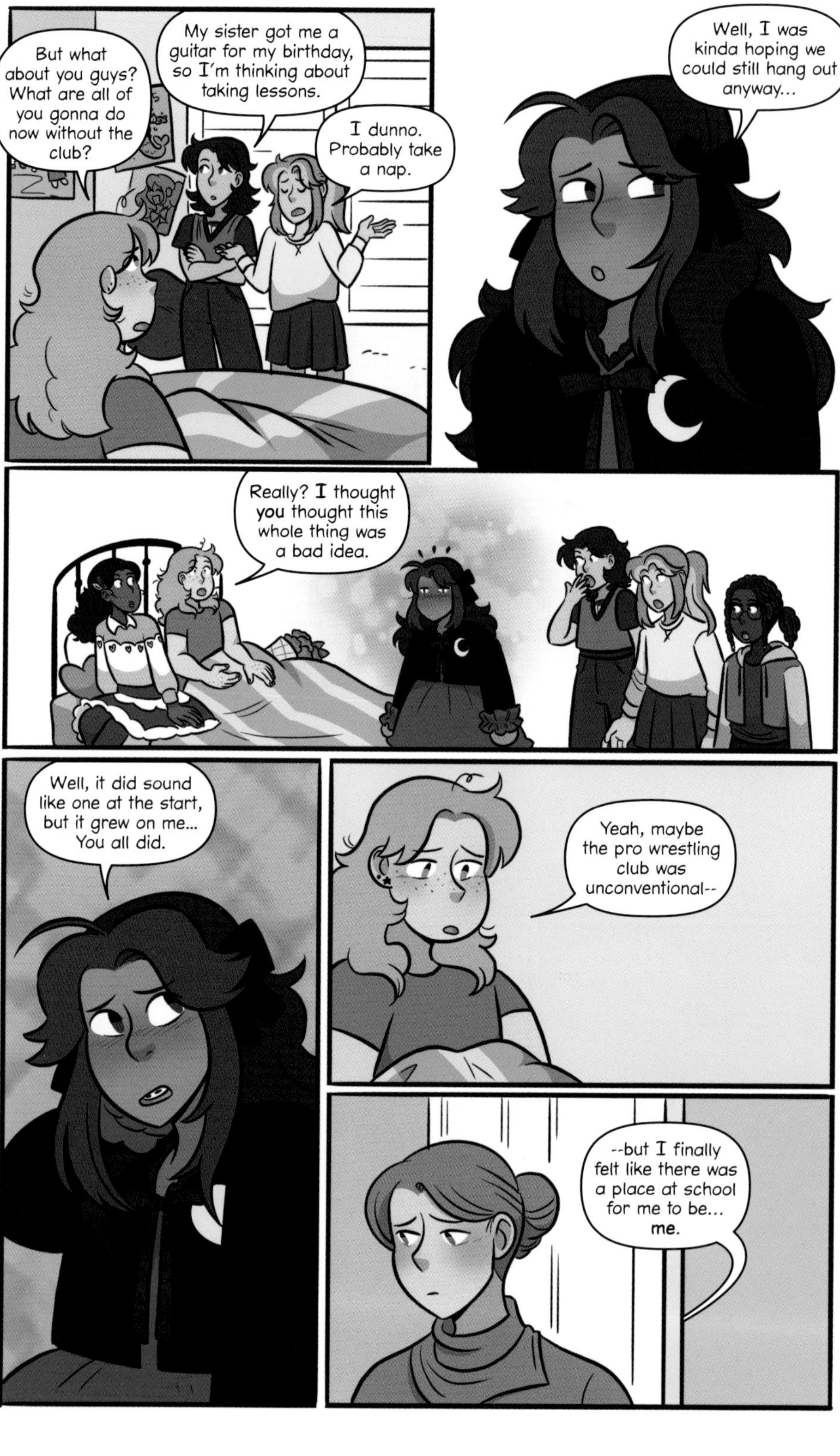
But what about you guys? What are all of you gonna do now without the club?
My sister got me a guitar for my birthday, so I'm thinking about taking lessons.
I dunno. Probably take a nap.
Well, I was kinda hoping we could still hang out anyway...
Really? I thought **you** thought this whole thing was a bad idea.
Well, it did sound like one at the start, but it grew on me... You all did.
Yeah, maybe the pro wrestling club was unconventional--
--but I finally felt like there was a place at school for me to be... **me**.

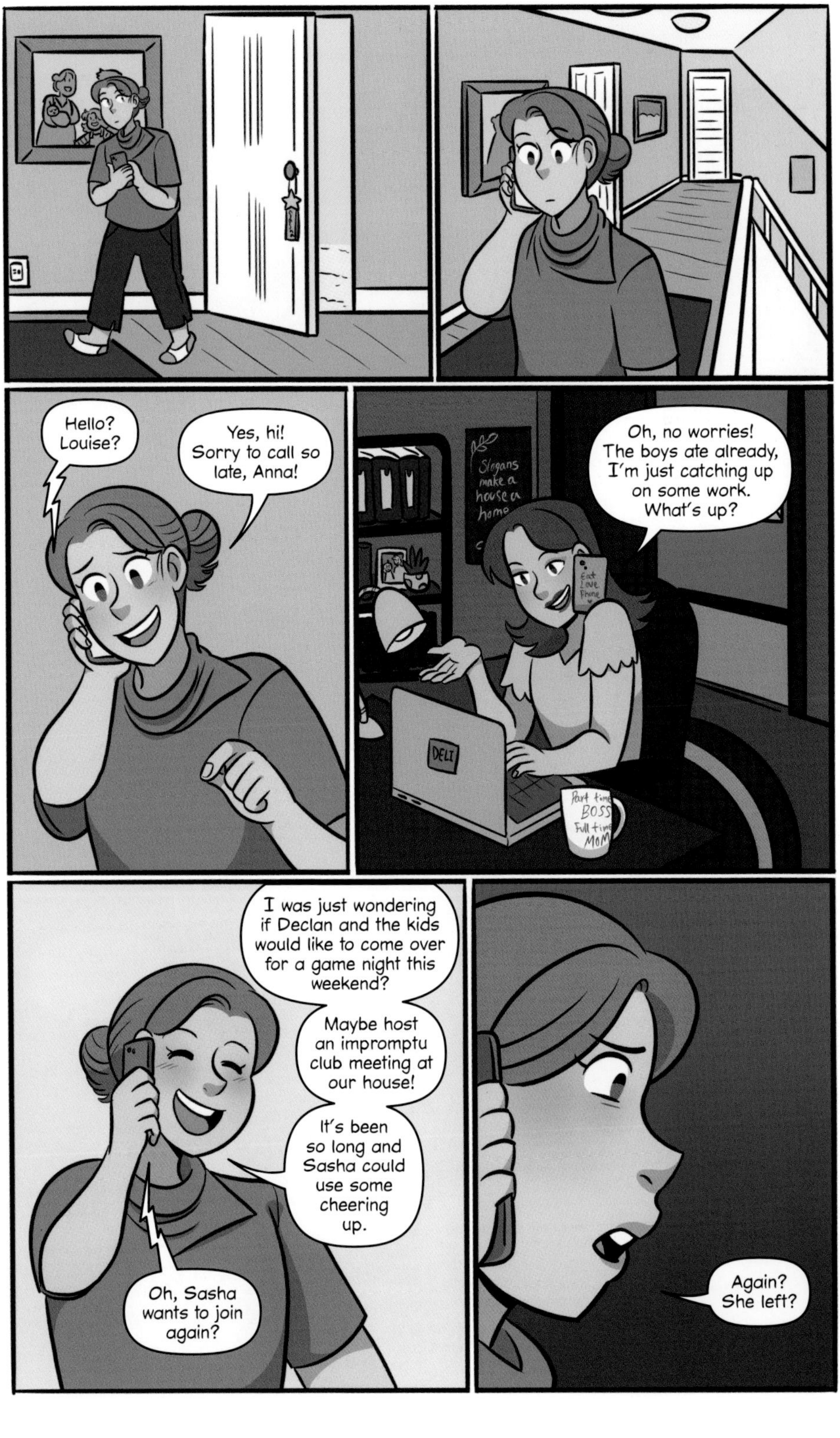
Hello? Louise?
Yes, hi! Sorry to call so late, Anna!
Slogans make a house a home
Oh, no worries! The boys ate already, I'm just catching up on some work. What's up?
DELI
Part time BOSS Full time MOM
I was just wondering if Declan and the kids would like to come over for a game night this weekend?
Maybe host an impromptu club meeting at our house!
It's been so long and Sasha could use some cheering up.
Oh, Sasha wants to join again?
Again? She left?

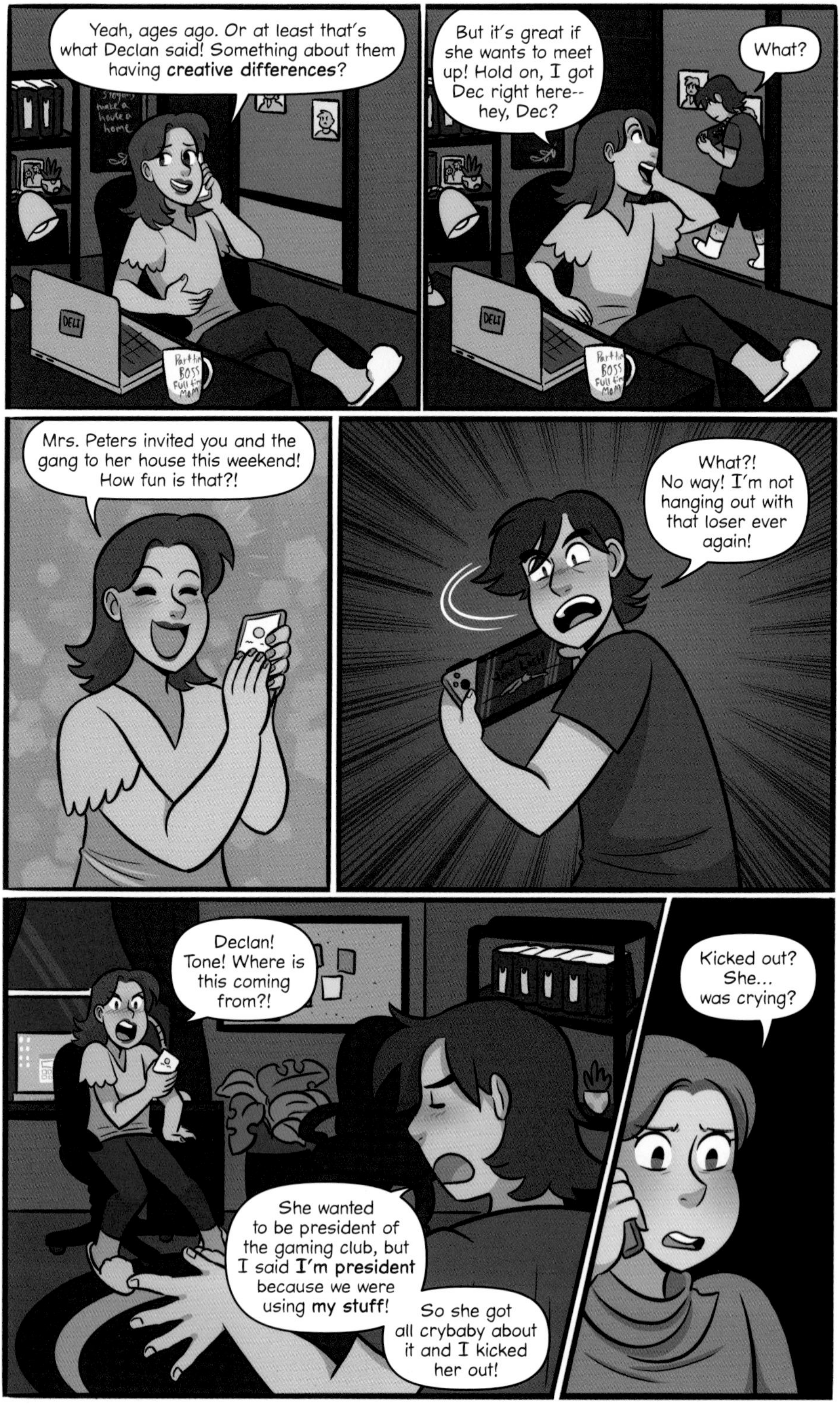
Yeah, ages ago. Or at least that's what Declan said! Something about them having **creative differences**?
But it's great if she wants to meet up! Hold on, I got Dec right here-- hey, Dec?
What?
Mrs. Peters invited you and the gang to her house this weekend! How fun is that?!
What?! No way! I'm not hanging out with that loser ever again!
Declan! Tone! Where is this coming from?!
She wanted to be president of the gaming club, but I said **I'm president** because we were using **my stuff**!
So she got all crybaby about it and I kicked her out!
Kicked out? She... was crying?

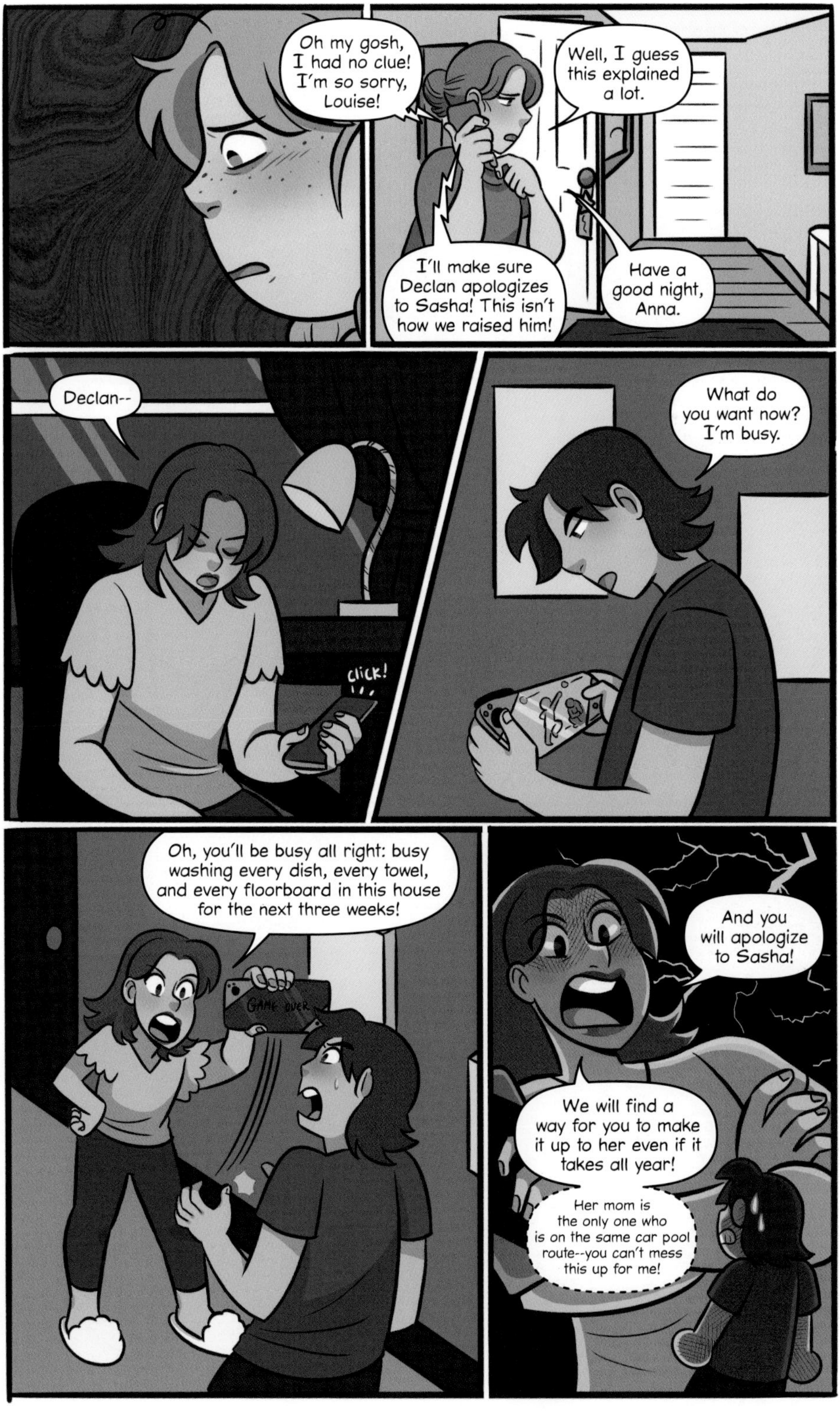
Oh my gosh, I had no clue! I'm so sorry, Louise!
Well, I guess this explained a lot.
I'll make sure Declan apologizes to Sasha! This isn't how we raised him!
Have a good night, Anna.
Declan--
CLICK!
What do you want now? I'm busy.
Oh, you'll be busy all right: busy washing every dish, every towel, and every floorboard in this house for the next three weeks!
GAME OVER
And you will apologize to Sasha!
We will find a way for you to make it up to her even if it takes all year!
Her mom is the only one who is on the same car pool route--you can't mess this up for me!

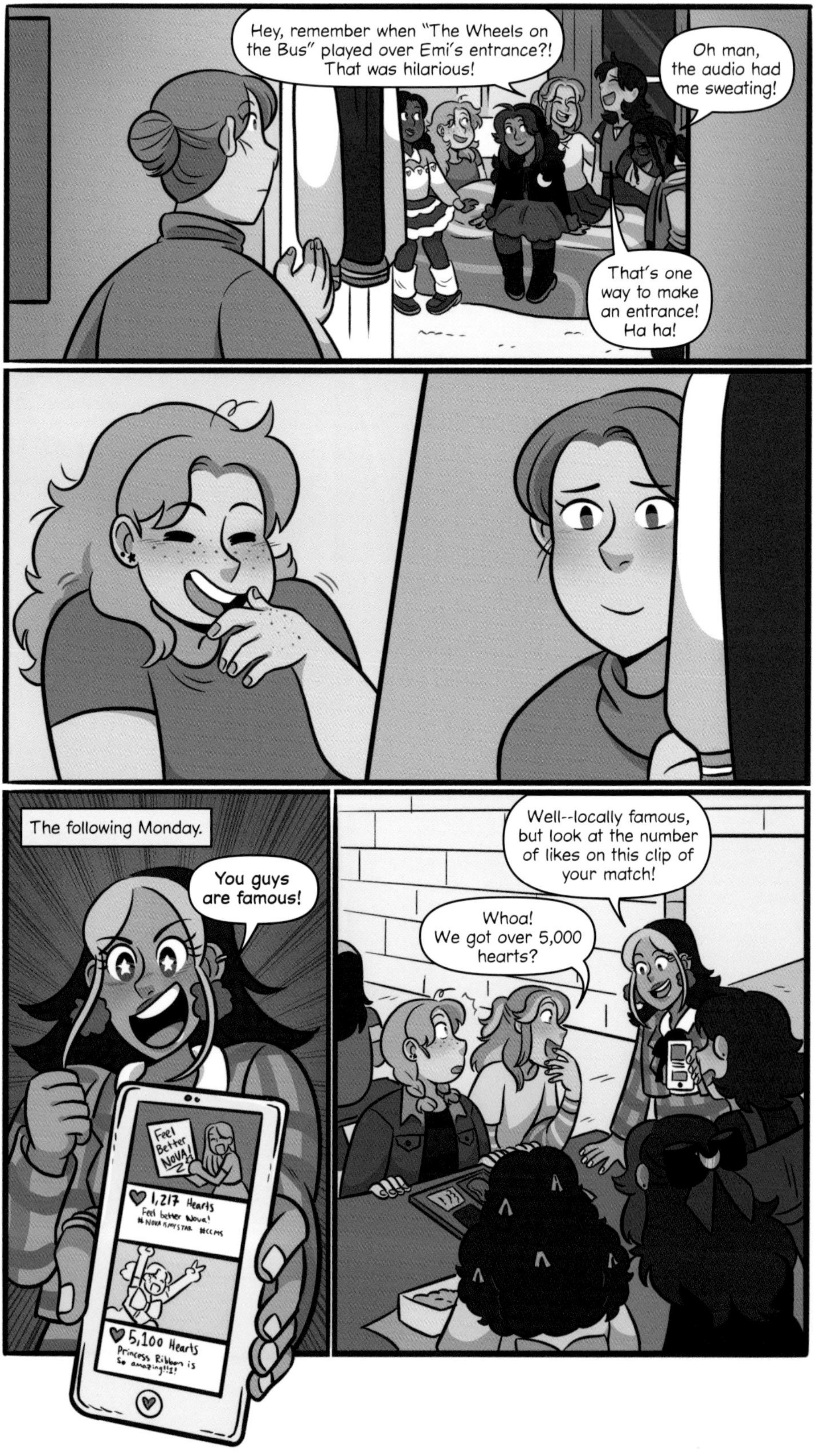

Hey, remember when "The Wheels on the Bus" played over Emi's entrance?! That was hilarious!
Oh man, the audio had me sweating!
That's one way to make an entrance! Ha ha!
The following Monday.
You guys are famous!
Feel Better NOVA!
1,217 Hearts
Feel better Nova! #NOVAISMYSTAR #CCMS
5,100 Hearts
Princess Ribbon is so amazing!!!!
Well--locally famous, but look at the number of likes on this clip of your match!
Whoa! We got over 5,000 hearts?

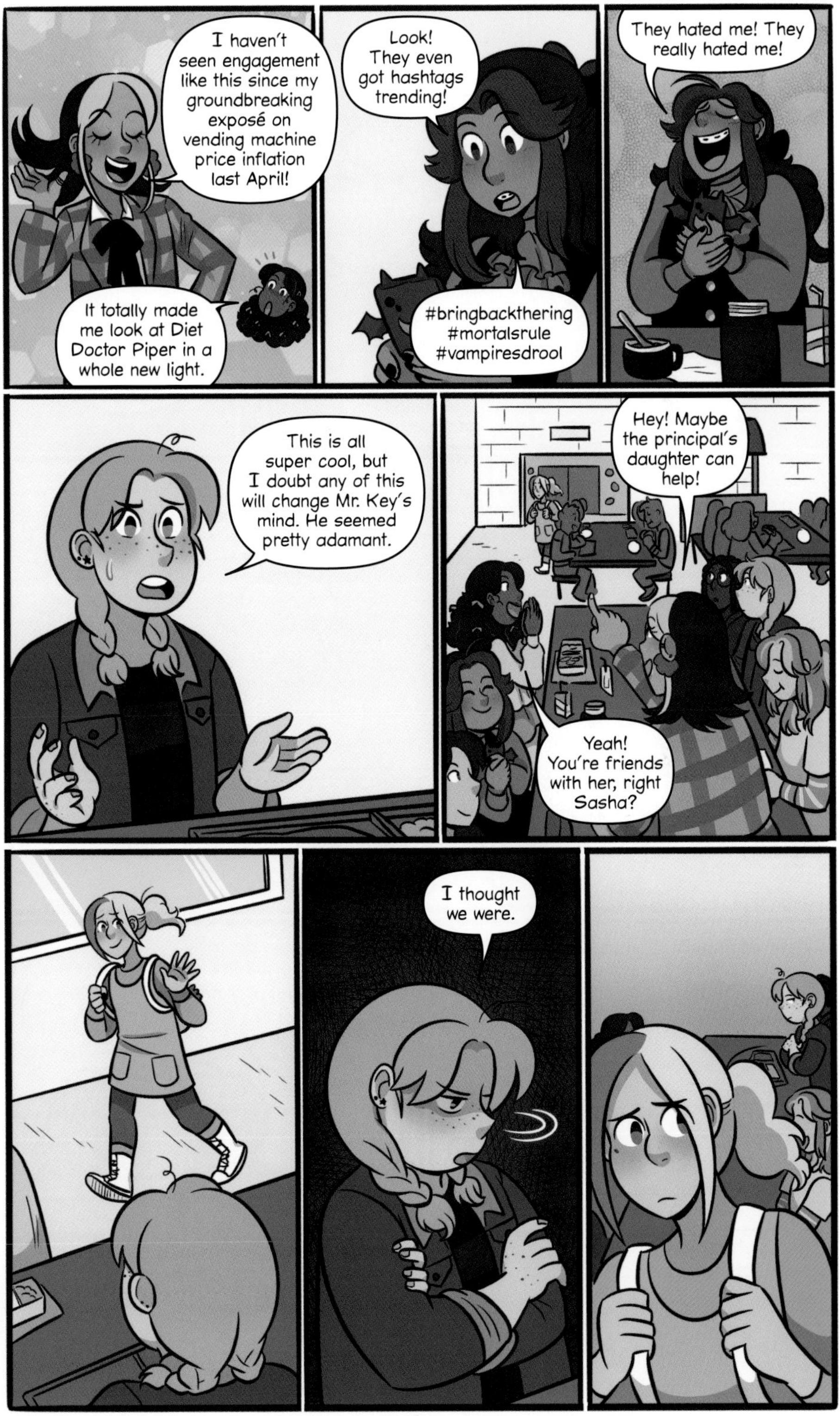

I haven't seen engagement like this since my groundbreaking exposé on vending machine price inflation last April!
It totally made me look at Diet Doctor Piper in a whole new light.
Look! They even got hashtags trending!
#bringbackthering
#mortalsrule
#vampiresdrool
They hated me! They really hated me!
This is all super cool, but I doubt any of this will change Mr. Key's mind. He seemed pretty adamant.
Hey! Maybe the principal's daughter can help!
Yeah! You're friends with her, right Sasha?
I thought we were.

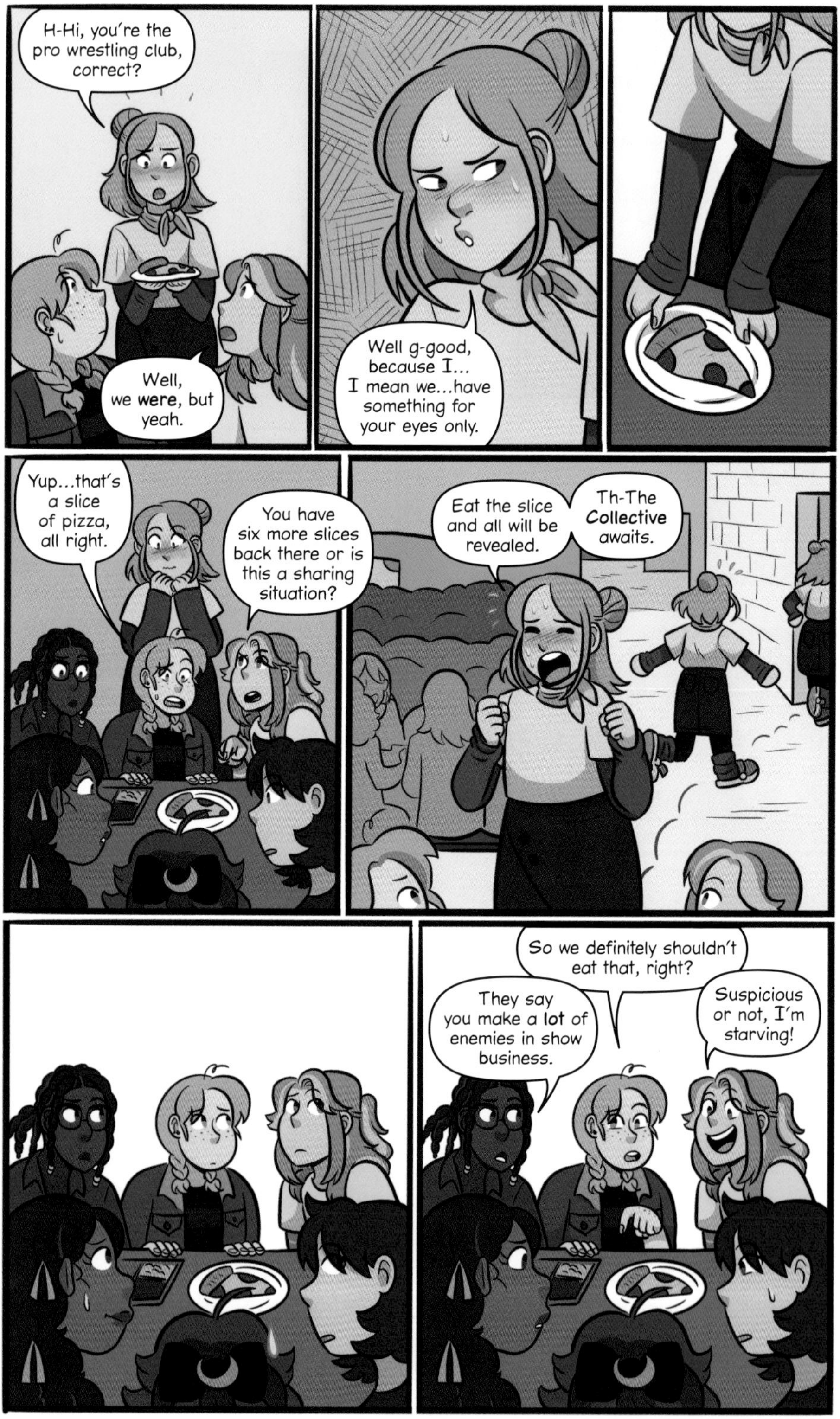
H-Hi, you're the pro wrestling club, correct?
Well, we **were**, but yeah.
Well g-good, because I... I mean we...have something for your eyes only.
Yup...that's a slice of pizza, all right.
You have six more slices back there or is this a sharing situation?
Eat the slice and all will be revealed.
Th-The **Collective** awaits.
So we definitely shouldn't eat that, right?
They say you make a **lot** of enemies in show business.
Suspicious or not, I'm starving!

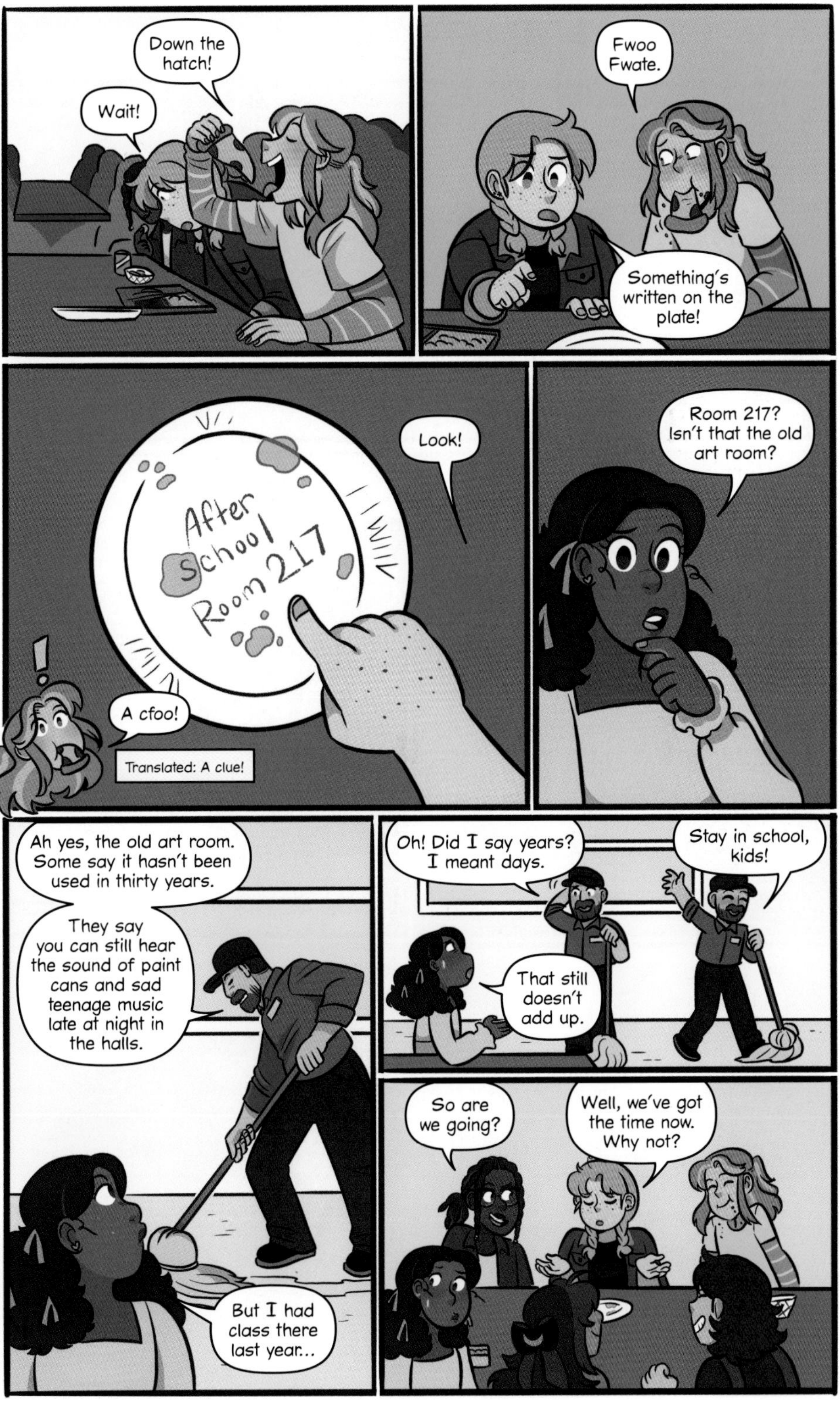
Down the hatch!
Wait!
Fwoo Fwate.
Something's written on the plate!
After School Room 217
Look!
A cfoo!
Translated: A clue!
Room 217? Isn't that the old art room?
Ah yes, the old art room. Some say it hasn't been used in thirty years.
They say you can still hear the sound of paint cans and sad teenage music late at night in the halls.
But I had class there last year...
Oh! Did I say years? I meant days.
Stay in school, kids!
That still doesn't add up.
So are we going?
Well, we've got the time now. Why not?

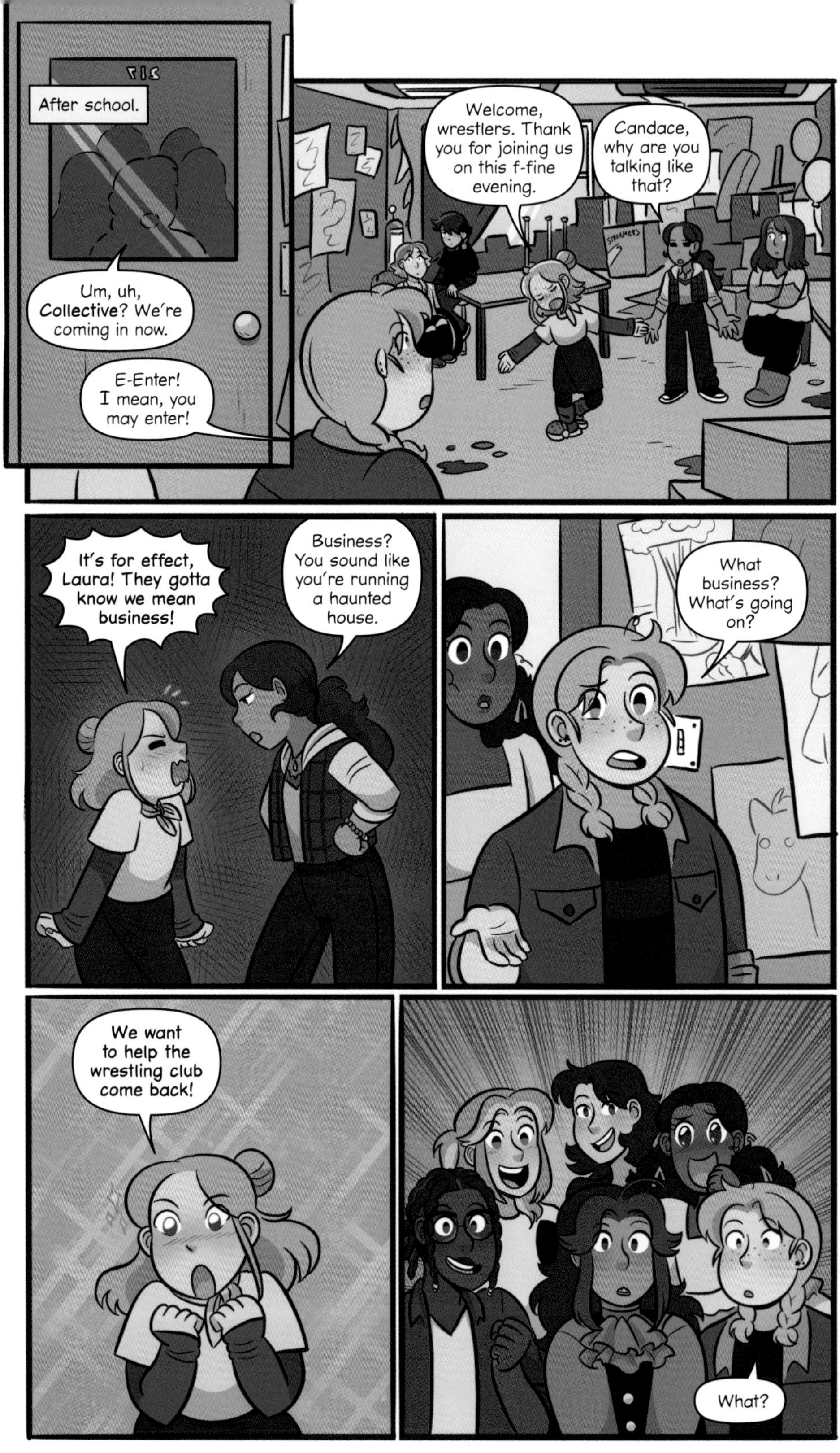
After school.
Um, uh, Collective? We're coming in now.
E-Enter! I mean, you may enter!
Welcome, wrestlers. Thank you for joining us on this f-fine evening.
Candace, why are you talking like that?
It's for effect, Laura! They gotta know we mean business!
Business? You sound like you're running a haunted house.
What business? What's going on?
We want to help the wrestling club come back!
What?

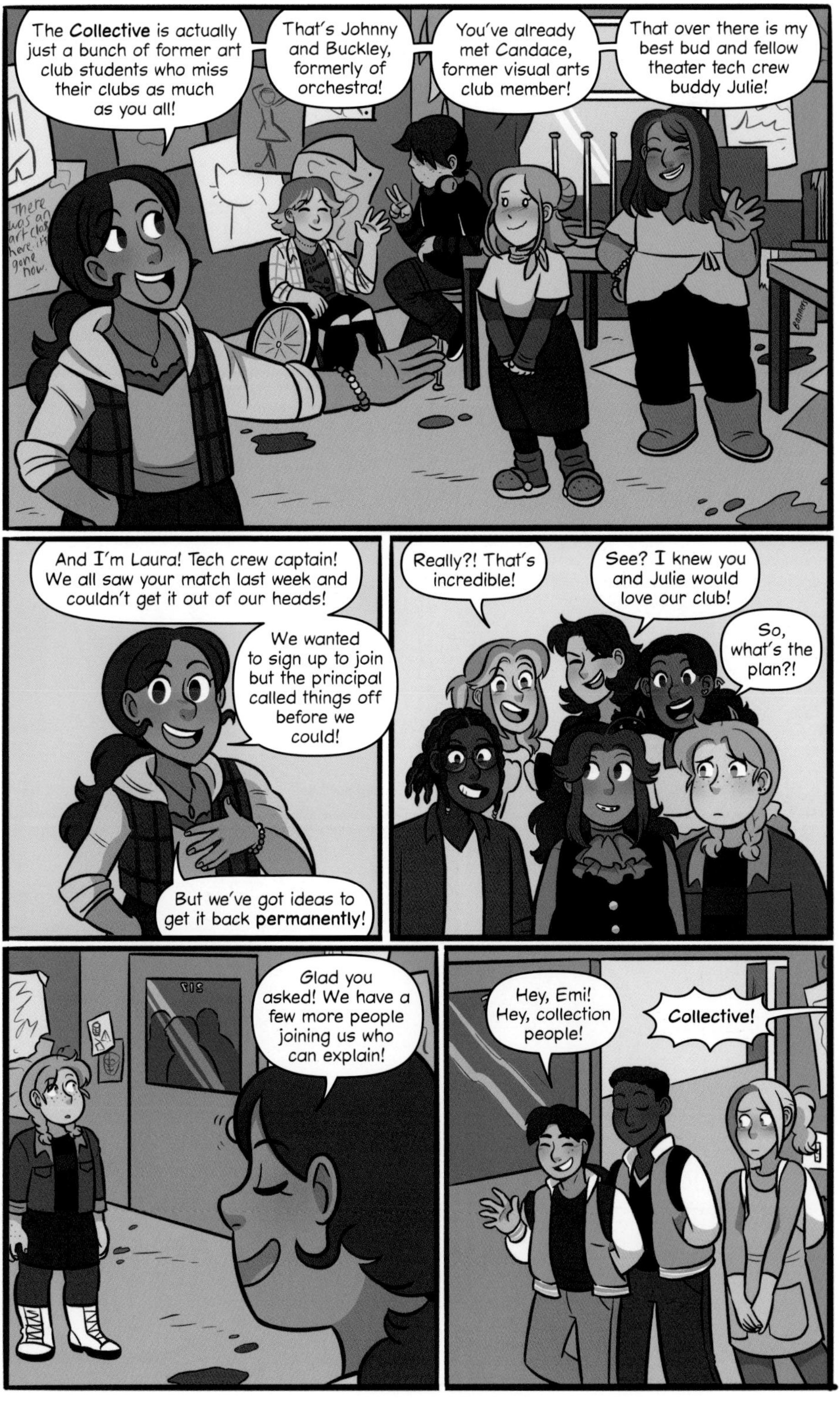

The **Collective** is actually just a bunch of former art club students who miss their clubs as much as you all!
That's Johnny and Buckley, formerly of orchestra!
You've already met Candace, former visual arts club member!
That over there is my best bud and fellow theater tech crew buddy Julie!
There was an art club here. It's gone now.
And I'm Laura! Tech crew captain! We all saw your match last week and couldn't get it out of our heads!
We wanted to sign up to join but the principal called things off before we could!
But we've got ideas to get it back **permanently**!
Really?! That's incredible!
See? I knew you and Julie would love our club!
So, what's the plan?!
Glad you asked! We have a few more people joining us who can explain!
Hey, Emi! Hey, collection people!
Collective!

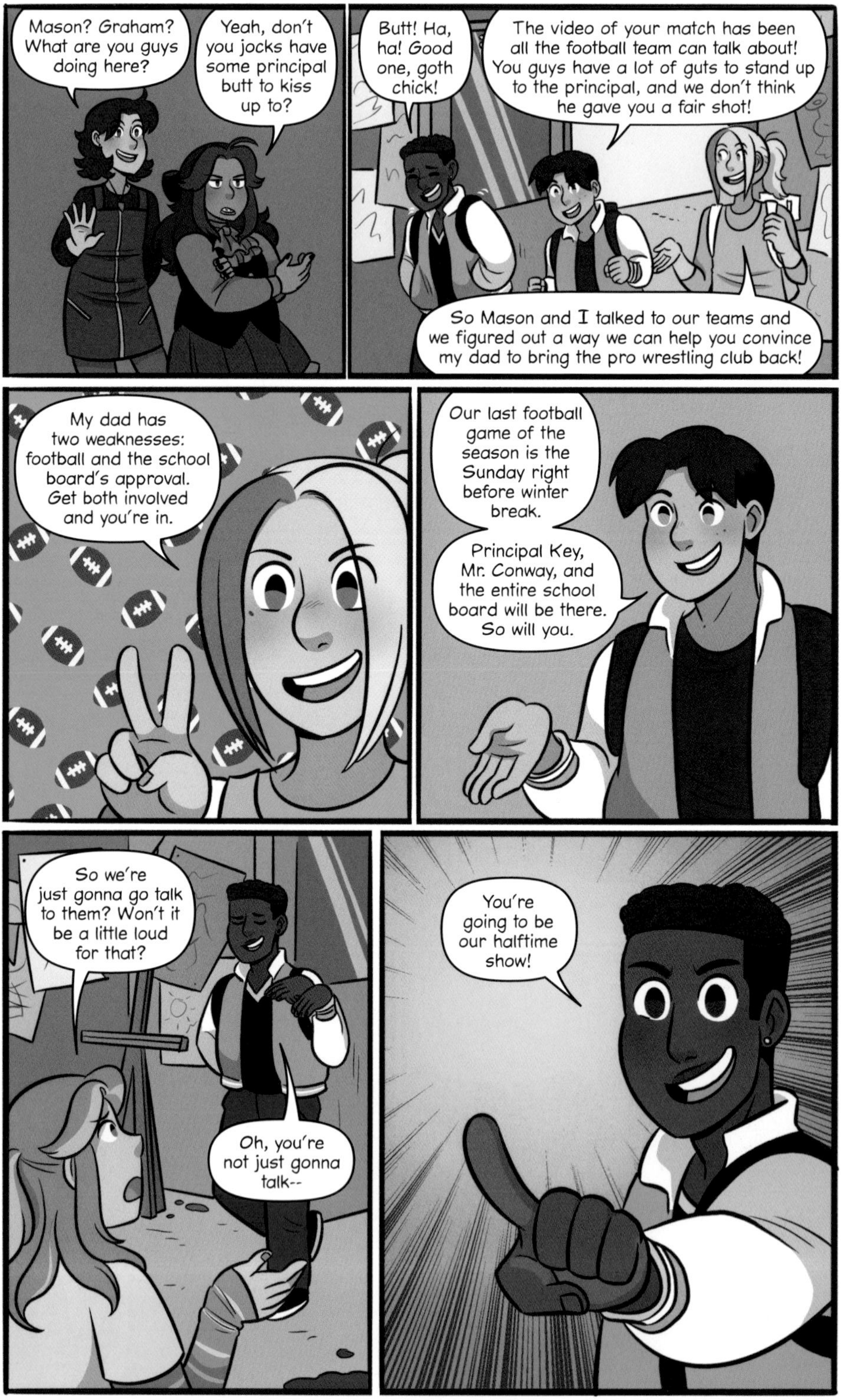
Mason? Graham? What are you guys doing here?
Yeah, don't you jocks have some principal butt to kiss up to?
Butt! Ha, ha! Good one, goth chick!
The video of your match has been all the football team can talk about! You guys have a lot of guts to stand up to the principal, and we don't think he gave you a fair shot!
So Mason and I talked to our teams and we figured out a way we can help you convince my dad to bring the pro wrestling club back!
My dad has two weaknesses: football and the school board's approval. Get both involved and you're in.
Our last football game of the season is the Sunday right before winter break.
Principal Key, Mr. Conway, and the entire school board will be there. So will you.
So we're just gonna go talk to them? Won't it be a little loud for that?
Oh, you're not just gonna talk--
You're going to be our halftime show!

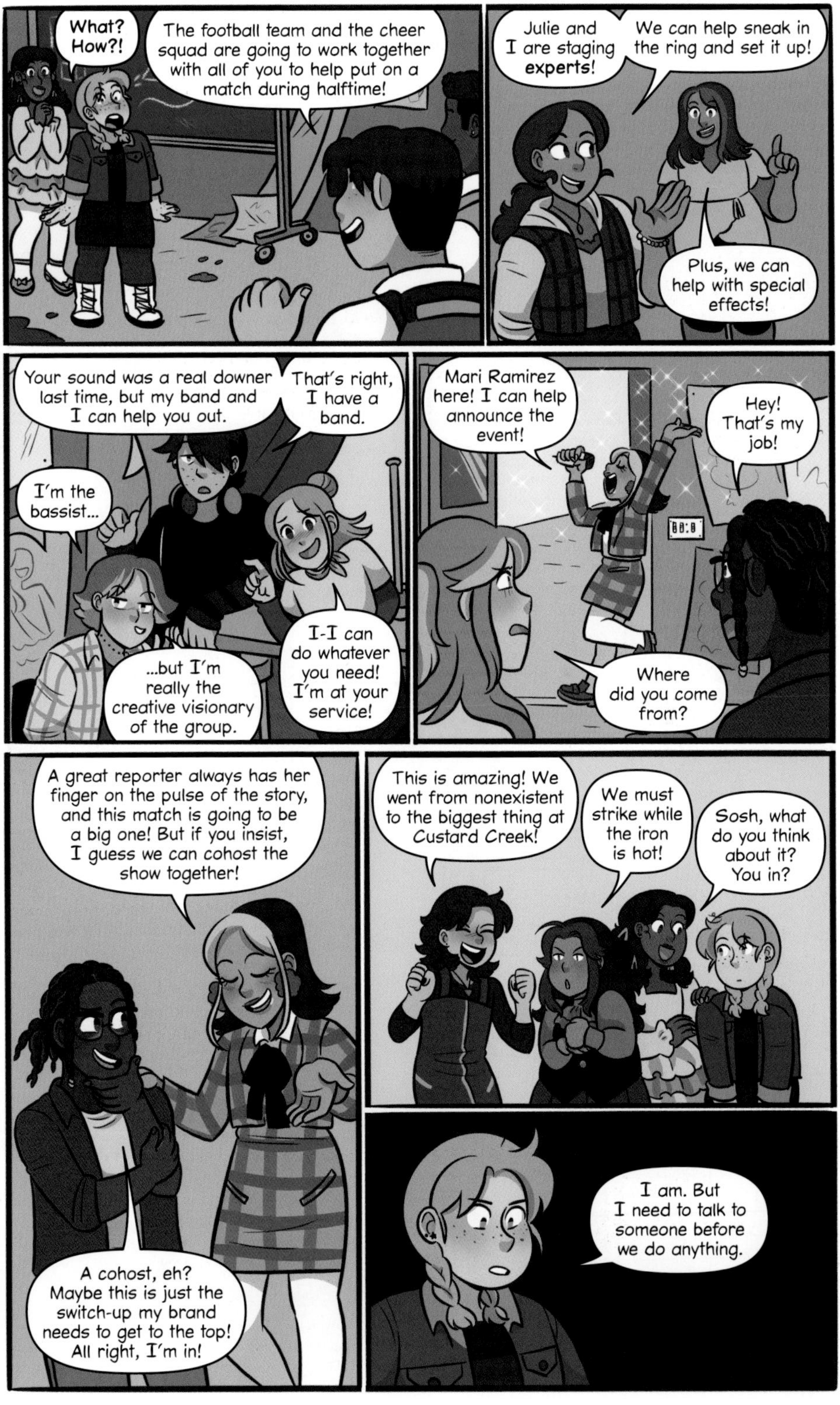
What? How?!
The football team and the cheer squad are going to work together with all of you to help put on a match during halftime!
Julie and I are staging **experts**!
We can help sneak in the ring and set it up!
Plus, we can help with special effects!
Your sound was a real downer last time, but my band and I can help you out.
That's right, I have a band.
I'm the bassist...
...but I'm really the creative visionary of the group.
I-I can do whatever you need! I'm at your service!
Mari Ramirez here! I can help announce the event!
Hey! That's my job!
Where did you come from?
A great reporter always has her finger on the pulse of the story, and this match is going to be a big one! But if you insist, I guess we can cohost the show together!
A cohost, eh? Maybe this is just the switch-up my brand needs to get to the top! All right, I'm in!
This is amazing! We went from nonexistent to the biggest thing at Custard Creek!
We must strike while the iron is hot!
Sosh, what do you think about it? You in?
I am. But I need to talk to someone before we do anything.

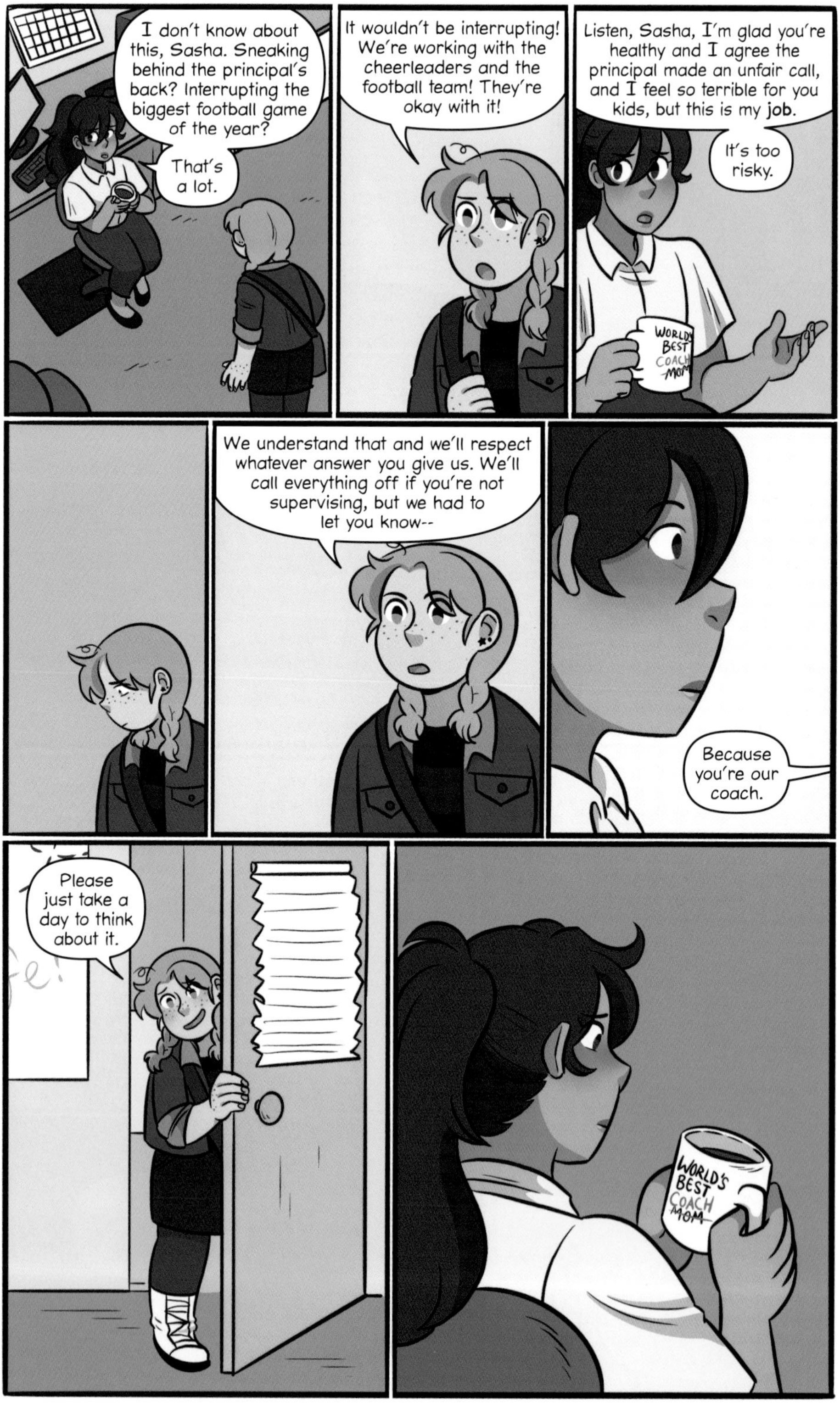
I don't know about this, Sasha. Sneaking behind the principal's back? Interrupting the biggest football game of the year?
That's a lot.
It wouldn't be interrupting! We're working with the cheerleaders and the football team! They're okay with it!
Listen, Sasha, I'm glad you're healthy and I agree the principal made an unfair call, and I feel so terrible for you kids, but this is my **job**.
It's too risky.
WORLD'S BEST COACH MOM
We understand that and we'll respect whatever answer you give us. We'll call everything off if you're not supervising, but we had to let you know--
Because you're our coach.
Please just take a day to think about it.
WORLD'S BEST COACH MOM

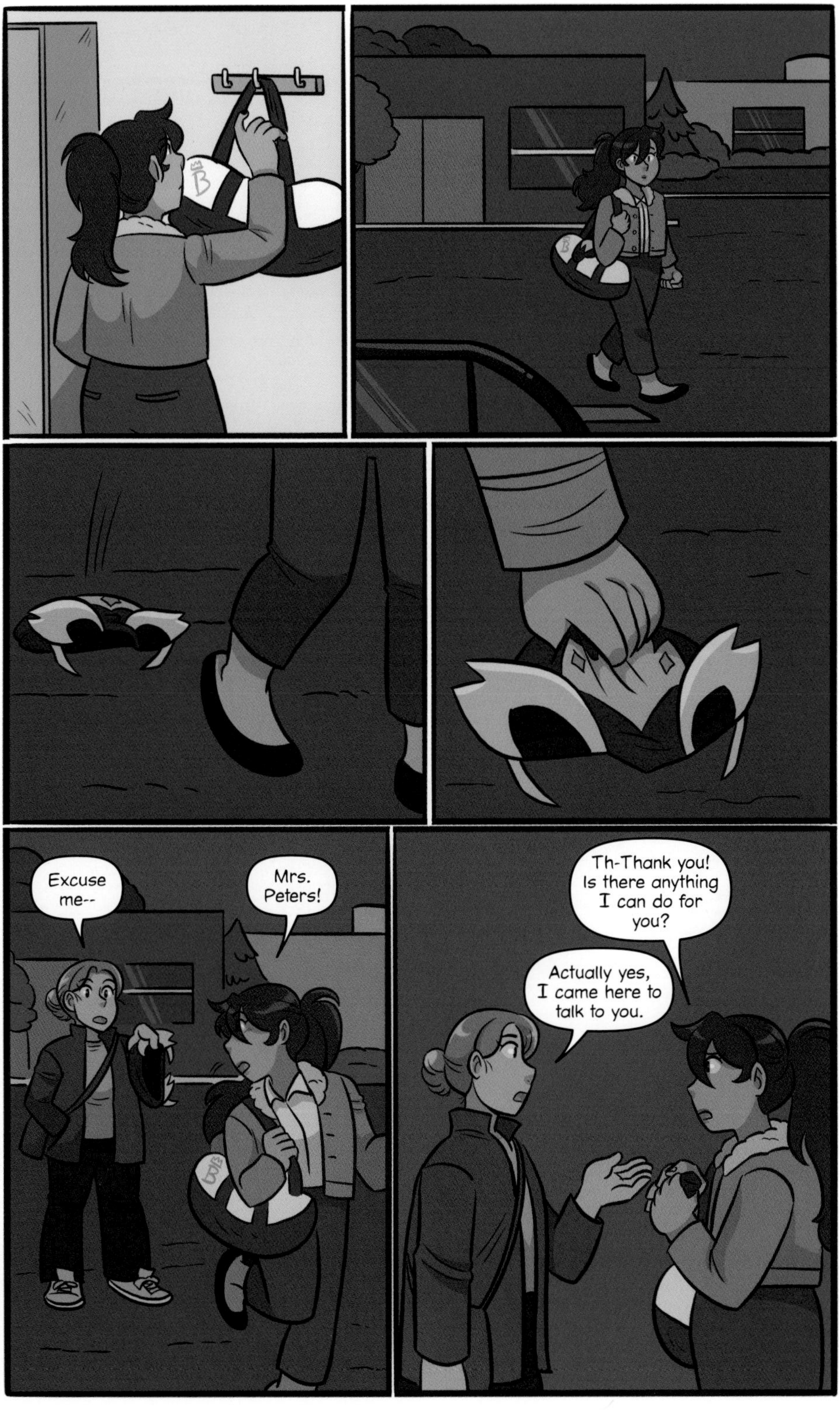
Excuse me--
Mrs. Peters!
Th-Thank you! Is there anything I can do for you?
Actually yes, I came here to talk to you.

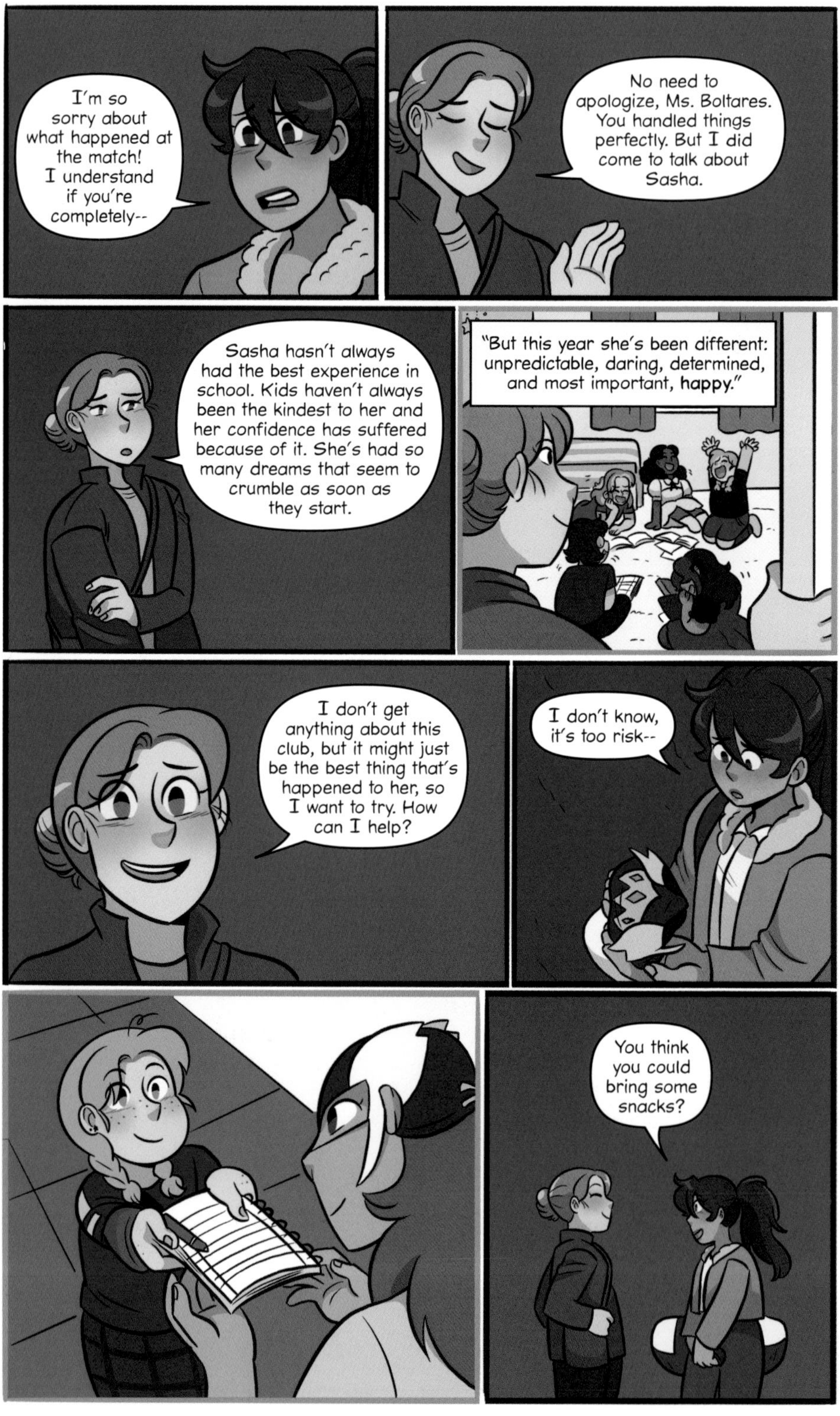
I'm so sorry about what happened at the match! I understand if you're completely--
No need to apologize, Ms. Boltares. You handled things perfectly. But I did come to talk about Sasha.
Sasha hasn't always had the best experience in school. Kids haven't always been the kindest to her and her confidence has suffered because of it. She's had so many dreams that seem to crumble as soon as they start.
"But this year she's been different: unpredictable, daring, determined, and most important, **happy**."
I don't get anything about this club, but it might just be the best thing that's happened to her, so I want to try. How can I help?
I don't know, it's too risk--
You think you could bring some snacks?

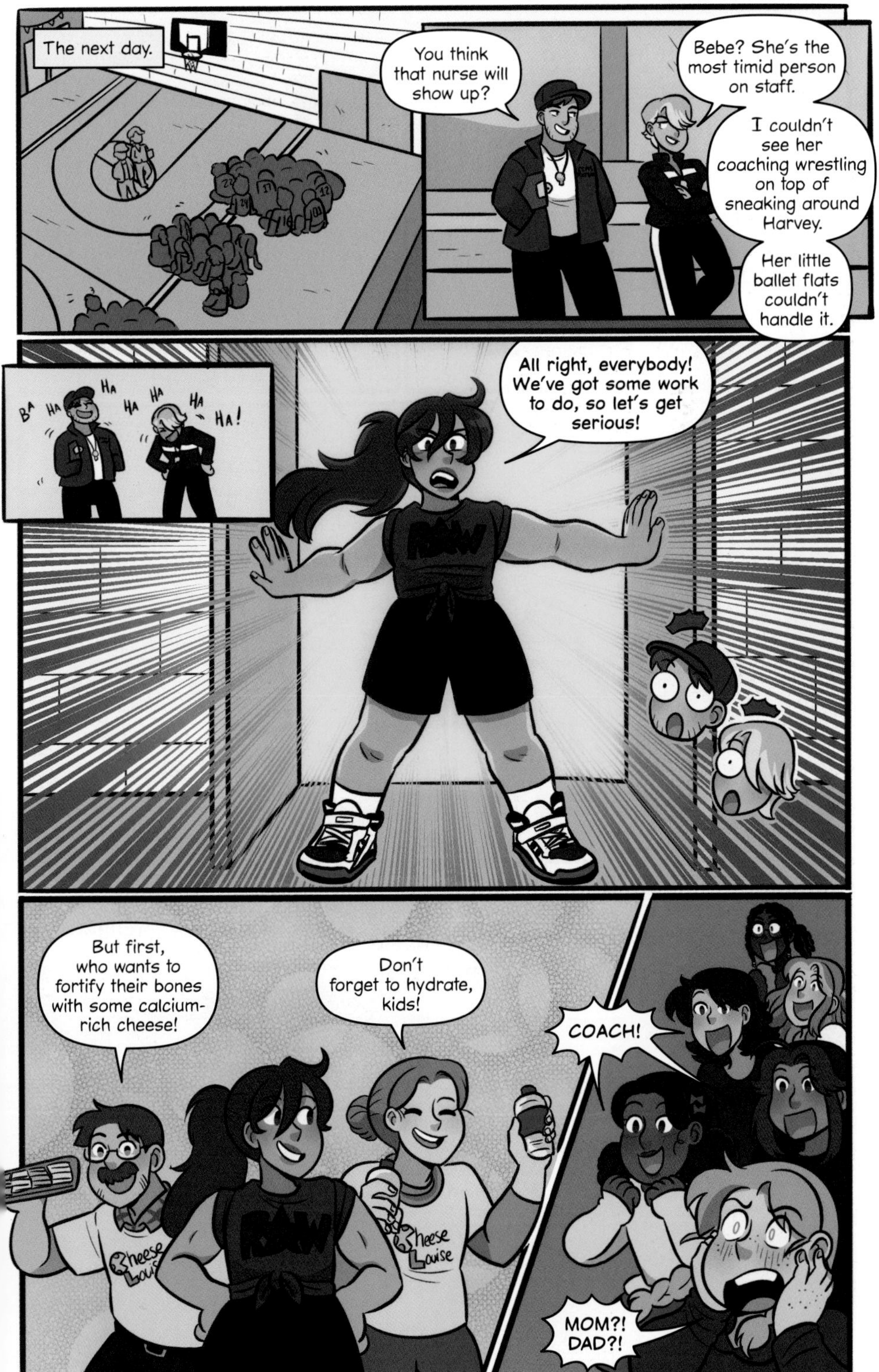
The next day.
You think that nurse will show up?
Bebe? She's the most timid person on staff.
I couldn't see her coaching wrestling on top of sneaking around Harvey.
Her little ballet flats couldn't handle it.
BA HA HA HA HA HA HA!
All right, everybody! We've got some work to do, so let's get serious!
But first, who wants to fortify their bones with some calcium-rich cheese!
Don't forget to hydrate, kids!
COACH!
MOM?! DAD?!

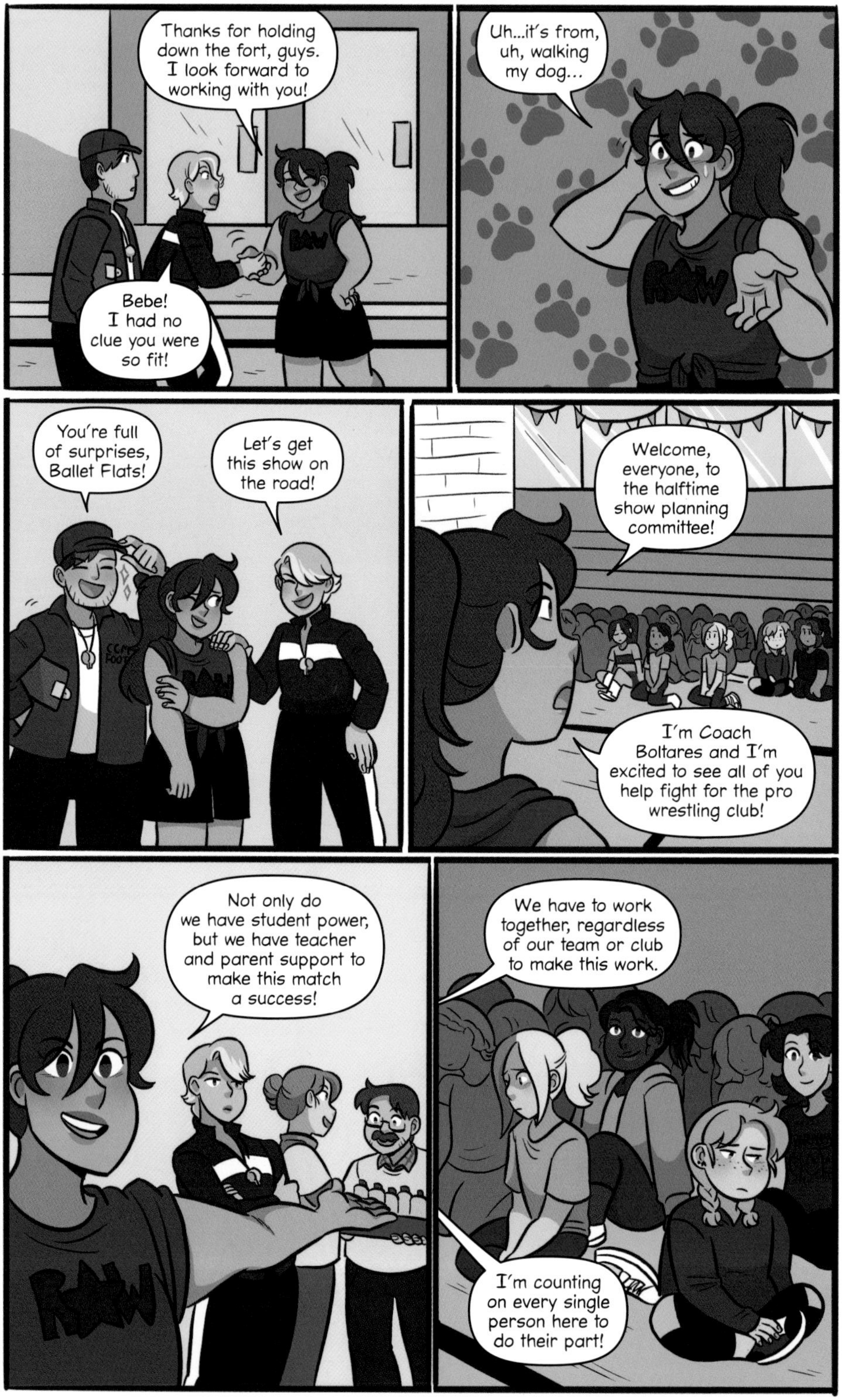
Thanks for holding down the fort, guys. I look forward to working with you!
Bebe! I had no clue you were so fit!
Uh...it's from, uh, walking my dog...
You're full of surprises, Ballet Flats!
Let's get this show on the road!
Welcome, everyone, to the halftime show planning committee!
I'm Coach Boltares and I'm excited to see all of you help fight for the pro wrestling club!
Not only do we have student power, but we have teacher and parent support to make this match a success!
We have to work together, regardless of our team or club to make this work.
I'm counting on every single person here to do their part!

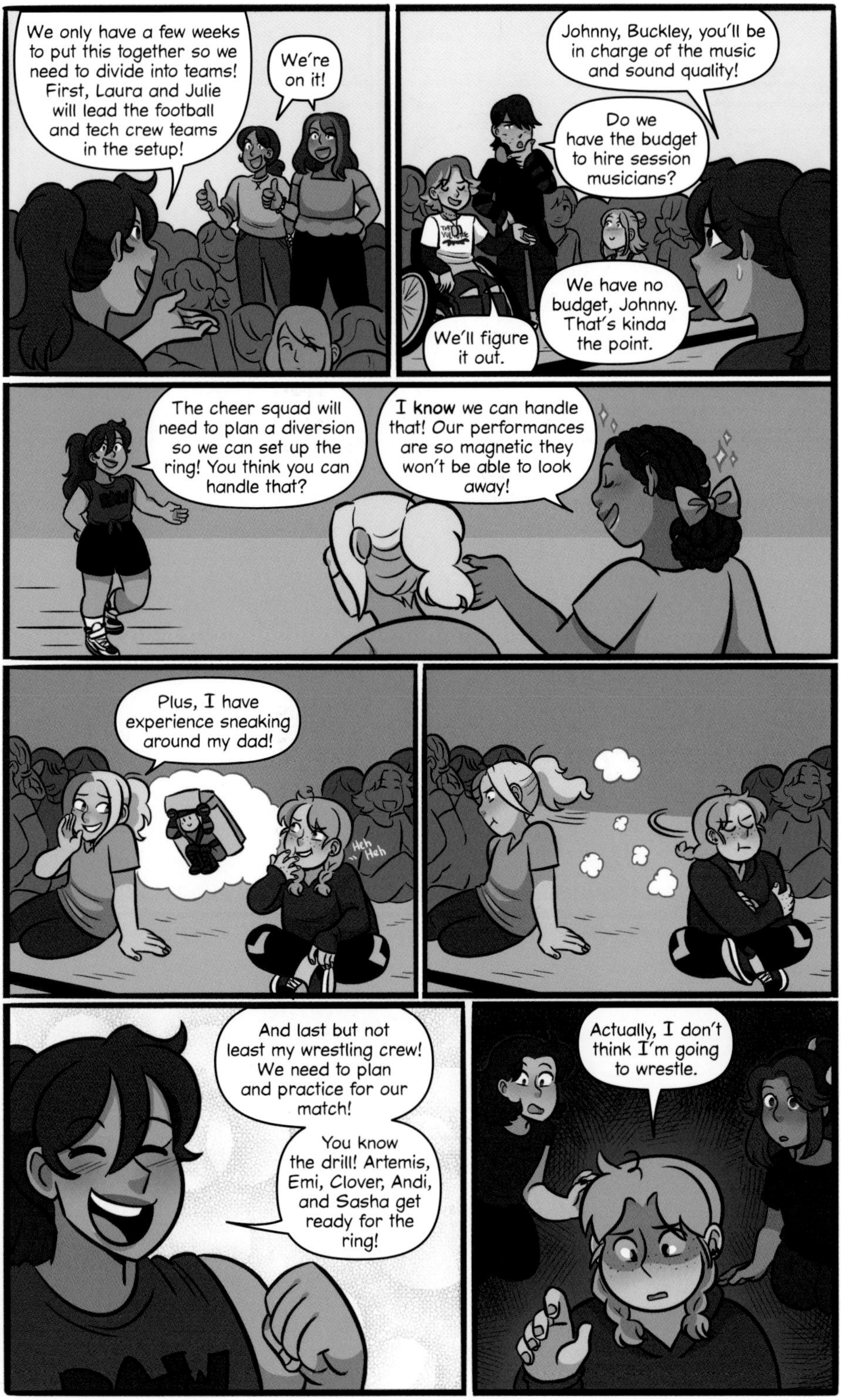
We only have a few weeks to put this together so we need to divide into teams! First, Laura and Julie will lead the football and tech crew teams in the setup!
We're on it!
Johnny, Buckley, you'll be in charge of the music and sound quality!
Do we have the budget to hire session musicians?
We have no budget, Johnny. That's kinda the point.
We'll figure it out.
The cheer squad will need to plan a diversion so we can set up the ring! You think you can handle that?
I **know** we can handle that! Our performances are so magnetic they won't be able to look away!
Plus, I have experience sneaking around my dad!
Heh Heh
And last but not least my wrestling crew! We need to plan and practice for our match!
You know the drill! Artemis, Emi, Clover, Andi, and Sasha get ready for the ring!
Actually, I don't think I'm going to wrestle.

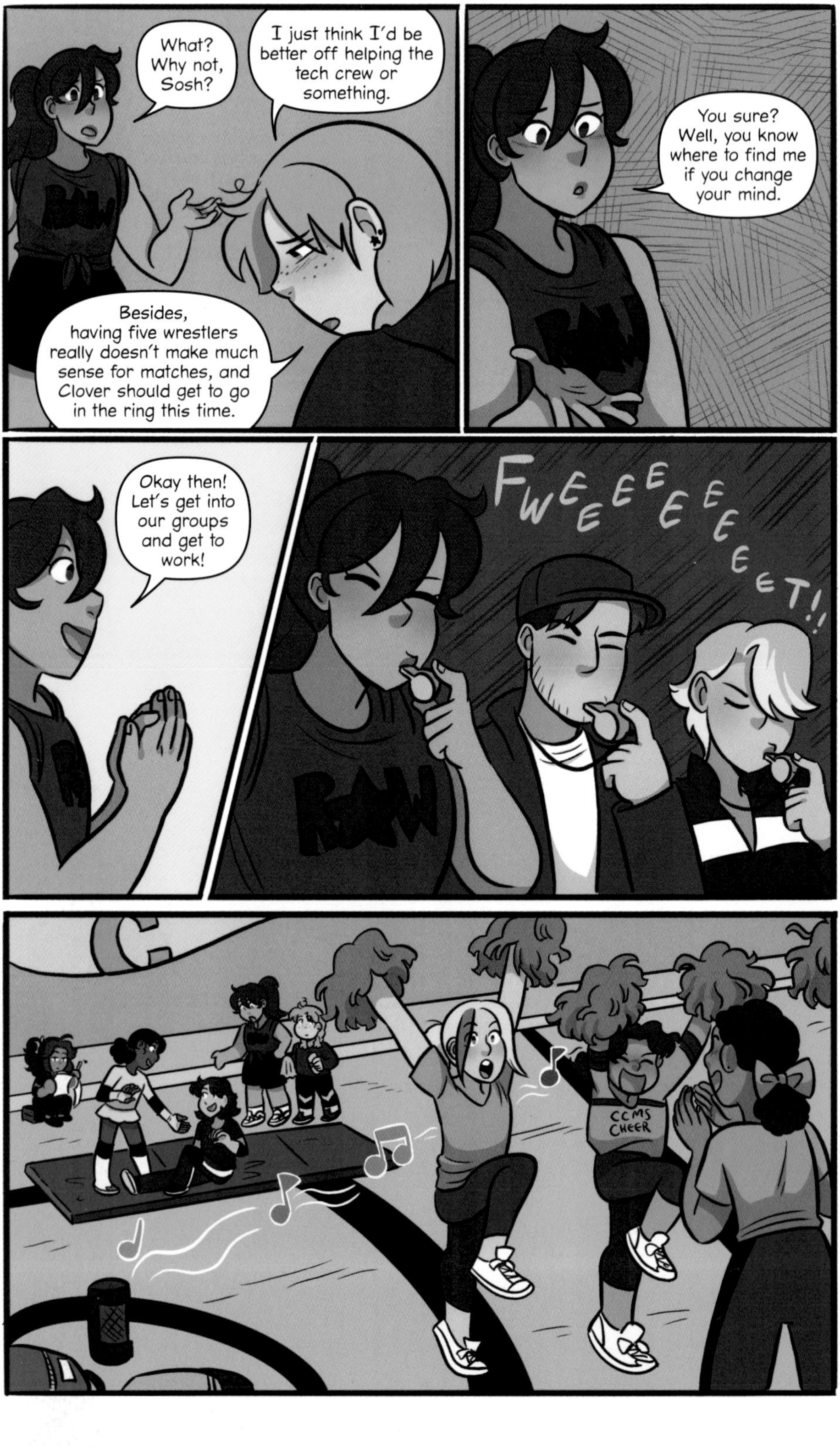
What? Why not, Sosh?
I just think I'd be better off helping the tech crew or something.
Besides, having five wrestlers really doesn't make much sense for matches, and Clover should get to go in the ring this time.
You sure? Well, you know where to find me if you change your mind.
Okay then! Let's get into our groups and get to work!
FWEEEEEEEEEET!!
CCMS CHEER

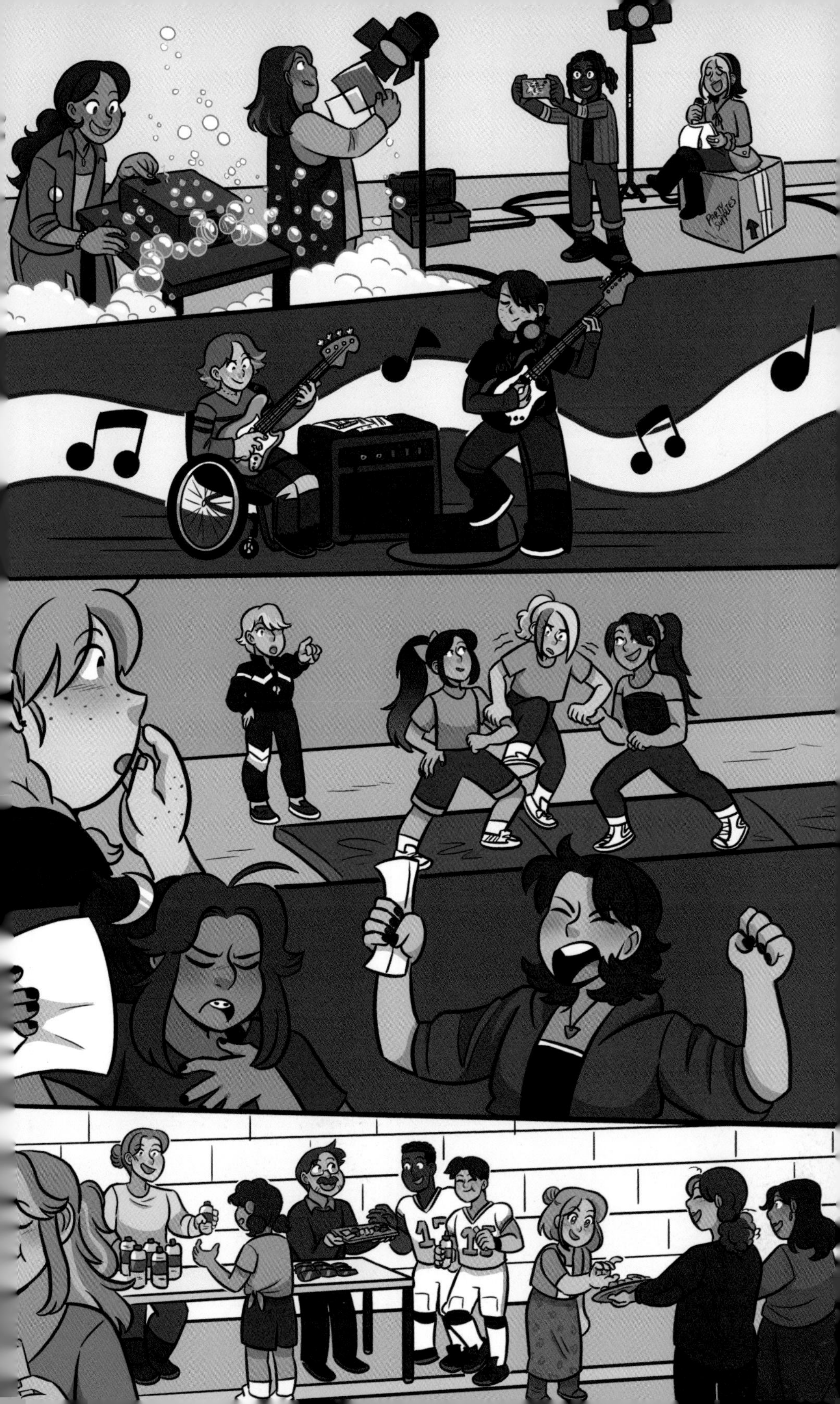
PARTY SUPPLIES

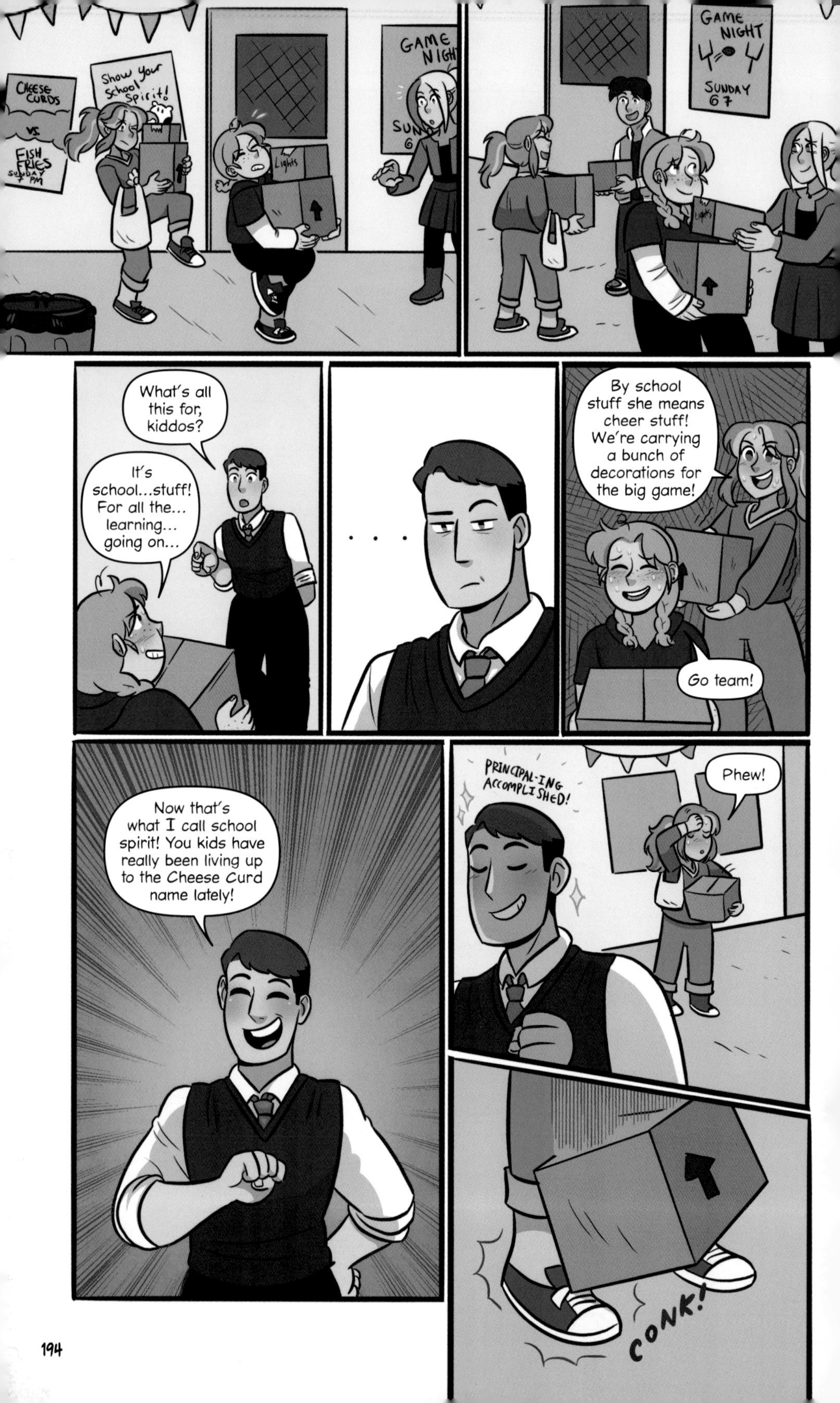

CHEESE CURDS VS. FISH FRIES SUNDAY 7 PM
Show your school spirit!
GAME NIGHT SUN 6
Lights
GAME NIGHT SUNDAY 6 7
What's all this for, kiddos?
It's school...stuff! For all the... learning... going on...
. . .
By school stuff she means cheer stuff! We're carrying a bunch of decorations for the big game!
Go team!
Now that's what I call school spirit! You kids have really been living up to the Cheese Curd name lately!
PRINCIPAL-ING ACCOMPLISHED!
Phew!
CONK!

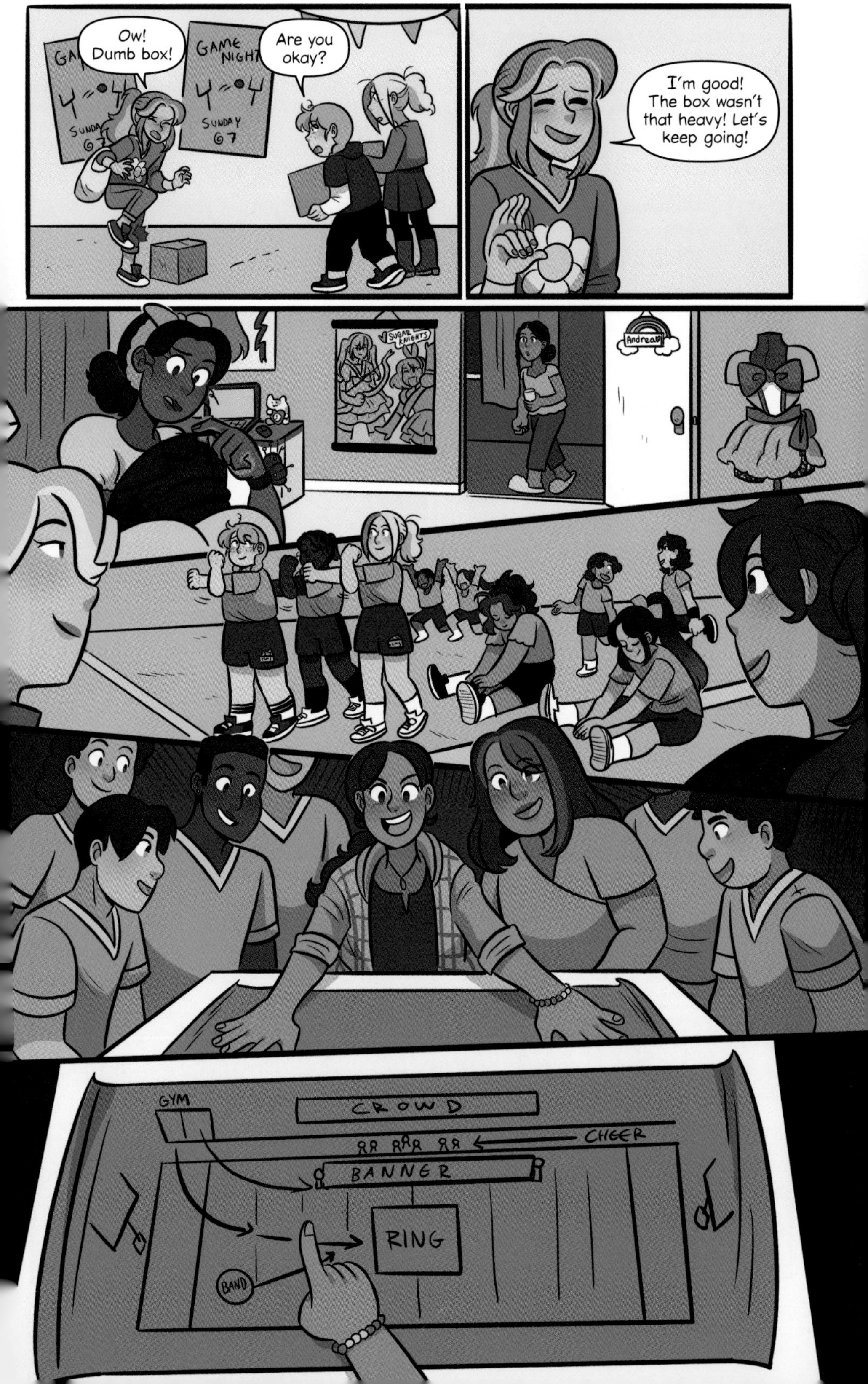

GAME NIGHT
4-4
SUNDAY
6-7
GAME NIGHT
4-4
SUNDAY
6-7
Ow! Dumb box!
Are you okay?
I'm good! The box wasn't that heavy! Let's keep going!
SUGAR KNIGHTS
Andrea
GYM
CROWD
CHEER
BANNER
RING
BAND

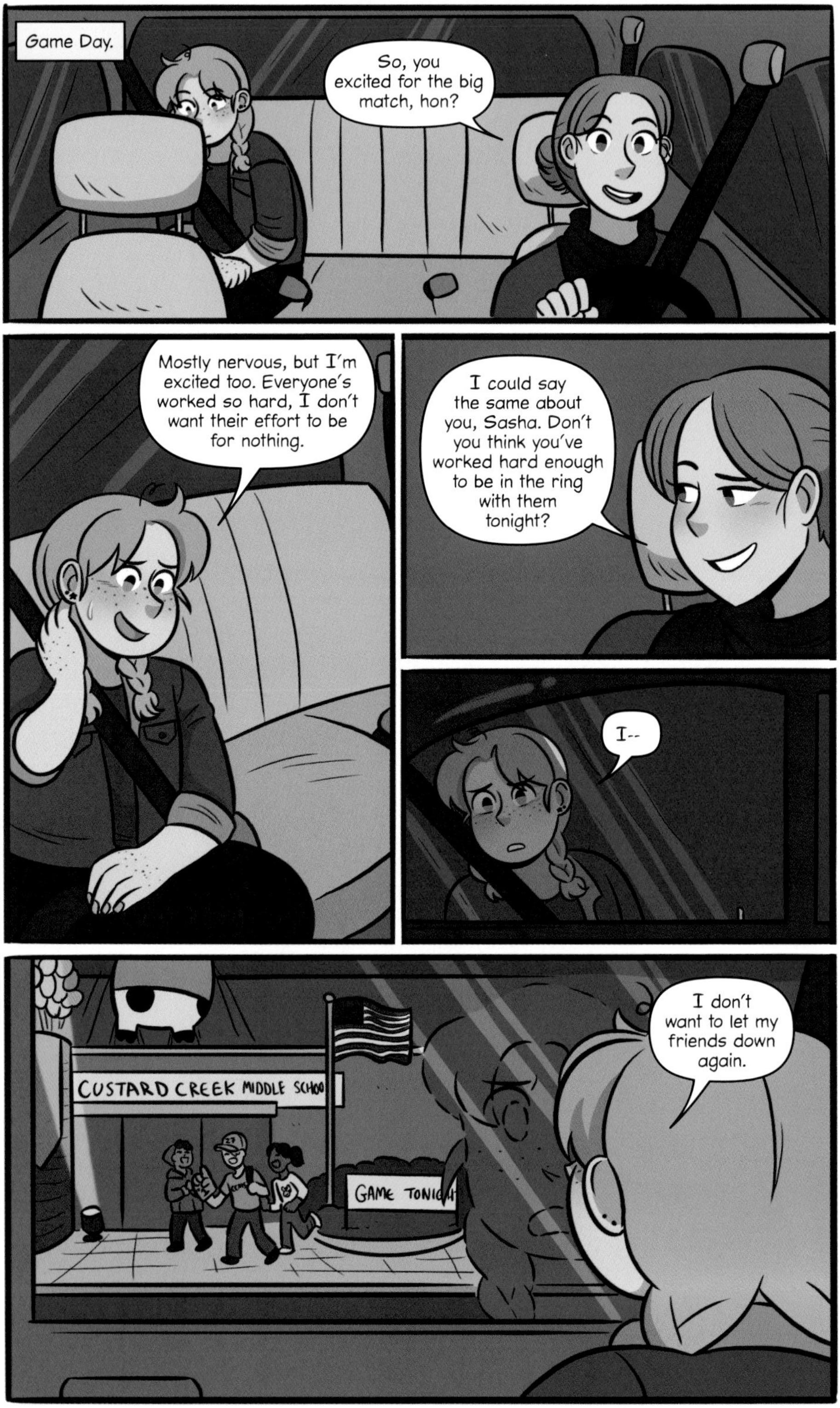
Game Day.
So, you excited for the big match, hon?
Mostly nervous, but I'm excited too. Everyone's worked so hard, I don't want their effort to be for nothing.
I could say the same about you, Sasha. Don't you think you've worked hard enough to be in the ring with them tonight?
I--
CUSTARD CREEK MIDDLE SCHOO
GAME TONIGHT
I don't want to let my friends down again.

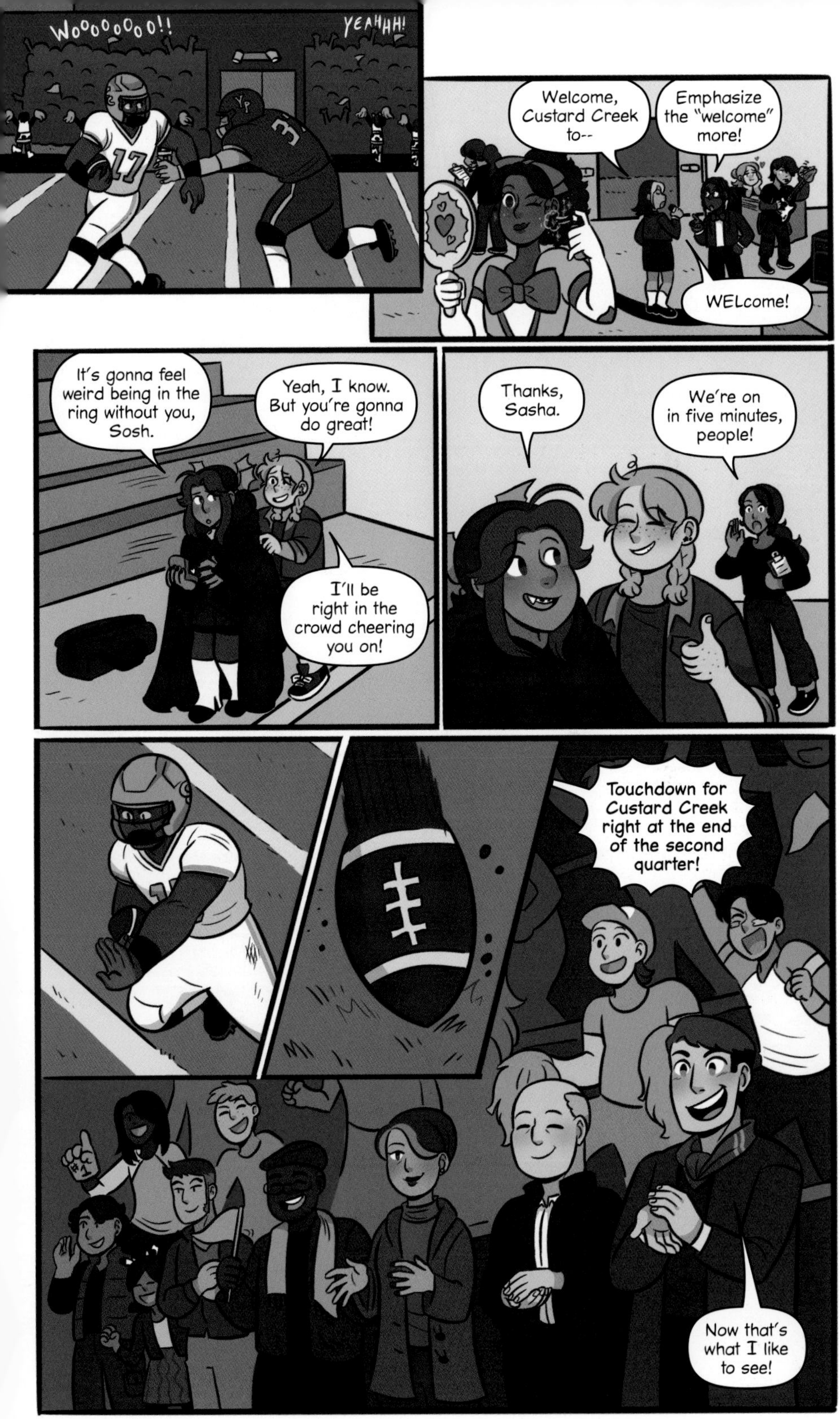
WOOOOOOO!!
YEAHHH!
Welcome, Custard Creek to--
Emphasize the "welcome" more!
WELcome!
It's gonna feel weird being in the ring without you, Sosh.
Yeah, I know. But you're gonna do great!
I'll be right in the crowd cheering you on!
Thanks, Sasha.
We're on in five minutes, people!
Touchdown for Custard Creek right at the end of the second quarter!
Now that's what I like to see!

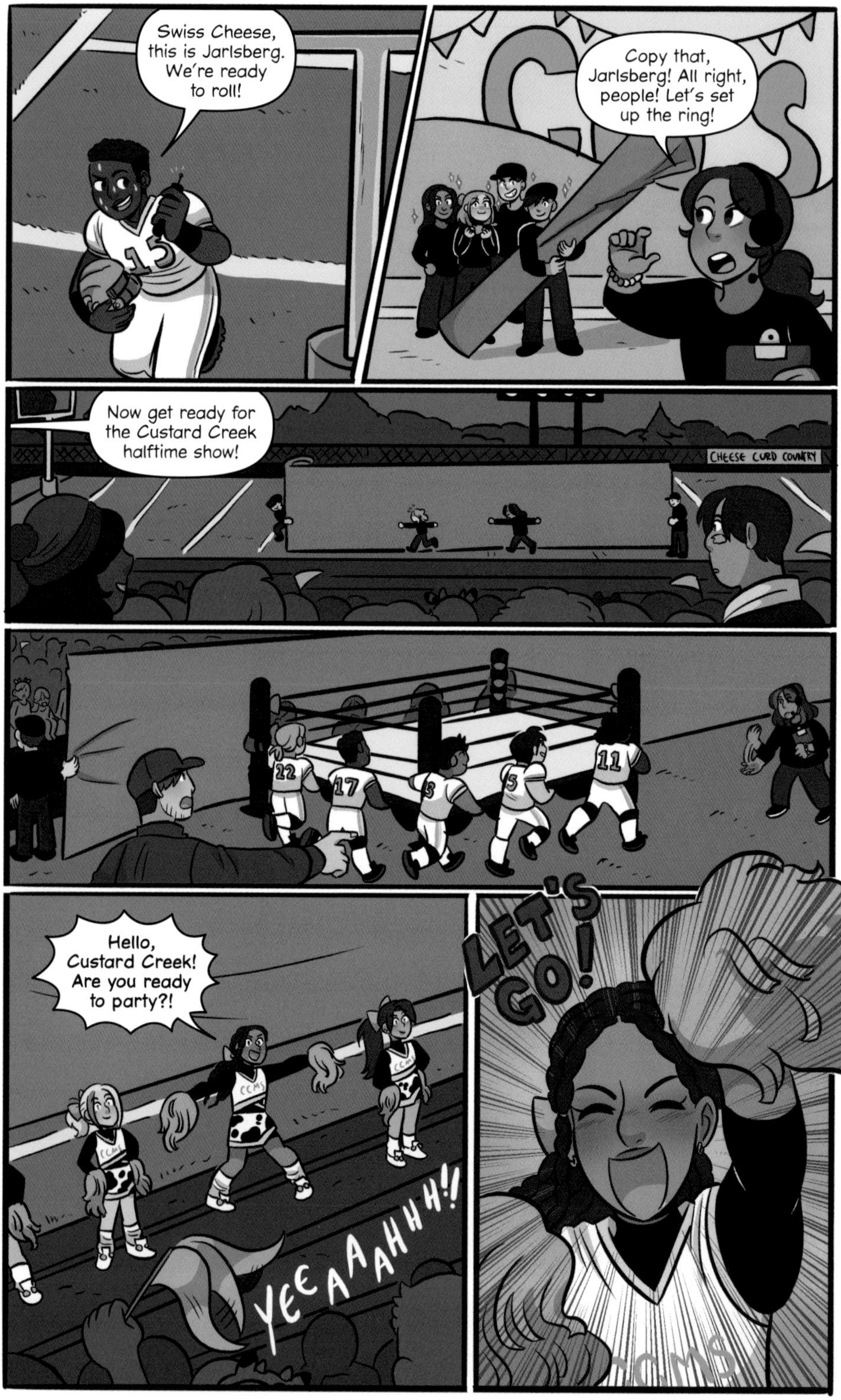

Swiss Cheese, this is Jarlsberg. We're ready to roll!
Copy that, Jarlsberg! All right, people! Let's set up the ring!
Now get ready for the Custard Creek halftime show!
CHEESE CURD COUNTRY
Hello, Custard Creek! Are you ready to party?!
YEEAAAHHH!!
LET'S GO!

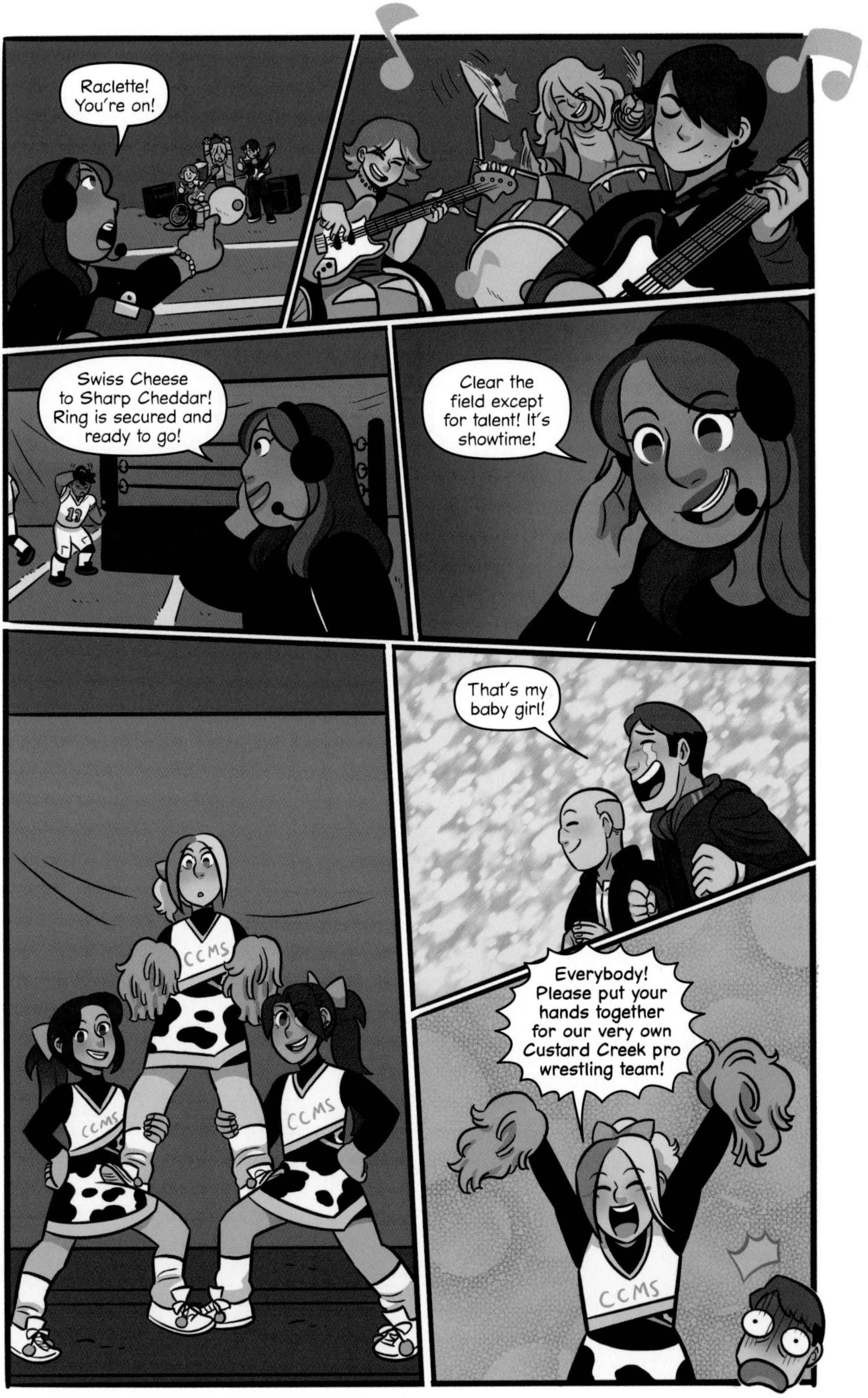
Raclette! You're on!
Swiss Cheese to Sharp Cheddar! Ring is secured and ready to go!
Clear the field except for talent! It's showtime!
CCMS
That's my baby girl!
Everybody! Please put your hands together for our very own Custard Creek pro wrestling team!

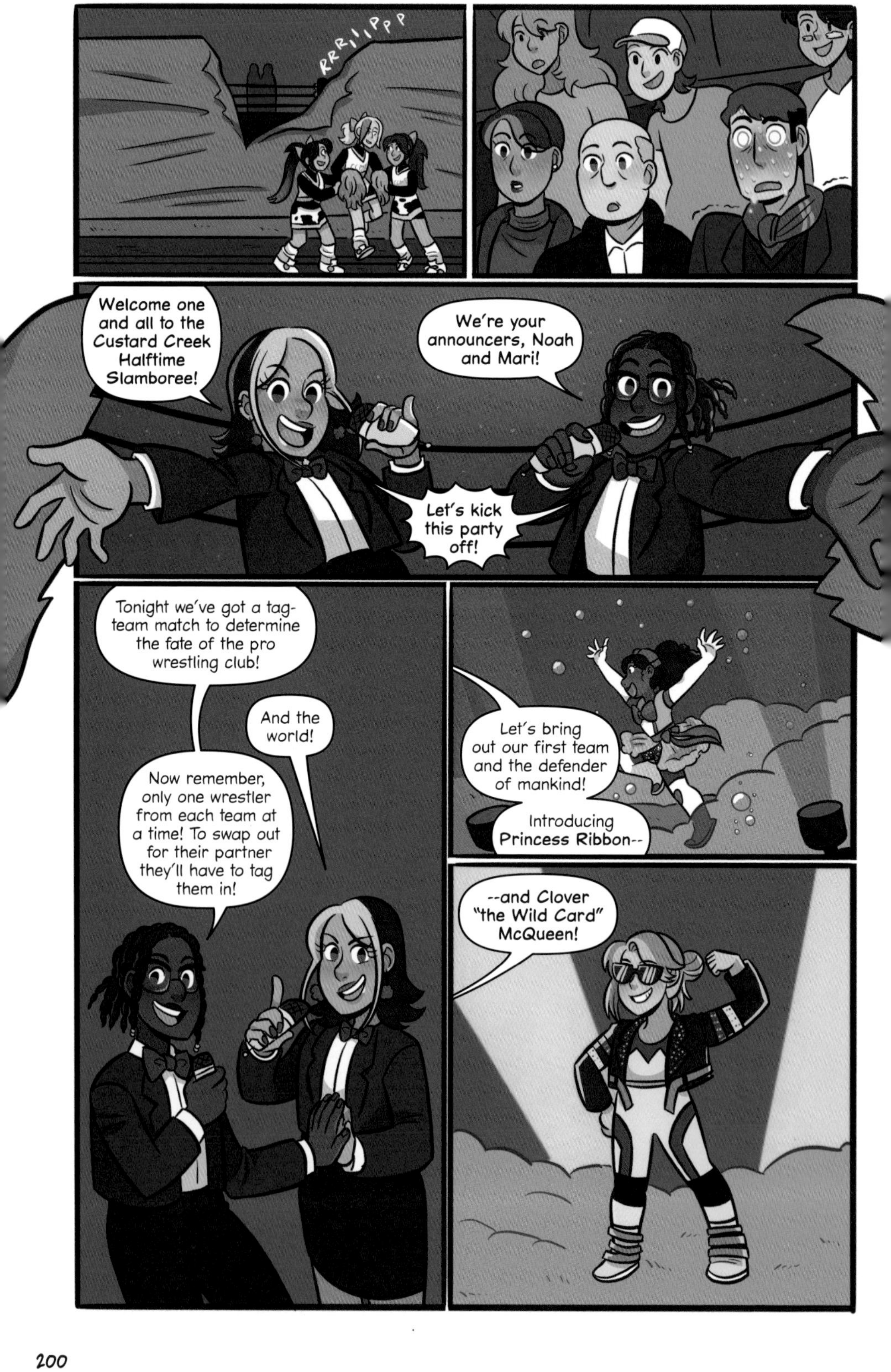
RRRIIPPP
Welcome one and all to the Custard Creek Halftime Slamboree!
We're your announcers, Noah and Mari!
Let's kick this party off!
Tonight we've got a tag-team match to determine the fate of the pro wrestling club!
And the world!
Now remember, only one wrestler from each team at a time! To swap out for their partner they'll have to tag them in!
Let's bring out our first team and the defender of mankind!
Introducing **Princess Ribbon**--
--and Clover "the Wild Card" McQueen!

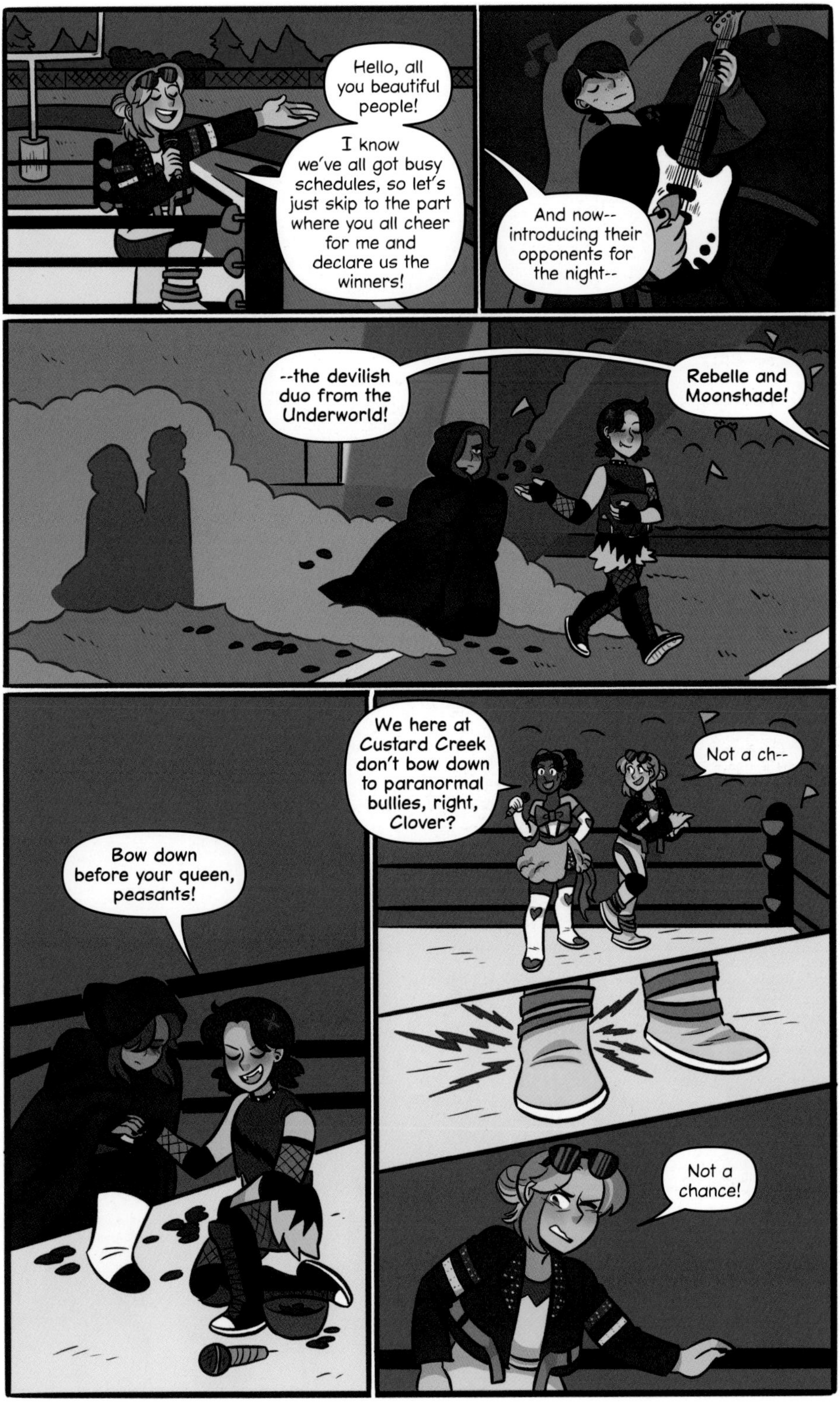
Hello, all you beautiful people!
I know we've all got busy schedules, so let's just skip to the part where you all cheer for me and declare us the winners!
And now-- introducing their opponents for the night--
--the devilish duo from the Underworld!
Rebelle and Moonshade!
Bow down before your queen, peasants!
We here at Custard Creek don't bow down to paranormal bullies, right, Clover?
Not a ch--
Not a chance!

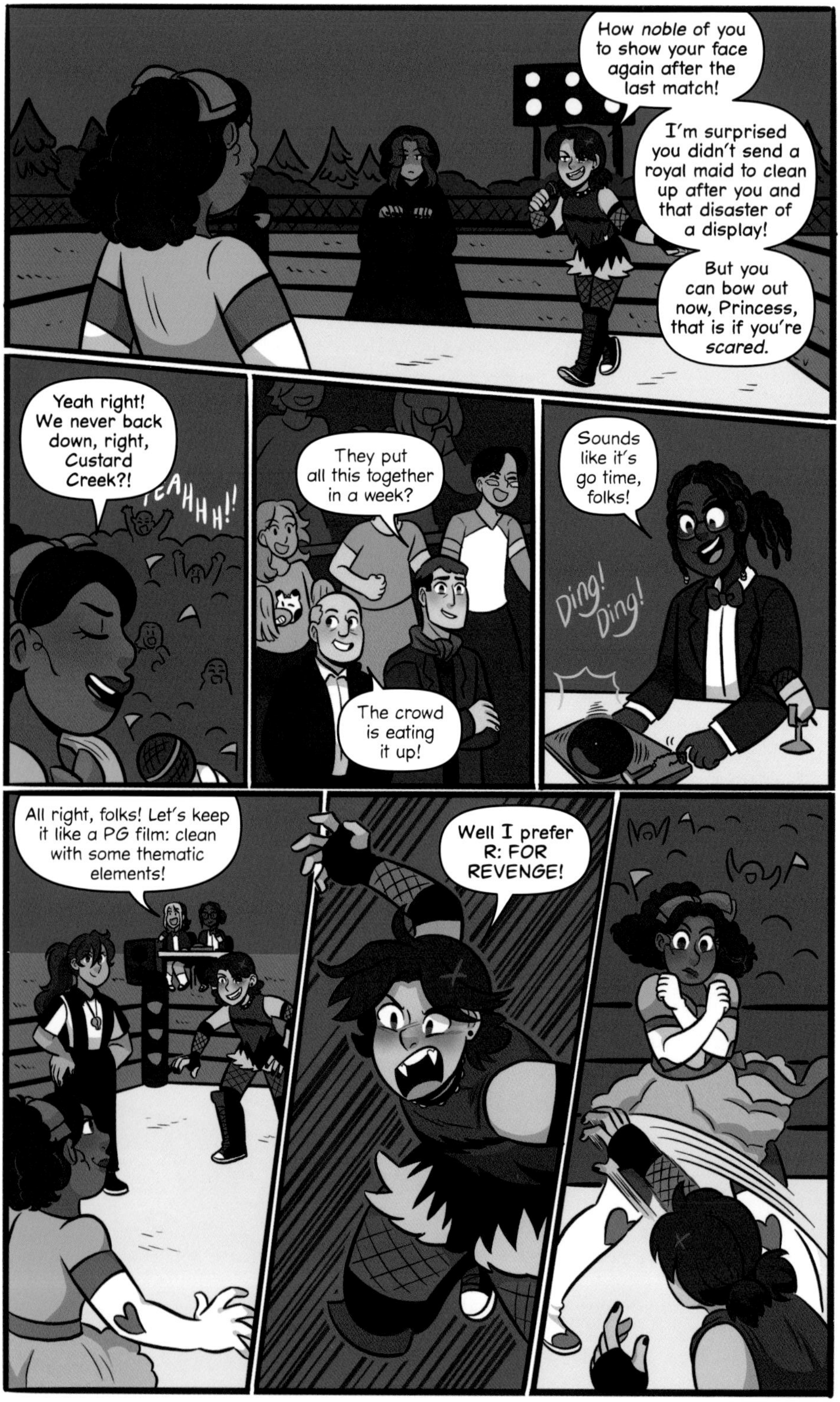
How *noble* of you to show your face again after the last match!
I'm surprised you didn't send a royal maid to clean up after you and that disaster of a display!
But you can bow out now, Princess, that is if you're *scared.*
Yeah right! We never back down, right, Custard Creek?!
YEAHHHH!!
They put all this together in a week?
The crowd is eating it up!
Sounds like it's go time, folks!
Ding! Ding!
All right, folks! Let's keep it like a PG film: clean with some thematic elements!
Well I prefer R: FOR REVENGE!

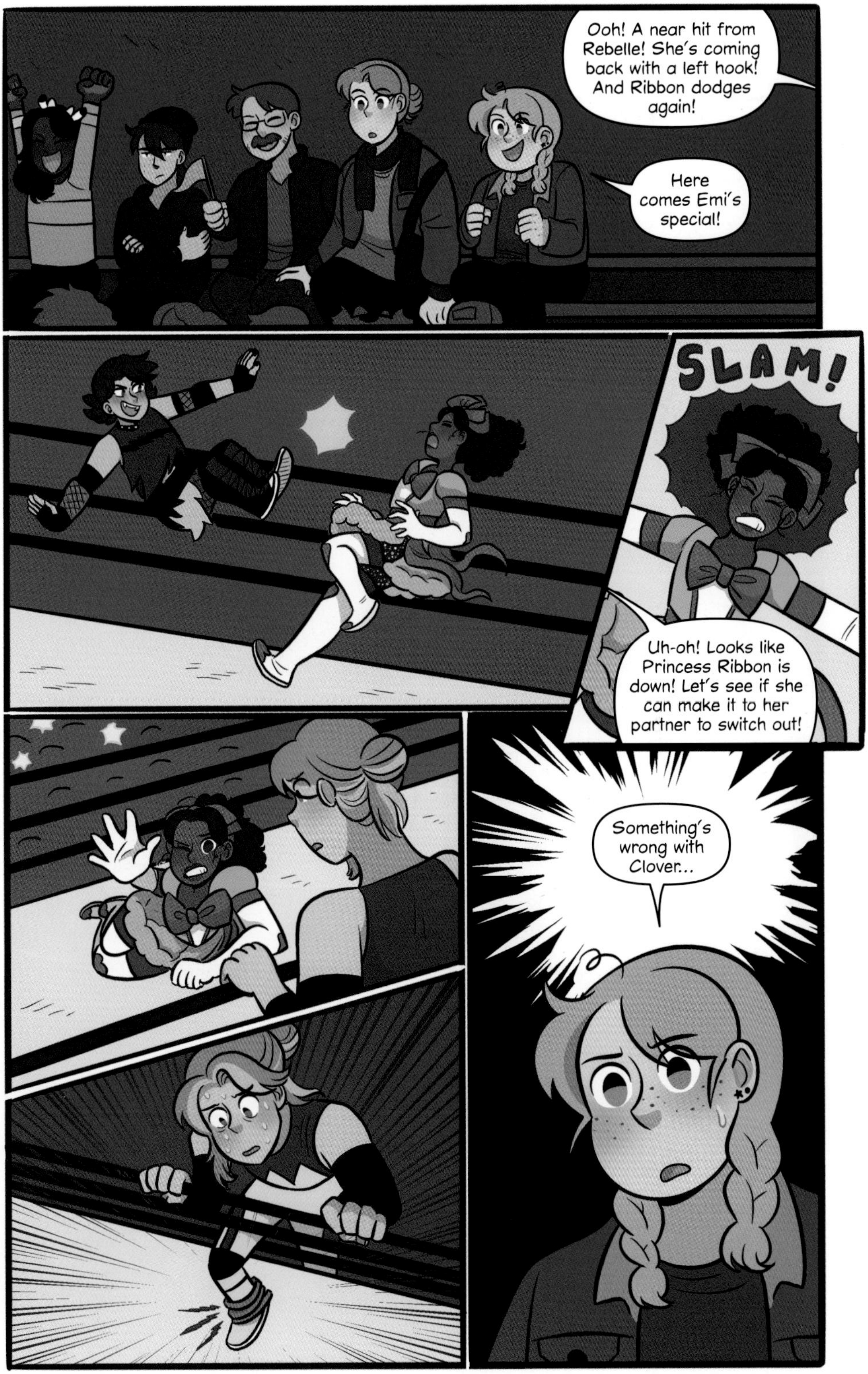

Ooh! A near hit from Rebelle! She's coming back with a left hook! And Ribbon dodges again!
Here comes Emi's special!
SLAM!
Uh-oh! Looks like Princess Ribbon is down! Let's see if she can make it to her partner to switch out!
Something's wrong with Clover...

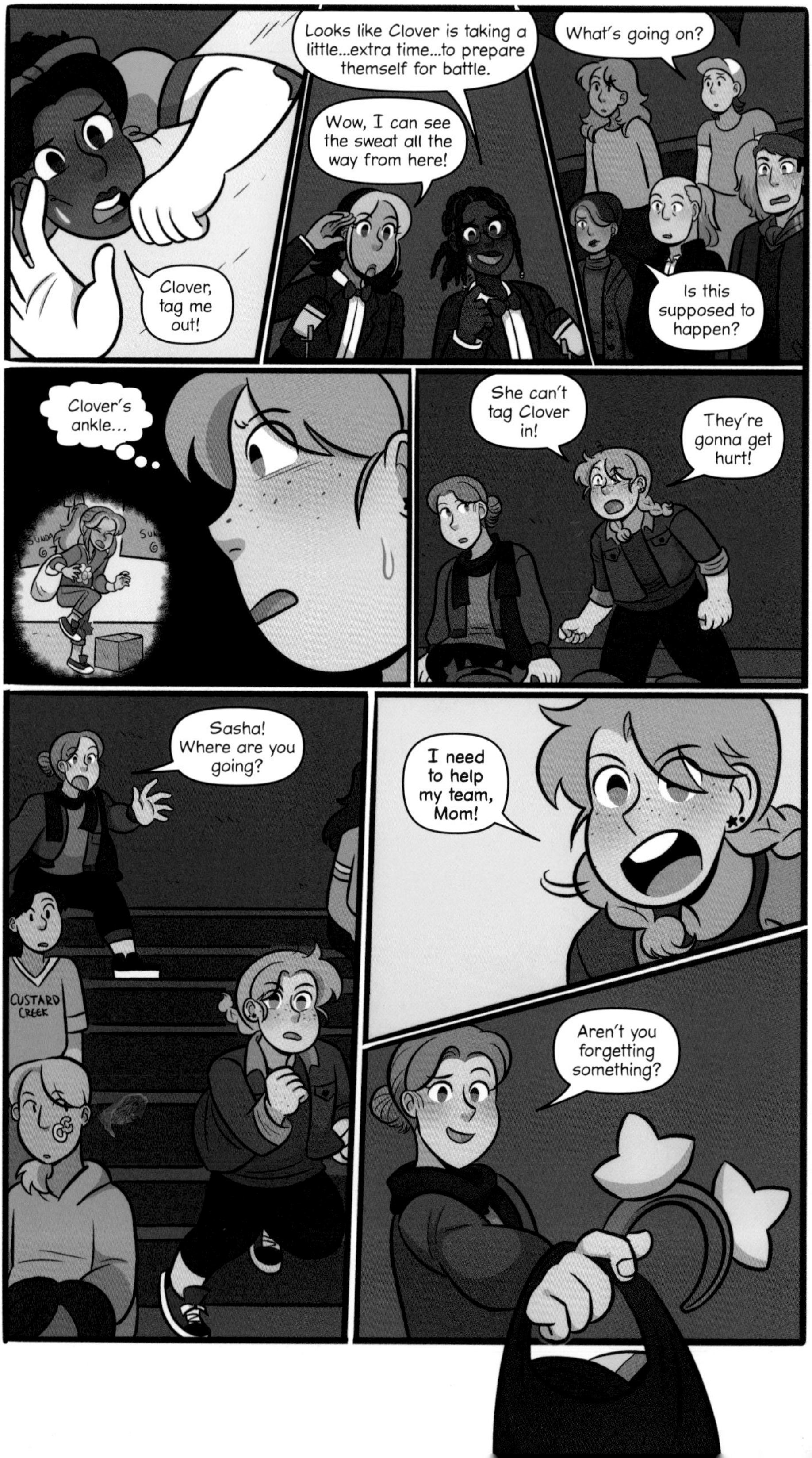
Clover, tag me out!
Looks like Clover is taking a little...extra time...to prepare themself for battle.
Wow, I can see the sweat all the way from here!
What's going on?
Is this supposed to happen?
Clover's ankle...
SUNDA
SUN
She can't tag Clover in!
They're gonna get hurt!
Sasha! Where are you going?
CUSTARD CREEK
I need to help my team, Mom!
Aren't you forgetting something?

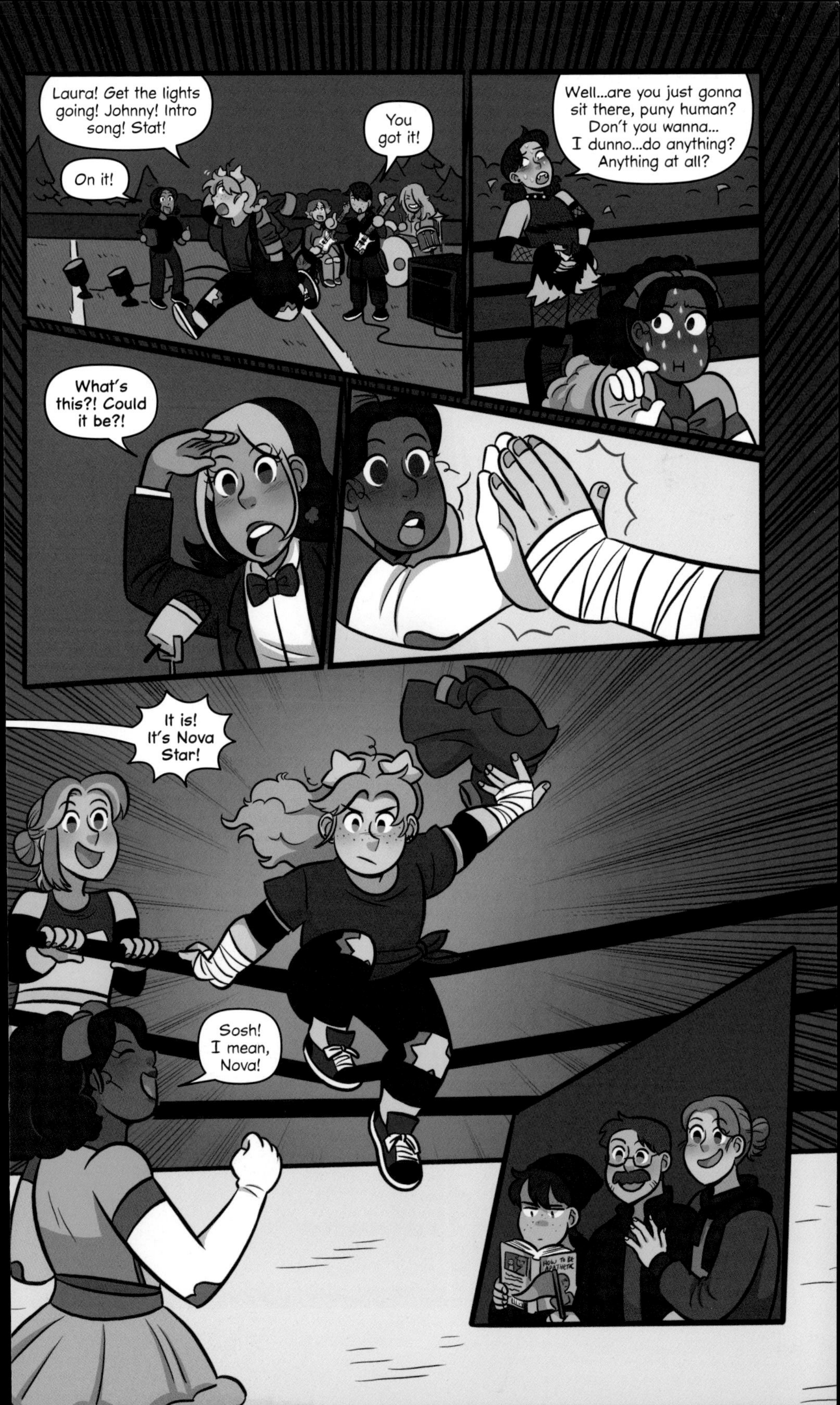

Laura! Get the lights going! Johnny! Intro song! Stat!
On it!
You got it!
Well...are you just gonna sit there, puny human? Don't you wanna... I dunno...do anything? Anything at all?
What's this?! Could it be?!
It is! It's Nova Star!
Sosh! I mean, Nova!

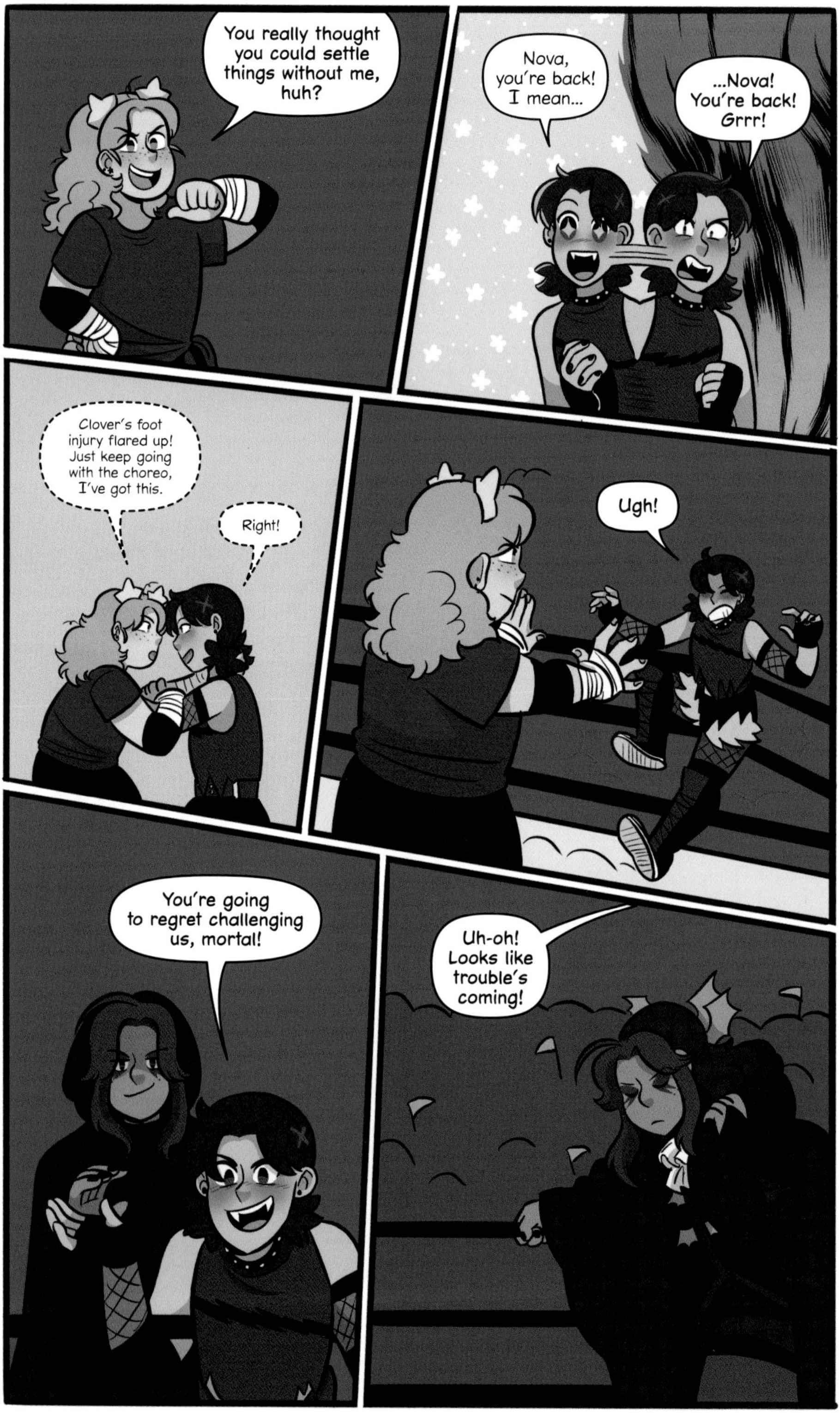

You really thought you could settle things without me, huh?
Nova, you're back! I mean...
...Nova! You're back! Grrr!
Clover's foot injury flared up! Just keep going with the choreo, I've got this.
Right!
Ugh!
You're going to regret challenging us, mortal!
Uh-oh! Looks like trouble's coming!

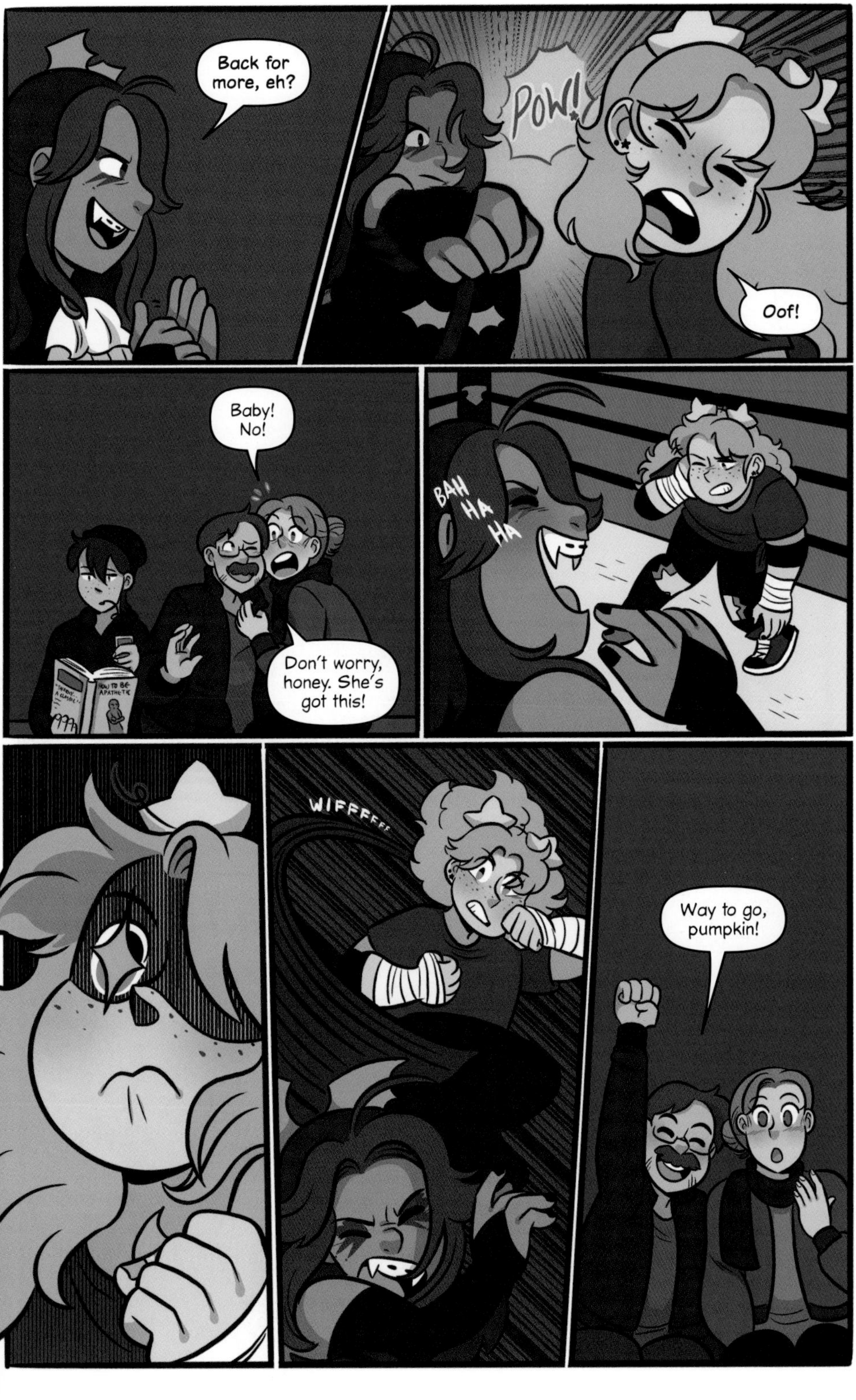
Back for more, eh?
POW!
Oof!
Baby! No!
Don't worry, honey. She's got this!
HOW TO BE APATHETIC
BAH HA HA
WIFFFFFF
Way to go, pumpkin!

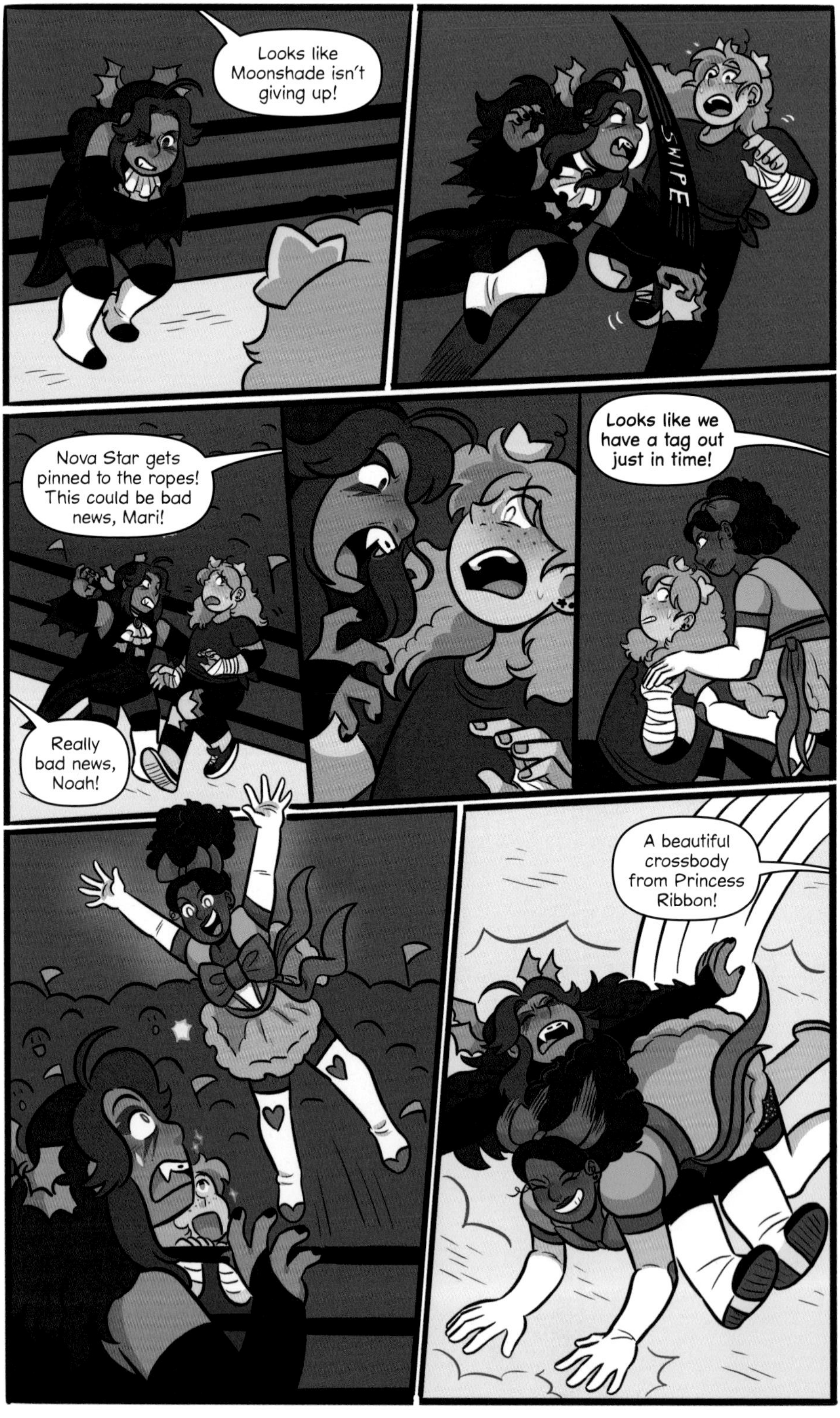
Looks like
Moonshade isn't
giving up!
SWIPE
Nova Star gets
pinned to the ropes!
This could be bad
news, Mari!
Really
bad news,
Noah!
Looks like we
have a tag out
just in time!
A beautiful
crossbody
from Princess
Ribbon!

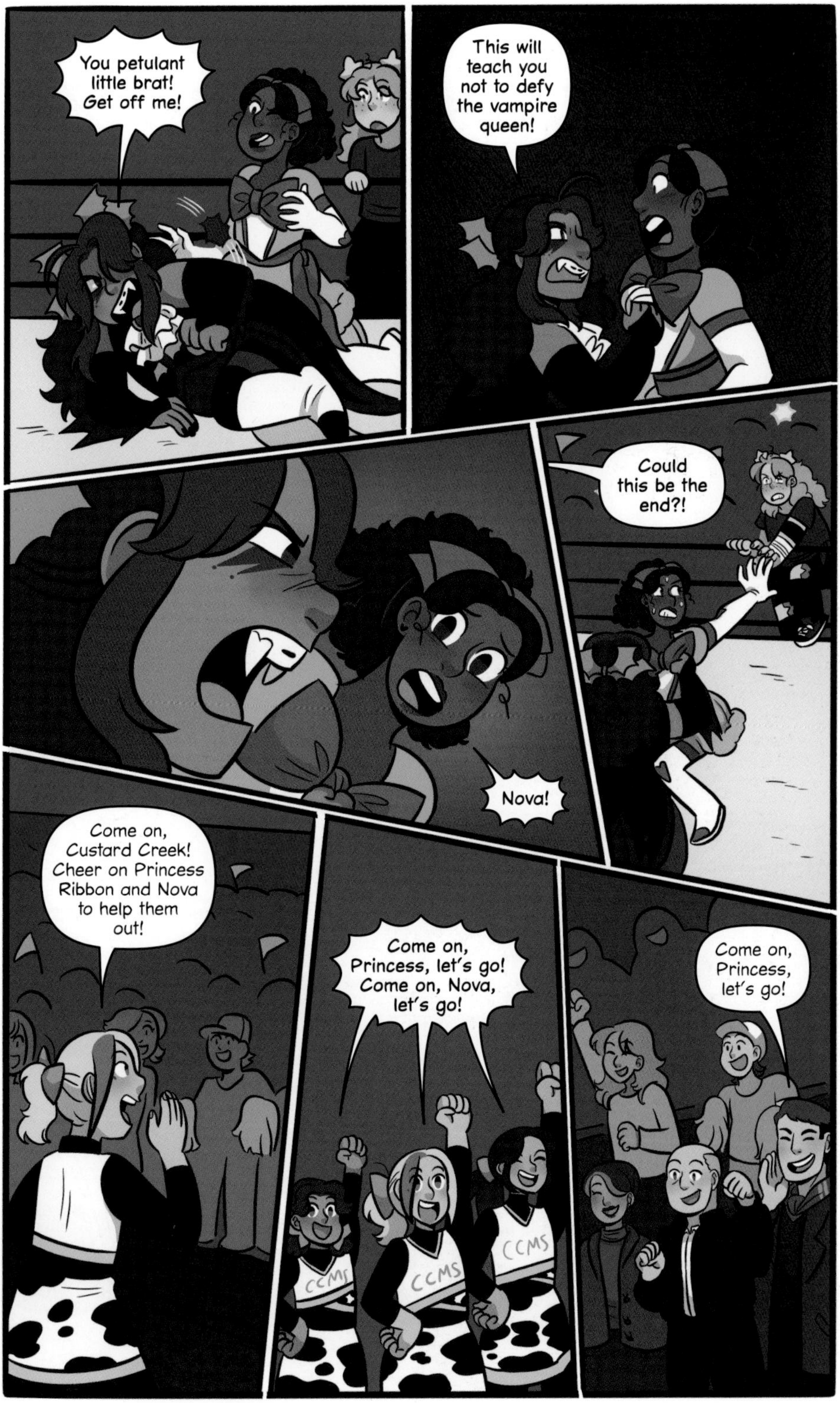
You petulant little brat! Get off me!
This will teach you not to defy the vampire queen!
Could this be the end?!
Nova!
Come on, Custard Creek! Cheer on Princess Ribbon and Nova to help them out!
Come on, Princess, let's go! Come on, Nova, let's go!
CCMS
CCMS
CCMS
Come on, Princess, let's go!

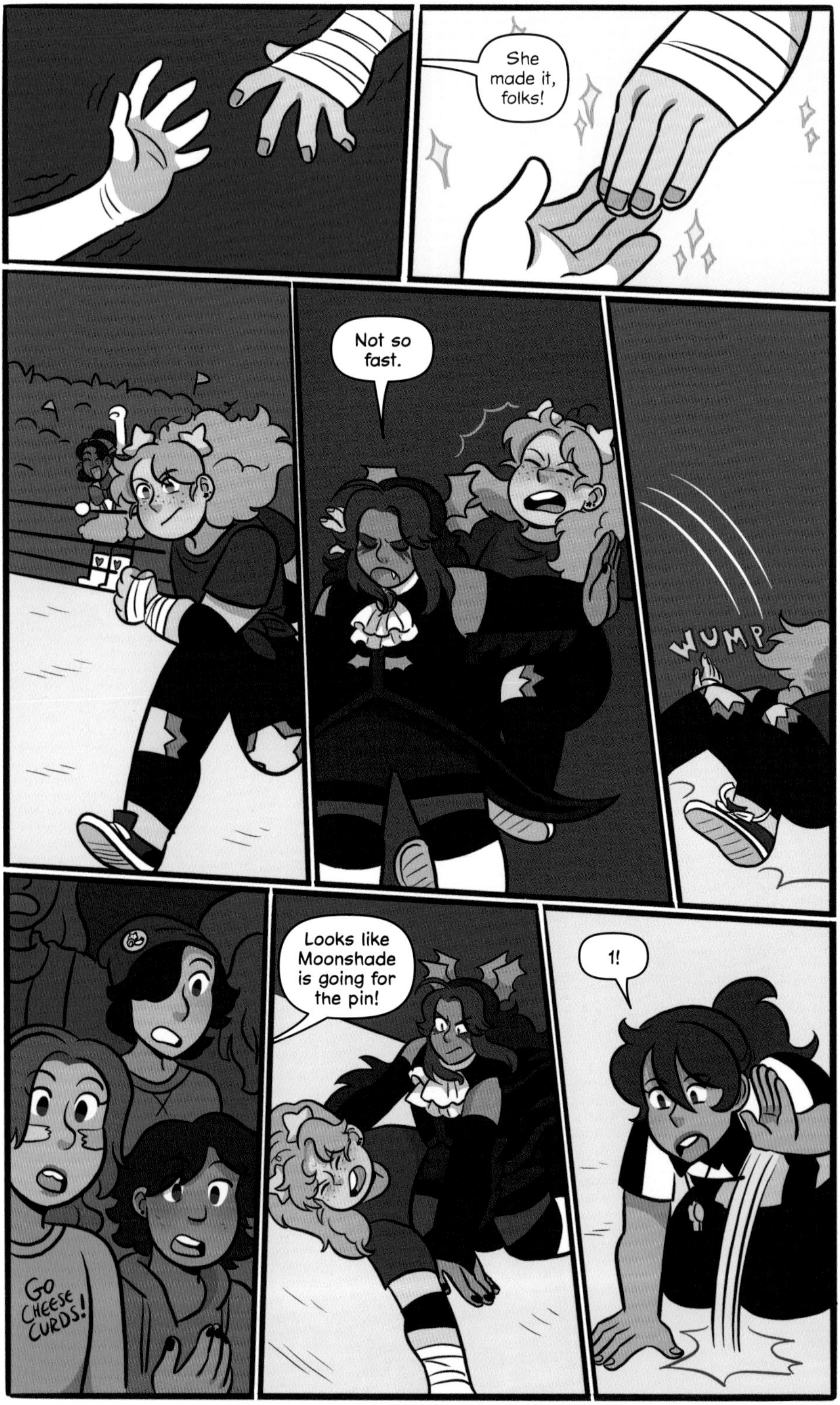
She made it, folks!
Not so fast.
WUMP
Looks like Moonshade is going for the pin!
1!
GO CHEESE CURDS!

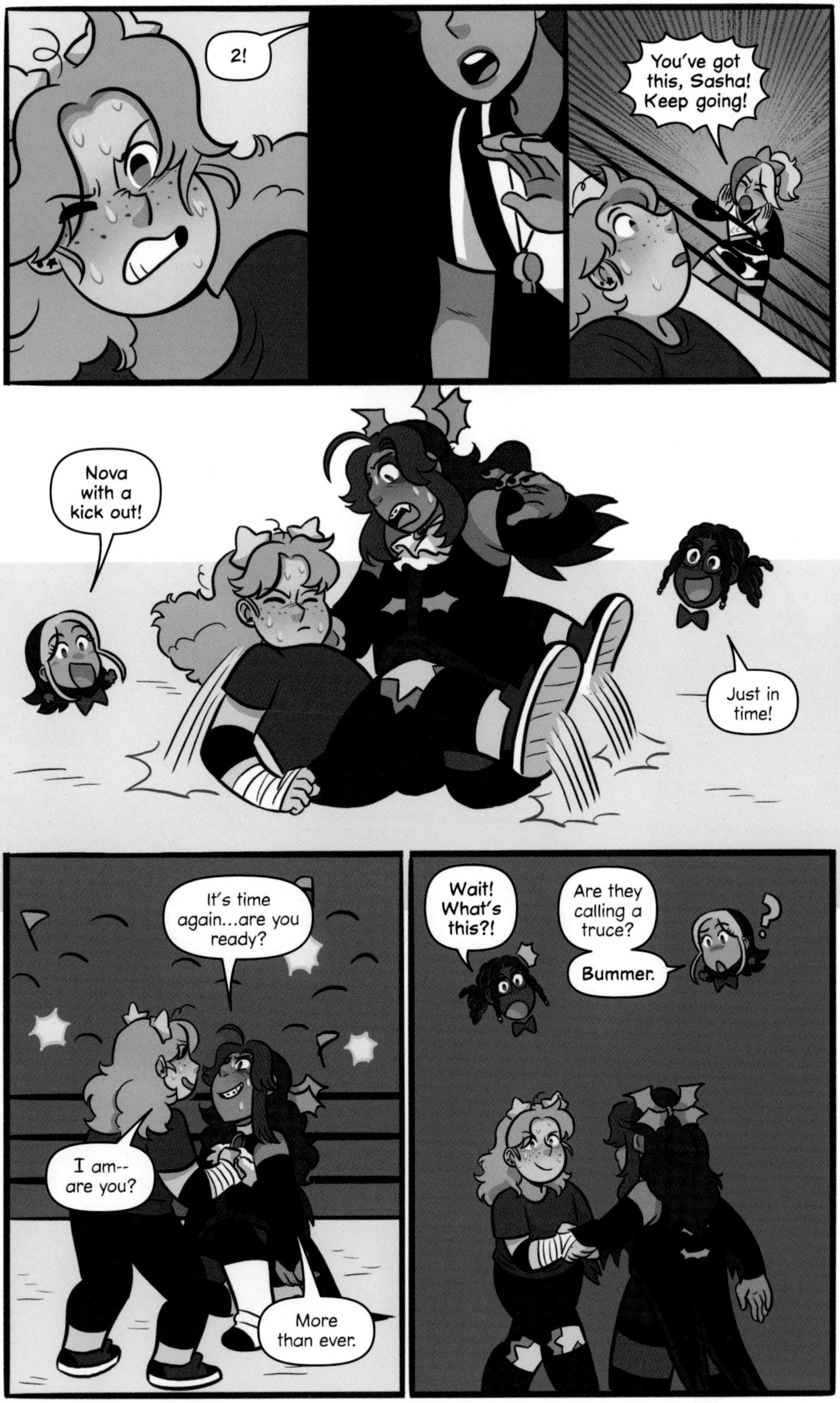
2!
You've got this, Sasha! Keep going!
Nova with a kick out!
Just in time!
It's time again...are you ready?
I am-- are you?
More than ever.
Wait! What's this?!
Are they calling a truce?
Bummer.

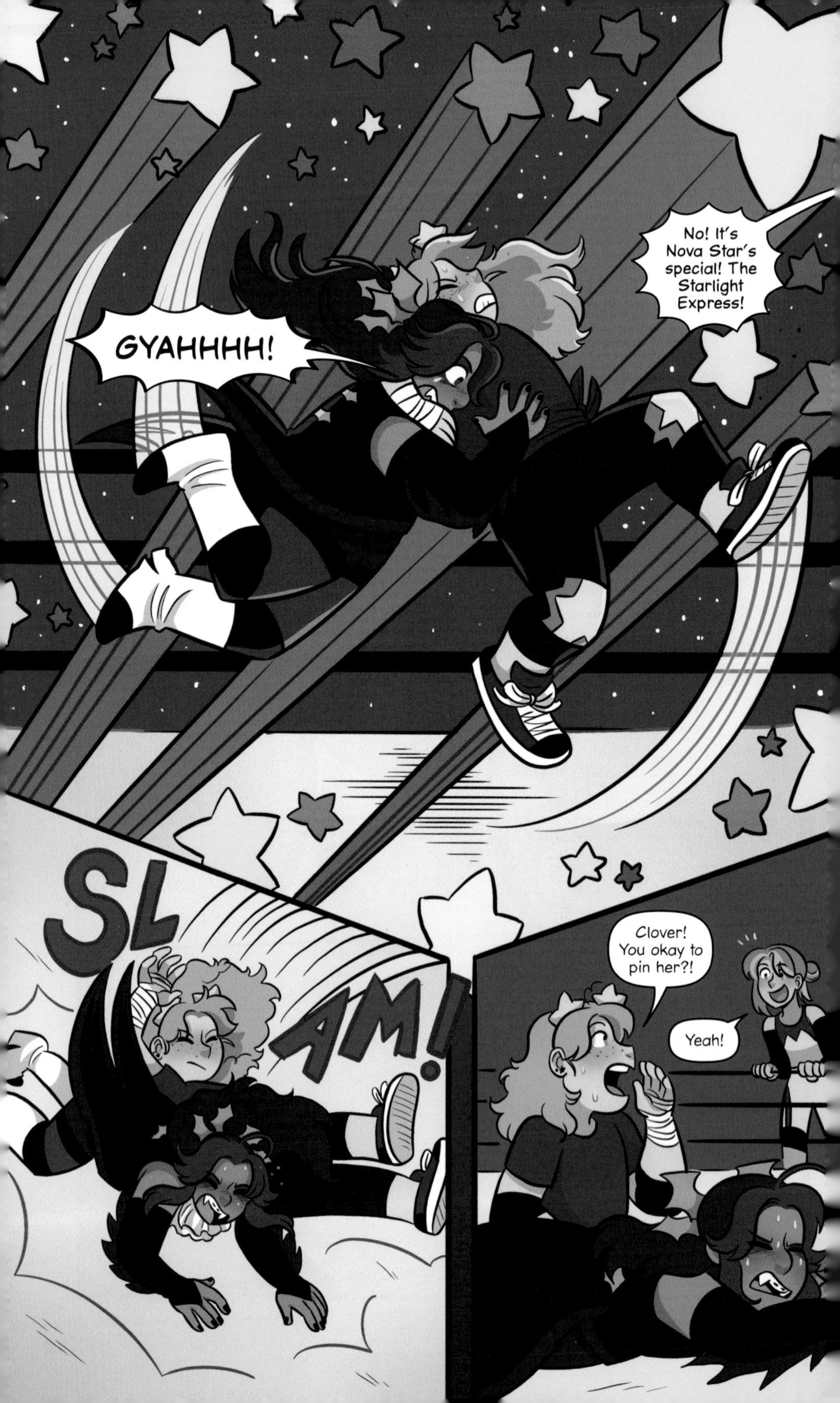
No! It's Nova Star's special! The Starlight Express!
GYAHHHH!
SLAM!
Clover! You okay to pin her?!
Yeah!

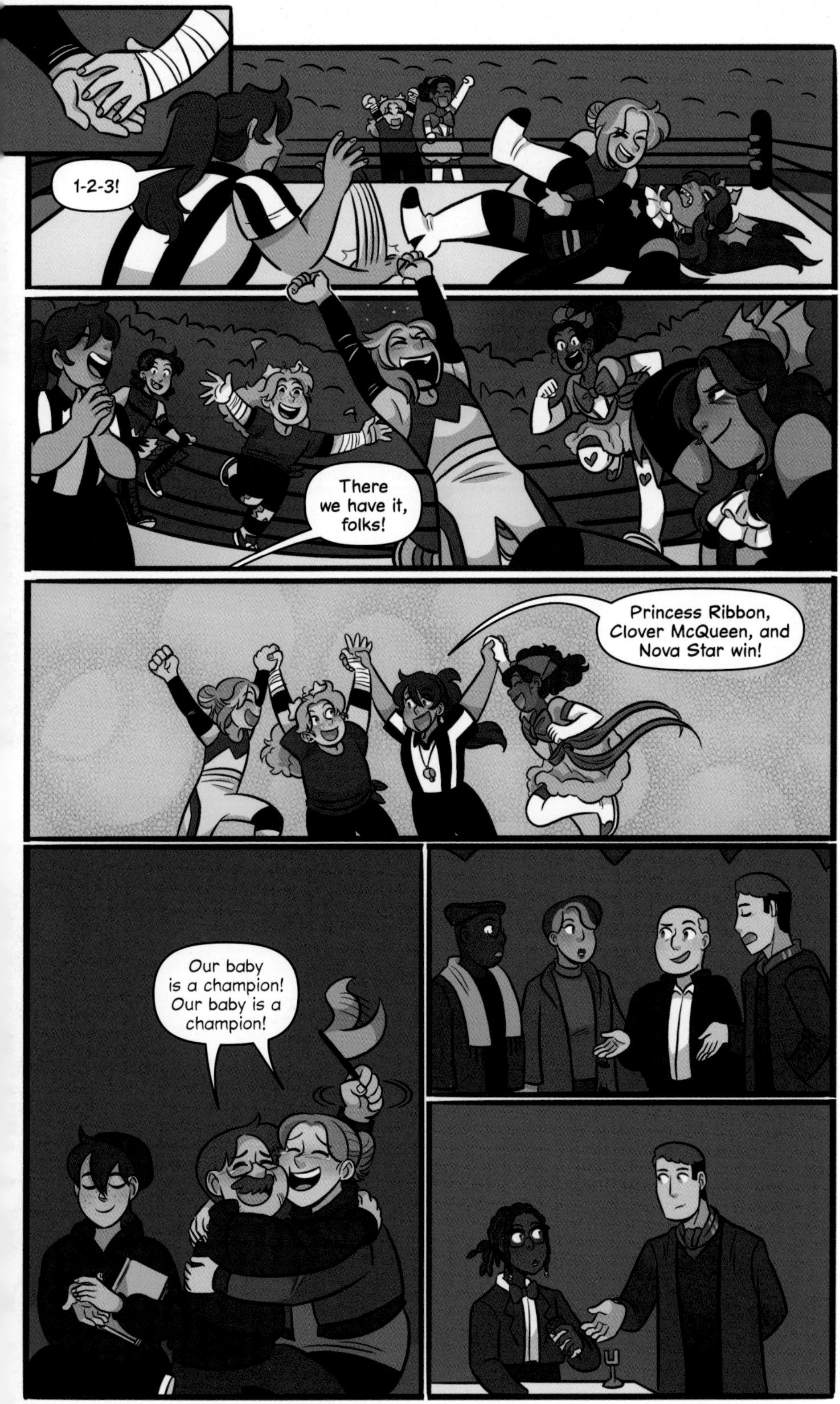
1-2-3!
There we have it, folks!
Princess Ribbon, Clover McQueen, and Nova Star win!
Our baby is a champion! Our baby is a champion!

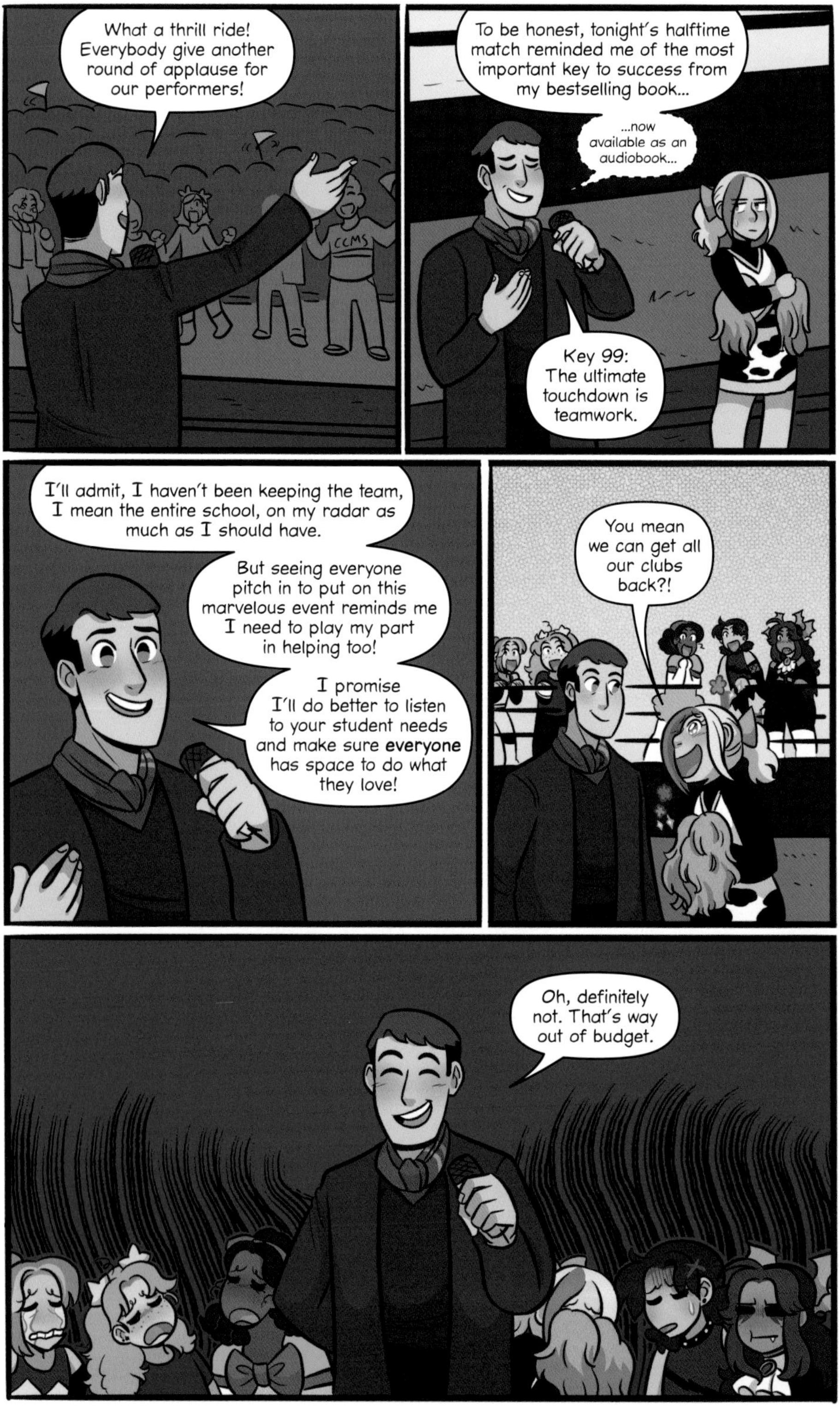
What a thrill ride! Everybody give another round of applause for our performers!
CCMS
To be honest, tonight's halftime match reminded me of the most important key to success from my bestselling book...
...now available as an audiobook...
Key 99: The ultimate touchdown is teamwork.
I'll admit, I haven't been keeping the team, I mean the entire school, on my radar as much as I should have.
But seeing everyone pitch in to put on this marvelous event reminds me I need to play my part in helping too!
I promise I'll do better to listen to your student needs and make sure **everyone** has space to do what they love!
You mean we can get all our clubs back?!
Oh, definitely not. That's way out of budget.

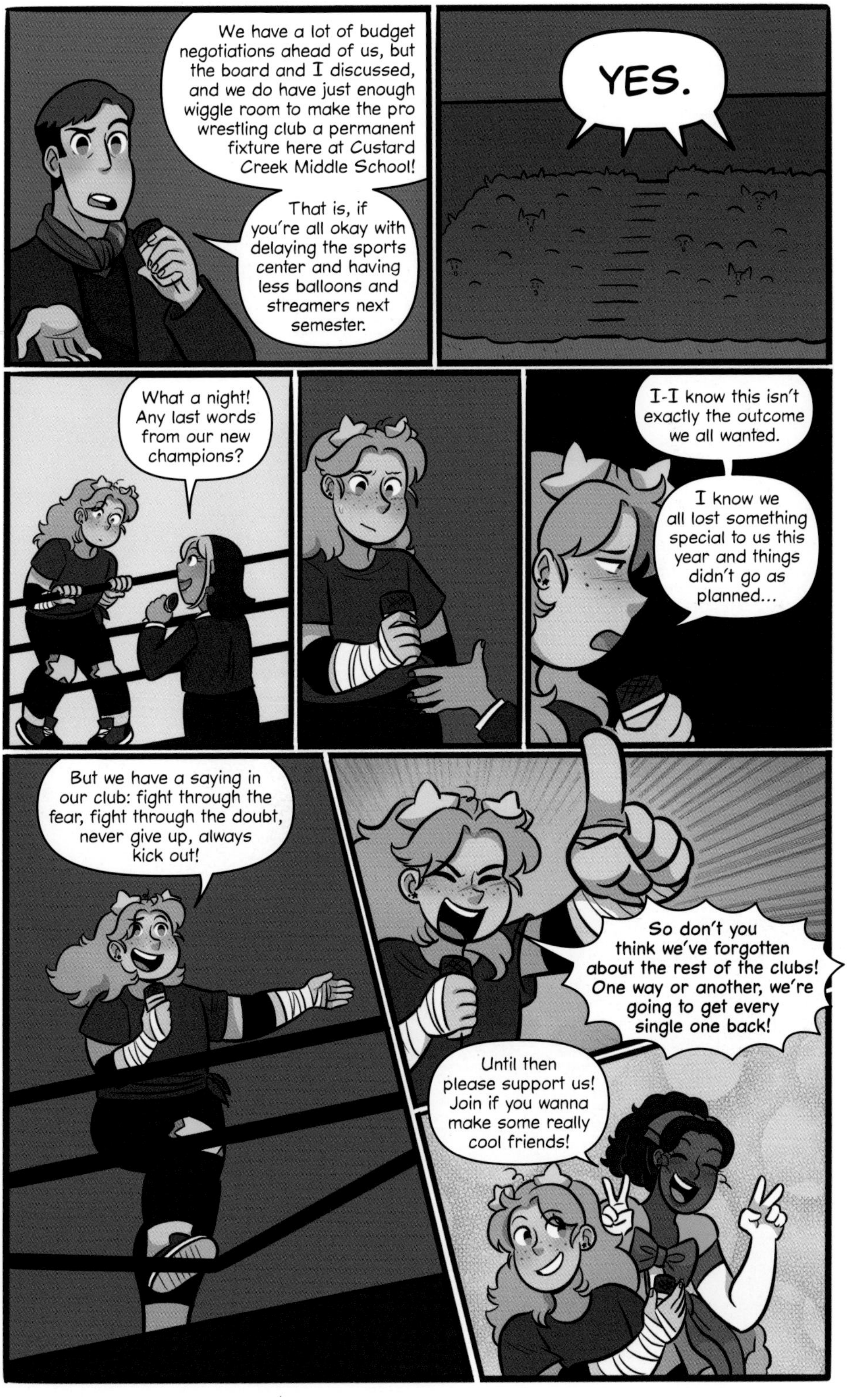

We have a lot of budget negotiations ahead of us, but the board and I discussed, and we do have just enough wiggle room to make the pro wrestling club a permanent fixture here at Custard Creek Middle School!
That is, if you're all okay with delaying the sports center and having less balloons and streamers next semester.
YES.
What a night! Any last words from our new champions?
I-I know this isn't exactly the outcome we all wanted.
I know we all lost something special to us this year and things didn't go as planned...
But we have a saying in our club: fight through the fear, fight through the doubt, never give up, always kick out!
So don't you think we've forgotten about the rest of the clubs! One way or another, we're going to get every single one back!
Until then please support us! Join if you wanna make some really cool friends!

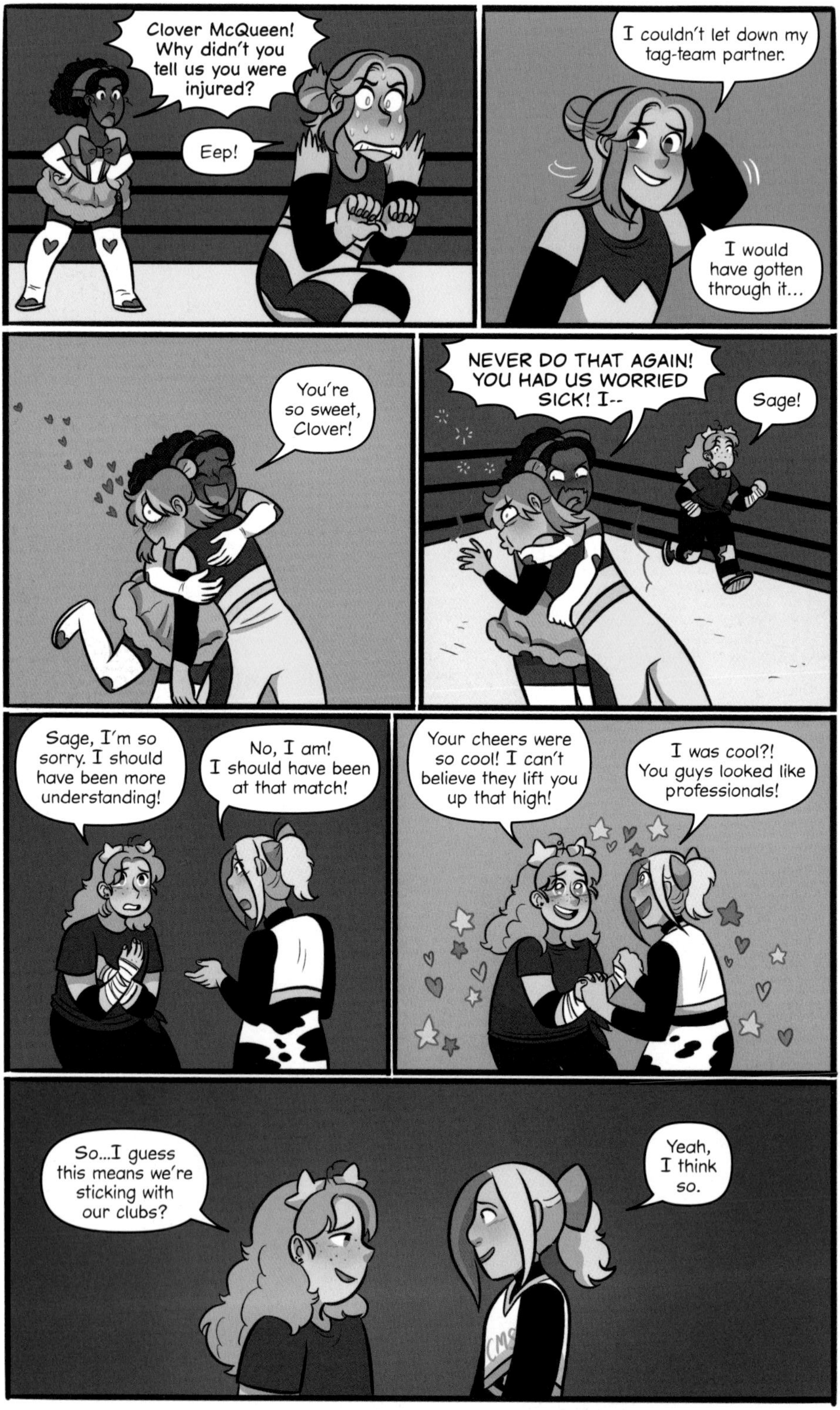
Clover McQueen! Why didn't you tell us you were injured?
Eep!
I couldn't let down my tag-team partner.
I would have gotten through it...
You're so sweet, Clover!
NEVER DO THAT AGAIN! YOU HAD US WORRIED SICK! I--
Sage!
Sage, I'm so sorry. I should have been more understanding!
No, I am! I should have been at that match!
Your cheers were so cool! I can't believe they lift you up that high!
I was cool?! You guys looked like professionals!
So...I guess this means we're sticking with our clubs?
Yeah, I think so.

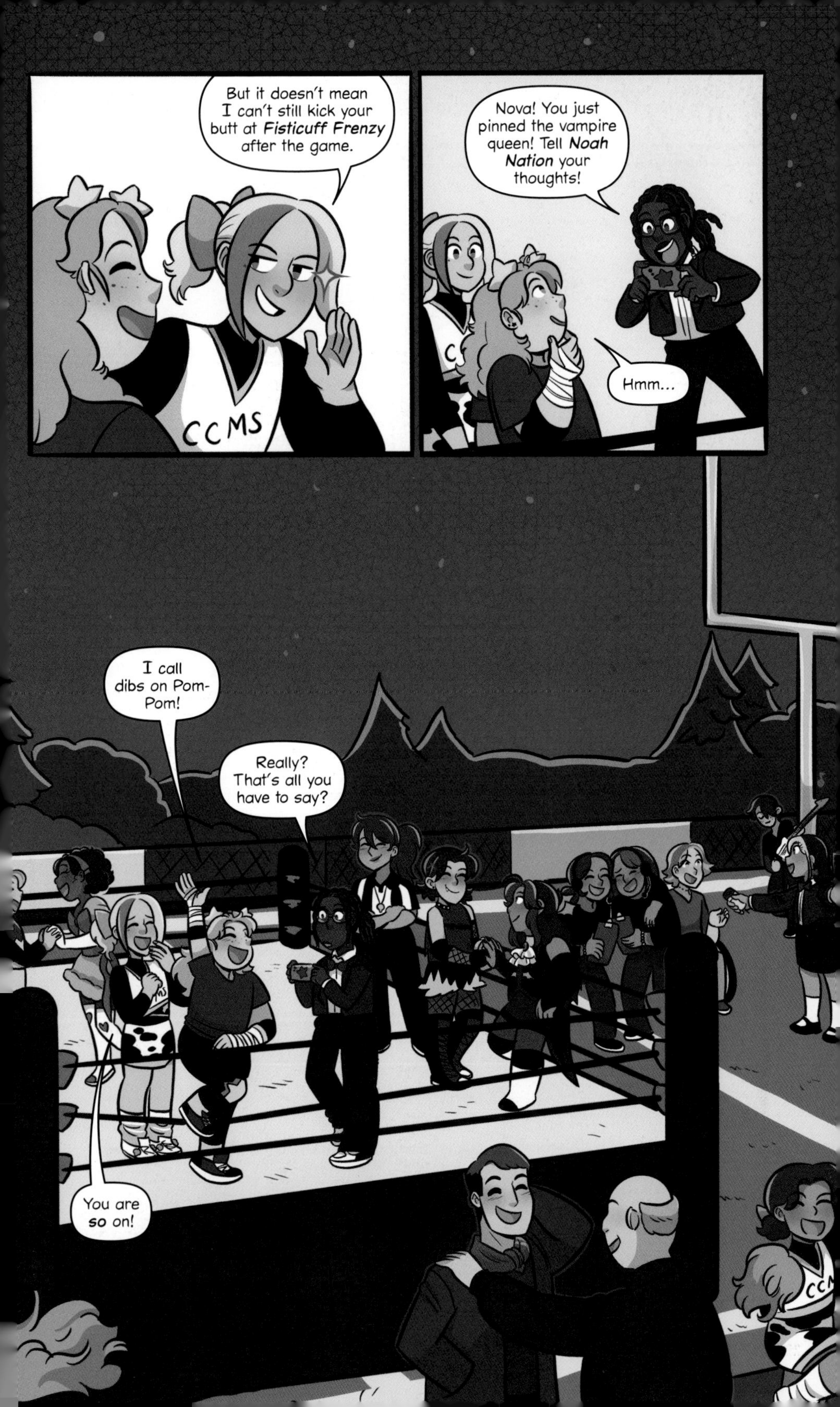

But it doesn't mean I can't still kick your butt at ***Fisticuff Frenzy*** after the game.
CCMS
Nova! You just pinned the vampire queen! Tell ***Noah Nation*** your thoughts!
Hmm...
I call dibs on Pom-Pom!
Really? That's all you have to say?
You are **so** on!

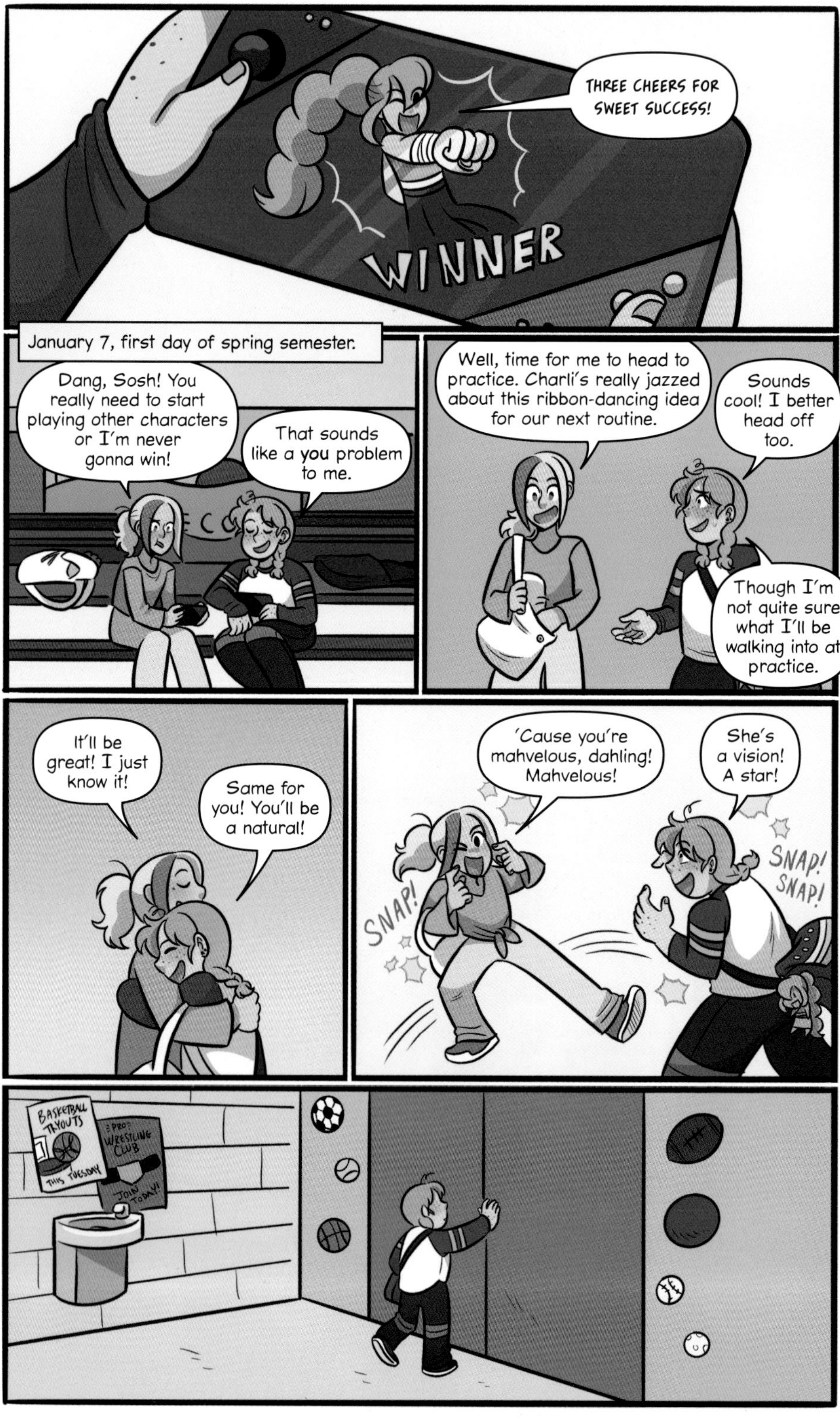
THREE CHEERS FOR SWEET SUCCESS!
WINNER
January 7, first day of spring semester.
Dang, Sosh! You really need to start playing other characters or I'm never gonna win!
That sounds like a **you** problem to me.
Well, time for me to head to practice. Charli's really jazzed about this ribbon-dancing idea for our next routine.
Sounds cool! I better head off too.
Though I'm not quite sure what I'll be walking into at practice.
It'll be great! I just know it!
Same for you! You'll be a natural!
'Cause you're mahvelous, dahling! Mahvelous!
She's a vision! A star!
SNAP!
SNAP! SNAP!
BASKETBALL TRYOUTS THIS TUESDAY
PRO WRESTLING CLUB JOIN TODAY!

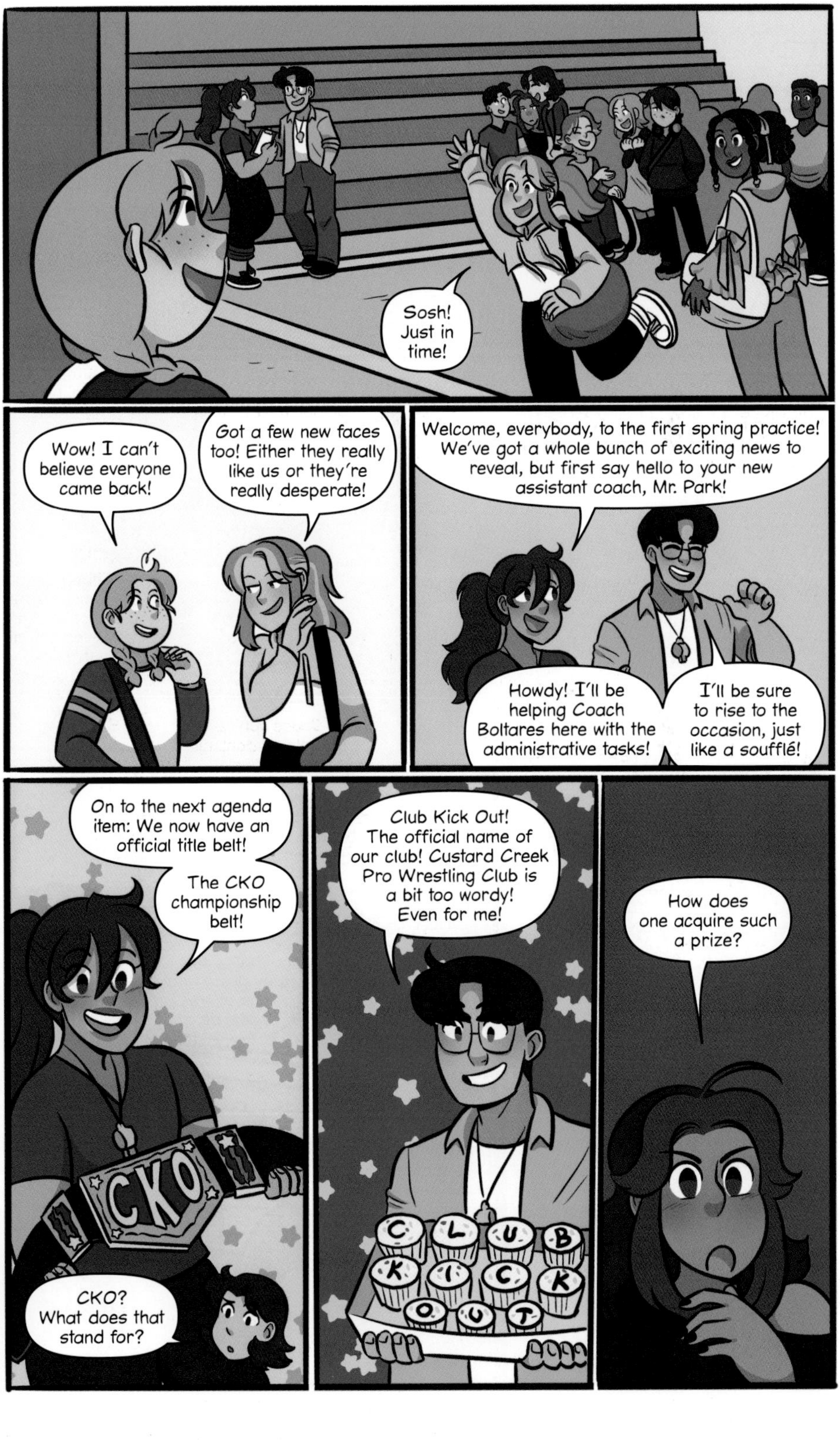

Sosh! Just in time!
Wow! I can't believe everyone came back!
Got a few new faces too! Either they really like us or they're really desperate!
Welcome, everybody, to the first spring practice! We've got a whole bunch of exciting news to reveal, but first say hello to your new assistant coach, Mr. Park!
Howdy! I'll be helping Coach Boltares here with the administrative tasks!
I'll be sure to rise to the occasion, just like a soufflé!
On to the next agenda item: We now have an official title belt!
The CKO championship belt!
CKO
CKO? What does that stand for?
Club Kick Out! The official name of our club! Custard Creek Pro Wrestling Club is a bit too wordy! Even for me!
CLUB KICK OUT
How does one acquire such a prize?

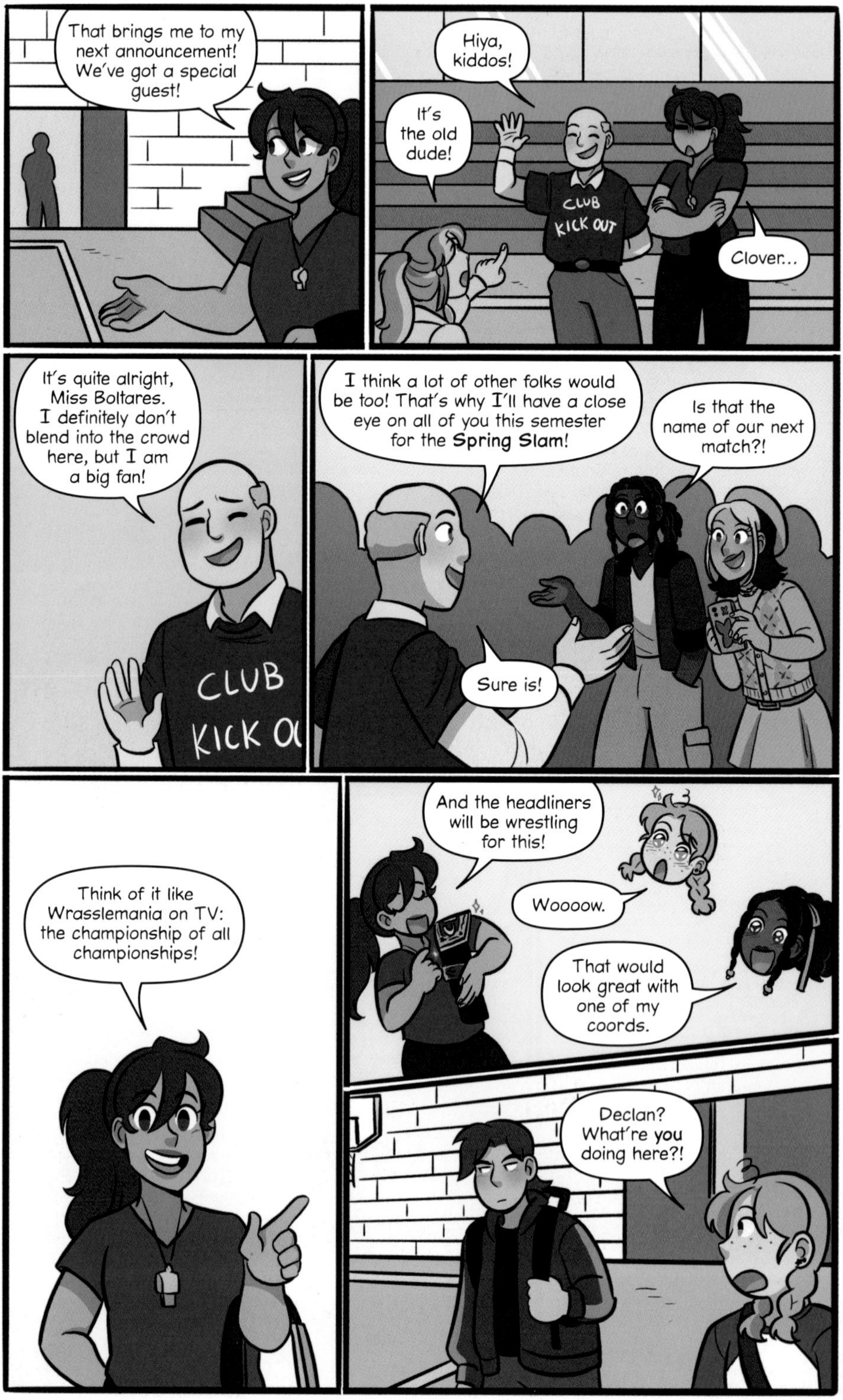

That brings me to my next announcement! We've got a special guest!
Hiya, kiddos!
It's the old dude!
CLUB KICK OUT
Clover...
It's quite alright, Miss Boltares. I definitely don't blend into the crowd here, but I am a big fan!
CLUB KICK OU
I think a lot of other folks would be too! That's why I'll have a close eye on all of you this semester for the **Spring Slam**!
Is that the name of our next match?!
Sure is!
Think of it like Wrasslemania on TV: the championship of all championships!
And the headliners will be wrestling for this!
Woooow.
That would look great with one of my coords.
Declan? What're **you** doing here?!

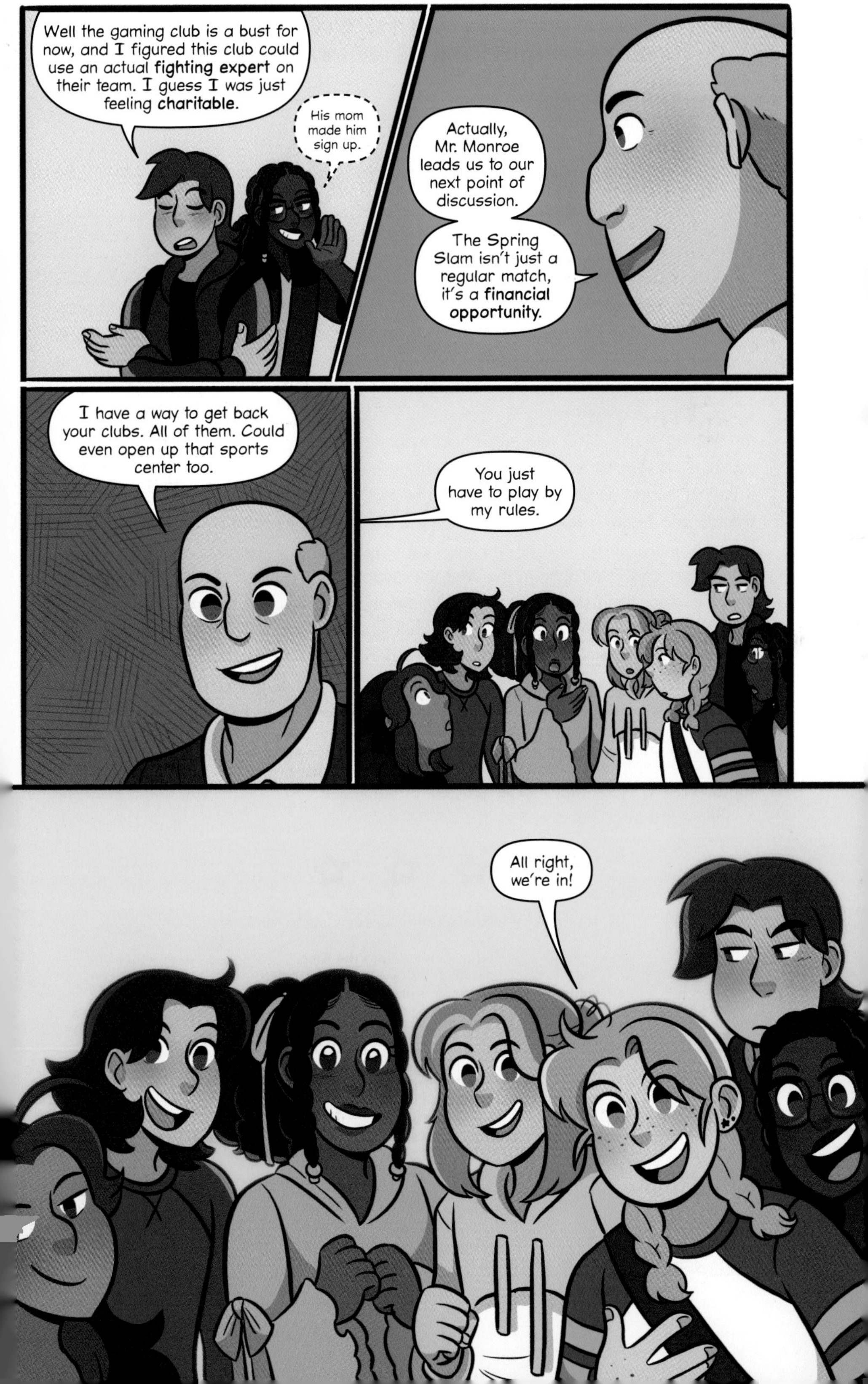
Well the gaming club is a bust for now, and I figured this club could use an actual **fighting expert** on their team. I guess I was just feeling **charitable**.
His mom made him sign up.
Actually, Mr. Monroe leads us to our next point of discussion.
The Spring Slam isn't just a regular match, it's a **financial opportunity**.
I have a way to get back your clubs. All of them. Could even open up that sports center too.
You just have to play by my rules.
All right, we're in!

DEDICATED TO MY TAG TEAM PARTNERS IN LIFE AND THE CHAMPIONS OF MY HEART—MY FRIENDS

Club Kick Out started as a little fire in my heart that I kept alive by sketching and dreaming, but over the course of years it became a flame far more powerful and bright than I could have ever imagined thanks to many, many people. First of all, thanks to my wonderful and caring agent, Britt Siess, who championed this book from the minute I dared to put it out in the world. A huge thanks to my editorial and design team at HarperAlley: Andrew Arnold, Rose Pleuler, Maddy Price, and my letterer, Chris Dickey, for helping shape CKO into something magnificent beyond my wildest dreams. Thank you to Kidd Riot for answering any wrestling questions I had; your insight into the pro wrestling world was amazing and beyond helpful! Thank you to my amazing group of art friends and fellow creators: Mat, Kristen, Stef, Georgeo, Shadia, Jenna, Hard Decora (and so many more), and all the inspiring creators at the agency who were a source of comfort and inspiration in my first solo journey into publishing. A big thanks to my mom, dad, brother, and sister-in-law for believing in my artistic aspirations from day one—this book wouldn't be here without your support! Thank you to my two goblin cats, Mooshie and Dipper, and a shout-out to my darling little niece, Piper, for being her little amazing self! Thank you to Kylie, Gabby, and all my friends at Wanderlust Archers, my home away from home. I also want to give a huge thank-you to my best friends in the entire world—Becky, Abe, Mikaila, Harmony, and Sam—you are my real-life Club Kick Out. Finally, thanks to you, dear reader, for giving this ragtag crew a bit of your time. I hope you all have a place that makes you feel at home like CKO, and if you don't—keep that fighting spirit to go out and find it!

HarperAlley is an imprint of HarperCollins Publishers.

Club Kick Out!: Into the Ring
Copyright © 2023 by Stephanie Mided
All rights reserved. Manufactured in Bosnia and Herzegovina.
No part of this book may be used or reproduced in any manner whatsoever without written permission except in the case of brief quotations embodied in critical articles and reviews.
For information address HarperCollins Children's Books, a division of HarperCollins Publishers, 195 Broadway, New York, NY 10007.
www.harperalley.com

Library of Congress Control Number: 2023931391
ISBN 978-0-06-311646-7 – ISBN 978-0-06-311645-0 (pbk.)

This book was penciled and inked digitally using Procreate, and the colors and screen tones were done in Clip Studio Paint. All of this work was done using an Apple iPad Pro and a lovingly worn Apple Pencil.

Typography by Chris Dickey
23 24 25 26 27   GPS   10 9 8 7 6 5 4 3 2 1
First Edition